Rebecca Shaw is a former school teacher and the bestselling author of many novels. She lives with her husband in a beautiful Dorset village where she finds plenty of inspiration for her stories about rural life. She has four children and eight grandchildren.

If you want to learn more about Rebecca Shaw and her novels, visit her website at: ww.rebeccashaw.co.uk

D1634797

Also by Rebecca Shaw

Rebecca Shaw

Three Village Novels

Village Gossip
Trouble in the Village
A Village Dilemma

First published in Great Britain in 2011 by Orion Books,
an imprint of The Orion Publishing Group Ltd
Orion House, 5 Upper Saint Martin's Lane
London WC2H 9EA

An Hachette UK Company

1 3 5 7 9 10 8 6 4 2

A CIP catalogue record for this book
is available from the British Library.

ISBN (hardback): 978 1 4091 3375 9

Typeset by Deltatype Ltd, Birkenhead, Merseyside
Printed in Great Britain by Clays Ltd, St Ives plc.

The Orion Publishing Group's policy is to use papers
that are natural, renewable and recyclable products and
made from wood grown in sustainable forests. The logging
and manufacturing processes are expected to conform to
the environmental regulations of the country of origin.

www.orionbooks.co.uk

Contents

Village Gossip

Inhabitants of Turnham Malpas

Nick Barnes	Veterinary surgeon
Roz Barnes	Nurse
Willie Biggs	Verger at St Thomas à Becket
Sylvia Biggs	His wife and housekeeper at the Rectory
Sir Ronald Bissett	Retired Trade Union leader
Lady Sheila Bissett	His wife
James (Jimbo) Charter-Plackett	Owner of the Village Store
Harriet Charter-Plackett	His wife
Fergus, Finlay, Flick and Fran	Their children
Katherine Charter-Plackett	Jimbo's mother
Alan Crimble	Barman at the Royal Oak
Linda Crimble	Runs the post office at the Village Store
Georgie Fields	Licensee at the Royal Oak
H. Craddock Fitch	Owner of Turnham House
Jimmy Glover	Taxi driver
Revd Peter Harris (Oxon)	Rector of the parish
Dr Caroline Harris	His wife
Alex and Beth	Their children
Mrs Jones	A village gossip
Barry Jones	Her son and estate carpenter
Pat Jones	Barry's wife
Dean and Michelle	Barry and Pat's children
Jeremy Mayer	Manager at Turnham House
Venetia Mayer	His wife

Neville Neal	Accountant and church treasurer
Liz Neal	His wife
Guy and Hugh	Their children
Tom Nicholls	Retired businessman
Evie Nicholls	His wife
Anne Parkin	Retired secretary
Kate Pascoe	Village school head teacher
Sir Ralph Templeton	Retired from the diplomatic service
Lady Muriel Templeton	His wife
Dicky Tutt	Scout leader and bar-manager at the Royal Oak
Bel Tutt	School secretary and assistant in the Village Store
Don Wright	Maintenance engineer (now retired)
Vera Wright	Cleaner at the nursing home in Penny Fawcett
Rhett Wright	Their grandson

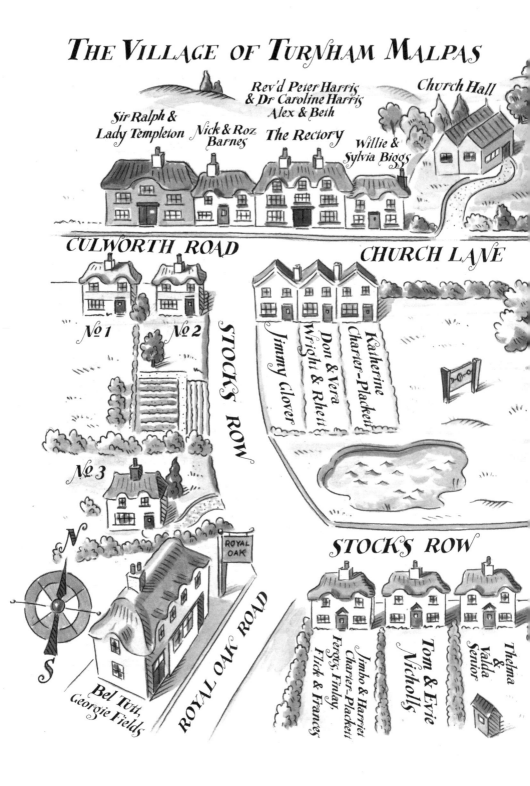

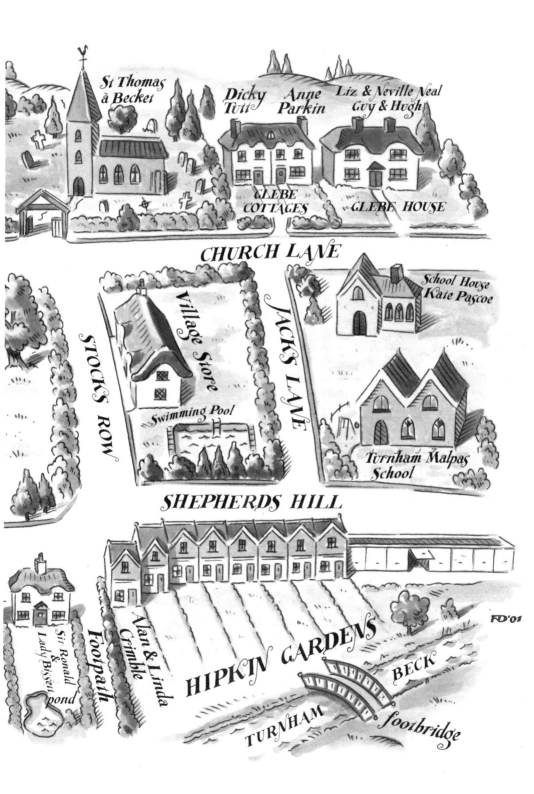

St Thomas à Becket

Dicky Tutt

Anne Parkin

Liz & Neville Neal
Guy & Hugh

GLEBE COTTAGES

GLEBE HOUSE

CHURCH LANE

Village Store

STOCKS ROW

JACK'S LANE

School House
Kate Pascoe

Swimming Pool

Turnham Malpas
School

SHEPHERDS HILL

Sir Ronald & Lady Bissett
pond

Footpath

Alan & Linda
Grimble

HIPKIN GARDENS

BECK

FD'01

TURNHAM

footbridge

1

His foot propped on the brass rail running along the bottom of the bar, a gin and tonic in hand, Peter toasted Caroline: 'Happy birthday, darling!'

She clinked her glass with his and smiled up at him. 'And the same to you.'

Peter bent down to kiss her. 'I say this every year, and I say it again; how many married people are there who celebrate their birthdays on the same day?'

'Somewhere, someone knows the answer to that, I suppose. Do you remember how sentimental you used to wax about our marriage being "written in the stars", "this was meant to be since the beginning of time", et cetera, et cetera, all because our birthdays were on the same day?' Caroline grinned up at him.

'Don't mock. I meant it and still do.'

'I know you do, and I'm eternally grateful that you do.'

'Always will mean it, no matter what.' Peter put his glass down on the bar and surveyed the crowded bar. 'I don't think we could have chosen a busier night.'

'You're right there.'

The Royal Oak had been in business since, as the villagers often stressed, the beginning of time. The thatched roof, the ancient white walls bulging slightly more than they had done five hundred years ago, the huge open fireplace which boasted a real log fire in the winter months, and the mighty oak beams all lent a feeling of timelessness, of permanence, of a kind of security which encapsulated the feeling everyone had about their village.

From the other side of the bar Georgie called out, 'I've just realised it's your birthdays, isn't it? Next drinks on the house, OK?'

Peter thanked her. 'Where's Dicky tonight?'

'Night off.' Georgie turned away to serve yet another customer. 'Yes, sir, what can I get you?'

Caroline, enjoying a birthday which some months ago she had thought she would not live to see, said to Peter, 'Harriet and Jimbo are late. I wonder if our table's ready? I'm starving.'

'So am I. I'll go see.' He threaded his way between the tables, stopping for a word now and again.

'Evening, Rector, 'appy birthday!'

'Thank you, Jimmy.'

'Your birthday is it, then? Many more, sir, many more.'

'Thank you, Don, Vera.'

'Many happy returns, Rector, and that's from Sheila too.'

'Thank you, Ron.'

He left a swathe of smiling faces behind him. Caroline, watching, smiled inside herself. He might have his ups and downs with them all but at bottom they were on his side. What a difference he had made to them since he had arrived. Stirred them up and no mistake. She hoped they'd never need to leave, because her roots had gone deep down here in this village and you couldn't ask for more than that. Her eyes lit up when she spotted Peter signalling from the dining-room doorway that their table was ready.

'But, Peter, what about Jimbo and Harriet? They're not here yet.'

'They've rung. Crisis with the children; they're just leaving.'

'Oh, brilliant. I wonder what's wrong?'

'No need to worry,' he smoothed away her frown with a gentle finger. 'Fran has had a temper tantrum.'

'Oh dear.'

Bel was in charge of the dining room tonight, a slimmer, more light-footed Bel of late. She beamed at the two of them and they couldn't help but notice what a lovely heart-warming smile she had.

'Good evening! We've given you the best table, seeing as it's a celebration. Jimbo and Harriet are on their way. Happy birthday to you both.'

'Thank you, Bel.' She handed them each a menu and padded away to attend to other diners.

The door between the dining room and the bar opened and Harriet and Jimbo walked in. Her dark hair damp and curling, her slightly sallow skin flushed with anxiety at her late arrival, Harriet waved when she caught sight of them. Jimbo stood behind her, smoothing his hand over his bald head which gleamed in the light over the tiny reception desk in the doorway. More round than he would have liked, Jimbo was a commanding figure. Energy, both mental and physical, exuded from every inch of him. 'Sorry we're late!'

Peter stood up to pull out Harriet's chair for her. 'Good evening, Harriet!'

She reached up to kiss him. 'Happy birthday, Peter. Happy birthday, Caroline! How useful of you to have your birthdays on the same day. It halves the remembering!'

'To say nothing of the cost!' Jimbo took Caroline's hand and kissed it. 'Happy birthday, my dear, and many of 'em.' He squeezed her hand and she knew exactly what it meant. A gesture of delight at her survival. Tears came into Caroline's eyes. She blew her nose and remained quiet for a while, listening to the chatter and pretending to study her menu.

'Fran Charter-Plackett! She's so amenable, fits in without a murmur with anything we plan and then suddenly wham! bang! she's on the floor drumming her heels and screaming like a hell cat!'

'Jimbo, darling! She did have good reason, or so she thought.'
Peter asked what the reason was.

Harriet explained. 'We've a guest coming to stay tomorrow, and Fran's having a practice go on the put-u-up in Flick's bedroom tonight. We'd talked about it and I'd put her favourite sheets on the bed, done all I could, but when it came to it ...'

The mention of a guest brought Caroline's head up from the menu. 'Who've you got coming?'

Jimbo wagged a finger at her. 'Wouldn't you like to know!'
Harriet protested. 'Jimbo!'

'If Caroline guessed until this time next week she wouldn't get it right!'

9

'You're teasing me! Come on, tell!'

Harriet laughed. 'It's a college friend of ours. Compared to Jimbo and me, who've only managed to rise to the dizzy heights of running a Village Store . . .'

Peter interrupted her, scornful. '*Only* . . . Considering the success you've made of it . . .'

Harriet silenced him with a finger to his lips. 'Hush now. Wait for it.' She intended to pause to increase the dramatic effect but couldn't wait to see their faces. 'His name is *Hugo Maude*.'

A silence greeted her announcement. Caroline stared open mouthed. Peter stared, not believing he had heard correctly.

Caroline, stunned, stammered out, 'Hugo Maude! Not *the* Hugo Maude!'

'The very same!' Jimbo smiled at her astonishment. It was lovely to see her so taken out of herself.

'You mean Royal Shakespeare-Broadway-Stratford-Hugo Maude?'

'The very same!' Harriet glanced at Peter, amused by his more controlled reaction.

Caroline, seized with amazement, said, 'How long is he here for?'

'As long as it takes.'

Bel came for their order.

'With salad?' They all four nodded. 'Jacket potatoes, sauté potatoes?'

Jimbo began to ask for sauté potatoes but hastily changed his order to jacket when he caught Harriet's eye.

'House wine, or something special?'

Peter asked for something special.

When Bel left, Caroline said, 'How long *what* takes?'

'The poor lamb has been terribly ill. Some ghastly virus he picked up when he went with the RSC to Tokyo, it came close to finishing him off. So Jimbo and I thought we'd ask him for a quiet stay with us away from the press and such, so he could recuperate properly.'

Caroline persisted with her questioning. 'How come we've never seen him before?'

'Too busy. Never stops. Acting dominates his entire life.'

Caroline nodded her head in complete agreement. 'To be able to act as he does it would, wouldn't it? Only to be expected.' She paused. 'Shall we have a chance to meet him, do you think?'

Harriet grinned. 'I expect so. In fact I promise you shall, but I'm not planning anything until he's been here a few days. I don't know just how ill he is.'

'Oh, of course. Yes. I see.'

Peter said. 'You know that's something we've never done.'

Jimbo looked puzzled. 'What is?'

'We've never used the stage in the Church Hall for serious acting. At least not while we've been here.'

Harriet thought for a moment and then said, 'We've been here three years longer than you and you're right, it certainly hasn't, not for years.'

Quickly picking up on her thinking processes, Jimbo wagged a finger and said, 'No, we are not. Definitely not.'

'Not what?'

Jimbo looked at Peter and answered him by saying they were not going to encourage Hugo to act in a play. 'The man has been very ill and he's here to rest. He's a dear sweet man and he doesn't deserve us begging him for help. It could be the last straw.'

Harriet replied briskly. 'Such a thought never entered my head. Just the same, a village dramatic society would be a very, very good idea, wouldn't it, Peter?'

'It would. A real challenge.'

Peter felt a tap on his shoulder blade. He turned to find Mrs Jones at the next table, twisted around in her chair, wanting a word.

'Good evening, Mrs Jones, and good evening to you, Vince.'

Mrs Jones, obviously bursting with information, stopped just long enough to greet him and then said, 'Sorry to be interrupting, Rector, but I couldn't help but overhear what you were saying.' Harriet snorted her surprise at such a monumental disregard for the truth. Mrs Jones turned her chair round and squeezed in between Peter and Caroline. 'The last time we had a play on the stage that wasn't done by the Scouts or the Sunday School was in 1953. It was the Queen's Coronation and we did an 'istorical pageant called . . . now what was it called, Vince? "Royal Progress" or "Queens Through the Ages", or something like that. Blinking good it was too. The old rector, Mr Furbank, was Prince Albert. I was Britannia, and Vince here was the Prince of Wales, wasn't yer, Vince?' Before Vince could reply she had launched herself into a list of the people involved, followed by an appraisal of the play's reception. 'Two nights we did it and they came from all over. Penny Fawcett, Little Derehams and even some from Culworth, would you believe. And you know what a stuck up lot they are.'

Their food came and they had to excuse themselves. Mrs Jones stood up and turned her chair back to her own table. The four of them ate in silence while they absorbed what she had said.

Peter broke the silence by saying, 'So you see it would be a good idea, wouldn't it? With or without Hugo Maude.'

Jimbo, helping himself to a lavish portion of butter for his jacket potato, said, 'Yes, but not until the winter, when Hugo's gone and then it'll give us something to brighten the long winter evenings.'

'But who the blazes in this village can act? Even more to the point, who the blazes would we get to direct?' This from Harriet who, despite Jimbo's warning, really longed for Hugo's help.

'Exactly. Who? Not me for a start.'

Peter looked at Caroline in surprise. 'Not you? But you did lots at Medical School and at school. Portia, wasn't it? And lots more which won't spring to mind.'

'We'll see. It's all so long ago. And there's the children. Baby-sitting and that. I can't always rely on you with your meetings and things.'

Peter patted her hand. 'Don't you fret about that. Sylvia and Willie would gladly sit in, as you well know.'

Jimbo, realising how much Peter wanted Caroline to be involved, agreed. 'Our boys are getting big enough to be left for a while looking after the girls, so long as we're not too far away. So between us we'd manage something. Rest assured.'

Peter flashed him a look of gratitude. 'It's settled then, a play we shall do. A serious play, not some amateurish cobbled together thing, but a real play.' He raised his glass and invited them to join him in a toast.

'To the play and the players.'

'That sounds terribly grand. When shall we have the inaugural meeting?' Harriet asked.

Caroline parried Harriet's question with one of more immediate importance to herself. 'When shall we be introduced to Hugo Maude?'

'At church on Sunday, if he's well enough. He never misses. Finds the whole thing movingly dramatic.' Harriet apologised to Peter. 'His words, not mine.'

'Sunday it is then.' Caroline drained her glass and asked Peter for more. He refilled it, thrilled to have lighted upon something which he hoped would fill Caroline's heart and mind and above all give her faith in her future.

Caroline stood gazing at him, dumbstruck. He was lean, too lean really, with a head of thick dark hair, left full at the sides which made for just a hint of curl above his beautifully shaped ears. He'd been introduced to Peter now and they were talking animatedly. There couldn't have been a bigger contrast between two men. Hugo was shorter than Peter, but then with Peter being six feet five, most men were. Not only was he shorter than Peter he was also much more lightly built. One couldn't imagine Hugo on a squash court or running three miles before breakfast like Peter did.

Caroline couldn't help but admire the profile which had been displayed on theatre billboards and in magazines and newspapers all over the world. Beautifully balanced, at once tender and arrogant, elegant and virile.

She was being ridiculous. At her age, swooning over an actor! Come on.

Harriet tapped her arm. 'I've never seen you so excited by a man. You've usually only eyes for Peter.'

Caroline looked at Peter and then back at Hugo. 'I can admire from a distance, can't I? After all, he is famous. You can see he's under strain.'

'He's been very, very ill. And I mean ill. It was a case of "will he or won't he?" at one stage. Lost a stone and a half in weight. It's left him very feeble.'

'I see.' By now Hugo was talking to Sheila Bissett, whose face was almost the colour of the dreadful purple hat she was wearing for church this summer. Above the babble of the congregation gathered about the church porch, Caroline heard Sheila say, 'Well, of course, you must come to one of my coffee mornings. It may only be a small village but we do know how to do things proper.'

This offer was greeted with enthusiasm by Hugo. 'My dear Lady Bissett, of course I shall be delighted to attend. It will be the highlight of my social whirl.' Hugo looked across at Harriet and made his excuses to Lady Bissett.

'Oh! he's coming over. I'll introduce you.'

Her eyes fixed on Hugo, Caroline muttered, 'I feel ridiculously nervous. Perhaps I shouldn't.'

Harriet did the honours and stood back a little to watch. Hugo took hold of Caroline's hand and raised it to his lips.

'My dear Caroline, what a privilege.' His voice, more suited to Stratford than Turnham Malpas, turned Caroline's knees to jelly. This gesture of his, this kissing of her hand and the holding of it for longer than was really necessary brought the eyes of the entire congregation to rest on her.

She blushed, and she hadn't blushed for years. When in her consulting room, people confided in her the most intimate details of their lives and she never batted an eyelid, never blushed, never ever. And yet here she was behaving like an empty-headed teenager.

'How do you do? I'm so sorry to hear that you've been so ill. We'll have to hope that the peace and quiet here will . . .'

'I shan't *hasten* to get well, not with charming people like you in the village.' Caroline appeared to have been pole-axed.

Harriet felt the need to intervene. 'Caroline's a doctor.'

'In that case, if I'm taken ill I shall be able to rely on you to cool my fevered brow.'

'I don't know about that, you see . . .'

Hugo dismissed her hesitation with a sweeping gesture of his hand. 'I won't hear of you refusing to come to my aid. I cannot forgo the thrill of your stethoscope pressed to my manly chest.' There were muffled giggles from someone way behind him and Caroline blushed even redder.

'I was going to say that it's not medical etiquette for me to attend another doctor's patient.'

Hugo struck a pose, one hand on his heart and the other clasping his forehead. 'Not even in an emergency! Am I cast out from all medical assistance to die miserably and alone for the sake of *etiquette*?' The last word, delivered with passion, and loud enough to wake Jimmy's geese on the village pond, fell on the delighted ears of the entire congregation. It had been some time since they had enjoyed so much free entertainment.

Harriet, catching the appalled expression in Jimbo's eyes, said abruptly, 'For heaven's sakes, Hugo, you're not that ill. Come on home, the children need feeding. Help me round them up.'

Hugo gave Caroline a huge wink, bunched his fingers, kissed them and trotted meekly after his friend.

With his mother on his arm Jimbo passed close by Caroline as Hugo left. Jimbo's mother wore severe disapproval across every inch of her perfectly made-up face. She and Caroline had long ago patched up their differences but it appeared that in one brief moment of time their friendship had been shattered. With a sharp nod of recognition replacing her normally gracious conversation she swept by. Jimbo raised his eyes to heaven and shrugged his shoulders apologetically.

The congregation began to disperse. Peter had disappeared inside to remove his surplice, Willie was waiting to lock up, the twins were chasing each other among the gravestones and Caroline realised it was time she remembered her duty.

'Alex, Beth! Come quickly now! We'll get the kettle on, Daddy will be wanting his coffee.'

'Mummy! That man kissed you.'

'Yes, Beth, he did.'

'What will Daddy say?'

Ever at the ready to pour scorn on Beth's statements, Alex replied, 'Daddy won't mind. After all, he only kissed her hand.'

'I know, but he shouldn't. He's cheeky. She's my Mummy.' Beth squeezed hold of Caroline's hand and kissed it herself.

'And she's mine, and I say he can kiss her hand.'

'Well, I don't. I shall ask Daddy if he minds.'

'No, darling, don't do that. Mr Maude is an actor and they're inclined to be a bit ...'

'Bit what?'

'Well, they're inclined to exaggerate everything. They go a bit over the top.'

Alex studied this statement while Caroline unlocked the Rectory door. 'It was only your hand. So it's nothing really.'

'You went ever so red, Mummy.'

'Did I?'

'Yes, you did. Red like a beetroot.'

'Thanks. Do you both want coffee, or orange, or what?'

While they argued with each other as to what they would have Caroline filled the kettle and began to get out the mugs. She heard the front door slam. 'Ready for coffee?'

'Please.' Caroline turned to look at Peter. He was standing in the kitchen doorway looking at her. Her heart flipped. She loved him so. Compared with Hugo ridiculous Maude he was a gem. His wonderful thatch of red-blond hair, his vivid blue eyes, his fair skin, the width of his shoulders, his energy and his love for mankind, all set her trembling with love for him.

Beth pulled out a chair. 'Sit next to me, Daddy. I'm having coffee too, Mummy, please.'

'And me!' Alex pulled out a chair the other side of Peter and sat on it. 'Daddy! Did you know that Mr Maude is an actor?'

'He is indeed. I've seen him once, a long time ago. In London. In *Macbeth.*'

'What's *Macbeth*?'

'A play by Shakespeare.'

'Was he good?'

'Oh yes, very impressive. In fact very good indeed, I think the best I've seen.'

'Mummy says actors behave like that.'

'Like what?'

'Kissing people and that.'

'Yes, they do. Very emotional they are.' Peter looked up at Caroline and winked as she handed him his coffee.

She had to laugh. 'He really did make me feel a fool.'

'I could see that. This coffee's welcome. What shall we do this afternoon? Do we have any plans?'

Hugo's plan to retire to his bedroom and lie down for the rest of the afternoon suited everyone. Harriet, because she'd had more than she could take of him at the lunch table; Jimbo, because Hugo had grated on his nerves and he was forced to admit to a tinge of jealousy which didn't sit easily on his shoulders; the children, because they couldn't get a word in edgeways as he wouldn't stop talking; and Grandmama, because she knew he spelt trouble with a capital T.

'Have you two girls finished? If you have your Grandmama has something for you in her handbag which you can take into the sitting room and play with.'

Five-year-old Fran jumped up and down with excitement. Flick, at twelve, recognised the subterfuge and wished she couldn't see through her Grandmama's every move. But it would only be boring conversation about Hugo and the threat he posed to one and all, so she might as well fall for it. 'Lovely, Grandmama. Come along, Fran.' They retired with some magic tricks in little plastic bags, . leaving the field clear for Grandmama's tirade.

'That man . . .'

Jimbo hastily said to his son, 'Fergus, close that door just in case.' When Fergus had reclaimed his chair, his Grandmama continued. 'That man is a charlatan, a chameleon and a sham. The sooner he leaves this house the better.'

Finlay chuckled. 'Wow! You're getting quite poetic, Grandmama.'

He received a withering glance. 'This is not a laughing matter, young man. Jimbo! You must get rid of him.'

Jimbo caught Harriet's eye and acknowledged the warning in them. 'As a matter of fact I quite like the chap. In any case, Mother, it's up to Harriet and me who stays in our house. He poses no threat here.'

'No threat? You must be blind.' She thumped the table with her clenched fist. 'Blind! He wants kicking out. Convalescing indeed. More like out of work or, as they euphemistically call it in the acting profession, resting.'

Finlay chuckled again. 'He is.'

'He is what?'

'Resting.' He pointed to the ceiling. Grandmama, as he was well aware, didn't have much of a sense of humour. She snorted. 'Sometimes you talk in riddles.'

'Mother-in-law! He almost died he was so ill. He lives alone, he needs a family to care for him. Don't worry. Before long he'll get an offer he can't refuse, he'll go dashing off and we shan't see him again for years. He's a close friend of Jimbo's, isn't he, darling?' Jimbo nodded. 'And of mine too. It's the least we can do.'

'Jimbo! Are you head of this house or not?'

'I am.'

'Then take my word for it, he is trouble. If you'll excuse me I'll be off now. I have two friends coming for afternoon tea and I need to get organised.' She collected her handbag and offered her cheek for Jimbo to kiss. 'Cast this viper out from your bosom, Jimbo. Listen to your mother for once. Bye bye, Harriet. Thank you for yet another delightful lunch, I do look forward to Sunday lunch with you all. Bye bye, boys.' She opened the dining-room door, went through it and then came back in. 'And another thing. Caroline Harris had no business to let him kiss her hand. Disgraceful behaviour outside church, with everyone watching. She blushed like a schoolgirl. I expect Peter will have something to say to her about that and no mistake.'

On summer Sunday evenings Peter and Caroline had dinner together after Peter returned from Evensong. With the children tucked up in bed they enjoyed an intimate meal, which Caroline always took a great deal of care over. The wine had been chilled, the steak was almost ready, the sauce bubbled very gently in the pan and the vegetables were already in the tureens in the oven keeping warm, when she heard Peter's key in the door.

'I'm back and I'm seriously in need of sustenance.'

'So am I! I've opened the wine. Won't be a moment.'

Peter came into the kitchen. He'd removed his cassock and was wearing his dark trousers and clerical collar with a grey short-sleeved shirt.

'Take your collar off, you look hot.'

He undid his back stud and peeled off his collar, placing it with the stud on top of the fridge freezer. 'Quite a lot there tonight.'

'Makes a change.'

'It does indeed. Just as I begin to think I shall suggest finishing with Evensong I get a good congregation and I have a rethink.'

Caroline gave Peter a cloth. 'Here, take the vegetables in. I've served the meat straight onto the plates.'

Peter put down the tureens on the dining table and picked up the bottle of wine. 'Where on earth did this wine come from? Chile! Oh my word.'

'If there's one person I don't like it's a wine snob.'

'Sorry! You're quite right. If I like it, what does it matter where it comes from.'

'Maybe you had a big congregation because they all hoped Hugo Maude would appear.'

'Well, he didn't.'

'I'm in trouble because of him.'

He looked up, his mouth full of steak, and mumbled, 'Why?'

'Grandmama Charter-Plackett doesn't approve of me any longer because of what happened outside church.'

'No wonder.'

'Living in an ancient village like this one, they can get too ... what's the word I'm looking for?'

'Don't know. Shall I finish the peas?'

'Yes, I don't want any more. Too narrow minded. In fact, almighty prim. They need their horizons widening. All he is, is a bit of fun. Liven us all up. I hope he stays for a while.'

'So do I. But, darling, please be very circumspect won't you? Rector's wife and all that.'

Caroline put down her knife and fork, drank a little of her wine and muttered, 'Here we go again.'

'I beg your pardon?'

'I said, "Here we go again." '

'Sorry, but you know ...'

'I know. By the way I'm going back to work as soon as I can get a job. I've decided. General practice. I like that best.'

He restrained himself from being protective, there was nothing more sure to make her go ahead finding a job than him putting the brakes on her. 'That's a good idea, darling, you must be feeling better.'

'I can hear the disapproval in your voice, but I am feeling better and it's ridiculous for an intelligent woman of my years with my professional qualifications not to be using them.'

19

'Of course. I quite agree. But Sylvia's cut down her hours. How will you cope?'

Caroline said, 'I wouldn't be full time, not like I was when the twins first went to playgroup. Probably just filling in for sickness and the like.'

'Well, that might be different then. You could do, say, three full days.'

'Well, I haven't got a position yet so we'll wait and see.'

'Are you sure? You've been so ill.' He reached across the table and took hold of her hand. 'I've only just got my confidence back about the chances of your survival. It has been a dreadfully challenging time for my faith, your illness.'

Caroline gripped his hand. 'I know, darling, I know. But I am well and, touch wood, I'm definitely here to stay. OK?'

'And the children, they haven't been the easiest of offspring, have they? Will you manage, do you think?'

'They take after their father, don't they?'

Peter pretended to scowl. 'Hey, less of that!'

Caroline laughed. 'Well, they do. Alex is so like you in his ways, and Beth just follows whatever he does. When I think of your stories about what you got up to when you were a boy, he's going to be just like that.'

Peter answered her abruptly. 'I would have preferred it if you'd spoken with me first, before you decided.'

'What?'

'Going back into practice.'

'What do you mean? I've just told you now. You knew what I would be doing. I should have gone back long ago. How long have I had off? A year? No, more than that. It's ridiculous.'

'No, it isn't. You don't have to work. If you want to be at home then at home you will be. I love it. You being at home.'

Caroline went to stand behind his chair and put her arms around his shoulders resting her cheek on his. 'Peter! I know you do, but there isn't enough for me to do.'

'There is, now Sylvia is doing fewer hours.'

'The children don't need me like they did. Not like when they were tiny.'

'I see. You've exhausted the mother bit so now you can wander off footloose and fancy free.'

Caroline, shocked by his attitude, drew away from him. 'That is absolutely uncalled for and quite untrue. You've upset me.'

Peter stood up and went to look out of the window.

'I beg your pardon. I shouldn't have said that. I'm ashamed of myself.'

'You should say it if that's how you feel.'

'I don't, not really. But I hate your preoccupation when you're working. You bring your problems home and I feel shut out.'

Mockingly, with half a smile on her face, Caroline answered, 'Oh dear! Poor little boy! Not got my full attention. Oh dear!'

Still looking out of the window Peter said, 'I suppose in part it's this old-fashioned idea that as the man of the house I should be the one earning the money. When you're in practice you earn far, far more than I do and could ever hope to do and it hurts, which is ridiculous but true. It kind of rankles. But I'm sorry for what I said.'

'And so you should be. If I want to work, I shall. I find it so *satisfying*, don't you see? You have a brain, you know how stultifying it can be not using it. Why do you think you do so much study and reading and writing articles for the papers? You're really a very scholarly man. The congregation hear only the tip of the iceberg of your learning. Well, it's the same for me, I need to use *my* brain too. And this business about the money. Your private income boosts your stipend enormously and we agreed when we married that your remuneration by no means equated with what you have to do, and that we wouldn't use it as a yardstick. Here you are doing that very thing.'

He didn't reply. Caroline went to stand behind him. She laid her head against his back and put her arms around him again. 'We musn't argue about this. I love you dearly. I love the children to bits. But I just need that something more to make life really worthwhile. And don't worry about my health. I'm fine and I wouldn't go back if I didn't feel up to it.'

'But before when you worked, the children were so distressed . . .'

'I know, darling, I know. But they're older now and they

understand better. But I'll give you the promise I gave you before. If they get upset I shall stop working. Right? They come first. So do you, for that matter. Can three people come first?'

Peter turned to face her. 'I want only the best for all the ones I love. I love you, so very much.' He looked her full in the face, adoring her fine creamy skin, the long straight nose, the deep brown depths of her eyes, and the way her dark hair curled almost childlike around her face. He pulled her close to him, bent his head and kissed her. A kiss which turned into a paroxysm of tiny kisses around her mouth, and then her throat. His eagerness for her was overwhelming.

'Peter! We musn't! Wait till we've eaten our pudding and I've cleared away.' Caroline tried to push him away but he had her held in a firm grip. 'Please! We can't come down in the morning to the kitchen in a mess. Sylvia will be absolutely appalled and will wonder what we've been up to. Please!'

Abruptly he released her. 'No, you're right. I'm sorry. Please forgive me. I beg your pardon.'

'Oh God! We have got our wires crossed. You haven't to apologise to me for wanting me! Right now *I* want *you*! It's just the timing that's wrong. Hey!' Caroline reached up to kiss his cheek. 'Am I forgiven?'

'For wanting to clear up in the kitchen?'

'No! Do I go back to work with your blessing?'

Resignedly Peter acceded the point. 'Of course you should go back to work if that's what you want. You don't need my permission to do as you choose. I'm not going to turn sulky about it. You wouldn't be you if you didn't want to go back to doctoring.'

'Exactly.'

'Yes, exactly so.'

Caroline thought she detected a sigh. She ignored it and cleared the table, then came back from the kitchen carrying a strawberry gâteau.

Peter's eyes lit up. 'That looks fabulous! Did you make it?'

'Of course. We'll have some now and then the children can help us finish it off tomorrow.'

As he finished the last mouthful Peter laid down his spoon and fork and sighed. 'That was brilliant. Superb. Let's do without the coffee. We'll clear up and then I'm taking you to bed.'

Peter left the dining room carrying the pudding plates and she stood gazing out of the window, listening to him stacking the dishwasher. However much he disliked it, she was going back, but she wouldn't let him suffer. He of all men needed support, because of the relentless, unrewarding, lifelong task he had undertaken when he was ordained. He deserved all her love.

Caroline carried their unused coffee cups into the kitchen. Peter turned to look at her. 'That was a lovely meal. It's fun eating with the children, but this meal on our own on Sundays is very pleasant.'

'Indeed it is.' There was a pause and then she said. 'You are right.'

'About the meal, you mean?'

'No, about me having to be circumspect.'

'Ah!'

'Sorry I let it happen. But he is fun.'

'He is. Great fun.'

'But I will be careful. Will this dish fit in the dishwasher or shall I wash it in the sink?'

'Leave it to soak. The cat flap's open, the back door is locked. Everything is shipshape and Bristol fashion and now we're going to bed.'

By the time Caroline had finished in the bathroom, having let Peter take first turn while she made sure the children were nicely tucked up and she had indulged herself remembering how once she'd longed to have children in bedrooms to check on before she went to bed, and how she wished she had more than she had, Peter was already sitting up in bed. As she walked towards him he swung his legs out to sit on the edge and began unbuttoning her shirt.

'I promise I won't let work get in the way of . . . damn it!' Caroline stood between his knees and pulled him close and kissed his mouth deeply and pleasurably, adoring his taste and the sharp, fresh smell of the soap he'd used. Heart and soul, mind and body she loved him. 'I love you so very much. I wouldn't willingly do anything to harm you and yours.'

'And I love you. Every single inch of your body, every single inch of your mind. Every single inch of whatever it is that's you, I love.'

By this time her shirt was off and he was unzipping her skirt. She kissed the top of his head. 'Somehow, every single centimetre wouldn't sound nearly so passionate and meaningful, would it?'

Peter pulled at her skirt. 'Wriggle out of it. That's it. Whoever invented tights?'

'A nun?'

'I'm sure stockings were much more fun. Just think of me undoing those lacy suspenders! One by one.'

'Gladly.' She helped him finish undressing her. He got back into bed, lifted the duvet for her and she slid under it and lay beside him. She relaxed against his naked body, enjoying the gentle exploratory touch of his fingers, and feeling amazed yet again that he never failed to create this wondrous sensation in her. She grinned and said, 'Peter?'

'Mmmmm?'

'I'm glad it was you I married, because I find your vigorous sexual appetite so gloriously satisfying.'

2

On Mondays Peter always went to Penny Fawcett, so it was Caroline who answered the telephone in his study when it rang just before half-past nine.

'Good morning, Turnham Malpas Rectory, Caroline Harris speaking.'

'It's me, Harriet. I'm in a hurry. What night are you free this week?'

'I'll check the parish diary. Hold on.' She gripped the receiver between her jaw and her shoulder and took a lopsided view of Peter's diary. 'By the looks of it, unless something comes up today, Peter's only free night is Wednesday. Why?'

'Wednesday it is. I'm having a dinner party. Will you come?'

'Love to!'

'Eight for eight thirty?'

'Lovely. Nothing special is it, not birthday or anything?'

'No, just for fun. See you.'

Caroline put down the receiver. Dinner party. Lovely. Just what she needed. What should she wear? Harriet and Jimbo had seen just about everything she had. Should she? . . . Yes, she would.

Sylvia was in the kitchen filling the washing machine with bed linen.

'We've had an invitation to dinner from Harriet and Jimbo. On Wednesday. Will you be able to sit in for us?'

'Delighted. It's ages since you went out to enjoy yourselves. What time?'

'Eight o'clock.'

'Fine. You won't mind if Willie comes too?'

25

'Of course not. I'm off into Culworth this morning. Is there anything you need?'

'Nothing I need, but you did say you'd see about some new sheets for the children's beds.'

'I did. I'll get those while I'm there. I shan't be back for lunch but I shall be home before you leave.'

'That's lovely. Have a good time, enjoy yourself. You could do with a change.'

'I'm looking dreary, am I?'

Sylvia contemplated Caroline. She looked her up and down, especially at her face, her lovely grey eyes taking in every contour. 'You're looking so well, so wonderfully well. But people your age need to be in the swing of things, and what with caring for the Rector and those two lovely holy terrors of yours and all the things you do for the church, you do get bogged down with good deeds. So go swing a loose leg and enjoy yourself. I'll answer the phone and things.'

'Thanks, Sylvia. I do appreciate all you do for us. How we would have managed without you when the twins first came I do not know.'

Sylvia switched on the machine and, with her face turned away from Caroline so she wouldn't see the tears beginning to rise in her eyes, ordered her off the premises quick smart.

Caroline took her bag from the hall cupboard, checked she had her car keys and her credit cards, and left by the back door to get her car out of the garage.

Driving to Culworth was the easy bit, parking when she got there was a whole different ball game. A huge new car park had been provided by the council a matter of only a year ago, but already it wasn't big enough to cope. Eventually she found a space in the station car park.

Culworth wasn't exactly a metropolis as far as fashion shopping was concerned, but there were a couple of dress shops still calling themselves 'boutiques' which she favoured, one in the market square and the other in Abbey Close.

Coming to the market square she tried that boutique first. Madame Marie-Claire could find nothing to suit her. Caroline left amidst a hail of apologies.

The other boutique, named 'Veronique', at least gave Caroline a choice. In the curtained cubicle with its gilt chair and wall-to-wall mirrors Caroline tried six dresses. One was red and close fitting and up-to-the-minute and outrageous. She remembered another red dress, not hers but someone else's, worn in defiance at a dinner party at Harriet's many moons ago, when she, Caroline, sick with longing to have Peter's children had offered him a divorce when they got home. The black? Too severe. The green? Bilious. The blue? Too safe. The other black? Too matronly. Silvery grey? Didn't suit her mood.

'Look, Veronica, I like this red the best, but I've got to have time to think about it. I shall be back, because I must have something new to wear, but it is a bit daring, isn't it, for me?'

'Maybe it's right for your mood, though. Whatever you've purchased here in the past has been elegant but cautious. But this ... this says something, doesn't it?' She held the slim red dress up in front of her and swirled it around and made it look as though it was doing a tango all by itself.

'It does. And that's the trouble. Dare I?'

'The colour is very flattering, your dark hair and eyes, you know. If you were fair like your daughter then I would say no because it would obliterate you. But this ... oh la la!'

Caroline loved it. 'I'll go have lunch and then I'll come back. Is that all right? Do you mind, keeping it on one side for me?'

'Not at all, for a valued customer like you, Dr Harris, anything is possible.'

'I'll pop into the Belfry for lunch and have a think.'

At twelve-thirty the Belfry Restaurant was rapidly filling up. A waitress signalled an empty table in the corner by the window. She wended her way between the tables, took off her jacket, hung it on the back of her chair and sat down facing the crowded room. She remembered sitting here at this very table when she'd tried to tell Peter she had cancer and realised she couldn't find the words. The menu didn't seem to have changed much. A shadow fell across it and she looked up ready to apologise to the waitress because she hadn't yet made up her mind. But it wasn't the waitress, it was Hugo Maude.

'It is Caroline, isn't it? What an amazing coincidence. I decided to come out this morning to get out of Jimbo and Harriet's hair for a while and they suggested here for a quiet lunch. They didn't say I should find you lunching here. May I?' He put his hand on the back of the other chair and raised his eyebrows at her.

'Of course.'

'Do you often eat lunch alone?'

'I can't remember the last time I had lunch alone in Culworth. I came in to . . .'

'Yes?'

'Have a change of scene.'

Hugo put his head to one side and studied her. 'And why not? Have you ordered?'

'No, not yet.'

'I'm having the lamb cutlets. I perused the menu in the window before I decided to come in.'

'I will too, then. Are you enjoying your convalescing?'

Hugo's face became bleak. 'I need applause, you know. Pathetic, isn't it? A grown man. I miss it very seriously indeed. It kind of feeds me.'

'It's applause you deserve, according to Peter. He saw you in *Macbeth* some years ago. He thought you were brilliant.'

'Peter? Who's Peter?'

'My husband.'

'Not the Rector?' Caroline nodded. 'Amazing. He has real presence, hasn't he? He should have been on the stage.'

'You're joking. The only place he wants to be is where he is. In the pulpit.'

'Truly amazing. But you've no children?'

'We have two, a boy and a girl.'

The waitress came and Hugo ordered for the two of them. 'Wine also?'

'No thanks. I'm driving.'

'No wine, then. Mineral water, please.' He smiled at the young waitress and she must have found it devastating for she blushed to the roots of her hair.

Caroline couldn't resist taunting him. 'You really are a charmer, aren't you? Do you do it deliberately?'

Hugo looked appalled. 'Of course not. I'm just naturally charming. But what about you? I find you very interesting.'

'How can you? You don't know me.'

'But I'm very sensitive to the people I meet. It's all part of being an actor. We have to get into the characters we play and the habit somehow creeps into real life. I can *feel* people's auras, and yours is reaching out to me. How did you come by the children?'

'What do you mean?'

'Well, I sense they're not yours. The emphatic way you replied and the slight hesitation as you chose your words.'

Caroline, avoiding his glance, said quietly, 'No, they're not mine.'

'Ah! Sorry. Obviously I've touched on a sore point. You'd feel better if you accepted it, welcomed the situation, faced up to it instead of covering up about it. It happens all the time, people adopting children, you know. But there's something different about this, isn't there? I can't quite put my finger on what it is, but you're shielding someone, aren't you?'

'I think you'd better eat both our lamb cutlets because I don't want mine. I think your behaviour is quite insufferably rude to someone you've only just met. You must think that your fame gives you *carte blanche* to offend, *carte blanche* to ride roughshod over people's feelings. Well, you're not riding roughshod over mine, thank you. I'll pay my half on the way out.' Caroline gathered her things together and rose from her chair, almost blind with rage.

Hugo rose too and held out a restraining hand. 'Please, please accept my apologies. I'm so sorry. Believe me, I really am.'

'Too late, I'm afraid.' Her anger infuriated her. How could she be so foolish as to make such an undignified exit from such a public place. That was twice now that he'd made her feel a fool. But he'd cut right to the core of her, for she was shielding Peter, let there be no mistake about that.

She strode lunchless into 'Veronique' and bought the red dress without even trying it on again.

'You'll love wearing it,' Veronica said.

'You're right, I shall.'

After a great deal of deliberation Caroline bought an elaborate Indian silver necklace in the ethnic shop at the corner of Deansgate and a lipstick in Boots, tried on several pairs of sandals hoping to find a pair suited to her new dress, but didn't, and went home to Peter.

She put her car away and entered the Rectory through the back door. One glance at the clock told her that Sylvia would already have left but that she still had half an hour before she collected the children from school.

Caroline dumped her purchases on the kitchen table and couldn't resist another look at the dress. She flicked it out of the carrier and held it in front of her. Her conclusion was that she must have had a brainstorm. What was she thinking, buying a dress like this? She would look a complete idiot wearing it at a dinner party in the country. Caroline flung it down on the table. She heard laughter coming from the study and went to stand in the hall to hear better.

It was Hugo talking to Peter. She hoped he wasn't using his amateur psychoanalysis on Peter. Better take the bull by the horns.

As she opened the study door she said, 'I thought I heard a voice I recognised.'

'Hello, darling, had a good day? Hugo's called to return your jacket, you left it in the restaurant.'

'Oh! Thank you. I hadn't realised. Thank you very much.'

Hugo bowed slightly. 'Not at all, my pleasure.' A silence fell.

Caroline filled it by offering to make tea before she went to meet the children.

Hugo refused. Peter accepted.

'I'll go make one, then. Won't be long.'

She could hear Peter seeing Hugo out and heaved a sigh of relief.

Peter came in the kitchen for his tea. 'You know he really is very pleasant. Considering his fame, he is a very modest chap, doesn't push it in your face like some would.' He saw her making a sandwich. 'That's not for me, is it?'

'No. It's for me.'

'I thought you'd had lunch with Hugo.'

'No, I walked out.'

'Walked out? Why?' He saw her shopping on the table. 'That a new dress? It looks extremely eyecatching.'

'It is. I walked out because he got me very angry and I'm not telling you why.'

'Oh, I see. I won't ask, then.'

'No, don't. Here's your tea. I'll move my shopping.'

Caroline devoured her sandwich with one eye on the clock.

Peter drank his tea. 'I'll collect the children, if you like.'

'Thanks. We've been invited to Harriet's on Wednesday. I checked the parish diary, you're free and Sylvia's promised to sit in.'

'Oh good, I shall look forward to that.'

'Yes, I expect you shall.'

'Shall I be taking you in that dress?'

'You shall. If I dare to wear it. Not quite the thing for a Rector's wife, is it, do you think?'

Peter heard the challenge in her voice. 'I don't see why not.'

'Oh good. Because I'm wearing it, and damn the lot of them.'

'My darling girl! What lot?'

'Your parishioners. Your prim, narrow-minded, gossiping, trouble-making parishioners, that's who.'

'What's brought this on? It's not like you to be so miserable. We'll talk about it, shall we, when the children are in bed?'

'We won't, you've a meeting.'

Peter stood up. 'Must go get the children. So I have. Damn meetings. Well, tonight then, when I get back.'

'Perhaps.'

Wednesday evening came round all too quickly. Sylvia had admired the dress, though privately she thought it unsuitable for a Rector's wife, but it appeared to be something Caroline needed and as far as Sylvia was concerned if Dr Harris wanted to wear it, it was all right by her. When she saw her actually wearing it Sylvia was very surprised, it was even more out of character than she had first thought. But the Rector seemed pleased with it, so it must be all right. 'Have a good time! Forget everything and just enjoy yourselves!'

When Caroline and Peter left the Rectory to walk to Harriet's they met a total of four villagers on their way. They all greeted them with something just short of surprise.

'Evening, Rector. Evening, Dr Harris.' This from Anne Parkin who typed for the parish.

'Good evening, Caroline! How lovely you look.' This from Muriel who was popping round with a cake for her new neighbour. 'Enjoy yourselves.'

Barry Jones heading for the pub gave Caroline a thumbs up, his face twitching with a grin. 'Good evening, Rector. Dr Harris. Nice evening!'

Jimmy also heading towards the pub raised his cap and at the same time eyed Caroline from head to toe. He grinned and commented, 'Going somewhere smart, eh? Wish I was thirty years younger! You're a lucky man, Rector.'

'I am. You're right.'

Peter and Caroline were the last to arrive. Gathered in the sitting room when they went in were Gilbert and Louise Johns, Craddock Fitch, Jimbo's mother, and Liz and Neville Neal. Their drinks were being replenished by Jimbo.

He broke off to greet the two of them and said 'Wow!!' when he saw Caroline's dress. 'Give us a twirl! Wonderful! Quite wonderful. Harriet will be jealous. What will you have to drink?'

'Vodka and orange, please. You like it then?'

'Like it? I should say.'

Peter said, 'So do I. It's revealed a whole new side of my wife, has this dress. I'm beginning to feel old-fashioned.'

'Well, you're not darling, you're just right. Thanks, Jimbo.' Caroline took her drink and went off to speak with everyone. Grandmama was barely civil, but Craddock Fitch made a great fuss of her and made her laugh which she badly needed.

Harriet came in to say dinner was almost on the table and where was Hugo?

'Not down yet.'

'Go give him a call, Jimbo. You know what he's like.'

'I'll just finish in the drinks department and then I will.'

Harriet sorted them out as to where they should sit and Caroline found herself between Gilbert and a vacant chair which she presumed was meant for Hugo. Trust Harriet to place him next to her. She was determined not to let him get under her skin. Never again. She would behave as if their contretemps in the restaurant had never happened.

Just before Harriet served the vichyssoise Hugo came in.

'So sorry. Am I late? I fell asleep by mistake.' It wasn't only Caroline who was charmed by his smile. She noticed Louise go gently pink and despite her misgivings about him Grandmama succumbed too.

Jimbo did the introductions. 'This is Hugo Maude, who requires no introduction to you. My mother you already know, this here is Louise, sitting next to Caroline is her husband Gilbert, county archaeologist and church choir master, this delightful creature is Liz Neal, wife of Neville Neal, right here, Neville is an accountant and the church treasurer, and of course you've met Peter, and last but not least Mr Fitch, the owner of the Big House you glimpsed between the trees yesterday.'

Hugo went around the table shaking hands and kissing as he thought appropriate. Caroline's hand got a small squeeze and she received a kiss on her cheek too.

Jimbo and Harriet were practised hosts, the food delicious, and the evening went by in the most enjoyable way. There was plenty of laughter and Hugo provided that extra bit of zest needed when it was a dinner party where everyone knew everyone else and the conversation might have become moribund. He told some splendid theatrical stories which everyone except Grandmama enjoyed. She was occupied casting scathing glances at Caroline, the last of which Peter had intercepted. Then it was Grandmama's turn to grow pink, because Peter, who could do no wrong in her eyes, gave her one of his sad smiles. Well, if he didn't mind Caroline dressing as though she was out to catch a man then who was she to complain. But that gown really was an eye stopper, not at all suitable for someone in her position. What was it Harriet was saying, she'd missed that. She watched her spoon some more raspberries into her mouth and heard her mumble, 'Don't you think it would be a good idea? In all the years we've been here we've never done a play. Have we?'

An energetic burst of conversation answered her query. Peter's powerful voice overrode everyone else's and they all stopped speaking and listened to what he had to say. 'I think it would be an excellent idea. It might be the beginning of the Turnham Malpas Amateur Dramatic Society. We have the stage in the Church Hall, we have the lighting, it's all yours for the asking. There's hardly ever been a show of any kind put on except the Gang Show each year.'

Harriet said, 'Hands up all the people who would be willing to take part.'

Grandmama refrained from volunteering and so did Mr Fitch. Another notable exception was Louise.

Caroline said, 'Well, the baby is very young. I can understand you not wanting to be in a play, it takes so much time rehearsing and things.'

Gilbert answered for her. 'It's not that. Well, it is in a way. We're expecting another baby, you see.'

Grandmama was scandalised. 'Another one. Good heavens, you've only just got one.'

'Congratulations!'

'That's wonderful.'

'You must be pleased.'

'Oh we are. Gilbert wants four.'

'Four! Good heavens. Does your mother know?' Grandmama downed the last of her wine and signalled to Jimbo she needed a refill.

The conversation broke up for a moment and it took Harriet some time to get it back to the play. 'I did think we might ask . . .' she nodded her head in Hugo's direction. 'How about it, Hugo?'

He'd been preoccupied entertaining Caroline and took a moment to realise he was being addressed. 'How about what?'

'How about helping us with the play? Directing it even? What say you?'

'Me? It can't be done in a fortnight, you know, and I wouldn't want to outstay my welcome.'

Jimbo charitably suggested that if he was helping with a village play then he wouldn't be outstaying his welcome. He could stay as long as it took.

Harriet, poised on the brink of victory, beamed at him. 'Well? Say yes. We'd be so proud to have you on board.'

'What play would you want to do?'

Suggestions flooded out across the dining table. '*Blithe Spirit*', '*Absurd Person Singular*', '*Arsenic and Old Lace*', '*Noises Off*', '*The Odd Couple*'. Ideas ebbed and flowed.

'Well ... what do you think?' Jimbo asked Hugo.

'Yes, yes, mmmmm, I'll have to think about it. If I say yes can I be leading man and producer?'

'If you wish. Why not?'

'We haven't asked you to do something which is kind of not the thing for a famous actor to do, have we? I mean, we wouldn't want to put a spanner in the works or anything.' Caroline smiled at him.

Hugo smiled back and for a moment the conversation came to a standstill. Caroline recollected herself and picked up her glass of wine intending to take a sip, but Hugo took it from her, held on to her hand and said, 'My dear Caroline, how thoughtful of you to consider me.'

Grandmama cleared her throat loudly and it broke the moment.

Hugo raised his glass to them all, drank from it, put it down and began speaking. 'It would be wonderful to do something just for fun. I don't mean to diminish the idea by making it sound as though I wouldn't be taking it seriously because I would, take it seriously, I mean. But just for once to work at something which didn't demand high profile action on my part would be wonderful. After all it isn't as if the whole world is going to know, not like they do when it's Stratford or the West End or something. We can just quietly get on with it can't we? Money isn't a problem ...?'

'It certainly isn't.' Mr Fitch shook his head. 'I should be proud to be associated with such an enterprise. Proud, yes very proud and I would like to commit myself here and now. I will underwrite whatever expenses you may incur. Yes, I certainly will. Who knows, this could be the beginning of something big.' He beamed at everyone around the table and accepted their thanks with delight. 'Now, Hugo, what do you think to that?'

'I am humbled by your generosity. Humbled indeed I am. We shan't be incurring massive expense, I would keep a stern eye on that side, believe me. Now, if I agreed to ...'

'Something quite appalling has occurred to me.' Caroline's strangled voice drew their attention. 'How on earth can we expect Hugo, who has worked with most of the famous names on the

British stage, how can we expect him to work with *us*, a load of complete amateurs? What presumption. We ought to be ashamed of ourselves even thinking of it. I'm sorry, so very sorry that we've put you in such an embarrassing position. Please accept our apologies. We all got carried away.'

A deathly silence greeted her outburst. Hugo was the first to break the deadlock. Very quietly he said, 'Please believe me when I say I would be honoured to work with you all. This business of the virus, I did have a virus certainly but it was exacerbated by the fact that I was also having a complete nervous collapse brought on by overwork. This rest I'm having, the media believe it to be because of the virus, which it is but also it's because I have run out of steam. After years of working like a maniac it is very difficult for me to do *nothing*, but I daren't, not yet, go back on the professional stage because it could be the end of not only me as an actor but the end of *me*. Producing this play would be heaven. You'd all be helping me to resuscitate myself. The decision is yours, but I hope you say you will.'

Jimbo raised his glass and toasted Hugo. 'Thank you for being so frank with us. Neither Harriet nor I had any idea how ill you have been. If we can help in any way then we will, and we'd all be honoured and privileged to work with you.'

'Coffee. I think I'll get the coffee. Anyone prefer tea?' They all wanted coffee. With Caroline's help Harriet swiftly cleared away the pudding and retreated to the kitchen to attend to the coffee making.

Harriet banged about making the coffee saying as she worked, 'God! that was awful. I'd no idea.'

'Awfully brave of him to admit to it, don't you think? I feel dreadful that I forced him into having to come out with it.'

'You musn't, you did right to bring us all up short. It was presumptuous of me. I can't think what gave me the idea. I must have been mad. I've put the cups out on the side there. We just need the spoons, they're in the cupboard in the dining room.'

'You have to like him, don't you?'

Harriet grinned. 'He's a darling. An absolute darling, but don't tell Jimbo I said that. I'm amazed he's so agreeable to the whole idea.'

'It must be Hugo's charm.'

'Well, he's certainly got plenty of that, so just watch yourself.'

'Me? Come on, for heaven's sake.'

'Yes, you. Carry the sugar in, will you?'

Caroline and Peter fell into bed at midnight, having left the party well before the end in deference to Sylvia and Willie.

'Peter, we can't both of us be in it, can we? That would be impossible, finding a sitter every time.'

'No, we can't, not both of us. But you could.'

'Do you think so?'

'Oh yes. With my height I'd be quite out of place on a stage.'

'Have you ever done anything on stage before?'

'Never, and I don't intend to.'

'Hugo says you have such presence he can't understand why you're not an actor.'

'Well, that's one bit of his amateur psychoanalysis that is way off the mark.'

'You think he does that too, do you?'

'Oh yes. He does. Has he been practising on you?'

She was on the brink of telling him about the incident in the restaurant but stopped herself just in time. 'I'm nearly asleep. It's the wine.'

Peter reached over to kiss her goodnight. 'God bless you.'

'And you.' Caroline was nowhere near ready for sleep but not for anything would she tell Peter what had made her leave the restaurant in such anger. Nor did she want to tell him how Hugo fascinated her. Nor that Hugo wanted her to be his leading lady in whatever play he decided upon. Nor that she was looking forward to the rehearsals with more enthusiasm than she had felt about anything for a long time. Not since ... well, she wouldn't think about cancer now. Not now. She would put that right at the back of her mind once and for all and get on with her life.

3

A note had been put through the Rectory letterbox addressed to Caroline. Peter picked it up and propped it against the vase on the hall table. He didn't recognise the writing, but then Caroline was always getting notes about one thing and another. When he heard her come back from seeing the children to school he called out, 'There's a note for you, darling, on the hall table.'

'Thanks.'

She came into the study with it in her hand. He watched her tear it open.

'It's from Hugo. There's a meeting about the play on Monday night. You're free aren't you, if I remember rightly?'

'I am. In fact I've three evenings free next week. Almost unprecedented. Shall we have an evening out together while we have a chance?'

'Why not?'

'There's bound to be seats going at the Royal. Culworth isn't exactly at the forefront where theatre-going is concerned, is it?'

'There might be rehearsals planned. Let's wait until Monday night before we book. Just in case.'

Peter patted his knee. 'Come and sit on my knee for a moment.' With his arms encircling her and her feet tucked into the kneehole of his desk he said, 'This play is really important to you, isn't it?'

'Yes, it is.'

'I'm glad. Something completely different from church meetings and children. There's a light come back into your eyes I haven't seen for a while.'

'Is there?'

'Yes. I hope, no, I *know* you'll do marvellously in this play. I shall be so proud of you. You must throw yourself into it and forget all about us. Go for it, you know. What an opportunity for you and for the village. He's such a generous man, doing this without a thought for his reputation.' They sat quietly for a few moments then he said, 'Love you, must get on.' He kissed her and tipped her gently off his knee.

Caroline had to make absolutely sure he didn't mind her being involved with the play.

'Of course not. Why should I mind?'

'You shouldn't, I suppose, I don't know why I asked. You hold me by the tightest of bonds and yet I am totally free.'

'Good. That's how it should be.'

'Do you feel free?'

He had to smile. 'No. I'm bound hand and foot to you. I'm not free and never will be, not even in the life hereafter.'

'Oh God! What a responsibility that is for me!'

'You musn't feel like that, because for me it's pure joy.'

She held his face between her hands, looked deeply into his eyes and briefly saw into his soul; he was alight with love for her. Right at this very moment, love like his she did not deserve. Why she didn't deserve it she didn't rightly know, but there were stirrings inside herself she couldn't analyse, and what was worse didn't want to analyse. It was as though she was at a crossroads, not knowing which way she would turn. Unable to find anything to say in reply to the look in his eyes, she tapped him lightly on his shoulder. 'I've some addresses to call at to collect jumble for Saturday, I'll be a while.'

'I'll have gone by the time you get back.'

After she'd left, Peter sat gazing out of the window. He watched Vera wave to Sylvia as she passed her house. Saw Jimmy setting out with Sykes at his heels. Caught sight of one of the weekenders in shorts and the briefest of tops setting off to the Store by the looks of the large shopping bag she was carrying. The busy life of the village went on, day in day out, despite the trials and tribulations which beset it. He thought about Hugo who could turn out to be a trial and a tribulation without doubt. Though what a lovely chap he was; friendly, caring, very charming, obviously in need of a respite from his demanding life and what better place was there than here in this village amongst friends? It was ridiculous to worry about the man, but somehow Caroline's enthusiasm for being in Hugo's play worried him.

Deep in his heart he became filled with a dark foreboding.

4

It had been quiet all evening in the Royal Oak until the crowd from the meeting came in. But then it was always quiet on Mondays in summer, a fact for which Georgie and Dicky were quite grateful. Summer weekends were hectic, good for business as Georgie always said with a laugh, but frantic nevertheless. Both she and Dicky were pleased with the way things had gone since Bryn left. In fact they were excessively pleased with themselves. The last eighteen months had been far harder work than Dicky could ever have contemplated, but with Jimbo Charter-Plackett teaching him how to keep the books and do the ordering and Bel helping at the bar when they were desperate, they were managing to keep their heads well and truly above water.

It was the first chance Dicky had had to get a close look at this newcomer they were all talking about. Georgie had swooned over his good looks and his reputation when she'd seen him in the Store, and he could see at first glance that she was right. He was handsome and not half.

'Good evening, mine host! Drinks all round on me. What shall you have?' Hugo looked at each in turn and they gave Dicky their orders. Georgie, unable to resist a chance to speak with such a famous figure, came to give Dicky a hand.

'Good evening, Mr Maude.'

'Mr Maude indeed! Hugo, please. I am amongst friends, surely. You are?'

'Georgie Fields.'

'Lucky man is Mr Fields, very lucky indeed.' He grinned at Dicky who let the mistake pass.

'Let's put two tables together then we can all sit round. Do you mind, Georgie?' Under the devastating beauty of his smile Georgie capitulated. Putting two tables together usually meant the group got very rowdy and she normally demurred if the idea was requested. It was the way Hugo's lips opened so generously, showing those immaculately straight teeth, with just one slightly crooked one which gave him the appearance of a boy, not a man.

'Of course. Dicky, give them a hand, will you?'

In no time at all Dicky had pushed two tables together and placed the tray of drinks in the middle. There was a lot of laughing and joking and sorting out of where to sit and whose drink was which. In the middle of it Caroline appeared from the lavatories. Instantly Hugo stood up. His expressive face broke into a warm smile for her which was observed by almost everyone in the bar.

'Caroline! What would you like to drink?'

'Just an orange juice, please.' Harriet pulled up a chair next to her and patted the seat. 'Sit here, look.'

Caroline's orange juice arrived in front of her with a flourish. 'Thank you, Hugo, that's lovely.'

Harriet nudged her. 'Well? What do you think?'

'About what?'

'The play!'

'I think it's going to be brilliant. A wonderful choice.'

'So do I. And it's really rather thrilling doing what is its first real outing on the stage in its present form. If it gets eventually to the West End, well . . .'

'Exactly.' Caroline sipped her drink leaving the others to make all the going with the one liners and jokes. She was in a quandary of the first order. Reading through the script which Hugo had so painstakingly photocopied on Jimbo's copier she had been appalled at the intimacy between herself and Hugo demanded by the play. Not that she had to be naked or anything like that, after all they couldn't go that far in a Church Hall. There were limits, even today. But they did have to kiss frequently, and mercifully the curtains closed on the scene where . . .

Heaven alone knew what the parish would think. If there was a moment to withdraw that moment was right now. This instant. Right now. She'd drop the bombshell immediately. As though in answer to her doubts there was a brief lull in the conversation. She put down her glass and said her piece.

'I'm afraid I'm going to have to withdraw, or take a different part. I think this part is beyond me. So, I'm sorry, but there we are.' There were gasps of disappointment all round the table.

Liz Neal said, 'Oh please, you're so right for the part, do do it, please.'

Neville agreed, 'You're so right for it, Caroline, you can't let us down.'

'I can and I will, I'm afraid.'

Hugo said loudly enough for the entire clientele to hear, 'Afraid. That's what the problem is. You've said far more than you know when you said, "I can and I will, I'm *afraid*." You are afraid, afraid of the challenge, afraid of Peter, afraid of what the parish will say. Maybe even afraid the bishop might hear what you've been up to. Tut tut.'

Caroline almost cringed at his words, they were so close to the truth.

Harriet was livid. 'Hugo! really. Be quiet, just shut up. If Caroline feels she can't do the part then that is that, it's not for you nor anyone else to query her motives.'

'Why not? This play could be the making of her.'

Harriet snorted. 'She doesn't need "making". Her life has been a complete success without your assistance. Now shut up and find yourself another leading lady.'

'I only meant the part would give her a chance to face up to herself.' He took Caroline's hand in his. 'My dear Caroline, I'm so sorry if I have upset you. I know I'm outspoken, and I apologise. You're not used to the cut and thrust of the theatrical world . . .'

Harriet interrupted. 'Not "cut and thrust". Bitchiness would be more accurate. You're making matters worse, so *be quiet.*'

'That's all right, Harriet, I can fight my own battles. I don't want to do this part because I . . . well I just can't do it.'

Hugo, seeing that bullying was getting him nowhere, changed his tactics. 'Go home and think about it. Sleep on it, as they say. You're so right for the part, you see. I can't see anyone else in it.' He addressed the other members of the cast. 'When she read tonight I knew it in my bones. You can all see her in the part, can't you?'

He looked at them each in turn and they half-heartedly agreed with him. 'You see. They all feel the same.'

Caroline said, 'I'll sleep on it then. Yes, I will. Give you a decision tomorrow. Though I'm quite sure Liz or Harriet would be just as good.'

'Oh no, we wouldn't.'

'I'll leave now, if you don't mind.' She stood up to go. 'Goodnight everyone.'

'Goodnight. Goodnight.'

Hugo followed her out. 'I'll see you to your door.'

'For heaven's sakes there's no need for that.'

'There is. I owe you an apology.'

'For what?'

'For trying to bully you. It wasn't fair.' He turned to face her and took hold of each of her hands. 'I know you will be great. You and me together, we'll make this play. I know it's only a small-time production, but that's no reason for not doing the best we can.'

'If that's all it is then I will think about it. I'll tell you in the morning. It's all very well you saying I ought to ignore my responsibilities to Peter and . . . the diocese and such, but they're there and I can't avoid them.'

By now they'd reached the rectory door. Caroline searched for her key. Hugo took it from her and put it in the lock.

'There. In you go. Sleep tight.' He gave her the lightest of kisses on her lips, stroked her arm comfortingly and pushed open the door for her.

'True as I'm 'ere I saw 'em. He'd been holding her hands and then he kissed her. I wouldn't be telling the truth if I said he'd made it last a while because he didn't, but he kissed her, right there under the Rectory lamp, plain as day for all to see.'

Sylvia sat up in bed appalled. 'Willie, are you sure? It's dark, you could have been mistaken.'

'I'm not. Shall I turn out the light?'

'Yes.' Sylvia snuggled up to Willie. 'I can't believe it of her, though when she went and bought that red dress I knew there was something afoot.'

'Holding her hands he was. Couldn't hear what they was saying but actions speak louder than words.'

'Oh I know. But there, let's be honest. You know what these actors are like, kissing and that. I bet they'd kiss someone who had the plague if it meant a part in a film or something.'

'Daresay they would, but what's he wanting from Dr Harris, that's what I'd like to know.'

'Willie! You don't think . . .'

'Maybe. Something to entertain himself with while he recups, or whatever they call it.'

'Whatever will the Rector have to say?'

'Whatever it is, he'd better say it quick before it's too late.'

'She's been in a funny mood for a while. That cancer business took her back and not half. It was the children, you see. She couldn't stand the thought of them being left without her, and her not seeing 'em growing up. She loves 'em that much.' Sylvia dug under the pillow for her handkerchief and wiped her eyes. 'And so do I, I love 'em too. I've never had a happier time in my life since I went to work there.'

''ere 'ere. What about since you married me?'

In the darkness Sylvia smiled. 'You're all part and parcel, aren't you? Went there to work, met you and that. It's all one and the same. If I suspect he's up to something more than producing a play I'll kill 'im. So help me I will. I'll kill 'im.'

'Sylvia!'

'I mean it, and I wouldn't care how many years I spent in prison, it'd be worth it.'

'Right scandal that'd be. What would you say when they asked you why you did it?'

Sylvia thought for a moment. 'I'd say it was a crime of passion, 'cos I'd fallen for 'im and he was ignoring me! It was jealousy, that's right, that was my motive. Jealousy.'

Willie was affronted. 'Sounds as though I'm not satisfying you as I should.'

'You're all right on that score, it's just a ruse so I don't have to tell the truth.'

'Which is?'

'I killed him to stop him ruining a very happy marriage. They love each other, at bottom. It's just that she's feeling trapped at the moment. If only . . .'

Willie rolled over and put his arms round her. 'Never mind, old love. It'll sort itself out.'

'Not easily, I'm afraid. You have to admit he's very appealing, very sexy and so good looking. There's something about his smile which is so attractive. He's kind of all male and all man and yet child all at the same time. It makes him very irresistible.'

'Any more of that and I'll be doing for 'im miself!'

'Oooo, Willie! You never would.'

'I would.'

'So, darling, what's this play called? Is it one I know or something Hugo's dreamt up?'

'Not dreamt up, no. It's a play written by a new playwright. It's been done once in Reading, or somewhere, and it flopped. Badly. It's been rejigged, bits cut out that didn't work, et cetera, and now Hugo is convinced the chap's got it right and he's dying to have a go with it. I read parts of it last night at the meeting and . . .'

'Yes?'

'Peter.'

'Yes?'

'Peter, it's quite . . . well, anyway, the part he wants me to take means a bit of kissing and that, and I wondered what you thought about it.'

'I see. What's it called?'

'*Dark Rapture.*'

'Mmmmm.'

'I know I'm being completely ridiculous and if I wasn't your wife it wouldn't matter two hoots really, but I am and that means complications and I've got to have you on my side before I say yes. Well, I did say yes and then I got cold feet last night in the bar and said I wouldn't do it.'

'What do the others think?'

'Hugo asked them and they kind of half-heartedly said yes, they wanted me to do it, so he took it as a definite yes, which it wasn't. You know how moral Harriet can get. She told him off.'

'Would you like to do it?'

Caroline nodded. 'Yes, I would. It feels like an affirmation that I'm taking life on again. I know it's only a village play, but ...'

'Then do it, so long as there's nothing you have to do which will be against everything you've ever stood for. There's no nudity or anything, is there?'

'Oh no, of course not. There couldn't be in a Church Hall, could there? There's the opportunity for naked flouncing about and it probably would be done that way if it got to the West End, but we're not doing it like that. And we're cutting out the worst of the swearing because I insisted it couldn't be said on church premises. Perhaps I'm being overly careful, I don't know. Nowadays anything seems to go.'

'Can I see the script?'

Caroline hesitated for a moment and then said, 'I'll go get it.'

Peter spent an hour going through the script. He had certain misgivings but that was only when he read it from the point of view of Caroline in the leading part. Otherwise the play was good, and in a strange, convoluted way had a strong moral theme to it. In the end good triumphed.

Peter could hear Sylvia singing as she worked upstairs, he called out 'Sylvia, where's Caroline?'

'Gone to the Store, Rector, she won't be long. Is there anything I can do?'

'No, that's all right. I'll speak to her when she gets back.'

Peter had a while to wait before Caroline returned. When she'd entered the Store a sudden silence had fallen and she became aware of sidelong glances at her, which she found puzzling.

'Jimbo, is Harriet here?'

'In the kitchens. Go through.' He raised his straw hat to her as she slipped past the till. At least he was looking her straight in the face if no one else was.

The kitchens at the back of the Store had been made by opening up a series of small rooms to become two big kitchens. One for outside catering and one for making the confectionery and savoury products with which they filled the Store freezers. Caroline herself had been grateful for their homemade quality on more than one occasion when she'd been too busy to cook.

Harriet, wearing her white overalls and the net cap she wore in deference to the hygiene regulations, was elbow deep in a huge mixing bowl.

'Hi! Come to see me? Won't be a minute. Go get a coffee from the machine and I'll be with you in a trice. There's a couple of chairs in the freezer room. Take a pew there.'

Caroline did as she was told, found the chairs and sat down to wait. She should have waited for Peter's opinion before she'd come to see Harriet, but she had the feeling that whatever he said she'd still agree to doing the play. Hang whatever anyone else thought, she'd a right to please herself for once.

'Right. I'll just pour mine into a cup. I hate these plastic cups but there's no alternative when it's for the customers – the washing up, you know. Here, let's pour yours into one too. There, that's better. Well?'

'Well?'

'Oh, I thought you'd come to tell me something.'

'Oh, I see. Yes. I've decided. I'm doing it.'

'Wow!! This coffee's hot! Jimbo must have just brewed it. I'm glad. Very glad. Really pleased. It's going to be so exciting.'

'Peter's reading the script.'

'Oh. Right. Is that a good idea?'

'We are doing it in the Church Hall, so . . .'

'Of course. Yes, you're right.'

'Hugo doesn't know, I haven't seen him yet.'

'He's not feeling too perky this morning so he's having a lie in.'

'Right.'

'Caroline, you are sure you're doing the right thing? I mean, don't say yes and then change your mind half way through, will you?'

'Of course not. I've decided I'm doing the play no matter what.'

Harriet looked at her, curiously surprised by her emphatic reply, said as though she was still convincing herself she was right to do it. 'You are sure, aren't you? I mean it's not . . . well it's not Hugo, is it, by any chance? I do know him for the absolute charmer he is.'

'I am almost forty, Harriet. For heaven's sake, a husband and two children whom I adore. I'm quite insulted really that you should think that I might be so stupid as to . . .'

'What?'

'Take a liking to him. I swear things will not get out of hand. Honestly.'

'OK then.' Harriet stood up. 'Sorry, got to get on, must go. Stay and finish your coffee.'

'Harriet, tell me, has Hugo ever been married?'

'No. But he's had dozens of female "admirers", believe me. He's far too gorgeous to have escaped someone's clutches, don't you think?'

'Of course. Yes. Here, let me rinse the cups.'

'Nonsense, they can go in with the rest.' Uncharacteristically for Harriet she gave Caroline a kiss on her cheek. 'Take care. Take care.' And Caroline knew she wasn't referring to her crossing the road.

Mrs Jones was working in the little mail order office when Caroline walked by on her way out.

'Hello, Mrs Jones. How's things?'

'Fine, thanks. And you?'

'Fine, thanks. Lovely weather.'

'It is.' She snapped off the sticky tape on a parcel she was wrapping and called Caroline back. 'Dr Harris!'

Caroline came back and stood inside the doorway. 'Yes?'

'I wouldn't mind giving a hand with this play. Backstage and that, of course. Our Michelle would like to help, too. There'd be plenty of things to do besides acting, wouldn't there?'

'Of course. I'm sure there would be. I'll tell Hugo. He'll be delighted to find things for you to do.'

'I'm a dab hand with a needle and sewing machine if it's costumes.'

'Right. Well, it takes place in the nineteen twenties so I suppose, yes, we shall need a wardrobe mistress. I'll ask Hugo if that's all right, I'm sure he'll be pleased.'

'Then that's that.'

'Oh, but I think we should check with ...'

'Michelle and me, we'll be in charge of costumes.'

'If it's all right with Hugo, yes, that will be lovely.'

'It's all right, is it, this play? I mean, it's not disgusting? I wouldn't want our Michelle to be involved if it was.'

'The Rector's reading it this very minute.'

Mrs Jones laughed. 'Oh, well, if he says yes then it's OK. My Barry's been roped in by Mr Fitch to do the scenery, did you know?'

'No, I didn't. He'll be excellent for that job, won't he?'

'Of course. And Mr Charter-P's put Pat in charge of refreshments, two nights you're doing it, eh?'

'Friday and Saturday.'

'Right. Well, I'll get to the library and I'll get some books out on costume. Charleston and that.'

'That sounds wonderful. We need all the help we can get.'

'If Mr Fitch has his way there'll be a play done at least once a year. And why not? Time we brightened ourselves up. All the talent we've got in this village, we could get famous.'

Caroline said she thought fame might be a bit too ambitious.

'Just wait till the press get onto it. The famous Hugo Maude, no less. And he's lovely, isn't he? Came in here the other morning and sat perched on that cupboard there chatting away as if we'd known each other all our lives. I told him things I've never mentioned to a living soul and he understood, truly understood how hard life can be.'

'He is very understanding.'

Mrs Jones gave her a piercing look. 'We'll have to mind our Ps and Qs, though. We're all taking a fancy to him, not just . . .'

'Yes?'

Rather lamely Mrs Jones said, 'Not just the young ones.' She neatly lined up the parcel she'd just sealed alongside the edge of the table, half started to speak again and then changed her mind, cleared her throat, picked up a list and began to study it.

Caroline wished her good morning and went through to the Store.

Dottie Foskett was standing, arms folded, propped against the chill counter listening to her cousin Vera Wright. 'So, just as I was closing the curtains — after all, you have to be careful these days even in a village, come to think of it, even more so in a village — when I sees 'em arriving at the Rectory door step. Believe it or belive it not he kissed her, and I don't mean a peck on the cheek like we've all started doing since we joined the Common Market — I mean, I blame the French for it – right on her *lips*. Then he stroked her arm and she went in.'

'But it was dark that time o' night, you couldn't see.'

Vera nodded her head. 'Oh yes I could, 'cos the light comes on when you stand by the door. Lutronic or something, it is. So I saw 'em right enough.'

Dottie gave her a nudge. 'You're only jealous. You wish it was you he was kissing!'

'Make a change from my Don, I must say. He's lovely though, isn't he? He's got a face to die for. That good looking I can understand anyone falling for 'im, I really can. And his voice all sexy and that. I fell for 'im when he was on telly in that saucy serial a while back. Saw 'im almost naked, not his vital parts o'course, but near enough. Strips real well he does.'

Dottie's reply was scathing. 'You're forgetting how old you are.'

'I can still dream, can't I?' She leaned towards Dottie and confidentially whispered, 'I'm thinking of volunteering me services, behind the scenes and that. Might get a chance for a quick cuddle if I play me cards right.'

Dottie chortled, and in a loud, scandalised voice she said, 'Vera! You are a one, you really are. Quick cuddle! It wouldn't be the likes of you he'd give a quick cuddle to.' Neither of them had noticed Caroline paying for her shopping at the till. 'From what you saw, any quick cuddles have already been spoken for!'

The two of them reeled with laughter. Caroline lifted her carrier from the counter, put her purse away and marched red-faced and embarrassed out of the Store. How dare they speak of her like that! Anyone would think she was some empty-headed teenager. What else could it be but a purely professional partnership? And she'd put her heart and soul into making a real fist of it. She'd show them.

5

Vera, having collected some cigarettes for an old gentleman at the nursing home, went to wait outside the Store for the bus to Penny Fawcett for her afternoon cleaning shift. She couldn't believe her good luck when only a minute after she'd arrived she saw Hugo heading up Stocks Row towards the Store. This could be her moment. Though her knees went to jelly and her tongue appeared to have stuck to her teeth she said, 'Good afternoon, Mr Maude.' She ran her tongue round her teeth to wet them again while she waited for him to reach her.

'I don't believe I've had the pleasure.' She found her hand clasped in his and as through a thick fog heard him say, 'Please, call me Hugo.'

'It's Vera Wright. I live opposite the Rectory with me husband Don and me grandson Rhett. He's a gardener up at the Big House.'

'Indeed. He works for Mr Fitch, then?'

'He does, and a harder taskmaster you couldn't hope to find.'

'A very generous benefactor though.'

'Oh yes. He is. He's footing the bill for your play, isn't he?'

'Not *my* play, my dear Vera ... may I call you Vera?' Vera nodded. 'Not *my* play, *our* play.'

Melting before his charm Vera pulled herself together sufficiently to say, 'I was wondering about helping. Behind the scenes, o' course. Not on the stage. Amongst all my other jobs I'm in charge of the sewing where I work. I could help with anything like that.'

'We shall be needing help with the wardrobe. Look, we're having a meeting, just for half an hour, for people willing to help behind the scenes immediately before the first rehearsal on Friday. How about coming along to that? I'll listen to your ideas and we can . . .'

'My ideas? What ideas?'

Hugo explained about the play and it needing nineteen twenties' costumes.

'All straight up and down and no . . . yer know.' She shaped her hands over her ample bosom and instantly wished she'd hadn't drawn attention to it.

'Well, yes, that kind of thing.'

The bus ground to a halt in front of them.

'I've got to go,' she said. 'What time?'

'Seven o'clock. Church Hall. Friday.'

'Yer on.' Vera climbed aboard and showed her weekly season ticket to the woman driver, who, as she stamped on the accelerator, asked her who her new boyfriend was.

'Jealous, are yer? I've just been taken on as his wardrobe mistress.'

Someone guffawed at the back of the bus. '*Bed* mistress'd be a sight more comfortable, Vera.' The bus was in uproar. Vera felt like crawling under the seat not sitting on it. Honestly, you couldn't have a decent friendship with anyone round here without they all thought you were going to bed together. That was the last thing she had in mind. Then she recollected the warmth of his hands as he'd held her own, the tenderness of his eyes and the way his hair grew in a widow's peak and the width of his proud forehead. A tremor ran down her spine. He really was gorgeous. Vera stared out at the passing countryside and pulled herself together. All those bloody sheets to put through the ironer today. And if that old bat in number seven did it in her bed again today she'd give her notice in. Well, perhaps not. She'd have a few days off sick instead. Anyhow, she'd got what she wanted, a chance to work behind the scenes.

At a quarter to seven on Friday evening Vera came downstairs ready for off. Don, who was finishing his tea and contemplating a good read of the paper before he went off to work, looked in amazement when he answered her remark that she was ready for off and could he clear the table when he'd finished.

'I thought you said you were going to a meeting at the Church Hall.'

'I am.'

'The last time you wore that suit was at our Brenda's wedding.'

'There's no point in it hanging in the wardrobe year after year. I might as well get me wear out of it.'

She went to stand in front of the living-room mirror.

'Yer 'air! Yer've had it done.'

'I know. Surprise surprise! He's looked at me!! I swear if I walked about naked yer wouldn't notice, because you never look at me. Not really look.'

She admired her hair, that mobile hairdresser who came twice a week to the village had done a good job, though she didn't expect it would stay like this for long, knowing her hair. This pink suit still looked smart. Well, if yer were wardrobe mistress yer had to let people know yer knew what yer were talking about. She'd show 'em. They'd all have a surprise.

'I look all right, then?'

'Yes, I've got to say you do. A bit of all right, you are. Definitely.'

Her delight at Don showing some interest in her braced her for the forthcoming challenge. She picked up her navy handbag which she'd already filled with notebook and pencil as well as her purse and the pink lipstick that matched her suit, slipped her feet into those excruciating shoes which had killed her all the way through Brenda's reception, and set off for the Church Hall.

Expecting that there would only be a small select band volunteering their help Vera had a shock when she opened the door to the Church Hall. At first sight it appeared that the entire village and then some had come to volunteer their services. The Jones family had arrived in its entirety, three generations of them, and it looked as though Mrs Jones meant business because she had some big books in a carrier bag and was about to put them on a table at the side. Then she spotted her Rhett. The cheeky little monkey! He'd said he was going out but never a word about coming to the meeting. Wait till she got a chance for a word. And there was Miss Parkin from Glebe Cottages, and Mrs Peel, well she needn't think Hugo would be wanting her to trill about on the church organ 'cos he wouldn't. Just behind her Rhett she spotted

Kate from the school and Dottie too, heaven alone knew what contribution Dottie thought she'd be able to make. She had to stop counting. This was ridiculous. Anyhow, Hugo had said she was wardrobe mistress and that was exactly what she was going to be.

Despite the pinching of her shoes she strode masterfully across to where Mrs Jones and Hugo were looking at the books. One glance over their shoulders and she realised that things were being taken out of her hands.

'What's this?'

Hugo turned to speak to her. 'Vera! You've come. Look at these ideas Mrs Jones has for the costumes. Aren't they brilliant? It's the colours we shall have to be careful with you know, Mrs Jones. Remember that black and white Ascot scene in *My Fair Lady*? That was so effective. Utterly divine!'

'Black and white, is that what you want me to do?'

Vera bristled. 'I don't understand this. I thought *I* was in charge of the costumes? Wasn't that what you said?'

Hugo, recognising that someone who came armed with illustrations of just the styles he was after was a much surer bet than someone who'd come with nothing, drew upon his considerable diplomatic skills.

'No, no. I merely used that to illustrate how important the contribution of the wardrobe mistress is. Mrs Jones, these designs are wonderful, now can I rely upon you and Vera here to source some materials, bring me snippets and we'll have a serious discussion next week about colours, et cetera? How about that, Vera?'

Disappointment flooded Vera's very bones and she could scarcely hold back her tears. One look from Mrs Jones' gimlet eyes, one glance at her triumphant posture, was enough. She drew back her handbag and swung it in Mrs Jones' direction. It missed, but caught Hugo on the shoulder. With the additional weight of the notepad inside it and rather a lot of loose change in her purse, it caused Hugo to stagger. He clutched at the table to save himself, and made one of the costume books slide off onto the floor and land noisily at Vera's feet.

Vera was devastated. 'Oh, Hugo! I'm so sorry. Look what you've done now, Mrs Jones. Look what you've made me do. It's all your fault, muscling in on my job.'

'It's not *your* job. It's not *my* job. I just brought these ...'

'Well, you can stuff the job right where it hurts. I'm not working with you, not at any price. It's either me or you, not both. You're a bossy interfering old bag, that's what you are. Think you're something special, don't yer? Well yer not. You're like the rest of us ... ordinary. I wanted this job and I bet you knew I did so you got them books on purpose to impress. You're a bitch.' She tapped Mrs Jones on her collar bone to emphasise her point.

'Well, really! All I've done is ...'

'Ladies, please. Please. Let's come to some amicable arrangement, shall we? I think ...'

But Vera wouldn't stay to listen to his pleas. She'd been made a fool of, and her distress was too much to bear. She kicked the book, twice, for good measure and then marched out with Mrs Jones' protests ringing in her ears.

'Well, Hugo, did you say she could be wardrobe mistress?'

'No, I didn't. I said she could come along to the meeting and give a hand, I never said she was it. That was her mistake. Somehow or other we've got to heal the breach, don't you know?' He put his head to one side and smiled at her, and Mrs Jones' heart melted. 'I'll sort something out. Don't you fret.' She rather boldly patted his arm. 'She can help me, be my chief assistant.'

'Good idea. Right, I'll start the meeting.' Shattered by the unexpected violence his project had brought about he strode more purposefully than he felt to the stage, sprang up on to it, and stood in front of the curtains with his arms raised.

'Ladies and gentlemen! Thank you. Thank you.' They all stopped talking and turned to listen to him. 'I'm amazed and delighted at the number of people who have turned up to volunteer their services. I have a list here of the backstage people we shall need. As I'm producing as well as acting I shall need really reliable people as back-up. Hands up anyone at all who has experience of theatre work, either amateur or professional.'

Hugo rather suspected there would be no hands put up and he was right. In that case then, here goes, he thought.

'Scenery. Barry Jones. Any ideas for an assistant, Barry?'

'I wondered about Sir Ronald, he's a very practical chap.'

'Is he here?'

'No, but you could have a word tomorrow, he's at home at the moment.'

'Right.' Hugo made a note on the list on his clip board. 'Lighting?'

With one voice they all said, 'Willie.'

'Willie it is. Are you here, Willie?'

'I am, and yes I'm willing. Long time since them lights was given a proper airing, but I'll do my best.'

Barry Jones gave Willie a verbal reference. 'You did wonders when we had that Flower Festival a few years back. Very subtle the lighting was. He'll do a good job, Hugo.'

'Willie. Lighting. Now, props. That means someone who knows every piece of furniture, every flower, every ornament, et cetera, needed for each and every scene, someone who can find all we need by begging borrowing or stealing – well, not literally, but you know what I mean. Any ideas?'

There was a silence and then a voice from the back piped up. 'I'll do that. I've finished my exams, be glad of something to do.' Dean Jones, Dean Duckett that was, waved a hand to everyone. 'If you'll tell me what you need.'

'Of course. You're . . .?'

'Dean Jones.'

'Excellent. You're stage manager, then.' Hugo jotted down Dean's name and continued on down his list. 'Now, publicity. This means programmes, posters, tickets, advertising. Who have we got? Any offers?'

There was a brief silence and then Anne Parkin spoke. 'I'm quite good at lists and things. I'm not creative, but I could do publicity and printing and such. If that's all right.'

'Wonderful. Your name?' He leant towards her in the most endearing manner and cupped his hand to his ear.

'Anne Parkin.'

'Anne Parkin it is. Now. Next. Costume is Mrs Jones and Vera Wright.'

A voice at the back said, 'You 'ope!'

'I can assure you it will be. A small contretemps, soon be ironed out. Now.'

'You'll have your work cut out sorting that little problem, believe me. How about it, Mrs Jones? Willing to let bygones be bygones?'

'You mind your own business, Jimmy Glover.'

'Mr Maude! I'm Sylvia Biggs. You'll need someone to make coffee and that when you have a break from rehearsing. How about me? Might not manage it every night, 'cos I may be needed at the Rectory. But I'd be glad to be involved, and I'd find a substitute when I couldn't.'

'You can have no idea what music that is to my ears. The cast rely deeply,' there was a lot of emphasis on the word 'deeply' and they all felt it in their bones, 'on cups of coffee to revive them. Absolutely essential. In fact the success of the play could be said to relate directly to the quality of the drinks provided during rehearsal! Wonderful, Sylvia.' He bunched his fingers and kissed them in Sylvia's direction. 'I'll put your name down.'

Willie nudged Sylvia and mouthed, 'Why?'

Out of the corner of her mouth Sylvia said, 'To keep my eye on what's going on, of course.'

'He's embarrassed you.'

'No, he hasn't.'

'He has. I'll come every night as well. Keep an eye on you.'

'You daft thing, Willie Biggs.'

'He's got a sight too much charm 'as Mr Hugo Maude. Just 'ope he doesn't turn out to be Mr Hugo Fraud.'

Sylvia giggled. 'You're in top form tonight I must say. But I can see you're jealous.'

'I'm not. Have you done? Let's go.'

'In a minute. Let's wait for instructions.'

Hugo had completed his list and wanted to get on with the first rehearsal. 'Thank you very much, ladies and gentlemen. I'll be in touch with all backstage people within the next few days and have some in-depth discussions with each of you regarding duties, expenses, what's needed, et cetera. We haven't much time left to get the show on the road, but we will do it if we all put our shoulders to the wheel! Thank you so much everyone.' He pointed to Michelle Jones standing at the back with Dean. 'Got a small part for you if you fancy it.'

Michelle looked around, realised Hugo meant her, blushed bright red and pointed to herself saying, 'Me?'

'Yes, you. Fancy it? Stay for rehearsal if you do.'

'Yes, please.'

Hugo searched the crowd and pointed to Rhett Wright. 'Hi there! You in the green top and jeans. Yes, you. Fancy a part?'

Rhett nodded.

'Not a lot to learn but every part is vital to our success. Fancy it?'

'Right. Yes, I'll do it.' Rhett rubbed his hands together with delight. 'Great, just great.' Then he remembered his grandma and some of the gloss went off the evening. She'd never forgive him.

And she didn't. When Rhett got home, Don had gone to his night shift and his gran was sitting in front of the electric fire drinking a shandy. By the looks of the cans on the table it wasn't her first.

'Where've you been till this time?'

'Well, Gran, Hugo offered ...'

'Shandy?'

'Thanks.' He waited till he'd sprung the can open and taken a drink before he continued. 'Hugo's offered me a part. Just a little one, like, but it's a part.'

Vera lunged at him and missed the side of his head by a whisker.

'You traitor, you. You should've left when I did. I've never been so insulted in all my life. Never. That Mrs Jones. Since she took over the mail order at the Store she's thought herself a cut or two above the likes of you and me. With her "Jimbo" this and her "Jimbo" that. I can remember when she was only too glad to clean at the pub when her boys were all little. How low can you get? Cleaning at a pub. I could tell her a thing or two about her Kenny and Terry that'd make her toe nails curl up. They are disgusting.'

Rhett eagerly demanded 'Are they? What do they do then?'

Vera scowled at him. 'I'm not telling you.'

'I am eighteen, nearly nineteen.'

'So you may be. What's this part then? Not that I'm interested.'

'I'm Dr Harris' son, and Michelle's her daughter.'

'Michelle? Another feather in Mrs Jones' cap. Is there no end?'

'Here's the script. Look.'

Vera gave it a sideways glance. Her lips trembled and she blurted out, 'Just once in my life I thought I'd grab the chance to work with someone who had genius. Real genius. They're few and far between are people with genius, do you know that? Your grandad and me, we've grubbed along all our lives, struggling just to make ends meet, not improve ourselves, but to keep the wheels oiled. Then yer mum went off the rails and we got you.' She patted his arm apologetically. 'I don't mean we didn't want yer Rhett, because we did, you were such a good baby, but just when we thought we could start to make progress you came along and I had to give up me job. I 'aven't regretted one minute having yer, but yer did 'old us back. Yer mum promised us money every month but o' course, as yer can imagine, that lasted for about six months and then . . . yer know the rest.' She wiped her eyes and gazed at the imitation flames curling round the imitation coals on the fire.

Rhett said softly, 'I'm sorry, Gran.'

'Nothing for you to be sorry about, love. But when the idea came to me to be wardrobe mistress I knew I longed to be involved with something beautiful. D'yer know what I mean? Something special, something people would admire me for. I know exactly where I am in the pecking order in this village and it's bottom. Bottom. Even Pat Duckett that was, she used to be at our level, talking over the fence and moaning about 'aving no money and now look what's happened to 'er. A new husband, a grand big house, a car now and a right good job with the Charter-Plackett's catering service. And where am I? Still at the bottom of the pile. I could truthfully say I yearned for that job with the costumes.'

'Look, if it means that much to you, how about eating humble pie, apologising and getting stuck in. Hugo announced that you and Mrs Jones were doing the costumes together.'

Vera looked at him through her tears. 'Not Pygmalion likely. Yer see you make beautiful things all day long in that garden. Yer in touch with beauty, and I never am.'

'You've flowers in your garden.'

His answer was a shrug of his gran's shoulders. 'Say a few of your lines for me, love, will yer?'

Rhett said he wouldn't, he'd be too embarrassed.

'All right then.' Wistfully Vera went back to thinking about the dresses. 'They'll have lovely materials for them dresses, I could right fancy handling materials like that. Touching it and holding it soft like against yer cheek. Lovely. All pretty and beautiful. All beads and embroidery. And the colours, them illustrations in 'er books! All pastel colours, yer know. Peaches and silver greys and soft greens and turquoise. Wonderful! And having that lovely, lovely man saying how pleased he was with them. That would be great. Yer see Rhett, yer grandad's a good man, faithful and that, never a word out of place, but he lacks sparkle. Yes, sparkle. And after all these years, so do I. But making them costumes, that'd make me sparkle and not half.' She stared into the distance and Rhett saw such a lovely smile on her face, a smile like he couldn't remember seeing before. Vera sighed. 'Still, there yer go. Mrs Jones has got the job and good luck to her. Go get me slippers, Rhett, me feet are killing me.'

Mrs Jones popped into the Store the next morning to finish off some orders she hadn't had time to do the previous day. Jimbo handed her a coffee as she swept through. 'Thanks, Mrs Jones. That's what I like to see. Enthusiasm. I hear you've had a promotion.'

'Promotion?'

'Yes. Wardrobe mistress. Hidden talents, eh?' Jimbo smoothed his striped apron, red and white this morning, raised his straw boater to her and bowed.

'Don't know about promotion, but it caused a commotion. That Vera Wright. Huh! Thinking she could do the costumes. That's likely!'

'She's had a hard time has Vera. She needs a leg up, you know.'

Humbled, Mrs Jones continued on to the mail order office. While she sorted and checked and packed the orders, one to Bristol, another to Newcastle, two to Devon, and yet another and another, she pondered on what Jimbo had said. The uproar had not been her own fault, but wild horses wouldn't make her go to Vera and suggest she helped despite the quarrel. Not likely. Never. The orders finished, she marched them to the post office counter and handed them to Linda.

'There you are, Linda. Six. There's your list. OK?'

'Thanks.'

'I'm off now. Off to Culworth on the lunchtime bus. Got some materials to look at. I know just where to go.'

'Exciting, isn't it? If I was more free I'd have a go too. Just imagine acting with that wonderful man. He could butter my bread anytime!'

'Linda! He's full of charm but he's not like that. It's only good fun and part of his lovely nature.'

'Oh yes. That's not what I've heard.' She leaned her elbows on the counter and put her face close to the grill. 'On Monday night . . .'

An old man from Little Derehams elbowed Mrs Jones aside. 'Hurry up. I need my pension. I'm catching the lunchtime bus to Culworth.'

'All right. All right. Keep yer hair on.'

She served the angry pensioner and by the time they'd argued about her rubber stamp not being clear enough and whether or not she needed a new one and she'd do better if she didn't gossip so much, Mrs Jones had to leave to make sure she didn't miss the bus.

Rhett, who'd gone round to see her about his gran's disappointment, missed her. He knew he owed his gran a lot. Everything, if the truth be known, because he might as well not have a mother for all she cared. And some days that hurt. Now he'd missed Mrs Jones so his idea had fallen on stony ground. He thought over his conversation with his gran last night and how she'd revealed more of herself than she'd ever done before. He thought about beauty. She was right. He touched and saw beauty every working day. Flowers, plants, fruit trees, vines. The scent of them after the rain, the mingled pleasurable aromas he inhaled greedily when he opened the glasshouses first thing in the summer. The smell of soil freshly turned with his spade, the crumbly moist feel of it; the new paths he laid, feeling his way, making the patterns with the stones; the satisfaction of . . . Then it hit him: energising shock waves ran through him right to his toes. Of course. The stones. He'd repair the crazy paving at the back of Gran's cottage, extend it a bit here and there and buy her a little plastic table and chairs so she could sit out. There were those old pots at the back of the kitchen garden wall that Mr Fitch wanted rid of. Greenwood Stubbs would let him have those for nothing and he'd buy some plants and . . . His head full of ideas, he pedalled furiously up the drive to the Garden House to find Greenwood. This would be the surprise of his gran's life. He'd see to it that she had some beauty.

6

True to his word, Hugo went to see Sir Ronald Bissett. He rang the bell and waited. Lovely old cottage, thatched roof, roses around the door, the lifelong dream of thousands of town dwellers. A cottage in the country for himself? No, not quite his scene.

The door opened and Sheila Bissett was standing there beaming, dressed as though expecting visitors.

'Hugo Maude, you remember me? Good morning, Lady Bissett.'

'Do please call me Sheila. Everyone else does.'

'Sheila, then. Is your beloved in?'

Sheila asked, 'My beloved?'

'The renowned Ron. His name's been volunteered to help backstage with the play and I promised I'd come to see him this morning. Told he's a very practical chap.'

'Oh he is. He does all our DIY. Every bit. Come in. Come in. Do.'

'Thanks.' He meticulously wiped his feet. He knew Sheila would notice that and like him for it.

'Do sit down. I'll tell Ron you're here, he's in the shed at the bottom of the garden.'

'You send him down there when you're fed up with him, do you?'

She was so flustered she didn't notice he was teasing. 'Oh no! Of course not. He's cleaning the mower. I won't be a moment. Coffee when I get back? It's not one of my mornings, but you're most welcome.'

'Why thank you, most kind.' He watched her open the french windows and trot down the garden. She lacked dress sense, she was

63

too fat, she'd no *savoir faire* whatsoever, she had an almost pathetic
desire to be liked, but there was something about her you couldn't
help but be drawn to. An honesty and a simplicity he had to
admire.

Sir Ron removed his garden shoes before he came in and Sheila
opened up a copy of the *Daily Mirror*, placing it carefully in the
easy chair before Ron sat down in it.

'You will excuse me, won't you? I'll leave you two to your men's
talk while I make the coffee.' With a coy little nod of her head she
disappeared from the sitting room.

'So, you're the Hugo Maude that's causing such a sensation.'

Hugo feigned surprise. 'Sensation?'

'Of course. Yes. They're all talking about you. Husbands as well
as wives. There's a few husbands who are being told they're not
coming up to scratch, you see.'

'Oh dear. I hope I'm not causing any trouble.'

'All in good fun. Now what can I do for you?'

'Barry Jones is doing the scenery for the play, but really it's a
two-handed job or even a three-handed one, and you were
recommended as a very able assistant.'

'Me?'

'You. I do hope you'll say yes. We're running short on time, you
see.'

'Well, now I don't see why not. I'd quite enjoy that and Barry's
very easy to get on with. Yes, I will. Thank you for thinking of me.'

'Don't thank me, everyone agreed you'd be a good choice.'

'Right. I'm well pleased with the idea.'

'Barry and I had a long chat earlier today and he knows exactly
what's needed. Mr Fitch has promised the wood and told Barry to
buy whatever paints et cetera are needed, so it's plain sailing really.
Just needs the time devoted to it and plenty of elbow grease.'

'Well, I've plenty of that. Turned this place inside out all by
myself, you know. Took a while but I made it in the end. I'm well
accustomed to public speaking but not acting, so backstage is all
right by me.'

He appeared to Hugo to be flattered that he'd been asked and he
wondered if the Bissetts weren't exactly accepted in Turnham
Malpas.

Sheila came bustling in. 'Here we are, then. Coffee for three. I didn't get to the meeting, did you get plenty of helpers?'

'I did indeed. More than I needed. Do you know Mrs Peel?'

'Of course, she's the church organist. Very nice person she is, she's really blossomed since Peter came. You see, Mr Furbank that was the Rector before Peter, had no idea about music. But Peter is an organist himself, you know, so he knows how to get the best out of her.'

'I see. Well, she came up with the brilliant idea that we could have live music instead of canned for the overture and during the interval. She has a repertoire of the most unbelievably suitable music and she has a genuine nineteen twenties' dress and the piano's just been tuned, she tells me. So right where you expect a desert you find an oasis.' Sheila handed him his coffee and placed the sugar bowl and cream jug at his elbow on a small side table.

'Of course.'

Hugo helped himself to sugar. 'So wonderful when gems like that fall into one's lap.'

'Indeed. I'm glad you got help like that. They're really very good in this village, but I expect it was your good looks and charm that carried the day.'

Hugo denied this by pursing his lips and waving a deprecating hand.

'Oh yes, it is, you can't fool me. I just wish there was something I was clever at that I could do to help.'

'But I believe there is. Flowers? Hey?'

Embarrassed, Sheila lowered her gaze. 'Someone's been telling tales out of school.'

'They have very justifiably too, I understand. Flower festivals and the like. Now, it means doing some research.'

'Research. Oh, I don't think I'm ...'

'Oh yes, you are. Perfectly capable. The set is that of a country house in about 1921, not a large one but certainly an elegant one and I want flowers, two vases full, on stage to go on the grand piano.'

Sheila's eyebrows went up in amazement. 'A grand piano? Where are you going to get that from? In any case it would fill the stage and there'd be no room for the actors.'

'A baby grand, actually, from Mr Fitch's flat at the Big House.'

'My word, he certainly means business, doesn't he?'

'Oh yes. He does. No stone unturned. Back to the flowers. One vase a winter arrangement and the other a summer one. Now, how did they do flowers in country houses then? I know they weren't done like I saw them in church on Sunday, all thanks to you no doubt.' He reached across and patted her knee and she had to restrain herself from clasping his hand. 'And they certainly wouldn't be Japanese style. Ikebana, isn't it? So could you find out and arrange them for me? What do you say?'

'Well.' Sheila took a deep breath. 'Well, yes I'll have a try. Yes, I certainly will. Research, yes. Of course. I'm honoured that you thought of me.'

'To whom should I turn but to an expert.'

'Oh! Really! Hugo. You're too kind. How about the hall itself, shouldn't there be some in there?'

'Well, of course that would be wonderful if you have the time. Within reasonable limits Mr Fitch is paying all expenses, so keep your bills. The flowers in the hall must be in keeping. And very, very important, the vases themselves *must* look right too.'

'Oh yes, of course. I can see that. Authenticity. Research. Right. Well, I never expected this when I opened the door. How exciting! The ladies in the flower club will be most impressed. I shall ask you to sign my programme.'

'Well, there'll be an acknowledgement in there.'

Sheila, to whom an acknowledgement meant an announcement in the paper thanking people for their floral tributes at a funeral, looked puzzled.

'You know "Flowers by Lady Sheila Bissett".'

'Oh, right, I see.'

Hugo could tell how delighted she was and he was glad he'd asked her and glad she was on his side.

'Dr Harris is in the play, I hear.'

'Yes, she's playing the leading lady opposite me. Lovely lady to work with.'

'Oh, she is. I'm a great fan of hers. She's always so pleasant, so kind and she hasn't had it easy. No, not at all.'

'Really?' He knew he'd learn a lot if he played his cards right.

'No, she's had cancer recently but she seems to have got over that now. Then her parents were very badly injured in a road accident – touch and go for a while. Then she had all the trouble about the twins, no that was before the accident and the accident was before the cancer, yes that's right. It wasn't easy, but what a gesture taking his children on like she did for his sake. Wonderfully loving that was. Of course we all love the Rector, he's quite simply wonderful. One look from those blue eyes of his and we're all his slaves. I don't wonder she . . .'

'I know they're adopted, so they're actually *his*, not hers, are they?'

Suddenly Sheila knew she'd said too much, but he was looking at her with such a sympathetic expression on his face she knew he wouldn't use what she was going to tell him.

As she opened her mouth to begin the story, Ron, much to her annoyance reminded her it was getting late and they were meeting up with those friends at the service station on the bypass and they'd better be off and he still had to get washed and changed.

'Are we?' A strained look about his eyes convinced her she had to play along with him. 'Oh yes, of course, I'd completely forgotten. Oh dear. Will you excuse us, Hugo? Another time, maybe.'

'Of course. Off you go. Have a good time. See me when you can about the flowers and your ideas, and you, Ron, get in touch with Barry, will you?' He took Sheila's hand in his, raised it to his lips and kissed it lingeringly whilst keeping his eyes fixed on hers. A tremulous smile lit her face. 'Dear lady!'

Ron stood up. 'Of course. Yes, leave it with me.'

Hugo left disappointed that he hadn't heard the full story about Caroline. He knew that he definitely wouldn't hear it from her, it would be too painful for her to resurrect. So, it must have been Peter she was protecting when she wouldn't open up. Harriet, that was right. Harriet. She'd know.

But Harriet wouldn't co-operate. 'Ask Caroline, but don't expect an answer. And you're certainly not getting one from me.'

'Fine. Fine. I get the message.'

'You'd better and while we're on the subject, Caroline is off limits.'

He didn't reply.

'I mean it, Hugo. Off limits. Definitely a no go area. OK? Flirt with whom you like, I'll recommend a few if you wish, but not Caroline.'

'Flirt! What a word to use about me! I'm thoroughly demoralised by the prospect that I would *flirt*! Well, really. Me?' He helped himself to a scone Harriet had not long taken from the oven. 'Why so protective?'

'She's a dear friend and I won't have her hurt.'

'She's a grown woman with a mind of her own.'

'You're right. She is and she has. But she is still *verboten*. I don't want to discuss it any more. I've got lunch to get, are you in?'

'Yes, and I'll lay the table for you as penance for upsetting you. In fact, I'll do it twice as double penance.'

Harriet gave him a quick kiss on his cheek. 'You're lovely, know that?'

Unashamedly he replied, 'Yes.'

They both fell about laughing, holding on to each other as they did so. Jimbo walked into the kitchen. 'May I share the joke?'

On Monday morning, having spent a rather chilly weekend with Jimbo looking glum most of the time, Hugo – partly to get out of the house and partly to have a chance to talk to Caroline on his own – decided to ask her if he could go round to the Rectory and run through her part with her in preparation for the rehearsal that night.

It was Peter who answered the phone. 'I'll get her for you. Just a moment. Darling! It's Hugo for you.'

'Oh right. Thanks.' She took hold of the receiver and said, 'Yes?'

'Good morning, Caroline.'

'Good morning.'

'Are you free sometime today?'

'When abouts?'

'Like now, for instance.'

'Yes, I am.'

'Could I come round and run through your part? Thought we could do some preparatory work, then tonight would flow more easily.'

'Very well.'

'In half an hour?'

'Fine. See you.' She put down the receiver and explained to Peter.

'I'll leave you to it, then. I'm off to Penny Fawcett, then I've some visiting to do, then I'm going into Culworth to take this article into the newspaper, and I'll call in at the hospital to see Lavender Gotobed, poor old thing.'

'Is she any better?'

'Not much. Bye, darling.' Peter put his arms round her and kissed her. 'Love you.'

'Love you. What about lunch?'

'I'll call back at the mini market before I leave and get it there.'

'Very well. Peter, I'm so looking forward to getting my teeth into this play, and thanks for helping me learn my lines last night.'

'It's a pleasure. I want you to do well, you see.'

'Thanks. I appreciate that.'

She stood at the front door to wave him off. The sun was shining on her, highlighting her dark curly hair and emphasising that happy look in her eyes which he hadn't brought about. It shone on her slender figure, and lit up the warm apricot-coloured dress she was wearing. God, how he loved her! He'd thought on his wedding day that he couldn't love her more than he did that day, but he did. Maybe love was self generating, the more one loved the greater the capacity for loving became. Peter raised a finger to his lips, kissed it and blew the kiss to her. He smiled at her delight but knew, in his heart, that the moment he drove away she would be thinking about Hugo Maude.

When Hugo rang the doorbell Caroline was on the telephone, so it was Sylvia who opened the door to him.

'Good morning, Mr ... Hugo. Do come in. Dr Harris is expecting you. She said would I put you in the sitting room and would you like coffee?'

'Later perhaps, I've only just had breakfast.'

She left him seated in an easy chair. He hadn't been in many rectory sitting rooms, in fact come to think of it he hadn't been in any but somehow he knew there weren't many rectors relaxing in sitting rooms of this standard. The almost oriental design of the curtains picking up as they did the warm gold of the carpet. And the chairs! So comfortable. Nothing well worn and dowdy in this room. He wondered how the other rooms must look and how she'd furnished their bedroom.

On the mantelpiece were framed photographs of their children, but the photograph on the window sill was of their wedding. Hugo got to his feet and went to look at it. He picked it up and studied her closely. She hadn't worn a veil, simply a circlet of fresh flowers on her dark hair. Her dress was an ageless classic. Long narrow sleeves, a neckline just low enough to allow her to wear a double row of pearls which glowed against her creamy skin. Modest. Maidenly. Virginal. He studied Peter and was devastated by the look of joy in his face. Envy, monstrous envy filled Hugo's soul. To love like that! If Peter wasn't so damned good looking perhaps things wouldn't be so bad, but those good looks *and* Caroline *and* to be blessed with a love like that! How he envied him.

'Like it?'

He'd been aware a moment before of a perfume in the room. Now, at the sound of her voice, he knew it was Caroline's.

Hugo carefully placed the photograph back on the window sill and turned to look at her.

'Hope you don't mind. Couldn't help but take a look. Got your script?'

'It's here.' She picked it up from the coffee table and went to sit on the sofa. He sat beside her with his script in his hand.

'I've already learned a lot of the lines, Peter's been helping me. This Marian character I'm playing, she's complex, isn't she?'

'Indeed. Tell me what you've learned about her.'

'Before the war, she was a dutiful wife. Usual thing, never had a job, married almost straight from school, the local boy everyone expected her to marry, had the prescribed two children, a boy and then a girl. The war came, he went into the army expecting her to be sitting tidily at home keeping the home fires burning and doing her bit by knitting balaclavas and mittens for the soldiers at the front. Well, she didn't. She got up off her backside, learned to drive, worked at the local big house which had been turned into a hospital for officers, became a nurse and saw more of the foul side of the war than most.'

'Yes, yes.'

'Then husband Charles comes home. He's not been physically wounded but emotionally and psychologically he's a wreck, but he manages to keep that particular problem well under wraps. Not even she has realised how badly damaged he is.'

'Excellent.'

'He is appalled at what she's been doing during the war and fully expects her to go back to doing nothing. Which she does, mainly because he is so adamant about it. I think there's a hint of cruelty in his attitude, and in addition it's almost as if he's afraid he might lose her if he doesn't keep her tied to the home. But she's so glad to have him back that she goes along with it. Then this man Leonard arrives. Am I getting it right? Is this how you see it?'

'It is.'

'He completely upsets the applecart. He upsets the husband and he upsets her. Stirs things up in her which she's never had stirred before. Husband Charles always insists on his conjugal rights but never quite gets it right. He's on a kind of "Oh! It's Saturday, so it's our night" routine. So rather surprisingly, to her, she finds herself ready for anything, as you might say.'

Hugo sat back watching her as she outlined her ideas to him. He'd a powerful idea that her husband had a completely different approach from the husband in the play, and that she knew he knew and she guessed he was jealous. Which he was. She moved on to the effect the newcomer, Leonard, had had on the wife. What was she saying ... 'So I can quite understand why she does what she does. Life with Leonard would be unpredictable. He's no job, just private money, and deeply in love with him though she is she can't cope with that so she opts for the safety of the husband and children. So sad Leonard gets killed the very night she tells him it's all over.'

'Do you think she's right?'

'To be glad he gets killed?'

'Yes.'

'It's never right to kill, no matter the provocation.'

'Do you think Charles kills him?'

'Oh! Definitely! Everything points to that.'

71

'It can't be comfortable, realising almost for certain her husband is a murderer.'

'Here, look, where she says to her friend Celia ...' Caroline leafed through the script till she came to the page she was looking for. 'Here it is. "It was doomed from the beginning, I see that now and I shall pay the price for the rest of my life, because I have to live with it every day".'

'You've studied it all out, haven't you?'

'If I'm doing something then I do it right and understanding what makes her tick is vital, surely?'

'Of course, of course. Let's do that scene where the chap first comes in. Act one, Scene two. Right. Off you go.'

'I haven't finished yet. Having an affair on the side was much more terrible then in 1920 than it would be today, wasn't it? You really do have to see it from their point of view to get the right message across.'

'Of course. That's the trouble with a lot of amateur productions, the cast don't have the width and depth of experience of life to get through to the essence of the part they're playing.'

Caroline, about to read her first line, looked up at him. 'I sincerely hope you're not suggesting that I've had experience of extra marital affairs and that's why I understand so well.'

Hugo who'd been lounging back on the sofa enjoying Caroline's company sat up straight. 'Oh no, of course not. With a man like Peter, what woman would want an affair? I'm sure you're quite satisfied on that score.' His slight hesitation before the word 'satisfied' angered her.

'Look here, I hope you're ... Look, let's get on, please. Have you found the page?'

They read through and discussed various points and only stopped when Sylvia said she was going to lunch and did Dr Harris want anything before she left.

Pulled back to reality by the request, Caroline had to think for a moment. 'No, nothing at all, thank you. See you later.'

'OK. Good afternoon to you, Mr Maude.'

'Hugo! Hugo!' His reprimand was spoken in such a pleasant way Sylvia had to smile.

'Yes, well, then, Hugo.'

'Good afternoon.'

Sylvia was clattering plates in the sink. 'Have you finished? Because I'm in a rush. I've got to get back, just in case. You were late, I've waited ages for you to come.'

Willie, who'd only had two bites of his sandwich, looked up, surprised. 'Come on, I haven't been in the house two minutes. What's the rush?'

'He's there.'

'Who is?'

'Who do you think. His lordship.'

'Oh, right.'

'I bet my bottom dollar he'll have stayed for lunch.'

'Put me a drop more milk in this tea, will yer? Look here, she's an upright, loving woman married to a lovely man. He's a priest, she's a doctor, she knows the position better than you and me. Stop worrying. She won't do anything wrong, believe me.'

'Won't she?'

'No, she won't. If he tries . . .'

'Which he will. I've seen that look he has in his eye before now.'

'Where have you seen it?' Willie picked up his cup.

'Dicky Tutt, for a start.'

Willie spluttered his tea over the cloth. He wiped his mouth, coughed a bit and then said, 'Honestly!' When he'd got over the choking fit Willie began to laugh. 'You're not suggesting there's going to be a real proper affair are you, like Dicky and Georgie?'

Faced with the question, Sylvia couldn't make herself voice her thoughts. If she said it, it might mean it would happen. 'No. not really. Well . . .'

'Give up, forget it. I know I'm right. You're worrying over nothing.'

Sylvia stood up. 'You finished?'

'I have now and I'll have indigestion all afternoon with hurrying.'

She cleared away, kissed him, reminded him to lock up after himself, and left him.

Their laughter reached her ears as she unlocked the front door. She called out, 'I'm back.'

They were sitting in the kitchen having lunch. A half-empty bottle of red wine on the table. An empty dish, which by the looks of it had held a cold beef salad and, waiting still to be eaten, two slices of her best fruit cake.

'You're soon back, Sylvia?'

'Lots of ironing to do. With not being in tomorrow I need to get on with it.'

'Of course. We'll take our cake into the sitting room. Bring the wine, Hugo, will you?'

Sylvia watched him follow her out. This kitchen belonged to the family. She thought about the times Dr Harris had sat in one rocking chair and she in the other giving the twins their bottles. She remembered when there'd been two high chairs round the table at lunchtime, with the Rector feeding one baby and Dr Harris the other one. What happy times they'd been. How much she'd enjoyed them. Lovely though he was, Hugo Maude didn't belong, he was dining-room company, not kitchen company. And wine at lunchtime! Now that was decadent. As she snapped open the ironing board Sylvia heard them laughing again. Caroline's laugh was joyous; happier than for some time. Well, at least that was a plus, she supposed.

7

Vera called in at the Store for a few vital necessities. Bread, milk, eggs, half a pound of bacon, some chocolate biscuits, a shaving stick and razor blades for Don. She was standing in front of the razor blade display trying to remember which kind Don used when she heard Mrs Jones' voice.

'There's ten parcels today, Linda. There's the list. Hurry up and we'll catch the lunchtime post.'

'Keep yer hair on! Shan't be a minute.' Linda finished sorting her postal orders, tidied the counter, put some paper clips back in her tray and tested the sponge she used for wetting her fingers when she was counting.

'Honestly! I haven't got all day! I've a costume to machine this afternoon when I get back. Beads to sew on as well. Hurry up!'

As Linda began weighing the parcels and writing down the cost on Mrs Jones' list Vera edged closer. Swallowing her pride because of her desperate need to help with the costumes she said, 'If you'd let me help I could be doing the beads. I've got a bit of 'oliday, time's getting on.'

'You! Not likely not after the way you spoke to me at the meeting. I wouldn't let you help, not for anything. I'd stay up all night first.'

'Would you indeed? You miserable old cow. I just hope Hugo doesn't like 'em and then you'll be in a fix.'

'Of course he'll like 'em. He's been with me every step of the way.'

'Oh! Very close, are yer? Hand in glove?'

'Don't be daft. We professional people have an understanding.'

Vera hooted with laughter. 'You professional people! I can remember the time when you were glad to clean at the pub when your boys was little. I don't call that professional.'

'So you think cleaning at a nursing home is a step up the ladder, do you?'

'Better than cleaning out stinking lavatories when they've all had too much to drink. And I don't stoop to nasty underhand tricks like you get up to, either.'

Mrs Jones grew belligerent at this accusation and looked ready to begin one of her famous tirades. Taking a deep breath she thundered, 'What do you mean, "underhand tricks"?'

'Like that time when you reported Carrie Whatsit to the Show committee for buying a pot plant at the garden centre and kidding on it was home grown.'

'I never.'

'You did. Or that time when your Terry beat up the husband of that girl what works at the Jug and Bottle and you swore he'd been 'ome all night. Don't think we don't know what you get up to.'

'You've a mind like a sewer, you have.'

'You might think you're superior but yer not. You're a scumbag, that's what.' Vera took her shopping to the till where Bel totted it up and asked her for nine pounds twenty-five. Her hands were shaking so badly she couldn't unzip her purse.

'Here, let me do it for you. There we are. There's your change look, seventy-five pence.'

Vera nodded her thanks. The aftermath of the argument was having its effect and Vera was bereft of speech.

Bel whispered, 'Take no notice. She's not worth it. Been right on her high horse since she got that job.' She lifted the carrier off the counter and handed it to her. 'There y'go, love.'

Vera was about to leave when the door crashed open and Grandmama Charter-Plackett came in.

'There you are, Vera. You'd better get home quickly. I've just seen Greenwood Stubbs and your Rhett pulling up in the van and they're unloading crazy paving and bags of cement and carrying them through your house.'

Vera's shock at this piece of astounding news brought back her voice. 'Crazy paving? I haven't ordered crazy paving. What's he playing at?' She hurried out of the Store, raced across the Green and peeped over her fence. Rhett was stacking the pieces of stone as Greenwood was carrying them through.

'Rhett, what do yer think yer doing? We can't afford all that. We've no need for it. Take it back.'

'Shushhh! Come in and I'll explain.' Vera walked round to the front door and went in.

'Before he went away Mr Fitch said that all the rubbish that was lying about had to be cleared before he got back. He said it was all old stuff he'd never use and it was making the place look untidy. When I saw the pots and the table and chairs amongst it I thought, well, if he doesn't want it, I know who does. So here it is. Then I remembered we'd a load of crazy paving left over from the new paths Mr Fitch changed his mind about, and I thought he wouldn't miss the few bits that would make all the difference to our garden. Greenwood here said we could have it. So we've brought it and the old man won't be any the wiser, will he?'

'But what's it for?'

'I'm repairing all this old crazy paving here at the back and extending it for yer. Yer know, bringing it right up to the lawn, then there won't be that nasty bit of rough ground between. It'll look really good. Then yer'll have a patio to sit out on.'

Vera was wreathed in smiles. 'Oh, Rhett. What a lovely idea!'

'Greenwood's said I can have the old table and a couple of chairs, wrought iron they are. They're old and they need working on but they're yours when I've cleaned and painted 'em. They were going to the tip anyway. Nobody'll miss 'em, they've been at the back of the kitchen garden for years.'

'So I can have a cup of tea sitting out here on me patio. I shall feel like lady muck. Oh, Rhett! Wait till yer grandad hears about this. You are a love.' She flung her arms round him and gave him a great big kiss.

'Steady on.'

'But is it all right, yer know? It's not thieving or anything, is it?'

Greenwood came through with some more paving. 'Keep mum about it, that's all. What the old man don't know won't do him no harm. What we're bringing here is a drop in the ocean to what we've used up there. He'll never miss it.'

Vera almost skipped for joy. Someone was at last doing something just for her, and the best of it was there was no price to pay because Rhett was doing it for love. Good old Rhett, worth his weight in gold.

Whilst he worked on the patio Rhett learned his part. Hugo had said it was a small one but it seemed big to him. He'd never acted in a play before and he'd no idea why he'd been chosen. At school he'd never had a chance, being in the bottom set of absolutely every subject you could name. Now he was older he regretted not having tried at school, but there really hadn't seemed any point in it, not him with a daft name like Rhett. With a name like that you were halfway down the field from the start.

At the first rehearsal he'd stuttered and stammered, got embarrassed, dried up, moved into all the wrong places till by the end of the evening he'd decided to resign. Hugo, however, had given him a pep talk.

'Look here, I don't know what you're worrying about. You're not giving yourself a chance. By the end of four weeks you won't recognise yourself. Give it a go. Believe me, I'll coax it out of you. I've had professional actors do worse, and that's the truth.'

'You're pulling my leg.'

'I'm not! That's God's truth. Your voice is strong, which it needs to be seeing as we've no amplification, so that's half the battle. Remember, Caroline is your mother, treat her as if she is. On stage she's no longer Dr Harris, try to see her as your mum. Mmmmm?'

'I see. Yes, I see.'

'Have you a younger sister? No? When you're working, or whatever, think what it would be like to have a sister. Get to know Michelle, build a relationship, learn your parts together, and then you'll react better to her on stage. Right?'

Rhett nodded. 'It's the bits where I have to put my arm round Dr Harris and kiss her. It's blinking embarrassing, that is.'

Hugo shrugged his shoulders. 'That's because you see her as Dr Harris and not as your mother. That's where you're going wrong. Caroline? Have you a minute?'

Caroline came across to see what Hugo wanted.

'Yes?'

'Look here, Rhett is having problems seeing you as his mother.'

'Right.'

'We'll have a mini rehearsal right here and now.' He flicked through his copy of the script. 'Here we are, look, page sixty-two. Half way down. Here's a chair, pretend that's the sofa. Go and stand behind her and say your lines. Sit on it, Caroline, that's it. Right, off you go, Rhett.'

Rhett stood behind her, put a hand on her shoulder and said his lines.

'*Why's Dad so angry about this chap Leonard? Seems all right to me.*'

'*You wouldn't understand, darling.*'

'*I'm not twelve you know, like Celia. I have got some idea about what goes on.*'

'*No, you haven't.*'

'*I do know things aren't right between you and Daddy.*'

'*Do you now? Even if it were true, which it isn't, it's none of your business.*'

'*It is if you're upset.*'

'*I'm not.*'

'*Very well, I know I'm right, but I'll have to take your word for it, I expect.*'

'*You do just that.*'

'*I just wish parents didn't lie.*'

'*I'm not. Goodnight, darling.*'

'*Goodnight, Mummy.*'

Hugo applauded. 'Well, done. Much better. But you're stiff. Look, this is how I would do it.'

He rested his forearms along the top of the chair and bent much closer than Rhett had. As he reached the last line, instead of kissing the top of Caroline's head like Rhett had done he leant further forward and kissed her cheek.

'Like that. Kiss her cheek as she looks up at you. See? Try again.'

Rhett had done it again, been more relaxed and had kissed Caroline's cheek as Hugo had done.

'Much better, wasn't it? Didn't you think so?'

Rhett nodded. 'Yes. I've to forget Dr Harris is Dr Harris and then that does the trick.'

'Exactly. What did you think Caroline?'

'Big improvement.'

'Agreed! Right everybody. Three rehearsals next week. Monday, Wednesday, Friday. You're all doing fabulously. Monday Mrs Jones will be here with costumes. Well, some of them at least. No scripts by Wednesday. Everyone word perfect, please.' They all groaned. 'You can do it! Goodnight.'

As Caroline called out, 'Goodnight, everyone', Hugo materialised beside her.

'I'll walk you home.'

She laughed. 'Honestly, walk me home. It's only two doors away.'

'Nevertheless. You're doing me a good turn actually. I'm in the doghouse at Harriet's, so the longer I'm out of the house the better.'

'What have you been doing?'

'Nothing. Nothing at all, but Jimbo's upset. Bit stuffy is Jimbo, did you realise?'

They'd reached the Rectory door. The light came on and they stood in its spotlight.

'He's very protective of his family.'

'His wife, you mean. No trespassing.'

'I should think not.'

'Harriet and I go back a long way.'

'That's no excuse.'

'It isn't, is it? You can know someone five minutes and feel closer to them than to someone you've known for twenty years.'

She studied his face, wondering how sincere or how significant that remark was. He was handsome. Every feature in just the right proportion. It really wasn't fair for one man to have so many of the right ingredients. Not only that, he had the charm to match.

Hugo leaned forward and placed a soft kiss on her mouth. Then he took hold of her hand, raised it to his lips, and said, 'Fair lady!'

'Hugo!'

'Caroline!' His eyes roved over her face as he murmured, ' "All days are nights to see till I see thee. And nights bright days when dreams do show thee me." '

The common sense part of her was angry with his dalliance, but there was something other in her which responded. She kissed his lips, patted his cheek, fumbled in her bag for her key, opened the door said 'Goodnight', and went in.

'I'm home! Where are you?'

'In bed.'

'I'm thirsty. Are you?'

'No thanks.'

'Won't be long.'

Caroline drank a glass of water and then went to check the children. As usual Beth had flung off her bedclothes and her nightgown was up round her waist. Caroline pulled the sheet up higher and thought about the innocence of this beloved child of hers. She stroked her face with a gentle finger and loved her deeply. There was nothing she would do to harm Beth. Nothing at all, and she must keep that foremost in her mind. That dratted Hugo. Quoting sonnets at her. Alex was fast asleep flat on his back, neatly covered up. She loved him just as much as she loved Beth. He was such a complete and utter darling. So like Peter. Damn that blasted Hugo.

'Had a good rehearsal?'

'Yes, thanks. Excellent. Rhett is really getting the hang of things.'

'Is he? He's changed then.'

'The thing is, Hugo can explain it so well. There's lots of actors I'm sure who know how to act, but getting it out of other people is beyond them. Like lecturers at college. Some were brilliant but their lectures were the pits. Hugo just has the gift.'

There was a short silence and then Peter said, 'Has he indeed?'

Caroline didn't reply. She walked naked to the bathroom. He heard the shower running and stopped the pretence of reading his book. It lay heavy on his legs. He knew he musn't trespass. This was her battle. He didn't know how to fight it on her behalf. Didn't know what to do to stop this runaway roller coaster. It was the light in her eyes, the spring in her step which frightened him. She may not know it, but Hugo was . . .

She came back in, wrapped in a towel and sat on the edge of the bed with her back to him. He always loved touching her skin when it was warm and damp and he couldn't stop himself from reaching across to feel her bare shoulder.

Caroline very slowly stood up, lingeringly rubbed herself dry, dropped the towel on the carpet, lifted the duvet and got into bed.

'Hugo can twist people round his little finger, you know. Even old diehards like Mrs Jones are eating out of his hand. Is he acting *all* the time, do you think? Or is he really the lovable person he appears to be?'

'Only time will tell. It certainly means he gets his own way with everyone, doesn't it?'

'Not with Harriet. She has him under her thumb. She tells him off as though he were a child.'

There was a short silence and then Peter said, 'Perhaps he is. I would find it hard having him living in my house.'

'Jimbo does a little. Apparently Hugo had rather a chilly weekend.'

'I can't think Jimbo will tolerate any dalliance.'

His use of the word 'dalliance' startled Caroline. 'No, I can't think he will.'

'I'm going to sleep now. Goodnight and God bless you.' He turned on his side, made his pillow more comfortable and closed his eyes.

'And you.' Caroline was quiet for a while and then she said, 'No matter what, you are my soul mate. You do know that, don't you?'

But it seemed Peter was already asleep for there was no reply.

Next morning Caroline took the children to school and didn't return immediately. Knowing her propensity to find someone in need of help, Peter eventually left a note for her when she hadn't returned after an hour and he had to go out. It said, 'I wonder where you are? Got to leave, going into Culworth to the hospital to see Lavender Gotobed and then on to lunch at the Deanery. I've left the answer machine on. My love to you. P.'

She found it when she got back around twelve o'clock. She hadn't meant to be so long but as she'd emerged into Stocks Row on her way home from the school Hugo had come out of the Store.

'Caroline! Hi!'

'You're up early! I thought you never rose before eleven.'

'I don't usually. I think it's this country air, it's doing devilish things to my internal clock. You look all rosy and excited. Is it me who has brought this about? Flatter me! Tell me I'm right!'

'You're not.'

'How can you be so cruel? Does not your heart beat just a little faster when you see me? When you look into these dark dark orbs of mine, are you not in some kind of a fluster? Mmmmm?'

'No.'

'I'm losing my touch. Oh, God, I am! My charms are diminishing by the hour.'

'You are a fool, Hugo Maude.'

'Now that is a part I have never played: the jester. The lover, yes, but not the jester. Come walk with me.'

'Where to?'

'By gentle glade and gushing ghyll. Where is that quote from? I can't remember.' He put his head on one side and pleaded with her. 'Please?'

'Very well then, just for a while. If you're wanting a gentle glade we'll go down the footpath by Hipkin Gardens and into the wood.'

'To the woods!' He proclaimed it as though he were on stage. The mothers leaving the school couldn't avoid hearing him. Indeed, his voice carried so well that Caroline was convinced the entire village must have heard.

She was angry, and hissed, 'Be quiet. My reputation will be in ruins.'

'We shall be like Hansel and Gretel going to meet our fate together, hand in hand, in the woods.'

'I can't see the woodman.'

'Nevertheless he lurks, ready to blight our lives. I am filled with fear. Hold my hand.'

'I shan't.'

He whispered in her ear, 'Wait till we're out of sight and then I shall claim you for mine own.'

He followed her down the footpath soberly enough but as soon as they were in the field he took her hand, kissed it and then held it firmly.

'Please, Hugo, let go.'

'Relax. I'm in need of comfort. I'm wondering if I've done the right thing by doing this play.'

'In what way?'

'A challenge before I'm ready for it. The real truth is I'm not sleeping at the moment. That's why I'm up so early. Must be my damned nerves playing up.'

'I'm sorry. Can you possibly hold out, do you think? Everyone's got so involved.'

'I know.'

'Perhaps steeling yourself to do it could be the best thing. Prove to yourself you really can still function. It's only a minor thing, isn't it? It's not as if there were thousands of pounds invested, like in a West End production.'

'Yes, you're right there.'

'If you only act at half cock it'll still be too good for a village play.'

'You underate yourselves. But that's what I can never do. Less than my best.'

'You're too hard on yourself.'

'Think so? Maybe I am. I sweat blood over my work. Did you know that?' Caroline shook her head. 'My life's blood ebbs away each time I go on stage.'

'That's why you're so good.'

'You think so?'

'The critics say so, and Peter says so too.'

'Ah! If Peter says so then it must be correct.' There was a hint of scorn in his voice and he looked at her with his expressive eyebrows raised.

She withdrew her hand from his clasp. 'I'm going back now.'

'Why? Too near the truth?'

'You're being insolent again, and far too intrusive.'

'I've guessed about the twins.'

'Have you indeed.'

'I know about the cancer.'

'Do you? And who's been letting the cat out of the bag? It wouldn't be Harriet, I'm sure.'

'Certainly not. She is without blame. No.' He gazed at the sky, wondering whether to tell her or not. 'It was Sheila Bissett.'

'I might have known.'

'But you do let him dominate you, don't you? His moral standards, his children, his life, his vocation. There's no end to your devotion.'

'There's nothing wrong with the principles Peter holds dear, and if it's what I choose.'

'Choose? Or has it been imposed?'

'My choice, because I love him so. He has supported me like no one else could. You couldn't have done what he's done for me, you're too much in need of support yourself all the time.'

They'd wandered into the wood and Hugo suggested that they sat down for a while. 'Here look, on this flat bit under the tree. You make me sound like a child and I wish you didn't. What are your children like?'

Lazily he helped her to sit down with her back against the tree and then he sat, with such elegance she noted, at right angles to her, leaned back, rested his head on her legs, and squinted up at her. 'The sun is coming through the trees and lighting your cheek bones in the most alluring manner. Is it love, do you think, that has made you look so beautiful? If so, would it were I who had inspired such love.'

'Hugo, for goodness sake, pull yourself together.'

'You're always so down to earth. Lighten up.'

'I shan't.' Caroline began to tell him about the children. She'd been talking for quite a while when she asked him if he regretted not having a child of his own. There was no reply, so she looked down at him and realised he'd fallen asleep. Poor man, it was true then that he hadn't slept well. She tentatively touched his hair, it was more silky than it looked, but very thick. His beautiful arching eyebrows tempted her to run a finger along them. No man had a right to look as devastating as he did. Nor so stunningly lovable.

She sat patiently waiting for him to wake.

It was their misfortune that Sheila Bissett had decided she needed to get healthier and had insisted on accompanying Ron when he took little Pompom out for his constitutional.

'You know, Sheila, Pompom isn't as young as he was. He can't go far.'

'Right into the wood and back isn't far, Ron. Do him good. I'm enjoying marching along. Hurry up, Pompom. There's a good boy.'

Ron sighed.

'Isn't it lovely this morning? So warm but so cool under the trees. Just the right place to be for a walk.'

'Right.'

'It's a pity more people don't get out and about. It does you good, blows the cobwebs away. We have this lovely field and woods and you hardly ever see anyone using it. You could be murdered in here and no one would know. It's so secluded. It's more friendly though than Sykes Wood, don't you think? That always seems so gloomy. This one at least gets the sunlight.'

'It does.'

Sheila stepped along ahead of Ron because the footpath had narrowed, so it was she who came upon Hugo and Caroline first. By now they were both asleep. Caroline with her head resting against the trunk of the tree and one hand on Hugo's shoulder. Hugo lay just where he'd fallen asleep. Sheila was aghast. She turned round to face Ron and gesticulated to him to pick up Pompom. She saw him about to ask why, so she placed a finger against her lips and urged him to be silent.

The two of them crept past as softly as they could. Pompom snuffling to get down and Ron gripping his jaws tight shut to stop him yapping. They scurried down the path fearing to speak in case they woke the sleeping couple up.

When Sheila thought she was safely out of hearing she said in a loud stage whisper, 'Well, really. Did you ever? I can't believe it. What can they be thinking of?'

'Best thing we can do is say nothing. Pretend we didn't see them.'

'But we did and it's not right. It most definitely isn't. I think Peter ought to know.'

'You must promise me not to say a word.'

Sheila hurried along beside him, her mind boggling at what she'd seen. Mind you, he was gorgeous. She could understand . . . If she was younger she could quite fancy him herself.

'Ron, how are we going to get home? We can't walk past again, they might have woken up. You never know what might be going on.'

'For heaven's sake, as if.'

'They're only human. How are we going to get home, then?'

'We'll turn left off the path and go out onto Shepherds Hill and go home that way.'

'Oh right, of course. I can't believe it. Fast asleep in a wood. Like something out of a film. They looked so happy. So romantic!' They looked like people who are in love do, so . . . well, beautiful. To tell the truth if she really faced up to it she felt quite envious. She and Ron had never fallen asleep in a wood, never been so much at peace with one another. There came a feeling of regret to Sheila, a terrible sense of having missed out on life.

Ron grumbled, 'I can't see the village calling it that, can you?'

'Romantic? No. What is she thinking of? I blame her for encouraging him. It's disgusting. It really is.'

'Mum's the word. Remember!'

But Sheila, already planning whom to tell first, never heard his warning.

8

Peter came back home around half past four. Instead of going into the kitchen and regaling Caroline with the details of his day he went straight to his study. The children called out to him but he took no notice of them.

Beth, full of sympathy for him, said, 'I'll go see to him Mummy, I expect he's had a bad day.'

'No don't, darling. Sometimes Daddy needs to be alone. Quiet, you know. Because he's from the Church, people tell him the most heart rending stories about their lives and he gets upset. He wishes he had a magic wand and could put it all right again for them. In a bit we'll go and dig him out.'

Alex said, 'I'm not going to be a Rector. I'm going to make lots and lots of money and buy you and Daddy a lovely house with a big garden miles and miles away from here, and then he won't have to listen to all these nasty stories.'

'That's extremely kind of you and I'm sure we'd both appreciate it. For the moment, though, that's what he does and he wouldn't want to be doing anything other.'

Beth declared, 'I do love my daddy. He could fight anybody, couldn't he? He's the biggest man in all the world.'

'He's not.' Alex stuck his tongue out at her.

'He is.'

Beginning to lose her patience, Caroline said, 'Get on with your jigsaws, please, there's good children. He is the best Daddy in all the world, he may not be the biggest but he is the best.'

But they didn't need to dig him out because he eventually came into the kitchen and stood watching the twins doing their jigsaws.

Beth shouted excitedly, 'Daddy! Look! I've nearly finished!'

Caroline, busy stirring a pan at the cooker, said, 'Hello, Peter. Had a bad day? Didn't it go well?' He was slow to answer, so she turned round to look at him. Instead of smiling at her, his eyes avoided her face and he quietly said, 'Bad day! I don't think it could have been worse.'

'Why, what's happened?'

Then he did look at her, and a dreadful sinking feeling began in her throat and found its way right to the pit of her stomach. Surely not. Please God, surely not. His unflinching gaze unnerved Caroline, and she dreaded what he would say next.

'You ask *me*?'

Alex shouted. 'Finished! I'm first. I'm first.'

'You're not, I am. Aren't I, Mummy? I finished just before Alex, didn't I? But I didn't shout.'

In a very controlled voice, with her eyes on Peter, Caroline said, 'I am not asking you, I am telling you to go play in the garden for a while. Chop. Chop. Quick now.'

Beth looked at her father and then at her mother and told Alex to go outside quickly.

'I don't want to.'

'You do. Come on.'

Alex looked at his mother and decided he would do as he was told. As the back door closed behind them Caroline asked, 'What is it, then?'

'I can hardly bear to tell you what the latest gossip is that's going round the village. It doesn't seem possible, but somewhere there must be a small element of truth in it.'

'You haven't been in the village today, so what can you possibly have heard?'

'Please, Caroline, don't prevaricate, we must have the truth between us at all costs. I can't believe it. In fact, I will not believe it because it cannot have happened as I have heard it, but I do need you to give me an explanation.'

Caroline, he noticed, was beginning to tremble. 'It's about Hugo and I, isn't it?'

Peter left one of those cold silences which his parishioners, frequently to their cost, knew all about. He never took his eyes from her face.

Her voice came out jerkily and barely audible. 'I didn't intend going to bed tonight without telling you.'

'Is that so?'

'Yes, believe me.'

'So?'

'I met him as I came out of school. He was feeling unwell, he's not able to sleep at night, his nerves and such. So I took pity on him and agreed to walk with him. We went down the footpath and on to the spare land and then into the wood. He got tired, so we sat down under a tree and I leant against it and he laid down, he asked me to tell him about the children, and while I was doing so, he fell asleep. And then so did I.'

Peter almost snarled his reply. 'What about the children?'

'How old they were, what they got up to.'

'I see. Thank you.'

Aggrieved at the defensive situation she found herself in Caroline asked, 'Who the blazes saw us? No one went past that I know of.'

'Well, someone *did*.'

In a shaky voice Caroline asked him if he knew who'd seen her.

'Sheila Bissett.'

Caroline threw her arms up in despair. 'I might have known. I just might have known. It would have to be dear old Sheila, wouldn't it.'

'It scarcely matters *who* saw you. You *were* seen.'

'But I've told you the truth, what was the version you heard?'

He turned to leave. 'It's not repeatable. Obviously it was perhaps something like fourth hand or even fifth hand by the time it reached my ears. By then it had been embroidered beyond recognition. I don't mind telling you the person who told it to me quite relished the idea. They thought I *ought* to know what was "going on". But nothing on earth will make me repeat to you what I was told. *Nothing*.'

'That blasted woman! Damn and blast her.'

'Had you not gone with him, had you not fallen asleep, then you wouldn't be blasting her to kingdom come right now.'

'At least I should know what they're all saying about me.'

'Not from me you won't. There's a pan burning.'

Under her breath Caroline said, 'Damn and blast.'

'However, thank you for telling me the truth.'

'It's this Rector's wife bit, isn't it?' She emptied the blackened remains of the stewed apples down the waste disposal and viciously switched it on.

Speaking loudly over the noise, Peter said, 'No, at the moment it's what is between husband and wife. That's what it's about. What the parish thinks will be next on the agenda.'

Caroline threw the pan in the sink, turned the cold tap on so hard that the water flung itself into the pan and back out again all down the front of her dress. In desperation, Caroline fled.

She got to the rehearsal early, coinciding with the arrival of Sylvia who was anxious to be there in good time to get her kettles boiling in readiness for the calls for coffee she knew would arise as soon as everyone came.

'Hello, Dr Harris. You're early.'

'Hi, Sylvia. Yes, well I've got some lines to run through. I used to be able to remember lines so easily, but not now. Hugo wanted us word perfect tonight.' As she said his name her cheeks flushed at the thought that Sylvia might well have heard the story going round the village, and she didn't want to lose Sylvia's good opinion of her. Although Peter believed every word she had said – she just knew he did because he was like that – she still felt his disapproval very severely. She knew he wouldn't ask Sheila Bissett not to repeat the story. That was pointless. The whole village would know by now, and Caroline certainly wasn't going to remonstrate with her. She wondered if Sylvia knew about the rumours and particularly whether she knew what Sheila Bissett had said was going on. She'd grasp the nettle, like her mother always said she should.

Following Sylvia into the kitchen, Caroline leant against the worktop, and asked her.

Sylvia took a moment to fill the first kettle and set it on the hob. As the gas flared into action she said, 'Oh, I've heard right enough. The Store was absolutely agog with the tale when I went in there this afternoon. Linda was really stirring it with a big spoon, and she had some very eager listeners.' She faced Caroline. 'Does the Rector know?'

'He does. But he's had the *truth* from me, not a load of lies and suppositions.'

'I'm glad they were lies. I'm very glad they were lies.' Looking sadly at her, Sylvia continued with, 'Just such a pity that people round about here are so happy to believe lies. That's where the damage is done.'

'What are they saying? Will you tell me?'

'I thought the Rector knew.'

'He does, but he won't tell me. Says he can't.'

'I'm not surprised, he must be very hurt.'

'Well?'

'They say ... you were with Hugo ... you know ... you know, making love on the grass in the wood.' She turned away, her face red with the embarrassment of not wanting to put it into words, but knowing she must. 'There, you know now.'

'Oh God!'

'You had scarcely a stitch on, apparently.'

'Oh God! I could kill that woman. I could, so help me I could kill her.'

'Not entirely her fault, I expect it snowballed after she told it. That's what happens, you know.'

They heard the outer door open and voices in the main hall. It was most of the cast, including Hugo, all arriving at the same moment.

They heard his resonant voice calling out, 'Coffee, Sylvia, I'm dying for a cup.'

'Very well, Hugo, won't be two ticks.' Sylvia remarked quietly to Caroline, 'Go join the others and brazen it out.'

'Right.' She squared her shoulders and marched in, focusing her gaze on Harriet and heading straight for her.

Harriet greeted her with a pursed mouth and raised eyebrows.

Before they had exchanged a word Hugo came up and, putting his arm round her waist, planted a kiss on her cheek. 'How's my leading lady tonight? In full voice, I hope. We're doing a straight run through act one, OK? Know your lines?'

Caroline extricated herself from his grasp. 'Almost.'

'Almost? Almost, she says, with that enchanting smile on her face. She I shall forgive, but anyone else who doesn't know their lines will be hung drawn and quartered. Liz?' She nodded. 'Neville?' He nodded. Hugo asked each in turn and they gave him an affirmative.

'Thank God! Private tuition for you, Caroline my love, if you're not word perfect tonight! Right! Beginners please. My coffee! You're an angel.' Sylvia got an arm around her shoulders and a kiss for her effort. She thanked him nicely but shrugged him away.

'Act one, scene one. Pronto. Pronto. Barry! Less noise with the scenery, please. Props! Some chairs to represent the sofa. Liz, are you ready? Rhett? Michelle? Good, good. Wagons roll. Hush, everyone.'

Rhett strolled on through the non existent door to the sitting room. He stood gazing out of the yet to be constructed french windows at what would be a back drop showing a lawn and well-tended gardens. He turned away and pretended to fiddle with the knobs of a radiogram.

'Stop! Rhett! You look as though you are walking about on the platform of a Church Hall.'

Surprised, Rhett replied, 'Well, I am, aren't I?'

Head in hands, Hugo moaned. 'Oh God! Oh God! Give me strength! No, you're not! You're in a drawing room, an elegant drawing room and you're the young man of the house thinking about going up to Oxford this autumn. You have the assurance – be it youthful, but you have it – that particular assurance peculiar to your class. You are monied!'

'Wish to God I was!'

'There you are, you see? You're still Rhett Wright, when you should be at this moment Julian Latimer with the world your oyster. Now come in again, and try harder.'

Harriet, standing close to Caroline, muttered, 'Well? I did warn you.'

'You've heard.'

'Couldn't help it. The world and his wife know, believe me. Jimbo's had the story ten times over today. Each time it got more lurid.'

'Nothing happened.'

'That's not what I heard.'

'Well, it didn't.'

'What does Peter think?'

'He knows it's all lies.'

'Next you'll be saying, "We're just good friends." '

'We are.'

'Oh, come on, Caroline. You're fooling yourself, and I've always admired your commonsense.'

'I haven't lost it.'

'You have. Once the play is over he will leave here and we shan't see him for years.'

Caroline watched Rhett and Michelle together on stage while she prepared her answer. 'That won't bother me.'

'Three months from now someone might, just might mention Turnham Malpas to him and he'll say, "Turnham what? Where's that?" '

'Think so?'

'Know so. You're on.'

'Oh, I am. Sorry, Hugo.' Caroline fled into the wings and stepped briskly on stage. ' "*Sorry, darlings, I've got to go out; Celia is having a lunch to introduce the new man in her life to everyone, Leonard someone or other. I expect he'll be devastatingly boring, her men usually are, and I wish I didn't have to go, but I must. I promised. Doris will get you lunch if you need it. Have you anything planned for today?*" '

She got through the evening needing only a few prompts. But it was hard going. The cold, uptight touch of Neville playing her husband left her unmoved. He was well cast because she always found him cold and uptight in real life. But each time Hugo touched her, declared his love for her, tried to seduce her, she wished it was for real. Harriet was right, she'd abandoned commonsense for this ridiculous idiocy and she couldn't put a stop to it.

By the time they reached the last line of the first act and Hugo had praised them to the skies for their efforts she was completely drained and in need of a stiff drink.

Hugo, in buoyant mood, called out, 'Right, everybody. You've done an excellent night's work and now we'll all retire to the Royal Oak and the drinks are on me.'

A cheer went up and they collected their belongings and rushed out in a frenzy of post-rehearsal chatter. Caroline made sure she walked alongside Harriet and Liz.

The pub was busy so they stood at the bar until a table became free. Caroline drained her gin and tonic as fast as she decently could and ordered another. Dicky served her and gave her a wink, which she ignored. As she paid him, a hand came out and pushed her money away. It was Hugo's. She could have recognised that elegant hand with its long tapering fingers and neatly clipped nails anywhere on earth.

'This is on me. Put your money away.'

'You can't pay for drinks for everyone all night.'

'I don't intend to, but I shall and will pay for yours. Here we are, Dicky. How's life?'

'Fair to middling, thanks.'

'Snap! Same for me. Fair to middling. Except I'm hoping this fair lady here will alter all that.'

Dicky grinned. 'You couldn't have made a better choice.'

Caroline spotted a table about to become free. 'Oh look, I'm going to sit over there.' Without waiting to see if he followed she went across, settling herself on a chair. In a trice Hugo was sitting beside her. He raised his glass to her and sipped from it. Looking at her over the rim, his eyes sparkled. 'Happy?'

'Not especially.'

'You turned in an excellent performance tonight. True feeling, not acting. Eh? Am I right?'

'You flatter yourself.'

'I feel you tremble at my touch.'

'For heaven's sake!'

'It's true, my love, and you know it.'

'I don't.'

'You're fooling yourself.'

'You're the second person to say that to me tonight.'

'I should guess the other was Harriet.'

'It was.'

'She knows me too well.'

'Is she right about you, though?'

He stared at Harriet still standing at the bar and then answered, 'Not always.' Hugo reached across the table and touched the hand holding her glass. 'Not this time.'

Caroline looked into his eyes, trying to judge the sincerity of what he was saying. His eyes left hers and looked behind her. His hand was withdrawn and she heard the last voice she wanted to hear at that moment.

'Darling, I thought I might find you here.'

She turned round to find Peter standing behind her. He was wearing a shirt she'd bought him only recently and his new linen trousers. He looked, as well he knew, a very appealing figure. Pure anger filled her to the brim but a lifetime of self-discipline enabled her to greet him civilly.

'Hello. What a surprise!' She pulled out a chair for him and then as an afterthought said, 'The children! Who's sitting in?'

'Sylvia.'

A thousand thoughts raced through her head as she realised that they'd made an arrangement so he could watch over her. Damn them both, she thought. How dare they? Before Peter sat down he put a hand on her shoulder and kissed the top of her head. He drew his chair nearer to her and sat with his arm nonchalantly along the back of her chair.

'How did the rehearsal go?'

Hugo, unfussed by Peter's appearance, answered, 'Excellently well. I'm very thrilled with them all. Your wife is proving herself tiptop where acting is concerned.' He put a slight emphasis on 'acting' which angered Caroline even further.

Peter, well practised at shouldering difficult conversations, chatted away to Hugo leaving Caroline to compose herself. Inside she was fuming. These two men were treating her as though she were a brainless chattel to be bandied about at their convenience. Peter doing his caveman act, all he needed was the leg bone of a mammoth in his hand, and Hugo playing the charming dilettante. Each of them recognised the other's role but spoke about every subject under the sun other than the one which really lay between them.

It was when Peter began saying how much he'd enjoyed Hugo in

Macbeth and Hugo had pretended to shudder at the mention of that dreaded word that she finally snapped.

'As the two of you appear to have lots to talk about I'll leave you to get on with it.' They both half rose in protest at her departure but she'd gone before they had a chance to speak.

On her way out she stopped to say goodnight to everyone and then coolly left, after a final wave to Harriet.

She greeted Sylvia with less than her usual courtesy. 'Hi there. Thanks for giving Peter a chance to come and have a drink with us. I've come home early because I'm tired.'

After Sylvia had left, Caroline checked the children were all right and then went to run a bath. She chose lavender bath oil to relax her and was just starting to simmer down when she heard Peter's key in the lock.

She listened as he checked the doors, shut windows, spoke to the cats, unlocked the cat flap and came slowly up the stairs. She'd imagined he'd come into the bathroom immediately but he didn't. Lying back in the hot scented water with her eyes shut, she contemplated where her feelings were leading her. Having arrived at the conclusion that she was infatuated with Hugo and it wasn't the real thing and she'd better get in charge of herself again quick fast, she became conscious of a movement close by and opened her eyes to find Peter in his pyjamas standing looking down at her.

Immediately the fury she had felt in the bar overcame her and she blurted out her anger. 'Satisfied, are you? You and Sylvia. That was a pathetic performance, Peter, and what's more it was beneath you and you know it. It was childish in the extreme.'

He knelt down beside the bath, laid his arms on the edge of it and rested his chin on them. 'I had to give the matter the stamp of my approval and it was the only way I could think of to get the message transmitted round the village that their soft-in-the-head Rector didn't believe a word of what they were saying.'

'Is that so.'

'Someone has to protect your reputation.'

'Oh, so that's what you were doing! And there I thought you were doing your caveman act.'

He trailed a hand in the water and she shifted her legs to avoid the possibility of him touching her.

'No. Though I can see it may have looked like it. But I don't want anyone looking at you as Hugo did tonight.'

'He has a massive ego and imagines every woman – excepting perhaps Harriet, who has his measure – will fall in love with him. He's probably quite right, most of them do.'

Peter flicked some water onto her shoulders and trailed his fingers over the wetness. 'He has no business to toy with your affections.'

'You make it sound as though I have no control over my own feelings. Well, I have.' She sat up, sploshing water over the edge of the bath and drenching his pyjama jacket. 'Sorry! I didn't mean to do that. Just leave it to me, will you? And don't ever again do what you did tonight. I am not a child. A jealous husband I don't need, because there's nothing to be jealous of.' Peter began touching her arm gently and persuasively. 'And you can take your hands off me, please, because I'm not having you going through the ritual of, as you see it, establishing your rights over me tonight. I am my own person and I won't have it.'

Peter sprang to his feet, angered by what she'd said. 'I have never done that. Ever. Not once. And well you know it. We have always been equal partners.'

The tremor in his voice appalled her. He was absolutely right. Damn and blast that Hugo. He was driving her to say things which in her normal mind she never would. She would not allow Hugo to make her throw away the one thing most precious to her.

Caroline pulled out the plug, stood up and slowly unbuttoned Peter's jacket, saying, 'Put it in the airing cupboard to dry.' She thought, what stupid comments people who love each other make when they really mean to say 'I love you'. She waited for him to close the cupboard door before putting her arms around his neck. She said in a shaky voice, 'I'm so dreadfully sorry, I really don't know what's come over me. Please forgive me. Now I'm making you all wet again. Sorry.'

He helped her out of the bath, wrapped her in a towel and, holding each other close, they left the bathroom.

9

Vera carried the tray out onto the patio and placed it carefully on the wrought iron table. She checked to make sure she had everything she needed and then sat down to wait.

The geraniums were growing wonderfully well and already she could just see tips of pink showing in the buds. By next week they'd be ablaze. The pots Rhett had found were ideal. She patted the table top and admired the chair opposite her. It was painted white just like she saw in those posh gardening magazines at the nursing home. In fact, truth to tell, the whole of the patio with its pots of plants and the table and chairs could have been from one of them. Identical it was. And the crazy paving! He'd mended the worst bits and then extended it right up to the grass. Smashing, it looked. If she'd paid a thousand pounds, which she wouldn't have, it couldn't look better. Who needed a mansion to have a posh garden? There was no doubt about it, their Rhett had an eye for gardens.

She heard the door bell. 'That'll be her.'

Dottie Foskett had already opened the door as Vera reached it.

'Thought you wasn't in, but you'd said half past three.'

'I was sitting out in the garden, it took me a minute. Go through. The kettle's already boiled, I won't be long.'

Dottie admired the garden while she waited. Their Rhett had turned out all right after all. Surprising in the circumstances, because she'd really thought he'd blown it with that witchcraft business the other year. Poor lad. What a start in life he'd had.

Vera came through with the teapot.

'New cups you've got then.'

'That's right. Got them from that china stall back o' Culworth market. I thought we needed something a bit different if we were joining the aristocracy.'

'Come on, Vera, you do give yourself airs.'

'I don't. Where could you find a nicer place to sit? There isn't a castle in the land with a lovelier patio than this.'

'They calls 'em terraces when they 'ave a castle.'

Vera pondered this for a moment and then agreed with her. 'You're right. Milk or lemon?'

'Milk, of course. Yer know they look God awful expensive to me. Are you sure they're not valuable?'

'Well, Greenwood Stubbs said they'd been laid about ever since he'd been there and nobody bothered with 'em so we got 'em. Pity for 'em to go to waste. Mr Fitch said they had to get rid of it all before he got back, so here we are.' Vera sipped her tea, put down her cup and asked, 'You weren't in the pub last night were you, Dottie?' Dottie, with a mouthful of buttered scone, shook her head. 'Rector came in, you know, and kissed her and that and sat beside her with his arm round her, talking to Hugo.'

'Bet you wished you were a fly on the wall when they got home.'

'No, I don't. I don't wish either of them any harm. They're a lovely couple. It's Hugo who's to blame.'

Dottie winked at her. 'Perhaps you should set your cap at him, take the heat off her.'

'Don't be daft. I can safely leave that to you.'

'Me!' Dottie made a show of being indignant. 'You've heard they're expecting another at Keepers Cottage?'

'Gilbert and Louise, yer mean. Yes, I have. Going great guns they are. Who'd have thought it, her being like she was.'

'The baby will only be eleven months when the next arrives.'

'Yer'd better have a word in her ear, then. Tell her all yer know. She can't keep this pace up. I expect Louise'll be wanting you to do more hours. More tea, or another scone?'

Dottie eyed her closely through narrowed eyes. 'You're enjoying this, aren't yer?'

'Wouldn't you?'

'Suppose I would. That miserable flat I have's neither use nor ornament. Can't swing a cat.'

'Good job you haven't got one then!'

They chortled together over the tea cups and Dottie told her a few more pieces of scandal which mainly involved the antics of Kenny and Terry Jones and herself.

'Honestly, Dottie, you are a one. You're disgusting. It doesn't go with my nice china at all it doesn't, a tale like that.'

'Is that your bell?'

Vera listened. 'It is. They'll be waking Don up. All right, all right I'm coming.'

Standing on her doorstep were two big men in suits. Before they opened their mouths she knew in her bones that they were police officers.

'Mrs Wright? Mrs Vera Wright?'

Vera nodded. They flashed their identification cards and asked if they could come in.

She opened the door wider and showed them into her front room. She asked them if they'd like to sit down. What on earth were they doing here? Was it Brenda? Had something happened to Brenda? Don had always said she'd finish up in the canal with the company she kept.

'Is it my daughter? Brenda. Is she all right?'

The taller police officer shook his head. 'It's nothing to do with a daughter. From information we have received we believe that you have stolen goods on the premises.'

Vera was shocked. 'Stolen goods? I haven't got no stolen goods. Do you mean shop lifting? 'Cos I've not been doing that. I'm honest and hard working like me husband.'

'Where is he at the moment?'

'In bed. He's on nights.'

'Could you wake him for us, Mrs Wright?'

'Why should I? He's only been in bed an hour.'

Dottie appeared in the doorway.

'Well, we need to speak to him.'

Vera, fearing Don's temper if she woke him now, asked, 'Can't you tell me what it's about?'

'Can we look in your back garden?'

'I haven't got no stolen goods in the shed if that's what yer mean. Me, my Don and our Rhett, we're all hard working people and we don't steal, so there.'

'It's not the shed Mrs Wright, it's . . .' he referred to his notebook, 'an antique wrought iron table, and two chairs, and a large quantity of crazy paving, two bags of cement and several highly-prized Victorian ornamental stone urns removed from the estate grounds in the last three weeks.'

Dottie gasped and reached out blindly for the nearest chair. 'Ohhh. Vera!'

Vera had gone white as a sheet. 'Oh no! Who's . . .' She was going to say 'split on us' but she was astute enough, despite the shock, to know that would give the game away. 'Dottie, get our Don.' Dottie disappeared up the stairs on feeble legs, every step a mountain.

'Your grandson? Is he home yet?'

Vera glanced at the clock. 'Won't be 'ome for a while yet. He starts at half past six in the summer and sometimes works till it's almost dark. What do you want him for?'

'He's implicated in the theft.'

'He got permission.'

'From whom?'

Despite her fear, Vera couldn't name names. 'Oh, nobody. But he wasn't to blame.'

'Then who was?'

'I don't know.'

'You mean you won't say?'

'Something like that.'

Vera stared at Don as he arrived in the sitting room with his trousers hastily pulled on, and his rolls of bulging fat clearly visible in the gaps between the buttons of his pyjama jacket. Was she married to *this*? No wonder they'd never made progress.

'Mr Donald Wright?'

Don acknowledged he was with a nod of his head. As the officer revealed his reasons for being in the house Don grew more and more furious and when the officer finished speaking he vented his spleen on Vera. 'You and your fancy ideas! I might have known no good would come of it. La di da on the patio with yer cups of tea and yer gossip. It's her fault, officer. She encouraged him.'

'Could we see the garden, please?'

Vera led the way and Don and Dottie brought up the rear. They made notes about the number of stone urns, the half bag of cement in the corner by the shed awaiting disposal, and took particular interest in the table and two chairs. Then they counted the paving stones Rhett hadn't needed, then the new stones he'd obviously laid.

Vera found she had tears sliding down her cheeks. She scrubbed at them with a corner of a tissue lying dormant in her skirt pocket. Just as she'd clutched her dream it was being snatched away. Why was there never hope? Other people had it but not Vera Wright. Oh no! Not her. Bottom of the pile again.

'Would you mind telling me how you came to know about all this?' Vera waved her arm vaguely around the garden. 'You know, who told you?'

'It was reported to us by the owners.'

'I see. Oh, I see.'

'Now, these articles may not be removed from this garden until we have arranged to do it ourselves.'

'You're taking up the crazy paving, are you then?'

'Well, perhaps not, but we shall certainly be removing the urns and the garden furniture. Probably later this afternoon.'

'What if we pay for it all?'

'Sorry, but the owners want to prosecute.'

At the word prosecute, Vera knew it was all up with them. She sat down heavily on one of the wrought iron chairs but immediately recollected it wasn't hers to sit on any longer and leapt to her feet. 'Don, it could mean jail for yer.'

'Me? I'd nothing to do with it. It was all you. If there's anybody going to jail it'll be you not me. I can't afford to lose my job.'

'Neither can I, Don.' She went in the house, closely followed by Dottie, Don and the police officers.

'We'll say good afternoon to you, Mrs Wright, Mr Wright. Nothing is to be moved from here at all. We've made a note and we'll be back either later this afternoon or first thing tomorrow. Sorry about this, but we're only doing our duty. We could do nothing else but take action once it was reported.' They shut the door and left Dottie, Don and Vera alone. For the first time since Brenda had got herself into trouble with Rhett, Vera sat down and howled. Don took the opportunity to stomp off back to bed.

Dottie patted her arm, handed her a fresh tissue from the purple plastic handbag she was clutching, and said, 'Look here, why don't yer go up to the Big House and see Mr Fitch and offer to pay for the crazy paving and give him back the pots and that. Surely if he's not out of pocket with it he'll let you off.'

Vera stopped sobbing. 'That's an idea. I could do that, couldn't I?'

'Of course yer could. I'll come with yer, if yer like.'

Vera decided she'd do better on her own than with her flashy cousin. 'It's very kind but it's my problem and I'll go by meself. Where's Don?'

Dottie, who'd always had a certain amount of respect for the man of few words her cousin had married, said, 'He's gone back to bed. The rat.'

'He is, isn't he? A blasted rat. I've stuck with him through thick and thin, but this time he's finally done it. Abandoning me like that. I'm going to get changed into something smart and I'm going up to the Big House and seeing what I can do about this. I'm damned if I'm going to prison.'

Dottie could almost hear trumpets sounding as Vera set off. She'd put on her pink suit from Brenda's wedding and carried with her her high-heeled shoes in a plastic carrier bag, having decided that her sandals would serve her better until she got within shouting distance of the Big House. She planned to change into them and leave her shopping bag under a bush while she went inside. 'Good luck, Vera. You'll win through.'

Vera went in through the main door. It had occurred to her that she ought to use the trade entrance but decided against it. She was here on business and she'd be at a disadvantage if she didn't use the main door.

Overawed by the dignity and beauty of the entrance hall, she hesitated, wondering where to go. A voice said, 'Good afternoon. Can I help you?'

It was a smart young thing behind a reception desk who had spoken.

'Mr Fitch. I want to see Mr Fitch.'

'Your name is . . .?'

'Vera Wright. Is he in?'

'I'm sorry, Mr Fitch is in the States. He won't be back for a while. Can I help? Or the estate manager, Mr Mayer.'

Relieved at hearing a name she knew Vera said yes, she'd see Mr Mayer.

'Sit down and I'll page him.'

Neither of them had to wonder if he was coming because long before he hove into sight they heard his heavy breathing and felt the vibration of every step he took.

Vera hadn't seen Jeremy Mayer for some time and was amazed at how much fatter he had become. Even worse, his breathing was so loud. He reminded her of an old bulldog who used to come to visit one of the patients at the nursing home.

He grunted and panted and then said breathlessly, 'Vera! Come into my office.'

She followed him into an office filled by a large desk, several filing cabinets, book shelves and Jeremy. He lowered himself into his chair.

'I know what you've come to see me about.'

'You do?'

'Yes, and I'm sorry but we shall be prosecuting. Mr Fitch is very serious indeed when it comes to staff stealing property.'

'But it was just lying about, and Mr Fitch had said he wanted it clearing away. No one had bothered with it all for years. It just doesn't seem fair.'

'Bothered with it or not it was, er, *is* estate property and is not to be removed.'

'If we return it all and pay for the crazy paving would that be all right? It wasn't done on purpose, kind of.'

'It didn't get into your garden all by itself, did it? When Mr Fitch finds out ...'

'That's what I want to know, who was it split on us?'

Jeremy shut up like a clam. He fiddled with a pen, straightened papers which were lying haphazardly about his desk, coughed and said, 'I'm not at liberty to ... Suffice to say I received information upon which I have acted on Mr Fitch's behalf.'

'Sounds like the bloody Gestapo to me. Does he have a torture chamber?'

Jeremy allowed himself half a smile. 'No, but we do have a very efficient information system.'

'Look. Could you speak on my behalf? Ask him to let us off. You know, not go to court. It wasn't done with any intent, not really. Just ...'

'The matter is in the hands of the police and that's that. I am acting under Mr Fitch's explicit instructions. Now, I'm a very busy man, if you'll excuse me.' He coughed and slipped a lozenge into his mouth.

'From what I hear that's just about all you do do, act under his instructions. A yes man, that's what you are. A yes man. He's got you right where he wants yer. Same as yer wife has yer, right where she wants yer.' As an afterthought she added, 'Except she doesn't want yer.'

Jeremy struggled to his feet. 'Madam, if you please.'

'We'll pay him for the crazy paving. He's getting everything back, everything. So if he's no worse off, do you think I might persuade ...'

'I do not, Vera. It's more than my job's worth to cancel the charges.'

The word 'job' jolted Vera. 'And our Rhett. What about his job?'

'He finishes today.'

'You wouldn't do that to him! He was only trying to cheer me up. That's all. Just cheer me up. A good turn, that's all. And this is his reward. He'll be heartbroken.'

'He shouldn't have stolen, should he?'

'He didn't, he just kind of did a long term borrow.'

'There's nothing more to be said.' Jeremy nodded in the direction of the door. 'Let yourself out.'

'Well, if you want to lose the best under gardener you've had in years then that's up to you. He's got his diploma, so I don't suppose he'll be out of a job for long.'

'No one will employ him if he has a criminal record.'

'Criminal record! You're prosecuting him as well?'

'Of course. You for receiving stolen goods and him for stealing. The estate has been driven into taking a stance on this. We lose thousands with all this pinching here and there, and it's got to stop.'

'Well, all I can say is damn your eyes. All this over a few stingy bits of crazy paving and he's a multi millionaire. We'll be ruined, but he'll go from strength to strength. It damned well isn't fair.'

Vera stormed out of Jeremy's office, sped down the drive as fast as she could and only remembered that night when she went to bed that her flat shoes were still under the bush at the Big House. Well, she thought, the dratted, dreary, boring things can stay there till they rot. Just like I'm going to rot.

The full implications of the situation didn't strike home until Vera went to the Royal Oak the following night. To her delight, Willie, Sylvia and Jimmy were at her favourite table and also Pat Jones, Duckett that was, waiting for her Barry to join her after the rehearsal.

'Vera!' Sylvia patted the seat beside her. 'Come and sit next to me. Willie, get Vera a drink.'

In obedience to Sylvia's request Willie stood up. 'What will yer have?'

'Arsenic?'

'Come on, it won't come to that.'

'Won't it? It's a police job yer know. In court. I could go to prison.'

Pat looked at her and said accusingly, 'It's all your Rhett's fault.'

Vera nodded. 'All he wanted to do was cheer me up 'cos I 'adn't got the job as wardrobe mistress. That Mrs Jones got there before me, as yer know. I know I was rude to her, but she cut me right out and I longed to do it.' A faraway look came in her eyes and Sylvia squeezed her hand. 'Poor lad, he's lost his job, yer know. Big fat Jeremy says even though he's got a diploma, with a criminal record he'll never get another job.'

Willie had come back with her drink and heard the last few words. As he put it down and pocketed his change he said, 'Yer mean he's being prosecuted as well?'

Vera nodded. 'Me for receiving and 'im for stealing. Just a few old pots and a rusty table and chairs. It's not fair. He worked hours on 'em cleaning the rust off. So now old Fitch gets 'em back like new.' She took a sip of her lager and sat shaking her head in desperation.

Pat said angrily, 'And what about me?'

'What about you, you're not involved.'

'No, but my Dad is.'

'So?'

'When old Fitch gets back from the States Jeremy says they're going to decide whether or not Dad loses his job, too. After all, the gardens are his sole responsibility.'

'He'd never sack your dad! Greenwood Stubbs sacked! Never!'

'Don't you be too sure. We're shaking in our shoes, believe me.'

'But where would he be without him? The gardens! The glasshouses! He'd never find another to replace him, not like your dad.'

'Old Fitch is in no mood for being sentimental, he's on the warpath and we're being used as an example. They steal like mad from the estate. Fencing posts, top soil, tools, wood, paint, electric drills, you name it. They all think old Fitch is fair game. He knows it and he's out to stop it. So now he's got actual evidence of stealing and the balloon's going up.'

Slowly Vera thought through what Pat had said. 'It'd just be a fine, wouldn't it though?'

Pat shrugged her shoulders. Willie gloomily contemplated his ale. Sylvia grew cold with the thought which had just struck her. Pat and her dad would be sure to lose the house which went with the head gardener's job, in which case Pat and Barry, Greenwood and Dean and Michelle would be homeless. She decided to stay sympathetically silent.

Jimmy spoke up. 'I may not have led a blameless life, but I've never actually stolen anything. It strikes me that you're all feeling sorry for yourselves and thinking how unfair it all is, when in fact yer guilty.'

A stunned silence greeted his remarks, followed by an enraged babble of noise.

'Jimmy! You of all people.'

'Well, I never!'

'Whose side are you on?'

'Turned capitalist, 'ave yer, now yer in business for yourself?'

'You're a traitor, you are!'

Jimmy raised a hand to silence them all. 'Just a minute. Answer me this question. Leaving aside the fact that the stuff was all lying unused around the estate, who does it belong to? Not you, Vera. Not your Rhett. Nor, Pat, does it belong to your dad even though he's head gardener. So who does it belong to?'

Reluctantly they all said, 'Mr Fitch.'

'Exactly. That's my point.'

Vera protested. 'But it was lying about doing nothing. He wanted rid of it, he said so. He wouldn't have missed it. What I want to know is who told him?'

They all agreed they didn't know. Vera smiled triumphantly. 'That's the point, he'd never have realised if someone hadn't told him. I've got to find out who it was.'

Jimmy groaned. 'Yer 'aven't got the point, 'ave yer. No matter who told him, yer still guilty of receiving stolen goods. Finding out who let on'll alter nothing.'

'I'd still like to know who it was, though.'

Sylvia didn't improve Vera's mood by saying, 'Anyone about that afternoon would have seen them unloading, you know. Anyone at all.'

Vera eyed Jimmy speculatively. 'It wasn't you, was it? Coming over all moral about theft just now, it makes me wonder.'

Jimmy snorted his anger. 'I wouldn't do a trick like that. I'm not that law abiding, I've no loyalty to that old Fitch, believe me. I'd rather see Ralph at the Big House, like he should be, than that old varmint.'

Pat said, 'And so would I. He wouldn't have minded Vera having a few stones and that, he'd have given them to her himself.'

Jimmy tapped the table with his forefinger, 'And that's why he isn't up there and old Fitch is. Men like Sir Ralph and those who went before him were too kind. They didn't watch the pennies, whereas old Fitch always has done and that's why he owns the Big House and old Ralph doesn't. Whatever yer say, Rhett, with your dad's connivance, stole that crazy paving and you're getting what yer deserve, hard though it may seem.'

Vera stood up. 'Well, all I can say is, Jimmy Glover, I shan't be drinking with you any more. I've always thought you were one of us, but I can see now you aren't and never have been. You're a traitor to your class, you are. A traitor. That's what.'

With what little dignity she had left after the battering of the last couple of days Vera left the bar, managing to hold on to her tears until she'd got through the door.

Sylvia filled the silence Vera left behind by saying, 'All this is Hugo Maude's fault. He's a lot to answer for.'

Willie asked, 'Yer mean *he* told old Jeremy?'

'Noooo! Of course not. If she'd got the job of wardrobe mistress, Rhett wouldn't have come up with the idea of cheering her up, would he? So at bottom, when all's said and done, it's Hugo that's caused it all.'

'Not only that from what I hear,' Jimmy said slyly.

Sylvia avoided Jimmy's eye and finished the last of her gin and tonic.

Pat asked, 'So what have you heard?'

Jimmy leant across the table and began to report the version of the tale he'd heard about Caroline and Hugo in the woods. He had just warmed to his story when the door opened and in came the entire cast of the play and the helpers. Barry came straight across to speak to Pat.

'Anyone ready for a refill? Be quick, I'm parched!'

They all agreed they were and he took their orders and eventually came back balancing a loaded tray. Barry sat down beside Pat, gave her a hearty kiss, shared out the drinks, toasted them all and downed half his glass at the first go.

'I needed that. By Jove, what a night we've had. Hugo's been losing his rag every five minutes.'

Sylvia laughed. 'He was firing on all cylinders when I left. He kept it up, did he?'

'I should say. He rants and raves and then next second he's as sweet as honey.' He shuffled closer to Pat, and whispered, 'Mind you, Dr Harris gets all the honey bit, it's the rest of us who get the ranting. That right, Sylvia?'

Sylvia gave a non-committal nod.

'In fact if I was Neville Neal I'd have resigned tonight. He couldn't get a word right.'

Pat asked 'Yer mean he hadn't learned his lines?'

'Learned his lines all right, just wasn't saying 'em like Hugo wanted him to. Give him his due, Neville stuck it out till he got it right.'

Pat recollected her responsibilities and asked, 'Barry, where's our Michelle? Who's taken her home?'

'Rhett.'

'Rhett? Oh, I see. Not our Dean?'

'No. Dean's over there, look, knocking 'em back. Michelle did real well tonight. Hugo's very pleased with her.'

Pat beamed. 'Well, I suppose that's something to cheer us up, there isn't much else, is there?' She looked across to where Hugo was standing beside Caroline toasting her not only with his drink but with his eyes. 'Dr Harris is skating on thin ice again by the looks of it.'

They watched Hugo put an arm around her waist and keep it there.

Pat asked Sylvia if the Rector would be coming again tonight.

Sylvia shook her head. 'Can't do that twice, once but not twice. I've an idea he caught it in the neck about that.'

Willie asked what on earth was up with Dr Harris? Something funny had come over her and no mistake.

When they'd all finished watching Hugo lead Caroline to a separate table for two they all looked at Sylvia. 'Well?'

'I can't understand it actually. Her and the Rector, well yer don't need me to tell you how much they think about each other. Sounds soppy, but they are very, very much in love with one another, like as if they'd married only yesterday. He worships her and her him. Yet he can stand by and give her the freedom to mess about with him.' She jerked her thumb in Hugo's direction.

Barry observed, 'Seems funny to me. If Pat was carrying on like that I'd have blacked both his eyes for starters, and broken both his legs for the main course.'

Willie grunted. 'Well, they're educated, aren't they? Different class o' people from us. They see things differently.'

Barry snorted his disgust. 'I bet it's true they've been having it off. See him running his finger up her arm? Sexy that. They're only the same as the rest of us when it comes to hanky panky.'

Jimmy's eyes twinkled.

Willie looked embarrassed.

Pat gave Barry a nudge to shut him up.

Sylvia became incensed. 'Barry! Really! What a thing to say!'

Barry leaned over towards her and said quietly so as not to be overheard, 'Well, admit it, that's why you're so worried. That's what you're dreading's happened. I'm telling you by the looks of 'em it has. When the Rector finds out then believe me it'll be Coronation night and Bonfire Night fireworks rolled into one!'

Jimmy intervened by changing the subject to the chances of the Turnham Malpas cricket team this week, and how was Barry's batting lately.

But Hugo's finger was still following a vein on Caroline's arm, and she was still enjoying the sensation.

10

In bed that night after Peter had gone to sleep Caroline grew too restless to settle and went downstairs to make herself a drink. Sitting in her rocking chair beside the Aga she sipped her tea and thought about temptation. She looked at her arm, remembering the feeling of Hugo's finger tracing along her skin. God, he was tempting. There was that indefinable quality which attracted her to him. The way his hand clasped hers, those fingers so strong and yet so elegant. He was truly a man designed for women to adore. She realised Hugo knew he was desirable, whereas Peter never realised for one moment how attractive women found him. Hugo knew women fell for him. He was arrogant, opinionated, egotistical, not at all the kind of person who in her right mind she would have liked, but at the same time he was gloriously fascinating. Damn him. The mature, experienced, commonsensical, well beloved Caroline had no need to crave for Peter's love; she had that always, forever. It was hers, whatever she did, whenever she needed it. But right now Peter's kind of unwavering love had become suffocating; she needed something different, something deeply exciting, before it was all too late. Some exquisite experience that would light her up whenever she thought about it in the years to come. In her heart of hearts the untried virginal Caroline of yesteryear lusted for Hugo. Coming as he did at this very moment in her life he was like the answer to a prayer.

Parallel to her thoughts about temptation and where it might lead ran her thoughts about her children. There was no way she could smash their lives to pieces, and that would be what she would do if she left Peter for Hugo. For Hugo? What was she thinking of?

A life of racketing about, never knowing who he was with, what he was doing, never being sure he would come home at night. And the children. In all conscience could she take them from their blood parent? But they were hers, Peter told her so, time and again. They loved her as she loved them. Their dear hearts would break.

How sure could one be of a person like Hugo? One couldn't. Not so entirely as she could Peter. With Hugo she would have wonderful, glorious, delirious, hilarious times but when it came to the real challenge of life, when the chips were down then where would Hugo be?

Her mind wandered away from reality and she was back in the wood with Hugo's head resting on her legs and her fingers entwined in his dark silky hair. She remembered how she felt about him in the role of Leonard and particularly his attempt at seduction in the second act. With her cup she toasted him as the actor, the lover, the man and wished she was drinking some exotic, madly expensive wine instead of dull, everyday, comforting, mundane tea. Her thoughts were broken by a cry. Instantly, she raced for the stairs.

'All right, Beth, I'm coming! All right!'

After she'd soothed away Beth's nightmare Caroline returned to bed and lay on her side looking at Peter in the glow of her bedside light. She could see just the faintest of lines around his eyes, and a very slight hint of a white hair here and there above his ears. He had one hand tucked under his chin, the fingers half curled, and she examined his well manicured nails and recalled the sensitivity of the touch of his fingers. She leaned over him and breathed in the familiar scent of him mingling with the faint aroma of the soap he'd used before he came to bed, and risked waking him by touching his cheek with her fingers and then kissing him. But it wasn't only his physical attributes which impressed. It was his courage, his all-adoring love and his steadfastness.

Unquestioning. Profound. Passionate. What more could a woman want?

Impatiently Caroline turned off the light and lay down again. Peter, feeling her presence even in sleep, reached out an arm and drew her close. How she wished he hadn't. At this moment she wasn't worthy of him.

*

The phone rang around half past nine the next morning. 'Turnham Malpas Rectory. Peter Harris speaking.'

'Oh! Good morning! Hope I'm not ringing too early.'

'Hugo! Good morning. What can I do for you?'

'It's Caroline really. Is she in?'

'She is indeed. I'll get her for you. Hold the line.' Peter went to the study door and called, 'Caroline! It's for you.' He picked up the receiver again and said, 'How are the rehearsals going?'

'Absolutely fine, thanks. Taking a bit of knocking into shape but very well really. Your dear wife is doing excellently. Really got into the part.'

'She's certainly enjoying herself, all due to you.'

There was a moment's hesitation and then Hugo replied, 'Good. I'm glad. How's life for you?'

'Couldn't be busier. Would you mind if I sat in on a rehearsal sometime? Just interested to see what goes on. Never seen a world class actor at work, you see.'

'Be delighted. Come any night you can get a sitter for those children of yours.'

Peter thought he detected a slight emphasis on the word 'yours'. 'Ah, here she is. It's Hugo, darling.' He made no move to leave the study so she could speak to him privately.

'Hello, Hugo! What can I do for you?'

Peter watched her listening to him: the restlessness, the barely disguised excitement, the slight huskiness of her voice. He turned back to the work on his desk.

'I'd love to. Yes, I really would. No, Peter's busy all day. I'd need to be back by three because of the children.' There came a pause as she listened to him. 'No, he cannot, he's working. See you about half past eleven then? OK. Bye.'

Peter watched the receiver being returned to its cradle, and waited.

'Darling, you don't mind if Hugo and I go out to lunch, do you? Just some things we need to talk over about the play. It's difficult when he's producing and acting at the same time, you see. There are important things he doesn't get a chance to tell me.'

Peter swung his chair round and faced her. 'Of course I don't mind. All I will say is *be careful.*'

'You're not suggesting he might seduce me over the lunch table, are you?'

Peter studied what his reply should be. 'That kind of comment is not fitting and well you know it. Of course I don't mean that.'

'Good, because there's no need for you to worry.'

'I'm not entirely blind to the effect he has on you. It's hardly surprising, even I can see he is a very attractive man.'

'Not to me he isn't.'

Peter sighed. 'You're fooling yourself, my darling girl.'

'Is this on the basis that the onlooker sees most of the game?'

'Something like that.'

'I'm not a complete fool.'

'I know. Indeed I do. Just a friendly warning, don't you know.'

'No, Peter, it isn't. You're doing what you always do, standing aside and allowing me to do whatever I want, pretending to be giving me my freedom but at bottom it's because you're so damn confident that your love for me will bring me to heel.'

'What would you prefer me to do? Go break his legs?'

Caroline gave him a slight smile. 'You could at that. At least it would be *something*.'

'Whatever, the warning still stands. *Be careful.* I don't want you hurt.'

'How about if I fancy being hurt? Fancy having a fling? Fancy doing my own thing? Fancy not doing the Rector's wife bit?'

'That's up to you. Do as you wish.' He swung his chair to face the desk and she took it as a dismissal. After she'd left the study, Peter tried to settle to his work, but on every page Hugo's face intruded on the words. He put a stop to the pretence of working and sat with his head in his hands thinking. He knew Caroline would realise the situation that was developing, she was too astute not to. What made it worse from his point of view was that she was going headlong into it with her eyes wide open. The play was merely the vehicle by which she gained access to the man. Damn and blast him. Why had he ever come?

The restaurant Hugo chose was one recommended by Jimbo. 'He says it's brilliant and just right for a tête-à-tête luncheon.' He took a moment from watching the traffic to glance at her. 'Happy?'

'I am. It's years since I had a ride in an open car. They really are fun, aren't they?'

'They are. Fun, that's just what you need. Fun and lots of it.'

'You're right. I do. Being a doctor all the people you speak to are people not at their best. It can be very draining. Then Peter has a similar kind of job in a way and between the two of us we have all the cares of the world on our shoulders. A bit of fun *is* just what I need.' Hugo pressed firmly on the accelerator as they turned onto the bypass and her hair began blowing about, bringing a stunning sense of freedom to her which she hadn't experienced in a long time.

'Did he mind?'

'Yes and no. He's like that.'

'Loves you very much, doesn't he?'

Caroline shouted back. 'He does. Too much sometimes.'

'Ah! I see. Cloying, is he?'

'Absolutely not. Well, just a little. What did you say this restaurant was called?'

'I didn't. Believe it or believe it not it's called The Lovers' Knot.'

Caroline laughed. 'That is just too obvious for words. Are you sure it was Jimbo's suggestion?'

'Why? Does the word "lover" have some significance for you and me?'

Quickly Caroline shook her head. 'Of course not, I don't know why I said it.'

Hugo smiled and pressed even harder on the accelerator. As the speedometer went up to a hundred he smiled even more broadly.

'It does for me. Have significance. I want you, Caroline.'

'Do you indeed.'

'Yes. I do.'

'Hard luck. How far is this place?'

'About twelve miles.'

'Twelve miles! Just for lunch? What are you thinking of?'

'I hug my thoughts to my breast, they are not for public declaration.'

'You are being ridiculous. I don't want to go twelve miles for lunch. Please turn round and we'll go to The George in Culworth. That's much nearer.'

'Too late.'

'That's what I shall be if you don't go back. I can't have the children coming home to an empty house, they would be devastated. In any case I'd never live it down if they had to sit on the doorstep waiting for me.'

'Tut tut. Your reputation in jeopardy again. Ring Peter and tell him you'll be late. He can be there.'

'No, he can't.'

'Yes, he can.'

'No, he can't.'

'This sounds more like Gilbert and Sullivan by the minute.'

'I mean it, Hugo. I want you to turn round and go back. There, look, half a mile there's a turn off.' This caused Hugo to speed even faster.

'You are upsetting me.'

'No, I am abducting you, my dear,' he said in the tones of a thoroughly ham actor, as he twirled the ends of his imaginary waxed moustache.

She had to laugh.

'That's wonderful, hearing you laugh like that.'

'You're right it is. I feel as though I've been deadly serious for far too long. Carry on.' She waved a carefree hand. 'Drive wherever you like. I don't care.'

At half past two she rang Sylvia on the hotel telephone to ask her to collect the children, but there was no reply. She rang the Rectory but there was no reply from there either. So she tried Harriet, then Muriel, and finally the school. Kate, the head teacher, promised to keep the children until someone came to collect them.

Hugo and Caroline arrived back at five o'clock. Hugo tooted the horn with a flourish as he pulled up outside the Rectory. 'There we are. Home at last. I have an apt quotation for this situation but it won't quite come to mind.'

'Good, because I haven't time to listen. Where's my bag? Oh, here under the seat.' As she brought her head up he kissed her ear. 'Hugo! For God's sake.'

'I know. Your reputation. Sorry.'

She didn't wait for him to open the door for her but got out, saying, 'Thanks for a wonderful day, it's been truly memorable. And the restaurant just as great as you promised.'

Hugo put his hand to his heart and murmured, 'I am desolate. My darling girl is leaving me.'

His unwitting use of a phrase of Peter's brought her back to earth with a crash. 'For God's sake just go.' As she fitted her key in the latch she heard Beth shouting. Relief flooded over her. Without even answering Hugo's wave she fled inside.

'Mummy!' Beth raced across the hall and flung her arms round her. 'You're back. Daddy came for us. We thought you'd got lost.'

'Not lost, darling, just busy talking to Hugo Maude about the play.' She bent down to kiss Beth and as she straightened up she realised Peter was standing in the kitchen doorway listening to her.

'You're back. At last,' he said.

'Of course. Did you think I wouldn't be back?'

'No, that wasn't what I was thinking at all.'

'We've had lunch.'

'You said.'

'Lovely place. Not somewhere to take children though, it's hideously expensive.'

'It would have to be. What's it called?'

Alex burst out of the sitting room where he'd been watching television. 'Mummy! Miss Pascoe let us play with her cats, Beano and Dandy. We had such fun.'

'Good. I'm sorry I'm late, I didn't realise the time.'

'Daddy came to find us.'

Caroline looked her thanks at Peter. 'Silly me. I shan't let it happen again.'

Peter said, 'I am glad. Just once is once too often, isn't it?'

The children disappeared. 'I did say it was just for lunch.'

'I know you did. What did you think I meant?'

She stood in front of the hall mirror and began dragging her comb through the tangles in her hair. 'He had the hood down on the car. It's ruined my hair.' Caroline tugged painfully at the knots.

'Here, let me have a try.' He took the comb from her and began gently combing her hair at the back. He caught her looking at his reflection in the mirror, and for a moment he looked straight back at her. Between two people who know each other intimately, a look can speak volumes. He was trying to assess how far things had gone that afternoon between her and Hugo; she appeared to be asking his forgiveness. But for what? Being late for the children?

Peter turned her round and began to comb the knots at the front. 'My word, you're brave, you're not even flinching.'

'Am I not?'

When he'd disentangled the last knot he straightened her hair and then, putting the comb down on the hall table, he took her face between his hands and kissed her mouth, a long slow massaging kiss. Then his arms slid round her and he held her close, but she wasn't part of it.

'My darling girl. I'm so glad you're home.'

'Have you started the meal?'

His arms released their hold on her. 'I have.'

'I'll carry on with it then.'

'You haven't told me where you went.'

Alex shouted from the sitting room. 'Daddy! It's that cartoon you like, be quick!'

Without looking at him Caroline answered, 'It'll keep.'

He watched her dash into the kitchen, leaving him no wiser. But surely she wouldn't have, would she? Not his beloved Caroline. He felt certain his instincts would have told him if she had. But then she wasn't herself at the moment. He damned Hugo yet again and went to watch the cartoon with the children.

11

Eating their supper seated around the table that night at the Garden House were Greenwood Stubbs, Pat, Barry, Dean and Michelle. They'd discussed what had happened during the day and had now got round to the subject of the theft.

Greenwood put down his fork, took a swig of his beer and commented, 'Well, Pat, from where I'm sitting things aren't looking too good. As I see it, Mr Fitch is bound to back old Jeremy's decision, and that means I'm out.'

Pat protested. 'But Dad . . .'

'No "buts" about it, love, I'm for the chop. I think you haven't realised what that means.'

Pat scooped up the last of her pudding, licked the spoon and asked, 'What does it mean, then?'

'Barry and me's been having a talk and we've decided that I shall lose my job and with it this house. He won't employ me any longer, he won't be able to trust me, yer see. Teach me a lesson.'

'What!'

'House goes with the job, doesn't it? Let's hope he gives us time to find somewhere.'

Pat was devastated. 'I never thought! Yer can't mean it? Does he, Barry?'

' 'Fraid so, love,' Barry replied: 'There's no way he'd allow me to have tenancy of this house. He'd need it for the new garden chap, it doesn't go with my kind of job. By the looks of it we'll be out sharpish.'

Michelle began to cry. 'I love this house. I love it. It isn't fair. I don't want to move.'

Pat lent her a handkerchief and Greenwood said, 'Come and sit on yer grandad's knee.' When Michelle had seated herself comfortably her grandad said, 'It's yer daft old grandad's fault and I'm sorry.'

Between sniffs, Michelle said, 'You were only being kind.'

Dean, who'd quietly been finishing his pudding while they'd been talking, remarked softly, 'It'll mean the end of that university scholarship old Fitch promised me.'

Pat burst into tears. 'Dean! I never thought. Oh, God! What shall we do? Barry!'

'Calm down, Pat. Anybody'd think we'd no money coming in. We have. You and me both. We'll see he gets to university, don't you fret. Don't give it another thought, Dean. I'll see yer all right. I shall be proud to have a son, even if he isn't my very own, at Oxford or wherever you go. Proud. That's what. We'll find the money somehow for whatever yer need.'

Greenwood apologised for the hundredth time.

'Just stop it will yer, Greenwood. You weren't to know. Let's face it, they do get stuff stolen day in day out and it is time they put a stop to it, and unfortunately it's you who's been caught out.'

'But it's not just me who's affected, is it? It's all of us. I'm that sorry, Dean, about yer scholarship. It's blooming rotten luck. Somehow we'll manage it, if I have to sweep the streets.'

Barry objected. 'There's no way you'll be sweeping the streets, you with your skills. No. I won't allow it. I reckon we'll manage fine.'

Michelle slipped off her grandad's knee and went to put an arm round Barry. 'You'll look after us all won't you, Barry?'

'Of course I shall. That's one good thing about me marrying yer mother, you've always got me at the back of you. I shan't let yer down.'

Michelle kissed his cheek. 'I knew you wouldn't. See Mum, you can stop crying now. You'd forgotten we've got Barry, hadn't you?'

'I 'ad, yer right. I'll take on more work with Charter-Plackett Enterprises, day and night if necessary and we shan't go short. How long before old Fitch gets back?'

Barry sipped his tea, put down his cup and looked to Greenwood for confirmation. 'They say Thursday after next, don't they, if nothing holds him up?'

Greenwood nodded. 'That's right. Thursday before the play on the Friday.'

'That gives us time, then.'

'Time for what?' Pat asked.

'Time to take action. Remember when old Fitch tried to steal the church silver that time? We all got together and showed him we wouldn't stand for it, didn't we? Well, how about a bit of action culminating on Thursday? He hates things going wrong. Likes it all moving along like a well oiled machine. Well, when he gets back it won't be a well oiled machine. It'll be chaos.'

Excited, they asked a million questions. Barry held up his hand to silence them. 'Be quiet! Right! I'll give it some thought and let you know. It can't be the central heating like last time, it's too hot for that to cause a problem at the moment. It could be the power, that'd ruin everything in the freezers.'

Pat interrupted. 'I don't want Jimbo getting hurt in this. It's all money to him is the freezers.'

'That's as may be. But I'll come up with something.'

Greenwood suggested he didn't have far to look. 'He's got that big directors' do day after he comes back. They're staying the weekend, country weekend and all that jazz. They've got seats booked for the play.'

Michelle looked horrified. 'You don't mean that, Grandad? Not Mr Fitch coming to see us?'

Grandad nodded. 'He's bringing the lot of 'em. Boasting, I expect, that we can attract such a big name as Hugo-the-big-I-am-Maude to the village. Fitch playing Lord of the Manor. I've flowers to provide for the bedrooms and that. Gardens to be looking spectacular and a tour of the glasshouses too. Me touching me cap to 'em all.' He imitated touching his forelock. 'He thinks!'

Barry clenched his fists and banged the table. 'That's it then. We'll sabotage that.'

Pat wagged a finger at him. 'Just a minute, I'm senior waitress that weekend. Friday dinner. Saturday lunch. Saturday dinner and Sunday lunch. Breakfasts as well. Blinking good money, it being the whole weekend. I don't fancy losing that. Not now.'

'Don't worry, love, I'll see you're all right.'

Michelle, excited by the thought of a bit of espionage, asked what Barry proposed to do. He tapped the side of his nose, 'Got to put my thinking cap on. Oh yes. If anyone comes up with any inspiration let me know. And not a word to anyone. This is our secret.' He pushed back his chair. 'Look at the time! Michelle, hurry up, you'll be late for rehearsal. And you, Dean.'

After they'd gone and Pat was clearing the table she asked her dad if he'd any idea who could have split on them.

'None at all. It's a mystery to me. Everyone in this village sees him and his belongings as fair game, they wouldn't mind us having a few bits of stone and some old wreck of a table and chairs, nor them old pots, some of 'em is cracked even. It's not someone getting back at me and Rhett, it's deeper than that.'

'Wish I blinking well knew who it was. I'd scratch their eyes out.'

'Don't fret, it'll all come out in the wash. Mark my words. Can I leave yer with all this?' He gestured to the washing up. 'I've had double the work without Rhett, it's nearly killed me today. The others are good lads and work hard but Rhett's taken a lot on his shoulders and we've really missed him.'

'Good lad, isn't he?'

'He is that. I'm going to try to get him a job in the Parks department. I still carry a bit of weight there.'

'Do you think there might be a chance that old Fitch will tell Jeremy he's a fool and cancel it all, and we'll be all right?'

'I doubt it. They stick together these folk. To save face he has to back him up, hasn't he?'

'I suppose so. It was me just hoping.'

'I know, love. I know. All our bright dreams gone. Thought Michelle would follow in my footsteps. We seemed so well set up, didn't we, all of us? Ah well. I can't say how sor ...'

Pat squeezed his arm. 'Like Barry says, that's enough apologising. Go and watch yer telly. Go on, off yer go.'

When Pat went into the Store first thing the next day to check Jimbo's catering diary with her own she found herself catapulted into a furious argument.

Jimbo, increasingly agitated because the ambience he strove so hard to maintain was being destroyed, called out, 'Ladies! Ladies! Please.'

The main protagonists were the two Senior sisters, Mrs Jones, who was already wearing her smart mail order office tabard with Harriet's Country Cousin Farm Produce emblazoned across the front, Linda, playing her part from behind the post office grille, Georgie Fields from the Royal Oak and Bel Tutt.

Valda Senior didn't heed Jimbo's request. 'When all's said and done, it's an unspoken agreement that if we can score off that old Fitch we do. Whoever it was who split on Vera deserves horsewhipping. We saw, but we didn't say a thing, did we, Thelma?' Her sister, with pursed lips, shook her head in agreement.

Georgie, small and pretty and looking as if an argument was the last thing she wanted, tapped on the post office counter and said through the grille to Linda, 'You ought to have more sense.'

Indignantly Linda answered, 'It wasn't me, I didn't tell. All I said was that they shouldn't expect to steal and then get away with it. That's all. I saw 'em unloading the stuff too but I didn't squeal. Not me.' She folded her arms as though to emphasise her innocence.

Bel Tutt pinged the till, gave Thelma Senior her change, and said, 'Well, if none of *us* has an inkling, who the blazes has?'

An uncomfortable silence followed this question which Pat filled with, 'By the looks of it Dad's going to lose his job, we're about to lose our house and Dean the university scholarship old Fitch promised him. If anybody would like to know, it's me.' She glared round. 'We're the ones suffering the most. Well, Vera is too and Rhett, but we could be losing the roof over our heads.'

Linda, coming out from behind the grille, said forcefully, 'In my opinion it's someone with a grudge against Vera. That's what's triggered it off. When they did it, they didn't see the consequences of it affecting you.'

'That's right. That could be it. So who's got a grudge against poor, harmless Vera?' Pat looked at each woman in turn, finally fixing her gaze on Mrs Jones, who flushed to the roots of her hair.

'Don't look at me. I've no grudge against anyone. Anyway, I've got work piling up.' She gave Pat a haughty stare and marched into the back of the Store.

Jimbo removed his boater, wiped his bald head with a

handkerchief, replaced his headgear and said, 'Well now, having sorted that out perhaps we could get on with our shopping? Can I help anyone? Good offers on the meat counter today and tomorrow if anyone's interested?'

The two Senior sisters ambled out, Georgie paid for her shopping and left, Linda returned to her counter and Bel Tutt waited patiently behind the till.

Disgruntled by the argument Pat said sharply, 'I've really come in, Jimbo, to catch up on my dates. In the circumstances I'm willing to work whenever and wherever. Looks like we shall need the money.' She brought a fat red diary from her bag and opened it up.

'Come in the back. I need a break.' He took her into his office, took off his boater and reached for his diary from the top of the filing cabinet.

Before he had found the right page, Pat, making sure the door was properly closed first, said, 'Jimbo, did you notice that dear mother-in-law of mine didn't say she hadn't split? Just that she'd no grudge, that was all she said. Do yer think it might be her?'

'No idea, Pat, she's *your* mother-in-law. What's done's done. It's too late now. Just have to limit the damage as best you can.'

'I don't suppose you'd have a word, would yer? Just for me?' As an afterthought she added, 'and Dad, and our Dean.'

'With Jeremy?'

'No, not him. He's just a yes man. Well, yes, perhaps with him before it's too late. Well, no, I meant with Mr Fitch really. He's very partic'lar nowadays not to upset everybody, ever since he let Muriel Templeton persuade him to reinstate Sir Ralph as president of the cricket. If you could let him know on the quiet that the whole village is upset ...'

'Well, they're certainly that. There's been no other topic of conversation in here but your bad luck and Vera's. Never known the village so worked up about anything.'

Pat frowned. 'That's what I'm worried about. They might take matters into their own hands. You know what they're like. I wouldn't want this director's weekend messed up.' Jimbo noticed that Pat looked as though she wished she hadn't said that.

He put his head to one side and looked at her. 'Do you know something I should know?'

Pat shook her head. 'No, no, nothing. No.'

'Because if this director's weekend is ruined I shall want to know who's at the bottom of it. It's important to me that the weekend goes well. They're all influential people with money to burn and it could mean an awful lot more business being put my way, which in turn lines your pockets as well as mine. We need to make a good impression, Pat. Right?!'

Pat nodded. 'Of course. About these dates.'

'Leave it for now. I'm expecting a rep any minute and I'm not in the mood. Why everyone has to choose my Store to air their disagreements I'll never know.'

Pat gave him a nudge. 'You know full well you like to be at the hub of all the gossip. You can't kid me.'

Jimbo grinned. 'You're right. I do.'

'It's good for business anyway.'

'Right again! See you, Pat.'

'See yer.' As she opened the door she turned back to ask, 'Will yer have a word?'

Jimbo nodded.

'Bye then.'

She left him staring out of the office window. What a mess. All because Rhett wanted to please his grandmother. Like a stone thrown into a pond, the ripples were far reaching. First Vera then Rhett and now the Joneses and Greenwood Stubbs. To save his own skin he'd better have a word. That fool Jeremy wouldn't listen, he knew that, but at least he could try.

He heard footsteps and found Harriet standing behind him.

He smiled at her. 'Darling! How's things?'

'Oh, fine, if only.'

'Mmmmm?'

Harriet ran her fingers through her hair in exasperation. 'It's Hugo. He's getting me very annoyed.'

'What's new?'

'I know I shouldn't have suggested he came to stay, but I did and we're landed with him. I told him that Caroline was off limits, but . . .'

'Mmmm?'

'I'm amazed you haven't heard. He took her out to lunch yesterday and went all the way to The Lovers' Knot, which you so kindly recommended, and it made her late collecting the children.'

'That must be the best part of a twenty-five mile round trip! For lunch! He is a fool. I didn't mean him to go there. Just mentioned it in passing.'

'What worries me is Caroline agreeing to it. He's absolutely captivated her, you know. I warned her about him and I thought she'd heed it.'

'Keep out of it. Peter will solve it, I'm sure.'

'Will he, though? You know how much Peter's into personal-freedom-in-marriage-our-love-is-strong-enough and all that.'

'One can't help liking Hugo, that's the trouble.'

Harriet sighed. 'I know.'

Jimbo looked hard at her. 'Harriet! Harriet!'

'Don't worry, not me.'

'Like me to have a word?'

'If you like. Diplomatically, of course. I can't stand atmosphere at home.'

'I could always ask him to sling his hook.'

'No, we've all worked so hard on this play, and not just us, but Anne Parkin with the advertising and ticket sales, and the props and things. No, we can't put the play in jeopardy. Be tactful, that's all I ask.'

'Tactful? What about?'

They both turned at the sound of Hugo's voice. 'I came to see if I could make lunch for you, Harriet dearest, and you too Jimbo if you can spare the time from your –' he waved an expressive hand round the office, 'emporium.'

He was wearing the briefest of white shorts with a tight fitting white tee shirt. The tan of his shapely legs was emphasised by the short white socks and white leather slip-ons he wore. He smiled at them both and said, 'Well?'

Jimbo cleared his throat. 'Look here, Hugo . . .'

'May I take a seat, it sounds like a dressing down is on the agenda.' With perfect poise he placed himself on a stool beside the filing cabinet.

'You're right it is. Harriet and I are very, very fond of Caroline and we are not prepared to stand on the touch-line without blowing the whistle once or twice. She is off limits. *Verboten.* Forbidden. Not available for . . .'

'Yes?' Hugo's eyes sparkled with fun.

'Damn it, man, you're too charming by half, and you know it. Please, leave her alone.'

'Or . . .?'

'You'll have me to answer to, to say nothing of Peter. He may be a man of the cloth but he is extremely fit and I wouldn't give much for your chances if he really blew his top. And, believe me, he can't be far from it.'

'You don't have to worry about Peter. He allows Caroline to do exactly as she wishes. He loves her so much, you see.'

'Is that so? I wouldn't bank on it. However, if you wish to remain in my good books, and Harriet's, you'd better cool it.'

Hugo looked humble. Just how much of his humility was genuine and how much an act Harriet wasn't quite sure, but she listened carefully to what he said next. 'For the first time in my life I'm in love. Don't spread that abroad, I don't want anyone to know.'

A deathly silence greeted his statement. Then Harriet broke it by laughing loudly. 'You! In love? You don't know the meaning of the word except where it relates to yourself. Come on, Hugo, pull the other one.'

Hugo got up and, with tears glistening in his eyes, he said, 'That's my trouble, you see, no one believes I have genuine feelings. Lunch it is, then. For three.'

When Harriet saw the lunch table she wondered if there was anything left in the fridge at all. He really had made an effort. He'd even poached some wine from Jimbo's secret store.

'Well, that's wonderful, Hugo. We shan't need another meal for a fortnight. Thank you so much.' Harriet kissed his cheek and he heartily kissed her back.

Jimbo stood in the doorway admiring the table. 'Thanks greatly. I usually have an out of date pork pie or left over sandwich in the office. It's really a treat to come home to this. Thanks.'

'Not at all. Your hospitality has been above and beyond, I had to do something in return.'

Jimbo smiled a little grimly. It hadn't cost Hugo a penny. Then he remembered not to be mercenary and thanked him again for all the trouble he'd taken. 'It makes no difference to what I said earlier. In love or not, you cool it. Right?'

'I heard.'

Jimbo left Bel and Harriet in charge at the Store and dashed up to the Big House straight after lunch. As he pulled up in front of the house the gravel spurted beneath his wheels and he narrowly missed one of the students taking a chance for a quick smoke between lectures. He called out cheerfully, 'Sorry!' The student waved his acknowledgement of Jimbo's apology.

Jimbo strode into the hall. 'Good afternoon! How is my favourite girl this afternoon? Firing on all cylinders? As usual?'

The receptionist beamed her pleasure at his arrival. 'Jimbo! You darling man. Lovely to see you. Favourite girl indeed! Mr Fitch isn't . . .'

'I know, it's Jeremy I need to see.'

'He's in his office, do go straight through.'

'OK.' Jimbo made off in the direction of Jeremy's office but stopped before he'd left the hall. 'You don't know anything about this prosecution, do you?'

In a stage whisper she answered, 'Only that he's hell bent on going through with it. I wouldn't like to be in his shoes when Mr Fitch finds out he's lost his head gardener and a first rate under gardener and from what I hear his estate carpenter too, because Barry's been in and threatened to resign. Tread carefully!'

Jimbo nodded. 'Indeed. Right, thanks.'

Jeremy hastily threw the wrapper of a Mars bar into his waste bin as Jimbo entered his office.

'Good afternoon to you. Got a minute?'

'For you, Jimbo, yes. How can I help? Catering problem is it? This directors' weekend causing probs, eh?'

'No. May I sit down?'

'Of course.'

Jimbo seated himself in one of the plush chairs and, leaning forward confidentially, asked, 'When is Mr Fitch back?'

Jimbo thought he detected Jeremy giving a slight shudder at his question. 'Thursday.'

'I see. Glad to have him back at the helm?'

'What's that got to do with you?'

'Nothing, except ...'

'Yes?'

'Have you got your bags packed in readiness?'

'In readiness for what?' His huge bulk shifted uneasily.

'Leaving. You and Venetia.'

Jeremy suddenly got the drift of Jimbo's questions and began to bluster. 'If you've come to persuade me to change my mind about prosecuting the lot of 'em, you're barking up the wrong tree. Mr Fitch knows full well the village takes every advantage of him they can, and he said before he went away, "From now on anyone caught red-handed will be prosecuted, no matter what the consequences." So all I'm doing is carrying out his instructions.'

'But it's so damaging! He may think it not worth the candle. Everything returned, the crazy paving paid for and no one, least of all Mr Fitch, will be any the wiser. Withdraw the charge. Honour restored on both sides.'

Jeremy's hand strayed towards the bottom drawer where he kept his supply of chocolate. He drew it back and said angrily, 'Someone has to be made an example of. What would you do if one of your staff was taking food home? Eh?'

'Sack 'em. But then kitchen hands are soon replaced, a talented gardener isn't. You haven't understood what it means, have you? A whole family out in the street. That'll look good in the paper. Mr Fitch will love that. Oh yes.' Jimbo paused for a moment to compose the most damaging headline he could but Jeremy got in first.

'It's none of your damned business. If you've nothing better to do, I have, so just leave.'

'I've rattled your cage though, haven't I?'

Jeremy pressed his hands on the desk and heaved himself to his feet. He stabbed a thick finger in Jimbo's direction. 'Your influence extends as far as that green baize door in the dining room and no further, so get back to your kitchens and leave me to attend to more important affairs.'

Amused, Jimbo stood up and, sounding rather more like an avenging angel than the entrepreneur he was, he said in sepulchural tones, 'Be warned! The oracle has spoken. Your end is nigh.' He left the room and quietly closed the door behind him. Grinning all over his face he waved to the receptionist and said, 'I've upset him. Take care.'

'Damn you for a nuisance, I'll have no peace all afternoon.'

Cheerfully Jimbo called, 'Sorry!' and left. He took the opportunity to call in at the kitchens to check that this rather important slice of his empire was in full swing. The staff were glad to see him and he enjoyed a ten minute chat with the chef about the arrangements for the directors' weekend.

Before getting into his car he went out through the back door of the kitchens to inspect the bins and check that they were being kept well disinfected. He'd planted bushes around the bin area to shield them from the bedroom windows at the back of the house and as he approached he sniffed the air and decided that despite the hot weather they were clean. What he hadn't expected to find beyond the bushes was Hugo's red sports car. He had half a mind to find out what Hugo was up to, but shrugged his shoulders and decided to mind his own business. A sneaking suspicion made him look up at the windows of the flat Venetia and Jeremy occupied. A curtain flicked back into place and he thought he caught a glimpse of Hugo's face as he quickly retreated from the window.

12

Caroline had been watching television while Peter had been at his Parochial Church Council meeting. As soon as she heard him coming in she called out, 'Peter, I didn't tell you. I've got six months' work at the practice coming up. Four days a week. Isn't that brilliant? They rang this morning and I accepted and then it went completely out of my head. The other woman doctor is pregnant and they need a stand-in.'

Peter bent over and kissed her. 'That's wonderful, truly wonderful and I'm very pleased.'

'Are you?'

'Oh, yes.'

Caroline frowned at him, suspecting some ulterior motive behind his delight till she remembered he wasn't made like that. 'You don't normally rejoice when I work, what's brought about the change?'

'I rejoice on the basis that what's good for you is good for us all.'

'I have the distinct feeling I'm being patronised.'

Peter shook his head. 'Absolutely not, as if I would.'

Caroline looked closely at his face as he leant over her. It was deadpan. He looked down at her and his eyes lit up with laughter.

Caroline returned his kiss and patted the seat beside her. 'Sit here. I need your advice.'

'About . . .?'

'I'm getting terribly worried about this play. What if I turn out to be a complete fool on the stage and ruin it for everybody. When I agreed to do it I was so full of myself I could have done it single-handed, but now I'm not so sure.'

'Hugo will see you through it.'

'Yes, he will. Of course he will. He's a brilliant actor, you know.'

'He is?'

'Oh yes, you can feel him rising to the occasion. He kind of puts on a mantle, you can visibly see him do it and he's no longer Hugo Maude, he's whoever he's playing. What a gift.'

'Indeed.'

'It's the most enormous privilege to work with him. He pulls everyone into his enthusiasm, draws them in, whisks them along. As a team leader he's amazing, he has them all eating out of his hand. The rehearsal tonight went wonderfully well. We are incredibly lucky, you know, to have him here. We're all well blessed.'

'I shall have to come to a rehearsal to see this great man at work.'

Caroline gave him a sharp look but his expression was completely innocent. 'Even Rhett, despite his troubles, is coming along splendidly. I watched him in the scene where he talks to his father about me and my new boyfriend and he almost had me in tears. It was very moving. Such a sensitive performance, all due to Hugo's coaching. You can't imagine Rhett being like that, can you?'

'No, you can't. It's surprising what talents people have.'

'It is. I do love it, all the rehearsing and such. It makes me quite skittish, kind of like a young foal in a field all excitement and jollity, capering about through life. Our lives – yours and mine – are so serious, aren't they? Always helping the lame dogs and such. There's not much time for laughter, is there?'

Peter thought for a moment before he answered. 'You're right, there isn't. But I can't change it. Not *my* life, at any rate.'

'Oh, I know, and I wouldn't ask you to in a million years. You're not in a job where you can decide to have a career change midstream, I know that. Yours is a vocation. And I fully accept that and always will. But I do think we should find time to laugh more. Don't you?'

'I shall give that matter my earnest consideration.'

'There you are, you see, all seriousness again. You should let up more often.'

'What's brought all this philosophising about?'

Impatiently, Caroline shook her head. 'Nothing. Nothing at all.'

She was silent for a while and then said, as though he were always at the front of both their minds, 'He's a little boy lost, you know. Needs a wife who's a mother as well.'

Peter didn't need to ask whom she meant. 'Like most men.'

'Only more so. The slightest thing can hurt him intensely. That's why he's such a good actor, so emotional. He's very touchy feely.'

'Oh! I'm sure he is.' He ran a lazy finger along her arm and as she watched it she wondered why nowadays he didn't ignite her like Hugo did with just the same gesture. Peter stood up offering her his hand. 'I'm ready for bed. Coming?'

'In a while.'

'I rather thought . . .' Peter shrugged his shoulders. 'Never mind.'

'Not tonight.'

Peter decided to fulfill his promise and make it possible for himself to attend the next rehearsal. Willie volunteered to sit in. 'Be glad to, sir, no trouble at all.'

'I shan't stay all evening, I don't think, but it's just a chance to see a great actor at work.'

'Oh quite. Yes, sir, you do right. Good idea. I'll tell them children a goodnight story and they'll be off to sleep in a trice.'

'About dragons as usual?'

'Oh yes, dragons is my speciality.'

'They make a big impression.'

'My dragons do! About quarter past seven, then?'

'That's right. Caroline likes the children to be asleep by eight at the latest.'

'You go and enjoy yourself, nothing like seeing at first hand.'

Peter wore his most relaxed looking shirt and shorts and wandered off in the steaming heat to the Church Hall. It was in darkness and the cast were standing on the stage listening to Hugo.

'. . . Four more rehearsals. Four more tries. Four more before lift off. You're doing brilliantly. Wonderfully. Fantastically well. I'm most impressed. But . . . that is no reason to give up trying to improve your performance. No one is ever perfect, least of all me . . .'

This last was greeted by hoots of derision. Hugo held up a hand for silence, 'No, I mean it. If ever you get satisfied with yourself then it's curtains. Kaput. Finito.' He ran a finger across his throat. 'You're dead. So ... all the stops out tonight and we're going straight through the whole of the first act. No interruptions. Remember! Never stop improving on your last performance. Remember how we felt our pace dragged a bit at the end? Don't let it happen tonight. We want the audience to be disappointed and not relieved that the interval has come. OK?'

They all nodded. 'Beginners, please.'

Peter seated himself on a chair at the very back in the shadows. He'd told Caroline he was coming but hadn't reminded her just before she'd set off for the hall. He rather hoped she'd forgotten.

They were good. There was no doubt about that. Talent such as he had never suspected from Liz and Rhett, from Michelle and Neville and from Harriet as the badly betrayed lover of Hugo.

There was a whisk of the curtains and a hushed minute of silence to denote the passing of time and then act one, scene two began. It was Hugo, now looking somehow like a nineteen twenties man about town, coming to return Caroline's umbrella. He hadn't got costume on, simply a pair of jeans and a tee shirt, but he looked what he was, a lounge lizard with a heart.

Peter listened to their dialogue. He admired Hugo's voice. Then it was Caroline's turn to speak. It was quite astounding to him how her voice had changed. At once languid and seductive, at once an ice maiden and a temptress. This Hugo had far more going for him than Peter had ever imagined. He sat fascinated. Every member of the cast was transformed. Even young Michelle was a changed person. When she cried there were genuine tears running down her cheeks.

Act one, scene two ended with a telephone conversation between Caroline and Hugo. Peter recognised restlessness, the need for excitement, the yearning in her voice and in her body language, she did it so well that although one couldn't hear Hugo's replies one knew exactly what he would be saying.

He couldn't help himself; he applauded.

Sylvia clapped too, and so did Barry, Ron and Dean. They couldn't help themselves either. Barry climbed onto the stage and gave Michelle a big kiss. 'Wasn't she marvellous, Hugo? Absolutely great. I'm that proud.' Michelle blushed and Rhett took her hand. 'And you Rhett, very powerful.'

Peter moved towards the stage. 'I'm exceedingly impressed. It was just wonderful.' He reached up and signalled to Caroline to jump down off the stage into his arms. He hugged her and whispered, 'Fantastic! I'm so proud. So very proud.'

'I'd forgotten you were coming. Are you just flattering me?'

Vehemently he answered, 'I'm not. You were excellent.'

'Thanks.'

Above the hubbub Hugo called, 'Right, that's it for tonight. See you next rehearsal, full scenery, full props. Goodnight! And thanks.'

They all retired to the Royal Oak except for Rhett and Michelle. The bar was moderately busy for a weekday night. Sitting like a peacock amongst a flock of sparrows sat Venetia Mayer, alone in a corner from which she had a full view of the whole bar. She wore her purple outfit, with matching slouch socks, trainers and headband. She didn't seem to have noticed that crushed velvet had been out of fashion for quite a few years now. Her hair, abundant as always, was blacker than ever, and her eye make-up would have been obvious to a blind man.

She waved vigorously to Peter and Caroline who headed the rush for the bar. They returned her wave and, having collected their drinks, went to sit at her table.

'May we, or are you expecting someone?' Venetia didn't answer, but simply invited them to sit by patting the seat alongside her and smiling.

Peter recollected he hadn't seen Jeremy for a while so he asked Venetia how he was.

'Jeremy? He's fine.'

'I heard you'd put him on a diet.'

Disinterestedly she answered, 'I did, but he wouldn't agree to it. It's a waste of time talking to him.'

'I see, that's a pity.'

Venetia wasn't making coy passes at Peter as she had done often in the past, instead she was scanning the crowd at the bar. He noted her satisfaction when she spotted whoever it was she'd come to see.

'You'll enjoy the play when you see it, Venetia. Hugo's done a wonderful job, everyone's quite excellent.' She wasn't listening, she was watching someone. He saw her face light up again and in a moment Hugo was sitting beside Caroline and opposite Venetia. There was a recognisable togetherness between Caroline and Hugo, the result of working on the play in such close harmony. Peter saw it and wondered if Venetia had too. He turned to say some platitude to her and saw the flinty look in her eyes. They were rapidly flicking between Hugo and Caroline, and for a moment he couldn't understand her anger, and then he did. It was the anger of a jealous woman.

Venetia, grimly keeping a hold on her temper said, between gritted teeth, 'Good rehearsal?'

Hugo asked Caroline to give her opinion. 'Excellent. It's all coming together quite brilliantly. Isn't it, Peter?'

'It certainly is. I was very impressed. You and Hugo here together are a dynamic duo.' Caroline and Hugo laughed. 'You should have joined the cast, Venetia. You could have had some fun.'

'Could I indeed? Well, well. Not my scene, as you might say.'

The four of them chatted together about many inconsequential things until Peter looked at his watch. 'I'll have to go, I promised Willie I wouldn't be late. You stay, darling, if you wish.'

'No, I'll come too. I've had a long day and I need my beauty sleep.' Caroline picked up her bag and squeezed out of her seat. Hugo stood up.

He took her hand and kissed her fingers. 'Sleep perhaps, but not beauty sleep, my love.' He held her hand a moment longer than he needed to and Caroline was forced to pull it free.

'Goodnight to you, flatterer!'

'Cross my heart and hope to die, I always speak the truth to my leading lady.'

Peter laughed at his flirting. 'No wonder all the girls idolise you, Hugo. You're too charming for words.'

Hugo turned to look at Peter. 'I mean it. It's true. You're a lucky man, though perhaps you don't know it.'

'I do, I do. I'm just unaccustomed to hearing other men say it, that's all.'

'Other men?' Hugo put a delicate hand to his brow. 'Other men?

Shame on you. Shame. Me! Other men! I am unique! Quite unique!'

He pretended to feel faint and slumped back onto his chair, dramatically prostrate. He withdrew a handkerchief from his pocket and mopped his brow.

Peter smiled while at the same time admiring Hugo's almost flawless physical beauty. 'You're right, you are unique, no one but you could have collapsed in such a stylish manner! Goodnight to you, and thanks, everlasting thanks for producing the play. It's going to prove to be truly memorable. Goodnight, Venetia.'

Her lips, tight as tight, only just allowed, 'Goodnight' to escape.

Caroline called out her goodbyes to everyone and closed the door behind them. As soon as they were out of hearing she said, 'What on earth is the matter with Venetia, she hadn't a word for the cat. Have we upset her?'

'Not us, no. Watching him just now the word "beauty" came to mind. Not a word I would readily use when referring to a man, but he has such classical beauty. For a split second I did wonder . . .'

'Have you got your key? Wonder what?'

As he reached to put his key in the lock, Peter said offhandedly, 'Is he straight?'

Angrily Caroline said, 'Of course he is. But what would it matter if he weren't?'

Peter pushed open the door. 'It wouldn't matter one jot, would it now?' He looked intensely at her face in the muted light of the hall and saw briefly in it a kind of naked passion, which she quickly veiled.

'No, it wouldn't matter. What *does* matter is his talent and his great generosity in making the play possible. We'll never have another chance like this, and we should take it with both hands and not dig for motives or stances or anything at all. Just take our opportunity eagerly.'

'Of course. Willie! We're back! Everything all right?'

Willie appeared in the sitting-room doorway and, looking directly at Peter, said, 'Yes. Everything all right with you?'

Peter forced a firm reply. 'Oh yes. Absolutely hunky-dory.' Leaving Caroline to say their thanks and goodnights he took the stairs two at a time and went directly to bed.

*

139

Caroline's enthusiastic support for Hugo would have been seriously diminished had she witnessed the conversation Harriet had with him the following day. Hearing him thumping about upstairs she went up and, looking into the tiny boxroom next to his own room, she saw he was dragging his cases out.

'Excuse me for asking, Hugo, but what exactly are you doing?'

Breathlessly he replied, 'Packing.'

'Packing? Might one ask why?'

He straightened up, pushed his hair from his forehead and announced, 'My agent, that was him on the phone. I simply can't turn it down.'

A very nasty, insidious dread invaded Harriet's brain. 'Explain yourself.'

Hugo perched himself on one of his cases. 'He wants to see me immediately. I've got the chance of Hamlet at Stratford. I've never played Hamlet, would you believe, never. That prize, that glittering, fabulous prize is within my grasp. Agreed I'm second choice, because Sir John is scheduled. But he's had a heart attack, so they've rung me. It should have been me to begin with, but Johnny's got a thing going with the director so that's how he got the job. Well, now he's got his just desserts.' Hugo shrugged his shoulders then dramatically clenched his fist and stared at it. 'I simply cannot turn it down. I've got to go.'

Harriet went from icy despair to total fury in the space of a moment. 'You slimy toad. You foul, thoughtless, self-centred pig. How *dare* you? How dare you sit there and say that to me? Now, I really know exactly what you are. Shallow. Vain. Mean. Jimbo's right, there's only one person in the whole world as far as you're concerned and that's Hugo St John Maude. You're an overrated, arrogant, egotistical, self seeking, swollen headed exhibitionist. How could you do this to us?'

She stormed downstairs and rang the Store. 'I don't care where he is or what he's doing, he is to come home immediately.' She listened for a moment and then shouted, 'This instant, whether he likes it or not and I don't care if he's signing the contract for Buckingham Palace garden parties, he's to come home *now*. You tell him from *me*.' She slammed down the receiver and paced up and down the hall, her anger intensifying as the moments passed.

Hugo came slowly down the stairs. 'Look, I know doing this makes me *persona non grata ...*'

'That's true! There isn't a quote in Shakespeare or anywhere else more apt, more apropos ... I should have had my head examined for asking you here. Never, never again as long as you live will I ever ...'

The front door burst open and Jimbo hurtled into the hall.

'My God! What is it? What the hell's happened?'

Harriet turned on him. 'You may well ask.' She pointed a shaking finger at Hugo who was sitting on the bottom step. 'That ... snake in the grass is leaving.'

'Leaving? What's he done? I'll kill 'im first and ask questions afterwards, shall I?' Jimbo's face flushed an ugly red.

Harriet shook her head. Arms akimbo she said scornfully, 'Tell Jimbo, then. Go on, tell him.'

Hugo, in a short speech full of self justification, told him why he was leaving.

Jimbo could scarcely contain his anger. In a cold fury, the like of which Hugo had never seen before, ashen-faced and visibly shaking with temper, Jimbo clenched and unclenched his fists, his lips set in a thin mean line. 'You misbegotten, arrogant, base, self-seeking low life. How can you leave everyone in the lurch like this? Have you any idea how much people are banking on you? You've come here, stirred us all up, agreed to produce the play, only a week to go and you do this to us all?' Jimbo strode over to Hugo and, grasping the front of his shirt, hauled him to his feet. 'I've a good mind to ruin your good looks once and for all. Then see where you'd stand as Hamlet. You'd be more fit for a second rate Richard the Third when I'd finished with you. You're despicable!' He unceremoniously released his hold on Hugo's shirt front and maliciously watched him clutch the newel post to keep his balance.

Hugo gathered about him the remnants of his self respect; physical violence always terrified him. 'That's rich, that is. I'm supposed to give up the opportunity of a lifetime for a *village* play? Come on! Be fair!'

Jimbo, his anger spent, stood surveying him silently. Harriet burst into tears. 'I feel so responsible! It was me who asked you in the first place.' Jimbo lent her his handkerchief.

'I know who could take my place. Peter! With that amazing voice of his, he'd be wonderful. Better still, he'd be freed of all his angst.'

Harriet hurriedly wiped her eyes and said, 'Angst? What exactly do you mean by that?'

Hugo shook his head. 'Oh! Nothing.'

'Explain yourself. Have you really given him cause for angst like they all say?' Jimbo took a step towards Hugo. 'I warned you!'

Striking a pose Hugo mockingly answered, 'Me? The cause of it all? Me? Of course not. As if I would. But when all's said and done, I'm going.' He turned to go back upstairs.

Harriet remarked, 'You're feeling up to it, then?'

'Oh, yes.'

'So staying here has done some good then?'

Hugo paused halfway up the stairs. 'Certainly it has.'

'You owe us all something then?'

'You could say so.'

'Well, repay your debt by staying and doing the play for us. There's no way Peter can take up the part at such short notice, he isn't an actor.'

From the top of the stairs Hugo looked down at her. 'Oh, but he *is*! His oratory from the pulpit and his behaviour towards me, especially, prove otherwise. He's doing an excellent job of being the supportive husband, the broad minded cleric, the gentle Christian, when underneath he'd like to beat me to a pulp and drag Caroline back to his cave. Believe me. Can't talk now, got to pack.'

Jimbo discovered he was still wearing his boater. He took it off and smoothed his hand over his bald head. 'Come here.' He folded his arms around Harriet and rocked her slowly. 'There, there. Don't fret. We'll have to cancel. It's unfortunate but we shall. Old Fitch will be bitterly disappointed. He'll go ballistic in fact, but he can't do anything about it.'

'Oh, Jimbo, they'll *all* be so disappointed. I know *I* am. It's heartbreaking.'

'You've known for years what he's like. I'm surprised he's lasted this long.'

'I shall never, never ask him here again. This is the end of a beautiful friendship.'

'Oh, good.'

'Jimbo, you are a baby!'

He gave her a tight squeeze. 'I know, but I'm nice with it.'

'For heaven's sakes! At least you're *reliable.*' She wiped her eyes. 'There. I'll make a start on ringing everyone up. I can't bear it. I just can't. It's all my fault, I should never have encouraged him.'

Jimbo tapped the side of his nose. 'I have an idea. Don't ring yet.' He left the house.

The Store had been full of customers when Harriet had rung Jimbo, so the news that something serious was afoot at the Charter-Plackett's had become the sole topic of conversation in his absence.

Linda, who'd answered the phone, avowed she knew nothing of what the trouble was, except that Jimbo had got the contract for catering for the garden parties at Buckingham Palace. That was all she knew, but wasn't it exciting, they might all get an invite if they played their cards right.

Bel knew nothing either, except she was doubtful about the contract Linda mentioned.

Mrs Jones, who'd been concentrating hard on her mail orders which seemed to flow in ever faster, reluctantly confessed she knew nothing, except that by the tone of the conversation Linda had repeated to her it sounded as though Hugo Maude might have a lot to answer for.

Miss Senior, the woolly hat she wore summer and winter madly askew with the excitement, raised an eyebrow. 'You don't think he's been ... you know ... making lewd suggestions to Harriet? You know what actors are like. First one and then another.' She rather relished the idea, and put her head on one side and winked knowingly.

Venetia Mayer was on red alert, her ears felt as though they'd grown to twice their size, and jealousy was getting the better of her.

One of the weekenders said, 'I wouldn't like to be in Hugo's shoes if he has. I reckon that Jimbo has a nasty temper when it comes to a showdown.'

Linda agreed. 'He was very nasty to me once, gave me my notice. Very sarcastic he was. Mind you, he soon took me back when he found he couldn't manage without me.'

Bel said bluntly, 'Don't overestimate your value to him, Linda. He's clever enough to learn your job in half a day.'

'Huh! Half a day? I should cocoa. It's taken me years to get it under my belt.'

Bel looked askance at her and Linda retired behind the grille, hurt and indignant.

Reluctantly Miss Senior left the Store but the little brass bell on the door had hardly settled into silence before she was back in again. 'The Rector's just gone across to Jimbo's, and Jimbo's coming here. Watch out!' Determined to hear all the news, Miss Senior pretended to be having difficulty choosing a birthday card.

The door bell jangled furiously as Jimbo slammed the door shut behind him. He surveyed the scene. Not a limb moved, not an eye met his. He smiled to himself, raised his boater, said, 'Good morning, everyone', straightened some peaches which had been tumbled into the apples by a careless customer, poured himself a coffee from the machine and, to their extreme annoyance, stepped quietly through into the back.

Peter had listened to Jimbo's impassioned pleas and at first had declined to offer his services.

'Look here, Peter, it's no good me trying. I've already had him by the throat . . . well, not literally, but nearly. We go back a long way he and I, so he's taking advantage of our friendship and I'm not having any effect. Please.'

Peter was staring out of the study window and didn't reply.

'Go over there, cassock and cross, the whole job and do your good Christian bit. It'll work, I know it will. Please?'

Still Peter didn't answer him. Jimbo stood waiting. Eventually Jimbo said, 'I'll be off, then. We feel so bad about it, Harriet and I. We're completely to blame, you see. If we'd had any sense we'd have remembered his selfishness and never encouraged him to do the play in the first place. Thanks anyway.' He waited a moment wondering whether to say what he had in his mind, and decided it needed saying. 'Man to man, I can fully understand you not wanting him to stay.' He opened the study door and closed it quietly after him, just as it clicked shut he heard Peter calling him back.

'Jimbo! Does Caroline know?'

'I shouldn't think so, he's only just had the phone call. Unless . . .'

'No one's rung here.' Peter continued staring out of the window. Jimbo felt himself dismissed. 'I'll be off then.'

'I'll come with you.' Peter went to the hall cupboard, took out his cassock and put it on. His cross he took from the pocket, placed the chain around his neck and tucked the cross itself into his leather belt. 'There, will that do?'

'Excellent. He'll love the drama of it, he's really into costume. Ooops, sorry! That didn't come out quite right, I didn't mean your cassock is a costume in the theatrical sense. I didn't tell you he fancied you taking over his role.'

'Did he.' Peter called up the stairs, 'Caroline, I've just got a visit to make, shan't be long.'

Faintly they heard Caroline call, 'OK. See you soon.'

Peter explained, 'Tidying the attic.'

Jimbo nodded.

They had parted company by the pond, Jimbo heading back to the Store and Peter to see Hugo. He was standing by the wardrobe taking clothes off hangers and laying them on the bed. Peter tapped on the door. 'Can I come in?'

Hugo was startled by Peter's arrival. For a moment he'd remained silent, recollecting what Jimbo had said about Peter's fitness and dreading any physical confrontation. Peter filled the doorway, his head bent to avoid the lintel, silent. Hugo had eventually said jokingly, 'Jimbo's brought in the heavy cavalry, has he?'

'What's this about you deserting your post?'

'To be shot for cowardice in the face of . . .?'

'No. For greed.'

'Certainly not, the money matters not one jot.'

'There are different kinds of greed.'

'I know of only one.'

'That's sad.'

'Sad? There's nothing sad about me. I'm on the threshold of . . .'

'No, you're not, you're beyond the threshold now.'

Hugo preened himself, for he adored praise. 'Yes, you're right I am.'

'You're so well established you could almost call any tune and they would dance to it, and well you know it.' Peter moved some of the clothes and sat down on the bed. Hugo dumped them on the chair and sat beside him.

'That's right. I could.'

'Then, Mr Hugo Maude, why are you leaving in such a hurry?'

Hugo didn't answer.

'Well?'

'Got to go. Arrangements to which I have to agree. These theatrical people screw you for the last drop of blood, believe me. There's no holds barred where contracts are concerned. Yes, must go.'

Peter raised a sceptical eyebrow. 'It's not because you've suddenly realised that you'll be taking part in a village play which will bring you no prestige whatsoever, which will not further your career, will not enhance your reputation and, if it got into the press, would make you look like someone who's finally flipped his lid? That couldn't be it, could it?'

Hugo shook his head indignantly.

Peter sighed. 'Come now. The truth, just this once. Look inside yourself and speak to me with complete honesty. It won't go outside these walls.' Still Peter got no reply. 'You see you can afford to do this thing. Someone still climbing the ladder couldn't, but the great Hugo Maude could and if he faces up to it he'll know he can. The press will be here like a shot once they know. I think, done right, it could be a superb publicity stunt.'

'How?'

'By explaining your motives for doing it. Be honest. Come right out with it all. Let them see the real Hugo Maude that's behind the actor.'

'Think so?'

'Oh yes. Tell them about your close shave with a nervous breakdown, the exhaustion of acting to such high expectations every time you're on stage, et cetera, et cetera. Such courageous honesty would be the headlines in every newspaper this side of the Atlantic and beyond.'

'You think so?'

'Yes. Go up to London today. See whom you must and then come back tomorrow. Jimbo has a fax, and e-mail, you can be in touch all the time. What a gesture on your part. You never know, the play could get to the West End! You in the leading role, and with that story behind it, it would be a glorious success.'

Hugo's face lit up at the prospect. 'It would, wouldn't it? There's a bit of an air of *Brief Encounter* about it, isn't there? That kind of pure love. Yes, it might, it really might. Especially with the right publicity. *Dark Rapture*. Brilliant title!'

'When do you expect rehearsals to start?'

The anticipation fell from his face and ambition took its place. 'Three, four weeks' time, but there's all sorts of preliminary meetings and things. I can't miss them.'

'You'll only miss the first week, and you must.'

'Who says?'

'I do. They'll wait for you. Man of your stature.'

'I'd rather hoped you'd step into my shoes and let me go with a clear conscience.'

'Absolutely not. You and she have the right chemistry. Everyone can see that. The combination is quite explosive, and it's not just in the play.' Peter stood up and went to look out of the window.

Hugo gave a sharp intake of breath. 'Knowing that, you've come here to beg me to stay? Most men would press me to go and good riddance.'

'Yes, of course they would. But I'm not most men. Sometimes these things have to run their course. It's no good asking me to act. I'd be no good playing the part of her lover anyway. I love her too much for that, you see. The thought of even a fictional lover like Leonard feels like slow strangulation.'

Hugo studied Peter's back view, for the moment lost for words. After a short silence he said softly, 'You've made me feel very humble. You just have no idea how much I envy you for the privilege you have of loving like you do, so unselfishly, so profoundly. I think if I loved, it would be a jealous love, an all consuming love which in the end would eat up both the giver and the receiver.'

Peter turned back from the window and looked Hugo straight in the eye. 'It doesn't feel like a privilege at the moment.'

'I can see that.' The need for an apology became paramount. 'I'm very sorry.'

'Are you?'

'Yes, I am.' Hugo shook off his moment of perception and said, 'I'll go and I'll be back tomorrow, that's my promise to you. They'll have to dance to my tune as you so rightly say.'

'Crisis over then?'

Hugo nodded. 'I'll be here to do the play come hell or high water.'

'This is just between us?'

'Yes. Not a word shall I disclose.'

'Nor me.' Peter looked at him. 'You'll never regret doing this for the village, it has that kind of effect. Only good can come of it.'

When he returned to the Rectory he climbed the stairs looking for Caroline. He found her still in the attic, sitting on a small stool surrounded by their mementos.

'Darling! Come and sit here and look at these with me. I keep finding fascinating things, things I'd forgotten all about. I'll never get tidied up at this rate.' She paused to clear a space for him to sit down and then realised how tired he looked. 'What's the matter? You look drained. Has something dreadful happened?'

Peter had no intention of revealing anything to her of his conversation with Hugo, so he simply remarked, 'I've been persuading Hugo not to desert us. What have you found?'

She looked up amazed. 'Why? Where was he going?'

'To London and then Stratford to do Hamlet.'

Caroline demanded all the details. To his response she alternated between delight at his opportunity and shock at his cavalier treatment of their play.

'You've *definitely* persuaded him to stay, then?'

'No rehearsal tonight, but he'll be back tomorrow.'

Caroline shuffled uncomfortably on her stool, torn between rushing over to see Hugo and not wishing Peter to realise how much she cared. 'Are you *certain* he'll come back?'

'As sure as I can be.'

'I can't quite believe it.'

'It's true.'

'How could he desert us all?'

'Well, he isn't, not now.'

'Thank you, Peter.' Caroline clasped his hand in hers. 'I know you don't ... appreciate him, but I do and I'm sure you had far more chance of persuading him than I could ever have had.'

Peter blurted out, 'I think you are deliberately understating your influence on him.'

Caroline paused to think about what he had said, realising that this was a turning point in the whole matter between the two of them. 'I don't want to hurt you.'

'But you have already, haven't you?'

The harsh note in his voice frightened her, and she bent her head to avoid his eyes, muttering almost inaudibly, 'Peter, one. Caroline, nil.'

'Don't joke, please. I'm finding all this extremely hard to bear.'

'I'm sorry to be causing you pain. I don't quite know why it's happening. Once the play is over ...'

'Then what? *Status quo*?'

'I don't even know that. Everything is all mixed up. I love both you and ...'

'Say it.'

Deliberately slowly and quietly, as though crystalising her feelings for the first time, she said, 'I love you and am bewilderingly bewitched by Hugo all at the same time. I know he's candy floss and you're permanent and such a wonderful support to me, and most of all that you adore me and I should have gratitude for your love always ...'

Peter snatched his hand from her grasp. 'Please! Not *gratitude*! I can't bear that.'

'... yet I can't shake off this fascination for him.' She paused and then added sadly, 'Sometimes the candy floss of life is very tempting.'

Peter painfully digested what she had told him and then, as a further challenge to her, declared, 'He wanted me to step in and play Leonard.'

Caroline was appalled. Looking into his bleak face she protested, 'Oh no, that would never do.'

'That's what I told him.'

'I couldn't, not in front of . . .'

Peter placed a finger on her lips to silence her, took her hand in his, kissed the palm and then pressed her hand against his cheek. 'Neither could I. Come what may, I shall still be here, like I promised on our wedding day, unto eternity and beyond. Now let's enjoy looking at what you've found.'

As he picked up the first photograph the door bell rang. He stood up abruptly. 'You answer it, I'm not in. The car's in the garage, they'll never be any the wiser.'

Caroline lurched downstairs, distressed and bewildered, and answered the door. Standing on the step looking contrite was Hugo.

His eyes looked her over, noting her old cotton shorts and the sleeveless tee shirt she wore and then came back to her face. She looked worn, like the shorts, and bleached white like the shirt. What had she been through to make her look like this? Was his leaving the cause of it?

'Peter must have told you, then?'

'What?'

'That I'm off to London.'

'Oh! Yes.'

'I'll be back tomorrow. Hamlet. I've had an offer to play Hamlet and I can't turn it down. Can I come in?'

Caroline opened the door wider. 'Of course, be my guest.'

'You don't seem surprised.'

'I'm delighted, absolutely delighted. Very, very, pleased for you. I shall expect a ticket.'

Hugo took her hand and held it against his cheek saying, 'Of course. And for Peter and Jimbo and Harriet too.'

'Thank you, I'll look forward to that very much indeed.'

There was a slight tremor in her voice and Hugo raised his eyebrows. 'Yes? Miss me?'

'Of course. *Dark Rapture* is all right then, even so?'

'Of course. I couldn't let you down, not my Caroline.'

'Thank you. It will make it all the more exciting, won't it?'

Still holding her hand, Hugo said, 'Darling!' The whole of her being clamoured for the thrill of his touch. He drew her into the study and kicked the door shut behind them with his heel. In a gesture reminiscent of Leonard in the play, he put his hand at the nape of her neck and drew her towards him. 'Darling Caroline!' The longed for kiss was deeper and more meaningful than they had ever experienced before. Her blood was pounding in her throat, her knees weak, and her body craved him. When they'd finished Hugo took in a deep breath and stepped back, releasing her as though he was almost afraid of the emotions he had stirred in her.

'Must go. Long way to drive. See you when I get back. Sorry about that just now, couldn't help myself.'

'Don't apologise. It was me as much as you.'

Gratefully Hugo asked, 'Was it?'

'Oh yes. Safe journey, and I'll be waiting your return, and want to hear all your news.'

'Thank you. That makes it very certain I shall be back, knowing you're waiting.' He kissed her forehead and squeezed her hand tightly. Fumbling behind him for the handle he opened the door, bunched his fingers, kissed them twice and left.

Caroline sat in Peter's chair, leant her elbows on his desk and wept.

13

'Well, then, Pat, 'ave yer heard yet when yer dad's case is coming up? Shouldn't be long now.'

'Not yet, it hangs over yer like a big black cloud, I wish they'd speed things up and get it out of the way. I'll thank you not to mention it, I'm trying hard to forget.'

Jimmy offered to get her another drink.

'Thanks, might as well. It's when yer on yer uppers you know who yer friends are.'

'I thought you'd stopped speaking to me after that row we 'ad about thieving. I was only trying to be fair.'

Pat half smiled. 'I know yer were Jimmy, but it didn't half hurt.' She paused. 'Old Fitch is back soon.'

'Is he indeed? Then yer should be hearing something. Be interesting to know who has the greater pull, yer dad or Jeremy. I reckon old Fitch could manage without Jeremy easier than he could without yer dad and Rhett and your Barry.'

Pat's head came up with a jerk. 'Without Barry? Is he getting the sack as well then?'

'Oh! I've let the cat out of the bag. Sorry.' He didn't say any more, but busied himself instead with collecting Pat's glass.

Pat laid a hand on her glass to stop him. 'Just a minute, why should Barry lose his job?'

'Didn't yer know, he's threatened to give his notice in if yer dad gets the order of the boot. Just trying to put some pressure on Jeremy, yer see.'

Pat stood up. 'The fool. The absolute fool. The blessed idiot. As if we're not in a bad enough state as it is. We'll all be on the social if we don't watch it. I'm going round to the Church Hall to give him a piece of my mind. Rehearsal or no rehearsal, he's going to get it in the neck.'

'Don't bother. There isn't one.'

'Isn't one? Then where's Barry gone to, and Michelle?'

'I understand that Hugo's done a runner.'

Pat sat down again. 'A runner?'

'Gone up to London, got the offer of Hamlet at Stratford and he's hopped it.'

Vera slapped her glass down on the table. 'Evening all. What's up Pat, just had yer purse pinched? Cheers.' She raised her glass to her friend.

'Hugo's done a runner. The play's off.'

Vera began to laugh. At first it was a slow chuckle then it turned into a gasping staccato laugh, then a rip-roaring guffaw.

Pat couldn't laugh with her. 'To be honest, Vera, I don't know what's so funny. They've all put such effort in, it simply isn't fair of him. In fact I'm downright disappointed in him. It's mean and thoughtless 'opping off like that.' Pat nudged Vera with a sharp elbow. 'Just stop it, will yer, they're all looking.'

Vera endeavoured to pull herself together. She mopped her eyes, coughed to clear her throat and said loudly, 'That's one in the eye for Mrs Jones, anyway. That'll have taken the wind out of her sails and not half, serves her right after the way she treated me. I haven't laughed so much in years.'

'You might find it funny but no one else does.'

'I know, but all them costumes she's made. What a laugh.'

Jimmy stood up to get Pat another drink. 'Don't mind admitting he'll cut a fine figure in them tights and that on the stage. He'll make a handsome Prince of Denmark.'

Vera scoffed at him. 'Hark at 'im! Gone all classical, 'ave yer?' Surprising what an effect that Hugo's had on this village.'

'It is,' Pat agreed and counted off on her fingers the people he'd most affected. 'Us probably being made homeless into the bargain. Your Don willing to let yer go to prison, who'd have thought that of him, 'im without a word for the cat. The rector in a right state over 'im. Dr Harris coming over all peculiar about 'im. Our Dean losing his scholarship, there's no doubt about that. You, Vera, in a stew about prison. The list is endless. Sooner he goes the better, I think.'

Vera sprang to his defence. 'Oh, I don't know. He's lovely. I could buy a ticket for Stratford just for the pleasure of seeing 'im in tights. He'll strip something gorgeous, I bet. Yer can forgive a man like 'im an awful lot. All them lovely costumes, too.' Vera stared into the distance thinking about her life and where it was going, and about Don. If only . . .

As though able to read her thoughts, Pat said, 'Well, begging your Don's pardon, he hasn't exactly a figure to die for, has he? Not meaning anything disrespectful like, but seeing as we're letting our hair down, he's not like my Barry.'

'But then your Barry's at least ten years younger. Though, come to think of it, even ten years ago Don didn't look like him. No, it could almost be said I've made a big mistake with Don. There's something to be said for living with someone, isn't there?'

'Oh, I don't know about that. Look at your Brenda, for a start. I wouldn't just have lived with Barry, I've got my children to think of. I want to keep their respect. It's not decent when you've got kids.'

'It must be lovely going 'ome to a handsome man, though.' Vera traced a pattern on the table with her finger and then asked, 'What was yer first husband like?'

'Useless. He did us all a good turn when he died. Lifting his elbow too often was his problem.'

'Can't say that about Don, that is one thing he doesn't do. I just wish he'd brighten up, though. Sparkle a bit, yer know. Your Barry's got plenty of sparkle, hasn't he?'

Barry arrived in time to answer before Pat could get a word in. 'He has, Vera, enough and to spare! What can I do for you, Vera?'

Vera giggled. 'Oh! Hark at him! Nothing, thanks, I'm off. Back to the ironing. I just wish he'd wear something exciting. I've been ironing his baggy underpants for over thirty years. Just like him they've got bigger and baggier as the years 'ave gone by. Ah well.'

Vera left Barry and Pat on their own; Jimmy was caught up in an argument at the bar.

Pat stroked Barry's arm. 'I'm so lucky. Poor Vera. Which

reminds me, where's our Michelle? And if you knew there was no rehearsal, why did the two of you set off together as if there was?'

'There's something I have to tell you. Don't fly off the handle will yer?'

'How do I know if I will or not?'

'You don't, but don't anyway. Michelle has gone to the cinema in Culworth with Rhett. I took 'em in the car.'

'You let her?'

Barry nodded.

'What were yer thinking of?'

'Two young people enjoying each other's company. She's got to grow up sometime and Rhett's promised to take care of her.'

'Has he indeed. I shall have something to say to her when she gets back. Cinema indeed, with a boy Rhett's age.'

'No, you won't Pat, you'll ask her how she enjoyed herself and what the film was like, and that's all.'

'She's my daughter and I'll . . .'

'She's mine too, now I've adopted her. I've vetted the film and talked to her about going out with Rhett, and I've told him she's precious and there's to be no hanky panky.'

'So that's something else we can lay at Hugo's door.'

'What's he got to do with it?'

'If he hadn't come Rhett and our Michelle would never have got it together.' Pat calmed down until she remembered the other bone she had to pick with her husband. 'So what's this about putting your job in jeopardy by threatening to resign over Dad?'

Barry looked uncomfortable. 'Just a try to help your dad, but it didn't work. So it's plan B now.'

'Look, Barry, this weekend is important to Jimbo, if it goes wrong there'll be *none* of us in work, and then where will we be?'

'Leave it all to me, my darlin'. Barry's in charge.'

With a slightly sarcastic note in her voice, Pat replied, 'Is he? Oh, well then. I understand the gorgeous lover boy has done a bunk.'

'Back tomorrow.'

Pat raised her eyebrows in surprise. 'That right?'

'The Rector got him to see sense.'

'Thank heavens for that. Our Michelle would have been

heartbroken if he'd cancelled it. She thinks the sun shines out of his ... you know what.'

'She's not the only one.'

'Yer mean Dr Harris.'

'I do. If I'd been the Rector I'd have let him go without a word. Glad to see the back of him.'

Pat giggled. 'Couldn't see you as a Rector! Heaven 'elp us!'

Barry laughed his agreement. 'Nor you as the Rector's wife! I've got Rhett and Michelle to collect. Coming with me?'

'Yes, I will.'

The first act in Barry's campaign to have the court action dropped was to head a delegation to the estate office. In Pat's opinion this was a pointless exercise, but Barry insisted that it was what they should do first of all. He checked with the secretary to make sure Jeremy would be in and assembled Greenwood, Rhett and Vera at the Big House as the stable clock struck two.

They'd agreed to see Jeremy in their working clothes and gave all the appearance of earnest people of the soil. As Greenwood said, a bit of kowtowing never did anyone any harm so long as they *knew* they were doing it, though he drew the line at touching his cap.

Jeremy had enjoyed a large, fattening lunch in the dining room at the small table reserved for senior management, and was contemplating a Mars bar to round it off when the secretary rang through to say that he had visitors. Reluctantly the chocolate was returned to the bottom drawer of his desk and he put on a welcoming smile. It swiftly left his face when he saw whom his visitors were.

'Yes?' he asked abruptly.

Barry, chosen to make the initial speech, took half a pace forward and cleared his throat.

'Good afternoon, Mr Mayer. I am well aware that you have already spoken to all of us in turn concerning this matter of the crazy paving and such, but we are making this last appeal to you before the court case and asking you to withdraw the charges ...'

Jeremy attempted to interrupt, but Barry held up a commanding hand. 'Let me finish, please. Even a condemned man has a right to be heard. Everything has been returned to the estate and Vera, as you know, is more than willing to pay for the paving and the cement which was used for her patio. We feel sure that Mr Fitch . . .' at the mention of his employer's name, Barry swore he saw Jeremy shiver, 'does not want to put himself in bad odour with the village yet again. In the past he's trifled with people's opinions to his cost and a further confrontation would do him no good at all. Therefore in *his* interest we have come to suggest – only suggest at *this* stage, you understand – that in Mr Fitch's interest and your own you inform the police that the charges are dropped. Mr Fitch need know nothing at all about it.' Barry stepped back and waited.

During the speech Jeremy Mayer had fiddled with his pen, straightened his tie, gone red, gone white, begun to sweat and then reassembled his confidence. After a short pause he declared, 'Mr Fitch is behind me in this. I have his full support. We are sick and tired of the thieving that goes on.' He thumped the desk with his fist as the assembly began to protest. 'No, don't deny it. He is intent on putting a stop to it. I had my instructions before he left and I'm carrying them out to the letter. I will *not* be moved. You're not the only ones who've been to try to change my mind, and I haven't and I shan't.'

Vera piped up with, 'Who's been to see you besides us, then?'

'Jimbo Charter-Plackett and . . .'

'Yes?'

'The Rector.'

Greenwood was shocked. 'You mean the Rector's been and you still haven't changed your mind? That's a first. He can charm a monkey out of a tree, he can. You must be rotten through and through not to do as he asked.'

Angry, Jeremy spluttered, 'I have my orders.'

Barry, also angry, replied, 'Your trouble is you're scared, running scared of old Fitch. Well, if that's how matters stand and you're not going to shift then we know what to do next.'

Heaving himself to his feet, Jeremy, furious that Barry had found his Achilles' heel, shouted, 'I will not be moved on this! The case goes ahead no matter what. When Mr Fitch gets back you'll see, he'll back me to the hilt. Now, please leave.'

'Oh, we will. But you've not heard the last of this, believe me.

We've other moves up our sleeves. One way or another, we shall win.'

The four of them left the office and didn't speak until they were out on the gravel car park.

His eyes blazing with missionary zeal, Barry said forcibly, 'Well then, it's stage two. We've got him shaking in his shoes, believe me. Old Fitch gets back next Thursday, dress rehearsal night. His weekend party arrives Friday and it's the first night of the play – bit awkward, that, so it'll have to be early teatime. Do we know what time they're expected?'

Greeenwood said he didn't, not exactly, but the domestic staff and the secretary would know and he'd find out for sure.

'Right then, we'll all be in touch. I'll muster the troops. You, Rhett, know what you've to do, seeing as you're not working. I'll get you the materials. Wood, nails, et cetera. Right?'

Rhett grinned and shook his head. 'Tut tut! I don't know, pinching from the estate. It's criminal it is.'

They all laughed. Barry offered Rhett and Vera a lift and they roared off down the drive in Barry's old red van. Greenwood watched them go and wondered where it would all end. He couldn't remember a job where he'd been happier. All those years with the Culworth Parks Department when he'd laboured away at the daily grind and thought he was fulfilled, but the satisfaction of working at Turnham House! Now *that* was something. His own master, a lovely home, his glasshouses, his flowers, the vegetables! Row upon row, bursting with life and beauty. And not just the gardens themselves but the people he worked with, too; loyal and hard working and happy. What a team. But, by the looks of it, it was all going to be snatched away. Life just wasn't fair. He turned on his heel and walked across the gravel back to his work. As he reached what he considered to be his very own part of the estate he paused to enjoy the sight of the bright splash of colour made by the Busy Lizzies flowering abundantly along the foot of the mellow terracotta red walls of his kitchen garden and his heart grew heavy.

Damn that Jeremy for his shortsightedness. Damn him!

Jeremy did feel damned. Damned if he did and damned if he didn't. But Mr Fitch's wrath was his worst fear. A pack of village people with scarcely a brain between them couldn't compare with the kind of wrath Mr Fitch was capable of. One scathing look from his employer and he, Jeremy Mayer, was reduced to jelly.

He reached down into the desk's bottom drawer and rustled about in the rubbish for a Mars bar. As he sank his teeth into it he relished for the third time that day the thought that a Mars bar always met his expectations: each and every one more faithful, more reliable than any lover could ever be. In the midst of his pleasure, without so much as a knock, the door opened and in walked Venetia.

He was too late to hide the chocolate bar from her. His joy turned instantly into a sin.

'Jeremy!'

'I know. I know.' He cleared his mouth as best he could and said, 'I need this, I've just had a drubbing from the estate lot.'

'What's new?' Venetia wandered across to the window and idly looked out across the gardens.

'You seem at a loose end,' he observed.

'Do I?'

'Lover boy done a bunk, has he?'

Startled by his outspokeness, Venetia rounded on him and brutally inquired. 'So? What's it to you?'

He cringed at her reply, he couldn't help himself. Whenever he saw her trim bottom, her slender, taut figure, her neat rounded bosom, her cloud of dark hair – even if it was darker than nature intended – it was his own Venetia who, despite everything she ever did, he couldn't stop loving in his own spaniel-like way.

He laid the Mars bar down on his desk without noticing that a trail of caramel had fallen on a letter he was about to sign. Head down, looking at his clenched hands, he muttered, 'It hurts.'

'Hurts?' Venetia stood opposite him and leant her hands on the desk. 'Hurts? Since when have you "hurt" about anything? Tell me that!'

'I might not protest, but it hurts all the same. How do you think it makes me feel?'

'You haven't got any feelings.'

'That's what you think.'

'You haven't been near me for years. When I think of the great times we had together, but not now ... Eh! not now.'

Helplessly Jeremy gestured at his body ... 'I can't, can I, like this.'

Venetia swept the remains of the Mars bar from the desk, and by chance it landed in the wastepaper basket. 'Stop eating these, then. I've tried to stop you, but you won't. It's disgusting.'

Jeremy bent down to rescue his treat but it was sticking to a tissue he'd used to clean his computer screen and was lost to him.

Venetia, savage in her desperation, shouted, 'If only you'd try.'

'What's the point? It's like a nail in my coffin every time you ...'

'Some nail. Some coffin. That's where you'll be if this snacking doesn't stop.'

Jeremy looked up at her. 'Fine Christian you're turning out to be. Lip service on Sundays and on Friday night at the youth club, but where's your religion now? If Peter knew what you get up to he'd be appalled.'

This statement brought Venetia up short and silenced her. It was the truth, as well as the shock of Jeremy speaking out. Not often troubled by her conscience, now long dormant, this last comment struck home. She swallowed hard. 'You're sticking the knife in and no mistake.'

'You stick it in me all the time with what you get up to ...'

'But you've never said. Never complained. I thought you didn't care, didn't even realise.'

'But I've known, I've always known. I'm not completely stupid. I've loved you from the first day I met you, but it's hard to cling to that when you throw it in my face time after time. And another thing, I've always known that's why we got this job here, because of you and *him*. Don't you think it sticks in my craw having *him* lording it over me?'

'Craddock's not been interested in me since before ... not since before he thought he would be getting married and then didn't.'

'I know, but the thought is always there in my head.'

'I didn't realise you knew all this.'

'Too wrapped up in yourself, that's why.'

Venetia stared at him as though he were a stranger. They'd been together for nine years now but she realised she barely knew him any more. So he'd known all along despite her being, as she thought, discreet. If Peter ever found out . . . She'd die. Literally die.

'What did that lot want?' she asked.

'Me to drop the case.'

'Why don't you?'

'Fitch would find out, somehow, and then where would we go? I'm in a cleft stick, me, a cleft stick.'

She slumped into the nearest chair and threw her head back so that her hair fell down the back of it. She closed her eyes. Immediately her conscience burst into life and she felt uncomfortable, disturbed. Leaping out of the chair, she said, 'I'm going into the village, shan't be long.'

She went to the church and sat in the little war memorial chapel where she knew Peter prayed every day. Venetia hoped that perhaps some of his crystal clear integrity might rub off on her if she sat there long enough. She waited an hour and came out feeling cleaner and purer than she had done for a long time, and vowed to behave better. None the less the moment she walked through the lichgate and out into the road her first thought as she slotted her key in the car's ignition was, 'He'll be back tonight.'

And he was. Bright, breezy and full of himself, Hugo burst into the rehearsal like a revitalised firebrand. With outstretched arms and beckoning hands he called out, 'I'm back! I'm back! Gather round.'

Everyone, props, stage manager, actors, lighting, music, hangers on, rushed to him, full of questions, eager to welcome him back and ready to listen open-mouthed to his news. His eyes found Caroline first and foremost and he told most of the story as though she were the only person in the hall.

'So I said to the director, I have a project in hand very dear to my heart and nothing short of an earthquake will drag me from it. So, old chap, you'll have to wait, I said. Yes, I know the RSC usually takes precedence, but this time it's the Turnham Malpas Amateur Dramatic Society that comes first. "The what?" he said. I told him, one day you'll speak that name with awe, for they're going to make a name for themselves! They are the dear, dear people to whom I owe a massive debt and they have first priority. So here I am, back in the bosom of my dear friends, in top form and so . . .' he paused as though searching for the right words and then his voice dropped to a soft whisper as he said, 'deeply, deeply glad to be amongst my friends.' Hugo sprang up on to the stage, faced them all and called out, 'To work, I say! To work!' His rallying cry was answered by a cheer.

'Act one, scene one?' Someone shouted from the back of the crowd.

'Exactly! Beginners, please!'

They'd never done it better than that night. Every move, every gesture, every word was perfect. Hugo was beside himself with delight and, after the curtains closed, he kissed everyone with whom he came in contact.

'To the Royal Oak! Anyone with the time to spare. Drinks on me, celebrate your success and mine! Come with me!' He took Caroline's hand and led the way. Everyone followed: an excited, exhausted, exhilarated band of players on a high because of Hugo's praise and their own success. They burst into the saloon bar like a whirlwind, setting it alight with their enthusiasm and energy. Dicky and Alan worked like slaves to get them served and amidst a lot of laughter and leg pulling they finally settled at tables.

By an unspoken agreement they always left Hugo and Caroline to sit by themselves once the initial serving of drinks was over. He took her to a small table beside the open hearth and, lifting his glass, saluted her. 'Glad to have me back?'

'Oh, yes. I did begin to wonder if we'd lost you for ever.'

His dark eyes glowed as he said, 'With you here, nothing could keep me away.' He drank his vodka in one go and flung the glass into the fireplace. The sound of shattering glass caused everyone to look their way in astonishment. Hugo was nonplussed.

'Another Vodka, Georgie, and I'll pay for the glass!'

'It wasn't Peter, then, who persuaded you to come back? It was me?'

Hugo hesitated for a moment before he answered, allowing Georgie to place a second glass in front of him, saying quietly, 'Don't make a habit of it, will you? It might catch on.'

His mind intensely occupied in finding a reply to Caroline's question, Hugo didn't answer. Then he looked up, gave Georgie one of his stunning smiles and said, 'No, I won't. Sorry.'

Turning back to Caroline he asked her if she knew everything Peter and he had said.

'Of course not. Just that he persuaded you to come back.'

'I see. Caroline! What can I say. You're married to a remarkable man. I have the greatest respect for him. In fact, I'm truly humbled by him and there are not many people who can do that to me. I'm jealous of him, too.'

'You are?'

'He has *you*, hasn't he?'

Quietly the answer came back, 'Has he?'

Hugo looked up and waited for Caroline to raise her eyes and look at him. 'Hasn't he?'

She took a sip of her drink, neatly replaced the glass on the beer mat in front of her and said, 'At this moment in time I don't really know.'

'You mean there's *hope* for me? For you and I?'

'I didn't say that.'

'You hinted.'

Caroline's hand let go of her glass and gently touched his fingers. 'I did, didn't I.'

They were so absorbed in looking at each other, in their desire to read each other's real meaning, that neither of them had noticed Harriet standing beside their table.

'You two! Georgie's called "time". Those who want to are retiring to our house. Are you coming? Caroline?'

Her voice was inescapably full of meaning. This was Harriet telling Hugo to call a halt, and warning Caroline to watch her step.

Caroline said she wasn't, thanks, she'd get home. Hugo ignored Harriet and said to Caroline, 'Please come.'

'No. I have things to do before I go to bed. Anyway, I'm tired. Good night.'

Hugo leant forward to kiss her cheek but she avoided him and quickly left.

Tight-lipped, Harriet whispered forcefully, 'You're damned selfish, that's what you are, through and through. Now git! If it wasn't for the play I'd get Jimbo to throw you out tonight. You have the morals of an alley cat.'

Equally quietly Hugo answered 'It's none of your business, darling. I love her, you see.'

'That doesn't give you the right to . . .'

'It does.'

'Being in love doesn't give one the freedom to do as one wishes with other people's lives.'

'You're taking this far too seriously.'

Angrier with him than she could ever remember being, Harriet pushed him out of the door and into the street. Facing him in the dark she asked, 'Are you behaving like this for your own amusement, then? Because if you are you're even lower than I could ever have imagined.'

The sounds of the others hammering on her front door came to her as she waited for his reply. 'Of course not. No. I am in love. And so is she.'

'She won't be when I tell her what I know about what you're up to. You're despicable.'

Jimbo called, 'Are you two coming in, then, or shall I close the door?'

Hugo's eyebrows shot up in surprise. 'You know? I didn't realise.'

'I do. Every breath you take is monitored by this village. You're a newcomer, you see, so they all keep an eye on you. If I tell her it will break her heart. I can't do that.'

'Well, don't. I'll deal with it.'

'It's your massive ego, Hugo. You can't cope without the adulation, can you? You're a child in a man's body. Sad really, when you've so much going for you.' Harriet stormed into her house leaving him standing out in the road. Within minutes she caught the sound of the throaty roar of his sports car zooming away, and fervently prayed he wasn't going for good.

14

'Don! Don! Are you up? Don! I'm back!' Vera flung off her cardigan and went to the foot of the stairs. 'Don!'

She heard the sound of the bathroom door being unlocked. 'Hold on! I'm coming down.'

Impatiently she filled the kettle, they'd have a celebration cup of tea, something stronger tonight in the pub. Wait till she told them all. At last, Vera Wright was on the up and up. She was so excited her hands trembled as she put out the cups, filled the milk jug, warmed the pot and brewed the tea. Don came down just before she finally erupted with the excitement of her news.

'Don! . . .'

'You're late, I'm wanting my tea.'

'You won't when you hear my news.'

Don dropped himself down onto a kitchen chair. 'Well?'

'You know the nursing home's been bought out?'

Don nodded. 'So?'

'Well, they're making sweeping changes. Bringing the nursing home right bang up to scratch. Obeying all the rules and that. More staff, higher fees, naturally, but a much better service, ensuite bathrooms, you name it. All them social workers who've been poking about for months can go back into their burrows now, 'cos we're going to be one hundred per cent politically correct. No flies on us!'

'So?'

Vera drew in a deep breath. 'So-o-o-o, now this is the exciting bit, so listen carefully . . . they've invited me to be assistant housekeeper!'

Don perked up at this. 'More money, then?'

'Well, kind of.'

He tapped the table, 'Now see here, promotion means more responsibility and that means more money. You're not doing it if there's no more money in it. I'm not having you exploited. They've had enough out of you over the years and it's time to call a halt.'

'Be quiet and listen. They've suggested and I haven't accepted yet 'cos you've to give the go ahead, I can't do it without you.'

'Me? What's it to do with me?'

Vera took another deep breath. 'I can have the position of assistant housekeeper so long as I'm willing to go live there. We'll have this beautiful flat, really beautiful flat, fully furnished, heating and lighting free.'

'There must be a catch.'

'Well, there is. Well, not a catch but . . . I'm to be the backup person on the premises during the night. So if there's an emergency they've always got someone on hand besides the night nursing staff. To help, like. A body, paid to be there. The flat, oh! Don, it's beautiful. Lovely furniture, newly decorated, lovely bathroom, a beautiful living room looking out over the side garden, and two *huge* bedrooms, so our Rhett's all right, he can come with us.' Vera sipped her tea with a faraway expression on her face. She could just see herself entertaining people on her day off. That carpet in the living room! The kitchen with all that lovely equipment! She looked round her old cottage, the cottage she'd been waiting years for Don to bring up to scratch and thought, 'Goodbye, you horrible dump. Goodbye.'

'They want us to move in first of the month. Just think, Don, it'll be nearer to work for you. Cut five miles at least off the journey. They might even have casual work for you, and if our Rhett doesn't get a job they might have him as gardener 'cos the grounds are "extensive", as they say in the brochure. Isn't it wonderful? Vera Wright no longer at the bottom of the pile!' She nudged his hand where it lay inert on the table, because he hadn't shown any enthusiasm. 'Well?'

He'd drunk his tea and now pushed his cup towards her intimating he needed a refill.

'And what would you do with this place, then?' He jerked his head and looked around the kitchen of the home he'd been born in and had never left.

'I've been thinking about that all the way back on the bus. Clean it up and rent it out, then when I get the order of the boot we can turn out the tenant and bob's yer uncle, we're back home with lots of lovely rent money in the bank. Well?'

'We're not going.'

The kitchen was filled by the heavy silence which lay between them. It was broken when Don slurped his tea, unconcerned by Vera's deep and puzzled frown. Finally, she found her voice. 'Not go? Not go?'

'*We're not going,*' he repeated with emphasis. 'I've lived here all my life and this is where I'm staying. I leave here feet first in a box.'

'But the money! To say nothing of the chance of a lifetime!'

'Money isn't everything.'

'You could have fooled me.'

'Say what yer like, I'm not going.'

'What if I say I am?'

Don calmly replaced his cup in its saucer and repeated, 'We're not going. I've said. So that's that. You can tell 'em tomorrow when yer go. Our Rhett said he'd be back soon, he'll be wanting his bloody tea, just like me, so get cracking, girl. It's no good looking at me like that, we're not going.'

All her years of struggle hammered one by one into her brain with the aggression of a pile driver. The insistent thud shattered any restraint she might have had in the past and she knew once and for all that she'd never climb out of the mire to the upland plains which were her just reward if he'd always be there to drag her back. Vera rose to her feet filled with hatred.

Don nodded his head at her and through a mist she heard him say, 'In any case, they won't want yer when they know you've got a criminal record, they won't want someone who's done porridge, will they? Stands to ...'

Standing on the top of the cooker was one of the cast iron pans Vera had inherited from Don's mother and never had the money to replace. She picked it up and hit him on the head with it. He sat looking at her, quite still and not speaking. Her temper boiled over even further at his lack of reaction, and she hit him again. He fell slowly sideways as blood oozed from the top of his head in a great trickle. There was a single grunt and then no more except for the thud of his body as it fell between his chair and the cooker. Vera put on her cardigan, picked up her bag and marched out of the house.

Where she was going she didn't know, but somehow the Store felt like a haven and she knew Jimbo would know what to do. He'd advise her. He was a businessman. He'd tell her how to go about renting the cottage out. She marched down Church Lane towards Stocks Row, breathing rapidly, still blind with rage. As she turned the corner she heard the jangle of the bell on the door of the Store and by chance it was Mrs Jones who came out. Vera's temper boiled over again and, like a flash of lightning, she suddenly knew it was her who'd blown the gaffe to the estate about her garden pots and her lovely table and chairs, all because of the wardrobe mistress business. Unaware of Vera's rage-inspired revelation Mrs Jones set off to go down Shepherds Hill, a loaded carrier bag in her hand. From behind she received a stunning blow from Vera's bag which caught her on the side of her head. She staggered, retrieved herself and twisted round to see who'd attacked her.

Vera, purple-faced, screamed at the top of her voice, 'You bitch, it was you, wasn't it? You told 'em, didn't yer? It'll be the end of me but I don't care. I'll go down fighting.' She grabbed Mrs Jones by the throat and began shaking her so that Mrs Jones' head swung back and forth violently. All the time Vera was shouting, 'You bitch! You bitch!'

At last, Mrs Jones struggled free of Vera's grasp, stumbled over her fallen shopping and tried desperately to escape by running back into the Store. Her way was impeded by Linda, Jimbo, Bel and a customer who'd rushed out into Stocks Row when they heard the shouting. Vera caught up with Mrs Jones and began hitting, punching and scratching her, anything to get her own back. Linda couldn't stop saying, 'Oh! Oh! Oh!' at the top of her voice, but Bel waded in and grabbed Vera, while Jimbo stood in front of Mrs Jones to protect her.

Vera, still screaming, fought like a wild cat to escape Bel, but the sheer weight of Bel's body prevented her. Finally Vera capitulated and began to groan, 'Oh! God! Oh! God! Oh! God!'

Jimbo and Bel took Vera inside, followed by Linda holding on to Mrs Jones who was trembling and so white they thought she was going to faint.

'Linda! First aid box, small brandy for these two. Come now, Vera, sit here and calm down. Mrs Jones, you too, sit yourself down. My goodness me, what a hullabaloo! What were you thinking of? Bel, ring Harriet. No, better still, ring the Rectory. Get Dr Harris. Tell her it's urgent. Quick sharp, please.'

Linda arrived with three brandies, one for each of the two antagonists and one for herself. She tossed it down, went weak at the knees, pulled out a stool and plumped herself down on it. 'Oh, Mr Charter-Plackett! I feel terrible. What's it all about?' she asked.

'Sip it, Vera. Steady now.' Jimbo, still supporting Vera, looked over to Mrs Jones, who was tossing back her brandy as though it was cola. 'Mrs Jones, steady with it, please. Do you know what's caused this?'

Mrs Jones shook her head. 'No more than you.' She took out her handkerchief and mopped her lips.

Vera, encouraged by the warmth the brandy was bringing her, said, 'She does know. It was her told Jeremy Mayer about my pots and that, just to get her own back.'

Mrs Jones opened her mouth to deny it but catching Jimbo's baleful eye she closed it again without a word.

Vera finished her brandy and gave the paper cup to Jimbo saying, 'It was her, I can see it now, to get back at me about them costumes. Well, she got more than she bargained for, didn't yer? Yer own son and his wife perhaps made homeless. Serves yer right. No wonder yer wouldn't confess.'

Linda, catching a whiff of scandal and emboldened by her brandy, said, 'No, really? Is this true Mrs Jones? Was it you?'

Mrs Jones didn't reply, but Jimbo looked sorrowfully at her and said, 'Better to get it out now and apologise before it's all too late.'

'Before it's too late?' Vera stood up, wobbled a bit, and then sat down again. 'It's already too late. The damage that old cow's done ... and now she's most likely lost me a blinking good opportunity to kick myself into a lifestyle above and beyond what I've got now.'

'The brandy's gone to her head. What on earth is she talking about?' Mrs Jones sniffed derisively. 'Lifestyle! What lifestyle can she ever expect?'

Caroline arrived in breathless haste. 'What's happened? Bel said there'd been an accident.' She looked from one woman to the next, then at Jimbo.

'We thought Mrs Jones was going to faint and Vera's not feeling too perky. There's been a disagreement, you see, between the two of them.'

'I see.' She looked more closely at Mrs Jones. 'You're going to have a lovely black eye.'

'Am I? That's all your fault, Vera. Hitting me like that.'

But Vera had suddenly gone very quiet. The blood had drained from her face and she was nervously plucking at her cardigan sleeve. Caroline bent over her, her arm around her shoulders. 'All right, Vera? Is there anything I can do for you? Get Don, perhaps? Walk you home, maybe?'

'I'd come to ask Mr Charter-Plackett how to go about renting out my cottage. That's all.'

'Are you moving, then? I didn't know.'

'No one did.' Abruptly she stood up, clutched her handbag to her chest and made a move to leave. 'I'll go to our Dottie's. She'll sort me out.'

'But that's in Little Derehams. There's not another bus now till nearly six o'clock.'

'I'll walk. Do me good, some fresh air.'

Jimbo raised his eyebrows at Caroline, who shook her head. 'Dr Harris says you're not fit to walk all that way. I'll take you in the car.'

Vera tried to smile at him, but it wouldn't quite come. 'Will you? Then we'll talk about renting out the cottage on the way. Got to get it straight for tomorrow.'

'Of course. I'll just have a word with Bel.' He winked at Caroline and left the office.

When Jimbo and Vera had gone, Linda went to pick up Mrs Jones' shopping and Caroline sat down facing Mrs Jones and asked her what it was all about.

There was a moment of indecision, then she said, 'It's all my fault. I'm the one who split to Jeremy Mayer about the garden stuff. I never let on, someone must have told her it was me. She's quite right. I should never have done it. I didn't think about the consequences, you know, about it affecting our Barry and that.'

'All over the costumes?'

Mrs Jones nodded. 'That's right. Then when it all blew up in my face I couldn't, just couldn't let on. Our Barry was so upset for the kids and that. I couldn't have faced him, just when life was going really well for 'im. My own grandchildren, 'omeless.' She dabbed her eyes with her handkerchief but it made her wince. 'But she just attacked me, didn't even speak, just hit out at me. Such a shock.'

'It must have been. You'll need to apologise, best to come out in the open, you know. Your eye's looking worse by the minute.'

'Never mind, I'll get my herbal stuff out, I've cured more bruises for my three boys than I've had hot dinners. I'll just go see if Linda's rescued all my shopping.'

'We'll both go, then. Vera did seem odd though, didn't she?'

Before Mrs Jones could reply they heard a commotion in the Store and Rhett shouting, 'Quick, Bel, ring for an ambulance – the call box is out of order. It's Grandad, he's fallen and split his head open. There's blood all over the place.'

Rhett wouldn't go inside the cottage again, said he couldn't bear all that blood, he'd wait outside in Church Lane and direct the ambulance when it came and would Dr Harris do what she could? Instinct told Caroline that something more than a bad fall had taken place at Vera's cottage: Vera's confused behaviour at the Store, and two cups and saucers on the table with the teapot still quite hot. Don, who never touched alcohol and hadn't ailed a thing all his life, falling off a chair? He was unconscious on the floor, looking for all the world as though he'd fallen and hit his head on the corner of the cooker as he went down. Lying on the floor in the pool of blood was a heavy pan. He must have clutched it as he tried to save himself, or knocked it off the cooker with his arm, perhaps. She moved it away to make a space so that she could examine him.

After making sure she'd done all she could for Don, and despite realising she might be interfering with evidence, Caroline quickly washed up one cup and saucer and put them away in the cupboard, rinsed the bloodstains from the saucepan and replaced it on the cooker.

It took twenty-five minutes for the ambulance to arrive.

'Dr Harris! How's things? Those two nippers of yours all right, are they? Good. Good. What have we here?'

'This is Don Wright. It would appear that he's fallen and hit his head on the corner of the cooker. He's not spoken since I got here, he's out for the count and no mistake.'

The ambulance man gently removed the clean towel Caroline had put on Don's head and examined the damage. 'Cor, he's bleeding like a stuck pig.'

'Well, you know head injuries.'

'I do. Certainly looks as if that's what's happened. Poor old fella.' He bent down to sniff Don's breath. 'Not been drinking, 'as he?'

Caroline shook her head. 'Only tea,' she gestured towards the teapot, 'he doesn't drink alcohol. Well known for it.'

'Wife, has he?'

'Yes. She's at her cousin's. I'll let her know, leave that with me.'

They expertly fixed a thick dressing to Don's head to absorb the blood and carried him off to casualty, leaving Caroline feeling guilty and distressed. She'd interfered where she shouldn't. She shouldn't have done it. Rhett had gone with his grandad, so she locked up the cottage with the key Rhett had given her and went back to the Rectory to telephone Dottie with the news about Don.

'I'll drive her in, Dottie, if she would like.' Caroline waited while Dottie explained her offer to Vera. But Vera wouldn't go.

'I'm sorry, Dr Harris, she doesn't want to go.' Dottie's voice dropped to a whisper. 'She's behaving real odd, I don't know what's the matter with her. Funny like, something about a fight with Terry Jones' mother, and she won't answer proper about Don. Insists on going to work tomorrow, says she's got business to attend to and can't have a day off.'

'Look, Dottie, I'll ring casualty and find out what's going on, and let you know. I'll make some excuse about Vera being ill in bed. OK? I'll be in touch. Take care.'

Don came home after three days and had only Rhett to look after him because Vera refused to go home.

The general consensus was that Don had dropped asleep at the table and fallen off his chair. In the Store, heads close together by the tinned soups, they nodded wisely and agreed, 'All that night work, can't be good for a living soul that can't, must upset yer body clock and it's caught up with him at last'.

'Drink isn't to blame like it could be with some.'

'Our Kev knows the ambulance chap who came for him, he said he hadn't been drinking and he should know.'

'Poor Vera. Taken real bad she is. Still 'asn't come home from their Dottie's. Going to work, though, she can't be that bad.'

'She'll be having a bit livelier time there than she's had for years with that Don!'

'What I can't understand is where Vera was. I saw her get off the bus when I was coming out of here – I'd been to collect one of Mrs Charter-Plackett's birthday cakes for my old man – and I called out, "Hello, Vera", she seemed real excited about something. So where was she between getting off the bus and beating up old Mrs Jones? Nobody's answered that one, have they?'

'One of life's unsolved mysteries, that is.' The gossip topped the list for days and even surpassed the talk about the play and the troubles Hugo Maude had brought upon the village.

15

Vera, disgusted by her cousin Dottie's nocturnal comings and goings and spurred on by her need to get her belongings together, eventually returned home after work. She stepped off the lunch-time bus, two plastic carrier bags she'd borrowed from Dottie in her hand. She cursed her bad luck as she saw Mrs Jones coming out of the Store. Vera turned on her heel and set off for home but Mrs Jones called after her.

'Vera! Just a minute! Hold on!'

Reluctantly she turned back.

'Vera! I'm sorry. Very, very sorry for what I did. Shouldn't have tried to get back at yer. I never should. My Vince is blazing.'

Vera studied over the apology, turning it over in her mind, pondering on the effort it must have cost Mrs Jones to make it, her being a proud woman. 'Not 'alf as sorry as me. However, I shall accept it. I owe you one too for going for you the other day. Perhaps you've learned a lesson from it. Barry and Pat don't deserve all this trouble, yer know.'

'I know they don't. I've been up and told 'em. Greenwood had a lot to say.'

'I bet.'

Mrs Jones had put down her bag and was twisting her hands together, looking down at them as though transfixed by their movement. 'I did wonder ... I 'ave to admit I'm getting nervous about the play. I don't suppose ... I mean, would you be free to ...'

'Yes?'

Taking a deep breath she said, 'I could really do with another pair of hands on the night, well Friday *and* Saturday. Back up, kind of. Would you ...?'

Masking her triumph as best she could, Vera replied graciously. 'Why, of course ... Greta ... I'd be delighted to help. It's more than one body can do, isn't it?'

Mrs Jones, smarting under Vera's use of her Christian name, agreed. No one ever called her by her Christian name except for Vince. 'It is, it gets very fraught.'

'I shall be moving into my new flat on Thursday but I'll make it somehow.'

Mrs Jones' eyebrows shot up in surprise. 'Your new flat? What new flat?'

'I've got the job of assistant housekeeper at the nursing home and a flat goes with it. When I've got straight you'll have to come one afternoon for a cup of tea and have a look round it.'

'My word, Vera, that's a turn up for the book and not half. What does Don think? He must be pleased.'

'He isn't coming with me. Staying where he is, is Don.'

Shock registered in every bone in Mrs Jones' body. 'Not going? You mean you're *leaving* him? Vera! After all these years. Yer can't be!'

Vera studied this question for a moment and then said, 'I suppose I am. Yes, I am leaving him. Yer right. In one way you did me a good turn refusing to let me help yer and then splitting on us. It made me take stock. Sometimes it does yer good to take stock, yer know. What time shall I be there?'

'Where? Oh, the play. Come to the dress rehearsal Thursday, if you can manage it, that is, I wouldn't want to put you out. Six o'clock. Learn the ropes. Well, I never.' She strode away down Jacks Lane shaking her head.

Vera became aware that the boost to her morale which her triumph over Mrs Jones had given her was steadily evaporating the closer she got to home. She prayed that Rhett would be in, he'd be glad to see her even if Don wasn't. His reaction to her return to collect her things was a definite unknown quantity. Would he remember it was she who knocked him unconscious? Would he remember about the flat?

She didn't need to use her key, the door stood open in the

afternoon heat. Don was sitting at the kitchen table on the very same chair, the same teapot and cup and saucer in front of him, a newly opened carton of milk to hand. It was as though the whole incident had never happened. She glanced at the cooker and saw the pan stood on the top as before. It was just as it was. Every blessed thing in the same place, even Don. Nothing had changed. Her heart jerked. Had she been given a chance to retrieve herself, time having taken a queer turn? Had it all been a dream? Then through the gloom she saw the massive bruising on Don's forehead, the shaved scalp and the stitched cut. So it was true, then.

'You're back.'

She put down her bags. 'I am. Any tea left?'

Don picked up the pot and weighed it in his hand. 'Enough for another one. Get yerself a cup.'

She sat at the table with him and poured herself some tea. It was stewed but for now it would do. In her mind's eye she imagined herself in the kitchen in the flat. All light and airy, the sun filtering through those lovely blinds framed by the matching curtains, all quiet and peaceful and glorious.

'How's things, then?'

She sipped her tea. 'Fine! Fine!' Didn't he know what she'd done? The stupid pillock. The stupid, dull, boring, useless, hopeless *pillock.*

Don sat without speaking and then burst out with, 'I've not been shopping. There's nothing in for tea.'

'I see.'

'I'll have to be off about seven. They want extra hours. Still, the money will be handy.'

'It will.'

'Rhett'll be back soon. Been out for a job interview, he has.'

'Right.'

His small brown eyes covertly watched her from beneath his thatch of grey disordered hair. 'Well, then, are yer going shopping?'

'When I'm good and ready.'

Don's eyes focused on hers. They looked steadily at one another, saying nothing but meaning a lot. She realised he wasn't going to mention what she'd done. He was going to ignore it. Shelve it. Pretend nothing had happened. Like always. Don't mention it and it'll go away, and Vera will carry on slaving in this tip like she's always done.

'I take over the flat on Thursday. Jimmy's giving me a lift with all my things. Are you coming?'

'I'm going nowhere, and neither are you.'

'I am. Don't say I didn't ask.' She stood up to put her cup in the sink, pouring away most of the stewed tea. There'd be no more stewed tea from now on. Rhett came in.

'Gran! You're back! Feeling better?' Vera nodded. 'Grandad tell you I've been for an interview for that garden job? Job's mine if I want it. Said I'd let them know.'

Vera smiled at him. 'That's good, I'm pleased, really pleased.' She paused. 'Rhett, I'm moving to the new flat, Thursday. Like I've said, there's a bedroom for you, and you're more than welcome. What do you say?'

Rhett nodded his head in his grandad's direction and raised his eyebrows.

'Grandad's staying here.'

'You're going without 'im?'

Vera thought about her answer. 'I am. Come with me tomorrow on the bus and have a look see. You'll love it.'

'I will. It's very tempting.' He looked round the depressing shambles that was his gran's kitchen. 'A real fresh start.'

'Oh, it is. Mrs Jones has climbed down and asked me to help with the costumes. I tell yer, there's a whole new life beginning for your gran right here and now. I'm off upstairs to sort some things out ready for moving. Here, take this ten pound note and go to the Store and get us something for our tea. There's nothing in. Get something we can just bung in the oven.'

Amazed by his gran's sudden generosity Rhett departed, his mind ranging over the selection of frozen meals Jimbo always kept in his freezer for emergencies.

Don sat impassively studying the design on the old teapot, his life being decided for him over his head.

As Vera went towards the stairs he said loudly, 'It'll be a different tale when they hear about your conviction. I'll tell 'em about what yer did to me, too, that'll put the frighteners on 'em. They'll be thinking yer might do it to one of them old bats yer talk so much about.'

Vera turned back and bent her head close to his unwashed, unshaven face. Her eyes only inches from his, through clenched teeth and with a steely purpose the like of which she had never known she possessed, she uttered a desperate threat. 'You'll keep your bloody trap shut, Don Wright. 'Cos if you utter one single word about anything at all to anyone I'll do for you once and for all. That blinking cut-throat razor of your grandad's with the genuine ivory handle yer keep prattling on about will suddenly find itself, after years of idleness, being put to good use.' She drew her finger across her throat. 'Get my meaning? Nothing and nobody's getting in my way. OK? Know why? Because something'll turn up and put things right for me, because now is Vera's moment. Not anyone else's ... Vera's. See? And if I don't take life by the throat right now, it'll be the end of me.' Her trembling legs carried her upstairs on the first step to freedom.

Not only Vera's legs were trembling. Jeremy Mayer's were too. Mr Fitch, having returned from abroad in the early hours and waking from a snatched and miserable sleep feeling totally disorientated, had come into his office wanting to catch up on the latest news about the estate.

'This damned jet lag plays havoc with me. What time is it?'

'Three o'clock.'

'It feels like ten o'clock. Where's my coffee?'

'I'll order some.' Jeremy pressed the number for the kitchen on his telephone, anything at all to delay telling him the crucial news about the court case. When he'd put down the receiver he shuffled his papers about, cleared his throat, shot his cuffs ...

'Well? I'm waiting. What's the news? Bring me up to date.'

'The new crazy paving path is finished, and looks very good. It was a commendable idea of yours, sir. Greenwood Stubbs has brought in the flowers for the main rooms in readiness for tomorrow, and the girl's arranging them. The training staff want to have a conference with you, some new ideas they've got, think you ought to give your approval. I've had Jimbo in and confirmed the menus for the weekend, so he's all set. The fencing is almost done.

Home Farm is having staff problems, two cowmen ill, but they're coping. The tickets are here for the play on Saturday night. First two rows centre. Everyone you invited has confirmed. Apart from that, nothing really.'

The girl came in from the kitchens with coffee for Mr Fitch. A nicely laid tray with silver coffee pot, cream and sugar and biscuits, just how he liked it. Jeremy thanked his lucky stars that Jimbo had well trained staff.

The girl carefully handed Mr Fitch his coffee and then said, 'Don't know if you need to know this, Mr Mayer, but the banners have arrived.'

His head shot up. 'Banners?'

'Yes, Barry's just fixing them up. Thought you might need to know.' There was a smirk on her face which boded no good.

Mr Fitch stopped sipping his coffee. 'Banners? What kind of banners. I didn't order banners.' He waited for Jeremy's explanation.

'I don't know what they're about, Mr Fitch. I'd better go see. Obviously there's been some mistake. You finish your coffee.' He lumbered to his feet and stumbled out of the office, his heart leaden in his chest.

Strung from the first floor windows were pieces of sheeting with lettering, huge lettering from one end to the other. He didn't read them because he couldn't: his eyes had clouded over as a result of the tremendous explosion of temper he experienced at the sight of them. There was a mysterious pounding in his chest and his ears throbbed. Sweat began to run down his face, the hair on his neck grew wet, his knees, already trembling, began to shake. Had he been able to see himself he would have seen that his whole body was shaking. Fear had him in its grip.

He roared at Greenwood Stubbs who was standing giving directions to someone in an upstairs window. 'Stubbs!'

Nonchalantly, Greenwood swung round and innocently answered, 'Yes?'

'Remove those at once! At once, I say! At once!' By now his face was beetroot red.

Greenwood's response was to laugh. 'Not likely! We've got to draw attention to the injustice of this prosecution you've brought. It's not fair and you know it.'

'Prosecution? What prosecution?' Mr Fitch had come out to the front, cup in hand, he turned round and saw the banners. 'What the hell's going on? Mayer! Inside. Greenwood, take those banners down this instant.'

Greenwood Stubbs ignored him and carried on giving directions to the person at the upstairs window.

'Do you hear me? I pay your wages, so I'm the one who calls the tune round here and I insist you remove them.'

'Not for much longer you aren't. Or so Mr Mayer gives me to understand.'

The coffee cup began to rattle against the saucer as Mr Fitch took on board what Greenwood had said. 'Mayer! In!' Jeremy stumbled after him, his heart pounding as never before.

Mr Fitch led the way to his own office, seated himself behind his desk, put down his cup and saucer, and waited.

Jeremy began to settle himself in the nearest chair, but a withering glance from Mr Fitch persuaded him it wouldn't be a very good idea in the circumstances, so he stood like a small boy in the headmaster's office.

Summoning all his strength Jeremy began, 'Before you went away three weeks ago you stated quite categorically that the next time any member of staff, either outdoor or in, was caught stealing from the estate they were to be prosecuted. The full works, police, the lot.'

'I did.'

'Therefore when I got information regarding the disappearance of a quantity of crazy paving, an Edwardian wrought iron table and two chairs, and several Victorian garden pots of considerable value, I apprehended the guilty party and they are being prosecuted. The case comes up on Monday and I am giving evidence.' Relieved to see an element of agreement in Mr Fitch's face he began to lower himself into a chair.

'Just a minute!'

Jeremy straightened himself up. 'Yes?'

'Who exactly is involved?'

Jeremy counted them off on his fingers, then while he waited for

Mr Fitch to speak he got out his handkerchief and wiped the sweat from his forehead.

'Have you interviewed these people?'

'Of course. I've seen Vera and ...'

'What did she have to say?'

'She said she would return everything and pay for the crazy paving and the cement if I would drop the prosecution, but I said no, I was under your strict instructions ...'

'And Rhett?'

'Well, he said something about his grandmother needing cheering up and ...'

'And Greenwood?'

'Stubbs agreed he'd used Jones' van for an hour to transport all the stuff, and that he'd been a party to the theft.'

'Knowing this village like I do, has anyone been up to speak on their behalf?'

Jeremy began to feel uncomfortable all over again. A sneaking suspicion that Mr Fitch was not entirely pleased with him began to permeate his subconscious, and he started to bluster.

'Now see here, Mr Fitch, I was only carrying out your orders. You said quite categorically that ...'

Mr Fitch tapped the desk with his pen to stop the tirade and bellowed. 'Who?'

'The Rector.'

'You sat here in this chair and . .'

Jeremy, clutching at straws, protested, 'Not that chair, my chair.'

'It bloody well doesn't matter which chair, what matters is you don't know when to let things go. I've spent years now building up a relationship with these people – why, I'm not quite sure, but it's something I know I have to do – and in one fell swoop you've destroyed all my work. When the Rector came you could have given in very gracefully indeed, made him think it was him who'd changed your mind and honour would have been satisfied, not just with him but the entire village. They set great store by that Rector. Come to think of it so do I. That would have been the end of the matter.'

'But you said ...'

'Never mind what I bloody well said, you fool. It'll look fine, won't it? Every newspaper in the county will be running the headline about greedy landlords and homeless workers.'

'Homeless?'

'Yes, if Greenwood's found guilty I've nowhere to go but to sack the man. I can't employ someone who's been proved to be an accessory to theft from the estate. Think of the example to the others. The house goes with the job, the whole family would have to vacate it. The best gardener any estate could hope to have, and the best carpenter . . .'

'Barry Jones is an idle layabout. If I didn't keep hounding him . . .'

Mr Fitch rose to his feet. 'That's your job, to keep him on his toes! He's a craftsman and there's not many of those about. To say nothing of Greenwood. I can't afford to lose him. There's no man alive who would keep those glasshouses in such tiptop condition for the money I pay him. He's a brilliant asset I can ill afford to lose. No, he's not the one to go, it's more likely to be you who goes. You're expendable.' He leaned across the desk as he fired this salvo and Jeremy could see the whites of his light blue eyes and the slight flush on each of his thin pale cheeks. His snow white hair appeared to crackle with anger.

'Me? What have I done?' The pitch of Jeremy's voice rose higher and higher. 'All I ever do is what you want, every decision, every letter I dictate is at your bidding . . . what more can I do?'

'For a start you can cancel that court hearing,' Mr Fitch snapped.

'If I do that I'll have no credibility left.'

'You have no credibility and never have had, that's why I need to tell you every move you make. You . . . bloody, blithering idiot.'

Jeremy opened his mouth to protest at Mr Fitch's ungentlemanly language but no words would come.

'You couldn't organise a chimpanzees' tea party, I should never have given you the job in the first place.'

Their voices were now so loud that there had grown quite a gathering of students and staff in the hall wondering whether or not they should intervene. The office door was partly open so they couldn't help but hear every word. Someone had gone to fetch Venetia and she'd appeared downstairs to witness the dispute for herself.

'I . . . I . . . I . . .' Jeremy clutched at his shirt collar and tried to drag it away from his throat, but his fingers had no more mobility than a bunch of carrots. He couldn't breathe and the sweat poured in rivers down his putty coloured face.

It was Venetia who rushed in first as soon as Jeremy began choking. The choking ceased, he gave three deep rattling breaths, then fell over backwards to the floor with the most tremendous crash and lay quite still.

'Oh, God! He's dead! He's dead!' Venetia knelt on the floor beside him, fitfully pounding his chest and then breathing into his mouth.

Mr Fitch went white and dropped like a stone back into his chair.

Later that evening Mr Fitch sat down at Pat's kitchen table. Pat, worried beyond belief by his unexpected arrival, inquired whether or not he would prefer to sit somewhere more comfortable.

'No, thank you, Pat, this is fine.'

'It's terrible news about Mr Mayer, isn't it? Have you heard any more? Is that what you've come to tell me?'

Mr Fitch studied his hands while he answered quietly, 'It's touch and go I'm afraid.'

'He's a bit of a chump but you can't help feel sorry for him with that Venetia . . . It can't be easy her being like she is.'

Mr Fitch didn't bother to ascertain whether or not Pat was scoring a point against him. 'Where is everyone?'

'Barry, Dean and Michelle are at the dress rehearsal and Dad's upstairs in his room watching telly.'

'Of course, yes, the dress rehearsal. Get him to come down, will you Pat? If he wouldn't mind.'

Greenwood Stubbs came downstairs and stood in front of Mr Fitch. 'Well, then, sir, what have you come for?'

'Sit down, man. Sit down. Tomorrow morning I am going personally to the court in Culworth and doing whatever is necessary to withdraw the prosecution against you. You must clearly understand that I do not approve of stealing, most especially from myself. If I had been asked, then I would more than likely have said yes, Vera could have all that stuff, but I wasn't and Mr

Mayer acted on my instructions. He is completely exonerated on that score. I know I said I wanted all that rubbish clearing away, but, well, I didn't realise it was antique stuff – not being well up in that area. But taking it and using it and pinching the crazy paving isn't quite the same thing, is it? Don't let it happen again Greenwood, will you? Wait and ask *me* first. Right?'

'Very well, Mr Fitch. I much appreciate your understanding . . .'

Pat, hope rising in her chest, asked, 'Does that mean we shan't have to leave? Does it?'

'Of course it does.'

'Thank you very much, Mr Fitch.'

Making up an excuse for his change of heart he answered, 'No, thank the Rector. If he hadn't been on your side, neither would I.' Mr Fitch stood up and looked around Pat's cheerful kitchen, admiring the sunny yellow walls and the bright flowers on the sill. 'You've made a lovely home here, Pat. Lovely.'

'Thank you, we love this house. You've just no idea how grateful I am. It would have broken my heart if . . .' Pat smiled at him nervously.

'Well, there's no need for you to worry. I know a good man when I see one and your father's one of those. Now . . .' he rose to his feet, 'I'm off to Vera's to tell her the good news.'

'Oh! But did you know Vera's moved to the nursing home in Penny Fawcett? She's got promotion and a flat goes with it. She moved in today. Oh no, I've just thought. She's helping at the dress rehearsal. She'll be at the Church Hall.'

'I'll see her there, then.'

Greenwood reached out to shake hands. 'Thank you, Mr Fitch. Thank you very much. I can't say how grateful I am.'

'Not at all, not at all. The least I can do. Can't lose hard-working skilled people like you, Greenwood. Don't worry about Dean's scholarship. If he gets in, the money will be in place like I promised. I'll be off, then, to see Vera.'

Mr Fitch stood at the back of the hall while he accustomed his eyes to the darkness. The stage was brightly lit, the body of the hall empty except for Barry, Sir Ronald and Willie Biggs who were conferring quietly in the far corner away from the stage. Barry was pointing something out to the other two concerning the stage, it involved a lot of arm waving and apparently denial on Willie's part. Mr Fitch became absorbed in the argument. He smiled to himself. It wasn't just big business, then, which caused serious disagreement. It happened in two-bit places like Turnham Malpas over a two-bit play. When he heard the powerful persuasive tones of Hugo Maude his attention was drawn to the stage.

The set was splendid. Far and away better than he could ever have expected. His baby grand piano had pride of place, with a bright Indian patterned, heavily-fringed silky cloth draped over it. His eye was drawn to a vase of flowers so totally in keeping with the nineteen twenties set he could hardly believe it. Seated at the piano was ... who was it? It was Caroline Harris! She wore a beautiful evening dress, light and beaded, and a jewelled band round her forehead. She was transformed; the sensible, caring Caroline he knew had been replaced by a siren out of the top drawer, no less. Her hands trailed along the keys, picking out snatches of tunes and then she began to play. Or was she? No, there in a corner was Mrs Peel, the organist, doing the real playing. How clever.

'*My dearest! That's the tune they played for us in the restaurant!*'

Hugo crossed the stage and stood behind her, his hands on her shoulders, his lips raining kisses on her head, tiny trembling kisses. His hands roved over her shoulders and arms. She looked up at him and, seeing him upside down, said, '*Dearest, you look quite strange this way up. I've never seen you like this before.*'

Hugo captured her hands and raised them above her head so he could kiss them. '*Beloved!*'

She clasped her hands behind his head and drew it down so they were cheek to cheek. His hands began roving over her, down to her hips and back up along her arms until he unfastened her hands from behind his neck. He pulled her to her feet, pushed the piano stool away and they stood locked together, kissing.

In the dark Mr Fitch found himself blushing: not because the acting was bad but because it was so good. Too good. He was stunned. Moved might be a better word to describe how he felt. He noticed the three arguing in the corner had stopped to watch, and no wonder.

He looked again at the stage and now Neville Neal of all people had entered. The other two had broken apart on his arrival and were looking genuinely appalled. That was nothing to what that cold fish Neville Neal had unexpectedly become capable of. It really was as though he'd caught his own wife in the arms of another man. For a moment Mr Fitch was confused, mixing reality with the play. He shook himself. By Jove! It was going to be a real corker, was this. Those chaps he had coming to see it on Saturday night would be mighty impressed. He had a further shock when he heard Caroline, well not Caroline in truth but ... She was giving her husband what for in no uncertain terms. 'Your constant, unwavering, everlasting love is sickening.' She pointed to Hugo. 'He's given me more excitement in two months than you have given me in twenty years. I never knew how thrilling loving could be till I met Leonard. Your feeble faithfulness, your self-righteous loyalty, your clinging to something which is no longer there! I'm weary of it. Weary! Do you hear me?'

Mr Fitch was spellbound.

'Will you never realise that I am not the person you left behind in 1914? You've come back to a new me. I've changed utterly and completely. That's what the war has done to me. Changed me for ever. But it doesn't seem to have changed you. You still have the same expectations of me.'

Neville Neal shook his head and wept.

Mr Fitch cleared his throat. It was all too realistic for words. He became convinced it was all true. Then he pulled himself together and remembered it was only a play. But what a play! Caroline was clinging to Hugo, her dress half off her shoulder, Hugo's arm around her waist, knee to knee, hip to hip, standing there watching Neville.

Then Rhett Wright came on stage. A transformed Rhett. A handsome, debonair, well dressed Rhett. And him only a gardener. What had happened to everyone? He couldn't wait to say nonchalantly to his guests, 'Oh, yes, that's one of my under gardeners. Talented lot, aren't they?'

Rhett and Neville left the stage. Caroline and Hugo kissed passionately and the curtains closed.

Mr Fitch crept out before anyone could see him. Vera would have to wait. He lit a cigarette, and stood outside looking at the stars and going over in his mind the tremendous excitement of the last few minutes. This only a village play and he'd financed it! Just showed what money could do. He walked down the path to the road to get in his car. Mr Fitch was well aware he was insensitive to other people's feelings and the incident with Jeremy that afternoon had proved that all over again, but right at this moment, excited by the play, he had a flash of insight and thought about how Peter would feel when he saw it. The light was on in Peter's study. He wondered if Peter knew what was going on? The Rector's wife acting her knickers off in a dodgy play in the Church Hall. Such good acting you thought it was real! Heaven's above. It wasn't, was it? Were they really having an affair? Surely not. They couldn't be. Or could they? He'd better warn Peter. The poor man. They couldn't cancel it now, it was all too late, but he'd better know, better be forewarned.

Peter answered the door. 'Why, good evening, Mr Fitch, how nice to see you. Do come in.' He led the way into the sitting room and invited Mr Fitch to sit down. Mr Fitch was glad Peter was in mufti, it made it easier somehow to talk man to man.

'I'm sorry, I know it's late but I had to come. I've just been watching a snatch of the play.' Mr Fitch cleared his throat. 'Have you seen it, by any chance?'

The light casual note in his voice amused Peter. 'I have.'

'Oh, right. I thought it a bit . . . *risqué* for a Church Hall.'

'In this day and age . . .' Peter shrugged his shoulders and smiled.

'Oh yes, I know. But Caroline, your wife, she's certainly putting her heart and soul into her part.'

'Unexpected talent!'

'Indeed. This Hugo Maude. What d'you make of him?'

'Full of charm, too much for his own good.' Peter laughed. 'But a brilliant actor. He's bringing out the best in the most unexpected people.'

Mr Fitch nodded his head. 'Oh! I agree. Rhett Wright, for instance. Whenever I see him he's got his boot behind a spade. Now, suddenly . . . well, it's quite unbelievable. And Neville Neal, crying real tears on the stage? Always such a cold fish. That Hugo must have something special if he can get him to do that!'

'Exactly, he has got "something".'

Mr Fitch took out a cigarette case and asked for approval.

'Of course, somewhere we have an ashtray.' He searched along the book shelves and found one. 'Here we are.'

'Thanks. Thirty years ago that play wouldn't have been staged in a Church Hall and, what's more, the Rector's wife wouldn't have been playing that part.' His voice had taken on a harder tone and Peter waited for the rest of what he had to say. 'Always admired you and the doctor. Wonderful couple, an example to us all. Married life isn't what it was though, is it? All this living together and divorce. Where do you stand on this divorce question?'

'For myself, marriage is for life. But for others I can see there are times when if it is a living hell, then ...' Peter shrugged his shoulders.

'For life. No matter what?'

'No matter what.'

'I admire you for that. This Hugo Maude, lady's man, is he?'

'Oh yes. They all love him.'

'I expect Caroline admires him?'

'She does. He's taught her a lot.'

Mr Fitch's eyebrows shot up. 'Has he indeed. None of my business, but ...' He stood up to go. 'This is a warning from a friendly bystander. He needs watching. You do realise that?' He looked up at Peter who'd stood too. 'Not got your scruples you see, the man hasn't, I should imagine. Besides which, the village is bound to be talking.'

'True. Leave him to me. I know what I'm doing.'

'Shouldn't be telling the Rector what to do, you're far wiser than I about such matters. But I just had to say something, that's really why I've called. Take some advice from an older man with plenty of experience.' He looked into the distance as though weighing his words very carefully indeed. 'That man is endangering your happiness, believe me. Don't leave it too late to take action. By the way the prosecution's off. Well, it will be when I've had my say. Never known anything so ridiculous.'

'I'm glad, so very glad. I couldn't manage to persuade Jeremy to drop it. Thank you. How is he? Have you heard?'

Mr Fitch looked anywhere but at Peter.

'Very, very ill. I wouldn't say this to anyone but you, and I hope it won't go further than this room, but I'm feeling guilty about the chap. I was so blazing mad at the way he'd handled it all, but really the poor fellow was only carrying out my orders. Pay peanuts, you see, and you get monkeys. Must go. Jet lag. Remember what I said about you know who! Goodnight to you.'

It was almost one o'clock when Caroline came home. Peter, ready for bed, was in his study reading. He carefully inserted his bookmark in his place, put the book on his desk and went into the hall to greet her.

Caroline looked shattered. Her hair was tousled, her stage make-up smudged, her clothes thrown on rather than worn and her eyes avoided his. She dumped her bag of things on the hall floor, saying, 'Don't say a word. I'm going straight to bed. I know I'm late, I know I should have let you know. I'm exhausted and, what's more, I don't think I can face tomorrow. Goodnight.'

She stood with her hand on the newel post, one foot on the bottom step. 'I don't think I can get upstairs.'

Peter didn't speak. He stood beside her, put his arm around her waist and began to help her up one step at a time. He left her in the bathroom and went down again to make her a cup of tea. He was carrying the tray upstairs when he heard her crossing the landing to the bedroom.

She was standing by the bed in her slip. Peter placed the tray on her bedside table, and undressed her. When he'd slipped her nightgown over her head he lifted back the duvet and she slid in, resting her back on the pillow he'd propped against the bed-head.

While she sipped her tea he got into bed beside her.

'Thank you, Peter, for this.'

'Rehearsal go well?'

'Excellently well. Couldn't have been better. This cup of tea has saved my life. I cannot remember when I have felt so tired, not even when the children were babies.'

'What are husbands for but to pick up the pieces.'

Caroline looked at him. 'What do you mean by that?'

'Nothing. Nothing at all.'

'You do mean something.'

'I don't. It was a perfectly innocent remark. You would do the same for me if our roles were reversed, I know you would.'

Caroline finished the last drops of tea, put the cup back on the tray, turned off her light and slid under the duvet. 'The trouble is I don't deserve you.'

'You do. What's more, you're stuck with me, like it or not.'

'Sometimes I wish ...'

'Yes?'

'Just sometimes I wish you'd *do* something instead of always being so sure.'

'About what?'

'About ... me and you ... you and me ... about Hugo.'

'That would be ridiculous, your attraction to Hugo being transitory. Which it is, isn't it?'

There was a silence. When she didn't reply, after a few moments Peter repeated, 'It is, isn't it?'

'Am I or am I not a grown woman?'

'You're a grown woman.'

'Then why don't I *know*?'

'Because even grown-ups can't always find the answers.'

'*You* always can.'

'Not always, Caroline. This one has me foxed.'

'Just hang on in there, Peter. Please.'

'I am trying.'

'What a stupid conversation. Why don't we say what we mean?'

'Want me to come right out with it?'

In the dark Caroline nodded.

'I think if I met him on a dark night and there was no one about I'd throttle him. In my most desperate moods that's what I want to do. An absolutely childish thing to be saying, but it's true.'

'I see. He loves me.'

'Does he indeed.' The sarcastic note in his voice didn't go unnoticed.

'That's what he claims. He made me an offer tonight.'

'Did he?' Peter turned on his side so that he faced her, and waited for her answer.

'I don't think the wife is supposed to tell the husband. It's all so ridiculous. I'm two people at the moment. I love you, but I don't want you to touch me, not in that way. And I love Hugo, and want him.'

The silence lengthened and eventually Caroline put her light on and looked at him. 'But is it love, Peter, or lust or just me in need of being told I'm still desirable by someone who doesn't love me unreservedly, like you do?' Her fingers fidgeted with the edge of the duvet cover. She gave a great sigh and then added, 'He wants me to go away with him, you see.'

Despite his shock at her almost casual announcement, very slowly, choosing his words with extreme care, Peter said, 'I wonder if the play is the root of your trouble. Emotionally you're very charged up, you're bound to be, it's a very emotional part. So why not wait until the play is over? It's not sensible to make life decisions when you're on a high and so exhausted.'

Petulantly, Caroline burst out with, 'That's right. Stand back. Leave it all to me, as always. The decision is mine, et cetera, et cetera. Let's all play at being reasonable adults.' Disdainfully, she added, 'It's all so painful.'

Peter's temper erupted. 'Painful! For whom? What do you think it's like for me watching all this happening? I'm not nearly so laid back about it as I give the impression of being. You just *looking* at Hugo like you do causes me such agony. Such jealousy. I hate it. Loathe it. I'm distraught by how I feel about him touching you. But I am determined to give you space, which at the moment is what you appear to me to be in need of most. However, don't underestimate what's going on underneath. It is flesh and blood beneath the clerical collar and the cassock, you know: vibrant, passionate, loving flesh and blood. It is beyond my endurance when you treat me like some kind of holy sounding-board, trying out your problems and indecisions about him on me. A servant of God I may be, but I am also a *man*, and don't you ever, *ever*, forget that.'

His outburst silenced her.

They lay in the same bed. But miles apart.

16

Jimbo's first customer the following morning was a stranger. He bought a newspaper and some chocolate, served himself a coffee, sat on the customer's chair and settled himself for a chat.

It wasn't long before Jimbo realised who he might be. 'You're from the *Culworth Gazette*, aren't you?'

He nodded. 'Eddie Crimmins. Short of news this week, thought I'd call round, see if anything was happening. Like "Vicar's wife had it away on her toes with the verger", or something of that ilk.'

'Sorry, nothing happens around here. You'd best get back to Culworth and do the courts, or something.'

'Not what I've heard. What's all the posters about the play. Anything there?'

Jimbo shook his head.

'Devastating new talent discovered? Some little milkmaid turns overnight into acting sensation?'

'You're behind the times, there aren't such things as little milkmaids any more. Milking machines, you know, or hadn't you heard?'

The reporter ignored Jimbo's sarcasm.

While Jimbo served his early morning customers, the reporter sat quietly listening to their exchanges. Then to Jimbo's annoyance in came Hugo, up earlier by at least a couple of hours than was his usual habit.

No one but a fool would have failed to recognise his commanding presence. Jimbo saw the reporter go on red alert and then carefully mask his excitement.

Hugo, unaware he'd drawn Eddie's attention, went straight to the bread counter. He called out to Jimbo, 'Jimbo! Croissants. I have a passion for croissants, do you have any?'

His wonderful speaking voice filled every corner of the Store, and the reporter knew he'd met up with his quarry. What luck!

'It's all right, I've found 'em. Brilliant!' Hugo took them across to the till. 'You weren't up when I got back last night. Did Harriet tell you what a superb dress rehearsal we had?'

'She did. She was so fired up she didn't get to sleep till around two o'clock she tells me. By Sunday morning she'll be a wreck!'

'Thanks for these. Need 'em for my breakfast.'

The reporter got to his feet. 'Mr Hugo Maude, isn't it?'

'It surely is.' Hugo eyed the stranger up and down. 'Mr Crimmins, I presume? Let's do the interview over breakfast. Have you eaten?'

Eddie shook his head.

'Come then.' As he walked towards the door with the reporter in tow, Hugo called over his shoulder, 'Harriet won't mind, will she?'

But before Jimbo could answer the little bell on the door jangled and Hugo and the reporter had disappeared.

The bell jangled again almost immediately and Jimbo looked up to see who'd come in.

It was Willie Biggs. 'Only me!' Having picked up his paper on the way from the door to the till, Willie slapped the exact money down on the counter and said, 'He's not the first. There's two already at the Rectory. What beats me is how they find out? Who tells 'em?'

'In this case I think it was the man himself.'

'Hugo? I 'spect that's quite likely. Folk like them don't hang about when it comes to publicity. Really putting Turnham Malpas on the map. Georgie and Dicky will be doing well out of it, yer know what reporters are like for drinkin'.'

'True. True.'

'Couldn't really expect to get away with it, could we? Stands to reason.'

'Good for trade!' Jimbo laughed.

Willie glanced round the Store, bent over the counter and confidentially whispered. 'What does your dear lady think to this

193

play? My Sylvia's a bit scandalised by it. Really wonders if it's suitable for a village Church Hall.'

Jimbo studied what Willie had said and then declared, 'We have to remember we're in a bit of a backwater here. Compared to some plays in the West End it's quite harmless and Caroline has insisted on some of the bits being cut. No, I think we're on the right lines.'

Willie looked indignant. 'I don't want to be disloyal, my Sylvia being housekeeper there and me verger, but I do think this business with Hugo Maude has gone too far.'

'In what way?'

'The Rector's very upset about it. I know. I can tell. He puts a smiling face on it but when yer catch him unawares he looks grim. Lost his inner peace, yer know, what comes from 'is faith. Course, being 'im he won't lay the law down, but it seems to me it's about time he did.'

'What goes on between the two of them is their affair, Willie, not ours.'

'But when you think about their position in this village . . . The Rector has standards to keep up and she's not keeping 'em, in my opinion. They should be setting an example, not acting like it's for real.'

Jimbo finished writing out a new slogan for the meat counter on one of his white plastic boards, then he said, 'Is that how it looks?'

'Oh yes. Time and again, it feels like for real. It's not right. Not right at all. And there's not only me who thinks that either.'

'Sunday morning it'll all be over. Storm in a teacup.'

'Will it, though? Will it all be over?'

Unbeknown to them Willie had not shut the door properly, so the bell hadn't rung when someone had come in.

It was another stranger, and by the looks of her a reporter. 'Do you do ready-made sandwiches? I'm starving.' She looked innocently at the two of them.

'We do. Above the chill counter. On the left. Freshly delivered every morning. All new in.'

Willie jerked his thumb at the reporter behind her back, pulled a face and left. Jimbo offered the reporter a coffee from the customer's machine.

'Oh! That'll be lovely. Thanks. Early start this morning, too early for me.'

'What brings you here, then?' Jimbo inoffensively inquired.

The reporter struggled to open the hermetically sealed sandwich and, before sinking her teeth gratefully into it, she asked, 'This play, you're doing. Heard it's good and a bit, you know . . . spicy?' She put her head to one side and smiled, inviting his confidence.

'No, no, all very low key. First time we've done anything of the kind so it's bound to be very ordinary.'

'Now come on.' She tried the coffee and approved. 'My word this coffee's good. And the sandwich too. Very good, in fact. Now come on, I've heard you've got Hugo Maude in it, so that's not what the world would call low key, now is it?'

Jimbo tried to be nonchalant about the whole matter to put her off the scent, not knowing how much she'd heard before he and Willie had realised she was there. 'That's correct.'

'Who else? Anyone I know?'

'You're not from the *Gazette*, so where are you from?'

'The *Fulton Examiner*.'

'No! Was it you who ran the big campaign against extending the bypass?'

'Don't try to change the subject! Who else is in it?'

Defeated in his attempt to divert her attention he replied, 'My wife, for a start. A local accountant and his wife, one of the gardeners from the Big House, a schoolgirl. That's about it.'

'How about that glamorous Rector of yours, is he in it? Bet he is, gorgeous man.'

'No, he isn't. Must press on, stay as long as you like.'

'Haven't paid you yet.'

'On the house.'

'It won't work, you know, giving freebies in the hope that I won't ferret about too much.' She wagged her finger at him and gave him a winning smile. 'My instincts tell me . . .'

'It's a blinking good play and you should stay to see it tonight.'

'Oh, I shall be back tonight. I'm reviewing it for the paper. Just thought I'd get some background detail this morning. What a feather in your cap. Hugo Maude, no less. How did it come about?'

'He's a friend . . .' He was going to say 'of ours' but changed his mind. 'He's a friend of mine from university. Came to stay and we persuaded him to produce the play. Well, he's acting in it, too.'

While he'd been speaking she'd been making notes. She looked up from her notepad and asked, 'And you are . . .?'

'James Charter-Plackett.'

'You don't seem quite the sort of person to be running a village shop.'

Jimbo winced. 'That's as may be but I've got to make headway this morning. Will that be all?'

'I'll leave a couple of pounds on the counter for the food. And thanks. I'll just finish eating this.' She waved her half eaten sandwich at him and sat down on the chair. Jimbo disappeared into the back just as Linda arrived to take charge of the post office.

'Oh! Good morning! Haven't seen you around here before, just moved in?'

The reporter picked up on the gossipy tone in Linda's voice and decided to make use of her. 'No, I'm a reporter.'

'No! Well, I never. You can interview me if you like.'

'I like. First of all we'll have your name, then I can quote you.'

'Oh never! Me with my name in the paper! How exciting! First time ever, except once when I was nine and won the egg and spoon at the Brownie sports. What do you want to know?' Excited to such an extent she was eager to throw caution to the wind, Linda propped herself against the counter and awaited her first ever interview.

The reporter got out her notebook and pen. 'First, who's in this play?'

Disappointed that the question she had been asked was apparently nothing to do with her personally, Linda straightened up and made to leave. 'I'm not in it and I've never been to a rehearsal, so I can't help.'

'Oh! I think you can. You're here at the hub of the village, and you seem to me to be a *very* sympathetic person. I expect you know, out of the kindness of your heart, of course, most of what goes on.' She smiled up at Linda and got the capitulation she'd worked for.

Linda resettled herself against the counter. 'Well, of course the highlight is having Hugo Maude here. He's been very ill, and he's come to stay with the Charter-Placketts to recuperate. Him being a friend from university of Mrs Charter-Plackett and ...' The tale wound on and before she knew it Linda had told the reporter about how scandalised the village was over the way Hugo Maude and Dr Harris had behaved.

'Dr Harris? Isn't that the Rector's wife?'

Linda nodded. 'Exactly! They've been seen kissing, and not just in the play. I mean, it's not quite the thing, is it? Kissing. What an example to set. Also, they were spotted in the wood together, you know, and ...'

'Linda!' It was Jimbo coming through from the back carrying a box of butter. 'Linda! It's past nine and you haven't opened up the post office yet.'

'But I was just being interviewed.' She made no move towards the post office and deliberately continued her conversation '... they do say that ...'

Jimbo banged down the box he was holding and said, 'Linda! I do not want to have words. Please do as I ask. Now!' To the reporter he said, 'Sorry about this but I am a stickler for opening on time. Can I help at all?'

The reporter closed her notebook, smiled sweetly, and left.

As he stacked the butter on the chill counter shelves, Jimbo said, 'Never have I been so angry with you, Linda. Telling a reporter all that. I bet three quarters of it wasn't true anyway.'

'It's no good speaking to me like that, Mr Charter-Plackett, and I was speaking the truth.'

'You were not. You were insinuating all kinds of things.'

'Were they or were they not seen in the wood together? Have they or have they not been seen kissing and holding hands, or him with his arm round her waist and her not objecting?'

Jimbo stopped stacking the butter and looked straight at her through the post office grille. 'I can't deny it.'

'Well, then.'

'But telling a reporter ...'

'Well, she kind of wheedled it out of me.'

'It makes me wonder what tales you tell that you hear in here. It should all be absolutely sacrosanct. Taboo.'

'Are you telling me, then, that you never tell anyone what you hear in here?'

Jimbo hesitated.

Triumphantly Linda replied, 'No, you see, you're as bad as me.'

'No, I am not.'

'You are. It's the kettle calling the pan black, that's what.'

'One more word out of you . . .'

'Yes?' Linda came out from behind the grille and, hands on hips, faced him squarely. 'Well, I'm waiting.'

'What you've said this morning is tantamount to putting an advertisement in the paper.'

'It is not. What's more you've no right to speak to me like this.'

Despairing Jimbo said, 'Haven't I? Any more and you'll be sacked.'

'Go on then, do it and then we'll see what the industrial tribunal will say. My Alan knows all about it.'

'I bet he does. Then do your damnedest.'

'Is that it, then?'

'Yes.'

'Right, I won't even trouble to take my coat off. That's it. Eight years of service to you and yours. Well, I can manage without you. And it won't be any good coming round and apologising and begging me to come back like you did before, because I shan't. So there!'

'Right! I'll send your P45 and the money I owe at the end of the month.'

'Right!' Linda flounced out, slamming the door with vigour.

Jimbo immediately regretted losing his temper. Linda might be annoying – she was a stickler for her lunch and coffee breaks – but she did know her job. Damn and blast. Now what? There was one thing absolutely certain, he wasn't going to beg her to come back, ever again. Once was enough. He'd manage somehow. Damn and blast Hugo Maude. The trouble he'd caused. Now this. He finished stacking the butter, threw the empty carton in the rubbish bin and shut himself in the post office with a heavy heart.

The reporter went straight across to the Rectory, knocked and waited. She quite fancied cajoling some more information out of the gorgeous Rector. She flicked a comb through her hair while she waited. She knocked again and to her disappointment it was neither the Rector nor the Rector's wife who came to the door.

'Yes?' Sylvia folded her arms across her chest and tried to look intimidating.

'I'm from the *Fulton Examiner.*'

'Yes?'

'It's about the play. I wondered if the Rector's wife would be able to give me an interview. I'm reviewing it tonight for the paper and I thought a little background information would be a good idea.'

'Not in.'

'Oh! That's a pity. I was hoping to see her. The Rector, then. Is he in?'

'No.'

Smiling her most gentle smile, her little-girl-in-need-of-help-and-sympathy smile, she asked, 'Are you in the play? You look as though you might be, you look the adventurous type.

'I am not.'

'I'll call back later, when they've both returned.'

'Don't bother. They've nothing to say.'

'Nothing to say? I can hardly believe that, not with the great Hugo Maude in it. Surely he of all people must have caused something exciting to happen! Such a handsome man, so charismatic. Every female heart aflutter, eh?'

'We're very level headed here, takes a lot to surprise us.'

With a twinkle in her eye the reply came back, 'I've heard one or two things.'

Despite the reporter's persuasive interviewing techniques Sylvia retained her resolve to let nothing slip. 'Well, I haven't and I work here.'

'Oh, I see. You'll know a thing or two about your delightful Rector's wife, then? Bet you've a few stories to tell. Leading lady, I understand. Who could play opposite Hugo Maude without being charmed, and he is a real charmer, don't you think?'

'That he may be, but it's nothing to do with the Rector's wife, believe me.'

'That's not what I've heard in the Store. Apparently, you're all scandalised about what's been going on.'

'I'm shutting the door. Right now.'

'Oh please . . .'

But the door shut with a crash. Knowing when to accept defeat, the reporter went off to the Royal Oak and Sylvia returned to the sitting room where Caroline was flicking through her script.

'Who was it at the door?'

'It's not my place to say it, but I'm saying it.'

'I beg your pardon?'

Sylvia, with her arm fully extended, pointed in the direction of the door. 'That *person* was a reporter. That person was asking me about you. She's found out, goodness knows from whom, what's been going on. I may lose my job over this but I won't stand by and watch the Rector being crucified any longer. You and the Rector and your children mean more to me than anything I can think of. At this moment you are tearing them apart.' Sylvia stamped her foot. 'Just what are you thinking of with this business with Hugo Maude? Tell me that.' She stood arms akimbo and waited for Caroline to reply.

Caroline stood up, her face taut, her eyes blazing. '*Nothing* is going on between Hugo and I. Nothing at all . . .'

'I don't know how you can stand there and *lie* like that. We all know. Every man jack of us in this village knows. You can't fool us, even if you're fooling yourself; which you are and make no mistake about that. I don't know how the Rector faces everybody each day, I really don't.'

'I'm afraid you're overstepping the mark now, Sylvia.'

'It's not me doing the overstepping, believe me, it's you and it's got to stop. Just think what you've got to lose. And the children. God help us, it would kill them if you left.'

'Who said anything about leaving? Not me! It's none of your business, none at all . . .'

'It is though! I've loved those children from the first moment I clapped eyes on 'em. They're like my own flesh and blood . . .'

'But they're not, and the whole business is entirely my concern and not yours. That is enough.'

'Right.' Sylvia began removing her apron. 'This is breaking my heart this is, but you have my notice as of now. This minute. I will not be a party to this kind of behaviour. Perhaps if you have to manage without me you might, just might come to your senses, because at the moment you've no sense left. Not one jot or tittle left. You must be out of your mind. I can't bear standing by and seeing the Rector ...'

'Always the Rector, what about me? Don't I have a life besides being his wife?'

'When you really get down to it, unfortunately you haven't. But then you knew that when you fell in love and married him, so it's no good complaining now. You weren't a young untried girl, you knew exactly what you had to face. He's the loveliest man any woman could hope to have, and there's dozens out there who'd jump into your shoes in a trice, but the pity of it is there's absolutely no one else for him, but you. It's the same for the children, no one else for them but you, you're their strength and stay. You're in danger of forgetting that and casting them aside, and all for what? All for *what*, ask yourself that! All for *what*?' Her lovely grey eyes full of tears, Sylvia turned away and left the room.

Distraught, Sylvia went about the kitchen picking up the bits and pieces which were hers; the comb she always left here, the apron she kept for the afternoons, the hand cream she kept by the kitchen sink, the old mac in case it rained. All treasures which she had thought were permanent belongings in the Rectory. Leaving the house quietly, she wandered off to the church in search of Willie to ask for the comfort only he could give at this appalling moment. She sat down on the seat he kept just outside the boiler house door where it caught the sun, and gazed out across the churchyard waiting for him to appear. The morning sun was creeping round casting lovely shadows over the grass. Such a peaceful, restful place and yet her mind was in turmoil, her heart was thumping and her legs felt like jelly. In the depths of despair Sylvia warmed her face with the rays of the sun; a face down which tears were falling.

I should never have said all that. But it's true. She's being led away by that ... mountebank. That womaniser. Now I've lost my job. Hang the money, I loved it. Willie'll be retiring soon and we definitely need it, but ... There'd be other places, other people who needed domestic help. The Rector would give her a reference ... but maybe he wouldn't, not after what she'd said. Caroline always came first with him. Like the reporter had said, he was a gorgeous man.

'Hello, Sylvia! I'm looking for Willie.' It was Peter, the sun catching his red blond hair making it resemble a halo. Sylvia tried to stem her tears.

Peter sat down beside her and quietly asked, 'Can I help?'

There was a silence and Peter waited, then Sylvia admitted she'd given notice.

'I see. Your immediate notice?'

Sylvia nodded.

Intuitively he answered, 'She's having a very difficult time.'

'I know, but so are you.' She patted the hand resting on his knee.

Peter studied Sylvia's face for a moment. 'Indeed.'

'You're being far too kind, far too considerate to all concerned.'

Peter sighed. 'What would you have me do?'

'Go for it.'

'For what?'

'Him.'

'You think so?'

Sylvia nodded. 'Oh, yes, I do. He's to blame. Catching her when she's so vulnerable. Her life up to having that cancer had been all glorious. You know, loving parents, happy family life, good at school, head girl, prizes and such at medical school, high praise in every direction. Then she marries you, then you give her the children and she dotes on them, she truly does, and then she got knocked sideways with the cancer thing. It came as a terrible blow. Really beaten into the ground she's been, and somehow this business is all part and parcel of getting over that.'

'Yes, I know.'

'I love your children, and I don't want to live to see them have their hearts broken. But ... well, that's what's going to happen if something isn't done and quick. But don't ask me what, 'cos I don't know. The pendulum's swung too far in his favour, and it's to be stopped. You see I can't believe he means all he says to her. At bottom he's a very lightweight person, a child, a kind of Peter Pan. She must be the only person in the village who doesn't know who else he's chasing – well, not chasing, he's already caught her from what I hear. Get my meaning?' Her voice caught in her throat and made her pause. 'I've said much too much and I'm very sorry. She'll never forgive me.' Sylvia wiped away a tear. 'Never!'

'We'll see. Like you, I do now believe something has to be done.'

'Oh yes. And quick, before it's too late.'

Peter stood up. 'I agree. But if she was to make a mess of this play that would be even more damaging. She's got to be successful in it, you see. If I step in right now, today, it could do untold damage. But, yes, you're right, I musn't stand aside once the play is over. Give this to Willie for me will you, please?' He dug into the pocket of his cassock and handed her Willie's wage packet, then walked away.

He'd left his car keys in the vestry so he entered the church by the main door, intending to retrieve them. Peter shut the door behind him and began to walk down the aisle, but paused by the tomb Willie claimed was haunted. Sleeping in his favourite place on the top was Jimmy's dog Sykes. Peter tickled him behind his ear, a practice Sykes adored. His short, stubby tail gently wagged his appreciation. Giving him a final pat Peter recommenced his walk down the aisle, but then stopped in his tracks.

Kneeling on the altar steps was Caroline, her head in her hands. He stood watching her, trying to decide whether or not to go and kneel beside her. Before he had decided what to do for the best she shuffled herself around and sat on the steps, her forearms resting on her knees, her head bowed, totally unaware of his presence. All the love he felt for her coursed through him right to his very feet and he longed to give her the comfort of his arms, to hold her, hug her, heal her. Yet he held back sensing that perhaps it was not *his* arms which could do any of those things at this moment. Space, like he'd said last night – was it only last night that he'd lost his temper? – space was what she needed and that was what he would give her now. So despite his surge of desire to hold her to him he turned and quietly left.

The keys could wait.

After an uneventful lunch prepared by Caroline, during which they'd exchanged small talk and nothing more, Peter left for the hospital to visit Jeremy in intensive care.

Slumped in a chair beside his bed was Venetia. She leapt to her feet when she saw who their visitor was.

Oh, Peter!' She made a hasty and useless attempt to tidy her hair, straighten her sweater, and generally pull herself together. He'd never seen her devoid of make-up, and seeing her now he realised just how devastated she must be about Jeremy's brush with death.

'I'm sorry I look such a mess, I've been here all night. It's kind of you to come.'

'Not at all. Any improvement yet?'

Venetia shook her head. 'Still touch and go. He's not conscious. Damn him!'

'It wasn't his fault!'

Venetia slumped back down in her chair and rubbed her hand across her face. 'I know.' Then she studied Jeremy laid there fastened up to all the paraphernalia of the seriously ill. 'Damn him! I've ignored his existence all the time we've been here. Laughed at him, scorned him, belittled him, taunted him ... shamed him ...'

'Shamed him?'

Venetia looked up at Peter and he saw the conflict going on behind the weary eyes. 'Yes, shamed him. I thought he didn't care about me and had never noticed what I was up to, but all the time he had. All the time he knew about me ... you know ...'

'No, I don't know.'

Venetia looked surprised. 'You mean that, don't you?'

Peter nodded. Venetia reached forward and took hold of Jeremy's hand, looking at him and not at Peter, she told him, 'I've been unfaithful to him time and again. *Time and again.* This time is the last time, the very last time ...' She stopped abruptly, looked at Peter for a moment and then continued. 'But if ... *when* he comes out of this, I'm going to propose. I never knew until yesterday, when I thought he'd died and it was all too late, how much he meant to me. He's been so loyal, despite everything I've ever done to him, a perfect gentleman all the time.'

'I see.'

'Together we're going to beat this weight business. It's comfort eating, you see, because he thought I didn't love him when he loved me so much. He was right. Well, he wasn't right, I *did* love him but I didn't realise, you see. So his weight is my fault, and my fault alone.' She patted the still hand and then looked at Peter. 'Cruel is the only word to describe me. I've never felt so full of sin in all my life. Do you think God will ever forgive me?'

'God always forgives those who truly regret what they have done.'

He saw hope in Venetia's eyes. 'Then He's even greater than I thought if He can forgive me for what I've done to Jeremy.'

'He is: greater than any of us can comprehend.'

Venetia pleaded with him. 'Will you remember us in your prayers?'

'Of course, we all will.'

'I've been praying all night.'

'Keep at it, he is still here.'

Still gripping Jeremy's hand Venetia said, 'I've had a lot of time to think. This last two years I've lived two lives. One at church and helping Kate with the youth club, and the other as the old Venetia, like I've always been. From now on there's going to be only one Venetia. The nicest and best Venetia, living in the world you live in.'

Peter smiled. 'The world I live in?'

'Yes. I'm going to belong to that respectable, kind, loving world where you and Caroline live. A relationship that's all crystal clear and straightforward with no intrigue and no confrontation. No pretence. No deceit. My world is going to be one where everything is in the open, no secrets, only truth.'

Peter, embarrassed by his marriage being held in such high esteem at this particular moment, simply touched her shoulder in sympathy murmuring, 'I'm glad, so glad.'

Venetia, on the brink of tears, acknowleged his sympathy. 'I'm jealous of the way you and Caroline love each other, do you know that? I'm going to try very hard to love like that. Strong and deep and loyal.' She smiled sadly at him, her lips trembling.

To avoid betraying himself he made to leave.

'Say a prayer for him and me before you go. Please.'

Peter took hold of Jeremy's other hand, said a prayer and made the sign of the cross on Jeremy's forehead and then on Venetia's. 'God bless you both.' Before he let go of Jeremy's hand he was almost sure he felt a very slight squeeze of his fingers.

17

Although the play did not open until half past seven everyone involved was at the hall by six o'clock. First night nerves were very apparent, from the stage hands scurrying about checking and rechecking to Mrs Peel worrying about her music, from the actors themselves to Sheila Bissett fluttering around checking her flowers.

'What do you think, Dr Harris, are they all right?'

'They're wonderful, Sheila, I told you so last night. Absolutely right. Even the vase.'

'Hugo likes them, too, in fact he raved over them, so I suppose they must be. The dear man. He's so thoughtful, isn't he?' She tidied the angle of one of her gladioli then stood back and admired her arrangement. 'So lovely, we shall miss him when he goes. You will too, I expect. Ron and I have been thinking of buying tickets for Stratford when he's on. We've never been, ever. Do you think it would be a good idea?'

Caroline agreed it would, and would Sheila mind if she left her to it as her first night nerves were at breaking point.

Sheila turned to look at her. 'Of course, off you pop, I've done here now anyway.' She glanced round to see if anyone was within hearing distance and then whispered confidentially, 'I don't blame you at all for falling for him, you know. We all have. I'm quite envious of you.' She gave Caroline a meaningful wink; a wink which bordered on lewd.

It served to categorise Caroline's passion for Hugo at the lowest level imaginable. What had been fine and beautiful and fullfilling was reduced in a moment so tawdry and commonplace by Sheila's gesture. She spun on her heel and went back to the minute dressing room she shared with Liz, Harriet and Michelle. All there was for her to sit on was a bathroom stool someone had brought from home. Caroline sat on it with her hands clenched, without speaking, letting the excited conversation of the other three swirl around her.

Harriet, knees bent so that she could see into the mirror she'd propped up on the narrow windowsill, broke off from combing her hair to admire Michelle's dress. 'Oh, that does look lovely! I'll say this for her, your grandmother knows her stuff.'

Michelle pirouetted in front of them in the dress she would be wearing in the first act. 'Just wish I felt as lovely as it looks! I don't know what made me agree to do this. It's not my scene at all. I've only kept going because Mum's so thrilled at me having the chance.'

Harriet wagged her finger, 'Whose leg do you think you're pulling! Rhett's the draw and no wonder! I can't believe he's the same boy, young man I should say.'

Michelle blushed. 'He is doing brilliantly, isn't he?'

'And so are you, isn't she, Caroline?'

Caroline looked up. 'Sorry, I wasn't listening.'

'And no wonder. You're going to do really well too, you know. Don't worry.' Harriet gently hugged Caroline. 'Hugo will see you through. He's an old hand at this kind of thing.'

There came a loud rap on the door and, as it opened slightly, they heard Hugo saying, 'Everyone respectable, can I come in?'

He cut such a dashing figure in his slacks, high at the waist in the nineteen twenties' fashion, an open-necked shirt with a dark cravat at his neck and his hair sleeked down with gel, they quite forgot they'd seen him the previous night at the rehearsal dressed just like this. Somehow there was an extra vitality about him, an added buzz which made him larger than life. The small room seemed scarcely large enough to contain him.

'All my favourite ladies prospering, are they?' But his question was really aimed at Caroline and the other three knew it.

She fell under his spell immediately and began to glow. 'We are.'

'Excellent. Fifteen minutes to blast off. Good luck!' He held Caroline's eyes for a moment and smiled especially for her.

'Good luck!' The four of them called as he closed the door.

Caroline acted stupendously well that night. Her performance was way beyond anything she had ever expected of herself. Congratulations flooded in, from villagers, from the press, from friends. When she finally arrived home at the Rectory she was on a high.

'Peter! Oh, Peter! It was brilliant! Marvellous! Wonderful! I can't find words to describe how well it's gone. Hugo is in his seventh heaven.'

Peter held his arms out wide and she went into them and he hugged her. 'I'm so glad! I can't wait to see it tomorrow night. I am prepared for being very impressed!'

She held her head away from his chest and looked up into his face. 'Oh! Make no mistake, you'll be impressed all right. We all of us acted our socks off! We really did. Michelle, Rhett, Liz, Neville, Harriet! The hall was full, every seat taken and the press were there, too,' she thumped his chest in her excitement. 'National and local! Hugo got them there in droves! What it is to be well known!' She flung herself down on the sofa and kicked off her shoes. 'I'm desperately thirsty.'

'Tell me what you fancy and it shall be yours.'

'Water. Cold, cold water. A jug full!'

After she'd drunk two glasses she said, 'We had one *faux pas,* that was all, but Hugo got us through it. There isn't any wonder that he's at the top of his profession! I can't wait to see him in *Hamlet.* He'll make a perfectly splendid one, I know. It's only because of him that we've done so well. Thank God for Hugo!'

'Indeed.' Peter sat down in the other chair and fidgeted with his wedding ring. 'I'm truly glad it went well, Mr Fitch will be glowing tomorrow night. He's quite childish sometimes about how his money can achieve things. He said to me last night how impressed he was with Rhett Wright. He made it sound as though it was he, Craddock Fitch himself, who'd got Rhett to act so well.'

Caroline sat up. 'Where did you see Craddock Fitch? I thought he'd only got home yesterday?'

'He did. He popped in to see me.'

'What did he want?'

'This and that.' Peter stood up. 'Finished? I'll clear away.'

'Well?'

He looked down at her and thought about Venetia believing that everything between him and Caroline was clear and open. 'Came to tell me he's dropping the prosecution.'

'That's a relief, he must be mellowing in his old age!'

But Peter had gone towards the kitchen. She followed him in. Her two cats were settled for the night in their basket so she kissed them on the tops of their heads, tickled their stomachs as they rolled over to wallow in her attention and then looked at Peter's back as he rinsed out her glass and got out a clean tea towel.

'Peter!'

'Yes?'

There was a pause. 'Oh, nothing. I'm going to bed.'

'Won't be long.'

'You deserve first prize for your ...' He turned to face her. '... loving patience.'

He turned back to the sink, put the well dried glass in the cupboard above the draining board and said, 'I'll follow you up in a while. Tell me more about the play tomorrow, you look completely whacked right now.'

Disappointed he hadn't taken up her remark she said, 'I'll say goodnight, then.'

'Goodnight. I'm so proud of you. God bless.'

'And you.'

Caroline fell asleep almost immediately and never realised that it was more than an hour before Peter, having spent an anguished time thinking over his situation, climbed the stairs to bed. He'd sat at his desk, head in hands, mulling over how he would handle the situation the following night. He'd smiled wryly to himself when he thought about the notion he'd had that morning of dramatically strangling Hugo in the wings at the end of the play as the final applause faded away. No, that wouldn't do! The publicity! And he didn't fancy a stretch in prison.

Appeal to Hugo's better nature? He didn't have one.

Threaten him? Not a suitable action for a pacifist to take.

Cajole him? Hugo would simply laugh.

Thump him good and hard? Even less of a good idea.

But somehow his exit from Turnham Malpas had to be brought off with the minimum of harm to Caroline.

Peter picked up the photograph he kept on his desk. It was the one he'd taken of her and the children on their first seaside holiday. She had a twin nestling in the crook of each arm and was nuzzling her cheek against Alex's head. He remembered how the people in the hotel had commented on how like him Alex was, and how Beth had a look of Caroline, hadn't she? He owed her so much. Her forgiveness alone was something he would never be able to repay, not if he lived a thousand years. Who was he to feel so desperately injured at this moment?

Peter replaced the photograph and knelt to pray for guidance.

On the Saturday night the play received a rapturous reception at the end of the first act. Mr Fitch's guests were incredibly impressed and told him so when they gathered for coffee during the interval.

'God! Fitch! You've boasted about this village of yours often enough, but bless me it's come right up to scratch and no mistake! It's like as if it's for real. Amazing!'

'Fitch! Where in heaven's name have you found such talent? Can't quite believe it in a village this size.'

'How come you cornered Hugo Maude? Even I've heard of him, so he must be good. Damn me! Introduce me, would you? My Angela will be green as hell ... Beg yer pardon, forgot I was in a Church Hall.'

'Congratulations, Fitch! Most impressed with the leading lady. Who is she?' The speaker bent his head to hear, balancing his coffee precariously within striking distance of Mr Fitch's country suit. Mr Fitch whispered in his ear. The inquirer was so astonished he shouted his reply. 'The Rector's wife! My God! The Rector's wife? Since when have Rectors had wives like that? Bet he needs to keep her on a tight rein.'

Peter, at Mr Fitch's request, had just come to join the group and overheard the last remark. He ignored the comment and tolerated being introduced to everyone with as good a grace as he could muster. Inside he seethed with despair. Accepting their congratulations on his wife's wonderful performance as cheerfully as he could, he longed for the interval bell to go so that he could slide back into anonimity in the darkness of the Church Hall and lick his wounds. He couldn't take much more.

When it came to the scene when Caroline told her lover that it was all over, Peter's flesh crawled.

'*I cannot go on. I have the children to think of. I suspect that Julian is ashamed of me, and I am too if I really think about it. Daisy hates it, too. She loves her father, you see, and knows how hurt he is. As a mother I have my duty to do. They didn't ask to be born, and they are flesh of my flesh and as such deserve the best of me. I have a husband who deserves none of this anguish . . .'*

'*But what about love? You haven't mentioned love. Surely it deserves a place in our lives. You've said yourself you don't love him any more.'*

Marian turned angrily on him. '*I've never said I don't love him. You're putting words in my mouth. What I am saying is I will not divorce my children's father, I will not. For their sakes, I will not!'*

Leonard went to sit beside her on the sofa and, taking her hand in his, he asked, '*Taking this course of action will slowly but surely destroy you. No one should have to make this kind of sacrifice. I'm offering you love, doesn't that count for something?'*

Marian kissed his lips greedily. '*Oh yes, of course it does, but it's not enough.'*

'*Not enough? What more can one ask? I shall love you to my dying day.'* He brushed her hair from her face and held her head between his hands, looking closely at her. '*If he loved you like I do he'd let you go, if that was where your happiness lay. It's all so easy, just come.'*

'*And live a life in corners, hardly daring to acknowledge each other. Perhaps in thirty, forty, fifty years things might be different but now I'd be classed as a wicked woman, make no mistake about that. I can't live that kind of life and he wouldn't divorce me anyway.'*

'*Make him.'*

Marian shook her head. '*It's against his principles.'*

Leonard mocked her. '*Divorce might be against his principles but torturing his wife isn't, then?'*

'*You're being ridiculous. In any case living your kind of life from one house party to the next wouldn't be my kind of life. I need stability, a structure, security. It sounds pathetic, I know, but it's true.'* She took his hand from her face, kissed the palm and whispered, '*Don't, please, don't make it hard for me to say goodbye. I love you like life itself. Since I met you . . . Before you, he and I trudged on, going through the motions but you . . .'* she traced his features with a trembling finger *'. . . you've made each moment of every day throb with life. The sun is brighter, the sky more blue, the world more entrancing. That's been your gift to me . . .'*

'But, darling . . .'

Marian placed a finger on Leonard's lips. *'So I shall have that gift for the rest of my life. I shall keep it locked away and take it out from time to time, unwrap it and enjoy it again and again. Kiss me, and then I'll leave. I shan't look back or I might weaken and take you in my arms and fly away with you like you wish.'* With great longing in her voice she added, *'You will be in my heart for ever and a day, my dearest.'*

Peter listened to the dialogue going back and forth between the two of them and writhed inside. There was still the scene to get through when she heard from the maid that there'd been a shooting accident at the Big House and did madam know it was Mr Leonard who'd died. He wished Hugo Maude in hell and longed for the play to finish.

When the curtains did finally close on the last line an audible sigh went around the hall, and then the applause began. Most of the audience stood to clap and they had curtain call after curtain call, until finally Hugo stepped forward to say his thanks.

With arms outstretched he opened his speech with, 'What can I say? Without your support where would we have been? You dear, darling people. Weren't the cast absolutely splendid?' He flicked his hands in the air, beckoning applause. When it had died down he continued. 'I came to Turnham Malpas a broken man, wounded by the hurly-burly of life. I leave to go to Stratford, refreshed, renewed, revitalised, re . . .'

'. . . charged?' Someone from the audience called out.

Hugo laughed, 'That's right. Recharged. I love you all . . .'

A voice from the back whispered hoarsely, 'Some more than others', and was instantly hushed by his neighbours. Hugo ignored the comment and followed on with, 'There are so many people to thank for this production, not least Mr Fitch who has sportingly lent us his piano and provided the wherewithal for the production. I give you Mr Fitch!'

Mr Fitch stood up and from his place in the front row turned to acknowledge the thanks.

Hugo quickly drew everyone's attention back to himself by signalling to one of the front of house helpers to step forward. They carried a bouquet. By West End standards it was huge, by Turnham Malpas standards it was colossal.

'For my leading lady!' Hugo leant down to take the bouquet into his arms and he dramatically kissed Caroline, handing the bouquet over to her. Massively stimulated by the success of her performance she thanked him with a big kiss. The audience cheered. This bouquet was followed by others from husbands, from families, from Mr Fitch, from well wishers. And then Neville stepped forward.

'I should just like to say how much everyone in the cast, and all the backstage helpers to whom we owe an enormous debt of gratitude, have learned under Hugo's tutelage. Me in particular. I know I'm considered a cold fish and that it's time I let my hair down and relaxed more, well now I well and truly have in this play and I quite like the experience!' Muted cheers came from the body of the hall. 'All our lives have been enriched by his work here and we're grateful for the time he has carved out of his busy life to work with us. He's a hard task master, believe me. He's kicked us, cajoled us, ordered us, badgered us, shouted at us, persuaded us, until finally we got it right. Hugo Maude, a present from us all.' He stepped to the wings and emerged with five bottles of champagne in his arms. 'With all our love and best wishes for the future.'

Hugo's eyes filled with tears as he accepted the champagne. 'What can I say, but thank you so very, very much.'

The speeches went on until finally Hugo called a halt. 'Goodnight! Goodnight! The cast still have a party to go to! Goodnight, everyone, and thank you once again from the very bottom of my heart for all your love and kindnesses. Goodnight!' He waved vigorously to everyone as they began to leave and then signalled for the curtains to close.

Turning, he enfolded Caroline in his arms and said, 'My darling!' He looked into her eyes and saw behind the excitement and the sparkle an unexpected wariness which he decided to ignore.

'Caroline! You were wonderful! Wonderful! Completely stupendous!' Bending close to her ear he whispered, 'Have you decided? Are you coming with me? Say you are!'

'Move over, Hugo, it's the husband's turn now.'

It was the sharp tone of Peter's voice which startled Hugo. Peter had only ever been polite and generous in his dealings with him, despite the delicacy of their relationship, so he released Caroline and looked up at Peter wondering what was afoot. 'Mr Fitch is anxious to introduce you to his guests, so you'd better go play your I-am-humble bit and accept their admiration.'

Hugo looked at Caroline but could read nothing from her face, he half thought of suggesting she went with him to see Mr Fitch, but changed his mind when he couldn't interpret her feelings. So he meekly did as Peter suggested. After all if he was to take *Dark Rapture* to the West End then he would need backers and all Mr Fitch's guests were influential people. It was only politic to go. Suddenly a sweet *au revoir* to Caroline didn't seem like a good idea and he left without a word.

'Brilliant! Quite brilliant. You were right. I was impressed.'

Eyes bright with success Caroline looked up at him. 'I told you you would be. And it wasn't just me. Michelle and Rhett and Harriet and Liz and Neville were brilliant too. Life will never be the same, will it? So I'm determined to enjoy every last minute of this day. You can stay for the party? Willie doesn't mind, does he?'

'He's sleeping in the spare room, so we can stay as long as we want.'

'Oh! I didn't know. Sylvia's not . . .'

'No.'

'Peter . . .'

He bent down and tentatively kissed the top of her head. 'Yes?'

'Nothing. This make-up feels uncomfortable. I'm going to remove it.'

'I'll help clear the chairs, then. Make space for us all.'

Apparently from nowhere, a trestle table was erected, and food and drink appeared as though by magic. Hugo, secretly extremely excited by the great impression he'd made on Mr Fitch's guests, having laid the seeds to take *Dark Rapture* to the West End, donated his gift of champagne to the party and opened a bottle. They all gathered round with their paper cups and waited for him to pop the cork. He gave the bottle a vigorous shake and the cork fired out, narrowly missing Caroline's face. She leapt aside, stumbled over Neville's feet and only saved herself from falling by grabbing Sylvia's arm.

'Sorry!'

'That's all right.'

'Sylvia!'

'Yes?'

'I'm really sorry, you know, about . . .'

Sylvia's eyes filled with unexpected tears. Caroline kept hold of her arm and said quietly, 'I'm so sorry. One day perhaps you might . . .'

'I'll see. I can't bear . . . It's the children, you know, I miss them.'

'I understand.'

'And you.'

'Yes?'

'And the Rector.'

Still holding her arm, Caroline kissed her cheek. 'We'll have a talk sometime. Yes?'

Sylvia nodded. 'Well, all right then.'

Hell's bells! Would nothing ever be right again? She'd accepted the maternity leave stand-in job, she desperately wanted to do it and now she might just have no one to see to the children. But would she be here anyway? Hugo caught her eye and smiled that special smile he kept for her. Her heart felt as though it was spinning in her chest, her blood pumped faster and faster and all she could see through the haze was Hugo's beautiful features and the smile which was only for her. For a moment they were the only ones in the hall. His glorious dark hair, his widow's peak, the strong beautifully moulded forehead and those eyes! Were there ever such expressive eyes as his? Then their moment was broken by someone standing in front of Hugo. It was Peter, blocking Hugo completely from view. Peter. Peter's children. Her children. Her darling Alex and Beth. They'd survive her going. Children were remarkably resilient and with her gone surely Sylvia would come back to give a hand.

The noise of the party grew, everyone was talking, running over the high points of the play, laughing, teasing, making plans for another production, returning borrowed jewellery, clothes they'd lent, pictures commandeered for the stage, her Indian throwover was returned to her, plans were made for storing the costumes Mrs Jones had run up, the chatter and the noise and the excitement went on. Someone had put on a tape and the music added to the excitement.

Then the door burst open with a crash and silence fell as they all turned to see who had come in. It was Don Wright. But not the Don they'd known all these years, for this Don was the worse for drink and unsteady on his legs. An audible gasp of surprise went round the hall.

'Wel-l-l now. Champagne, ish it? Don'll 'ave one!'

'Now, Don, is this a good idea?' This from Mrs Jones.

''Ello, Greta! Give us a kish.' He went forward weaving his way between the chairs. 'You've known me a long time, but it doeshn't give you the righ' to tell me wha' to do. Come on, then, I like a nicesh plump woman I do. Round, like, and cuddly.' He lurched forward and grabbed her, giving her a resounding unwelcome kiss. His hands clutched her bottom. 'My word, but you're a . . .' Mrs Jones fought him off and then smacked his face.

'Oh now come on, that'sh not kind to an upright good living man li' me. My Vera never lifted a hand to me.' His bleary eyes peered at everyone. 'Where ish she? Where'sh my Vera?'

But Vera was hiding behind Rhett. 'Don't let him see me, Rhett, please.' Rhett stood his ground. 'Oh, Rhett! Whatever have I done? I've driven him to drink, that's what. Him that's never done me a wrong turn all these years.' Vera peeped out from behind Rhett and, seeing him, realised he was still the same old Don. 'He won't change for me though, will he? It's just a load of sentimental old tosh he's saying. His problem is he's got no one to wash his socks and iron his shirts. But I shouldn't have done what I've done.'

When Don couldn't spot Vera, he said, 'Anyway it'sh not only her I've come to shee, it's that Mr Hugo Maude. I've come to knock his block off.'

Hugo pushed forward into a gap and faced him. 'I'm here.' Summoning all his acting techniques, despite the prospect of a physical attack, he assumed an air of authority and said, 'I suggest you toddle along home, Don, and sleep it off.'

'Home? I haven't got a home no more. Not now my Vera'sh left. You've driven me to drink! Me, a lifelong teetotaller! Thish champagne's good, gi' me some more.' He held out his cup and someone dribbled a drop in to pacify him. 'That's not enough, fill it up, go on fill it up. That's better!' Don staggered slightly, steadied himself, took a slurp of champagne from his paper cup then pointed with his free hand at Hugo. 'This is a toast to that shnake in the grassh. Mr Hugo Maude. The man who parts women from their lawful husbands. He started with my Vera. Thirty-six years of married bliss we've 'ad, and he comes along and whizz bang wallop she leaves me. Three daysh and it feelsh like three yearsh.' Don placed his champagne on the trestle table and, taking out a grimy handkerchief, mopped his bleary eyes.

'Oh Rhett, he really is missing me. What have I done?' Vera whispered.

Don put his handkerchief away and continued with his tipsy monologue. 'But he wasn't content with just one woman, was he? Oh no. When my Vera left me because of him, he didn't tell her he already had another string to his bow, did he? Oh no! Up at the Big House getting his oats, he was. She was only too ready and willing; anything in trousers, that's her motto. He's a two-timing black-guard. Now 'er 'usband's had a 'eart attack! It was the shock that did it! Lucky if he lives.'

'Someone get him out!' Hugo snarled his request, but no one moved to comply; Don's performance had mesmerised them all.

Don picked up his cup again. The champagne appeared to have cleared his head, for now his speech was not nearly so slurred and his eyes were taking in everything: the blank, horrified faces, the incredulous ones, the embarrassed ones, and in Caroline's case the appalled one.

Don went to stand in front of her. 'It's you my heart bleeds for. You're a lady, and he shouldn't have done it to you. You've been duped.' Don liked the sound of the word and said it again, 'Absolutely duped. How many more he's had while he's been here I don't know, but he's rubbish, he is. Don't take no notice of him,' he jerked his thumb in Hugo's direction. 'Don't listen to his sweet talk, it's all acting. Go home to the Rector and them lovely children of his, 'cos all that rat will do is drag you through the mud, believe me.'

Peter, horrified by what Don was saying, at last mobilised himself as Don paused to toss the last of his champagne down his throat. He forced his way through the crowd, pushing aside those rooted to the spot by the horror of what they were witnessing. He intended to take Don by the arm and frog-march him out, but as he reached him the door opened again and everyone turned to look at the newcomer. This time it was Venetia.

Unaware of her arrival, Don pursued his point, emphasising it by stabbing the air with a shaky finger. 'Yer see it's all right for Mr Hugo Maude to mess her about, 'cos that Venetia's a . . . tart. An out and out *tart*. But not you!'

Someone switched off the tape and in the profound silence which followed everyone stared at Venetia.

The evening was full of shocks, for this was a Venetia they'd never seen before. A broken reed battered by life's storms, she wore a grubby sweater, wrinkled trousers, no jewellery. Her hair was straggly and unkempt and, for the first time since they'd known her she wore no make-up. She looked completely done in. It was Venetia who spoke first.

'Thanks for the character reference, Don. That's all I needed to hear, tonight of all nights.' No one answered her, all they could do was brace themselves for her news. 'I saw the lights on and I had to talk to someone before I went to bed.'

Harriet broke the spell by walking towards her. Assuming the worst, she said, 'Of course you did. We're all so very, very sorry about Jeremy. Such a great loss for you . . . and for us. Look, come and sit down here.'

Venetia shook her head. Looking directly at Hugo she said quite steadily, given the circumstances, 'From this day forward I shall not be the Venetia everyone's always known. I regret deeply all the things I've done which have caused harm, and from now on things will be very different because, hopefully, I've been given a second chance. I may have been a . . . tart, like Don said, but not any more.

'My Jeremy's not dead, you know.' An audible sigh of relief went round the room. 'I proposed to him tonight. I don't know if he realised what I was saying, I hope he did. I hope it gives him the strength to keep on fighting because I want him to live. It's still touch and go, you see.' Venetia half lifted her hand in a sad farewell. 'Goodnight. God bless.'

No one spoke for a while after the door closed behind her. Peter's first concern was Caroline. He looked down at her and knew he'd never seen her so distressed. She visibly trembled. Her eyes were closed. Sweat beaded her top lip. Her hands were clenched so tightly the knuckles were white. Peter didn't know what to say or what to do. One wrong move and he could blow it for ever.

He stood beside her watching people self-consciously begin clearing up: saying nothing, just busily occupying themselves to cover their embarrassment. Slowly they began to exchange a few words. Don weaved his way across to the collection of empty champagne bottles and, putting the top of one of them to his mouth, he sucked the last drop from it and from the next and the next. He staggered wildly and then lurched forward, falling across the end of the trestle-table. It collapsed with a mighty crash and he with it.

The noise caused Caroline to open her eyes. She looked up at Peter and said softly, 'Please take me home in as dignified a manner as possible.'

'There's just one question I want to ask you. Did you know he was seeing Venetia?'

Peter shook his head. 'Not until yesterday when something Venetia said at the hospital made me think he just might, you know ...'

'Because if you'd known and said nothing ...'

'I truly didn't know.'

'It wasn't news to everyone else. They all knew, I could tell from their faces.'

'Apparently so. Here, drink this.' He handed her a small brandy. 'You need it.'

Caroline placed the glass on the coffee table. 'Not now, I need a clear head. I never thought it would be Don Wright who would cut me down to size.'

'It's been a night of surprises.'

'You can say that again. What I can't understand is why I never guessed, why a grown woman like me, well experienced in dealing with people from all walks of life, never realised. Not a glimmer. Not a hint.'

'He's a very complex character.'

'I can't believe he didn't mean what he said to me. He can't have done, can he?'

'I think he did at the time he said it.'

She looked up hopefully. 'You think he did?'

'Oh yes.'

'I see. Can I be honest?'

'What else?'

'That phrase Marian used in the play, "throb with life", every moment. That's how it was for me.'

'I know.'

'Every moment to be treasured. It was gloriously reckless. Miraculous. Enchanting. He cast a spell over me.'

Peter knelt on the hearthrug to put himself on a level with her.

'Now, damn him, all that fine, uplifting love is smashed to smithereens. All those wonderful times ground under his heel, like the finest crystal, shattered and never to be, no more.'

She sat quite still for a moment just looking at Peter, remembering gratefully how, despite her crying need for him, she'd told Hugo she couldn't in all conscience sleep with him until she'd definitely left Peter. At least she didn't have that stumbling-block to face. Then she thought of Hugo and how he'd captivated her and she asked pleadingly, 'It was true what Don said, was it? About Venetia? It wasn't just him being drunk for the first time in his life?'

'Judging by Hugo's face it was true.'

'Damn! Damn! Damn! How could he do it to me? How could he?'

'I'm sure that when he was with you he did love you.'

'If he did, how could he go from me to her?'

'Because he's several people all at once, and all of them crave adoration. It feeds his genius, you see.'

The door bell rang.

Caroline's eyes were wide with pain as she begged, 'Peter! Don't answer it.'

'I must. It could be someone in need of help.'

'Not at this time of night.'

The bell rang again. Peter stood up.

'Please don't answer it.'

They heard Willie coming down the stairs, complaining.

Peter went into the hall.

'Oh, you're back, sir. Thought it was you forgotten your key. Will you see who it is?'

For the first time in his ministry Peter decided to ignore what might be a call for his help. 'No. Ignore it. Go back to bed, it's half past one. Whoever it is can wait till tomorrow. Thank you.'

Willie turned back and climbed the stairs. Peter went to the sitting room window and moved the curtain slightly so he could see clearly. He could just make out Hugo's silhouette walking away down the road back to Jimbo's. 'Whoever it is has gone away.'

'It would be him coming to apologise. Full of remorse. I can't bear to take any more of his sweet talk. Never any more of it. I must have been the only one completely taken in by it. Perhaps I needed to be taken in, needed to believe he loved me. It was so . . . let's face it, it was so flattering. It inflated my ego, boosted my morale, gave me such a kick. What a fool I've been!'

Peter shook his head. 'Don't, don't. You're being too hard on yourself.'

'Not hard enough. To think I nearly threw everything away, everything . . . You. Alex. Beth. When I think of their distress if I'd gone, I can hardly believe I could even *think* of putting their happiness in such jeopardy.' She was looking down at her hands, twisting them together back and forth in her lap when she said this, so she didn't see the searing pain in Peter's face.

She raised her eyes and looked straight at him. 'Because of my job I thought I knew the human race, but I don't. I'm an amateur, a complete amateur. You're streets ahead of me in that. I've made an utter fool of myself. I wish he'd never come here. The damage he's done!'

'He's done some good too, you know.'

Scathingly Caroline asked, 'Such as?'

'He's made Venetia, for one, think about herself and her lifestyle and made her put Jeremy first. He's brought Mrs Jones to heel; she had far too much pride, far too much self-importance. Mr Fitch has been humbled and about time, too: he's almost sick with worry about Jeremy. Vera's struck out for a better life for herself all because of her disappointment over the costumes. Don has learned Vera's value to him, to the extent that he is most probably going to do as she wants. People working on the estate have had a salutary lesson, which was sorely needed, about appropriating estate property. I'm also completely certain that Sylvia will be back. It might take a week or so, but she will. And when she is back, your regard for each other will be strengthened not diminished. And look at the cast of the play! Who would have thought that Rhett and Neville could act like they did? Superbly too! Their lives will never be the same again. So, in a way, the village is a better place for him having been here.' He smiled at her, one of his gentle encouraging smiles: full of strength and support.

She was silent for a while, then raised her eyes to his, and with a voice clearly at breaking point, asked, 'How can you ever want me back?' Having dared to ask the question uppermost in her mind Caroline began to cry. It was like a storm breaking. Peter daren't even touch her in case his embrace would be unwelcome, so he sat on the rug waiting. She howled like an injured animal caught in a trap, desperate with pain, and it cut his heart to pieces, but he knew he must wait for her; for her to show her need of him. Wait and wait for her.

He heard Willie creeping down the stairs. He came to stand in the doorway, clutching his clothes, and signalled he was going home for the rest of the night. Peter nodded. 'Goodnight and thanks. See you in the morning.'

Willie nodded towards Caroline. 'She'll see things straighter tomorrow.'

'I know. I know.'

It was fully ten minutes before Caroline held out her arms and begged him to hold her. The time he'd sat waiting for her to ask for his help was the most tortured he had ever known.

'Oh Peter! I'm so sorry! Can you ever forgive me for what I've done to you?'

'There's nothing to forgive.'

'Where would I be without you?'

'My darling! You won't ever need to be without me.'

Turnham Malpas Amateur
Dramatic Society

presents

DARK RAPTURE

by

Digby Clarke-Johnson

on

Friday 10th and Saturday 11th July

in

ST THOMAS' CHURCH HALL

at

7.30 prompt

Tickets £5 including refreshments
Concessions £4

CAST

Marian Latimer	Caroline Harris
Charles Latimer	Neville Neal
Julian Latimer	Rhett Wright
Daisy Latimer	Michelle Jones
Leonard Charteris	Hugo St John Maude
Doris Jackson	Liz Neal
Celia Tomkinson	Harriet Charter-Plackett

Produced and directed by

Hugo St John Maude

The action of the play takes place
in the drawing room of Rocombe Manor,
home of the Latimers.

ACT ONE

Scene 1

A summer morning

Scene 2

The following evening

Refreshments will be served in the interval

ACT TWO

Scene 1

Sunday morning four weeks later

Scene 2

The same evening

ACKNOWLEDGEMENTS

The Society wishes to thank all those who have contributed in any way towards the production of this play. Most especially our thanks go to Mr Craddock Fitch, our President, without whose enthusiastic support this play would not have been presented.

Stage Manager Dean Jones

Lighting Willie Biggs

Scenery Barry Jones and Ronald Bissett

Costume Greta Jones

Flowers Sheila Bissett

Music Dora Peel

Publicity Anne Parkin

Sound effects Barry Jones

Box office Anne Parkin

Refreshments Charter-Plackett Enterprises

Trouble in the Village

Inhabitants of Turnham Malpas

Nick Barnes	Veterinary surgeon
Roz Barnes	Nurse
Willie Biggs	Verger at St Thomas à Becket
Sylvia Biggs	His wife and housekeeper at the Rectory
Sir Ronald Bissett	Retired Trade Union leader
Lady Sheila Bissett	His wife
James (Jimbo) Charter-Plackett	Owner of the Village Store
Harriet Charter-Plackett	His wife
Fergus, Finlay, Flick and Fran	Their children
Katherine Charter-Plackett	Jimbo's mother
Alan Crimble	Barman at the Royal Oak
Linda Crimble	Runs the post office at the Village Store
Georgie Fields	Licensee at the Royal Oak
H. Craddock Fitch	Owner of Turnham House
Jimmy Glover	Taxi driver
Revd Peter Harris MA (Oxon)	Rector of the parish
Dr Caroline Harris	His wife
Alex and Beth	Their children
Mrs Jones	A village gossip
Barry Jones	Her son and estate carpenter
Kenny Jones	Barry Jones' brother
Pat Jones	Barry's wife
Terry Jones	Barry Jones' brother
Dean and Michelle	Barry and Pat's children

Jeremy Mayer	Manager at Turnham House
Venetia Mayer	His wife
Neville Neal	Accountant and church treasurer
Liz Neal	His wife
Guy and Hugh	Their children
Tom Nicholls	Retired businessman
Evie Nicholls	His wife
Anne Parkin	Retired secretary
Kate Pascoe	Village school head teacher
Sir Ralph Templeton	Retired from the diplomatic service
Lady Muriel Templeton	His wife
Dicky Tutt	Scout leader
Bel Tutt	School secretary and assistant in the Village Store
Don Wright	Maintenance engineer (now retired)
Vera Wright	Cleaner at the nursing home in Penny Fawcett
Rhett Wright	Their grandson

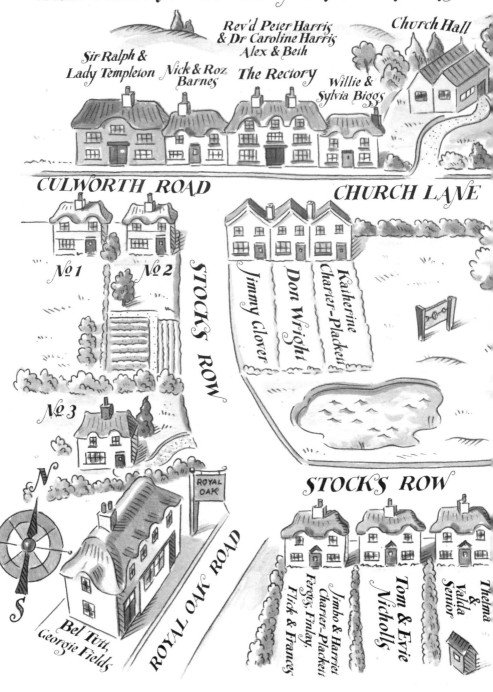

THE VILLAGE OF TURNHAM MALPAS

Rev'd Peter Harris
& Dr Caroline Harris
Alex & Beth

Church Hall

Sir Ralph &
Lady Templeton

Nick & Roz
Barnes

The Rectory

Willie &
Sylvia Biggs

CULWORTH ROAD

CHURCH LANE

No 1

No 2

STOCKS ROW

Jimmy Glover

Don Wright

Katherine Charter-Plackett

No 3

ROYAL OAK

STOCKS ROW

N

S

ROYAL OAK ROAD

Bel Tutt,
Georgie Fields

Jimbo & Harriet
Charter-Plackett
Fergus, Finlay,
Flick & Frances

Tom & Evie
Nicholls

Thelma
&
Valda Senior

1

Muriel glanced at the dining-room clock as she put the last of the salad on the table. Only half past three and all was ready. Would she never learn? All her life she'd been ready too early for everything and here she was still at it. But it did give her half an hour to sit quietly and contemplate life, Ralph's birthday and all these people coming to help him celebrate. How lucky they'd been to have so many happy years together. Just think, if she hadn't taken hold of life by the scruff, how much happiness and excitement she would have missed. Muriel had to confess she was an entirely different person from the one he'd married. She laughed at the memory of how precise and uptight she had been, so meticulous in all aspects of life, and tragically so afraid of it too.

She cocked an ear for Ralph and heard his light step coming down the stairs. So he was ready early as well. Dear Ralph! The sight of him could still make her heart miss a beat. The door opened and there he stood. The birthday boy. He'd decided against his sports coat then and gone for the pale blue shirt and trousers with the dark blue spotted tie she'd given him at Christmas. The shirt emphasised the sparkling whiteness of his hair and flattered his lightly tanned face.

'My dear! You look delightful!' He came across to kiss her cheek.

'Handsome as ever, Ralph! How do you do it?'

Ralph studied her face. 'Only in your eyes, my dear. I fear others see me as a crusty, short-tempered, elderly man with a somewhat old-fashioned penchant for "doing the right thing" ...'

Muriel protested, 'Never! Never! You're courteous and kind and understanding and a pillar of the community. And much loved, not just by me.'

Ralph bowed with a mocking grin on his face. 'You're too kind.'

'What do you think to the table? Have I forgotten anything at all?'

Ralph inspected the magnificent spread, and decided she'd forgotten nothing. 'This is wonderful. Quite wonderful. I must say, Muriel, you've really excelled yourself today. A wonderful feast. How shall we sit everyone?'

'If you look out of the window you'll see that while you were out this morning everyone brought their garden chairs and tables.'

Ralph went to the french windows to look out. He had to smile. He guessed the imposing teak set would be Jimbo and Harriet's, the green plastic would be Willie and Sylvia's because he could see those in their garden from the attic window, and the white set with the elaborate twirly pattern on the backs of the chairs and the impressively flowered seat-pads must be Ron and Sheila's or Ronald's, as Sheila called him when she remembered; she thought it common to shorten his name. The plain white with the embroidered cushions foxed him. Ah! Yes. He guessed they might be Tom and Evie's.

'Evie's coming, is she?'

Muriel answered him with a hint of apprehension in her voice. 'She is. Poor Evie. I hope she can face it.'

'Is there anyone not coming?'

'Craddock Fitch. He's in Warsaw.'

'I shan't miss him.'

'Ralph! How unkind of you! He has improved so much since he nearly killed Jeremy.'

'One can scarcely say he nearly killed him.'

'Well, he escaped death by a whisker and we all know he collapsed in the middle of their most tremendous row. It's that scathing, icy temper of his. It's quite scary.'

'He doesn't scare me!'

Muriel smiled to herself. 'Oh! I know he doesn't. You're a match for him any day.'

'Self-made men are all right if they acknowledge that they are, but he tries to pretend he's a gentleman, and one can't. One either is or one isn't.'

The bell rang and Muriel panicked. 'Oh! They're here! I should never have organised this. What a fool I am. You answer the door. Go on. Please! I feel quite dreadful.'

Muriel appeared to fade into the wallpaper so apprehensive was she, the effect heightened by her being small, pale-complexioned and fair-haired. Briefly Ralph felt concern for her but then he saw her summon up her courage and she re-emerged from the wallpaper with a smile on her face. He patted her arm and hastened to the door.

They'd said four for four thirty but by ten past almost all their guests had arrived. Presents were given, drinks accepted, kisses exchanged, chairs occupied, children commended on their smart appearance, greetings given and in the midst of it Muriel was in a complete flurry. She should have accepted the help she'd been offered, she knew that now. There was Evie in the corner without a drink in her hand. Oh dear! 'Evie, what would you like to drink?'

Straining to hear Muriel had to guess she'd said, 'Orange juice, please.'

'Certainly.' In her mind and conversation Muriel always prefixed Evie's name with 'poor' because that was just how she always looked, and even more so today. Not poor in the sense of being without money but, rather, poor in spirit. Oddly dressed in a big emerald green wool jacket with beneath it a skimpy navy skirt and a black polo-necked T-shirt. Surely Tom could help her with her clothes? 'Here we are! There's plenty more. Help yourself. I'm so glad you could come.'

But Evie wasn't for answering and in any case Katherine Charter-Plackett was demanding Muriel's attention. 'Muriel! I've been away! I'm looking to you to keep me up to date with the news.'

Katherine always brought out the worst in Muriel and consequently their relationship was delicate. Muriel looked up and sighed inside. The holiday had done nothing to soothe Katherine's domineering manner and certainly nothing to diminish that jutting jawline which appeared to jut out even further when she was on the warpath. How she came to have a son as charming as Jimbo Muriel couldn't imagine.

'You must come for coffee next week and I'll bring you up to date.' Muriel immediately regretted her invitation but she couldn't stop to talk now, still less face Katherine's detailed interrogation about the smallest detail.

Katherine thanked her graciously, saying, 'I'll keep you to that.'

Muriel fled, intending to stand by Ralph's side while she recuperated, but on the way across the hall she met Caroline. 'Caroline! We're so glad you could come! Where are the twins? Have they got a drink? I've put out Coca-Cola specially, I know how much they love it.'

'You spoil them. They're in the garden with Peter.'

If anything Caroline was thinner than ever. Anyone, even someone with a turnip for a head, could feel the unhappiness emanating from her. And from Peter too. In her heart Muriel damned that actor fellow Hugo for almost persuading Caroline to run off with him. He'd gone on to magnificent triumphs at Stratford leaving this girl behind with her marriage in tatters.

'Enjoying getting back to general practice?'

Her question sparked Caroline off as Muriel knew it would.

'Indeed I am. I'd no idea how much I missed it. One feels to have such purpose in life.'

'Indeed. Purpose is so important.'

'Three days a week suits me fine. I don't feel too guilty about the children, you see.'

'It must be hard coping without Sylvia. Can she not see her way to coming back to help?'

Caroline's face shut down. Her eyes searched around to see if Sylvia was within hearing. 'Apparently not. Harriet has them until either Peter or I get back. It seems to be working quite well. Though the holidays ...' Caroline shrugged her shoulders.

'Muriel! Have we any more ice, my dear?' She hastened off to answer Ralph's request with yet another bucket of ice cubes from her new American fridge-freezer. It was so hot. She paused a moment to pat her handkerchief to her forehead and run the cold tap over her wrists to cool her down. There! Now she had a wet patch on her skirt. No one would notice, they were all too busy enjoying themselves. There was such a hubbub of conversation, always a good sign that people were relaxed and happy. That was her problem with entertaining, worrying about whether the guests were enjoying themselves. On her way into the dining room with the bucket of ice she found herself enveloped in a bear-hug by Jimbo Charter-Plackett.

'Just listen to that racket! Everyone's having a wonderful time! Congratulations, Muriel! May Ralph see many more birthdays!' Jimbo gave her a smacking kiss, which almost made her drop the ice. 'Give that to me! I'll take it. Wonderful party! We're so lucky to have you and Ralph.'

He strode off and Muriel decided to seek the shade of the garden and make sure at the same time that everyone out there was happy.

The back door from the hall was open and through it Muriel could hear loud chatter. She loved this view from the doorway. It lifted her spirits in a way no other aspect could. Framed by the door was the giant beech tree at the end of the garden under which Ralph had buried her dear, dear poodle, Pericles; his little memorial stone only served to enhance the view. Between the beech tree and the terrace was the lawn now dotted with the tables and chairs and the bright umbrellas and, best of all, dotted about also were her dear friends, laughing and talking. The rectory twins interrupted her reverie.

'Moo! Moo!' They both rushed at her and little Beth flung her arms around her waist. 'Moo! Can Alex and I have some more Coke? Daddy says we may, if it's all right with you.' Her ash-blonde hair and those lovely rounded cheeks, what a stunning combination they were! Alex took her hand. 'Moo! May we?' So like Peter! They could be his eyes looking at her.

'Of course you may, as much as you want.' She really must stop this dreaming and enter into the hurly-burly. Muriel targeted Peter, who was standing under the beech tree alone. There was far too much of that nowadays. Peter, alone.

He gave her his lovely smile and she looked up at him and smiled back. 'I do believe, Peter, you get taller every day! Or maybe it's me who's shrinking!'

'Neither! I think it's you standing a little lower than me.'

Muriel looked down at her feet. 'So I am. How foolish of me.'

'Aren't we lucky with the weather today, though? They say the sun shines on the righteous.'

Muriel ignored his joke. 'I worry about Caroline. Is there no way we can get Sylvia back? Do you want her back? I wondered if I could –'

'Nothing would please me more, but they've had such a fall-out, she and Caroline. I think it's something they have to sort out for themselves.'

Being warned off so abruptly Muriel stepped back to see his face more clearly and her heart trembled for him. He might be the Rector and have answers to lots of other people's problems but . . .

'I see. Your glass is empty, come and get another drink.' Muriel slipped her arm in his and drew him into the house. She subtly handed him over to Ralph and as she left the two of them she heard Ralph asking if he'd had any answers to his advertisement for a new verger. That would keep him busy.

Glancing at her watch Muriel decided it was time to eat. She checked she had the matches at the ready for lighting Ralph's candles and went into the kitchen to make the tea. She'd had kettles from the church kitchen gently simmering since before everyone had arrived and now she put the tea-bags into the giant teapot she'd borrowed and turned up the gas under the kettles.

As she filled the teapot to the brim she felt a surge of triumph. It really was going well. She'd planned and schemed to get things just right this afternoon and her hard work was being rewarded. Full of success, she bounced into the dining room with the teapot.

It was the scandalised tone of Caroline's question which gave her the first hint that all was not well. 'You have what?'

Grandmama Charter-Plackett's chin jutted but her mouth smiled. As far as the village was concerned that boded ill. 'I have agreed with him. It should be done.'

'*You* have agreed with him? What have *you* got to do with it?'

'I just happened to be having a cup of tea with him and he mentioned his intentions.'

'But it's none of your business.'

'Are you saying that village affairs are nothing to do with me?'

Caroline's eyes blazed. 'I suppose I am. You've hardly been here two minutes and you're interfering yet again, as if you haven't caused enough trouble since you came. He's getting away with this over my dead body.'

Grandmama drew herself up. 'I think you're taking this far too seriously. It's perfectly ridiculous to be making such a fuss.'

Jimbo intervened. 'Mother! I think –

'Well, then, don't. I'm quite capable of looking after myself, thank you, Jimbo.' Turning to Caroline she said, between clenched teeth, '*I'm* not digging it up, I only agreed with him that it should be done.'

Jimbo opened his mouth, intending to pour oil on troubled waters, but Caroline put a hand on his arm. 'No, Jimbo, leave this to me. This village needs dragging into the twenty-first century. There are some things I agree with, but this, however, is beyond belief. What is it, three years you've been here perhaps nearly four? Most of the families here this afternoon have lived here for *centuries*. If anyone has a right to agree or disagree it is them and not you. How dare you!'

Muriel's question, spoken in a small voice, gently cut through the bristling silence which had fallen. 'What is it we are talking about?'

Ralph quietly explained. 'Mr Fitch has decided to dig up the hedgerow behind our houses and replace it with a fence.'

Every word of Ralph's fell like a stone on Muriel's heart. Appalled she said, 'You mean Rector's Meadow hedge? Why?'

Grandmama Charter-Plackett replied, 'Because he can't find people either willing or able to maintain it, and he thinks a nice well-made wooden fence would be more economical.'

'What has economy to do with it?'

'He runs a tight ship and he can't bear for there to be waste. That's why he's rich.' She nearly added, 'And that's why he's at the Big House and your Ralph isn't any more,' but even she realised that would be a tad too far.

Muriel took a deep breath, amazed by the insensitivity on display. 'Waste? What about all the creatures who make their homes there?' Her eyes filled with tears as she thought about them.

Grandmama, genuinely surprised by the thought that anyone, four-legged or otherwise, would choose to live in a tatty overgrown hedge, almost smiled but the sight of tears in Muriel's eyes stopped herself smiling. 'They'll soon find somewhere else. It's all a storm in a teacup and I would have thought, Caroline, that you of all people would have welcomed progress. Muriel, of course, as we all know, always prefers the status quo.'

Indignant at being dismissed as a stick in the mud Muriel declared, 'I do not!' But she did about the hedge. 'But in this instance I do. There must be nearly half a mile of hedge and it belongs ... to us.'

Caroline agreed with her. 'I shall not stand by and let that – that – hooligan ruin the village.'

Katherine ignored Caroline, preferring to answer Muriel. 'To be exact, Muriel, the hedge belongs to Mr Fitch, he bought it and he has a right to do with it whatever he wants. Considering how this village benefits from his generosity with his money, the least we can do is let him get on with it. Otherwise what has happened to liberty? It is being eroded on every side. Well, this time I think he's right.' She turned to give Jimbo her empty glass. 'Put that somewhere appropriate, if you please.'

Jimbo, white with temper, smoothed his hand over his bald head and said, 'Mother, you're spoiling the party and that's not good manners.'

'You're right, it isn't. I apologise, Ralph, even though the upset is not my fault.'

Suddenly Muriel was aware she was still holding the tea-pot and her arms were beginning to ache. She handed it to Ralph and looked at him for assistance as he took it.

Ralph placed it on the stand by the teacups and said smoothly, 'Shall we all begin to eat? Muriel has provided such a banquet for us and I can't wait to cut my cake. Come, Katherine, here's a plate for you. May I help you to salmon or do you prefer the cold chicken, or perhaps a little of the stand pie?'

Grandmama always fell victim to Ralph's accomplished charm and today was no exception. 'Why, thank you, Ralph, the salmon, I think, with just a little of the mayonnaise. No cucumber.'

Though the matter had been shelved as far as general conversation went, it burst out in quiet outraged huddles all over the house and garden.

Jimbo and Harriet were incensed. 'Your mother! When will she learn? I should never have agreed to her coming to live here, I knew she'd cause trouble.'

'God! Wait till I get her home.'

'Caroline's right, it would be criminal to uproot that hedge. If she starts a campaign I shall support her.'

'Careful, Harriet. Think about Mother.'

Harriet looked scornfully at Jimbo. 'You would do well to remember the pledge you gave me before she came. Remember? You and I stand together.'

Jimbo raised an eyebrow. 'How much of Caroline's anger is directed at Mother rather than the hedge? Hmm? Ask yourself that.'

Thoughtfully, Harriet chewed on a stick of celery while she framed her reply. 'I agree they've had their moments, the two of them, but I genuinely believe she is also very angry about the hedge. I wondered how long old Fitch could manage without being a thorn in the flesh yet again.' She looked across at her mother-in-law, who was conversing with Peter as though nothing upsetting had taken place. 'I shall tread carefully. But, like Caroline said, over my dead body does he put up a fence.'

In the garden things were being said which were much less polite. 'That blasted woman! Here, Ron, tilt the umbrella different, I'm right in the sun and if there's anything I hate it's eating food in full sun. Pig ignorant she is. Pig ignorant, for all her airs and graces. She's really upset Caroline and it won't do.'

'She could be right, Sheila.'

Sheila glared at him, 'Right? That woman's never right. Ever. As we well know. If they get up a petition I shall sign it at every opportunity.'

Ron cleared his mouth of his pork pie and said, 'Watch it.'

'Why?'

'Mr Fitch has been very kind in the past sponsoring the Village Show and the Flower Festivals and that. You could stand to lose a lot if he takes his bat home over this. You keep out of it.'

'When principles are at stake a stand has to be taken, no matter what.' She'd read that in a book and had been storing it up for just such an occasion.

Ron shook his head in despair.

Muriel heard none of this as she was in the kitchen patiently lighting the candles on the cake and trying her best to take delight in doing so. Bracing herself she carried the cake aloft into the dining room and, as through a thick cloud, heard them all cheer at the sight of it, for it really was quite splendid. They made room for it on the table and Ralph invited the children to help him blow out the candles. Peter lifted them up on to chairs, Beth, Alex and little Fran Charter-Plackett.

Alex shouted, 'You must make a wish, Sir Ralph! Go on, make a wish.'

They all waited in silence, the children hopping up and down on the chairs. 'Right! I've done it. Are we ready? One, two, three, blow!'

Cutting up the cake with Caroline's help, Muriel whispered, 'I'm so angry, but I don't want to spoil Ralph's party. We'll have clean plates. Here they are, look.'

'So am I. That beautiful hedge! How could he? I'm working on Monday otherwise I'd go straight up there first thing.'

'He's not here, though. Oh, this slice has broken in half. Never mind, I'll have it. He's not back till Tuesday night.'

Caroline groaned. 'I work Wednesday too.'

'Don't you worry, I'll go up to the Big House myself. I've worked miracles with him before. Let's hope I can do it again. I'll take the cake round. I'll let you know how I go on.'

In the end the party was a success, despite the disagreement, and while Ralph helped Muriel to clear up he told her so several times.

'You have no need to worry, my dear, it was perfectly splendid. I have so enjoyed myself.'

Muriel kissed him. 'I'm so glad.'

'I know what you're thinking.'

'You do?'

'Yes. You're planning to tackle Fitch about the hedge.'

'Well, yes, I am. Will you help?'

'Frankly, no.'

'But, Ralph, I was relying on you.'

'All my support will achieve is his absolute determination to do exactly the opposite of what I want. He and I have crossed swords too many times for me to be of any value to you at all. Can you see that?'

Muriel thought about what he'd said and finally agreed. 'You could be right at that. You'd simply be a red rag to a bull.'

'Just like Katherine is to you.' Ralph had to laugh, and when he caught Muriel's eye, so too did she. 'So I shall keep out of it.'

'Thank you for distracting Katherine so tactfully. We could have had a full-scale row and that would have been unforgivable. Right now I'm going down the back garden, crossing the lane and giving the hedge a pat. And I'm going to tell it it needn't worry because Caroline and I are going to save it.'

Ralph smiled indulgently. 'Off you go then. I'll finish in here, you've done enough today.'

Muriel clipped shut the gate which separated her garden from Pipe and Nook Lane, checked there were no cars coming up to the garages at the top end and went over to the hedge. It was all of three feet wide and five feet tall now, in places even taller, not having been touched since Mr Fitch had bought the house. Just where she stood a wild rose was flowering, wide single petals, of the palest of pale pink, it fluttered delicately in the evening breeze. How could he? How could he even think of destroying all this beauty?

A wren, unaware he had an audience, was hopping briskly about amongst the twigs. His pert, upstanding tail amused her and for a moment, his head on one side, the wren studied her. They looked at each other eye to eye, two living beings, in form as unalike as it was possible to be and yet ... He flew off with a flick of his soft brown tail. As Muriel studied the hedge she spotted deep inside it an abandoned nest, a perfectly round scoop of a nest still beautifully lined with soft feathers, and wonderfully and intricately woven grass by grass, fine twig by fine twig: a miracle of construction. How could anyone think of destroying this? If only they could all see it through her eyes as she saw it now in the mellow evening light.

Trailing her fingers amongst the leaves Muriel said out loud, 'Don't worry, that monster isn't going to get rid of you. I'll see to that even if ...' rather rashly she concluded with 'I have to throw myself in front of the diggers.' Having acknowledged she might perhaps have to do that very thing, her heart quailed at the prospect. 'But I shall. Oh, yes. I shall.'

Muriel inspected first one leaf and then another, realising that though she had lived here with Ralph all this time, apart from the wild rose she didn't know any of the other plants growing there. Shame on you, Muriel, she thought, it's time you did, and she marched inside purposefully, intent on seeking out a countryside book of Ralph's to find out exactly what it was she was being called upon to defend.

2

That night the bar of the Royal Oak hummed with the news of the disagreement over the hedge. Those not privileged to be guests at the birthday party had had the story told them, and each and every one had an opinion to express.

Sylvia having been a guest had already told Willie she thought that Caroline and Muriel were right. 'Lovely old hedge that. Been there long before you and I saw the light of day. He's no business to be uprooting it.'

'He does own it, though.'

'I know he does, but landowners have obligations in this day and age. They can't ride roughshod over everyone just because they have bright ideas about increasing their crops.'

'Well, at least it'll give Caroline something to concentrate on.'

Sylvia fell silent. She sipped her gin and orange and wished, how she wished ... Caroline. It had been painful seeing her. Right at that moment she deeply regretted resigning in such a temper. 'The children ... it was lovely talking to them.'

Willie took hold of her hand. 'See here. Eat humble pie and ask for your job back. She's in a fix and she needs your help and it's what you want.'

Sylvia, glad of a chance not to answer, waved to Don who was just coming across to their table with an orange juice in his hand.

'Evening, Sylvia, Willie. Enjoy your party this afternoon then?'

'Yes, thanks. You know, it still seems funny seeing you in here without your Vera.'

Don didn't answer, he simply ran a stubby hand through his coarse grey hair.

'Have you been to see the flat she's moved into?'

'No, and I shan't.' He tapped the table with a thick forefinger. 'Nothing and nobody is moving me from my cottage. I was born in that front bedroom, in the very bed I sleep in still, and that's where I'm staying, and I'm not moving out to some poncy flat just to please her.'

Willie put his spoke in by reminding him about the dreadful condition of his cottage. 'You really can't expect any woman to put up with that dump in this day and age. I'm surprised she hasn't moved out sooner than this. You haven't done a hand's turn in years to improve it. No wonder she grabbed her chance when she could. You should have hightailed it after her to that flat if you'd had any sense. Shouldn't he, Sylvia?'

Sylvia nodded.

Don remained silent. But then they were used to Don being a man of few words. Trouble was, when he did speak he was, on occasion, far too forthright.

Sylvia reached forward and encouragingly patted Don's arm where it rested on the table. 'Nice little job that nursing home offered her. It's just a pity you didn't see it that way. She had the right idea, doing up the cottage and renting it out while you both lived in the flat.'

When he didn't answer she remarked how stubborn some people could be when the right thing to do was staring them in the face.

Willie agreed. He glanced at Don. 'Another orange juice, Don?'

'No. Thanks. I'll be off. Early shift tomorrow. When you're footloose and fancy-free there's jobs to be done before yer can go to bed. But don't you fret, Don Wright 'ull survive without 'er, just you wait and see. Who needs women?' Don fixed his beady brown eyes on Sylvia and said, 'Before I go, as it seems to be a night for 'anding out advice, my advice to you, Sylvia Biggs, is to hightail it yourself, back to the Rectory, and apologise and ask for your job back because at bottom that's what you really want to do. You've never looked the same since you left and it's time to make up. Good night.' He squeezed out of the narrow gap between the settle and the table and left them alone.

Sylvia, red-faced and furious, folded her arms across her chest and said angrily, 'That Don is having a sight too much to say for himself right now. The cheeky devil, him handing out advice to *me*. What does he know about anything anyway?' Scornfully Sylvia added, 'He'll manage without Vera! Huh! And pigs might fly. I just hope that mucky cottage 'ull tumble down on top of him, and it'll serve 'im right.'

Willie gave Sylvia a sly glance. 'Seems to me he could be right about you.'

'Hmm. Thanks, anyway, for not letting on the Rector had been round to persuade me to go back.' She paused, recollecting Peter's kindness and the gentle way he'd given her the opportunity to change her mind without loss of face. 'He's hard to resist he is.'

'Then you shouldn't have resisted, you could have given in graciously to him, everybody knows how persuasive he is. You're stubborn, you are.'

Emphatically Sylvia shook her head. 'No, I'm not stubborn, I just know what's right. She came within an ace of deserting those children for that Hugo actor man,' briefly her face softened for she'd been caught up in his charisma too, just like everyone else, 'within an ace, and couldn't see where it was all leading. What I said I meant. Someone had to speak up 'cos one thing's for certain the Rector wouldn't. Seeing as you're on your feet get me another gin and orange, there's a love.'

'Will yer think about it though, to please me?'

Sylvia paused for a moment. 'I might. Then again I might not.'

Willie smiled into her large grey eyes, those eyes which had attracted him to her so powerfully those few short years ago. He bent his head to kiss her and smiled inside himself as he straightened up, certain that if he knew anything at all she'd be back at the Rectory very soon and all would be right with the world again.

While Willie waited at the bar Sylvia thought about what he'd said. She loved those children as though they were her own grandchildren, but as for ... No, she wouldn't. Caroline would have to do the asking, not her. Willie, walking towards her now, suddenly looked older somehow. Strange that: you lived your life with someone and didn't see what was happening under your very nose. He'd been right to say he would retire.

'Thanks. Funny Tom applying for your job. Doesn't seem quite right somehow, him wanting to be verger.'

'That's what the Rector says, but he's the only applicant and to be honest I shall be glad to be shut of the job. It's all too much being at everyone's beck and call. He's coming for an interview on Monday.'

By twenty minutes to nine Tom Nicholls had his ear to one of the panels of the vestry door listening to the Rector and Willie talking. The door was too thick for him to make sense of what they said, and in any case he remembered there was no need to sneak about, not like he used to have to do. When they paused he tapped on the door.

'Come in!'

Tom snapped the door open and entered in his usual get-up-and-go style. Peter looked up at him from behind his desk. 'Good morning, Tom, take a seat.'

'Thank you, sir.' As he seated himself Tom hitched his trousers at the knee forgetting he was wearing his country scruff outfit. This consisted of a tweed hacking jacket, which had seen better days, fawn cavalry twill trousers, which had also seen better days, a tweed cap at an angle which could only be described as breezy, and well-polished brown oxfords. They were a bit out of kilter with his clothes but he couldn't abide dirty shoes. His shoulders were too narrow for his height and this made him appear much taller than he was. He had a long pale hollow-cheeked face, and when he took off his cap from his high domed head, a thick covering of larger than life gingery hair was exposed. He put up his hand to tidy his moustache, forgetting he'd shaved it off just before he came to the village. Old habits die hard, he'd have to watch himself.

'Thank you for coming, Tom. I've read your letter but I need more details than you've put in it. I must be quite frank, yours is the only application and whilst Willie here is prepared to carry on until a replacement is found I'm anxious to find someone soon, even if it's only temporary. I have to confess I'm somewhat surprised to receive an application from you. It doesn't seem quite your line of country, if you see what I mean.'

'Hit the nail on the head, Rector, but I've decided on a change of lifestyle. Spent too many years dashing here and dashing there, buying this, selling that, and it's time I gave up this entrepreneurial lark and did something more worthwhile. Something where I can get job satisfaction. So, if you'll have me, I'm giving all that up. Evie agrees "Tom," she said "I –" '

'This might sound like an impertinence when I've known you for, what is it, three years now? but I must ask, have you any references? A formality, you know.'

'I have. Indeed I have.' Out of the inside pocket of his old tweed jacket he pulled two spanking new envelopes. Handing them across the desk to Peter he said, 'You'll be well satisfied with those, I can tell you. Tom Nicholls can always find people willing to testify on his behalf.'

Peter opened the envelopes and studied what they said. He handed them to Willie, who read them with a little less belief than Peter had. Willie, having promised himself he'd leave the interview to the Rector, changed his mind and decided to speak up. 'It's unrelenting work, yer know. Locking up, unlocking, day after day. Security's very important nowadays, more's the pity. Sometimes we have bookings back to back for the hall and they all expect it to be just how they want it. Used day and night it seems, some days. Would you be prepared for that? It's very tying.'

'Evie's very amenable. If I got called away, which isn't likely, she'd stand in, very capable is Evie, she always says –'

Peter interrupted with 'If I did agree to recommend you to the Church Council they would have the last word. I can't appoint you without their approval. Why not have a look around with Willie, let him explain what has to be done, then see how you feel? We'll meet again at two, here, this afternoon and have another talk. The job is very much concerned with integrity, you know, Tom. There's things you will be privy to which must not be divulged, like people wanting to get married secretly, or a conversation you unwittingly overhear. The big plus in your favour is that you are, and always have been since you came here, a regular communicant. Nothing less would be permitted.'

Tom fidgeted self-consciously. 'Thank you, Rector. I'll be pleased to go around with Willie, have a look, get the lowdown on things. I just hope that in the future should I have any queries, which I'm sure I shall, Willie will give me the benefit of his experience. He must be a fount of knowledge. That is if I get the job.' Tom smiled at them both, that disarming smile they'd come to like. You couldn't help but like Tom: there was that something about him which drew on your sympathy: in a trice you were on his side, and you couldn't understand how it had come about. 'And I'm good with people as you know. Old and young. I've changed since I came to this village. I don't know what it is about it but it kind of gets you in its grip and makes you want to be, well, noble. Must be all that history which hits you in the face every morning the minute you open your eyes. Brings out the best in you, kind of. That's how I feel anyway.' Tom stood up. 'Shall we be off then, Willie? Let the Rector get off to Penny Fawcett like he always does on Monday mornings. There, you see? I'm getting into my stride already!'

Willie put down his cup, wiped his mouth and said, 'Question is, is he the man for the job? I can't decide. What do you think, Sylvia?'

'Oh! I like Tom. You can't help yourself, and he's always ready for a laugh. More tea?'

'Yes, please. You see, I'm a steady chap not always gallivanting off, but he's always off here, there, everywhere, whatever opportunity comes up. How he's going to settle to a rigid timetable, I'll never know. Look at Wednesdays. I'm backwards and forwards all day with one thing and another and it's eleven before I can lock up, nearer midnight sometimes. He reckons he's changed, but I don't think he's going to settle for that. I'm ready for my pud.'

'Last of the strawberries. Ice cream?'

Willie shook his head. 'It'll be nice to have more time for the garden. I've often fancied growing asparagus.'

'Then grow it you shall. I've no idea how to cook it, but I can soon look it up. If he's not right for the job it won't need an Act of Parliament to oust him, will it, so don't worry yourself.' Sylvia put a dish of fat ruby red strawberries in front of him, fresh from the garden that afternoon, sprinkled with sugar more than an hour ago so it was melting and making juice in the bottom of the dish. Fit for a king, she thought. 'Get yourself outside that lot and stop fretting and leave it to the Rector.'

*

Not long after Willie had slipped out to unlock the church hall for an evening meeting, Sylvia heard a tap on her back door. When she opened it she found Alex and Beth standing there. A broad smile lit her face, she held wide her arms and they both ran into them and she held them close to her.

'My little darlings!' They hugged and kissed her and she hugged and kissed them, and then she stood back to admire them. 'Well, well, what a nice surprise. Does Mummy know you're here?'

There came a slight pause before they answered, but then they said confidently that, yes, Mummy knew, and could they come in?

Sylvia ushered them into the kitchen and asked, 'Either of you ready for a drink?'

'Yes, please.'

She bustled about getting them drinks and they seated themselves at the table and without speaking drank their orange. Sylvia, her heart melting with love for them, knew she'd have to go back to the Rectory, like it or not: she just couldn't miss out on their company any longer. She'd never have another chance at having substitute grandchildren and she might as well face the fact that that was what they were.

Beth wiped her mouth on the back of her hand and said, 'Sylvie! How's Willie?'

'He's very well, thank you.'

Alex asked, 'And how are you, Sylvie?'

'I'm very well too.'

'Don't you miss seeing us every day?'

'Well, Alex, yes, I do.'

Beth said, 'We miss you. Are you looking after some different children now?'

'No.'

'I'm glad, because you belong to us and other children wouldn't be the same, would they?'

'No, they wouldn't, Beth.'

Alex finished his drink and wiping his mouth on his handkerchief said, 'I expect like Mummy said now Mr Biggs is retiring you want more time to spend with him, going out and things.'

'Well, it would be nice.' She guessed what this was leading up to and felt angry that Caroline had permitted them to come to ask her back instead of asking her herself.

'I expect we shall have to learn to do without you.' Beth struggled to get her handkerchief from the pocket of her shorts. 'Mummy's a doctor again now and it being the school holidays . . . And we don't want any mouldy old person looking after us, do we, Alex? We want you!' Fat tears rolled down her sweet rounded cheeks and she brushed them away with her handkerchief, but they wouldn't stop coming. Leaping from her chair she flung her arms around Sylvia's shoulders and wept.

'There, there, Beth, don't cry, I only live next door and you can come to see me as often as you like. In fact I could invite you to tea sometimes, couldn't I?'

Beth brightened up, lifted her head from Sylvia's shoulder and said, 'Really?' Then cold reason made her see sense. 'But it's not quite the same, is it? I like it when you meet us from school and we sit in the kitchen at home and talk and things. Next to our mummy you're my very best person. Except for my daddy, that is.' Beth looked at her apologetically for adding that.

Sylvia smiled and said, 'But of course, that's understood, it's only right. I'm very proud to be third best.'

Alex got up from his chair. 'Come on, Beth, it's no good. We'll go.' He tugged at Beth's arm, took her handkerchief from her and wiped her eyes. 'Come on. 'Bye, Sylvie. See you soon.'

Beth put her hand in his hand and the two of them left the kitchen by the back door, wandering slowly down to the back gate like two lost souls. Sylvia watched them, remembering how many times she'd ironed those red shorts and the red and white shirt Alex was wearing and how she'd had to mend the split in Beth's shorts because they were her favourites and she couldn't bear to throw them away. And that little T-shirt Beth was wearing was the one Willie had chosen for her when he and Sylvia had taken a holiday in Spain last year; sunny yellow with a wavy white stripe, it really suited Beth's fair colouring.

The two dear little things. It was no good. She'd have to go back: she'd accused Caroline of almost breaking their hearts and here she was doing the very same thing all because of anger and pride. First thing tomorrow she'd go next door and ask for her job back. Yes, definitely she would.

Sylvia didn't tell Willie what she intended because if they didn't want her back she'd look a right fool and she wasn't having that. But school holidays! Just how would those children cope, passed about everywhere? That mustn't be allowed to happen.

Sylvia had had a key for the front door all the time she'd worked at the Rectory but, of course, now she hadn't and she wasn't sure if knocking on the front door was quite the right thing to be doing in the circumstances: it made it all official like and one thing she didn't want was the Rector answering the door and taking her into the study. No, she preferred the kitchen and as it was Tuesday Caroline would most likely be around.

The back door was standing open when she got there so Sylvia called out, 'Helloooo! Anyone at home?'

Chang and Tonga, the two cats, came out of their basket and condescended to weave around her legs mewing. Well, at least the cats remembered her. No one was about so she called out again, 'Helloooo! It's only me.'

The door from the hall opened and there was Caroline. A short silence followed and then Caroline greeted her: 'Why, Sylvia, how nice. Do come in. I was just going to make coffee for Peter, would you like some? Do you have time?'

'That would be nice. Thank you.'

'Do sit down.' But Sylvia remained standing, uncertain and nervous.

They were silent while Caroline filled the kettle and got out the mugs. Sylvia had almost offered to make it, but thought better of it. Take things steadily, she reminded herself.

With her back to her Caroline said, 'Lovely long summer we're having, aren't we?

'Yes, we are. We could do with some rain for the garden though.'

'We could, you're right. The pleasure of watering it every evening soon palls.'

'It does. Your roses are looking wonderful.'

'I've really made an effort with them this year, pruned them back hard and fed them well. Here we are. I'll just take this to Peter, won't be a moment. Please, do sit down.'

'Where are the . . .' but Caroline had gone. Perhaps they'd manage better if the issue wasn't clouded by Alex and Beth being around. When she came back Caroline sat opposite her at the table. They sipped their coffee without speaking. Well, the silence couldn't go on for ever so Sylvia cleared her throat and said, 'Are you serious about getting Mr Fitch to change his mind? About the hedge?'

'Oh, yes. I am. It's tantamount to sacrilege to destroy such a wonderful old piece of village history.'

Sylvia hadn't seen it quite like that but she agreed it was. All went quiet again and Sylvia knew she must brace herself and come to the point. She flushed bright red and then out it all came in a rush. 'I was wondering what arrangements you had made for the school holidays. For the children, I mean.'

'Patchy at best.'

'I see.'

Caroline looked directly at her and said, 'What have you come to say? Something special?'

Sylvia shifted uneasily in her chair. 'If you can forgive me . . .'

Head down so her face was hidden Caroline didn't answer.

'If you can forgive me and have me back I would be pleased.'

Caroline still didn't answer.

'I should never have shouted at you nor deserted my job so abruptly. I can only say I'm very sorry.' Was Caroline even listening to her? She really couldn't tell. 'I was so worried, you see, about you and the children. And the Rector, come to that. I thought you were going to leave them, you see, and I couldn't bear it. We'd all been so happy.'

Caroline's head came up and Sylvia was appalled by the drained look of her face. 'We were, weren't we? If you will come back it will be such a relief to me. I just didn't know what to do about you.'

'Then I will. Three days, is it?'

Caroline nodded. 'That's right. Monday, Wednesday and Friday, all day in the holidays, of course. But schooldays perhaps you could pop home for a couple of hours in the afternoon.'

'Then you can rely on me. I shall be glad because seven days a week living hand in glove with Willie now he's retiring . . . much as I love him, absence, you know. Doesn't do to live too close, you lose the spark if you're not careful.'

Caroline stood up. 'When shall you start?'

'How about tomorrow? Eight o'clock?'

'Yes.'

Sylvia smiled, warmed and thankful that peace had been restored between them.

'Friends again then?' Caroline came round the end of the table and stood in front of her.

'Oh, yes!'

'You've no idea how pleased I am. All water under the bridge. Eh?'

'Of course.'

'I'll give you your key for the morning.'

'Thanks.' Tears came into Sylvia's eyes as her fingers closed over the key that had been hers for so long. It still had her name on it so . . . 'It's the children, you know, I have missed them. I love them dearly.'

'I know you do, and I've missed you. And thank you for coming to heal the breach between us, I'm so grateful, please believe me, I really am. It puts my mind completely at rest.'

3

To get on to the estate land Muriel used the small gate at the back of the churchyard instead of walking all the way down Church Lane and in by the main gates. No one was supposed to take advantage of the short-cut, but this morning, somehow, it was all part of her defiance to do so. In any case Mr Fitch wouldn't know, he scarcely ever used it as his short-cut to church because he hardly ever attended.

The morning was cloudy and chill, and a stiff breeze came up once she had left the shelter of the trees which ran along the church wall. Muriel was wearing a jacket and skirt, having decided that a skirt and cardigan would categorise her as a country woman, when this morning she couldn't have felt less like one. She'd rehearsed her approach to him time and again, but knew full well that despite her preparations she would say the first thing that came into her head at the time. She'd have to tread softly: Mr Fitch was an intimidating man, and a head-on confrontation would be the last thing that would achieve her objective.

The grounds were looking particularly beautiful this morning but then so they should for Mr Fitch spent thousands on their upkeep. Thousands more than Ralph would ever have been able to find. In the distance she could hear a mower swirling about cutting grass but here where she was it was peaceful. Into view came the Big House, amazingly immaculate, almost too immaculate: it rather took away from the ancient beauty of the building.

She crossed the Tudor garden and reached the gravel laid to make a car park immediately in front of the house. How incongruous. Muriel, concentrate, she told herself. The huge ancient front door stood open, and Muriel walked straight in savouring the beauty of the door by trailing her fingers along the old weathered wood as she went.

The receptionist recognised her. 'Good morning, Lady Templeton. Mr Fitch is ready for you. I'll take you straight through.'

Muriel, though she knew which way to go, allowed the girl to lead her and inform Mr Fitch she'd arrived.

He got up from behind his desk and came round to greet her. Taking her hand in his he didn't shake it but held it between both his own, saying, 'My dear Muriel, what a pleasure. May I offer coffee? No, don't answer that. I have no other appointments this morning so I think we'll be much more comfortable upstairs in my flat. Charlotte! Ring my housekeeper and tell her coffee for two immediately.'

This morning he was dapper in the shining black shoes on his small feet, the light grey pinstripe suit, the white shirt, putting the seal on his efforts with a remarkable tie which, for some reason, reminded her of Isadora Thingummy who used to dance with scarves. He was still as lean as the day he arrived in the village though the hair was whiter than ever, and the blue eyes still as icy.

He led the way up the beautiful Tudor staircase taking each step with great precision as though he'd practised time and again to make his ascent as perfect as he could for a film. Muriel trotted after him, uneasy and tense, well aware he was doing this to intimidate her. Did he know her reason for coming?

He unlocked the door of the flat and ushered her into the sitting room. It was inclined to be a dark room and the cloudy day made it worse. He indicated a chair and then went round switching on lamps on the low tables so the room was flooded with a soft glow.

Mr Fitch sat down, placed his elbows on the arms of his chair, put his fingertips together and said, 'Well, now, Muriel. All on your own? Ralph's not ill?'

Muriel knew full well he didn't care how Ralph was, nor come to that how she fared either, but she answered him politely, assuring him that Ralph was in good health.

'I'm sorry I missed his party on Saturday. Did it go well?'

'I was sorry you missed it too, but it did go well, thank you.'

She hesitated and he filled the gap with 'So . . .?'

'I have heard something which I truly cannot believe, so I have come to ask you for the truth.'

'Am I to get a roasting?'

Muriel smiled as cheerfully as she could in the circumstances. 'Certainly not. Nothing of the kind. I'm not that kind of a person.'

'I see.'

The housekeeper came in with the coffee at this point. She offered to pour but Mr Fitch declined. 'I'll attend to that myself. Thank you.'

He busied himself with the coffee, placed a table beside Muriel's chair and put her cup on it.

'Thank you. I'll come straight to the point. Katherine Charter-Plackett says you are intending pulling up the hedge around Rector's Meadow and replacing it with a fence.' Muriel put such scorn into the word "fence" that Mr Fitch could have been in no doubt how she felt about the idea. 'I'm sure, we're all sure, she must have misunderstood.'

Mr Fitch sipped his coffee and looked at her over his cup. The icy blue eyes seemed to bore straight through Muriel.

'She's right. I am.'

'Why?'

'Because I am.'

'But you can't.'

'It is my hedge. I bought it. I do own it. Do you ask permission of me before you uproot a rose tree or dig out a lupin in your garden? No.'

'But . . .'

He held up his hand to silence her. 'No, Muriel, I won't listen to you appealing to my better nature. My mind is made up. I have bent over backwards to accommodate the wishes of the people in the village time and again, but the hedge I shall have my own way about. That is the end of the matter.' He stood up in a dismissive manner, and Muriel felt compelled to stand up too and make ready to go.

'It's such a beautiful hedge. I'm very disappointed in you, I had thought . . .'

'No matter how much money I give to one cause or another, no matter whose jobs I save, no matter who benefits from my

Education Fund, no matter how I support the church I still can't get it right with you all, so I'm calling a halt, and doing as I like for once.'

Muriel had to agree with what he said: it was all true, he had done all those things. Just the same she'd try once more. 'When you come new to a village like this you have to tread carefully, so very carefully, and this is one instance when you could prove your good intentions by changing your mind. Like over the presidency of the cricket team, you stood down and it won you countless Brownie points. This is another case in point. Please say you'll change your mind. Once it's gone that will be the end of it. It's all the wildlife, you see, the plants and the birds and such, I've even seen wild violets growing in the shelter of that hedge. Could you think about them, please? They're all so precious.'

Mr Fitch glanced away from her pleading eyes and said, 'This might work with Ralph but not with me.' Sarcastically he added, 'After all *he* is a gentleman. You can't expect the same response from me.'

Mr Fitch's answer stung Muriel and left her with nothing more to say.

'I rather imagine from the look on your face he has pointed that out to you, so I'm amazed you should think I would be subject yet again to your particular brand of genteel persuasion.' He moved towards the door. 'You can tell everyone you meet that I am adamant that hedge is coming down. The fence will be in good taste, I assure you. Even I can manage that.'

The cold smile on his face made Muriel shudder. She picked up her handbag and left, finding her own way to the front door, having declined his offer to escort her. She wouldn't let the receptionist see her tears, but as soon as she was in the Tudor garden they did come, mostly brought on by the thought of that little wren losing his stamping ground and the wild rose being pulled up by its roots.

Well, he wasn't the only one who could be determined. Oh, no! She'd see Caroline tonight and report to her. By the time Muriel had reached the little gate in the church wall she had pulled herself together, stiffened her shoulders and determined she wouldn't tell Ralph what Mr Fitch had said about being a gentleman – well, about not being a gentleman. Which he wasn't, and couldn't be, but it needn't stop him from behaving well, now, need it?

'Well, my dear, how did you get on? Worked your charm on him as usual?'

'No. Nothing worked.' Muriel told Ralph everything they'd said except that bit about ... 'I can't help feeling that he is very hurt somehow. He's blaming it on people never being grateful, and he's right, they'd die first before admitting to being in his debt for what he does for the village, but I don't think that's the real reason. There's something else. However, I shall ask Caroline round tonight and we'll discuss tactics.'

Ralph smiled ruefully at her. 'I did tell you he wasn't a gentleman.'

Muriel blushed.

'He wasn't rude to you, was he?'

'No, of course not. No, he wasn't.'

Muriel went round to the Rectory that night to discuss strategy. When Caroline had rung to invite her she'd been told that Peter was out and could Muriel come to the Rectory. So she did.

They sat comfortably in the sitting room, with a bottle of wine between them.

'This seems awfully naughty for a business meeting, sharing a bottle of wine. I mustn't have more than two glasses or I shall not manage to get home. It tastes wonderful.'

'Why not? It might get the brain cells working.'

'Well, mine certainly need some stimulus. One gets very rusty if one is not careful. *University Challenge* defeats me completely nowadays.'

Caroline had to laugh. 'Really, Muriel! Come along then, tell me what happened.'

So Muriel did, and included the bit about him saying he wasn't a gentleman. 'I tried my hardest but had no success and am completely stumped about what to do next.'

'So am I.'

'I had thought Peter might have some ideas. He is on our side, isn't he?'

'Of course. More wine?'

'That will be sufficient for me. Thank you. Have you had a chance to discuss it with him?'

'No, I haven't. The only thing I can suggest is contacting the environment people. They'd advise, wouldn't they?'

Muriel clapped her hands. 'Oh, Caroline, of course. How sensible you are. Peter always admires your common sense and here it is again.'

'Neville Neal, now he's a councillor, isn't he on the environment committee?'

'I do believe he is. Of course. Yes. The very man. It doesn't affect his house but he's got to see things done right, hasn't he? Even if he isn't on that committee he could perhaps point us in the right direction.'

Caroline didn't appear to be paying attention. She was fiddling with her wine-glass, turning it round and round and round in an abstracted fashion.

'My dear, you seem ... not well.'

'Worried. You know.'

'Would it help to talk to me? I'm very discreet.'

Caroline half smiled at her. 'I know you are. It's Peter. He's gone.'

Muriel, appalled at her news, tried in vain to keep the shock from her face. 'For a little holiday, you mean.'

'Kind of. Just needed to get away.'

'I see.'

'It's me you see. Can't quite cope. Not since I made such a mess of things.'

'But you need him more than ever, then, surely?'

'He's been under a lot of strain.'

Muriel went to sit beside her on the sofa and put a tender hand on hers. 'Of course. Of course. He'll be back, my dear, believe me.'

'He has to come back because of the church, but ... I don't know ... Enough of my troubles. Will you see Neville or shall I?'

'I will. You've enough on your plate without all this.'

'I need to keep my mind occupied.'

Muriel stood up. 'I'll see him at the weekend then, and let you know. If you come up with any more bright ideas share them with me.'

'There's the conservation people too, of course.' Caroline made a fist and thumped it into her other hand with gusto. 'He's got to be stopped. I can't think what's got into him, he must have gone mad.'

'There's certainly something the matter, I know that.'

'I thought we'd do a leaflet and put it through people's doors, and posters for the trees and the noticeboards in the church hall and in the Store, in the Royal Oak and such. What do you think?'

'Oh, excellent! Of course. We make a good team, don't we?'

'We've got to move smartly. Knowing Mr Fitch he'll have the diggers in before we have a chance to protest.'

'I hadn't thought of that. He could, couldn't he?'

Caroline nodded. 'He will, without doubt.'

'Ralph knows someone who does posters. I'll get him on to it straight away.'

'We'll have to hold a protest meeting. I'll see Tom about that.'

'Of course.' Muriel put her hands to her temples and groaned. 'My head's in a whirl.'

Caroline laughed. 'I'm determined we'll win.'

'So am I.' Heading for the door Muriel turned back to say, 'You've got Sylvia on track again, I hear? That must be a help.'

'I have. Thank goodness. She's saved my life.'

'Good. Things will work out, I'm sure. He'll be back, you wait and see. Good night, my dear. God bless.' Muriel leaned forward and kissed Caroline's cheek.

As Muriel walked between the Rectory and her house she chanced to meet Neville Neal walking home with Liz.

'Hi, there, Lady Templeton! How are you?'

'Very troubled, Neville, and it's lucky that I've met you. Good evening, Liz. Have you heard about Mr Fitch insisting upon digging up the hedge round Rector's Meadow?'

'I heard a rumour.'

'Well, Caroline and I are organising some opposition and we thought, well, Caroline did, that as a councillor you might be able to point us in the right direction for mobilising some official support.' Muriel put her head on one side and smiled sweetly at him. In the fading light she thought she saw a momentary glimpse of guilt in his face but then he was saying, 'I'm afraid there's nothing we can do, Lady Templeton. Quite out of our hands. It is his hedge, you see.'

'Oh, I know that, but I would have thought . . .'

'He is putting up a fence which will be very sympathetic to the environment, not some ghastly white plastic picket fence so . . .'

'Oh I see. You know his plans then.'

Caught on the hop by this innocent-looking member of the aristocracy – and one mustn't forget that was exactly what she was and had Sir Ralph influence? By Jove, he had – Neville stuttered a little, and then said, 'Well, I did happen to meet him in the Conservative Club the other week and we were discussing it.'

'Ah! I see. I'm very sorry you can't help our campaign.'

'Campaign?' Neville appeared to shuffle a little uneasily.

'Oh, yes! Caroline and I are determined he shan't do this to our village. Whatever his reasons. We shall fight him every step of the way, and believe me, we mean it, so if you see him . . . by chance . . . in the Conservative Club you can tell him just that. I'll say goodnight then. Good night, Liz.'

'Good night!'

Muriel reported her evening's activities to Ralph, not forgetting to mention the look of guilt on Neville's face.

Ralph muttered with disgust, 'Our esteemed councillor is, to put it bluntly, a slimy toad.'

'Ralph!'

'I beg your pardon, my dear, but he is. There's something else behind this fence business which has yet to be revealed.'

'I shall bypass Neville and go straight to the fountain head.'

'Who is that?'

'I don't know but I shall soon find out and I shall unashamedly use my title to gain access to whichever pompous, self-satisfied council official can do the trick.'

'My word, Muriel Templeton on the warpath is someone to be reckoned with.'

'I hope you're not laughing at me, Ralph, because I am willing to do anything to stop that man from committing this terrible deed.'

'Anything?'

Muriel nodded and answered, with a firm nod of her head, 'Anything.' After a moment's pause she added, 'Within reason.'

4

On the first Monday morning that Tom and Willie were working together Willie made sure he got to the church five minutes early. But even that was not early enough, for Tom was already there sitting on the old wooden bench outside the boiler house drawing eagerly on a cigarette. He had on what looked like a new pair of overalls, bright orange with the words Constable Construction Company printed up each leg and in larger letters across the middle of the back. On his feet were a pair of steel-capped boots, in pristine condition. His unnaturally red hair was covered by a baseball cap, also bright orange with a logo of three capital Cs intertwined above the peak.

'Morning, Tom! I like punctuality! Like the outfit, pity about the cigarette. No smoking whatsoever anywhere on the premises. Church, church hall, churchyard. Nowhere at all. Insurance, yer know.'

'As you say, boss.' He heeled the butt into the soft ground at his feet and stood up. 'Nervous, you know. Sorry.'

'That's OK. So long as you remember. On Mondays I always get the logbook out and see what's what for the week. What bookings we've got, what grave to dig if need be, what gardening jobs there are an' that. It's the verger's Bible, as yer might say. That plastic box.' Willie pointed to the smart box lying on the bench.

Tom smiled and bent to pick it up. 'That's my lunch. Evie's out today so she made it up for me. My Evie always says –'

'Bring it with you into the vestry and leave it there. We'll have a brew up while we study what needs to be done this week. In the winter, with no grass to cut and no gardening to do, life gets a bit easier, but in the height of summer like now it's one body's work keeping everywhere looking smart.'

He unlocked the side door of the church and switched on the lights. 'And don't think for one minute that because the Rector's a gentleman he won't speak out if needs be. Right shaming he can be, if things aren't as they should be. Likes the churchyard looking neat, between every grave, all the paths, all the land not used yet, no weeds growing at the foot of the walls, no overturned urns or vases, no sunken gravestones. Well, that is except the very old ones, he doesn't mind those, says they've a right to topple a bit but anything less than two hundred years 'as to be straight, like soldiers on parade. He likes the bedding plants by the lych-gate to be well weeded and colourful in the summer. I can help out with that 'cos I always have plenty growing on in my greenhouse so don't be spending church money in garden centres ...'

Tom raised a hand to silence him. 'No need to worry about that. I grow plenty myself, and I've a good source for bulbs too. Don't you fret.' He tapped the side of his nose knowingly. 'Tom Nicholls knows a thing or two.' He laughed confidingly. 'I take two sugars in tea. Thanks.'

'Here you are then.' Willie handed him a mug of tea and pushed the sugar bowl across the table. He looked round the vestry for a moment, took a sip of his scalding hot tea and said, 'Every inch of the church has to be dead clean, every statue dusted – I'll show you the long-handled feather duster I 'ave for 'em – every inch of floor swept, every brass cleaned down each aisle, every tomb, every surface, the altar, the pulpit. You name it, you clean it or else he'll know.'

'The Rector or the Almighty?' Tom laughed, till he noticed Willie's disapproving face. 'Sorry. Didn't mean that.'

'It's not funny – well, to me it isn't. I've watched over this church for sixteen years and I shall be on the look-out every Sunday and any other time for lapses. And don't think I shan't notice 'cos I shall. It may not pay well but it's still to be done right and if you don't want to do it right, say so, and we'll put an end to it. I might be getting older but I'm not going blind and I'm not going daft either.'

'I know that. I'm just surprised you're taking early retirement.

Fifty-five's no age for retiring, not for a man with plenty of go in him.'

'You know full well I'm a lot more than fifty-five so save your flattery for them as appreciates it.' He turned to point to a padlocked cupboard. 'That's where we keep the cleaning materials. Brushes, cloths, disinfectants, polish. I polish all the woodwork once every two months. Between polishing yer dust. Carefully. When yer need more supplies the Rector has the petty cash and he needs receipts for everything. Everything, mind.'

'Of course, I wouldn't have it any other way. Show me some of the keys then.'

Willie pushed a heavy bunch of keys across the table. 'Each one's named. No problem there.'

Tom took it up and began to examine the keys. He queried some of Willie's shorthand on the varying tags and then asked what the heavy ornate key with no name was for.

'Ah! That's for the music cupboard. It's a spare just in case Gilbert Johns comes without his. I haven't named it 'cos I never use it.'

'Funny chap for a choir-master. Never seen him wear a coat even in the depth of winter, always looks half starved. Thin as a rail.'

'Thin he may be, but he's well looked after and he's a first-rate choir-master.'

'Never said he wasn't.'

'You don't touch that cupboard, he knows exactly what's in there and exactly where it is so don't go reorganising it for 'im.'

'I shan't. This one? What's it for?'

'That's the key to the safe.'

'Safe?'

'Don't kid on yer didn't know we had a safe. Everybody knows that. Rector bought it after we had the church silver stolen.'

'Stolen! Who the blazes would steal from a church?'

'A teenage girl, daughter of the licensee of the Royal Oak before Georgie. Poor girl. She met a grisly end, believe me.'

'Before my time, that. What happened to her then?'

'Stabbed straight through her innards with a carving knife trying to escape the police. A holy retribution.' Willie pointed skywards and nodded knowingly.

Tom shuddered theatrically and hastily put down the key. 'I shall need to know the combination, though.'

'There's two keys and they're both needed to open it. The Rector has the other. So both of yer have to be there.'

'Seems a big fuss for a few bits of silver.'

'Bits of silver! Few bits of silver! Don't let anyone hear you say that. The whole village got together to stop it all being sold. It's a long story but, believe me, that silver's precious to us all and you're not a true villager if you don't subscribe to that either. So watch your step.'

'Sorry! Sorry! I didn't realise.'

'It's not just its sale value it's its value to the village as a whole. We're very proud of it. Most churches have had to sell their silver to keep going but we have benefactors who make sure we don't need to. Like Mr Fitch at the Big House, and Sir Ralph too.'

'Of course. A real gentleman he is, is Sir Ralph. Got the common touch.'

'Indeed. Real aristocracy. Finished?' Tom nodded and Willie picked up his cup, opened the vestry door and threw the dregs out on to the grass. 'Not much on this week, it being almost August. We'll take a good look at the logbook and study it properly another day when I'll show you how to manoeuvre things to get the best out of the bookings. For now we'll go to the shed and get the gardening stuff out and get a move on while the weather holds.'

Almost too casually Willie thought, Tom asked him, 'The Rector's wife? Does she have much say in things?'

Willie looked at Tom and wondered what was behind the question. Somehow there seemed to be a reason he couldn't fathom behind everything Tom asked. 'The Rector's wife keeps a low profile. You've no need to worry about her.'

'Oh, I'm not worrying. Just wondering. Tales going about. Wish I'd been at the party after the play when old Don spilled the beans.'

Willie couldn't help but chuckle. 'I was and, believe me, it wasn't pretty. Never seen him drunk before. Teetotal all his life and then that exhibition. Yer could have laughed if it hadn't been so awful.'

'There was some truth in it, then? Her and that actor fella? It wasn't just the beer talking?'

'You know as much as me. Let's get on.'

'My Evie says . . .'

'With all due respect I don't give a damn what your Evie says, I'm being paid to work, so let's get on.'

Tom followed him out into the sun and meekly mowed and weeded all morning. Willie couldn't fault his application and he took orders and started the mower first time even though it was temperamental and sometimes took ten or more goes before it started, and altogether proved a willing pupil. When it got to lunchtime Tom sat on the bench ouside the boiler house and opened up Evie's tempting packed lunch saying a bright 'See yer later,' to Willie as he left for home.

Half-way through his lunch Willie heard the latch lift on the front door and Ralph calling out, 'With Peter being away, thought I'd call to see how things went today.'

'I'm in the sitting room.'

'Sorry to interrupt your lunch, I won't be a moment. I've seen Tom, had a word and he seems quite happy. Very appreciative of your help and advice.'

'He's quick to learn, I'll say that for 'im, and he's got the hang of the mower in no time at all. If he can keep his trap shut I think he'll do very nicely.'

'Keep his trap shut? He's got to ask questions.'

Wryly Willie answered that, yes, he had, that was quite true.

'You think he'll be satisfactory then?'

'Well, we've no choice, have we? But, yes, I think he will. I 'aven't had an opportunity to go through the book work with him, though.' Willie nodded at the window. 'Got to take my chance with this good weather and get the outside work done first. Bookings for the hall could be a different matter. Money an' that.'

'He's been in business for a long while, he should be *au fait* with accounts.'

'Yes, I expect he should.'

'Altogether then seven out of ten so far.'

Willie grinned. 'Hit the nail on the head as Tom would say.'

Ralph stood up to go. 'We could do with having a review of what we charge for letting the church hall. Whilst we don't want to appear greedy, we mustn't be running at a loss. Perhaps Tom would have some input about it.'

'I'm sure he will. We'll have to get the signwriter out to alter the board outside. Verger: Thomas Nicholls, Orchid House,' Willie sniffed derisively, 'Stocks Row, and his telephone number.'

'It'll be strange not having the name Biggs on the board. How long was your father verger?'

'Forty years almost to the day, I believe. So it's fifty-six years there's been a Biggs on that board. If I'd had a son he wouldn't have wanted a job like mine, he'd have been off into Culworth or London even. The young don't settle for jobs like mine nowadays.'

'But do they lead happier lives?'

'Ah!'

'I'll be off.'

The signwriter's arrival two weeks later was cause for comment in the bar that same night.

As he waited for his orange juice Don said, 'I see Willie Biggs has got his marching orders. Where is he by the way, Georgie?'

'On holiday in Torquay. That'll be eighty pence. Thanks, Don.'

Jimmy called out, 'Come over and sit with me, Don, I'm lonely without Willie and Sylvia and I never see hide nor hair of your Vera nowadays. How is she by the way?'

Don slid his plump backside on to the settle opposite Jimmy and took a drink of his orange like a man reaching an oasis after a long hard slog across a desert. 'It just fits the bill does this, sitting 'ere with an old friend in pleasant surroundings, drinking my favourite tipple. Six shifts a week I'm doing now – this is me only day off this week.'

'Yer should be taking it easier not working harder at your age.'

'Less of the "your age". A man's as young as he feels. But I have to say that night work is stopping soon once they've finished this big order. They're going to be cutting right back, so I shall be working eight till five, five days a week. Shan't know meself! I see the signwriter's made it official. Lord Tom's been installed.'

'Official. I can't fathom out why he wants it, 'im with his import-export lark, settling down to a two-bit job like verger.'

With a dead-pan face Don answered, 'Don't let Willie hear you say that. According to him the verger at St Thomas's is a mainstay of the Church of England. I have heard said the Archbishop consults him on theological matters from time to time.'

Jimmy looked at Don in surprise. 'Come on, Don, be careful, yer nearly made a joke. It does my blood pressure no good at all.'

'Did I? Perhaps I did. Grand chap is Tom. You can't 'elp but take to him. Right laugh when you get him going. He can't half tell some tales about the East End when he was a boy. Like another world.'

'That's just it, he doesn't fit just right, does he? What's the son of an East End barrow boy doing being verger in Turnham Malpas?'

'Come to that, what's Jimmy Glover Esquire, late poacher and ne'er-do-well, doing owning a taxi, eh? Jimmy?'

'Yer right.'

Gloomily Don reflected on his life. 'Come to think of it, what am I doing shifting for myself with no Vera? I wouldn't want you to think I'm missing her 'cos I'm not, I'm as happy as a sand-boy, and I don't want her back, not if she begged me. No arguing, no nagging, only one mouth to feed ... I tell you, there's a lot to be said for the single life.'

Jimmy stared into the distance. 'Not much from where I'm sitting, but then you've only been on your own a matter of weeks. Tell you what, you've lost weight and look better for it.'

Don looked down at the gap between his big stomach and the edge of the table. 'You could be right. By the way, they tell me Tom's put up the charges something ridiculous for the church hall. The Flower Club are, as Sheila Bissett put it, "outraged". Doubled, she says, but pay early and you get a discount.'

'Who says?'

'Tom. He's warning people before the notices go out.'

'Speak of the devil. He's just come in.'

Tom took off his tweed cap as he entered and waved it in general at whoever cared to acknowledge him. 'Evening, Jimmy, evening, Tom.' Jimmy, looking forward to a bit of sport at Tom's expense, called out, 'Come and sit with us, Tom. Two lonely bachelors, we're in need of cheering up.'

Tom chatted up Georgie while she got his order and then came across to them carrying a tray with his own lager and a drink each for Don and Jimmy.

'Here we are then, lads. Drinks all round. One thing, you don't cost much, Don. Orange juice!'

Don nodded his thanks. 'Evie not with yer?'

Tom took a sip of his lager after he'd toasted the two of them, placed his glass neatly on the beer mat in front of him and said, 'Evie doesn't take to life in a bar. She always says –'

'Nice woman, your Evie, you're lucky to have her.'

'I am. What about you then, Don? Not got Vera back yet?'

'There's no yet about it, she won't be back, and as I'm not going to live in that tarty flat of hers, that's how matters stand. Married all these years and she's marched off without so much as a backward glance. Women!'

'Nothing quite like a woman to cuddle up to on a cold night though. Evie always –'

'What's this about putting up the charges for hiring the church hall. Whose idea was it?' Jimmy asked, before Tom could tell them what Evie always did or said.

'The Rector's.'

'The Rector's! Doubling 'em! It doesn't sound like the Rector.'

Tom leaned across the table and tapped a thin finger on it several times. 'Do you know when the prices last went up? Five years ago. Time they were increased, with costs as they are.'

'But double!'

'Double. But discount for cash and early payment.'

'That doesn't sound like the Rector either.'

Tom had the grace to blush. 'No, that's Tom Nicholls bringing the church into the twenty-first century.'

Don sniggered. 'It's hardly into the twentieth century, never mind the twenty-first. Doesn't seem right somehow.'

Jimmy looked straight into Tom's eyes and said, 'Don't look now but Sheila Bissett's just come in with Ron. From the looks of her she's got the light of battle in her eyes. Too late, she's spotted yer. She's ordered Ron to get the drinks. 'Ope you've got some good reasons 'andy ... Yer going to need 'em.'

Tom stood up, the only one of the three to do so. 'Good evening, Sheila. Let me get you a chair.' He went to another table and asked permission to remove their spare chair. 'Here you are. I'll put it on this end where there's more room. Ron won't mind the settle, will he? Move up, young Don, make room for Ron. I'm a poet and didn't know it!' He beamed at Sheila, patted her shoulder and seated himself again.

She wagged her finger at him. 'I'm glad you're in here tonight, it gives me a chance to put my case. Don't think playing the gentleman will undo the harm you have done, because it won't.'

Tom looked shocked. '*Playing* the gentleman. I *am* a gentleman.'

Sheila snorted. 'You might appear to be one but how can you be when the moment you take charge the price of booking the hall doubles? I shall have to put up our membership fee for the Flower Club and it's going to be hard for some of them to find the money.'

'It isn't my responsibility, putting it up. The Rector came up with the idea and he's waiting for confirmation from the committee.'

Taken aback Sheila said, 'Oh, I see. The Rector.'

'So I'm not to blame. I'm only the poor geezer in the firing line.'

'Yes, but I bet it was you who sowed the seed. Yes, I can just see it, all comfy over a cuppa and . . . Thank you, Ron.'

Ron placed her drink in front of her and eased himself on to the settle beside Don. 'Evening, everyone.'

Jimmy greeted him with 'Your Sheila's getting stuck in about the charges for the hall.'

'I've told her it's only reasonable but she won't listen.'

'I do listen, Ron, I do, but I don't have to agree with you, do I?'

Tom said vehemently, 'The church can't afford to subsidise everybody.'

'No, but I bet you've had a hike in salary. I bet my bottom dollar you're getting more than Willie did.'

'Now, Sheila . . .'

'"Now, Sheila" nothing, Ron, I bet he is. Go on, deny it.'

Tom spilt his drink and made a bother of wiping his jacket and the pool of lager on the table. 'Just look at that. What a mess. Evie will have something to say about this. "Just back from the cleaners," she'll say. I'll get a cloth from Georgie.' He got up and went to the bar, leaving Jimmy and Don laughing quietly.

Ron said, 'You nearly nailed 'im there, Sheila, but he's too quick even for you.'

'I'm right, though, aren't I? Otherwise he'd have denied it.'

Tom came back and made a fuss of wiping up the lager. 'How clumsy of me, what a mess! Evie says I'm –'

'Never mind, don't make such a fuss. I jogged yer elbow, didn't I?' Jimmy said slyly.

'You didn't do it on purpose, though, did you?'

'Oh, no.'

'Well, then.' Tom took the cloth back to Georgie and stopped for a chat. 'Where's Dicky tonight?'

'Everyone knows and so should you. It's Scout night.'

'Of course! Grand job he does, you know. A grand job. The two of you no nearer being able to marry?'

'No. We still haven't tracked down that husband of mine. He's probably dancing the night away under some southern sun with that disgusting Electra clinging to him. If only he knew the heartache he's causing.'

Tom placed a sympathetic hand on hers as it rested on the bar. 'Never mind, one day he'll turn up and you'll be able to get him sorted out. Dicky's the sort of chap who's worth waiting for. And wait he will, with you as his prize.'

Georgie blushed. 'Now, Tom!'

'In fact if I wasn't well and truly married I'd be elbowing him out!'

'Would you indeed!'

'I would! You're a gorgeous woman, Georgie. A fitting tribute to womanhood!'

'Get away!'

Tom laughed and went back to his table. While he'd been away the others had been silent.

On Tom's return Jimmy said, 'Now Willie Biggs isn't verger I'm hoping for some inside information from you. Never uttered a word about any secrets he learned as verger, played his cards too close to his chest for my liking. People, including himself, got married on the quiet and he never let slip a word. At funerals, and we all know the bother they can cause, all sorts 'appened and he never let on.'

'What can happen at a funeral, for goodness' sake?' Tom asked.

'Well, there was a funeral once and the deceased's bit on the side turned up looking really dramatic, in black, with a black veil over

her face and shoulders, and there was a terrible row and almost a
fight at the graveside when she tried to take her turn throwing soil
on the coffin like yer do. Willie never let on, never told us a word.
Another time someone stood at the graveside and fell in as the
Rector was praying, sprawled dead drunk on top of the coffin he
was. You should have heard the screams. He went spark out and
they had to hold everything up till they'd managed to haul him out.
'Nother time the wrong person got buried in the wrong grave.
Right dust-up that was. They'ad to dig 'em up and rebury 'em.
That was before this Rector's time too. All that 'appening and
Willie never let on.'

'Sounds as if I shall be having an interesting time.'

'We shall gather here on a night waiting for any snippets of
gossip.' Jimmy winked at Don who, keeping a poker face and quite
unable to see what was funny in Jimmy's stories, said, 'Remember
that time when the Rector, this one, that is, was conducting a
wedding? Great big do it was with a carriage and horses for the
bride and groom and the church full and a big reception at the
George in Culworth. Top 'at and tails. Church bells ringing. You
name it, money no object, and when the Rector got to the bit about
any just impediment why these two should not be joined in
matrimony someone stood up at the back and shouted, "I'm the
impediment, me and my four kids," and she turned out to be the
bridegroom's first wife and they weren't divorced. She marched the
kids down the aisle and presented 'em to the hopeful bride. "Now",
she said, "what are you going to do about this lot?" The father
caught the bride just as she fainted. They'ad to call an ambulance
for the bride's mother. Had a heart-attack she did, right there in
the front pew. 'Bout six months ago it was, maybe a year.'

Jimmy drew a little closer to Tom and whispered, 'For a start
what do you know about the Rector?'

'Being on holiday, you mean?'

Jimmy scoffed at Tom's comment. 'Holiday! Holiday! That's a
laugh. You see? You've started being secretive already and you've
not been in the job scarcely a month.'

'Honestly! God's truth, that's all I know.'

'Is it indeed! You know and I know and we all know he's left
home.'

'Never! No, no, he's not. He's taking a break.'

'Well, keep your ears and eyes open and let us know. He's our Rector and we've a right to know what's going on, and we can't ask Sylvia 'cos she'd die first before tell us.'

'He went unexpected, I can say that.'

'Exactly! Usually he has it all planned out, meetings postponed, clergy from Culworth to take the services, and that, but not this time. So don't you keep your mouth buttoned like Willie did. *We want to know.*'

'I have promised not to divulge –'

'Well, I 'ope yer 'ad your fingers crossed behind your back.' Jimmy looked him straight in the eye. 'Nothing, and I repeat *nothing*, goes on in this village without someone finding out. Eventually. That includes any tales about you, Tom Nicholls, and any tales about anyone at all, so you might as well tell all as not. Got the message?'

5

Muriel Templeton had come to the conclusion that cleaning the church brass on alternate weeks was therapeutic not only for Muriel herself but for whoever happened to be in the church at the time. It so often happened that as she polished she met someone in there who needed to talk. She'd counselled Louise Bissett when she'd had that dreadful time falling in love with the Rector, she'd talked with Venetia when she'd been unfaithful to Jeremy. Though as it turned out they weren't even married so could one be unfaithful if one wasn't, and should one be living as though married in the first place when one was not? Morals nowadays had become so confusing: perhaps they were best left to the people themselves to square it with their own consciences, if they had any, that is.

From the understairs cupboard she got out her neat wooden box, which Ralph had made especially for her; she loved the old dark wood he'd made it from and best of all the curved handle to hold it by. Before leaving the house she checked she had all she needed. Spotlessly clean yellow dusters, her pieces of old towel cut into neat squares for putting on the polish, the old toothbrush for the wiggly corners the duster couldn't reach into, her household gloves to protect her hands, yes, they were all there.

As Muriel was about to shut the front door she remembered. The brass polish! How silly could she get? The new tin stood on the kitchen worktop. She went back in, picked it up and put it in her box, but not before she'd taken a glance around her kitchen and admired it for the umpteenth time. Despite Ralph's opposition she'd been right to insist on this deep gold colour for the walls above the tiling. It gave that added warmth and provided a good background for those icon things she'd bought at the craft fair. Artistically they deserved only four out of ten but she loved them. Muriel paused to recollect where Ralph was. Good heavens, he was in the study and she hadn't told him she was going out.

Muriel opened the door and said, 'I'm going now, Ralph dear, back for lunch. Don't work too hard.'

Ralph looked up from the post he was opening. Muriel's heart flipped. He was so good-looking. How did he manage to keep his looks? Those frank, intelligent dark brown eyes, that proud forehead, the snow-white well-barbered hair, and that aristocratic nose! She wondered sometimes if that was the real reason she'd married him: her attraction to his arrestingly handsome nose combined as it was with his well-tanned fresh complexion.

'Enjoy!'

It was his voice too. So deep but not rumblingly deep, and his top-drawer accent, now that really could set her heart-strings vibrating and no mistake. Muriel rushed across the study carpet on winged feet and planted a kiss on his cheek.

Ralph laid his hand on hers as she rested it on his desk. 'My dear!'

'I love you so. So very much!' She gave him another kiss on the top of his head and fled. Having slammed the front door behind her she found she'd left the brass-cleaning box on the hall chair and had to go back in to pick it up. After such a disastrous start would she ever get the brass cleaned?

This morning she decided she would begin with the cross on the altar. She spread a clean duster on an altar chair and stood on it so she could reach. Now which hymn should she hum while she polished? 'Jesus Wants Me for a Sunbeam'? The rhythm fitted just right. As she hummed she paused to wonder how long the cross had been standing on the altar. One of her favourite phrases was 'time immemorial' but she didn't think that applied to the cross, not like it did to the tombs, especially the Templeton tomb at the back of the church, or the stone flags of the church floor or the old uncomfortable pews. No, she rather felt it was much younger than that.

Having brought the cross to a fine high glow Muriel stepped

down from the chair and stood back to judge if she was satisfied. Yes, she was. Now for the lectern. She replaced the chair, removing the duster from its tapestry seat and carried the box to the lectern. This eagle holding the Bible she had never really liked, she watched birds-of-prey programmes on the television and tried hard to like eagles but she couldn't. Nevertheless it had to be cleaned. The eagle's beak was slightly open and she had to be careful not to leave brass polish in it. Muriel turned to pick up the toothbrush and heard a sound. It wasn't the sound of the heavy outside door opening nor the sound of a footstep, just the old building creaking. She expected she'd creak too if she was as old. The wind under the tiles perhaps. Or Willie in the vestry. Oh! but it wasn't Willie now, was it? It was Tom. At the thought of his name Muriel smiled. He really was a delightful man. Rough diamond, true, but always so polite and considerate and very amusing.

Just as she had grudgingly polished the eagle's outspread wings and attended to his feet Muriel heard the noise again. A rustling kind of noise. Not mice. Oh, no! Not that! She stopped to listen. There it was again. 'Tom! Is that you? Tom!' But there was no reply. The sound stopped. Muriel gave herself a talking-to. 'Get on with the job, Muriel, and don't be so pathetic. If Ralph had been here you wouldn't even have noticed there was a sound.'

Now for the brass plates on the altar: one depicting the risen Christ, the other His ascension into heaven. She noticed that there was old brass polish in the folds and creases of the moulding of the plates. Oh dear! Sheila Bissett had slipped up last week. Working away, absorbed in thought, Muriel missed the second spate of creaking and rustling but not the third: this time they were so loud they made her jump. She dropped the tin of brass polish and a great splash of it ran down the side of the altar. It trickled steadily down the oak wood like a great putty-coloured tear. Quickly Muriel grabbed a duster and rubbed it away. Concerned about staining the wood she rubbed furiously and didn't notice until she'd finished that it was her polishing cloth she was using and not the putting-on cloth.

'Oh, no. Now, what a mess I've made! My lovely yellow duster all smeared and horrid. What a nuisance.'

There came a creak and muffled rustlings and all thoughts of the ruined duster went from Muriel's mind. 'Now, see here! Who is it? Is it you, Tom? Tom!'

But the only reply was the familiar deep silence of the church.

I really must pull myself together. I'll finish the polishing then straight away I'll find Tom and tell him. It must be mice. Those scamps of angelic choir-boys will have left crisps and things in some corner and a mouse has crept in and decided to make a home in here. That'll be it. If I get Tom to put out traps, by the time it's my turn again to polish they should be caught and the traps gone, then I shan't come across them by mistake.

Muriel put 'risen' and 'ascension' back on the altar and then she went to the rear of the church to polish the brass decoration on the font. She loved the stone bits of the font and the two angels which decorated it, but the Victorian addition of the brass with its pompous inscription rather annoyed her, but who was she to ... there was that noise again but this time much closer. Then there came a loud bang, as though something had been dropped. From the Templeton tomb not three yards from where she stood.

Her flesh crept, goose pimples rose on her skin, her scalp prickled and her knees went to jelly.

The church was ice cold and so too was she.

Her hands chilled to the marrow. And trembling.

Her mouth bone dry.

The silence now was almost worse than the noise.

Who moved and then didn't?

Who wouldn't reply to her calls?

Was it haunted like Willie had always said?

But one of Ralph's ancestors? Surely not.

Her ears caught a slight scratching sound.

Dear God!

Muriel lifted the heavy handle of the main door and escaped out into the sunshine, running, running for the safety of Ralph and his sane no-nonsense world.

She croaked, 'Ralph! Oh, Ralph!' as she shut her front door behind her.

Startled, Ralph stood up and went out into the hall to find Muriel sitting on the chair, breathless, speechless and shaking.

'My dear! Whatever is it?'

Muriel tried to speak but couldn't.

Ralph put his arms about her, and hugged her. 'You're safe now, my dear, but whatever's happened? Tell me!'

Muriel pointed to her mouth.

'Glass of water?'

She nodded.

She drank half the water and then gave a great shudder.

'Tell me, Muriel. *Please!*'

'Oh, Ralph! I've been so frightened.'

'By whom?'

Muriel shook her head. 'By mice. It must be. But they couldn't make a big bang, could they?'

'You're not making sense.'

She explained what had happened, ending with 'And I've left all my polishing stuff there and I've got to go back to get it and I daren't.'

Ralph said, 'We'll both go. The two of us. If it's mice, well, Tom will have to do something about it.'

'If it's not?'

'Well, if it's not . . . it could be a tramp gone in there for the night out of the rain. Or . . . Muriel's vivid imagination?' He looked gently into her face and she felt both foolish and indignant.

'I'm not in my dotage, Ralph. I heard those noises. I'll finish this water and then we'll go and we'll sit quietly in a pew by the tomb and we'll listen together. If you'll hold my hand that is and I put my feet up on a hassock just in case.'

'Gladly.'

Ralph pushed open the heavy door and there was Tom in his bright orange overalls busy dusting round the heads of the statues with Willie's special long-handled feather duster. Everything so ordinary and commonplace it was alarming in itself.

'Good morning, Sir Ralph, Lady Templeton! Lovely morning. If you're wanting a quiet moment I can come back later.'

Tom's cheerful greeting flinging her pell-mell back into normality somehow worsened Muriel's fear. Ralph, clasping her hand firmly in his, found she'd started trembling again. 'That's all right,

Tom, you carry on. We've come for Muriel's brass-polishing box. She thinks she left it by the font.'

'She did. I've put everything back in it, Lady Templeton. You'd dropped it.' Tom sounded slightly puzzled but was too polite to ask why she'd obviously run away in haste. He went up to the font, picked up her box and took it across to her. 'There we are. If you feel it's getting more than you can fit in I'll gladly take over and do the polishing myself.' Tom's smile was so kind, Muriel felt quite restored.

'That's very kind of you, Tom, but I do enjoy my polishing. There's not much I can do for the church but this is something within my capabilities and I should hate to give it up. Thank you all the same.'

'That's fine.'

'Have you been in here all the morning?'

'No, I came in about five minutes ago. Before that I was clearing the weeds away from the old gate at the back that leads to the Big House.' He went to the main door and opened it for them.

Ralph carried the box in one hand and held Muriel's hand with the other. She was gripping his fingers so tightly he had no circulation in them.

When they were safely out on the path she whispered, 'I wish he wouldn't wear those orange overalls. They make him look like some kind of malevolent insect, made huge by a mad scientist in a laboratory somewhere and released to take over the world. Do you think there are more of them?'

'Muriel!'

'It's true, they do. But you see I *was* in there by myself and I did hear those noises, but we couldn't very well sit there to listen for them with Tom working, could we?'

'No. Are you sure you heard noises?'

'You have never doubted my word before, Ralph, so why do you doubt it now?'

'I'm sorry, my dear. I'll go back and ask Tom to put down some traps just in case. We have had mice in before, some years ago, so you could be right.'

'Thank you. I'll go home and get the lunch.'

*

Muriel went into the Village Store after lunch to collect the video of *Shakespeare in Love* which Jimbo had ordered especially for her.

'Jimbo rang me yesterday and said it was in, Bel.'

'Right, Lady Templeton. I expect he's put it in the back office. I won't be a moment.' Bel trotted away into the back, leaving Muriel with Linda behind the Post Office grille doing her accounts and Sheila Bissett occupied with choosing a birthday card.

'Good afternoon, Sheila.'

'Good afternoon, Muriel. I was hoping to see you. Is it possible you could do my brass cleaning next week and I'll do the next two weeks instead? Ronald is going up to London for a few days to some union meetings and I'd love to go with him, shopping and things, you know.'

Somewhat disconcerted, Muriel hesitated before she replied. Sheila, who easily took offence, said, 'If it's not convenient . . .'

'It's not that. I've been polishing today and I was sure I heard mice in the church moving about, you know, and I hate mice or . . . rats and such and I've not really got over it.' She trembled again at the thought. 'But I'll get Ralph to sit with me and read or something just in case. Tom's going to put traps down and I hate them too, but there's no other way is there?'

Sheila drew her confidentially to one side. 'I don't think he's doing all that good a job, actually.'

'You don't?'

'Night before last the lights were left on in the church. I got up to make a cup of camomile tea because I couldn't sleep and while I waited for the kettle to boil I looked out of the window and the lights were on. Some of them, not all. And if we've got mice in then . . .' She shook her head as though despairing of Tom. 'I can see straight across the green down Jacks Lane between the school and the old oak and there was no doubt about it. Lights had been left on. And obviously, if there's mice, he's not cleaning properly, is he?'

Muriel, hating to agree with her for really she liked Tom, replied, 'I wouldn't go as far as to say that . . .'

'Willie was much more conscientious. However, if you are able I would be grateful.'

'You can rely on me.'

Muriel realised that Bel was patiently waiting for her, 'Oh, thank you. I paid when I ordered it.'

'That's right, that's what it says. Is it good then?'

'Oh, yes. We missed it when it went the rounds of the cinemas and I did want to see it.'

Sheila joined in with 'You've missed the last two Flower Club meetings too. We need all the people we can get now the hire charge for the room is going up.'

'I know, we just seem to have been so very busy lately, but I will make an effort.'

'It's that Tom. It's all his fault the charges going up. Bring back Willie, I say.'

'I understand it was the Rector who broached the idea first.'

'Spurred on by Tom, I've no doubt, and he's got more salary than Willie got.'

Somewhat primly Muriel said, 'We don't know that.'

'I do.'

'Well, then, Sheila, I'll do next week and you can do the next two weeks and then we shall be straight again. That right?'

'Fine. Everywhere I look there's posters about the protest meeting. Very stylishly done and very eyecatching. Who's made them for you?'

'A friend of Ralph's. Will you be there? We're very keen to get everyone on our side. Almost everyone I speak to is sympathetic to our campaign, except for ...'

'I know, except for Grandmama Charter Plackett. I think she's the only one on his side. But I'll do my best to drum up support wherever I go. I'm so glad Caroline is at the forefront of it all. She carries such weight with her opinions. Do her good too. She's never looked the same since ...'

Muriel hastily diverted Sheila from saying any more. The Village Store was not the place to air one's views about anything, least of all about the upset at the Rectory.

'Thank you, Sheila, I shall be glad of your support, and Sir Ronald's if he can see his way.'

'He won't dare to do any other than support you once I've had a word with him,' she patted Muriel's arm, 'and don't worry about the mice, I'm sure they'll have been caught by next week.'

*

283

Muriel debated about taking Ralph with her the following week when she went to clean the brass. In fact she even thought about not going at all. Was it perhaps a little excessive to clean it every week? Perhaps every other week would be sufficient? But Muriel recognised the coward in herself and brushed her weakness aside. The Christian martyrs had had far worse things to face than a few mice and she, Muriel Euphemia Templeton, was not one for weakness. No, she'd go all by herself and face the music.

There was a chance Tom had already caught the little horrors. She'd find him and casually introduce the subject. What she didn't want to happen was to come across a decapitated mouse still in a trap awaiting Tom's ministrations. Maybe even with the cheese still in its mouth. Or did the trap smack shut before it had actually – No, she wouldn't think about that.

Tom was getting rid of the cobwebs on the underside of the lych-gate. 'Good morning, Lady Templeton, overcast today, isn't it? I've never seen so many cobwebs as this in my life. It must be a real good summer for spiders.' He stood in her way energetically brushing with a soft, long-handled brush. 'They're sticky, you know.'

Muriel kept well out of the way of any spiders running from Tom's murderous intentions. 'Tom. Talking of spiders, have you caught any mice?'

Tom, hands behind his back, crossed his fingers. 'Two the first night. None since, so I reckon we've got the all-clear.'

Muriel put a hand to her heart and said, 'Oh, I'm so relieved. I was dreading ... I know you'll think I'm silly but ...'

'Not at all. I see you've got your brass box with you. I wouldn't go in just yet, I've been spraying in the church for spiders too. Best let the air get clear a bit first. Not good for the lungs.' He held up a spray can with evil pictures of spiders and ants on it. 'Brilliant stuff this, if you have any problems, but very potent for the breathing. Stand clear, I'm using it on here now.'

Muriel stood away and watched him squirting the spray on the old beams. He stood on the seat at one side and sprayed right into the corners, and then stood on the opposite seat and did the same. Tom appeared to Muriel to over-egg the pudding a little but she supposed there was no point in doing it at all if one didn't do it well. A waft of the spray reached her and she waved it away. It was certainly potent. She'd better not go in the church for a while.

'I'll sit on the seat by the old oak and wait ten minutes.' Muriel planted her box beside her and set herself to wait. She checked her watch because she was never any good at guessing the passing of time. Twenty minutes to eleven. Right! Seated there Muriel looked like an elderly lady taking a nap, but she didn't feel elderly and she most certainly wasn't taking a nap. She was admiring the old church and thinking how lucky they all were to have one kept so beautifully. Tom had gone round to the side door, and out of it, through half-closed eyes, she saw Kenny Jones emerge.

The sight was so startling! She couldn't believe what she saw. Kenny Jones coming out of church! It was such a shock to her, but it didn't appear to be a shock to Tom for they were talking quite amicably. Tom took his cap off and scratched his red hair, Kenny wagged a finger at him and then waved goodbye and came down the side of the church, wearing his old navy anorak, which Muriel knew would tell a rare old tale if it could speak. Wearing an anorak on such a humid day.

If Muriel wasn't mistaken he glanced round as he came out into the open as though looking for someone, or was he checking no one was watching? Well, that was understandable: considering how many years it was since he'd been in there he'd surely be embarrassed for anyone to see him. Muriel guessed that the last time Kenny had visited the church was when he was at the village school, and that must be at least twenty years ago.

Kenny marched briskly down the church path. Muriel pretended to be asleep. As she heard the lych-gate creak shut she opened her eyes just a slit and through the veil of her eyelashes glimpsed him marching towards Jacks Lane to go past the school, down Shepherds Hill and home.

When her ten minutes were up Muriel wended her way up the path and into church. It was only when she was applying the brass polish to the wings of the lectern eagle that it occurred to her that Kenny Jones hadn't given a thought to his lungs being affected by Tom's spider spray. She hoped he'd be all right.

6

'You there, Mum?' Kenny pushed open the house door, shutting it at the same time as hanging his anorak behind it, all in one swift practised movement.

She was sitting in her chair, head down, crying.

'What's up?'

Mrs Jones endeavoured to make herself look as though crying was the last thing on her agenda but she wasn't successful.

'What yer crying for?'

'Yer dad's just rung. He's lost his job. Finishes end of the week.' She sniffed loudly and wiped her eyes again.

'Aw! Mum! How's that come about?'

'Council put the road-maintenance work out to tender, company from the other side of Culworth has won it and they don't want him. Too old, they say. He can shovel with the rest of 'em, it isn't fair. I don't know whatever we're going to do. He'll never get another job at his age. Oh, Kenny.'

Kenny lay down on the sofa, not knowing how to cope with a mother he'd never ever in all his life seen crying. 'Something 'ull turn up.'

Mrs Jones snapped out in her distress, 'Don't be bloody daft, nothing will. All we'll have coming in will be my money from the Store. We can't manage.'

'There's our Terry's wages.'

'And how much do I see of that? Tell me. Go on. Tell me.'

'Nothing.'

'Exactly. Well, things will have to change.'

'They will?'

286

Mrs Jones' head came up and she looked him straight in the eye. 'For a start ...'

'Any tea going? And I wouldn't mind a sandwich.'

'No, Kenny. You're collecting the social every week and what does your mother see of that? Zilch! It's supposed to be for you to live on. So by my reckoning that means paying for your food and laundry and the roof over your head. I'm keeping you no longer. In fact, I can't no more, neither you nor our Terry.'

'Just as you like, but when I come into money –'

'You come into money! And pigs might fly! You'll have to move out. Get your own pad.'

Kenny pretended to be shocked. 'Mum! How can you say that to your little boy? Your little boy who's –'

'Who's been a pain in the whatsit since the day he was born.'

'Mum!'

'I mean it, Kenny. Why should your dad and me keep you, a grown man? Just get a real job, please! Either that or you're out. Full stop! The estate's always wanting help of one sort and another. Our Barry 'ud put in a good word. Ask him.'

Kenny lifted his feet from the sofa arm and sat himself up. His keen brown eyes looked at his mother's back. 'Don't, and I mean don't ever suggest again that I should work for that old faggot Fitch. Our Barry can kow-tow to 'im if he wants, but not me. I'm made of different stuff.'

'You're right, very different. He's got a nice wife and family, a nice house, a steady job, money coming in regular, you name it.'

Kenny sneered at the prospect. 'Who wants a life like his? Boring. Boring. Boring. Coming home covered in sawdust and smelling of glue with thick fingers and swollen hands from working outside. Not even the kids are his own.'

'Only because they both felt they were too old to start another family, that's all. Families cost money and with Pat having two already ...'

'There's one thing, though. I know for a fact I'm firing on all cylinders don't I? He doesn't.'

'Don't bring that up. Two children you don't own up to, and I can't acknowledge. Not a single real Jones grandchild. It's not right.'

'There's always our Terry.'

'Fat chance.'

'You're hard, you are. Not long since you'd have given me your last ha'penny.'

'I've seen the light.'

Mrs Jones turned to switch on the iron and while it heated up she looked at him. Her three boys had been the joy of her life for years, she'd defended them against all the odds, no matter what they did, and sometimes done it against her better judgement for their sakes, but she'd finally run out of steam. She didn't know who was worst, their Terry or him laid on the sofa, idle as they come. If it wasn't for her job doing the mail order at the Store they'd all have been in the cart. Vince had always done his best, but labouring on the roads wasn't exactly the sort of job that brought the money rolling in.

'If you had some money you and Terry could rent from Sir Ralph. One of his houses is coming up empty. That would be nice.'

Kenny ignored her remark. He knew better than to latch on to an idea like that: before he knew it she'd have him and their Terry installed and then where would they be? No meals cooked, no shopping done, no shirts ironed, no clean sheets, and if there was one thing he approved of it was clean sheets on a regular basis. There was nothing quite like sliding into bed with the sheets all fresh and smelling nice and feeling smooth and sexy. In fact it could be said it was one of Kenny Jones' passions. The word passions brought on a daydream about the barmaid at the Jug and Bottle in Penny Fawcett, and his mother's next words simply fell on deaf ears.

'However, from now on, no money, no food. Two weeks of that and if there's still no sign of money you're out. Lock, stock and barrel. Including your air-guns and all that exercise paraphernalia you bought last time you were in the money. I've dusted round it for two whole years and now that's it, it's going, and you with it, and our Terry. I've finally reached the end of my tether after all these years. You've been conspicuous by your absence this morning, where've you been?'

Kenny didn't answer; he'd just remembered the feeling of getting the barmaid up against the counter in the empty lounge bar and was about to kiss her luscious tempting lips to see if she was as good as their Terry had claimed. You don't answer daft questions like that from your mother when you're occupied like that.

His mother pursued her theme. 'I'll ask about it tomorrow.'

'Ask what?'

'Ask Lady Templeton about the house coming up. See what the rent is.'

Kenny's daydream was replaced by the picture of Muriel sitting nodding on the new seat the parish council had had constructed round the foot of the oak on the Green. Daft old thing she was. None dafter.

A big stumbling block to the scheme sprang into his mind. 'We've no furniture for it.'

'Oh, God! Yes. Ah! but I've just had a thought. They're having a right turn-out at the nursing home where Vera works. I could have a word. Good stuff being thrown out, I understand. I'll ask.'

Kenny cackled. 'Your friend Vera! After what you did to her she'd be more likely to choke yer than give yer furniture. No, sorry, Mum, that little scheme isn't going to come off.' He lay back on the sofa smiling a self-satisfied smile as only Kenny could.

His mother, enraged at the memory of how close Vera had come to going to prison over the stolen paving stones because of her and more so at his disregard of her terrible dilemma, suddenly retaliated. She clenched her fists and began beating him about the head and shoulders. He put up his arms to protect his head as the blows rained down on him. His mother's face so close and so venomous turned him into a child again and he feared her. 'Hey! Mum! Don't! Don't! Please don't!'

'I'll give you don't! Get a job! Go on! Get a job! I'm sick to death of yer. Sick to death!' Her energy drained, she flopped on to the sofa Kenny had vacated and wept again.

Restored to adulthood now she'd stopped beating him, Kenny turned away from her so she couldn't see what he was doing and extricated a thick wad of notes from his back pocket. Peeling off five twenty-pound notes he rammed the rest back into his pocket and turned to give her the hundred pounds.

'All right, Mum. Stop the yelping. Here, take this towards the housekeeping.'

Mrs Jones, silenced by the shock of what he'd said, looked at the money in astonishment. 'Why, Kenny! How much is that?'

'Hundred pounds. Now can I have a sandwich?'

Alerted by his nonchalance Mrs Jones asked, 'Just where did you get that from?'

Kenny tapped the end of his nose. 'Ask no questions . . .'

'Well, thanks very much. It's not left you short, has it?'

He used up another of his guises and played the part of the martyr. 'Don't you worry about me, I can manage, I don't need much to live on.'

'But where did you get it?'

'Business deal, with a chap in the market in Culworth. Owed me a favour.'

'Oh! Right. It's not illegal, is it, Kenny? I wouldn't want you to get into trouble just because we're desperate.'

'As if I'd be so daft. Come on, Mum. Use your brains. Kenny Jones in trouble? Huh! I'm not stupid. Not a word to our Terry that you're flush.'

'No, of course not.' She tucked the money into the pocket of her apron and went into the kitchen to make him a sandwich. Kenny lay on the sofa again, berating himself for allowing her to dominate him like she'd done when he was a kid. There'd be no end to her demands now she knew he had money. Might be better if he did move out. In fact after his sandwich he'd get the car started and go see the Templetons himself about the house.

After half an hour messing about with jump leads and with the help of their Terrry's old banger, Kenny eventually got the car started and drove off up Shepherds Hill into the village.

Yes, Sir Ralph was at home and, yes, of course he could see him, do come in. He followed Lady Templeton into their sitting room and there sat Sir Ralph in an imposing winged armchair, *The Times* open on his knee, his gold-rimmed reading glasses in his hand, wearing a smart checked suit, gleaming brown shoes and a welcoming smile on his face.

'Come in do, Kenny. Long time since I saw you. What are you getting up to nowadays?'

'This and that, Sir Ralph, this and that.'

'Me too. This and that. What can I do for you?'

'I've heard you've a cottage in Hipkin Gardens coming free. I wondered if I could, well, me and our Terry, could rent it from you?'

'Have I? I didn't know.'

Kenny, surprised that a property owner was so disinterested in money as not to know, patiently explained. 'Yes, it's the Nightingale's cowman at number seven, he's been dismissed and he's got a job somewhere in Devon so he's off. Next week. So Mum says anyway.'

'He didn't tell me. If it's true, which I expect it is, I have to say I am very particular about my tenants. I won't have unreliable people. I won't tolerate tenants who neglect or abuse the cottages and the lease is for six months in the first instance and if I'm not satisfied then it's out. I mean that, Kenny. I'll ring my agent, if you'll excuse me, and ask him what he knows.'

While Sir Ralph went to his study to use the telephone Kenny looked around the room. This was just the sort of décor he'd like in his house. Mellow, friendly, welcoming, quality. Yes, that was it. The key was quality. Not a thing in poor taste. He quickly leaped to his feet and tried out Sir Ralph's chair. The suppleness of the leather upholstery was stunning. Your hands wanted to stroke it, to enjoy the lovely expensive pliable stuff, to caress it almost. Oh, yes! This fitted the bill all right! Kenny sat back enjoying the comfort and the sensation of importance the chair gave him. This was what he lacked, possessions which gave him prestige. No wonder Sir Ralph could be the sort of person he was: sitting in this chair would without doubt bolster his feeling of authority. Kenny felt envy trickling along his veins. One day! One day! A chair like this could be his. He leaped up at the sound of the study door opening and was seated back in his original chair before Sir Ralph had set foot in the sitting room.

'You're right, Kenny. He is going and the agent hasn't got a tenant in view as yet.' He seated himself back in his chair. 'But what about money? I don't usually have anyone who can't provide references from their employer. Why should I make an exception for you?'

'I'm self-employed, Sir Ralph, sir.' A bit of deference never did anyone any harm and what's more it cost nothing. 'I can give three months' rent in advance if you prefer.'

'Self-employed doing what, might I ask?'

'Like we both said, this and that. But I'm on to a good thing at the moment and there's no likelihood of the market drying up. In fact I'm well pleased with how things are going.' He delved into his back pocket and hauled out the thick wad of notes, which looked not at all depleted by his gift of one hundred pounds to his mother. He loved the action of peeling notes off a wad with his thumb. So he did it rather slowly and dramatically but with a carelessness meant to signify it was all nothing to him. He'd reached the fifty-pound notes now, peeled off twelve of them and swaggered across to give them to Sir Ralph.

He shook his head. 'I haven't said yes yet and I don't touch the money. That's for my agent to deal with.'

Kenny could have kicked himself. Of course, Sir Ralph wouldn't be touching *money*, not he. The first he knew about it would be when it arrived in his bank statement. That was what being a gentleman was, if indeed he ever bothered to look at his bank statements. Kenny put his money away in his pocket and found himself apologising.

'Please don't apologise. Your gesture has reassured me that you do have money, for now. So, seeing as you're a village person born and bred, I'll let you rent it for six months. After that if you wish to stay longer, then you can, subject to how you have behaved yourself in the meantime. Is that agreeable?'

Kenny nodded.

'Nothing is confirmed until you've seen the agent, paid the first two months' rent, or more if you wish, and you've signed the contract.'

Remembering his new status as a businessman Kenny asked, 'If I pay for six months all at once do I get a discount?' The moment the words were out of his mouth he knew he shouldn't have asked. He realised by the look of disapproval on Sir Ralph's face that they had very nearly undone the whole arrangement.

Sir Ralph rose to his feet and said rather coldly, 'It is not negotiable. If you wish to proceed, then see the agent and get it signed and sealed. If not, someone else will. Rented accommodation hereabouts is hard to find.'

Kenny held out his hand. 'Thank you for approving of me. I shan't let you down. I was thinking ...'

Sir Ralph shook his hand saying, 'Good afternoon, Kenny. My kindest regards to your mother.'

It was a dismissal, kindly done, but it was there. Kenny hurtled into Culworth and got it all signed and sealed, using a telephone call to Sir Ralph as his reference. He rushed home to his mother to tell her and to tell their Terry, who nearly collapsed when he heard. Terry's comment to Kenny was 'You shouldn't have.'

Ralph's comment to Muriel was 'I can't help feeling I've made the kind of decision I shall live to regret.'

'I saw him coming out of church this morning, so perhaps he's turned over a new leaf. You have to give him the benefit of the doubt.'

Kenny and Terry kept out of the Royal Oak that night to avoid any questions, for they knew, the village being what it was, that everyone would know by now and if they didn't they would before the night was out. But seated in their usual places were Jimmy, Sylvia, Willie and, unusually for her, Vera.

'Is this Kenny Jones we're talking about? The idle good-for-nothing womaniser we all know and love?' Sylvia asked.

'The very one, Sylvia.'

'Well, I never. Where's he suddenly got money from?'

'That's the question, isn't it? Where has he got it from?'

Vera chuckled. 'Maybe he's done someone a good turn and they've left him it in their will.'

'Good turn! He wouldn't know what a good turn was if it jumped up and bit 'im!'

The four of them roared with laughter.

Jimmy related a story he'd heard about Kenny and so too did Willie, and before long they'd agreed he'd paid his way into the cottage with dirty money but from what source they'd no idea.

Sylvia, having dried her eyes and pulled herself together, said, 'I'm amazed at Sir Ralph! Letting Kenny have a cottage. We all know his mother's waited on him hand and foot all his life and that he won't know where to start with anything domestic. The cottage will be a tip from day one. I reckon Sir Ralph's made a big mistake.'

'So do I. So do I.' Willie nodded his head in agreement. 'But yer never know, maybe it could be a turning-point for him. Out from under his mother's wing, fending for himself, it might do him good. It's not often Ralph makes a bad judgement where character's concerned.'

'They say their Terry's moving in too.'

Vera spluttered into her vodka. 'Terry! A right den of iniquity that'll be then. But with Vince having got the push, I expect they'll be glad to see the back of those two boys.'

'Either that or they can't take any more of her bossiness.'

Sylvia, seated alongside Vera on the settle, said, 'You know, Vera, this is nice having a drink with you, quite like old times. It seems ages since I saw you.'

'Is it? I've been so busy settling in I haven't had time to think.'

'You like it then?'

'Like it! I should say so. What a pleasure it is to go upstairs into that flat after work, all bright and airy!'

Willie asked her how many times she had to get up in the night to give a hand.

'I suppose it's about two nights a week on average. So it's not that bad. They've two nursing staff on, you see, so they only want me if they've several crises all at once. I change sheets, make tea, ring for the doctor, sit with the old dears when they've had a fright, go looking for them when they've gone missing, that kind of thing. Nothing medical, thank God!'

'So it's been worth it?' Jimmy wanted to reassure himself that she didn't regret it.

Vera nodded. 'Definitely.' She took a sip of her vodka and tonic and, almost casually, asked how was Don, had they seen him at all?

'Don't you worry about him, he's as happy as a sand-boy. He says. Don't quite believe it meself but there you are. He mentions you a lot, yer see.' Jimmy smiled at her.

'Don't grin at me.'

'I wasn't.'

'You were! It isn't funny. I never thought I'd finish up a single woman after all these years.'

Sylvia reminded her it was she who'd left him.

'I know that, but I thought he'd follow meek as a lamb and he didn't. Right called my bluff he did. But I was determined. I couldn't take any more of that house. The trouble is he can't see what I mean. He thinks it's lovely.'

Willie nodded wisely. 'It's a tip. Even I can see that. Mine was till I met Sylvia and I realised I couldn't ask her to visit me like it was, so I did it up.'

'Did you? Just for me?' Sylvia's face lit up at the thought of what he'd done for her sake. Her lovely grey eyes, which unbeknown to her were what had attracted Willie in the first place, brimmed with tears.

Willie squeezed her arm. 'Just for you.'

Sylvia stood up and leaned across the table to kiss his cheek. 'Thank you. I'd no idea.'

Vera watched this private moment between Sylvia and Willie and her heart almost burst. It was Don more than the house that she was sickened of. More loving consideration had passed between Willie and Sylvia in that moment than she'd experienced in years from Don, and she was envious. She looked up to see Don at the bar and his arrival at a moment when she had been made so vividly aware of his shortcomings put her in a steaming temper.

'Oh, no! Just look! The fool's come in. What does he want to come in for right now, spoiling everything when I'm enjoying myself?'

'Comes in a lot nowadays. He must be lonely.' Jimmy's wry grin did nothing to assuage Vera's temper.

Don spotted Jimmy's back view and, picking up his orange juice, drifted across. He stopped abruptly when he saw that the smartly dressed woman opposite Jimmy was Vera. In her new jacket and skirt he hadn't recognised her. And she'd had her hair cut shorter and made curly and she looked altogether more ... well, sort of different, and she made him feel shabby. He hadn't changed his shirt all week because he couldn't be bothered to iron the ones he'd washed and he remembered he hadn't had a bath since ... How could she put him in such a fix? Without any warning she turns up and ...

Jimmy leaned over and pulled a chair across from the next table. 'Sit down, Don.'

'In the circumstances, I won't bother. Thanks.' He turned his back and, because all the other tables were occupied, went to perch uncomfortably on a bar stool, drank his juice as fast as he decently could, said good night and left.

Vera watched him depart and very briefly felt sorry for him, then remembered that pigsty of a kitchen; the only shining thing about it was the fridge-freezer which she'd got from the nursing home when they were throwing it out, and even that was speckled with pinpoints of rust. As for the rest, if they needed a kitchen for a museum it would qualify hands down. Victorian most likely, or even earlier. But worse she remembered his unattractiveness, his neglect of her, his disinterest, the boring life his inertia forced her to lead. No. She'd struck out for a better life and if he didn't want it, well, it was bad luck, Don. She was better off where she was and so long as she closed her mind to what she would do when they retired her, things were pretty good.

7

Tom helped Kenny and Terry move. Not that there was a great deal apart from the exercise equipment Kenny had bought and never used. It took three car loads and a lot of heaving and pushing to achieve it, though. The beds came from a second-hand furniture store in Culworth, and their mother gave them two easy chairs she was glad to see the back of, and the dining table and chairs she'd appropriated via Vera from the nursing home.

Just before he went to bed that first night Kenny stood in the little kitchen drinking his nightly tot from a mug and thought, this is only the beginning. From now on Kenny Jones is on the up. He'd had nothing to buy in the kitchen because it came fully fitted and looked really good. He wandered into the sitting room and his heart sank. There was no two ways about it, he'd have to graft to get this looking anything right. He recollected the feel of Sir Ralph's leather armchair and yearned for it. His envy set him on a path from which he determined there would be no turning back until he'd achieved his objectives.

Being new to housekeeping he went round securing windows, locking doors with almost religious fervour and then meandered up to bed. Pity about his dad losing his job; at least with the two of them out of the way they'd manage better, and he'd see them right, his mum had no need to worry, even if he gave them money just to show how successfully his new business career was progressing. They'd be proud of him from now on. He'd no idea where their Terry was at the moment, but he guessed it was the barmaid at the Jug and Bottle who'd enticed him away tonight. From now on Kenny Jones was aiming higher than her. She no longer suited his lifestyle. Quality was his watchword from now on: there'd be no more scuttling about in the gutters with tarts and fleabags, oh, no!

Tom, climbing into bed beside Evie that night, said, 'They've no furniture to speak of and no stuff like pans and dishes and such. Just a mug and a cereal bowl each they've borrowed from their mother.' He put an arm round Evie's thin waist. 'Like it here, do you, Evie? I do. Like as if I've come home, and this job as verger, it's given us respectability. Lovely that. We've been accepted. Haven't you noticed people's attitude is different now? We've arrived as you might say. They do say it takes fifty years to become a true villager here but, well, I reckon as far as Tom and Evie are concerned we've reduced that to three!'

He gave her a squeeze. 'All those years of worry, all finished with.' He nuzzled her with his chin. 'Orchid House. I'm glad we chose that name. Better than Lilac Cottage or Chez Nous. Orchid House. Has a ring to it. And we do, grow orchids I mean. So it's genuine. Honeysuckle growing round the door. Like a picture book. Always dreamed of a house with honeysuckle round the door. There isn't a house in Turnham Malpas with such style as ours. Long may it remain so. Buying all Sadie Beauchamp's furniture did the trick. We'd never have made it like this, would we, buying the stuff ourselves? We don't come from the right background, you see, you and me, to know what to buy. It takes class to furnish a place like this is furnished.'

He took his arm from Evie's waist and lay on his back. In the light of the full moon creeping round the edges of the curtains he surveyed the bedroom and remembered other rooms he'd slept in, and he decided that here in Turnham Malpas, in this room in his dream home, he felt the safest, most secure and happiest he'd ever been for many a year. Yes. Here was pure heaven.

'Shall we start doing a bit of entertaining? Ask people round, casual-like for a meal. Let's see. I know, we can start with Sheila and Ronald. What about it? Eh? What do you say? They're our kind. Cut our teeth a bit with someone we feel happy with. Ask them for Friday night, Evie. Just knock and ask. If they say, "No," well, OK, it's not the end of the world. Who else could we ask? I know: Vince Jones and his missus. They're our kind. But we'll start with Sheila and Ron. Sir Ronald and Lady Bissett, oh, yes! I'll look forward to that. Something special to eat. Yes, that's what we'll do. You do the food, I'll see to the drinks. We'll show 'em!'

Tom rolled on his side and put his arm round Evie again, kissed her earlobe, pulled the duvet up around her shoulders seeing as the night was chilly, and fell asleep. But in the small hours of the night he woke sweating and fearful. Kenny! Oh, God! Kenny. Kenny was his only threat.

'Come in, come in! Let me take your jacket, Sheila. You don't mind if I call you Sheila, do you? Good evening, Ron.' They shook hands even though they'd seen each other only that morning, because Tom couldn't kiss Ron's cheek as he had Sheila's and other than that he was at a loss to know how to greet him.

Ron handed over a bottle of wine. 'Thought it might be useful. I know a little man in London, you see, and he always makes sure I buy only the best.'

'London! My word! We are privileged! Do come in. Evie's busy in the kitchen, she won't be a moment. Come in, sit yourselves down.'

Sheila took a brisk look around the sitting room. Just as she'd thought, they'd bought Sadie's furniture and pictures and done nothing at all to imprint their own taste on the house since they'd moved in. Oh, well! She would have liked the odd little touch which said, 'This is mine and this is how I like it.' She seated herself carefully, hoping not to crease her skirt. This suit was an absolute pest for creasing. She'd worn it to a dinner with Ron and when she got home she'd realised she must have looked a perfect ragbag all evening. Ron was looking quite handsome tonight. His dark lounge suit, with that tie with the hot air balloons on it that added just the right touch of colour, made him look debonair. She looked at Tom and decided he'd gone a bit over the top with his smart country suit like Sir Ralph wore sometimes but not a quarter the quality of his, oh, no! You couldn't fool Sheila Bissett where clothes were concerned.

'Thank you, Tom.' The sherry was just how she liked it. Sweet and cloying and restorative. What she was waiting for was a sight of Evie. Evie the silent. Evie the elusive. Evie the shadow.

'Can I give Evie a hand in the kitchen at all?'

'That's very kind but she's happier coping on her own.'

'I had hoped Evie would join the village Flower Club. Is she a flower person?' Privately Sheila thought Evie wasn't a person at all.

'No, not really. Embroidery, yes. But not flowers.'

'Embroidery! Oh, my word. I wonder if we could start an embroidery class. Culworth is such a long way to go for things like that. A class here in the village would be excellent. I'll ask her.'

'I don't think ...'

At this moment Evie came in carrying two dishes of nibbles. Sheila often categorised people by naming the animal most akin to their personality. Evie was definitely a little dormouse. Or could it be she was more like a shrew? No, a dormouse: she hadn't got it in her to be a shrew.

At a signal from Sheila, Ron, reminded of his manners, stood up to greet her. He'd intended giving her a kiss like Tom had Sheila but Evie shrank away and he ended up with empty arms, kissing the air.

Evie placed the two dishes of nibbles on the coffee table beside Sheila, then with a nod at Tom, she scuttled out. He apologised and darted after her.

They were left to themselves for such a long time that Sheila began to wonder if she should alert the rescue services. She and Ron tried to make conversation but it was difficult as all Sheila wanted to talk about was their hosts and to question whether or not Evie would ever be heard to speak. She'd known right from the start when Tom first knocked on their door to invite them that they should have trumped up an excuse, but taken unawares they hadn't thought fast enough.

Tom reappeared. 'Right, we're ready. Do come through.'

Sheila noted that the dinner service was a popular line in Boots kitchen departments, but even her sharp tongue couldn't fault the laying of the table, nor the presentation of the starter: pâté with small green bits of salad, a thin quarter of tomato on top and tiny triangular pieces of toast. Very tasteful.

Tom and Ron talked trade-union affairs almost continuously and left Evie and Sheila to make the best of it. Sheila began by saying she'd heard Evie was an embroiderer. Evie nodded.

'I was wondering if you might be able to start an embroidery class in the village? Although we're all busy people a class like that would create a lot of interest.'

Evie looked up startled, as though confronted by a large and threatening cat. After a pause she answered, 'I could.' Sheila was surprised by Evie's voice. For such a small, quiet person it was amazingly deep and strong.

'Really? Would you? That would be wonderful! Have you got some embroidery I could see? Just to look at.'

'Yes.'

'After we've eaten then?'

Evie nodded.

When Evie took her into the study which had been converted into a workroom Sheila was astounded. She'd been expecting only mediocre talent or even none at all and perhaps having desperately to wriggle out of her idea about the embroidery class. But no such thing. The walls were hung almost from floor to ceiling with embroidery. Well, was it embroidery? Sheila asked herself. Evie had used lots of fabrics to make the pictures, sewn it down with embroidery stitches and in some places padded it for extra effect. Some framed, some used as simple wall hangings but each and every one an outstanding example of the craft. The colours she'd used almost made Sheila's head spin. They were strong and vibrant but so subtly chosen that they didn't clash at all.

'Why, Evie, they're wonderful! Such skill. You're an artist. This one, and this one, and *this one*! They're wonderful. Quite wonderful! Did you design them all?'

Evie shook her head. 'That's a copy, and so's that.' She pointed to two wall hangings, which appeared to Sheila to be medieval originals. 'The rest are my design.' She stood hands clasped in front of her with no emotion showing on her face.

Sheila, stunned by the sheer beauty of the work, said, 'Why have you never let on about all this?'

Evie shrugged her shoulders.

There was a large, square, floor-standing antique embroidery frame to one side with a white cotton cover over it. Sheila pointed to it and said, 'May I?'

Evie nodded. Two-thirds finished, it was a religious collage depicting the Nativity. The glorious choice of fabrics, glowing and almost sparkling in the intensity of their colour, was stunning. The robes of the Three Kings were superb, their crowns and their gifts padded underneath to make them stand out, and with gold thread embellishing them. Yet the rough simplicity of the manger and the animals, and the dryness of the spiky hay so cleverly depicted and the tiny mouse going about its own affairs were captured quite beautifully. And Mary, so cool, so still, dressed in a soft pale blue gown, which might have been overshadowed by the richness of the colours about her, but which actually drew the eye as much and more as the vivid colours did. Joseph, still to be finished, was already looking homespun and earthy.

'What's this for?'

'Church.'

'Our church?'

Evie nodded.

'When the Rector sees this he'll be amazed. Absolutely amazed. Such talent, Evie.' Sheila patted Evie's arm. 'Talk about hiding your light under a bushel. I've never seen anything so beautiful. How do you do it?'

Evie simply smiled, pulled the cover over the frame and invited Sheila to return to the sitting room, to join the two men.

She'd enthused to Ron and Tom before they'd decided to play a game of cards but that was nothing to her enthusiasm when they got home.

'How can such a mousy person produce work like that? If it was in an exhibition up in London it wouldn't go amiss. It is sensational! I wish you'd seen it, Ron, I was speechless with admiration. All that from a . . . well, let's face it, she's as mad as a hatter, isn't she? Hardly a word for the cat. Not exactly someone you'd choose as a dinner guest. I wonder if she'd do something for me? I've that space in the hall between the kitchen door and the cloaks, wouldn't have to be too big or it wouldn't fit, and the colours would have to be just right, I wouldn't want it to clash. I'll ask her. But what a triumph for us if I can persuade her to do a class.'

Riffling through her handbag looking for her reading glasses, Sheila clicked her tongue in annoyance. 'Drat it, I've left my reading glasses in the chair where I sat. It's too late to go knocking now! I'll go back tomorrow to get them and make it a chance to thank them again for a nice evening. And such good card players too!' The doorbell rang. 'Oh, that must be Tom bringing them for me, how kind of him. Such a very nice man, so thoughtful. You go answer the door while I put the kettle on.'

From the kitchen she listened to Ron answering the door, and hoped he'd demonstrate real gratitude to Tom; sometimes he could be so off-hand. She heard the door bang shut, then heard Ron grunt, and after that a thud as though something heavy had crashed to the carpet, breaking by the sound of it her entire collection of delicate glass ornaments that had taken so long to get together.

'What on earth –!'

But by then two men, with black balaclavas over their faces and evil menacing eyes peering through the slits, were in the kitchen wielding their coshes on her and she went down, the kettle bouncing across the rush matting, spewing its contents as it went. Before she fell unconscious under their repeated blows Sheila squinted a floor-level view of black trainers and, mysteriously, drops of blood spraying across the floor close to her eyes.

Well, there was one thing for certain, Muriel declared to herself after a whole hour of tortuous struggling, she was going across to ask Sheila Bissett to give her a hand: if anyone could put things right it would be Sheila. She pushed back her hair from her face, pulled out her handkerchief from her skirt pocket and dabbed her forehead and top lip. It really was all too much and she'd never ever attempt this again.

All this angst had come about because Muriel had volunteered to arrange the church flowers for the weekend. A series of unusual coincidences had brought the situation about and here she was deputising for an official flower arranger and wishing to heaven she wasn't. The greenery was limp and wouldn't hang right, the oasis kept crumbling, and the tape holding it in place was not doing a proper job of it at all. Now she couldn't push in the stems of the flowers, and whoever had chosen roses that had no intention of standing straight? Muriel stood back to assess her arrangement and could have wept. A child of seven could have done better.

Leaving everything as it was Muriel stepped as quickly as she could across the Green towards Sheila's house, hoping against hope that though it was Saturday they would be in, and she'd get Sheila to help her. Muriel never got on very well with Sheila, but give her her due, where flowers were concerned ... She knocked lightly on the door. Rather apologetically she knocked again and then to her surprise found that the door appeared to be knocking back at her. How odd! Low down, there it was again. How peculiar. Maybe it was Sheila's new cat playing games. But then she thought she heard a quiet groan.

Muriel lifted the latch and tried the door; she could open it a few inches but then no more. Cautiously putting her arm at shoulder level through the gap she had made she could feel nothing, so she went lower still waving her hand about in the hope of coming into contact with something. Then, low down close to the floor, she did. Exploring but not able to see what she explored, she felt around and came to the conclusion she was actually feeling someone's knee. Embarrassed, she stopped, retrieved her arm and knelt there wondering what on earth to do next.

She stood up, dusted off her knees and gave the door a heave. Something gave way and it opened a few more inches. Muriel, being slim, pressed her way through the enlarged gap. There at her feet lay Ronald Bissett, curled up like a baby. Muriel stuffed her knuckles into her mouth to stop herself screaming. He looked horrific. His head and face were bloody, swollen and so badly bruised he was barely recognisable, and his suit and shirt looked as though someone had stood on him in dirty shoes. Great splashes of blood had sprayed across his shirt front in a wild psychedelic pattern. Beside him his glasses had been ground into the carpet, and his bloody hands were in a claw-like grip grasping the fringe of the hall rug.

Ron groaned.

'Oh, Ron! Whatever's happened? Where's Sheila?'

But she got no reply. Fearing what she might find, Muriel tiptoed around the ground floor in search of Sheila. She tried the sitting room first, then the dining room and all that was left was the kitchen so she pushed open the door and found her. Surely no one could take a beating like that and not be dead? She must be. There was blood all over the place, up the cupboard doors, on the dishwasher, even as high up as the worktops. In fear and trepidation, for she'd never before touched a person she thought might be dead, Muriel stepped over the kettle to put her hand to Sheila's ghastly bruised and battered neck and found, she thought, a slight pulse. Oh, Sheila! Oh, Sheila! An ambulance! With hands scarcely able to hold the receiver she tremblingly dialled nine nine nine on the kitchen telephone, but there was no life in it at all. Glancing at her hand still furiously tapping the number nine button Muriel saw it was red with blood. Sheila's blood, thick and dark and congealed. Oh, God! Oh! God!

Ralph! No, he wasn't at home.

Peter! Neither was he.

Jimbo! Of course!

The door stood wide open so Muriel was in the centre of the Store without any warning at all, distraught, hands and dress streaked with blood shouting as loud as she could, 'Police! Quick! Ambulance! Dear God!'

Silence fell. Everyone there was transfixed at the sight of this terrible apparition. What on earth was she talking about? What on earth had she done?

The first to gather his wits was Jimbo. 'Muriel! Muriel!' He put an arm around her shoulders and asked, 'Who for? Who do you want the ambulance for?'

'Sheila and Ron.' Bel just managed to get a chair under her as she collapsed.

'Nine, nine, nine, Linda. Quick.'

Bel grabbed a bag of frozen peas she'd just sold to a customer and put it to Muriel's forehead, hoping it might calm her down and stop her fainting.

Tom raced out and headed for Orchard House as fast as he could.

Linda said, 'Are they murdered, do you think?' and promptly fainted.

The two Senior sisters began chanting like a pair of demented nuns. 'Oh, God! Oh, God! Oh, God!'

The two Charter-Plackett boys, Fergus and Finlay, having been commandeered for shelf-filling that morning, ran out after Tom. Within seconds they were back ashen-faced and Finlay had to rush back out again to be furiously sick in the grating outside.

'Dad! You should see. It's terrible,' Fergus shouted. 'Just terrible. I don't think they'll live.'

At this the remainder of Jimbo's customers squeezed out of the door and ran round to Orchard House, leaving Bel to get a glass of water for Muriel and one for Linda. Jimbo, still holding Muriel, muttered dark threats about coming to the village for peace and security for the children and then this happening, but he reproved himself when he recollected that Ron and Sheila were probably at death's door.

It was on the regional TV news that night and in the papers the following morning. Trade-union leaders, eager for the exposure the media would give them, spoke grimly of this atrocious crime, of in what high esteem this elder of their movement was held, how shocking and apparently motiveless it was. Potted histories of Ron's career appeared, hastily pulled together by journalists taken by surprise.

In the village the reaction to it was more sincere. For those who'd lived alongside them these last years this wasn't just a ten-day wonder to fill the newsreels and the papers in the dying days of a newsless August. In the Store Jimbo did a brisk trade in newspapers, having to double his order of some to satisfy demand. In the Royal Oak Georgie, Dicky and Alan worked like slaves to keep up with the meals and drinks all the journalists and sightseers demanded. At night the village was as quiet as the grave. The nonchalant attitude most of its inhabitants had had about locking their doors was tossed to the wind and every door and window was locked and checked both day and night.

But for heaven's sake why? Sheila and Ron had never done anything to deserve such a vicious attack. Mild, innocent lives they'd led. Mind you, Sheila couldn't half be provoking and verging on abandoned with her outspoken comments, as most of them knew to their cost, but to deserve such a beating? No. This was some outside job, but what was the motive?

Louise had searched through the house but found nothing of her parents' possessions missing, so far as she could tell. Agreed there'd been a bit of vague throwing about of drawer contents to make it look like a burglary but it was obvious that murder had been the intention or at the very least a serious warning.

Sheila was the first to speak. Muriel and Ralph were visiting the two of them in the hospital and talking to her about the village. 'So you see, Sheila,' Muriel said, 'we're having the meeting tonight to mobilise everyone. We can't let Mr Fitch ride roughshod over us all, can we? I'm just sorry you can't be there. But I'll let you know what goes on. We have to move quickly, you know, or else. You've not to worry about anything though, just you get well. All the things you are responsible for are being attended to. All you've got to do is get better. Grandmama Charter-Plackett has taken over the Flower Club,' at this Sheila stirred, 'just temporarily, of course, and she's going to oversee the Harvest Festival for you, so there's no need to worry about that. She's . . .'

Sheila's mouth opened and she whispered hoarsely and almost unintelligibly, 'She'd better not 'ave.' Her false teeth having been removed Sheila appeared to Muriel to be extraordinarily vulnerable, and she felt more moved by the intimate glimpse she'd had of her helplessness than she was by her injuries. Ralph had to chuckle: apparently just the mention of her old adversary taking over had penetrated her unconscious mind and stirred her into a reaction.

8

Muriel and Caroline had been tempted to book the small committee room for their protest meeting but as an act of faith had chosen to book the hall. 'We shall look foolish, Muriel, if there's only a handful there – they'll be lost in the big hall – but we've got to think big. Tom's putting out twenty chairs and having the others ready as and when. Shall you want to speak?'

Muriel shook her head. 'Only a small speech in support of you. I get so nervous.'

'Very well. We'll have coffee afterwards then you and I can circulate. I've rung up quite a few people and they've promised to come.'

'Caroline, are we doing the right thing, do you think?'

Caroline looked surprised. 'Of course we are. Are you getting cold feet?'

'I always do. It is his hedge, you see, just like our garden is ours. It's just that his is bigger.'

'I know, but he has responsibilities to the land. After all, it is his in trust during his lifetime, in the end the land belongs to itself. He's simply privileged to look after it for a while.'

'I hadn't seen it like that, but of course you're right.'

'See you tonight then. Sylvia's sitting in for me and she's coming round at seven so I'll be there in good time.'

'Peter not back yet?'

'No.' Caroline turned away saying, 'See you tonight,' and leaving before Muriel could ask another question.

When Muriel walked into the hall at five minutes past seven she was surprised to find it a hive of activity. Posters were up round the walls, a leaflet on every chair, and six of the chairs were already occupied.

They all turned to look at her. Arthur and Celia Prior were there, two of the weekenders, Miss Pascoe from the school, and Georgie from the Royal Oak.

'Good evening! So good of you all to come.'

Arthur, Ralph's so-called cousin, stood up. 'Good evening, Muriel. Celia and me, we've come to give you our full support. Someone's got to put a stop to him and I for one am willing to stand up and be counted.'

'Thank you, Arthur, Celia. I do appreciate that.'

Georgie patted the chair beside her, 'Do sit with me, Lady Templeton.'

'I'm supposed to be sitting at the front with Caroline, thank you, Georgie. I've a speech to make.'

One of the weekenders called out, 'We're right behind you. The man's a monster. We can't let him get away with it.' He clenched his fist and raised it in the air. 'Down with Fitch, I say!'

Gently Muriel reminded him, 'It's not Mr Fitch himself but rather what he's doing that we're protesting about.'

'Same thing in my book. We haven't bought a house here in this lovely village to have it spoiled by a man with no understanding of what the countryside is all about. I and my wife have taken time off work to stay on specially to attend this meeting and, please, count us in with any protest you intend to make.'

'There are people who think he should be allowed to dig it up, you know.'

'Are there indeed! Just show them to me and I'll give them a piece of my mind!' He laughed loudly and nudged his wife, who almost toppled off her chair. 'Sorry, pet, but I'm so incensed.'

At this point Grandmama Charter-Plackett came in. Muriel thought she heard a slight booing sound but sincerely hoped she hadn't.

Grandmama went to sit on the front row, ignoring the murmur of protest, calmly placed her bag beside her and folded her arms. 'Good evening, Muriel!'

'Good evening, Katherine.'

'Is Mr Fitch coming?'

'He has had a leaflet but not a personal invitation.'

'And what about the council? Anyone from there daring to face the flack?'

'Those concerned have been invited but they have not replied.'

'I shall be the only one then?'

'Only one?'

'The only one on Mr Fitch's side.'

Muriel's heart quailed at the prospect of answering her, but that dear little wren needed her support. 'We'll have to wait and see.'

'Hmmmph.'

The hall was beginning to fill and Tom had to find more chairs. Caroline was already there, standing behind the table on which she had placed her notes. Muriel, whilst highly delighted at the interest their meeting had attracted, shook with nerves as she took her place beside Caroline. Why on earth had she said she would spearhead a protest they hadn't a hope of winning? Ralph smiled at her from his scat at the back and she gathered courage. There must be forty people at least already and there were bound to be latecomers. At seven thirty prompt Caroline tapped the end of her pen on the table and brought the meeting to order.

'Good evening, everyone. First I should like to say how pleased and impressed Muriel and I are to see so much interest in this protest of ours. Obviously it isn't just Muriel and I who have taken this threat to our village to heart, apparently you all have too. I shall begin by . . .'

Muriel listened to Caroline's well-reasoned argument and felt proud to be associated with her. Observing the reactions of the crowd she noticed that most kept nodding their heads in agreement and at one stage some shouted, 'Hear, hear!' or clapped their hands in approval.

Then suddenly it was her turn and Muriel, knees knocking, stood up as the applause for Caroline faded.

'I'm a country woman at heart though not a very knowledgeable one. But what I do know is that we have to fight to preserve our countryside. It simply will not do for us to stand by and bow to the destruction of it. I have been to the county records office and I have seen with my own eyes ancient maps and there, as large as life, is that hedgerow, already well established by the seventeenth century.

Living in that hedgerow are dozens of wild creatures and wild flowers and plants which must not be left homeless.'

Muriel picked up her notes. 'There are holly, yew, hazel, wild rose, dogwood, blackthorn and ash as well as flowers such as wild violets, to say nothing of birds and small mammals which rely upon it for food and for bringing up their young. So determined am I to stop the destruction of this hedgerow that I am prepared to stand in front of any tractor, any digger, any tree-destroying equipment, at the risk of my *life*, to stop this happening. If it comes to it, how many of you will join me?'

Her challenge was greeted by cheers and the noisy weekender stood up and called out, 'Me for one! I'll be right beside you, shoulder to shoulder!' He faced the crowd eyeball to eyeball. 'Well?'

'And me!'

'And me!'

In the midst of the excitement the door opened and in came Mr Fitch. The proverbial pin could have been dropped and everyone would have heard it. The whole room froze into silence.

Mr Fitch paused for a moment and then marched between the chairs towards the table. He stopped in front of it and faced the meeting. 'Permission to speak, Madam Chairman.'

Muriel couldn't answer him, but Caroline could. 'Of course, it's a public meeting.'

He glared at each and every one sitting in front of him. 'In all the years I have lived in this village I have bowed to your wishes. Because of your opposition I have stood down from being chairman of the cricket club whose pavilion and equipment *I* financed, I have paid for the church bells to be rehung, I have paid for the church central heating, I have set up an educational trust to help talented children and young people, I have underwritten the Village Show, the like of which has never been seen in this county before, and I have hosted the Bonfire Night party. I employ nineteen workers of one kind and another from this village and the surrounding ones, and I am always a soft touch when it comes to donating to charitable causes. Now this time I want my own way. A simple thing, the replacing of a hedge by a stout wooden fence. That is all. I have come simply to inform you of my intentions. I *will* remove the hedge and I *will,* despite your opposition, erect a fence.'

Mr Fitch turned on his heel and left the hall.

The silence, which had fallen when he arrived, was nothing compared to the deep silence he left behind him. Muriel felt ashamed. Caroline questioned her own motives. Grandmama Charter-Plackett smiled smugly. Ralph looked grim and an awful lot of them were embarrassed.

'He is right, he has done a lot for us. We'd miss him in more ways than one if he sold up.'

'He's paid half our Lynn's ballet-school fees. We'd never have been able to let her go if he hadn't.'

'Look at that time when he . . .'

'And when he paid . . .'

'We owe him a lot.'

'Perhaps we shouldn't oppose him. After all it is his hedge, isn't it?'

Muriel, realising that in another minute her cause would be totally lost, was about to stand up to implore them to back her and Caroline, when the door opened again. Who was it this time? Not Mr Fitch come back?

Heads turned to see. 'Why! It's the Rector!'

'Hello, sir, glad you're back.'

'Just the person we need.'

'The man for the moment.'

Muriel sneaked a look at Caroline. Her eyes were fixed on Peter. He was wearing that royal blue pullover which picked up the colour of his eyes and emphasised his blond good looks in a way no other colour could. His jeans hung on him a little, but otherwise he looked the same except that the peace and joy which normally emanated from him was missing. Finally, after a long stare, Caroline smiled at him and he smiled at her.

Muriel said quietly, 'Glad you've come. We do need your help.'

Ralph stood up and gave Peter a brief résumé of what had taken place. 'So we have stalemate. We're all well aware of what he has done for this village but at the same time . . .'

'One thing we have to be careful of is to be sure we're not objecting simply because it's Mr Fitch being high-handed again.

There must be some legal way of stopping him. Have we investigated that?' He put the question to Caroline directly.

Taken so completely off-guard by his sudden appearance Caroline stammered, 'W-w-we've been advised that the – council can't stop him.'

'Officially?'

'Not in writing.'

'That's what we need then. Cannot Neville Neal advise us?'

Muriel told him of her conversation with him. 'So we assumed we'd drawn a blank.'

'I think there must be something somewhere we can use. But first I shall go visit Mr Fitch myself. Tomorrow. First thing. If I might suggest, seeing as you are all obviously very much concerned about this matter, that you leave your names and addresses before you go so that you can be contacted and told of future developments?'

Muriel clapped her hands when she realised that the fight might not be ended. 'What a good idea! Of course. How splendid.'

Hastily she found clean pages in her notebook and laid it out on the table alongside her pen. 'Here we are! Here we are!'

Grandmama, who'd felt herself to be on the winning side for a moment, forbore to add her name to the list and strode towards the door, distinctly put out by the turn of events.

Peter went to sit down at the back of the hall and wait for the meeting to close. By the time Caroline had had a word with people, collected her papers, thanked Tom for getting the hall ready for them and for locking up, and coped with her emotions at Peter's unexpected reappearance, she was exhausted.

It was Peter's key in the lock, Peter who thanked Sylvia for babysitting, Peter who made a hot drink for them both and Peter who carried it into the sitting room. He placed the tray on the coffee table and handed Caroline her mug.

'Thank you. You're back then?' She looked up at him as she spoke, not knowing whether she should be glad or not.

'I am. This problem of the hedge. I certainly don't want it uprooting. It's a delightful sight and precious too. I'm glad you've decided to do something about it.'

'I was incensed when I found out.' She explained about Ralph's party and how furious Grandmama Charter-Plackett had made her.

Peter, having listened attentively to her explanation, said, 'As one of his tenants she has a lot to lose if she opposes him and so have a lot of other people in this village – Jimbo with his catering contract, which I understand is a sizeable percentage of his turnover, and all Mr Fitch's employees. It will be very difficult for them to come out in protest, especially workers like Barry Jones and Greenwood Stubbs so soon after their last scare about losing their jobs.'

'I hadn't quite seen it like that. Harriet didn't come and I thought perhaps she might.'

'Like I said, many will have divided loyalties. That's why I think it might be best to approach it from the legal direction. I'm amazed –'

'Peter! Have done!'

He put down his mug and looked at her. 'Have done?'

'Have done! Where have you been? I daren't tell anyone that you'd disappeared off the face of the earth. If they asked where you were I said you were taking a holiday. You appear without warning and wonder why I'm ... *hurting* like I am. I need an explanation.'

'I've been walking in the Dales and I've come back because the Bishop will shortly be making enquiries as to my whereabouts and so ...' he looked down at his hands '... but I needed to be back anyway. Couldn't manage, you see, without seeing you.' He looked up and smiled apologetically.

Caroline got up, walked across to him and knelt in front of him, a hand on his knee. 'I have wept bitter tears for what I've done to you. Bitter tears. A thousand years of saying sorry won't be enough.'

'Darling!'

'Hush! Let me finish. I know now that given a little more time the old Caroline you once knew will be back. Can you wait for her?'

'I can. I'm sorry to have left you like I did, but I couldn't cope any longer.'

'You'd every right, I behaved abominably. I must have been out of my head. In fact today I am positively cringing about what happened. When I went to church the morning Hugo left and I saw the love and the compassion you were offering me in front of everyone . . .' Caroline shook her head. 'It was only because I had died inside that I couldn't accept it, and it's only everyone else's love for you which has saved my bacon over this.'

'They love you too.'

'Only because I stand in your shadow.'

'Leaving you was selfish, I thought only of myself and my own pain.'

'Not before time. Everyone needs to put themselves first some time or other in their lives.'

Very tentatively he stretched out his hand to touch her hair. He fingered the soft dark curls above her forehead, trailed the back of his finger along her jawline, traced the outline of her mouth; his finger excessively gentle.

'Whatever happens, you are the great love of my life and always will be. I've read somewhere the line "you are the beat of my heart" and you are, just that. I've pined for your touch.'

Caroline pushed his knees wider so she could kneel between them and get closer to him. 'Pine no more.'

They put their arms around each other and held each other close, not speaking. The simple humane gesture of hugging each other made them both feel cherished, and it comforted and nourished each of them more than words could ever have done.

After a time Caroline said, 'It'll be a while before things are as they were before, but we'll get there, I know that now, given time.' She sat back on her heels and asked, 'You love me still despite everything?'

'Of course.'

'And you're on my side about this hedge business?'

'Of course.'

'God bless you then. Welcome home. Had the children gone to bed when you got back?'

'No. I saw them both.'

Caroline placed a hand on his cheek. 'They have missed you.'

'Have you?'

'Now you're here I realise I have. But, like I said, it's going to be a while before I get my life with you completely sorted out, you understand what I'm saying?' Very tenderly Caroline saluted him by kissing his mouth, then in a business-like tone said, 'However, first things first. This campaign ...'

First thing the next morning Peter went up to the Big House and insisted upon seeing Mr Fitch. He held up his hand when the receptionist said he was too busy saying, 'I insist. It's important.'

'Very well, Rector. I'll go plead your case.' Succumbing as always to his masculinity she twinkled her fingers at him and disappeared into Mr Fitch's study returning in a moment saying, 'He'll see you now.'

Peter towered above Mr Fitch but in no way at all did it intimidate the man. They shook hands and Peter seated himself in a chair.

'Good morning, Rector, nice to have you back with us again. Had a good holiday? Good. Good. What can I do for you?'

'I came home last night to find Caroline was at a protest meeting. I understand you had left just before I arrived so you don't need me to tell you what it was about.'

Mr Fitch nodded. 'I know. So they've sent you to persuade me otherwise, have they?'

'No one sends me anywhere I don't want to go.' Peter left a silence.

Mr Fitch tolerated it with an amused smile on his face until eventually it was he who gave in. 'One of your well-known silences won't trick me into giving in. I'm not one of your parishioners.'

'Oh, but you are, Craddock. You live here and if you never darken the door of my church you are still in my care. Like it or not you are.'

Mr Fitch shuffled in his chair and settled himself more comfortably. 'So?'

'As it is obviously a commercial decision, what is there in it for you pulling down this hedge?'

Peter knew instantly from the momentary startled look in Mr Fitch's eyes that he'd hit the nail on the head.

'What possible commercial benefit could I get from pulling down a hedge which is good to neither man nor beast and for which I can't find anyone with the skill to attend to it as it should be attended to? It's fast becoming an eyesore and it needs dealing with.'

'You tell me.' Peter waited and so too did Mr Fitch.

Eventually Mr Fitch said, 'All at my expense, please note. I did intend putting the fence a little further into Rector's Meadow so that your access to the garages would be wider and it would make life easier. Of course, the fact that I am losing two or three feet of my own land is nothing in anyone's eyes I expect.'

'We like it as it is. That end of Pipe and Nook is perfectly adequate for our needs. We enjoy the cut and thrust of squeezing our cars past if someone else is in the lane.'

Mr Fitch shrugged his shoulders. 'Stuff and nonsense.'

'So, I can't change your mind. Not even if I find someone who could tackle the hedge and put it to rights?'

'No. I'm sticking to my guns on this one.' But he couldn't meet Peter's eye and Peter guessed he was getting too close for comfort to Mr Fitch's real reasons.

A wider lane, better access, what did that add up to? For the moment he couldn't answer his own question so Peter decided to fire his broadside and leave. He stood up and leaned his hands on the desk. 'Please think again. There are more things in life than money; qualities like love and affection and admiration and loyalty. The village is intensely loyal as I have found in the past, isn't that worth something to you? It is to me. Ask yourself what your relationship with them really is right now.' He didn't get an answer. 'I can tell you if you don't know. They will take with both hands anything you offer, they'll thank you and then go home and mock at your generosity, simply because they don't care a fig for the man who is doing the giving. Wouldn't it be immensely worthwhile to have their enduring affection and admiration?'

Peter shut the door behind him as quietly as he could.

9

Since the attack on Ron and Sheila the whole village had appeared to be swarming with police officers, some in uniform, most in plain clothes. Men in white overalls had trawled through Orchid House testing for this, and testing for that, and an interested group of spectators appeared to have taken root around the front door curious to find out what on earth they could be doing all this time.

'Them in white overalls 'ave been through it three times now. I reckon they suspect something serious.'

'Couldn't be more serious, could it, with Sheila and Ron nearly killed?'

'One thing for certain they won't find any dust. Sheila, bless 'er, might have her faults, but dust isn't one of 'em.'

'All right you saying "bless 'er", that wasn't what you said that time when she put the flower arrangement you'd done for the festival right at the back and no one couldn't see it.'

'Well, I know, but she 'ad a cheek, 'adn't she?'

'Comes to mind you called 'er something disgusting.'

'You would have to bring that up right now, wouldn't you? Just show some respect.' A large car pulled up and out of it stepped the well-dressed man who'd been interviewing everyone since the first day.

To the assembled crowd he said, 'Excuse me! There's nothing to see, I think it might be best to move on.' He went into the house without waiting to see if they did what he asked.

'That's Detective Superintendent Proctor from Culworth CID. Our Kev says ...'

Someone raised their eyes to the sky and said scathingly, 'As if we didn't know. He's practically lived here since the attack.'

'That's 'im what came when the Baxter sister kidnapped poor little Flick, isn't it? Remember? 'Cept he was Inspector then. I don't think he's got anyone left he could interview. Course, he could always start questioning Sheila's cat if he's short of clues. Just think what Topsy could tell if she could talk.'

'Where is her cat, by the way?'

'At the Rectory. Dr Harris took her in. They aren't half taking it seriously, yer know. After all, it was only a burglary that went wrong, not like it was a gangland revenge for something. I mean, Sheila and Ron aren't those kind of people, are they? Come on.'

'I 'ave 'eard a rumour that they're thinking of opening up the police house and us 'aving our own constable again.'

'Really? Well, not before time. That Kenny Jones and their Terry need a policeman all of their own.' She nudged her companion and winked significantly.

They drew closer together. 'What d'yer mean?'

'You know my Amanda? Well, she goes clubbing up in town – them in Culworth think they've got brilliant clubs but she says they're nothing to the ones she goes to – and she's seen the two of 'em these last few weeks hanging about, two and three o'clock in the morning.'

'No! That's where . . .' She thrust out her chest and, hand on hip, imitated a provocative walk. 'Isn't it?'

'Exactly, and they have had a lot of money just lately, haven't they? Renting the cottage and that and buying furniture. So are they pimps or what?'

'A bit of stealing's all well and good, but pimping! 'Ow low can yer sink?'

'Might as well be off, there's nothing going on 'ere. We've run out of Ovaltine and our Amanda loves a cup before she goes to bed. Coming?'

'Might as well. Pimping though. I bet their mother doesn't know.'

'And if Mrs Jones did know, what could she do about it?'

They both wandered into the Store, one to the shelf where the Ovaltine was kept and the other to look around to see what kind of a treat she could buy for her lunch, both of them relaying their conclusions about Kenny Jones and their Terry to anyone who would listen. It was their misfortune that Mrs Jones had come through from her mail-order office to collect a jar of apricot preserve. 'I've run out, Mr Charter-Plackett, so is it all right if I take one from the shelves in the Store?'

'Of course. I thought you'd rung the woman who makes it and told her we were running short?'

'I have, last week, but it's not arrived.'

Jimbo's lips tightened. 'It won't do. That's the second time she's let us down.'

Mrs Jones slipped past the post office counter with a nod at Linda through the grille and headed past the soups to the preserves. As she reached up to pick out the jar of jam she was looking for she caught the tail end of a sentence. '. . . so what other conclusion can you draw but that Kenny and their Terry are pimps?' Swinging round in fury Mrs Jones spotted the customers nodding their heads in agreement.

The listener nearest to her burst into hysterical laughter, which Mrs Jones immediately choked at source by bringing her arm back and smacking her hard across her face. What had been a bustling cheery morning, busy with customers from Little Derehams and Penny Fawcett as well as Turnham Malpas, turned instantly to chaos. Tins flew from shelves, packets cascaded to the floor, customers clutched the freezer cabinets as they tried to prevent themselves from being knocked down by Mrs Jones' flailing arms. Her intended victim scuttled between the shelves desperately trying to avoid being caught by this friendly neighbour turned raving lunatic. Linda, safe though she was behind her grille, took to screaming; at the till Bel made for cover as the customer she was serving took a lunge at Mrs Jones, who was hurtling by in pursuit of the woman who had maligned her boys. 'How dare you! How dare you! My boys aren't pimps! I know they're not.'

The attack continued right the way around the Store: hardly a shelf or a display escaped destruction. Finally by the stationery Mrs Jones caught hold of the front of the woman's cardigan with both hands and shook her violently. 'That's disgusting that is. Disgusting! You foul-mouthed old *bitch*!' Bursting into tears, Mrs Jones fled from the chaos she'd created into her office at the back, and left behind her a stunned and shattered collection of shoppers.

For a moment there was complete silence and then uproar ensued. The customer on the receiving end of her wrath cried, heartbroken, on Bel's shoulder. 'I wouldn't mind, I never said a word! Not a word!' The two who'd started the ball rolling by accusing the Jones boys of being pimps crept quietly out, while others began picking up the tins and packets which had flown from the shelves and the rest pulled themselves together and tried to continue collecting their shopping.

Jimbo stood arms akimbo, for once lost for words. His straw boater askew, his moustache bristling with temper, he viewed the ruin of his beautiful Store and vowed Mrs Jones would have to go. He went to go in to the back to tell her so before he changed his mind.

The Store was a shambles. Linda came out from the post-office section and began putting the stationery back on the shelves, Bel went to start tidying the fruit and vegetables: apples and oranges and pears had rolled all over the floor to say nothing of the grapes, which had been stamped on and flattened and therefore posed a danger. Anyone coming in at that moment would have thought the fight of the century had just taken place.

'Go out through the back. I don't want to see you on these premises again. Never!' Jimbo's loud voice boomed round the mail-order office and Mrs Jones cowered. 'Never, do you hear? A brilliant career in mail order has just ended. I will not have my business ruined in this manner. I shall send what I owe you at the end of the month. After that your name will be *expunged* from my records, never to be seen again. You understand? You're not even to shop here.' He turned on his heel and left her perched on her beloved stool, quivering with the shock of what her temper had brought about. The humiliation! Mrs Jones fingered the marking pen she was so fond of, the address book she loved with the glorious roses in full bloom on the cover, the fancy sticky labels with the pattern of summer fruits around the edge which she'd introduced, and the stapler, red and business-like, which had always given her such pleasure when she used it.

She picked up her cardigan and bag, looked round her well-stocked shelves and remembered Jimbo always lodging his boater on top of the jars of chutney while the two of them had a policy meeting, and her eyes filled with tears again. Such an understanding man, but where his business was concerned ... All this lost because she'd sprung into action, as usual, in defence of her boys. What mother wouldn't? But suggesting they were pimps!

She marched round to Hipkin Gardens and shouted through the letterbox of number six, 'It's your mother. Come on, open up, I know you're in!' While she waited for one of the boys to open the door she had a good squint at the inside. She could see they'd had carpet laid and that looked like a new table to the right of the door.

Peering through the letterbox at the same time as hammering on the door she eventually saw Kenny's stockinged feet coming down the stairs.

'About time!'

She did him the courtesy of waiting until the front door was safely shut before she began her tirade rounding it off with 'So now because of you I've lost my job. Them saying something like that about my boys! I was wild.' Kenny shook his head. 'Saying you and our Terry were pimps! As if my boys would be involved in such a filthy business. Pimps! I almost died of shame. What your father will have to say I don't know.'

'Well, he's never said anything all my life so I don't expect he'll start now.' Kenny leaned forward and with his eyes only inches from hers he said, 'We are not pimps! Right! So you can go and put those nosy old besoms right on that score. See?'

'That's what I said. I said you weren't. But I've lost my job for ever. He meant what he said. Nicest job I've ever done. I'm not allowed in there even to shop, let alone to work.'

Kenny rubbed his eyes and then his face to wake himself up. 'Coffee, Mum?'

'Oh, yes, please.' She went to sit in their living room and her jaw dropped when she saw the latest addition; a huge leather armchair with wings. Mrs Jones sniffed it. Yes, it was, it was leather, none of your imitation. The real thing. This had cost a packet and not half. She gently lowered herself into it and practised resting her head against the right-hand wing. My! This was comfortable.

'Kenny! What did you pay for this new chair?'

'Too much!'

'All right then, don't tell me if you don't want to. But I bet it wasn't a penny under a thousand pounds. You are doing well. Wait till your dad sees it, he will be proud. I 'ope you're making our Terry pay his way.'

Coming in with the coffee Kenny replied, 'Don't you fret, our Terry's doing well for himself too.'

'Him too? Brilliant. I'm that proud. Getting this house has changed you both round. Time you were making your way in the world.'

'I've forgotten the sugar.' Kenny went back to the kitchen and when he returned not only did he have the sugar in his hand but two fifty-pound notes. 'Here, add this to your housekeeping. Say nothing to no one. Right? It's a thank-you for defending me.'

'What we'll do now I'm out of work as well as your dad I don't know. It won't be any good me crawling back and apologising, 'cos he's that blazing mad with me. Thank you for this. Thank you very much, it won't half 'elp. I'm that grateful.'

'Shut up, Mum. Take it and say nothing.'

'Well, thanks. Thanks very much.'

When she was leaving she turned back to say, 'You're not doing anything wrong, are yer, Kenny? Yer know.'

'Course not.' But he didn't look her in the eye as he said it.

With Sheila in hospital it fell to Muriel to polish the brass every week. She'd got over her fright about the mice, with Tom reassuring her he'd caught two, and went off happily to do her polishing thinking she would say a prayer for Sheila and Ron while she was there. Ralph she left studying the *Financial Times*, with a pot of coffee beside him and a small fire lit as autumn was creeping in and the mornings could be cold.

Tom had been hosing down the path leading up to the main door of the church so when Muriel got inside she made a point of wiping her feet well on the doormat before she walked down the aisle. She heard a sound and stopped. But to her relief it was only the Superintendent. He was standing looking at the Templeton tomb.

'Why, good morning, Lady Templeton. You look as though you're going to be busy.'

'I clean the brass alternate weeks with Lady Bissett, but I'm doing her turn for her.'

'Of course. I've been to see her this morning and been able to speak to her.'

Muriel's pale face lit up. 'Oh, how lovely! How was she? Could she tell you anything? We'd be so glad to get it cleared up. It has been such a worry, Sir Ralph has been most concerned. So unlike our village to have anything quite so ghastly happening. The odd argument, the occasional bit of bad feeling, but this! Of course, there was poor Sharon McDonald and Toria Clark. Now that was dreadful! But it's all been so peaceful since. I expect it's an everyday occurrence for you, Superintendent, but for us, well, it's so puzzling. I've racked my brains for an answer to it and the only thing I can come up with . . .'

'Yes?' Mr Proctor, his stern world-weary face grey with fatigue, stood looking down at her waiting, hoping, for some dynamic clue.

'Mistaken identity. They were beaten up in mistake for someone else. But then who else? Oh dear. Maybe that's not grammatically correct but you understand me, don't you? If they were not deserving of a beating up, then who was? Who in this village is less than well behaved? Kenny and Terry Jones spring to mind but that's just petty thieving and car crime . . .'

'For which we've only once managed to catch them. Very fly young gentlemen, Kenny and their Terry.'

'Exactly, but . . . they live down Shepherds Hill, or they did, there is no way their house could be mistaken for Sheila and Ron's. So whose house could be mistaken? Anyone around the Green. They're all thatched and they're all white with black timbers, most have roses around the door, except for Glebe Cottages and Glebe House. So I went round the Green in my head the other night and there isn't a single person who could possibly be in need of a beating.'

Muriel picked up her polishing box from where she'd rested it on the flat bit of the tomb. 'While I polish I'll have another think.' She turned back to say, 'You see, our houses are not numbered. The Post Office wanted to number us all a few years back but we all said we wouldn't use them if they did. I can tell you there was quite a row about it and an official came down, but we stuck to our guns. One must, you know, about such things. The same with the street lighting. They said it would help to cut crime. Crime? we said. What crime? Now I am beginning to wonder. If there'd been lights perhaps Sheila and Ron would . . .'

'I'll say good morning, Lady Templeton, pleasure talking to you.'

'I've just thought, what did Sheila have to say?'

'While you polish think of all the people around here who wear trainers. Black trainers.'

Muriel's eyes opened wide. 'She saw them then?'

'Only the trainers.'

'I see. Were you wanting time for prayer? I could come back later.'

The Superintendent smiled. 'Not much in my line of country, but maybe I might solve crimes quicker if I did.'

Muriel patted his arm and smiled. 'Maybe you would, maybe you would.'

Being such an ancient church it was much visited by enthusiasts for church architecture so she was accustomed to strangers wandering about while she worked. But this morning no one was around and she hummed and polished in solitude. Muriel was in the corner by the font, working on the brass decoration. It was the Victorian brass addition to the font she'd taken exception to. She heard the main door open. She couldn't see who had come in and she was hidden by the wall anyway so she worked away ignoring them. Then, standing back to inspect her handiwork, Muriel missed her footing and slipped down the shallow step which separated the font area from the main aisle.

'Oooh!' She saved herself from falling by grabbing the staff of a saint in the niche by the font. 'Oh dear!' Muriel rubbed her ankle and hopped about for a moment till it felt better. She packed up her cleaning box and went to walk towards the main door.

Standing by the Templeton tomb was Kenny Jones. His tatty anorak had been replaced by a black leather jacket, his grubby T-shirt by a royal blue shirt and a tie with a dazzling design on it, his old jeans by black twill trousers and on his feet were smart leather brogues. And always before he'd worn . . . Oh! No! Black trainers!

Kenny was so surprised to see her you could have thought he'd imagined she'd simply materialised from behind the tomb.

'Oh!' He recovered himself and said, 'Good morning, Lady Templeton. Nice morning. Been busy, I see.'

'Yes, that's right. I always take my turn to polish the brass, and now I'm doing Sheila Bissett's turn too. How are you, Kenny?'

'Very well, thank you. Nasty that. Beating 'em up.'

'Sheila's come round. That nice Mr Proctor told me. He's been talking to her. I'm glad to see you coming to church. There's nothing quite like a sit-down in here for sorting yourself out. Worries, you know. Problems and such.'

'Not my cup of tea really, but yes, I thought I'd come in.'

'Of course. There's nothing like it for calming the soul. Such a solace.'

'Indeed. Wouldn't know much about that, but it's worth a try. How's Sir Ralph? Keeping well, I hope?'

'Oh, yes, very well. Are you settled into your house? I hear tales of you making it very habitable.' She looked at him with a teasing grin on her face, though that was the last thing she really wanted to do. Black trainers? Surely not.

'Doing our best. We're glad of the chance, all thanks to Sir Ralph 'aving faith in us. Our Terry and me, we know what everyone thinks of us, and it doesn't help you to pull yourself up out of the mud, and that's what I'm doing by hook or by crook. I'm sick of being at the bottom of the pile.' He looked round the church. 'All this history. Wonderful old place. We're always so busy-busy, aren't we? But here it's so calm.'

'Exactly.' Muriel was surprised by his thoughtfulness; there was more to him than she had realised. 'I'll leave you to it then. Bye-bye.'

'Be seeing yer. Take care.'

Kenny opened the door for her and watched her going down the path. If she knew, he thought, if she just knew. Gracious old bat, though, but so, what's the word? That's it, naïve.

Muriel, having seen such a nice side to him, decided not to mention about the black trainers, for he couldn't really be the kind of person who would attack Sheila and Ron, not when he was so thoughtful. What's more, it wouldn't do to throw suspicion on him because there must be dozens of men wearing black trainers besides Kenny. She wouldn't even tell Ralph.

10

The bar and dining room of the Royal Oak were always first-rate places for learning what was going on in Turnham Malpas, as well as all the happenings in Little Derehams and Penny Fawcett. By nine o'clock on the Saturday night the dining room was full, and the bar was filling up nicely. Dicky and Georgie, with Alan's help, were busy supplying the drinkers and Bel was standing in for the dining-room manager who had flu. Most of her diners were from outside the village, a lovely mellow autumn evening having tempted them out from Culworth and some from as far away as the other side of the motorway.

In the bar it was mainly the local people who filled the chairs. There was a full house at the table which had the settle down one side of it. Jimmy was there with, under the table, his dog Sykes, who knew he wasn't supposed to be in there and who kept quiet because past experience had taught him that if he did keep quiet he would be rewarded with a long drink from Jimmy's beer before the end of the evening. Sitting with Jimmy were Sylvia and Willie and also Vera, making one of her rare appearances.

Vera, feeling flush with the bonus she'd received, said, 'Next round's on me. Busy tonight, ain't it? Any more news about the hedge? 'As that dratted old Fitch decided to climb down?'

Sylvia shook her head. 'The Rector's has been up to see him as well as Lady Templeton, and neither of them have budged him an inch. So they're planning a petition and I shall be the first to sign it.'

Vera placed her glass neatly in the middle of the beer mat and said knowingly, 'I reckon this hedge business is only the first step in a bigger scheme.'

Scornfully Willie asked, 'What bigger scheme?'

'I reckon he's wanting to build houses on Rector's Meadow and thinks if he gets the hedge question out of the way there'll be nothing to stop him. I have heard that he's widening the lane when he does it, so the council can't put a stop to it because of access.'

'Vera! Sometimes . . .'

Sylvia stepped in with her support. 'She could have a point. He's a devious one you know, and he's never done anything with that field, has he? Never planted it, never had the cows in it from Home Farm, never nothing. I think Vera could be right.'

Willie and Jimmy laughed. 'You two, you get worse.'

Vera tapped the table with her finger. 'Mark my words. He's coming round to it step by step. You can laugh, I shall remind you about this when it all comes to pass. Any news about poor Sheila and Ron? Have they got anybody yet?'

'No. The police are baffled, as they say.'

'Glad enough to take a fat rise, but not so enthusiastic about getting crimes solved. Our Rhett thinks it's a gangland revenge.'

Jimmy laughed. 'Aw! Come on, Vera! What on earth have Ron and Sheila to do with gangs?'

'He reckons someone's after silencing Ron. He did make that speech, didn't he, about workers' rights and the right to strike not being taken from them? He got a lot of publicity in the papers an' that.'

'Yes, but –'

'Yes, but nothing. You never know. Them in high places don't want unions getting up on their hind legs and making a fuss. They're all earning big, big money nowadays and they're committed to big mortgages and that and high living and they don't like the idea of doing without, so they sink to beatin' people up.'

Willie looked sceptically at Vera. 'I reckon those old dears you look after are addling your brains.'

Sylvia, shocked by his remark, nudged him. 'Willie!'

Vera looked hurt. 'I may not have much up top, Willie Biggs, but I'm not daft. Those people who've come up from the bottom rung are enjoying a lifestyle they never thought possible in their wildest dreams and they've no intention of losing it all. They'll stick at nothing. Lying in their teeth, cheating, fraud, anything.'

Jimmy tried pouring oil on troubled waters. 'I'm ready for a refill.' He pushed his glass towards Vera.

She stood up saying, 'Rightio. Same again, everybody?' They all nodded.

Sylvia watched her walk towards the bar. 'You shouldn't pour scorn on her, it's not right. She's doing her best to improve things for her ... self ... Well, I never!'

Jimmy and Willie, their backs to the door, turned round to see what or who had caught Sylvia's attention.

Together they both said, 'Blimey!'

'It's Don, isn't it?'

He'd used too much hair dye and the result was an over-exaggerated head of jet black hair, but the barber had given him a very good cut, well tapered into his neck, parted and thinned, and it had taken years off his age. He'd been shaved immaculately: even the tufts of hair he always kept missing around the cleft in his chin had been banished. His skin, instead of being muddy and looking suspiciously as though it hadn't been washed properly in weeks, was positively glowing. He was wearing a smart checked sports jacket with dark trousers, a sober tie and matching shirt. Conversation came to a standstill as the entire bar gazed in amazement at this unbelievable spectacle.

Vera hadn't seen him, with her back being to the door, and he hadn't seen Vera and he went straight across to their usual table.

'Can I get anyone a drink?'

Sylvia was the first to answer. 'Well, my word. I have to say it. You do look so smart, I am impressed.'

He tried to pass off her remark by shrugging his shoulders and showing them a ten-pound note. 'Well?'

Willie found his tongue. 'You've lost weight too. By Jove, Don! I could nearly think you were courting.'

Sylvia nudged Willie again. 'Take no notice, Don. We're all right for drinks, thanks, Vera's just getting us a refill.'

Don glanced across to the bar. 'Didn't realise she was 'ere.' They watched him pinch the knot of his tie to make sure it was just right and as he marched across to Vera their eyes followed him.

Jimmy whispered, 'I swear I can smell aftershave.'

Willie agreed. 'So can I. This could be interesting.'

'I've never seen him in that outfit before, have you?' Sylvia asked, with her hand over her mouth so he couldn't possibly hear her. 'Let's hope he isn't meeting someone in here tonight.'

Jimmy finished the last drops of his beer and said, 'No, I reckon it's Vera he's courting. We could have some fun.'

Sylvia tapped Willie's arm. 'And just you watch your tongue. We don't want to upset things, not when he's making an effort.'

At the bar Don took hold of the tray. 'I'll pay for these, Vera. Add an orange juice, would you, Alan, please?'

'Certainly, Mr Wright.'

Vera hadn't seen him yet, but she'd smelt the pungent aftershave. She wondered how it could be Don's voice she heard, but not the old musty smell of the Don she remembered. At the sound of his voice she hesitated and then very slowly turned to face him. Conversation fell away. Everyone in the bar knew the state of affairs between Vera and Don and most agreed Vera had been justified in leaving him in that pit he called home. They watched quite openly to see her reaction.

But there was none. She looked at him in complete silence, her face composed and giving nothing away. No surprise. No amazement. No pleasure. No consternation. Without a word she walked back to the table and sat down. Jimmy got up and pulled a chair across for Don. There was a quiet hum of conversation while everyone waited to see what would happen next. Vera sat mute. Don handed round the drinks, returned the tray to the bar and came back to sit at the end of the table, his knees almost touching Vera's where she sat at his right hand on the settle.

Don asked her, 'Gin and tonic now, is it?'

'Any objections?'

'No, no, none at all. Bit different from your usual port and lemon, that's all.'

'It is. But then I've moved on, you see.'

'Of course. Job working out all right?'

'Yes, thanks.'

'Rhett liking the flat, is he?'

'He couldn't but. Nice room overlooking the gardens. He's well set up.'

'He hasn't called to see me.'

'Not surprising, is it? You've not been to see him.'

'I am still his grandad.'

'Are you now?'

'What do you mean by that remark?'

'Nothing.'

'Have you stopped him coming?'

'No. He does as he likes, like I do.'

'I can see that.' Don looked her up and down, noting the flattering dress she wore and her smart hairstyle. 'You look nice. How do you manage to get your hair done in that dead-alive hole?'

'The hairdresser who comes to do the patients' hair does mine in exchange for a nice meal and a sit-down in my flat before she leaves.'

'Got it all organised, haven't you?'

'Oh, yes! My life's got style now. I'm off on holiday in a fortnight. Torquay. I've always wanted to go. 'As just that air of distinction which I quite fancy nowadays.' She stood up. 'I'll be off now, the company doesn't suit.'

Don stood up. 'Can I give you a lift?'

His suggestion put the torch to her temper. 'Lift? You? Give me a lift? I wouldn't accept a lift from you if I had a hundred miles to walk. A lift? In that stinking uncomfortable sidecar I've put up with all our married life? Why I've stuck with you I'll never know. But at last, thank Gawd, I've come to my senses.' She gestured at his new clothes. 'Another thing whilst we're on the subject, you've no need to think you're making an impression on me with this lot, because you're not. Underneath you're still the same old Don. Selfish! Inconsiderate! Dull! Boring! Hidebound! Yes, hidebound. You'd no more think of going to Torquay than – than . . .'

Vera picked up her bag and pushed him full in the chest so she had room to get out from the settle. His chair fell over but he managed to remain upright. 'See! Stolid from head to toe. Immovable! That's you! Immovable. You haven't that much spark in you, not that much!' She held her finger and thumb a centimetre apart close up to his face. 'Good night to you!'

Don bent to pick up his chair and he sat down in it, his head lowered, giving the remains of his orange juice close scrutiny. Jimmy, to cover his embarrassment, put his glass under the table for his dog Sykes to finish.

After a few moments Sylvia shuffled along the settle and sympathetically laid a hand on his arm. 'She's just a bit upset, you see.'

In a very subdued voice Don replied, 'What about?'

'That's just it, Don. It's like she says. You don't *think*.'

'About what?'

'About *her*.'

'But this is for her.' He gestured towards his jacket. 'I thought she'd be pleased.'

'She is. But she won't let on because it's like she says, nothing's changed. You've made a good start, but it's only skin deep, you see.'

'Tell me then, Sylvia, what can I do?'

Needing to get the position absolutely clear Sylvia asked him, 'About what?'

'About getting her back.'

Willie intervened: 'It all depends on how much you want her back.'

Don looked up at him. 'Well, I do. It was all right at first, the novelty yer know, but now, well, I miss 'er and it's not just the cooking an' that. I miss 'er. I want things like they used to be.'

'Nay, Don.' Jimmy sighed. 'Nay, Don. Yer haven't listened to a word what Sylvia said. Vera doesn't want things like they used to be, that's what she's rebelling against.'

'But look at me, I've tried. What more can a fella do?'

Sylvia took hold of his hand. 'How could you expect her in all conscience to want to have a lift in that rackety old sidecar, dressed like she is and with her hair newly done? Answer me that.'

'But it's a classic! Worth a lot.'

Scornfully Jimmy muttered, 'Then sell the damn thing.'

Don reacted violently to Jimmy's suggestion. 'Sell it? It's my pride and joy.'

'But,' said Jimmy, 'it doesn't make your meals, or iron yer shirts, ui keep yei company, or keep yer warm in bed, does it? So make up yer mind.'

Sylvia gave him an ultimatum. 'It's Vera or the bike, Don.'

'It's make-yer-mind-up time.' Jimmy stood up. 'I've to be off. They'll all be wanting taxis soon and outside Culworth Station is where I've to be pronto, pronto.' He popped a mint in his mouth from a packet he kept in his pocket, called a cheerful goodnight to everyone and left with Sykes slinking along beside him, licking froth from his lips and trying to look as if he didn't exist.

'Night, Jimmy.' Don turned to look at Sylvia. 'I'm going to have to do better, aren't I?'

'Yes, you are. After all, she's only wanting you to live at the nursing home while ever she has a job there. She'll go back to the cottage when she retires. It's not for ever, is it?'

'That's it though, she won't. That's the problem, my cottage.'

'Well, that's for you to decide, because you're the one who'll have to change things.'

Don looked up at Sylvia and gave her one of his very rare smiles. 'She did look nice tonight, didn't she?'

'Yes, she did, very nice. Come on, Willie, that programme'll be starting in a minute and if we don't see the beginning you'll be asking me who's who and what's what all night. Good night, Don. Think on what we've talked about.'

Don sat a while longer contemplating his orange juice. He'd never been a sociable man so no one bothered to come over to keep him company. After a while if they'd been watching him they'd have seen him almost visibly come to a decision. He got up, drank his orange juice right to the bottom, banged down the glass and marched out, leaving the swing door crashing back and forth behind him.

It must have been close to eleven o'clock, because the last of the Royal Oak customers were leaving for home, when the village became aware of loud noises coming from Don's cottage. There were horrendous hammerings, vicious bangings and huge thunderings as though someone was taking a fourteen-pound hammer to the entire contents of his cottage.

Grandmama Charter-Plackett, sitting up in bed in her silk nightgown and matching bed-jacket enjoying her nightcap of whisky and water, leaped out of bed with alarm, convinced that very soon, if not sooner, Don would be appearing through a hole in her bedroom wall. She put on her fluffy mules and her winter dressing-gown and marched down the stairs preparing for war.

When she saw the crowd gathered outside she tightened her belt and joined them. 'Someone,' she said, 'must go in there and do something. The man has gone mad.'

There were murmurs from the crowd but no one stepped forward. It was as well they didn't because the front door flew open and Don came out of it backwards dragging large pieces of wood, which jammed in the doorway and brought him to a halt. Willie, who'd been on his way upstairs to bed and had just come out to tear a strip off the person about to disturb his sleep, offered his help.

''Ere, let me give you a hand.' Between them they freed the wood and got it out in the road. 'Now, what's all this? You can't be a-doing of this now. It's eleven o'clock. We're all off to bed.'

Don simply climbed over the wood and back into the house where the banging began all over again.

Grandmama asked, 'Is the Rector in?'

Willie shook his head. 'Gone to a meeting in Gloucester. Should be back any time, though.'

'Then who's going to put a stop to it? He's gone mad. Quite mad.' She looked imperiously around the crowd to find several of them avoiding her eyes and others looking very sheepishly at her. Windows were opening, voices calling out asking what was going on and could they keep quiet. Two weekenders came out to see which of the local yokels had finally gone mad, and were obviously looking forward to some good entertainment.

'In that case, then, I shall have to go in. Though what you men are made of I cannot begin to imagine.'

Sylvia protested. 'Mrs Charter-Plackett, I don't think it's fit for you to ...'

But she was already climbing over the wood.

The front door led straight into the sitting room, a sitting room stacked on every surface with the contents of the kitchen cupboards. Don was in the kitchen at the back. Inside the house the noise was ear-bending. She couldn't actually get into the kitchen because pieces of wood were flying off his hammer in her direction as he attacked the dresser right by the door, but she recognised the terrible desperation which had triggered his lunatic attack: telling him to stop would only increase the frenzy. Sweat was rolling down his face, a puce-coloured face which caused her extreme anxiety about whether or not he would see the night through without having a heart-attack. Telling him off would be like putting a match to a very short fuse. When he paused to get his breath she shouted, 'Mr Wright! It's me from next door. I've just called to see if everything's all right?' Looking into the kitchen she added, 'My word, you have been busy. What a good idea. Just what it needed. Shall I give you a hand getting it all out? Here, you get the other end of this piece and between us we'll take it out, then you'll have more room to work.'

When the banging stopped those outside had smirked at each other, imagining the dressing-down Don would be receiving, but when Grandmama appeared backwards out of the door heaving another large piece of wood out on to the road they couldn't believe their eyes. She threw it on to the pile and marched back in without a word.

Taking their cue from her there followed a glorious united effort from everyone to rid Don and Vera's kitchen of every single last inch of shelving and cupboard: the sink and the cooker and the fridge-freezer were all dragged out too. Under Grandmama's instruction some marched in and out removing the results of Don's manic attack, others stayed outside stacking the remnants of the kitchen as they were brought out, while Don continued to swing the hammer. Finally the entire kitchen was outside on the road.

'Well,' said someone under their breath, 'that lot's what I call rubbish and no mistake. That cooker isn't even good enough for Culworth Museum. As for the cupboards! And that table and chairs! Every leg ready to fall off any minute, and not a decent lick of paint left on 'em!'

'Wait till Vera hears!'

To their final astonishment they heard Grandmama inviting Don round for breakfast. 'You can't even boil a kettle in there now, so, I breakfast at eight thirty prompt on Sundays and you'll be more than welcome.'

For the first time since the whole episode had begun Don spoke. 'Thank you, Missus, eight thirty it is. Goodnight.'

It had always been recognised that they broke the mould after Mrs Charter-Plackett was born, but to their total amazement as the church bells rang out for the ten o'clock service on Sunday morning and everyone was making their way to church, she topped even her Saturday night performance. They were stunned to see Grandmama Charter-Plackett, a scarf tied over her summer going-to-church hat to secure it against the wind, graciously waving to them from Don's sidecar and the two of them steaming down the Culworth Road as though the hounds of hell were after them. And, yes, it was true then, they had cleared Don and Vera's kitchen out, right to the bare walls, because there was the evidence for all to see, still stacked outside the door.

11

Kenny Jones walked into the Store on the Monday morning. It was too early for Bel to have finished her caretaking duties at the school so it was Linda behind her post-office grille to whom he spoke.

'Boss in?'

'If you mean Mr Charter-Plackett, yes, he is.'

'Can I have a word?'

She looked him up and down. 'Heck! What's happened to you? Surprise, surprise! Quite the country gent, aren't we?'

'Cut the sarcasm, Linda. You should have married me instead of that creep you call husband, then you'd have been sharing in my good fortune.'

Linda flushed. She'd always known people thought of her Alan as a present day Uriah Heep but to have it said outright, on a Monday morning too, was a bit much. 'Nasty sod! I'd a lot rather be married to him than a no-good like you.'

'Watch your tongue, you. I might need a stamp or two and I'm not having a cheeky bitch serving me.'

'Didn't know you could write.'

'Eh! Watch it.'

'There's no law that says I'm compelled to serve you.'

'No? We'll see about that.' Being securely locked in her post-office section, according to regulations, he'd no means of getting to her other than unlocking her door. He slotted his fingers through the wire triangles around the door lock as though intending to gain entry. His furious rattling alarmed her and she pressed her panic button.

Jimbo, busy in the mail-order office in the absence of Mrs Jones, sprang into action picking up as he ran the rounders bat he kept for the purpose. When he saw Kenny collapsed with laughter propped against the stationery shelves Jimbo felt disappointed. He was just in the mood for confrontation.

'What the blazes, Linda? It's only Kenny.'

'Only Kenny! He was rattling the door trying to get in here.'

'Were you?'

'Only kidding, just to get her going.'

'It's not funny, Kenny, not funny at all.'

'Sorry. But she was impudent to me. Refused to serve me.'

'I didn't, you didn't ask.'

'I said I might.'

'Well, there is no law that says I must.'

Jimbo interrupted, 'There's the law according to Jimbo. That says you must.'

'Does it indeed? Insulting he was to my Alan. Real insulting, and I won't stand for it.'

Aware that another row with Linda was looming, which might end with him sacking her yet again, Jimbo turned his attention to Kenny. 'What's the reason for your appearance at this early hour?'

Kenny nodded his head in the direction of the back office. 'Can I have a private word?'

'If it's about your mother getting her job back, no, you can't. She isn't. Full stop.'

'But −'

'Sorry, but no. I've put a notice in the window advertising her job and the first suitable applicant to walk through that door gets it.'

'But she's done a good job here. I know she has.'

'Agreed. But she isn't coming back.'

'You can't sack people like that nowadays.'

'I have done.'

'We'll take you to a tribunal.'

'You will? Try me. Behaviour prejudicial to the good conduct of my business.'

'Sod off! You think 'cos you've got money you can throw your weight around, well, just you wait and see. Next it'll be Kenny Jones with money and then I'll get my own back on you.'

'That's likely. What money I have I've got through sheer hard graft and that's something you know nothing about.'

'Then you're daft. There's ways!' He tapped the side of his nose. 'Anyway, you'll regret sacking my mother, just you wait and see.' He prodded the air with his index finger and stepped closer to Jimbo.

Jimbo raised the rounders bat. 'Are you threatening me?'

'Me? No! Threatening you? Certainly not.' He laughed, made a rude two-finger gesture to Linda and slammed the door behind him.

'Oh, Mr Charter-Plackett, you are brave. The no-good disgusting slob that he is. Wait till my Alan hears about this!'

'I should advise your Alan to steer clear. He isn't a match for someone like Kenny Jones.'

The slight on her Alan's capacity for standing up to that loathsome slob upset Linda and she burst into tears. 'Let me out! Let me out!'

'You've got the keys.'

'Oh, yes!' She unlocked herself and fled into the back. Jimbo threw his hands up in despair.

'God! What have I done to deserve this? Linda! Linda!' He locked the post-office door and, taking the keys with him, followed her through and put the kettle on. A cup of tea always did the trick with Linda.

Kenny, angry because he'd hadn't succeeded in getting his mother's job back for her, realised he'd gone about it in totally the wrong way. Men like Jimbo appreciated good manners and civility and he should have remembered that, like he had done when he asked Sir Ralph to let him rent the house. He really would have to curb his tongue. No good wearing the smart new clothes if the man inside didn't fit them.

He wandered across to the church. Pushing open the main door he recalled his conversation with Muriel. That had been pleasant and he'd managed it very well. Given her such a good account of himself that he'd made her feel better about him. Almost sympathetic she'd been.

He went to sit in the church to wait for Tom.

*

Tom had a big rubbish bag in his hand and was going round the churchyard collecting up the dead flowers from the graves, and generally casting his eye about for any imperfections which might offend the Rector. He hadn't had a chance to speak to him yet but no doubt he'd be in later this morning to see what was what. Of course he'd have been in for his early prayers before most people had opened their eyes and then off for his morning run. Such discipline. Such dedication.

He leaned against a headstone and thought. Thought about how much he loved this place. Never imagined in all his life he'd come to such a position. Verger of St Thomas à Becket! Men he'd worked with in the past would have reeled about laughing at the thought. Let 'em. He had the last laugh. He had the peace, the comfort. The trees waving in the breeze, the flowers flowering, the grass growing, the pulse of life at his fingertips. Yes! He wouldn't swap it for all the money in the world. There'd felt to be something so right about buying the house in this sleepy village. He likened himself and Evie to a ship crossing the stormy oceans, plunging through wild waves as high as mountains and finally coming into a safe haven at last. He liked that idea and ruminated on it for a while.

The only fly in the ointment was Kenny. A blast from the past. He shook his head and decided not to dwell on him.

Straightening himself up he went off to the very back of the churchyard to try out the gate which led to the grounds of the Big House. It swung easily on its hinges now he'd used WD40 on it, useful stuff. Satisfying that. He stroked the old timbers of the gate. Nobody used it now, but it was nice to keep such a lovely old gate in good fettle. Better get on. According to Willie's schedule, it was the day for polishing the pews. With the rain just beginning to come down it seemed an appropriate time for doing it, and he was looking forward to it.

The huge tin of furniture polish awaited him in the cleaning cupboard, with the cloths beside it. The label on it showed a dear old chap wearing a green apron, lovingly polishing a shining table; there was an aspidistra on a stand close by and old paintings on the wall. He smiled to himself. He hadn't got the green apron but he did have his orange overalls. He felt a twinge of conscience when he remembered where he'd pinched them from. All in a good cause though.

He went through into the church, faced the altar and bowed his head as part of his ritual for keeping Lady Luck on his side. He prised the lid off the tin and dipped a cloth into the polish. Must take care to rub it all off, otherwise they'd all be complaining about polish on their clothes. Absorbed in his task he whistled a hymn tune and looked forward to a rewarding morning's work. The church clock struck quarter past ten. Nice that. Glad they'd got it mended. He pondered what Evie might have put in his lunchbox. If it was one of her good days it would be appetising, if not he wouldn't fancy anything she'd put in and he'd have to tip it in the bin and say nothing ... He smelt smoke. Cigar smoke. He looked up and there was Kenny, sitting at the back, his feet propped on the pew in front.

'Morning.'

'Have some respect, Kenny, if you please.'

After a pause Kenny very slowly removed his feet from the pew and sat up, taking another drag on his cigar as he did so.

'And the cigar. You know we're not allowed to smoke in here.'

'I haven't finished it yet.'

'Well, stub it out.'

'On the pew?'

'For God's sake, don't be so stupid. Here, stub it out on this lid.' Tom walked up the aisle and offered the lid of the polish tin to him. He sat down on the pew in front of Kenny and said, 'Well?'

'Well?'

'What's up?'

'What's up? You tell me.'

'I've nothing to say.'

Kenny leaned an elbow on the top of the pew in front of him to get closer to Tom. 'What the blazes *are* you doing here?'

'Making a real life for myself. All I want is leaving alone.'

'You call this a real life? God! Tom, you must have lost your marbles.'

'No, I haven't. It's what Evie and I want. We've never been happier.'

Kenny shrugged his shoulders. 'Each to his own.'

'Exactly. Now buzz off and let me get on.'

Kenny leered. 'Pity about Ron and Sheila.'

When Tom looked closely into Kenny's eyes he found they were giving nothing away. 'Surprising how you can get beaten up and you've done nothing at all to deserve it. Not fair, is it?'

'No.'

'Could have been killed.'

'Yes. They could.'

'Good morning, Tom.' Kenny got to his feet, picked up the parcel beside him on the seat and left.

Tom eased the collar of his overalls away from his throat, and felt the sweat trickling down his neck. Picking up the lid of the polish tin he carried it to the outside wheelie-bin and tipped the stub in. There were flecks of ash left behind so Tom brushed them away, and wished he could brush Kenny away as easily.

Tom took his lunchbox home. Evie was eating silently on a seat in the garden.

'Thought I'd have mine at home with you.' He put his box beside her and sat down. The sun, though warm, wasn't really quite warm enough to sit outside but that was Evie all over. If she wanted to eat outside she would, even in the depths of winter.

'Bit cold for you.'

Evie nodded.

'Happy?'

Evie nodded again, shielding her eyes against the sun to watch a robin pecking at crumbs.

'Grand little chap. Nice to have time to watch him.'

Evie smiled.

'Been working this morning?'

Evie gave him the thumbs up.

'Good. Nearly finished the Nativity?'

'Yes.'

Rewarded at last with an answer Tom said, 'Good. Good.'

'I've got an idea for the next one.'

'Excellent. You could have an exhibition.'

'No, not an exhibition.'

'Why not? It could trigger off this embroidery class Sheila's keen on.' Remembering Sheila brought Kenny to mind. Tom, impatient with himself, stood up and headed towards the house. He put the kettle on, made them a coffee each and went back to Evie.

'Is it your sugar day? It had better be because I've put it in without asking.'

Evie gave him one of her infrequent smiles.

'Kenny's been round to see me.'

Evie began to shake. Her coffee spilt out of her mug and scalded her hand.

'Don't worry, now. You're not to get worried. Here, let me take your mug. There, there. Now, now.' He put an arm round her shoulders. 'I wish I'd never said.'

'You won't, will you, Tom? You won't.'

'No. You've got my promise on that.'

'I can't bear it starting all over again.'

'It won't. I made a promise.'

Tom kissed the side of her head, smoothed her hair back from her face and kissed her cheek. 'You and me's all right, Evie, believe me.' He sank his teeth into a piece of Evie's flapjack. It was so hard he thought for a nasty minute he'd broken a tooth.

When Tom returned to church after his lunch Peter was in the vestry. 'Ah! Tom!'

'Good afternoon to you, Rector. Had a good holiday? Nice to see you back. Never quite the same without you in the Rectory.'

'Yes, I have. Thank you.'

Tom looked at him and decided he'd got some of his old energy back. 'Nothing happened since you went. Downright dull it's been.'

'Not dull enough. I smelt cigar smoke in here when I walked in. You don't smoke, do you, Tom?'

'Must have been someone in while I was at lunch. Went home to eat it with Evie.'

Peter looked hard at him and Tom had difficulty keeping his gaze steady. 'Mmmmmm. Because, you know, we cannot afford to have a fire started by someone smoking. If it was proved we wouldn't get a penny on the insurance – these old timbers would go up like kindling. If you catch someone smoking turn them out.'

'I would, immediately, you can bank on that.'

'Good. This funeral on Thursday. Everything in order?'

'Willie's run through it with me, and I'm all set. Grave dug already.'

'Good. I'll get off home for some lunch then.' Peter got to his feet and, towering over Tom, he looked down at him. Those intense blue eyes of his shook Tom a little; he thought they could see right inside him. God help him if they could. 'You seem to be doing a good job, Tom. I'm glad you applied, I think we're going to get on well together. You've already got yourself organised and that's excellent. Evie well?'

'Yes, thanks.' Peter went out of the vestry, crossed himself as he passed in front of the altar and left Tom to get back to his polishing. Somehow the swish of Peter's cassock as he strode down the aisle tugged at Tom's conscience. All he longed for was to be truthful like Peter was with him, and he couldn't, not to save his life he couldn't.

12

Ever since Don had thrown out the contents of his kitchen the whole village had been on red alert, waiting to see what would happen next. The story being told at coffee mornings and in that convenient corner by the tinned soups in the Store and by the crowd of waiting mothers at the school gate was that Grandmama and Don had been into Culworth DIY and ordered a complete new kitchen. They found this hard to believe as Don and Vera had always been so very short of money. Maybe, someone slyly suggested, Grandmama had lent him the wherewithal for his services in a completely different direction. After the initial burst of laughter at the idea, they scoffed at such fantasy.

The other matter occupying their idle tongues was where was Don eating? No kitchen, no cooker, no food. They'd speculated on an arrangement between Grandmama and Don, but dismissed that because someone volunteered they'd twice seen him coming out of Willie and Sylvia's. One or two brave souls had dallied with the idea of asking Jimbo outright but at the last they'd got cold feet. It was Vera who, in shock at the sight of her kitchen in pieces outside the front door, finally asked him the million-dollar question one afternoon when the rubbish had still not been moved and people were growing tetchy about it. She'd cadged a lift with the man who delivered groceries to the nursing home and to the Store and gone straight in, wedging the door open for him so he could get in and out more easily.

She found Jimbo standing by the till, idly casting an eye over his empire. 'Seeing, Mr Charter-Plackett, that you know most of what goes on in this village due to the fact you love listening to gossip,'

Jimbo pulled a face at this remark and tried to look innocent of the charge, 'no good pretending you don't because you do, can you tell me what's going on?'

Eyes round with innocence Jimbo took off his boater and smoothed a hand over his bald head. 'About what?'

Vera gave him a nudge. 'About my kitchen being out in the road. I've been to look. It's true, it's just like they've said. So? I understand your mother is to blame.'

'Blame? I wouldn't say that. Not blame, she's aided and abetted, yes, I agree.'

'Well, then, what are they up to?'

Jimbo bent towards her and spoke in a low voice. 'Don't know if I should be telling you this, but he's ordered a new kitchen. Coming at the weekend and Barry Jones, and the electrician and the plumber from the Big House, are spending the weekend fitting it. Under Mother's supervision, so you know it will be done right.'

Vera was aghast. She drew in a couple of deep breaths while she studied over what he'd said and finally came out with 'Ah! But where did he get the money? That's what I want to know.'

Jimbo shrugged his shoulders. 'Got to go. Customer.' And he fled to attend to his business leaving Vera none the wiser.

All his life Don had been virulent about people who bought on credit. Go to hell sure as maybe will all them what borrow money. A sure and certain path to damnation is borrowing. So although he'd appeared to be doing some strange things since she'd left him, borrowing money almost certainly wouldn't be one of them, because Don had always had a very healthy respect for hell. A terrible suspicion began to dawn on her. Maybe all these years when she'd been scrimping and saving he'd been saving too. Maybe he earned an awful lot more at work then he'd ever let on. She cast her mind back and thought about always getting a proper payslip from the nursing home telling her how much she'd earned, how much the thieving government had taken from her in tax and things, so she knew for certain how much she'd have in her pay packet. But had she ever seen one of Don's slips? No! She had no more idea how much he earned even after all these years than she had had when they married, and what's more she'd never thought to question him. Come to that, had she ever seen a bank statement?

There'd never been one come through the post, that she knew for certain. In a flash she knew Don wouldn't trust a bank anyway. So just what had he been keeping from her? How much, and where was it? The lowlife, the stinking rotten lowlife.

Vera stood in the middle of the Store so carried away with her thought processes that she didn't realise she was in everyone's way. Someone bumped into her and apologised. She moved her bag to the other hand and felt the hardness of the cottage key as it banged against her leg. The message it gave travelled from her leg up to her head. She looked up at the lovely old clock Jimbo had on the wall behind the till. The beautiful shapely brass hands were saying half past four. Don 'ud be another half an hour before he got home. The key was in her bag as her leg had just witnessed, that huge key more fit for a castle than a cottage. Here was her golden opportunity to find out. Vera marched home, heart beating fast, too fast, but she didn't care: she had to find out before he got back.

She glanced quickly up and down Church Lane: the only living creatures in sight were Jimmy's geese waiting outside the Rectory. Vera swiftly put the key in the lock, turned it and disappeared inside. The sight which met her eyes horrified her. Every inch of space was taken up with the contents of her kitchen shelves. Only one chair was free, and that was placed directly in front of the telly. She smiled grimly to herself. Typical. Under the mattress was the usual place for people of Don's kind to hide things. She climbed the tiny twisting stairs; on every step some item was laid which Don should have put away in the bedroom but which had never got further than the stairs.

The bed was unmade and it looked as though the sheets had not been changed since she'd last slept in it. She wrinkled her nose with distaste, but pressed on with her quest.

Lifting up one side of the feather mattress she splayed her fingers and patted as far as she could under it, spreading her arms as wide as possible, but found nothing. She went round to his side of the bed, the one nearest the window, and did the same. Her fingers closed on a fat envelope. Inside were loads and loads of banknotes. Vera pulled them out. They were all fifty-pound notes. Neatly bundled with pages torn from an exercise book and fastened with sticky tape. Feverishly she made a hasty calculation. Over seven thousand pounds! Sweat rushed from every pore. The shock of it! So where had he kept all this lot when she lived at home? Certainly not in the bed. She'd have noticed. But it didn't matter. What mattered was the deception. Making her use all the money she'd earned to keep them and contributing as little as he could, so he could save. But she couldn't understand how *much* he'd managed to save. What really hurt was the thought that she could have had the new kitchen years ago.

The throb-throb of his motorcycle engine sounded outside. He was back from work. Vera raced down the stairs, picked up the first thing which came to hand, which by chance was the very cast-iron pan she'd hit him with the day she left, and charged outside.

Don, his back to her innocently unaware of his fate, was calmly immobilising his bike and still wearing his crash helmet, so he didn't hear her breathing heavily behind him. Despite her anger she knew it would be pointless hitting him whilst he still wore his helmet, so she bided her time.

Don, having read outside a bank somewhere that helmets should be removed before entering the premises, always took his off before going in the house. His leathers creaked as he turned. If she hadn't been so furious with him she'd have burst out laughing at the expression on his face when he saw her standing there, the pan held in both hands, raised ready for attack.

'Vera!'

'You thieving little runt! I've found yer money! That nice little hoard you thought you'd keep for yourself. All that money and me living in poverty! Where've you been keeping it? Eh? Tell me that!'

'I haven't been keeping it! Let me tell yer! Just listen!'

But she wouldn't. She aimed a great swipe at him and, with memories of the last time she'd hit him with that same pan, Don dropped his helmet and started to run with Vera in pursuit. Jimmy's geese, still grouped around the Rectory door in the hope that the children would be coming out to feed them, began honking loudly and followed in a stream behind the two of them, half flying half running in pursuit. Neither Don nor Vera was as fit as they would have liked and Don, hampered by the weight and the restriction of his motorcycle leathers, lumbered awkwardly past Jimmy's cottage and round the Green, with Vera shrieking the worst words she knew as she chased him. Fortunately she'd never learned really bad ones, so when the the children came out of the Rectory and Jimbo's four poured out of their house and the early birds at the Royal Oak came out to see the fun they didn't need to cover their ears. By the time they reached the Store every customer was out cheering in Stocks Row to see them go by.

'Go on, Vera. Give him it!'

'Run, Don! Run!'

'Now, Vera! Give it up! The poor chap!'

'What's he done?'

Running and shouting at the same time meant Vera was panting heavily as they passed the school, and by the time they reached their cottage again she was completely out of breath.

'The money! You rotten dog! The money! You thieving, lying hound!' She lunged at him yet again with the pan but he had just enough breath left to dodge out of her way. 'All that money!!' They both looked at the open cottage door, at each other, shouted, 'The money!' in unison and tried to squeeze through the door together. The geese, still in a state of extreme excitement, were pecking at Don's legs as they tried to join the crush at the door so Don paused to kick at them and consequently Vera won. As she clambered up the stairs, on her hands and knees, too exhausted to walk upright, she made up her mind that half that money at least belonged to her.

Don almost had a heart-attack when he saw all the notes laid out on the bed. At the top of his voice he shouted, 'You daft beggar! Leaving the house unlocked and all this money about! If you'd just stop to listen.' He gasped for breath and sank on to the eiderdown, his head down, heaving great gulps of air into his lungs. Vera collapsed into the Lloyd Loom chair that had been so dear to his mother's heart and began to laugh. Quietly at first and then more and more hysterically until tears began running down her face and she sobbed. Sobbed for her lost years, for her yearning for a better life, for being married to a man who loved her so little.

'You've got the wrong end of the stick, Vera. I meant to tell yer.'

'Shut up! Shut up!'

'If you'd just calm —'

They heard a voice downstairs. 'Hello! Hello! It's Peter from the Rectory. Is everything all right?'

Don hastily pushed the money under the mattress and called out, 'Coming down, won't be a minute.'

When he reached the bottom of the stairs Don said, 'Vera's been a bit upset.'

'I guessed. Is she feeling better now?'

'She will in a bit. It's a misunderstanding, and she doesn't want to hear.'

'I see. Would she like a lift home?'

'That's all right, I'll take her.'

Peter raised his eyebrows.

'Well, perhaps not.'

'I'll take her. Tell her come to the Rectory and knock when she wants to go and I'll drive her.'

'Thanks.' Don looked up at him, hesitated a moment wondering whether to confide his troubles to him and decided this wasn't the time.

'You've blotted your copybook, I think, Don.'

'Yes. That's right.'

'Tell Vera I'll take her as soon as she's ready. I'm working at home the rest of the day.'

Peter glanced round the little living room, looked long and hard at Don and left. Don sat down on the empty chair in front of the TV and switched on. Damn me! if it wasn't one of those home-improvement programmes. He switched it off and flung the remote control into the farthest corner. It clattered to the floor behind the Be-Ro recipe books stacked on top of his mother's green enamel casserole dishes and it took Don a whole week to find it.

He couldn't remember feeling so low. The exhilaration of smashing the kitchen to smithereens had long since passed and now Vera was so wild with him she'd probably never speak to him again. He'd been in a mess for some time but this beat all. If only she'd listen to what he had to say.

He heard her footsteps coming down the stairs. She arrived at the bottom and he turned to speak. For a brief moment his heart swelled with a loving thought. 'The Rector'ull take you home, he says. Will yer let me explain? Please.'

Without addressing another word to him Vera left and crossed the road to the Rectory. Caroline answered her knock, swiftly closing the door behind her because of Topsy.

'Come in, Vera. Peter's on the phone, he shouldn't be long now. There's tea in the pot. Would you care for a cup?'

Vera nodded.

'We're in the kitchen.'

Alex and Beth were still finishing their meal. Alex shouted, 'Hello, Mrs Wright! You didn't catch Mr Wright then?'

Caroline hushed him, but Vera didn't seem to notice his question. Caroline sat her in the rocking chair beside the Aga, and handed her a cup of tea.

'Sugar?'

Vera shook her head.

The children found her silence unnerving, and soon asked to be excused. Caroline sat at the table finishing her pudding. Feeling the need to express her sympathy she said, 'I'm sorry you're having such trouble.'

Vera looked at her, then at the table which, despite the ravages of a meal almost done, still looked inviting and wished, oh, how she wished. 'All I ask for is some consideration from him, but what do I get? An almighty kick in the teeth. You're so lucky. So very lucky. We only have to see the Rector look at you and we know how much he loves yer. Don't ever do anything to lose that, because you'll regret it as long as you live.' Vera blushed for having been so familiar, and longed to go. 'Will the Rector be long?'

'That sounds like him now.'

'Has he finished his meal?'

'Yes.'

Vera stood up ready to leave.

They drove all the way to Penny Fawcett in silence. Peter looked at her occasionally but her face was so set in misery he couldn't bring himself to disturb her.

He pulled up outside the nursing home, opened the car door for her, and as she got out she said, 'Rector, I think I've reached an all-time low today. I was so excited when they told me Don was having the kitchen done. I thought, at last he's taking some notice of what

I want. At long last. But after what I've discovered today . . . I know just how little he thinks of me. Zilch. Nothing. Zero. Nought.'

'Look, Vera, I don't know, obviously, what caused that furore just now but whatever it is, if you feel the need to talk to someone about it, the Rectory door is only locked to keep Sheila's cat Topsy in, not you out. You only need to knock and either I or Caroline will listen, and we'll help you all we can.' He took her hand in his as he said this and made the sign of the cross on her forehead. 'God bless you.'

'Thank you, Rector. Thank you. I'm grateful for that.'

A week later in the post came a communication from a bank informing her that she needed to call at their Culworth Branch with some documents they specified to sign papers for the opening of an account in the joint names of Donald Isambard Wright and Vera Renee Wright. She had to read it twice before realisation began to dawn. Never having received a letter from a bank before, it took some understanding. Had he put all the money into the bank and she had a share of it then? He couldn't. He wouldn't, wouldn't Don. Or had he? How could she find out? She puzzled over this all morning till finally she became so confused someone asked her if she wasn't well. 'Oh! I am. It's to do with money. I've got to get to the bank today, it says so. I'll work extra tonight to make up.'

So she trundled to Culworth on the lunch-time bus with the letter in her bag, wearing her newest jacket and skirt. She didn't have to see the manager, someone else, a nice young girl who didn't look old enough to be working, let alone managing customers' accounts, dealt with it. She showed them her birth certificate and a letter from the council addressed to her at the nursing home, signed the papers, nodded that the address was correct, and then asked, 'Excuse me, is it all right for me to ask how much is in the account? My husband set it up, you see, and forgot to tell me.'

'Seven thousand five hundred pounds.'

Vera never let her face slip, not an inch, not even one of those new-fangled millimetres. 'And if I want to take money out?'

'By cheque, or by a cash card with a pin number, but that will take a while to set up.'

'You mean one of those machines in the wall?'

Sitting on the Penny Fawcett afternoon bus Vera was forced to the conclusion that Don was a far nicer man than she had thought. Still, time would tell, a leopard doesn't completely change its spots, not all at once anyway. She'd bide her time, but she would send him a little note to thank him for what he'd done. When the bus pulled up outside the Store, out of habit she rose to get off then remembered she was going on to Penny Fawcett. Her mistake triggered off the thought that however kindly she might come to think about Don she wasn't giving up her job and going back to live in the cottage. He'd have to come to her at the flat. She thought about his dyed hair and giggled. Who'd have thought it?

13

Muriel was at Orchard House to welcome Ron and Sheila back from the hospital. Vera's cousin Dottie had cleaned the house and changed the beds and generally titivated everything for their return. Ralph and Muriel had been to the Store to get in some supplies for them, Caroline and Sylvia between them had baked cakes and made a trifle to help tide them over the first couple of days, and Jimbo had sent round a bottle of Sheila's favourite sherry. Several of the villagers had arrived with flowers and, much to Muriel's despair, she'd had them to arrange. The thought of Sheila's skill with flowers had inhibited her and she'd made a poor job of filling the various vases.

Still, as she stood appraising the sitting room just before they arrived she decided that, yes, it did look welcoming, and the small table set with the necessities for morning coffee looked very attractive.

She heard a toot and saw Gilbert's car slide gently to a stop outside. Sheila walked in as though she'd just been out for a stroll, but Ron moved awkwardly and his face was white with pain.

'Oh, Sir Ronald, do sit down, you look to be in such pain!'

He grunted, which she took to be a yes, and gently lowered himself into the nearest armchair. Muriel took his stick from him and propped it against the wall.

'There, Sheila, where are you going to sit?'

Sheila gave a great sigh. 'It is so lovely being home. I thought at one time I wouldn't want to come here ever again but I do. I thought we'd have to sell up and go somewhere else, but how could

I?' She beamed at Gilbert who was coming in with their belongings. 'I couldn't leave my dear Louise and her lovely Gilbert, could I?'

Gilbert grinned at her and said, 'Now, now, Mother-in-law, less of the flattery. Where shall I put these?'

'I mean every word. You're the best son-in-law anyone could hope to have, isn't he, Ron?'

Ron nodded. 'He is. The best. Thanks for this morning, Gilbert.'

'The least I can do. Louise will be round tonight, she's leaving me in charge while she comes. Just sorry the baby's too poorly to be left.'

'Upstairs, Gilbert, please.'

He went to do as Sheila asked, leaving a silence behind him.

Muriel filled it by asking if they'd like coffee.

Sheila groaned. 'Would I like coffee! I certainly would. That stuff at the hospital tasted like lavatory cleaner.'

'But they've looked after you quite splendidly, haven't they?'

'Oh, yes. The medical attention is first-rate. Couldn't be bettered if we'd paid a thousand pounds a day, but the food . . .' She looked round the room and noticed the flowers. 'Where have all these flowers come from?'

'The roses are from Nick and Ros Barnes, the Michaelmas daisies and chrysanthemums from Dicky, Bel and Georgie. Tom and Evie sent this wonderful pot plant with a little note and –'

'How are they? Tom and Evie?'

Gilbert came down and said he'd have to get back to work, and anything they needed they only had to ring, and on no account was Ron to cut the lawn, he, Gilbert, would do it at the weekend. Ron moaned at the prospect, and Gilbert left in a flurry of laughter.

Sheila smiled. 'Such a lovely boy, Gilbert. I don't know where we would have been without him these last weeks. So Tom and poor Evie?'

'Very well, so far as I know.'

'It must have been a shock for them, that happening to us after such a lovely evening.'

'I'm sure it was. Tom took it very much to heart.'

'That nice superintendent is absolutely foxed as to why we got beaten up. It wasn't as if it was a burglary and we'd interrupted them. They beat us up full stop.'

'It must have been dreadful.'

Sheila quietly began to cry. Ron gestured to her in sympathy but couldn't face heaving himself out of the chair, and Muriel went into the kitchen to make the coffee. There was nothing she could find to say. It must have been terrifying and then coming back had inevitably revived all the horror.

Muriel carried the coffee pot in. Sheila was wiping her eyes. 'I'm sorry about crying, it's not like me.'

'Don't be sorry, it's only to be expected. You've had a dreadful time and then you come home and have it to face all over again.' As Muriel poured out the coffee she said, 'There's post in the kitchen, I'll get it for you, that is if you want to bother with it.'

'Oh yes, I love getting post. Yes, I'll open it.'

Muriel finished serving the coffee and went into the kitchen to pick up the letters. The topmost one was addressed to Orchid House. Oh dear! That relief postman was getting himself all confused. Orchid House. Orchard House. Orchid House! Why? Surely not. It couldn't be, could it? Had the attackers got themselves confused just like the postman? It was dark, and with no street lighting ... Why ever hadn't she thought of it before?

Muriel rushed back into the sitting room. 'Sheila! This letter is addressed to Tom and Evie at Orchid House. Don't you see? Orchard House. Orchid House. That was the mistake! In the dark. They meant to hurt Tom and Evie, not you. It wasn't you at all!'

'Let me see.'

Ron struggled to his feet. 'Of course! It was *them*, not us.'

Sheila scoffed at them both. 'Don't be ridiculous. What have poor Evie and Tom done to deserve it any more than us?'

Muriel felt very silly. 'Of course, it's just as impossible, isn't it? I'm sorry, I really must stop jumping to conclusions. Who'd want to batter a harmless verger?'

Sheila, her mind working furiously, suddenly began to find very good reasons for supporting Muriel's theory. 'Ah! But he hasn't always been a verger, has he? Let's face it, we none of us knew what he'd been up to before he became verger. All that supposed wheeling and dealing. Import, export. That covers a multitude of sins, or it could.'

Ron sat down again. He battled with the pain for a moment and then said, 'Well, I feel too ill to bother. At least we're alive and we know it's not happened because of something we've done, so let the police get on with it.'

'No,' Sheila protested,' we can't let the matter drop. Can we, Muriel?'

'I feel very silly actually for even thinking it. Ralph won't want me to get involved, so I for one am not going to say any more. I'll take the letter to Tom's and not say a word. In fact, I'll pop it through the letterbox and I won't knock, because I feel too embarrassed.'

'Well, if you won't take it further, I will.'

'But we don't know, do we, what they could possibly have done to deserve it? You have to be very careful.'

'Poor Evie. Makes you wonder what she's had to put up with all these years. All that terrible silence must mean something. Perhaps she daren't speak because she's afraid of giving secrets away. That'll be it. He's silenced her.'

'But Tom's not like that.' Then Muriel remembered how she'd told Ralph she didn't like Tom wearing those orange overalls, and how he'd pooh-poohed it. Maybe Tom really was a malevolent creature planning to take over the world, or at least their part of it and Ralph was wrong.

The doorbell rang in the midst of all these suppositions and when Muriel answered it there stood Ralph.

Him having been uppermost in her thoughts at that moment Muriel was startled to find him on the doorstep. 'Oh! It's Ralph!'

He looked surprised at her greeting. 'Yes, this is your husband here. I live with you across the Green, you know, next door but one to the Rectory.'

Muriel laughed. 'Don't be silly, Ralph!'

'Can I come in?'

She stepped back and opened the door wider. 'Of course. Sheila and Ron are in the sitting room.'

Sheila winced. If only she'd called it the drawing room, in front of Sir Ralph too. 'Come in, Sir Ralph, please do. Here we are, all cosy in our lovely drawing room again.'

Ralph bent to kiss her cheek. 'Welcome home, Sheila, and you too, Ron.' He shook hands with Ron. 'Lovely to have you back all in one piece. I must say you're looking remarkably well considering what you've been through.'

Sheila smiled her hostess smile saying, 'Lovely to see you too. Can we offer you coffee?'

'Thank you, no. Muriel and I are out to lunch today and we must be leaving shortly, but I felt I must come to say welcome back.'

'That's so thoughtful of you. Do you know, Sir Ralph? Muriel has come up with an answer as to why we were attacked.'

Ralph raised his eyebrows at Muriel. 'Have you?'

'No, I haven't not really, dear.'

'You have, Muriel, hasn't she, Ron?'

'Well, I'm not convinced . . .'

'It should have been Tom and Evie who got beaten up not us. In the dark they confused Orchard House for Orchid House. Why did they change the name to Orchid House? Just to cause this kind of confusion, do you think?'

Ralph shook his head. 'No. Tom specialises in growing orchids. I've seen them. He's quite an expert.'

'Oh, that's what the fancy greenhouse is then? I wondered what it was for.'

'That's right.'

'Still, it means we were on the receiving end of whatever was intended for them.'

'Now, Sheila, you do not know that. You only surmise. Please be careful, you know what rumours are like in this village. A seed becomes a monstrous tree in the course of a day.'

'But don't you think the police should know?'

'Possibly they have already thought that out for themselves.'

'Well, Sir Ralph, if that is true why haven't they done something about it?'

'They may have and drawn a blank like they have about you and Ron.'

Ron, too weary to tolerate Sheila's persistent questioning, said, 'Look, let's leave it for now. I'm quite sure the police can manage perfectly well without our assistance. I'll have more coffee, if I may.'

Muriel poured it for him and then said, 'I'll wash up before I go.'

Sheila shook her head. 'No need. That Dottie Foskett is coming back to make the lunch. She's at Louise's at the moment. We're going to share her for a while till I feel better, which won't be long if I've anything to do with it. How our Louise puts up with Dottie I'll never know. Louise says she's conscientious and punctual and never asks to go early. But the gossip! Louise says sometimes she's had to send Gilbert out of the room so he won't be embarrassed. Such an innocent is Gilbert. However, she did tell . . .'

In case Ralph got treated to a sample of Dottie's gossip Muriel decided to leave. 'You have my number, Ralph and I will be only too pleased to help, any time, don't hesitate. I'll pop in tomorrow just in case.'

'Thank you, Muriel, very much. Everyone's been so kind.'

Muriel popped the letter for Orchid House through the letterbox and as they crossed the Green she said, 'You know, I'm sure I'm right.'

Ralph tucked her hand into the crook of his arm and held it there. 'You well could be, but don't say anything. Like Ron said, the police know what they're doing. That Proctor chap has more than his fair share of brains. He'll sort it out.'

'It's the orange overalls. I did say, didn't I?'

Ralph stopped by the pond and watched the geese with their broods of young ones preening themselves by the water's edge. 'I love your imagination, Muriel. It gives me great pleasure, so childlike, not childish, childlike, but you've got it wrong.' He finished what he had to say with an emphatic 'So please say no more about it.'

'I'm not used to you laying down the law to me.'

'I know you're not, but I am, just this once. Your thoughts transmitted to anyone else will grow in their minds and before we know it it will turn into a witch hunt, and we shall be rolled back three centuries in a single decisive moment. So for everyone's good, forget it, my dear.'

'Like when they stoned the Baxter sisters' house.'

Ralph nodded. 'Exactly. I can't quite find the right words to describe it, but whatever it is, something gets called up from way back in time and makes them erupt into quite violent action. Very alarming really when it happens. Lunch, I think.' He looked at his watch. 'Ten minutes and we've to be off.'

'Oh, Ralph, I'll never be ready in time!'

Sheila had plenty of visitors that first morning, which quite exhausted Ron and he had to retire to bed after lunch completely worn out. Dottie stayed long enough to make the lunch and clear away and then set off on her bike again for Little Derehams and Louise's, but not before Sheila had tested her new theory out on her.

'It was Lady Templeton who twigged what had happened, she was very convinced.'

'Well, she should know what's she's about, her a Lady.'

Sheila nodded. 'Yes, you can rely on her.'

'But what's he been up to?'

'Ahhhh! That's it, isn't it?'

'Yes.' Dottie shifted her weight to her other leg and lifted the corner of Sheila's nets to peep outside. 'Does the police know? 'Cos they're just about to knock on the door.'

'What?' Sheila straightened herself up, patted her hair and regretted not having repaired her lipstick since eating her lunch.

They heard the doorbell ring.

'That's them. Shall I let them in?'

'Of course.'

Dottie hovered in the hall listening to them talking. The upshot of the conversation with the police was that they would prefer it if Sheila and Ron, in the circumstances, had a police officer on duty at the house at all times, only as a precaution, of course.

'Dear heavens! Whatever for!'

'We'd prefer to move you to another house. Is there anywhere local like Penny Fawcett or . . .'

'My married daughter lives in Little Derehams but their cottage is full. They've two babies, you see, we'd get no peace and Ron isn't at all well. We don't want to go a long way away because Ron's still having treatment.'

'In that case we'll do as I first said and you can have a police officer here at all times.'

Panic set in and Sheila began to tremble. 'I'm not at all well myself and now you've frightened me. I don't know if I can cope with anything more.'

'There's no need to worry, it's just a precaution.'

'But I am worrying. Why on earth do you think we need someone here? Are they going to come back?'

'As I said, it's just in case.'

'What have Tom and Evie done?'

'Tom and Evie?'

'Yes. You've got to come clean about this. It was them not us they were after, wasn't it?'

Superintendent Proctor got to his feet. 'The less you know the better.'

He left behind a charming woman officer, who looked too fragile to prevent a manikin attacking them never mind a gang. 'Are you sure she's . . . capable?'

'Judo black belt.'

'Oh, I see.'

'She'll give you the run-down on what to do. Take care, Lady Bissett. My regards to Sir Ronald.'

'For how long do you think?'

'Few days.'

That night Ron had a very restless sleep. He'd got worked up about having a police officer in the house, about his injuries, and damning to hell whoever'd kicked him because the internal bruising was taking so long to go away, his pain-killers were ineffective and altogether he wished himself anywhere but where he was. 'Sheila! Could I ask you for a cup of tea?'

Sheila struggled awake. 'What? What?'

'A cup of tea. I'm having such a bad night, you've no idea.'

'Oh, I have! You keep grunting and shuffling about.'

'I can't help it, love. I'm sorry. I'm just so uncomfortable.'

She flung back the duvet and found her slippers by shushing her bare feet about the carpet till she located them. 'Right. I'll have one myself. Don't go to sleep, will you? I won't be long. On second thoughts, I'll put my bedside light on, it'll keep you awake.'

'Fat chance I have of falling asleep.'

Sheila wended her way downstairs, filled the kettle, got out the small tray with the Portmeirion pattern on it, and laid it elegantly. If a job's worth doing, she thought. While she waited for the kettle she went into the sitting room and stood by the window looking out. It was so good to be home. So very good. She loved the view from her window. The stocks, the pond, the old oak tree . . . at the height of the summer the tree somewhat obscured her view of the church but she didn't mind because it was so beautiful. She smiled to herself about the old legend, if the oak tree dies so too will the village. A likely story. Take more than a dead tree to finish this village off.

The deep silence of the middle of the night was broken by the sound of a car. Who on earth could that be at this time? Surely not the – Oh, God! The car was coming round Stocks Row past the pub. And no headlights. Dawn was just beginning but it still wasn't light enough to drive without . . . They were stopping! Outside Tom and Evie's! Oh! Not another beating up. Sheila froze. But they wouldn't stop right outside, would they, if they were up to no good? The driver got out. By craning her neck she could see him open up the boot, then the sound of a door, then . . . surely not! It was. Tom and Evie! He had his arm round Evie's waist and a case in the other hand. Another man appeared out of the car and then the case Tom was carrying was put in the boot. Evie seemed close to collapse and was shaking her head in refusal. It appeared to take all Tom's efforts to persuade her to get in to the car. He shook his head at one of the men as though despairing and then they all got into the car and drove away. Poor Evie! Poor Tom! Had they been kidnapped? No, they went easily enough in the end and the men weren't forcing them in. She was sure Tom would have put up a fight, even if it was only for Evie's sake. But perhaps they had guns and he'd no alternative! They were in a hurry because the car engine had never even been switched off. They were expected, because the case was already packed. Such haste. And what for?

Ron's tea! She made the tea and rushed as fast as she could to tell Ron. Half-way up the stairs she remembered the policewoman. Some good having her in the house, lying there fast asleep and all this happening. Sheila put the tray on her bedside table saying to Ron 'Let it brew. I won't be a minute.' She scurried along the landing to the policewoman's bedroom.

'Claire! Claire! Are you awake?' Tapping on the door brought no response so Sheila opened the door slightly and called again.

'Yes?'

'Tom and Evie have been taken away in a car. Do you think they've been kidnapped?'

Claire sat up with a start. 'Have they? Are you sure?'

'I saw them being driven away.'

'God help us!' She fished under her pillow for her telephone and dialled a number, waving Sheila away as soon as she made contact. Quite put out Sheila closed the door thinking, I expect she didn't want me to hear her getting a dressing-down for being asleep when she should have been on the *qui vive*. Still, she couldn't keep awake twenty-four hours a day, could she? They should have sent someone else to relieve her. No, they shouldn't, thought Sheila, I don't want the entire police force in residence when not even one is necessary.

Ron had sat himself up in bed and was waiting patiently for his tea. 'It took a long time. Did you forget to switch the kettle on?'

'No, I didn't. Here, get hold of it tight, we don't want tea all over the bed. You know what a long way even a drop can go.' She gingerly climbed back into bed, remembering how the slightest wrong twist or turn could cause her pain. 'No, it's Tom and Evie, they've been taken away. In a car.'

'Sheila!'

'It's true, I saw them.'

'God! What next? Bang goes the quiet-English-village-where-nothing-happens theory.' He sipped his tea. 'Maybe the police-woman is a good idea after all.'

'Fat lot of good she is fast asleep.'

'Well, at least she's reassuring.'

'I suppose so. Make sure the duvet's pulled well up, we don't want her embarrassed, she might come in with a message.'

Each one of Sheila and Ron's visitors the next day went away with a dramatised version of the great escape of the Nichollses.

'I saw them with my own eyes. Believe me, they were hustled into the car, Evie's feet barely touching the ground. You should have seen! Terrified she was! Weeping heartbroken. What I should like to know is who were they and why were they removing Tom from the scene? Tell me that. Of course the police will tell me nothing. We might as well not have this Claire Thingummy here, complete waste of time she is. The only thing she's useful for is answering the door and saving me getting up out of the chair. Strict instructions we have, *don't answer the door*. In fact after the last time Ron answered it I don't think I want to answer it ever again. Well, would you?'

That second night when they guessed Claire would be asleep, Ron quietly opened the front door and went for a stroll. A very careful, guarded stroll, one foot placed slowly in front of the other, one hand clutching the side where the worst of the kicking had been, breathing in the fresh air in deep gulps, appreciating it all the more after the clinical smells of the hospital and enjoying the peace of the midnight hour. Thank God for it, thought Ron, I'd go mad if I didn't get out, and that damn bossy Claire wouldn't hear of it, but he needed it for sanity's sake.

It was Sheila's idea to wait until everyone had gone to bed and truth to tell he was glad he'd waited, because he was forced to walk so slowly he felt an idiot; an old fellow in his dotage, no less and – My God! Just by his shoulder he thought he caught a glimpse of the net curtain at Tom and Evie's sitting-room window moving just slightly. No lights, but the curtain had certainly moved. So it was all a tale about them being kidnapped. Honestly, why did Sheila have to exaggerate everything so? He passed their other window and was creeping round the corner down Royal Oak Road when he felt a hand on his shoulder.

It clamped down, gripped him fiercely and a voice whispered, 'What are you doing out?'

His heart went completely out of control, thudding so erratically he was convinced his chest would explode. When he found his voice he said, 'Taking the air. Who are you?'

'Police. Shushhhhh! Home, if you please.'

Disgruntled at having been found out like a small schoolboy misbehaving, Ron grunted, 'All right, all right. But why can't I take a walk?'

'Because. Here, let me help you.'

'I can't hurry. It's the bruising, you know.'

The two of them turned round and started back home to Orchard House. Squatting in the front of the Royal Oak under the window of the lounge he spotted a shadowy figure and he could just make out someone else standing behind Jimmy's fence in the shade of his chicken house. My God, the place was full of police. Wait till he told Sheila.

14

Kenny and Terry had not been home all that night having, unbeknown to each other, each found himself a woman. Terry, the barmaid from the Jug and Bottle, and Kenny, someone he'd picked up in a Chinese restaurant in Culworth. Consequently it was something like twenty-four hours before both their cars were parked once more in the drive of number six Hipkin Gardens. By curious chance Terry arrived home within a moment of Kenny.

Terry didn't bother to lock his car, it being, as he well knew, quite valueless and anyone wanting to steal it was welcome to it. 'Where've you been?'

Kenny replied, 'Ask no questions get told no lies. Got yer key?'

Terry put his hand on the front door to steady himself while he put the key in the lock only to find that the door swung open of its own accord. 'That's funny. You must have left the door open yesterday.'

'I never did.'

'Oh, God! Damn and blast it! We've been burgled!'

Kenny pushed Terry aside and marched in. It was difficult to find a place to put your feet for all the carpet downstairs had been heaved up and every stick of furniture pulled out of its place. Shouting expletives his mother would not have known the meaning of, Kenny rushed from sitting room to kitchen, from stairs to bedroom to bathroom then back downstairs and up to his bedroom again. He stood in the doorway confused as to why nothing appeared to have been stolen yet ... Kenny looked round the crash site that had been his bedroom: everything had been overturned including the bed. His clothes, his beautiful, fashionable new clothes which he'd left hanging neatly in the wardrobe, were heaped on the floor, every drawer emptied, every picture off the walls. They'd done a thorough job. A cold sweat broke out on his forehead, ran down his neck, trickled on to his shirt collar and some of it poured down his spine. This wasn't petty robbery, this was ...

He could hear Terry howling in the kitchen about some discovery he'd made then his footsteps racing up the stairs to view his bedroom. It was the same all over the house. Their possessions thrown about in a cruelly systematic search.

Kenny scrambled down the stairs and slumped down in his big leather armchair to think. Think what? Who? Why? What for?

Terry asked in anguished tones why their house had been picked on.

Kenny looked wryly at him.

Terry exploded with an idea. 'Ring the police!'

'For God's sake, Terry! Sorry, Mr Plod, but our house has been done over and we can't think why. Oh, yes! They'd love that, wouldn't they? They'd be laughing all the way from the station.'

'Who's done it then?'

'Use yer brains, Terry. Who do you think? Them what have toes that we've trodden on.'

'What d'yer mean? Who did it to us?'

Kenny looked scornfully at his brother and wondered how he'd managed to be burdened with such a fool. 'Turkish Delight?'

Terry paled at the thought. 'Oh, God! It'll be 'im, you're right.'

'We'd better stay low for a while. He's given us a warning, that's what this is all about. If he'd found our money ...' He gestured at the mess. 'This is 'im telling us he knows. This is only for starters is this warning.'

Terry laughed, but there was a tremor in his voice when he replied, 'You and me! Come on, us compared to them! You've got ideas above your station you 'ave. You and me a threat to 'im? That's a laugh! Why should Turkish Delight bother with us? We're small fry in comparison.' He sat down in the more meagre chair allocated to him by Kenny.

''Cos he's heard about our activities up in town and he's not having us trespassing. Safest thing we can do is get the money and make a fast exit for a while.'

Terry sat up abruptly. 'You mean leave Turnham Malpas? Go somewhere new? Leave everything behind?'

Kenny mocked him. 'Yes! Next time we might be at home when they come.' He blanched at the thought of their narrow escape. 'I'm not into violence and that's what it's going to be if we aggravate old Turkish Delight any more. Violence with a capital V.'

'Just when we're building up a good business. Blast it. I'm never going to make it big, am I?'

'We will, one way or another. We've been too cocky trying this. We've watched enough serials on telly about drug-dealers being buried in concrete overcoats to know when to do a bunk.' Kenny shuddered. 'I'm going to church. Right. Won't be long. The money's not safe there anyway with Tom gone. Willie's not so . . . amenable.'

Terry, scared though he was, sneered at the word 'amenable'. 'You mean you 'aven't got a hold over him.'

Kenny gestured at the chaos around his feet. 'That's right. Tidy up, OK? Shan't be long. I want to leave it spick and span. Don't want Sir Ralph upset with us.'

'Won't matter if he is, we shan't be here.'

'Just do as I say. See yer.' He left then came back in again. 'While I'm gone pack a couple of bags for us, and put my new clothes in mine and don't forget your toothbrush, if you can find it that is. And don't forget to rescue the white stuff from under the shed.'

Willie was devoting his time to a thorough cleaning of the memorial chapel. He'd just got used to his freedom and here he was back again doing the verger's job. Poor Tom. Still it was enjoyable, made yer feel needed, and the money would be useful for their holidays. Who'd have thought it, him, Willie Biggs, swanning off to outlandish places like Minorca? He only did it for Sylvia's sake, or pretended he did. Let's face it, he thought, as he wrung out his cloth in the bucket, I enjoy it as much as she does. The hot sun, the new sights, the company, the hotel. Yer came back renewed. He got up from his knees and settled himself on a chair facing the altar to ease his cramped legs for a moment, to his left the huge carved memorial screen shielding him from the main part of the church, in front of him the altar where the Rector said his prayers each day.

Times had changed and not half. He looked at the names on the brass memorial tablet beside the altar, and tried to imagine what the village must have been like all those years ago when things like beatings for no reason at all simply didn't happen. A cart track into Culworth, no TV, scarcely even a telephone. A motor car, he supposed, up at the Big House. No washing-machines. No videos. Nor this new-fangled Internet they all talked about.

As he sat there thinking, the opening of the church door barely touched his consciousness. He belonged to the history of the village. Two of his uncles on the memorial plaque and there'd been Biggses living in his cottage since ... well, heaven knew how long, certainly a hundred years but in the long life of the village that was a mere moment. Domesday Book they'd been mentioned in. He'd seen it in a book. And them Roman ruins up at the Big House before ... What was that?

A strange noise he couldn't relate to anything. It didn't sound like visitors: they usually whispered loudly and crept noisily about. He cautiously stood up and moved towards the screen. Finding a hole through which he could see into the main body of the church, Willie put his eye to it. By turning first right then left he had a view of most of the church. The only bit he couldn't see was the font right at the back. His scalp prickled and he felt as though his hair was standing on end for, as he looked towards the Templeton tomb, he saw someone rise up from the narrow end of it. They'd actually come from inside it. A ghost, was it? A ghost like he'd always said! He'd been right, it was haunted. Had he gone completely mad? Then the world righted itself and he saw it was Kenny Jones standing there. Grave robbing! Whatever next?

Willie leaped out of the memorial chapel like a man possessed, his desert boots making no sound as he pounded down the aisle. 'Kenny Jones! What you up to? Eh? Tell me that!'

Kenny looked up, startled out of his mind: dusty and dishevelled, in his hand a Tesco's carrier-bag.

'What's that you've got there, you thieving runt, you? Grave robbing! Whatever next!' As he reached Kenny, Willie met Kenny's fist head on. It smacked him straight between the eyes and he fell on the stone floor unconscious, blood pouring from his nose. Breathing heavily, Kenny carefully replaced the marble end panel of the tomb, dusted himself off and headed for home, his car and anonymity.

Willie regained consciousness very slowly. First he couldn't think where he was, till he felt the chill of the stone floor penetrating his sweater. Then he realised his face felt peculiar and when he tenderly tested it with his fingers he found blood everywhere and he remembered. Kenny Jones! Kenny Jones had hit him. Willie sat up, his head throbbing. Curiously everything appeared to be in order yet he could have sworn ... Yes, he was right, Kenny had been interfering with the tomb. He pulled himself up by the tomb using the foot of the marble knight laid atop of it. He could tell just by looking that the end panel had been moved. Robbing a grave. How could he? Surely it was a criminal offence.

Willie struggled up the aisle determined to get to the Rectory. He locked the main door so no one could interfere with his evidence, and with a handkerchief pressed to his face as his nose was still dripping he hammered on the Rectory door.

Peter knew instantly who it was as Willie always knocked in that way even if what he had to say was something quite innocuous.

Peter gasped when he opened the door. 'Heavens! Willie! What on earth has happened? Come in.'

Willie's voice was thick and unrecognisable. 'No, I won't, thank you, sir. It's Kenny Jones what's done it. Hit me he did. I caught him grave robbing.'

'Grave robbing? Kenny Jones? I don't believe it! Whose grave?'

'The Templeton tomb in the church. Come and see for yourself. Come on.'

'Shall we wash your face first and inspect the damage? It looks incredibly painful.'

'No. We need the police. Come and see, I caught him red-handed.'

Peter locked the Rectory door behind them and followed Willie into the church. 'But what did he steal?'

'I don't know, but he had a plastic carrier-bag in his hand with something in it and he was dusty.'

'I can't see Kenny being keen on opening up a tomb, can you?'

Willie took the handkerchief from his face and said 'Look, there you are.' He pointed to the panel that had been replaced. 'It was open when I saw him and then he socked me one and when I came round he'd gone and the panel was back in place. I tell you he deserves all he gets. Will you phone the police or shall I?'

Peter inspected the panel, observed it wasn't quite, just not quite, fitted back correctly and he looked at the fine particles of dust on the floor. 'Better not touch anything.' Peter straightened up and dusted his hands together. 'It does seem extremely odd. What on earth is he thinking of? I'll phone the police.'

'Muriel told me he'd started coming into church, but being Muriel, kindly like, she thought it was to pray. Fat chance. It was something to do with this 'ere tomb. It gave me a fright I can tell yer.'

In the bar of the Royal Oak that night the attack on Willie was the sole topic of conversation. The man himself had returned from Casualty with Sylvia at eight o'clock and insisted on a meal in the dining room and then a drink afterwards.

By then his face was black and blue, and the strips of plaster they'd used to hold the lacerations together while they healed, created an interesting criss-cross pattern on it. There was also considerable swelling, one eye being closed and the other just a slit.

Sylvia patted his arm. 'You're not well enough to go out, Willie. You look a real sight.'

'That Kenny Jones isn't keeping me away from my ale. 'Elp to dull the pain it will. Come on. You need feeding too as well as me.'

'All right, then, but it's madness. Here, take my arm, because I'm blessed if you can see a thing.'

A cheer went up as they entered.

'Come on, Willie, let's see the damage.'

'My, that Kenny can punch.'

'You'll be a fortnight before you're right.'

'Break yer nose, did he?'

'They've phoned Mike Tyson to let him know you're available!'
This last was greeted with hilarious laughter.

'Must have given you a shock, Willie, 'im dressed all in white
stepping out of a tomb! You've always said it was haunted.'

Willie laughed off the teasing as best he could. He wasn't feeling
quite so full of life as he had been, and the pain felt to be getting
worse. Truth to tell, it was bravado which had got him into the bar,
and he didn't know if it would carry him through the rest of the
evening.

Two people got up to go, saying as they shrugged on their
jackets, 'We'll go play spot the policeman.' This witticism was
greeted with another outburst of mirth.

A chap sitting at the bar shouted, 'No wonder the rates keep
going up. It's to pay for that lot hanging about doing nothing all
night.'

'They wouldn't do it if they didn't think it was necessary.'

'But just what are they expecting to see? That's what I would like
to know.'

'But just think, that Kenny opening up a tomb.' The speaker
shuddered. 'What on earth must it be like after two hundred years.'

'Is it that long since it was opened up then?'

'Says so on the side. Eighteen hundred and one.'

'But robbing a grave! How low can you sink?'

The conversation broke up after that, and Willie was allowed to
go for his meal and eat it in peace.

When he and Sylvia had finished they returned to the bar to find
Don Wright and Barry Jones seated at the table where they usually
sat. 'Evening, Don! Barry! Mind if we join you?'

Don moved along the settle to give Sylvia more space. 'Here. Sit
yourselves down.'

Barry looked embarrassed. 'I'm dead sorry about your ...' He
gestured towards Willie's face. 'I don't know what got into him.'

Willie, beginning to find it painful to speak, said, 'He might be
your brother but you're as different as cheese from chalk, so don't
worry yer 'ead about it. No' your fault.'

'At least let me get you a drink.' Barry got up. 'What will it be?'

Sylvia smiled up at him. 'Gin and tonic for me and a glass of
Dicky's home brew for Willie, please.'

Barry strode away to get the drinks and Sylvia said, 'Different, aren't they, him and their Kenny and Terry? Barry has all the vigour and they . . . well . . .'

Don agreed. 'He's working that hard for me. Says he won't take any payment for it but he will.'

'Nearly done?'

'Kitchen's finished and the plumber's tiling the bathroom. White it is, snow white from top to bottom. Even got a shower over the bath, and it's not one where the water dribbles out, it comes out in a rush. I can't wait to 'ave a go. Smashing. Wait till Vera sees it. Thrilled she'll be.'

Privately sceptical that Don might ever get under that shower with any enthusiasm Sylvia decided to speak up on another matter. 'We're all getting a bit fed up of looking at that mountain of rubbish outside your door. Time it was moved.'

Barry came back with the drinks. 'Here we are then.' He handed out the glasses then raised his to Willie. 'Thanks for being so nice to me about our Kenny.'

'That's all right.' Willie sipped his ale with relish. 'Sylvia's right about that rubbish, Don. What are you going to do about it? The pile gets bigger every day. Spoiling the village it is.'

Barry wiped the froth from his top lip. 'I've an idea about that. Harvest Festival next week, before we know where we are it'll be Bonfire Night. So . . . I think all your stuff would make a good basis for the fire. I'll ask Mr Fitch if we can use the van to carry it up to the field. If we cover it with plastic sheeting anchored down, it'ud be all right.'

Willie laughed as best he could. 'One time you'd have used it and not asked old Fitch. Things have changed.'

'Been decent to me, has Mr Fitch just lately. In fact, he's been decent to everyone just lately.' Barry grinned. 'So I've decided to behave myself. Given us all a rise, and he's much more nice now. As head gardener my father-in-law can't put a foot wrong if he tries. Got a rise and an extra week's holiday. When they meet it's Greenwood this and Greenwood that. All very friendly. And as for Jeremy! Well! Buddies, they are. Buddies.'

Surprised at the prospect of Mr Fitch being buddies with anyone at all Sylvia asked, 'How is Jeremy, then? We haven't seen him since he was in hospital.'

'If you did you wouldn't know it was him. He's lost four stones.'

'Four stones!' Sylvia couldn't visualise Jeremy four stones lighter.

'Still more to lose but he's looking so much better. Started swimming now.'

'Swimming!' Sylvia couldn't visualise that either. 'Jeremy swimming? The mind boggles.'

Barry laughed. 'Not a pretty sight, but he's doing it every day. To get back to our Kenny, I'm blinking sorry about what he's done. Heaven alone knows what he's up to. Mother's heartbroken. Losing her job over him, Dad without a job too and then what Kenny's done today, it's nearly finished her.'

'Tell her it's not her fault. Heaven alone knows she's tried to bring the three of you up well.'

'She has indeed.' Barry shook his head.

Sylvia decided to ask Barry about the hedge while he was in such a reflective mood. 'Barry, if ever you hear any news about the hedge could you let me know? You being up there every day I thought perhaps you might, you know . . .' Sylvia cupped her hand around her ear and pretended to listen. 'Dr Harris is determined to stop him pulling it up and I'd like to help.'

Barry winked. 'I shall be on the blower as soon as I hear. The Rector's had no effect on him at all. The news is old Fitch will have it done before the winter sets in.'

Sylvia's eyes opened wide. 'No! He's definitely going ahead with it, then?'

Barry nodded. 'Don't know exactly when. When I do I'll let you know.'

'Thanks. They do say that Lady Templeton is all ready to throw herself in front of the digger.'

Barry laughed. 'No-o-o-o! She's always so ladylike I can't quite believe it. She means business then.'

Sylvia nodded vigorously. 'Oh, yes! we all do. It amazes me that he can be so much nicer to all of you and yet takes us all on yet again about the hedge. I know I go on about it but I can't help feeling that there's more to it than just the hedge. They say he's after widening Pipe and Nook Lane at the same time, and there must be a reason behind that. Why else should he give away a long strip of land like that?'

'I reckon he'th got the counthil in hith pocket.' This from Willie who was finding speaking increasingly difficult.

'For what, though?' Barry asked.

'Houtheth?'

'What? Oh! *Houses.*' Barry laughed. 'On Rector's Meadow! He'd never get planning consent.'

Willie pretended to tap the side of his nose. 'Oh, no? He'd get blood out of a thtone he would. Money talkth. I'm off home.'

'Good night, Willie. Hope you feel better tomorrow. Sylvia, soon as I hear a whisper I'll be in touch.'

'Thanks.'

By eleven thirty not a single human being was about, Jimmy's geese were sleeping, the occasional owl swept across the village over towards the motorway embankments searching for mice, not a light shone, the only disturbance being that caused by the wind ruffling the leaves of the old oak and the roses and honeysuckle growing around the cottage doors. The moon came out from behind the clouds and briefly illuminated the village, making the white walls of the cottages appear almost fluorescent, but then flirtatiously it disappeared behind the clouds again. Still waiting behind Jimmy's chicken house, and in the shelter of Misses Senior's garden and over the wall in Tom and Evie's were the policemen, and in the early hours silently and swiftly, just like the owls, they struck, captured their quarry and stole them away.

15

Vera not visiting the Royal Oak as frequently as she had when she lived in the village kept up to date with Turnham Malpas news by questioning anyone and everyone who called at the nursing home and might know any gossip. This morning she was keeping an eye out for Jimmy whom she knew was booked to take a patient on a shopping trip into Culworth. As the bonnet of his red Sierra came into view round the rhododendrons she dashed to the front door.

'Good morning, Jimmy! How's things at 'ome?'

'Still call it home, do yer? Well, now, there's a chap called Don going to take a fortnight off to do some decorating,' said Jimmy. 'You won't know your house when you see it.'

'I don't want to see it.' Vera turned away, then turned back to ask, 'The kitchen? Is it good?'

'Good! What a question. Barry's done a wonderful job, lovely new cooker, smashing cupboards like something out of a magazine, I tell yer. And the bathroom! Well!'

'He's done the bathroom as well?'

'Vera! You didn't have what could rightly be called a bathroom before, did yer? But you have now. Snow white from floor to ceiling. All gleaming and a shower an' all. Yer should go see it.'

Vera shook her head. 'Not likely.' She hesitated and then said, 'He'll expect me to go back there and I won't. First chance we've had to make real money renting out that cottage while we live 'ere, and I'm not going to give in. In any case I don't know if I want him back.'

Jimmy saw his fare coming tottering out of the front door of the home and made ready to depart. Before he opened the taxi door he said, '*He* wants *you* back. I understand he's putting all the furniture on the bonfire. Complete clean sweep he's 'aving.'

'What?'

Jimmy grinned at her, and having stowed the old gentleman safely in the front seat he swept out of the gates still grinning.

On her first afternoon off after this conversation with Jimmy she caught the lunch-time bus into Turnham Malpas to see for herself. Confident that Don would be at work she marched round Stocks Row and slotted her key in the lock. There was an old car parked outside and she thought, What a cheek, someone parking their car right outside our house. But at least it was clean and polished even if it was old. It'll be one of the weekenders, just like 'em.

The cottage was quiet. She ignored the living room still stacked high with the stuff out of the kitchen, and went through into the back and stood there amazed. Their Rhett would have said gobsmacked and she was. The sunlight was coming in through the window and illuminating, that was the only word for it, illuminating the kitchen, the cupboards a kind of pale oak colour, she knew there was a fashionable word for it but she couldn't think of it at the moment, the knobs so elegant, and there under the shiny draining board a brand new washer. The cooker! Well! It was way beyond anything she had ever dreamed of.

Vera opened a drawer and let it slide smoothly closed, she did it again then tried a cupboard door, and then the new blind over the window and the one on the back door. A kitchen for the future and not half. Give her her due, Grandmama Charter-Plackett had made a good job of the kitchen, for nothing was more certain than that it hadn't been Don alone who'd organised this.

Back in the living room she opened the door at the bottom of the stairs and began climbing. The tiny bathroom had been transformed. Somehow they'd fitted in a basin as well as a toilet and bath. The whole effect was of a glimmering, shimmering paradise. Her mind was in such turmoil at the changes Don had wrought that she didn't become aware of the swish-swish of his decorating brush as he painted their bedroom walls until she'd completely studied every last inch of the bathroom. Standing in the bedroom doorway she gasped. Without looking at her at all he said, 'This is all for you.'

'How did you know it was me?'

'Saw you looking at my car.'

'Your car?'

'My car.'

'Since when?'

'Saturday. They brought it today.'

'But where did you get the money from to buy a car? There won't be a penny left.'

'I've kept telling you how valuable that motorbike and sidecar were, but you wouldn't have it. A classic I kept saying. Well, I got eight thousand for it.'

Vera had to clutch the door frame to keep herself upright. She was speechless.

'Polished it up and that, put a new clutch in and that, had the seats restored and that's what I got so I could well afford the car. Will you have a ride in *that*?'

'I might be tempted. I like the kitchen. So where *did* you get the money from, Don?'

Don climbed down from the ladder and stood his emulsion brush on the lid of the clover pink paint he was putting on and sat down on the old bedroom chair. 'Remember the old allotment me dad had in the war?'

'That one you always talked about resurrecting after he died, but never did? What happened then? Did they strike oil?'

Don grinned at her joke. 'No, not oil, but the allotment association got an offer from a builder wanting it for posh houses. Grand spot, looking out over Havers Lake. I used to fish there when he took me up to the allotment when I was a boy.'

'So ...'

Don paused to reflect on the happy times he'd had fishing by the lake. 'So they had a vote and I never thought they'd all agree, thought there'd be someone who'd put a spanner in the works preferring to escape her indoors and 'ave a quiet smoke and a game of cards in their huts, but they did and we got paid out. Twelve and a half thousand pounds I got, and I've spent five of it on the kitchen and the bathroom.'

'Well, I never. So Dad turned up trumps at last.'

Don answered, 'Yes, he did.'

'Thanks again for putting it in a joint account. I haven't taken anything out.'

'I know.'

'It was nice to be trusted.'

'That's all right. Only fair.'

Vera inspected the painting. 'Nice colour. It'll look good.'

'Hope so. Time for a cup of tea?'

She was tempted to have a go at making tea in that wonderful kitchen but feared she might take a liking to it. 'No. Thanks. I'll be going.'

'OK.'

'Jimmy says all the rubbish outside is going on the bonfire on Guy Fawkes night. Make a great blaze. I shall be glad to be there to see it all go up in smoke.'

'And the furniture too.' Don gazed innocently about the room, half a smile on his face. 'It'll let better unfurnished.'

Vera took umbrage. 'I don't know where you think you're going to live.'

Don felt the ground giving way beneath his feet. 'I had thought . . .'

'You'll have to wait and see, won't you?'

Very quietly Don said, 'There's not much more I can do to make amends, Vera. I've missed you that much.'

Vera felt a small sliver of interest. 'You'd have to let that dye grow out. I liked yer better with iron grey hair not that funny black. Anyway we'll see. Bye.'

Her heart fit to burst with delight, Vera made her way to the bus stop calling in at the Store first to get something nice for her and Rhett for their tea. She mustn't appear too eager, well, just a bit perhaps, because he had worked hard. The decision did appear to be hers, though. Rent for the cottage, she'd ask Jimbo.

Linda was on duty in her post office as usual. 'Hello, Linda. Bet you were glad it wasn't your house got trashed. Them Hipkin Garden houses all look the same – they might have made a mistake.'

'You should have seen it! What a mess. Nothing damaged really, just everything thrown about. You don't miss much though, do you, even though you live out in the wilds?'

Vera scoffed at Linda's remark. 'Can't call Penny Fawcett out in the wilds, now, can you?'

'No regular bus service, no church, no school, no shop. Come on, Vera!'

She had to laugh. 'You're right! It is. But I love it.'

Slyly Linda enquired if she'd be coming back to Turnham Malpas now Don had got the cottage to rights.

'Mind your own business, Linda Crimble. You're worse than Jimbo for gossip and that's saying something. Is he in?'

'Find out for yourself.'

'Thanks, I will.'

Rhett and Vera had finished their evening meal and were washing up when there was a knock at the door.

'Not another crisis! Go answer it, Rhett.'

She half listened to the conversation and suddenly recognised Don's voice. It couldn't be! Not Don. Vera caught a quick reflection of herself in the mirror by the kitchen door and wished she'd had lipstick on and her hair fresh combed. Too late now.

Rhett came back. 'It's Grandad. I couldn't say he weren't to come in, could I?'

'Of course not. I'll just finish tidying away and then I'll be in. See if he wants a cup of tea or something.'

Back came Rhett. 'He doesn't. He's sitting by the window gawping at the garden.'

Vera snapped at him, 'Don't make him sound as if he's in his dotage, 'cos he isn't.'

'I know that. I only told you what he was doing.'

'You off out tonight?'

'Why?'

'Are you?'

'I could be.'

'Well, buzz off then. Sharp.'

Rhett smirked at her. 'I see, courting are you?'

She aimed a hasty swing at him with the wet tea-towel and he ducked and laughed. Vera did wonder how near the mark he might be with his joking.

'Hello, Don. Nice surprise.'

In his hand Don had a bunch, no, a bouquet of flowers.

Beautifully wrapped in Cellophane like Jimbo always did the special flowers. Carnations and lilies and roses. They'd cost a packet.

''Ere, these are for you.'

Tears brimmed in Vera's eyes. He hadn't given her flowers since their Brenda was born. 'Thank you, very much. I'll put them in water and arrange them properly later.' Vera got out her plastic bucket, filled it with water and put them in it. Lovely they were. Lovely. Things had changed.

Back in the sitting room she said, 'Would you like to look round?'

'I would.' So she took him round, showing him the bathroom and separate toilet, the lovely bedroom with the huge window looking out over the garden, the bright kitchen with its view of the drive, Rhett's bedroom and the big airy storage cupboards and wardrobes she had.

'We get a good view from up here. These rooms were part of the servants' quarters and the nurseries, you see. Lucky, aren't we, Rhett and me?'

Don looked at her properly for the first time. 'It's done you good coming 'ere.'

Vera almost blushed at his close scrutiny. 'Yes, it has. I love it. It's the furniture and that, and the lovely big rooms, elegant like, and that lovely kitchen. Should really be for the matron but she's got four kids and it wouldn't do.'

'I fancy going to the pub –'

Quickly Vera interrupted him, 'Not the Royal Oak.'

Don was disappointed because he wanted to show her off, but he agreed and suggested trying the Jug and Bottle.

'Not the same standard but it'll do. I'll get changed. Put the telly on if yer want.'

What was she doing getting changed to go to the Jug and Bottle for a drink? Anything would do in there so long as yer weren't stark naked. She wished she hadn't thought that. It made her remember a time long ago . . . Fifteen she was. In the hay barn at Nightingales' Farm after helping with the harvest . . . her and Don. It hadn't been the clumsy fumbling of two virgin adolescents, for the gift of glorious passion had been theirs that night and their Brenda had been the result of all that tenderness and joy. Her father had threatened to kill Don, till her mother pointed out that if he did

Don couldn't never make an honest woman of their Vera. Sixteen with a baby. How did she cope? Those were the days.

She'd stand out like a sore thumb she would in this outfit in that dump, but stand out she would. That was how she wanted to be tonight, standing out from the crowd. Don looked good too. That new sports suit and that tie! She wondered who'd persuaded him to buy that tie, or was it that the spark he'd had years ago was returning?

When they got back, Don didn't go up to the flat again, he said goodnight to her at the front door. 'Give us a kiss to be going on with.'

'A kiss. Huh!'

'Go on, Vera. You know yer dying for one.'

Indignantly Vera denied she was. 'There's a long way to go before I want a kiss from you. You've ignored me for years and now all of a sudden you want a kiss. Come off it.'

'Don't I even get full marks for trying?'

'No. You're not having your way with me as easy as that. I'm not saying I'm not impressed, but . . .'

'Yes?'

'Good night, Don.'

'With my cottage done up I might find there's more fish in the sea than you. A well-modernised cottage could be tempting for a woman.'

Furious at the prospect Vera said, between clenched teeth, 'Well! Who is there who'd be tempted by you?'

Don smiled one of his rare smiles. 'Dottie Foskett?'

He could be right. She'd better be a bit more flexible. 'Go on then. One kiss. Here on my cheek.' She proffered her cheek but his knuckle under her chin turned her face so he could kiss her mouth.

Vera went all trembly and fled inside.

That week, with help from one of the weekenders recruited by Grandmama Charter-Plackett, Don had the living-room furniture outside by the front door ready for Barry and the estate van.

Now that the bedroom furniture was back in place and she'd had the chance to inspect it more closely, Grandmama was struck with an idea. 'You know this bedroom furniture, Don?'

'Yes.'

'Well, I think it's far too good for the bonfire. The three-piece suite and that old sideboard thing are only fit for burning, but I think those wardrobes might be Georgian, and that chest of drawers and the bed-head. They all match. Let's ask Sir Ralph, see what he thinks.'

'I'm not having Sir Ralph poking about in my old furniture. Heavens above! He wouldn't want to.'

'Not even if he thinks it's worth a lot?'

'What d'yer mean? Fifty pounds like?'

Grandmama shook her head. 'If I'm right it could be worth a whole lot more than fifty pounds.'

'It's been in that bedroom for years. Never moved till I started decorating. How the blazes we'd get it out I've no idea – couldn't go down that twisty staircase and through the door.'

'There's ways like taking windows out. After all they didn't build the house round it, did they? It must have got in somehow.'

'No, yer right.'

The prospect of more money to dangle in front of Vera rather excited him and he strode off post-haste over the road to speak to Ralph.

'It's Grandmama Charter-Plackett's idea, sir, that my ... our bedroom furniture might fetch a rare penny or two, so before it goes on the bonfire she wondered if you'd care to have a look, you being in the way of antique furniture.'

'Why not? I don't profess to be an expert by any manner of means but, yes, I'll have a look.'

'The bedroom's newly decorated or otherwise I wouldn't ask.'

Ralph looked at Don with new eyes. 'Pleased to see the effort you've been making. I'd be glad to have a look, see your alterations too. Could Muriel come?'

'Of course. If she wants. I'm off to the DIY in about an hour, if you'd like to come over before then ...'

'I'll get Muriel, she's tidying the garden at the moment. We won't be long.'

Don went home to wait. He occupied himself making a list for his shopping expedition. Sunny yellow for the small bedroom, he thought. White paintwork, make it look bigger. Nice new curtains with a touch of the yellow in them. Those magazines Grandmama had lent him came in useful for ideas. He'd better measure for the curtains and the curtain rail before he set off. Now everything was out of the sitting room he could make a start on that too.

There was a tap on the front door. It opened and Muriel put her head round. 'It's us! Can we come in?'

'Of course. This way.'

When Ralph saw the bedroom furniture he was amazed. 'My word, Don! You've got a treasure trove here. How do you come to have such wonderful stuff?'

'My grandma used to say it all came from the Big House, but I find that hard to believe. Your Big House, that is. She said her grandmother had it given to her as a wedding present. Why, I've no idea because she wasn't in service there. When I asked why her grandmother had been given it, my grandma just tapped the side of her nose.'

Ralph opened drawers, looked at the dovetailing, inspected the door hinges, peered at the bed-head, ran his finger along the mouldings. 'Oh, yes. They'd fetch a pretty penny in an auction house.'

'They are Georgian then?'

'I'm fairly sure they are. But do you want to sell them when they've been in the family such a long time?'

'Yes.'

'What does Vera say?'

'She doesn't care. Hates 'em cos she can't . . . couldn't . . . move the wardrobes to clean. How do I go about it then?'

'If you'll permit me I'll contact the auction house in Culworth and get someone to come out and take a look.'

'I want them out of the way, yer see.'

Muriel, dismissing from her mind the idea that the furniture seemed familiar to her, asked to be allowed to view his alterations. When they'd admired everything Ralph said as they left, 'And Vera. What about her?'

'I'm thinking she's right. I started all this for her to make her come back, but she's that stubborn.'

'She has got a point. A good tenant in here paying rent, you'd have a little nest egg by the time Vera retires.'

'Shall I give in then and go live at the nursing home?'

'Why not? You've got wheels, so it's no problem.'

'Will she have me? That's the other question.'

Muriel, who'd been listening sympathetically to their conversation, said, 'I'm sure she will. Play your cards right and offer to do as she suggests. Take her on holiday, treat her well. She'll come round.'

'She's only just back from Torquay.'

'What does that matter? Ralph and I are always going away. It does you good. Even if it's only two or three days. Come along, Ralph, Don wants to get on. It's beautiful what you've done, an absolute transformation. It's nice to see someone achieving something worthwhile after all we've gone through these last few weeks. No news of Kenny and Terry?'

'Not that I know of. No news of Tom either. Pity that. I liked Tom and poor Evie. Strange woman.'

'Indeed. But happy in her own quiet way. Bye-bye, Don. Thank you for the tour of your home!'

Pointing at the contents of Don's house still out in the road Ralph's parting shot was 'You'll be getting all this stuff out here moved, will you? Makes the village look unsightly.'

'Tomorrow. Make a grand bonfire, won't it, and shall I be glad to see the back of it all!'

'Good. Good. Got to keep up standards.'

As Ralph and Muriel opened their own front door Muriel said, 'How odd him having such wonderful stuff. Do you suppose it's true?'

'True?'

'About it coming from your old home?'

Ralph locked the door behind him, something they'd all started doing since the trashing of Kenny's house had made them nervous, and then said, 'Muriel! I have a sneaking suspicion it might have been given for services rendered to the master at the Big House, or one of his sons perhaps.'

Muriel's eyebrows shot up. 'Ralph! You don't mean ...'

'I do. Why else is it there? Don's great-great-grandmother being given that kind of furniture as a wedding present, she was being bought off, don't you think? The price for her silence? The Wrights have been poor for generations, they certainly would not have been able to afford such good stuff, ever.'

'Well, well!'

'That's the only reason I can think of for it being in that cottage. Far too grand for it.'

'Oh, Yes! Even I can tell that. You don't want to buy it, do you, seeing as perhaps it was once yours, so to speak?'

'No, I do not. Reminders of my ancestors' immoral misdeeds I do not need! But thank you, my dear, for being prepared to take it on.'

Muriel was silent for a moment and then she said speculatively, 'You know the antique washstand we have on the landing, and you don't like the colour of the marble top, you don't think it might belong . . . ?'

Ralph's eyes widened as he contemplated Muriel's idea. 'You could be right. Surely not . . .'

They both rushed up the stairs and Ralph turned on the landing light so he could see more easily.

Muriel snatched at the flowers and the runner she kept on it. 'There, we can see better.'

'My dear! I do believe you're right. When we were looking at Don's stuff I thought it was familiar. It belongs, doesn't it? It's part of Don's suite.'

'Look, the moulding's the same and the handles on the drawers.'

'Well, well! I'm sure we're right. It is identical.'

'Maybe there just wasn't room for it in that bedroom and it had to go back to the Big House.'

Ralph smoothed his hand over the marble top. 'Can you imagine the gossip when it all arrived at that cottage of Don's? I've never liked this colour. Too red somehow. It seems a shame for it to be separated from everything else.'

Muriel sighed. 'It must have been so lonely all these years wondering where everything that belonged to it had gone.'

'Oh, Muriel! My dear. Of course. When the chap comes from the auction house I'll show him this first then Don's suite and see what he has to say.'

Muriel slipped her hand into the crook of his arm. 'Let's do that. It's only right it should be together with the rest, where it belongs. I think Don's going to be amazed at the price he'll get for it. I don't think he's any idea how valuable it is.'

16

Peter heard Sylvia answer the knock at the Rectory door and guessed it was the one he'd been expecting: Tom Nicholls. He had to admit he wasn't exactly relishing this meeting, but at least an explanation of all the weird and incredible happenings in the village just lately would be more than welcome.

Sylvia tapped at the door and ushered Tom in. Peter shook his hand, and pulled out a chair for him.

Tom cleared his throat and said abruptly, 'I haven't brought Evie back, not yet, not till I get things straightened out with you, Rector.'

'I'm glad you've come. The village has been seething with rumours ever since you left so mysteriously and since then with the police popping out from behind every wall. We'd no idea where you'd gone, you see. Look, if it's a long story . . .'

'Which it is.'

'Then we'll have coffee and sandwiches, if you don't mind. Would that be all right with you? I haven't had lunch yet and I breakfasted what seems like years ago.'

Tom nodded his thanks.

'I'll ask Sylvia to make two lots and then we can settle down.' Peter closed the study door behind him and sought out Sylvia in the kitchen. 'Before you go for lunch, Sylvia, could you make another set of sandwiches? I think Tom's going to be a long time and I'm starving.'

'Back, is he? I hope it's not permanent, we've suffered enough because of him.'

'I am reserving judgement until I've heard the full story.'

She looked up at him and seeing the honesty of those eyes of his, she retracted her statement. 'You're right, of course. But the story had better be good.'

'We'll see. Coffee as well, please, and a slice each of ...'

Laughing, Sylvia flapped her hands at him. 'Get on with you! I'll bring it in.'

'Thanks.'

Tom didn't begin his tale until the sandwiches were in front of him. He poured sugar into his cup as though he needed every ounce of support he could get, had a good drink and began. 'I'm sorry there's been all this trouble. I never intended it to be so. We thought we'd escaped into paradise when we came here, but it didn't work out that way, did it? You see, the root of all our problems is that I've been a police officer since I was eighteen. Loved the job, I did. Truly felt I was making a real contribution to the world. Evie and me, we married at twenty, but unlike you and the doctor we weren't able to have children. Evie had several miscarriages, just couldn't carry, and they couldn't find out why. Broke her heart it did, but such is life. We can't order these things, can we?'

Peter shook his head.

'Started as a constable and then I moved up to sergeant and then got a chance to go into plain clothes, Detective Sergeant Nicholls. That was a proud day I can tell you. London was a rum place to work in. There was a taste of every criminal activity under the sun there. Somehow one fateful day when they were short-handed I went out on a job with the drugs squad. That was the first day of the rest of my life. Like an idiot I enjoyed the adrenalin rush, the sheer bloody thrill of it all. The surge of power it gave yer when it came off and you'd made an arrest and put another pig of a dealer behind bars. There were the bad days, days when you failed and they got away to ruin dozens more lives, when you sank so low in spirits you nearly gave up.'

'More coffee?'

Tom held out his cup. 'Yes, please. This was when Evie began being ill. She'd had another miscarriage, five months she was so we'd just begun to feel hopeful, but she'd lost it yet again. I was up to my neck in the squad, coming home at all hours and her never knowing if I would come home at all. I didn't see the signs, thought it was losing the baby that was the trouble, which it was, but it was anxiety over me that compounded the problem.' He paused a moment, shook his head as he remembered how it had all been.

'Anyway, came home about two o'clock one morning and she'd cut all the curtains up, and was laid eyes wide open staring into space in the middle of a heap of shreds. Lopped them off just below the curtain hooks she had and set about cutting them up. So I had to insist she got help. It nearly finished me, the pain, oh dear! The pain.' Tom swallowed hard. 'She wasn't communicating at all so you never knew what she was feeling. Like a dummy she was. So docile. So terribly, terribly sad.'

'I'm so sorry, Tom. I'd no idea.'

'I asked them to take me off the drug squad, which to give them their due they did. Eventually Evie came home and her mother came to stay with us to give her a hand, keep her company like, and she'd begun to accept that children would be out of the question. She seemed so much better that daft Tom here decides he can take the risk and get doing what he loved best, undercover work. This time I worked at getting accepted into a gang on the fringe of the big stuff. It was like being an actor but being yourself all at the same time. Two lives lived in the one body. Living a life which was against all your better instincts with the objective of pulling in the gang and getting them off the streets.'

'You don't seem like a man who could do this.'

'Like I said, two people in one body. Funny existence. Sometimes when you woke up you couldn't remember what you were, him or me. I'd be days away from home, unable to communicate with Evie, except an officer at the station would phone her from time to time to say I was still in the land of the living.'

'Poor Evie.'

'Indeed. Yes. Poor Evie. Then things began to get too hot. I was very close, very involved, well accepted, but I had this sixth sense that someone was becoming suspicious of me. Nothing positive, nothing I could put my finger on, just a feeling. But I stuck to it, knowing how close we were to getting to the big boss. Then the balloon went up. We got it all together one night, and we arrested the big boss just leaving for an important dinner in the City, Rolls-

Royce, dinner jacket, chauffeur, the works. What a triumph. They arrested me too to keep my cover, but you're not safe in prison, you know. If you want to get beaten up that's the place to go. Some prisons, the prisoners rule not the screws, believe me. I feigned an epileptic fit and they rushed me to the prison hospital, then took me to an outside hospital for treatment, they said, but that was the excuse. In fact they whisked me and Evie away to a secret address.'

'Tom!'

'We kept having to move. New identity, new names. It wasn't easy. Evie had another breakdown, more serious than the first. The only plus was that we'd got our man and broken up the ring. Millions of pounds they were making from selling drugs. Coming in from all over the world. If you saw the lives torn apart like I've seen them . . . you'd understand the triumph of getting the beggars behind bars. You'd sacrifice anything, anything at all.'

Something about the despair in Tom's voice prompted Peter to ask, 'To look genuine, to blend in kind of, you didn't have to take drugs too, did you?'

'No, no, I made them think I did, I'd seen enough to know how to behave. The one plus about Evie being in hospital for a second time was that while she was there they taught her to do embroidery and it saved her life, literally. You should see her work! You'll be amazed, such talent, it's unbelievable. She's going to have an exhibition when we get back, Sheila Bissett says she'll organise it – well, she said she would but maybe by now she mightn't be so keen.'

'I didn't know that. She's never said anything about it. So how did you come to be here?'

'Well, we were watched and guarded in the safe houses, I dyed my hair, shaved my moustache, Evie had always had short hair so she grew it long, and spent hours and hours and hours and hours embroidering without speaking, never going out because she was too afraid. However, prisoners are not prisoners for ever and I started getting twitchy about things. Thought I was being followed, you know the sort of thing.'

'Well, no, I don't.'

'Of course not, sorry. Well, I didn't think Evie could take any more. She'd come close a few times to suicide and as it was all my fault I decided we'd strike out, independent like, and give our minders, the police like, the slip. We couldn't be worse off than we were. Eventually we found here, I bought Mrs Beauchamp's house, lock, stock and barrel, and we moved in. But ...'

Tom looked up with a rueful smile on his face.

'Yes?'

'Who should I meet? Kenny Jones. By a million to one chance, I'd met him briefly while I was in prison. I didn't know him from Adam, but for some reason he'd remembered me. So, round about the time I got the verger's job he went into the drugs scene to make his fortune, quick, and he made me let him use the Templeton tomb to hide his money because he knew if anyone got on to him the first place they'd look would be his own house. He's been going into town at weekends selling drugs, so he's done well out of it.'

Peter was horrified. 'Kenny? Selling drugs! Kenny Jones! And using the church to hide his drugs money? Dirty money? Tom, how could you? In God's house!'

Tom couldn't look Peter in the face, he was just too ashamed. Head down he said, in a quiet voice, 'He had a hold over me, you see, said he'd blow the gaffe if I objected, so for Evie's sake I kept quiet hoping that one day I'd sort it out ... It made me feel really bad and I longed to tell you but I couldn't. I couldn't bear for Evie to be ill again. I've been so happy here and so has Evie. The thought of moving again, well, I couldn't even begin to think about it.'

Peter was speechless.

'Kenny, finding I was becoming awkward 'cos my conscience was troubling me, decided to put it around in the right quarter that I was living here and who I was. After Ron and Sheila got beaten up in mistake for us, the police whistled us away during the night and then kept watch.'

'So where did they take you?'

'To a safe house.'

'And Sheila thought you'd been arrested!'

'Over-active imagination! But she's been so kind to Evie. However, during one night they came back again to get us but the police were waiting and arrested them.'

'So that was why they were hiding everywhere. And Kenny and Terry? Where are they?'

'No idea. They've disappeared off the face of the earth. But they'll be found eventually. On the other hand, though, they might be under a couple of feet of concrete.'

Peter shuddered. 'Do you mean that?'

'Oh, yes. You don't start trading on Turkish Delight's patch without suffering the consequences.'

'And you? What about you?'

'Well, I'm prepared to take the risk of staying here in comparative ease until the lot I've put away are let out, and these henchmen who've just been arrested will be in for some time, believe me, including their bosses. Ten years at least. What I really want is to ask for my old job back.'

Peter shook his head. 'I shall have to think very seriously about that, Tom. You betrayed my trust. I know there were mitigating circumstances, but I'm afraid . . .' he shook his head again . . . 'you co-operated in the hiding of tainted money on church premises. That really was very wrong.' To change the subject and give himself a breathing space to make up his mind Peter asked, 'Are you here to stay now?'

'We shall be very shortly, the sooner the better. Next week, I think. Evie's pining for home.'

'Leave me a contact number or an address, whichever. The village feel you've brought great danger to them all, so there could be a lot of opposition to your return. They can't stop you living in your own house, of course, but as for the other . . .'

Tom looked Peter straight in the face and pleaded, 'For Evie's sake, if nothing else, I'd love to stay and get on with my job. She's been better here than she's been for years. This village is so healing, you see. Me getting the job as verger just seemed to put the seal on our safety, to say nothing of her happiness. But, of course, that's up to you.'

Peter stood up and reached out to shake hands. 'Thank you for being so candid about things. I shall do my very best for you.'

Tom shook hands. 'Thanks for listening and thanks for the lunch.'

'My pleasure.'

'There's my phone number. I'm going to collect a few things from the house then I'll be away.' Peter went to see him to the door and they shook hands again.

'I shall quite understand if you can't work the miracle. I know there'll be a lot of opposition and perhaps I've no right to be asking after all that's happened.'

'What would you like best to happen?'

'Me and Evie back here, which we shall be shortly, her having an embroidery exhibition and me as verger again. That would be the very best that could happen. Right where we can feel safe again and welcomed, for a while anyway.'

'I'll do my best.' Peter watched him stride away over the Green to his house. What a man. What a predicament! Could he see any way in which he could give Tom his job back? No, he could not. There was no way he would allow him a position of trust within the church ever again. It quite simply was not to be. Tom had broken the trust he had in him in every way: lying about his past, understandable in the circumstances but not excusable, and letting Kenny get the upper hand. Peter cringed at the thought of money tainted by filthy greed and agony and very possibly murder being hidden in his church.

A week to the day after speaking to Peter, Tom and Evie came home. Willie had locked up the church hall after Scouts and had just turned into Church Lane when he saw their car turn right from the Culworth Road into Stocks Row.

Willie hesitated outside his cottage, his hand poised to lift the latch and go in to his Horlicks and bed. But something of Peter's compassion filled his heart and he decided to follow them round Stocks Row and give them a word of welcome.

Evie was unlocking their front door while Tom was lifting a heavy box from the back of his car.

'Tom! Evie! Welcome home!'

Evie gave a little shriek and dropped the door key. Tom put the box down again and turned to speak, his face alight with appreciation. 'Why, Willie! Thank you! We've come late because we wanted to get settled in, in peace, kind of.'

'Well, I for one am damn' glad to see you back. This verger

business is for a much younger man than me and I'll be glad for you to take the reins over again.'

Tom shook his head. 'I don't know about that, Willie. We're back but I'm not sure I shall have my job back.'

'Why ever not?'

Evie said softly, 'I can't find the key in the dark.'

Willie pulled his torch out of his pocket. 'Here, let me look. I always carry a torch when I'm locking up, just in case.'

He bent down to shine the torch around Evie's feet. To his surprise she was wearing calf-high fur-lined boots, which seemed a little excessive at the height of an Indian summer, but he made no comment. 'Here it is! Look!' He picked it up out of the honeysuckle, dusted it off and presented it to her with a bow and a grin. Evie gave him a shy smile, thanked him, slotted the key in the lock, turned it and went in.

To Tom's relief Willie offered to help unload. 'Thanks, that'll be great. This one's heavy. I'll take it, if you could bring this, and this with the shopping in.' Between them they emptied the car, and Tom asked Willie to have a drink before he left. 'Least I can do.'

'Thanks, I will.'

Leaving Evie to wander about the cottage and acclimatise herself, Tom dug in the Sainsbury's carrier-bags and brought out a four-pack of Guinness.

'You couldn't put a good word in for me, could you, Willie?'

'I could always try but it's not up to me.'

'They can't stop me living in my own house.'

Willie nodded in agreement. 'They can't, but they can turn very funny in this village. They take umbrage and nothing stops 'em . . . Well, the Rector can but he's about the only one. He's stepped in more than once when things have got nasty.'

'Nasty? I can't believe it. You all seem so kind.'

'Oh, we are, but just now and again . . . Like when they made an effigy of Mr Fitch, and when the Baxter sisters got their house stoned for kidnapping Flick Charter-Plackett, and Dicky and Bel got attacked because –'

'Good heavens. For Evie's sake I don't want . . . Oh, there you are, love. All right?'

394

Evie stood in the sitting-room doorway, her face alight with joy. 'Oh, Tom! Willie! It's lovely to be back home!'

Tom, so full of delight at her pleasure, agreed with her, his voice breaking as he answered, 'You're right, it is. Lovely!'

At that moment Willie made up his mind that, for the sake of gentle Evie and her very obvious joy at being back where she felt secure, he would do all he could to make certain they stayed and Tom was verger again.

It might be an uphill task. He enlisted Sylvia's help. 'The most positive thing we can do,' she said, 'is have that exhibition of Evie's embroidery. I know Sheila Bissett exaggerates but she really was impressed with how beautifully Evie embroiders, and she's bursting to have an exhibition for her. That way they'd all see what a clever person she is, and she and Tom would have to be there and meet everyone and people couldn't be rude to their faces, could they? What do you think? In aid of charity, and with cups of coffee and gâteau. How about it? One Saturday morning? The exhibition in the small meeting room and the refreshments in the big hall.'

Willie nodded. 'It wouldn't take long to organise – it's not like a village show or something, is it? I'll get the diary out tomorrow and check the first free Saturday.'

Stirring her Horlicks to rid it of the last bits which hadn't quite mixed in Sylvia said, 'But we shall only succeed if we do a lot of quiet propaganda – you know, when we meet people and that. A word here and a word there.' A thought struck her. 'What does the Rector think?'

'He had a word with me yesterday, saying he hoped when they got back there wouldn't be any trouble. I just hope he gives Tom his job back, I can't keep up with it all any more.'

Sylvia patted his hand where it lay on the blanket. Putting her empty beaker on her bedside table she snuggled down saying, 'If there's one thing I've learned in life it's to live every minute to the full. We're neither of us getting any younger, you know. We never know when we might get called to higher service, do we?'

Willie was appalled. 'Called to higher service! I'm not about to pop my clogs, you know, far from it.'

'I wasn't meaning it like that, I meant we should do all the things we want to do and see all the things we want to see before it's all too late. Dying with regret must be –'

'Just shut up, Sylvia, I don't like talk like that.' Willie slapped his beaker down and looked into those grey eyes he so loved. 'Sorry for that, but you mustn't. We've years yet together enjoying ourselves and you've not to think we haven't. You know, I saw tonight how much Tom loves Evie and seeing her pleasure at being as she called it "back home" I thought, they're just like my Sylvia and me, in love with each other, and it made me decide to do my best for 'em. And I do love you, and every minute is precious and perfect and . . .'

'Willie, you're sounding quite poetic.'

'That's how it gets yer.' Willie settled down in bed and took Sylvia's hand in his. 'She's a strange woman is Evie, but you can't 'elp but like her. There's an innocence about 'er that's rare nowadays. Childlike, almost, and yet all that talent. She had her fur boots on. In this weather her feet must have been near casseroled!'

'Never mind her boots, did you get a chance to see her embroidery?'

'I carried a box of sewing stuff into her workroom for her. Stunning it is. Stunning. Wait till they all see it. Just wait.'

When the posters advertising the exhibition appeared in the window of the Store and on the church noticeboard there was a great deal of comment, not much of it favourable. The Charter-Plackett children did a leaflet drop all around the village too, so when the villagers found it on their doormats there it was staring them right in the eye: the Nichollses were back and intending to stay.

Despite their opposition to Tom and Evie returning, curiosity finally drove them to visit the exhibition, their excuse being that after all it was in a good cause: all them refugees, and the money given to someone who was going out there with medical supplies for the poor beggars, that made the difference; you weren't just handing out money to some vast faceless organisation, this way the person concerned was accountable.

The exhibition opened at ten. Sitting at the entrance taking the money was Sheila Bissett, a broad smile on her face.

'Thank you, that'll be four pounds, please, for the two of you.'

'*Two pounds*! For a few pictures on a wall.'

'It's in a good cause. You'll be amazed, it's worth every penny.'

'I should hope so.'

'Oh, yes. It was me discovered her talent. We've got plans for classes. Sign up when you come out, I've got the list here.'

'They're intending to stay then?'

'Of course.'

'I'm surprised you're so keen after what happened to you and Ron.'

Sheila stifled a shudder. 'They'll all be behind bars for years to come, and I for one am not going to let what happened affect me.'

'Well, I reckon you're brave. I really do. You're an example to us all. We'll let you know if we think it worth it.' The ticket buyer leaned over the table and whispered, 'Are Evie and Tom here?'

Sheila nodded. She wasn't feeling nearly so brave as she made out, because this was the first time she'd taken part in village life since ... well, anyway she was here but it had been a real effort to come out and sit taking the money. But, as Ron said, you couldn't spend the rest of your life frightened of your own shadow, and he for one, now he was feeling so much better, was going to put it all behind him. So Sheila agreed with him for once, not because she was brave but because she couldn't bear the thought of allowing herself to be stuck in the house too nervous to go out.

Sylvia was wielding the coffee-pots and Willie was fidgeting about in the exhibition room, nervous that his lighting arrangements might not be showing Evie's work off to its best advantage. My, but they were splendid were these pictures: they lit the heart up with their beauty. Willie couldn't imagine how one small quiet person could have such skill, such an eye for colour, such splendour in their very soul. He listened to the exclamations of delight from the villagers and convinced himself that Tom and Evie would be here to stay and he wouldn't have to be verger any more. Relief covered him like a rash and he realised he was grinning like a Cheshire cat.

Caroline was serving gâteau and putting in a discreet good word for Tom and Evie as she did so. 'Two more coffees, Sylvia, please. Chocolate, lemon or almond? Lemon, that's Harriet's contribution.

It looks lovely, doesn't it, so tempting? What do you think then? Isn't Evie clever?'

'She most certainly is. Not a word for the cat, yet all that going on inside her head. So beautiful!'

'Such an asset to the village, aren't they, the pair of them?'

'Oh, yes! Such an asset.'

Sylvia winked at Caroline and they both smothered their laughter. To have such a success on their hands was more than they could ever have hoped for. The door opened and Peter came in, his eyes searching for Caroline immediately. Having found her he smiled and her heart went instantly into overdrive; for one blinding moment she couldn't see a thing except his eyes and the whole of his face glowing with love for her. He raised a hand in greeting and she almost choked with love for him. I'd forgotten how handsome he is! And he's mine! All mine! All that love is mine!

'Dr Harris! A slice of the chocolate for Willie, please. Dr Harris?'

All mine! I'd forgotten how much I love him. And there he is. All splendid and wonderful. She smiled back, but he'd turned to answer Sheila and the chance to show that her feelings for him had sprung back to life was lost.

'I'll cut it, shall I?'

Caroline was trembling with shock, her beloved Peter was there, still loving her, still supporting her after all he'd been through. Well, this was the end of making him jump through hoops, because . . .

Sylvia said, 'Shall I serve Willie?'

Caroline looked down at the cake slice in her hand. 'Oh, right, which would you like, Willie? The chocolate's very popular.'

She cut him his slice then excused herself, saying her hands were sticky and she'd wash them in the kitchen. Standing at the sink letting the cold water rush over her hands and wrists, Caroline hoped Peter wouldn't come after her. She needed time to catch up with her feelings. Three months since Hugo had left, and now at last she'd become wholly herself once more. To think she'd even considered going away with Hugo, he who was a shell of a man compared to Peter. She must have been out of her mind. She'd be indebted to Peter for ever for not asking for more than she was able to give.

'Mummy! Alex is wanting another piece of cake. I've told him he can't. He'll be sick.'

Caroline dried her hands, took her bag out of the cupboard where she'd put it for safe-keeping and handed a pound coin to Alex, who straight away rushed off, and offered another to Beth.

Beth patted her stomach. 'I don't think I can, Mummy, thank you. He will, you know, he'll be sick, he's so greedy. Sylvie's wanting you, she's says she's rushed off her feet.'

'I'll be there in a minute tell her.'

'Your voice is funny, are you all right?'

Caroline bent down and kissed her cheek. 'Oh! I'm absolutely fine. Daddy's here somewhere.'

'Is he? I'll go find him.'

Caroline wished *she* could go find him and take shelter within his love as she had no doubt Beth would do, but for now she had to take time to realign herself. The relief of finding her life had value again was overwhelming her and –

'There you are, my dear! Are you all right? Sylvia's anxious in case you're not well so I've come to ...' Muriel studied Caroline's face and could not interpret the look she saw there.

'Muriel! Couldn't be better! Just needed to wash my hands, they were sticky, you know.' She fled back into the hall to help Sylvia reduce the length of the queue. Muriel stared after her, still puzzled by Caroline's expression, but then Muriel didn't know that Caroline, not five minutes ago, had fallen in love.

Sheila had ten names on her embroidery class list, added her own and felt she'd had a very worthwhile morning. 'Evie! Evie! Come here! Look! Eleven names! Isn't that wonderful?'

Evie came across to her, a glass of water in her hand. Without speaking she picked up the list and studied it.

'Isn't it encouraging? I'm so excited. I have a little place in my hall where a picture would just fit, I was going to ask you to do one for me, but if I come to your class I could do it myself, couldn't I?' Sheila looked up at her, eagerly awaiting her reply. But she saw a tear begin to roll down Evie's cheek.

'Now, Evie, come along, we've had a lovely morning, everyone full of admiration. There's nothing to cry about.' She fished in her bag and brought out a clean tissue. 'Here, use this.'

At a loss to know how to tackle the situation Sheila looked around for help, and to her relief Tom came. He put an arm around Evie's shoulders and hugged her. 'Now, come on. It's all been great, hasn't it? You said so yourself.'

Evie dabbed her face with Sheila's tissue and pulled herself together. In that strange deep voice of hers Evie said, 'It has and it's all thanks to Sheila. It'll help me if you come to the class.'

'Oh, I will, I'm on the list.'

'Then I shall do it, immediately, seeing as it's October. I've never done anything like it before but we can always give it a try.'

Tom took his arm away from Evie's shoulders and beamed at Sheila. 'I told her it would be all right and it has been. All we need now is for the Rector to persuade the others to let me have my job back. Then everything in the garden will be lovely. The meeting's on Tuesday night so we should know then, I hope.'

17

Muriel put down the receiver and held on to the chair for a moment to steady her nerves. Well, she'd said she would do it and now was the time to stand up and be counted, but she was trembling so much she'd have to sit down. Why did she make these pronouncements in the heat of the moment then so deeply regret them? But she had said she would, and if she was ever going to hold up her head again, she'd have to do it. Stand there and *do it.* Surely there must be another way, but there wasn't, was there? She'd tried, Peter had tried, Jimbo had tried, but Mr Fitch had remained adamant.

Ralph! Where was Ralph?

'Ralph! That was Barry on the phone.' Dear God! Help me. 'Ralph! Oh, there you are!'

Ralph looked gravely at her. 'It's D-Day, is it? I never thought for one minute he'd go ahead with it. I really didn't. As the weeks slipped by I was sure he'd changed his mind. Damn him! Damn him!'

Muriel nodded. 'First light tomorrow morning they're moving in. Oh, Ralph! Am I brave enough?'

'None braver.'

'Shall you have one last try?'

Ralph shook his head.

'No, you're right, it would only make him more determined.'

Ralph stared into space for a moment then said, 'Sit down again, here's your list of people to ring. I have to go into Culworth, on business. I shan't be in for lunch.'

Muriel looked up at him and anxiously enquired if he really needed to go.

'I do, yes, I do. Don't worry I shall be back, hopefully by the middle of the afternoon. Things to do, you know.' His lips tightly pressed together and his eyes intensely preoccupied, Ralph stared into the distance.

'I shall need you tomorrow for moral support.'

'And you shall have it, all you need.' He bent to kiss her, squeezed her shoulders, picked up his car keys and disappeared through the back door calling, 'Bye, my dear. Good luck with your phoning.'

She wished he hadn't gone, she wished he'd stayed and braced her for what was to come. It was an odd thing for Ralph to do. He'd said nothing yesterday about having to go into Culworth. Still, she was clever enough to organise things without anyone's help, it would be tomorrow when she needed ... The telephone began to ring and when she answered it was Caroline, consumed with enthusiasm. 'You've heard from Barry? Good. So, we have lift-off. I'm about to start on my list of calls. I'll ring you back when I've completed them and tell you what support we can expect. Muriel? Are you there?'

'I am. We've got to be brave, haven't we?'

'Of course. I can't wait to get at it. He has got to be stopped.'

'Oh, I know. I know. Right, here we go. Come round with your list, instead of phoning. We'll have coffee and compare notes and plan our strategy.'

Muriel was encouraged by the enthusiasm of her supporters. They all promised to get neighbours and friends to come too if they could, and by the time she'd gone through her list Muriel was beginning to feel more confident. If it came to it, with a *crowd* lying down in front of the diggers she wouldn't be quite so obvious, would she? The newspapers! Of course! She'd ring and get them to come. A big splash in the local paper would do nothing but good. If she kept the thought of that little wren with his bright brown twinkling eyes in her mind she'd be all right.

Muriel didn't sleep that night, of course. Mad, scary scenes of confrontation and police and being arrested raced through her mind. Of course she might be arrested, that would be a distinct possibility, causing a breach of the peace. What would her dear mother have said? Frankly she would have been appalled. 'No real lady would do such a thing,' she would have said. Well, Mother wasn't here so Muriel could do as she wanted, within limits.

Ralph rose first before it was light and went downstairs to make breakfast for her.

'No, Ralph! Let me do it.'

'It's the least I can do. Put warm sturdy clothes on and bring a brave heart with you. Come down when you're ready.'

'I don't think I can eat anything.'

'Oh! You must.'

He stood over her while she ate a bowl of cereal and drank a cup of tea.

'Here's your banana.'

Muriel shook her head. 'No, Ralph, I really can't manage that at this time in the morning. Thank you all the same.'

'Put it in the pocket of your Barbour then, for later when there's a lull.'

'Very well. The most terrible thought has struck me. Will Mr Fitch be there, do you think?'

'He goes abroad such a lot, he most probably won't be.'

'I can't bear the thought of him seeing me behaving ridiculously.'

'Is that how you see it?'

'Yes.'

Ralph took hold of her hand and put it to his cheek. 'You have too much innate dignity, Muriel, ever to be accused of behaving ridiculously. Now, where are your placards?'

'At the Rectory.'

'Then off you –' He was interrupted by a knock at the door. 'That's probably Caroline, I'll go.'

Muriel discovered it was a bright, very crisp autumn morning when she went outside. Going through her gate at the end of her back garden and out into Pipe and Nook felt symbolic: a moment of change, a moment when Muriel went from being a quiet, shy, back-room support type of person to becoming a front runner, a stand-up-and-be-counted person. She braced her shoulders, smiled at Caroline and marched sturdily towards the entrance to the field.

It wasn't directly opposite her house but below it on the way out of the village. The entrance was blocked by a huge old farm gate, with a chain and padlock on it.

Caroline propped the placards against the hedge and she and Muriel stood in front of the gate. They'd only been there a moment or two when their supporters began arriving in twos and threes. There was Sheila and Ron, Tom and Evie, Anne Parkin, Mrs Jones, two of the weekenders in what they considered to be appropriate country wear, Liz Neal, and trailing on behind were the two Misses Senior, their woolly hats suited to the chill morning air. A chorus of 'Good morning' ensued, and there was an inspection of the placards with praise for their apt wording, a rubbing of hands to ward off the chill and above all an air of anticipation and excitement.

After a lull came more supporters, eager for the fray, Linda Crimble with her little Lewis on a trike, Georgie Fields, Jimmy Glover and Willie and quite a few of Mrs Jones' neighbours from down Shepherds Hill. Arthur Prior, Ralph's cousin, came as promised escorted by his bevy of granddaughters. What they hadn't expected was the arrival of some members of the local Environmental Studies group from Culworth.

Their leader called out cheerfully, 'Morning, all! Never fear now we're here!' Under their arms they carried placards at whose inflammatory slogans Muriel quaked.

'I didn't know anyone else knew.'

'Ha! Ha! Nothing much goes on in the environment that we don't get to hear of, and we rather felt this was a situation which required not just the foot soldiers but the cavalry too.' Looking down the lane he asked, 'So where are the –' he spotted the look of distaste on Muriel's face and changed it to – 'beggars?'

Muriel said firmly, 'I want it absolutely understood that this is our village and our protest, and it will be conducted with dignity and restraint.'

'Dignity and restraint! These greedy landlords don't know the meaning of the words. They'll ride roughshod over you and anyone else who gets in the way, four-legged or two.' He nodded his head towards Rector's Meadow. 'Got this lined up for housing, and it's not on.' He took off his glove and exposed a hand the size of a gorilla's. 'Gareth Edwards.'

Muriel's hand disappeared inside his and was gripped painfully. 'Muriel Templeton.'

'Well, Mrs Templeton ...

Tom hissed, 'It's Lady Templeton, actually.'

Gareth bowed mockingly. 'Beg pardon, milady.'

'That's quite all right, you weren't to know.' As she spoke the rumble of heavy machinery was heard in the distance. 'Housing? We didn't know that.'

Gareth winked at her. 'We have a mole in the planning department. Not much goes on we don't know about.'

The word 'housing' flew round the lips of the protestors and served to heighten their determination.

Muriel asked, 'Are you sure?'

'Positive. Old Fitch has them under his thumb.' Gareth pretended to count out banknotes with his fingers.

'I don't believe it! Mr Fitch!'

The rumble of the equipment grew louder and Caroline hastily shared out the placards and they made a double line of defiance across Pipe and Nook Lane.

Chin up, but with trembling knees, Muriel faced the enemy. Great yellow giants they were, impressive and very threatening. Muriel felt her breastbone shuddering with the vibrations caused by their mighty engines. Surely they must stop. The driver of the foremost vehicle had enormous protective earphones on his head, there'd be no use shouting to him he would never hear, so she waved her arms above her head, palms towards him and the others joined her.

The digger tested her resolution for it ground to a halt only six feet from her. Muriel went round the side and gestured to him through the open window to take off his earphones. He did, but the noise of the engine made it almost impossible to shout loud enough for him to hear, so she pointed to what looked to her like an ignition key though she wasn't sure, for the cab appeared to be full of gadgets and levers.

'We're here because we don't want to have this hedge taken down. We're sorry to be interfering with your work but we feel so strongly about it that we are compelled to stand here and do what we are doing. Please, could I ask you to agree not to dig out a hedge which has been growing for something like three centuries that we know of?' She smiled up at him, this strong healthy young man, a product of an age she had little in common with, and didn't expect to get any sympathy from him at all.

'Now, little lady, we're going to be paid a lot of money to do this job, and I've got men to pay, and they've their children to feed, and a roof to keep over their heads. Do you really think I'm going to refuse to do it?'

'We can't let you. I'm sorry but there it is. You will have to run us over to get into that field, and I know you can't possibly work from this side because the lane is too narrow for you to manoeuvre.' She tried the sweet smile again, and for a moment thought she'd melted his heart.

From a shelf below his windscreen he picked up a mobile phone, pulled a piece of paper from his top pocket and began to dial the number written on it.

He said, 'Thank heavens for mobile phones.' He listened for a moment.

Caroline asked, 'Who are you ringing?'

'Mr Fitch. Hello, sir. Good morning to you. Blair here, we've arrived but half the village has turned out to stop us getting into the field.'

From where she stood on the road she could hear Mr Fitch going berserk. The digger driver held the phone away from his ear. It went dead and he switched it off. 'He's coming.'

Nonchalantly he climbed down from the digger and stood leaning against one of the enormous wheels lighting a cigarette. The protestors went into a tight circle muttering about their situation and should they this and should they that.

Muriel looked at Caroline with raised eyebrows. 'This is the last thing I wanted. He will think I've gone off my head.'

To encourage her Caroline gripped her elbow. 'No, it's him who's gone off his head. We've got to stand firm. How can they run us over? We just must not break ranks.'

Gareth was smirking. 'Good. Good.'

'Good?' Muriel said, 'Good?'

'Of course. There's been no abuse from that Blair, so that's a victory.'

'I don't see how.'

'If they're abusive then you're in trouble. He's being reasonable so that's a plus.'

'Oh, right, well, I expect you know more about these things than I do.' Quietly to Caroline she said, 'I do wish Mr Fitch had been away. I shall feel such a fool.'

'It's all for a very worthwhile cause. Why should you worry what you look like?' Caroline quite fancied having an opportunity to stand up to Mr Fitch. They'd all taken so much from him in the past.

Mr Fitch roared up the lane in his Land Rover, dust flying from his wheels. He'd leaped out almost before he'd braked, and charged up past the machines to confront them all. He stopped short when he saw Caroline and – surely not! – Muriel at the front of the group.

'Muriel! Go home at once. This isn't a suitable place for you to be at all. Go along, go home.' He waved a hand at her expecting her to capitulate immediately, but Muriel didn't. In fact the way he treated her, as though she was a child and ought to be in school, stiffened her spine.

'Had you not decided on this cruel and heartless action I would not need to be here at all. The fact that I am here is entirely your fault, Mr Fitch.'

'My fault?'

'Of course. I cannot stand by and allow you to ruin my countryside – no, our countryside, it belongs to us all.'

Caroline stepped in, fearing for Muriel. 'Mr Fitch! We beg you not to go forward with this plan. Someone has told us that you are intending *building* on Rector's Meadow. Surely that cannot be true?'

If Caroline had thought she would shame him into surrender by the disappointed tone in her voice, she was mistaken: he had a lot at stake. The only thing which troubled his conscience was Muriel being there, for he valued her principles enormously.

He stood on the step of the digger and raised his voice so they could all hear. 'Now see here, I'm not getting rid of the hedge as such –'

Gareth shouted him down 'What is digging it up by its roots but getting rid of it?'

'There'll still be a fence there, and Rector's Meadow will still exist.'

'Oh! Yes!' shouted Gareth. 'Who yer kidding? Birds and plants can't grow in a fence. Our heritage is at risk!' This statement proved a rallying cry and all Gareth's group waved their placards and shouted, 'Our heritage! We shall not be moved! Down with greedy landowners!'

Scathingly Mr Fitch said, 'Your heritage! You don't even live here!'

'No, but we're here to support our brothers ... and sisters!' Gareth put an arm around Muriel's shoulders and squeezed them.

Muriel thought she would die. 'Mr Fitch, this is all most unseemly.'

'It is.' His shoulders drooped and Muriel thought, Victory!

Ron stepped forward to speak. 'In view of my experience in negotiations on behalf of the union could we perhaps retire for a discussion? I would willingly offer my expertise.'

'Hear, hear!' some of them shouted.

Mr Fitch glared at him, and momentarily Muriel saw disdain in his ice cold eyes. Speculatively he appraised the scene and appeared to come to a decision. 'Well, if you're so determined, far be it from me ... these great machines can't turn round in this lane, though, and it's too far for them to reverse all the way down into the Culworth Road. We'll unlock the gate and they can turn round in the meadow and then when they're sorted we'll have that discussion, Ron. All right, Muriel?'

Out of the corner of her eye Muriel could see Caroline furiously shaking her head. But he was right, they couldn't turn round, they were far too big, so yes, she agreed, they'd better turn round in the field. For the moment half a victory seemed better than none. 'Very well. We agree, and then we'll talk.'

Gareth almost exploded. 'No. No. No. We can't allow it.' He thumped a big fist into the palm of his other hand and shouted, 'It's a trick. A dastardly scheming trick! Don't you see?'

Muriel calmly patted his arm and declared, 'Mr Fitch is doing his best to accommodate us, I'm sure he is a man of his word. We have got him to talk haven't we? and as you would say that is a plus.'

The driver had the key and they all stood back to allow him through. The huge gate swung open and the driver secured it with a stone. He climbed back into his cab, and in a moment their ears were filled again with the horrendous noise of his engine. The other two vehicles revved up and followed on into the field. Immediately, Muriel saw what was happening. He'd got the diggers into the field by the most reprehensible trick, but before she could do anything about it Mr Fitch had swung the gate shut and snapped the padlock closed. He was out in the lane, smiling to himself. Muriel who, though small, was about the same height as him, strode forward to stand in front of him. For the first time in her life she was shaking with temper. 'I am ashamed of you. Ashamed. You wish everyone to think of you as a gentleman, well, let me tell you here and now, you are not and never will be.'

He couldn't meet her eyes.

Gareth girded his group together and surrounded him. Muriel sensed an ugly feeling in the air, and when she saw Gareth beginning to shoulder Mr Fitch and shout abuse at him, she thought, There's going to be a lynching here. She wasn't quite sure what a lynching actually involved but the threat was there for all to see. She pushed her way into the mêlée surrounding Mr Fitch and shouted, 'This must stop. This instant. I will not have it! Do you hear me? Stop it.'

Ron, Arthur, Willie and Tom squeezed through to stand beside her, just in case. Caroline ran to get Ralph, but he was already there in the lane. Muriel went to climb over the gate and was in such a state of high dudgeon that she climbed over it without the smallest difficulty. Landing safely on the other side she beckoned the others to follow suit. 'Lie down front and back of them, then they can't move.'

In a trice the Senior sisters were over the gate and rushing to lie down with Muriel. They were closely followed by Caroline and all the others. Three vehicles: there were at least four people to every one of them and effectively they put paid to any movement. Muriel stared up at the sky, her heart beating faster than she thought possible. Never, never as long as she lived would she give Mr Fitch the benefit of the doubt again. He was a craven liar and trickster in her book, and she'd said to his face what Ralph had long declared . . . Where was Ralph? She could hear all the commotion going on, Gareth shouting a lot and, oh dear! that sounded like a police siren. So it had come then. She was about to be arrested. Did she care? No, the whole world had a right to know what a perfectly dreadful man Craddock Fitch was.

A flash from a camera almost blinded her. Oh, no. Now her picture would be plastered across the front of the paper. Muriel determinedly closed her eyes, and didn't care a damn that the dry spiky grass was pricking into her legs nor that there was a distinct feeling of dampness creeping into her bones. What was that compared to a wren losing its home and those dear shy violets being destroyed for ever? The sacrifice was well worth it.

In the ensuing struggle Muriel heard Ralph's voice, then, above all the chaos, Mr Fitch yelling '*What!*'

A stunned silence fell, so Muriel sat up to see what was happening.

Ralph, with a posse of men in suits standing behind him, was facing up to Mr Fitch. 'You *will* listen to what they have to say, Craddock. Right?'

'I shall not. They know what they have to say, and that is that I am at liberty to tear up this hedge, and neither you nor anyone else is going to stop me.'

A man whom Muriel assumed must be from Culworth Council stepped from behind Ralph. He cleared his throat, always a sure sign, thought Muriel, that someone is nervous. His voice at first was squeaky with panic and then as he went on it deepened. 'Mr Fitch, the council insist you must not take down this hedge. If you do you will be prosecuted and fined and will also have it to replant, every single metre of it.'

'That's not what you said when I gave –'

The man from the council held up his hand. 'I'm sorry, but under the Hedgerow Regulations of 1997 this ancient hedgerow cannot be removed.'

Mr Fitch, seething with temper, took the man aside. 'What are you talking about? You knew, I knew, I couldn't take it down but you agreed I could.'

The man from the council took Mr Fitch's hand from his arm and said, 'Well, now I've changed my mind.'

'Had it changed for you, you mean.' Mr Fitch, boiling and almost speechless with temper, turned to Ralph a fist raised, and Muriel, through the bars of the gate, could see that things were getting even uglier. She leaped to her feet, scaled the gate and was beside Ralph ready to defend him before Mr Fitch had sufficient control to speak.

'You supercilious sod, you.' He drew in a deep, shuddering breath. 'Been throwing your aristocratic weight about, have you, down at the council offices?'

'Be careful what you say, Craddock, the press and the police are here. I merely showed these council officials the error of their ways. Money, after all, you see, cannot buy absolutely everything.' The council officials had the grace to look embarrassed.

'Damn and blast you. You bloody interfering old has-been.'

Muriel said, 'Mr Fitch, please.' Her quiet protest brought a semblance of control to him. His fist was put at his side, his breathing slowed.

He turned to speak to the council officials, taking them aside for a muttered conference. Muriel slipped her muddy hand into Ralph's and squeezed his fingers. She whispered, 'Thank you, dear.'

Mr Fitch's parting words were spoken with a finger stabbing at the three men from the council. 'You owe me! And don't you forget it.' He walked away down the lane to his Land Rover and they watched it reverse rapidly and erratically down the lane to where it joined the Culworth Road. A cheer went up. The Environmental Studies group, still in the meadow, danced a celebratory jig, shouting and laughing, slapping each other on the back. The rest of the Turnham Malpas supporters shook hands with each other and congratulated themselves on a victory well won. The council representatives went off to speak to the police and the press, and Blair unlocked the gate and asked for space to drive out.

Gareth came to Ralph, shook his hand and said, 'Thanks for

that. We knew about the Hedgerow Regulations, and suspected he'd bribed someone.'

'Oh, he had, well and truly. They were very busy lining their pockets. Now I think it's time I took my dear brave wife home.'

'She's been a splendid fighter this morning, all credit due to her. I don't suppose you would consider joining our group, would you? You'd be a fantastic asset with your ... connections?'

Ralph shook his head. 'No, thank you. It's not quite my thing. But I do wish you every success. Come, Muriel, my dear. 'He raised his voice and asked for silence.' Thank you to everyone who turned out this morning. I wish it had never been necessary, but I wasn't entirely sure that the council would come this morning so I had to let the protest go ahead just in case they didn't. We've won! We've saved this precious hedge! Thank you, everyone, thank you very much indeed. Splendid job you've done!'

They gathered round and shook his hand, thanking him for his intervention. 'Not at all, the least I could do.'

Caroline called out, 'Three cheers for Muriel!'

'And for you, Dr Harris,' Willie added.

Muriel had decided to go to bed early that night, because she was emotionally and physically exhausted: having summoned up so much of her resources there seemed to be nothing left of Muriel at all.

'My dear, why not get ready for bed and I will make us a drink and you can come downstairs to drink it before you finally expire? Sitting in front of the fire will be very calming.'

'They won't use that picture of me laid in front of the tractor, will they?'

Ralph smiled. 'I expect they most likely will.'

'I said unforgivable things to Mr Fitch, you know. But I meant them. They were true.'

'You told me.'

Muriel shook her head. 'It was such a dastardly trick after I had believed him. I must be a complete simpleton not to have realised what he was up to.' Muriel sighed. 'I'm going to get ready for bed like you suggest. I'll have Horlicks tonight, please, dear.'

She was half-way down the stairs, wearing her best dressing-gown and matching nightgown when the doorbell rang.

'Ralph! Who can that be at this time of night?'

When Ralph opened the door the very last person she ever expected to see was standing on the doorstep.

'Craddock! Good evening, do come in.'

Muriel half hesitated and debated about whether to turn tail and run back upstairs again, she couldn't face him not after what she'd said, but Mr Fitch caught sight of her and called, 'Please, Muriel, I need to see you.'

'But I'm . . .'

'That's of little consequence tonight. Please.'

Ralph courteously invited him to sit down, and after having seated Muriel in her favourite chair he sat down in his own winged chair and waited.

Mr Fitch fidgeted with his hands for a moment, head down. He crossed his legs, raised his head and said, 'I have come to offer you both the deepest of apologies. I behaved in a disgraceful manner this morning and I am deeply ashamed. You, Muriel, said I wasn't a gentleman and never would be . . .' Muriel cringed at his words. 'You were right, I'm not.' Mr Fitch held up his hand to silence Muriel, who appeared about to interrupt him. 'No, let me finish. I am thoroughly ashamed of myself. I always will try to bring the business world to Turnham Malpas and, of course, that's not right. It has no place here. Only loyalty and affection and understanding have a place. Those three qualities will achieve far more. How I could ever have contemplated building houses on Rector's Meadow I will never know. I've been for a walk right round it this afternoon, by myself so that I could think, and I had a revelation. Don't laugh, I did, even hard-boiled old Fitch can have his weaker moments!' He smiled wryly. 'I saw all of what it was you people talk about. I concede that I am merely a custodian of the land, for the land will still be here centuries after I am dust, therefore I must do my best by it, like so many men before me.'

Ralph nodded his agreement.

'Well, I understand that fully now. I apologise most sincerely to you, Ralph, for calling you what I did, I was seriously at fault and I have no excuse for it. I apologise to you, Muriel, for my behaviour, it was unseemly, as you said. Will you forgive me?'

Ralph stood up and went across to shake his hand. His voice was rough with emotion as he said, 'I accept your apology. Let's forget it, shall we?'

'No, not forget, but let's put it behind us, perhaps.'

Ralph nodded.

Mr Fitch got to his feet and went to Muriel. He took her hand from the arm of the chair where it was resting and put it to his lips. 'You are not only a lady by name but by nature too. Next time I face a moral dilemma I shall consult you. It will be your job to keep me on the straight and narrow.' He smiled down at her, and she smiled up at him.

'I'll say good night then.' Mr Fitch nodded his head at the two of them and let himself out.

18

When he got back from the meeting about Tom that night, Peter found Caroline stretched out on the sofa with a bottle of wine and two glasses waiting on the coffee table, warming her bare feet at the fire.

'Hello, darling. I've made a start on it, I'm afraid. Long, exhausting day and I needed to relax.'

Peter leaned over the back of the sofa and kissed her several times. This was as far as they had got since he'd come back from Yorkshire. There were times when he felt he was too reserved and more eagerness on his part would bring them closer more quickly, but since her brush with cancer and the need for his reticence because of it, and then Hugo, he'd willingly fallen into the habit of acquiescing to Caroline leading their relationship.

'Good meeting? Did you get the result you wanted?' She handed him his glass of wine.

Peter looked grim. 'No, I did not. I've told them all that nothing short of one hundred per cent agreement will satisfy me, as I feel they should all bear the responsibility of Tom. I am the only one to object to him being verger again. I've taught them to have compassion and now it's backfired on me.'

Caroline wagged her finger at him. 'They could have a point.'

'They have not got a case. He cannot hold a position of responsibility within the church ever again.'

'Peter!'

'He has lied, he has withheld the truth, and he has connived, whatever his reasons for doing so, to assist a drug-pusher to hide

415

his ill-gotten gains, and I'm sorry, but it's not on. He was an excellent verger, none better, but ... I won't have him back.'

'Here, drink this. Put like that I'm sure you're right, but it doesn't stop him living in the village, does it?'

'No, it does not. He'll have to exist on his police pension.'

Peter, sitting in the armchair opposite her, sipped his wine with approval. 'Good choice this.' He took a moment to admire Caroline's beauty. It was the clean lines of her he loved. A tad too thin since her cancer but at the same time it had brought a greater beauty to her face: heightened her cheekbones and brought her jawline into a prominence which flattered. But best of all he loved her dark eyes: her deep compassion for people, her shining honesty were still there in them despite her troubles. She caught his glance and, for a brief moment, he thought he saw her love for him shining out too, but she quickly turned her face towards the fire and the impression was lost. His blood was drumming through his veins though, and to cover his emotions he took another drink of his wine. 'This is very good.'

'Poor Tom, he wouldn't have known which way to turn.'

Peter nodded his head in agreement. 'It must put you in a terrible dilemma when you know your wife's sanity depends on your actions. You know the trashing of Kenny's house, that wasn't anything to do with Tom. It was done as a threat to Kenny and Terry, for muscling in on Turkish Delight's patch in Culworth.'

Caroline burst out laughing, a rip-roaring joyous laugh he hadn't heard from her in months. It completely took over and she abandoned herself to it. The laughter became so infectious that Peter caught it and joined in.

Caroline hugged her side. 'Oh dear! I shall have to stop, I've got a stitch! I cannot believe I have heard you say that. I thought Big Harry and Mack the Knife and names like it only belonged in nineteen fifties Ealing comedies. Oh, God! I've got such a pain!' She rubbed her side. 'Is it really true what you said? Do they call them names like that still?'

'Of course – well, that's what Tom said anyway. Turkish Delight is very big in drugs.'

'What I can't understand is, if you know this then the police must know it, so why don't they arrest him?'

'They have.'

'Oh, right! And Kenny? And Terry?'

'Tom says they'll find the pair of them eventually, but possibly under a couple of feet of concrete.'

Caroline sobered up. 'Poor Mrs Jones. She has idolised those boys all their lives, I can't begin to imagine how she feels.' She stared into the fire for a few moments and then said, 'We have so much to be thankful for. Haven't we?' She took her eyes from watching the flames and looked at Peter. He was holding his glass close to his lips, his eyes shut, enjoying the warmth of the fire and the peace after a long day.

For such a big man he had very slender fingers, strong but slender, it would be possible to describe them as elegant. She admired his face, half in light, half in shade. She tried to decide which half she admired, no, loved the most. There again that twin impression: his features strong but at the same time so gentle and just lately so vulnerable. She watched him take another sip of his wine, his eyes still closed. Caroline wished he'd open them because she wanted him to look at her. Wanted him to see that all her love for him had mysteriously, and unbidden, come flowing back on Saturday when he'd come through the door and looked for her. Wanted him to see her gratitude for his understanding and, above all, longed for him to witness her bodily need of him.

She poured herself another glass of wine. This was her third, she'd better stop otherwise she'd never get up the stairs to bed. She looked at her watch, half past ten, looked at Peter. Swiftly she got to her feet and gently removed Peter's glass from his hand for he'd obviously fallen asleep and the remains of the wine were threatening to spill on to his cassock.

The thought crossed her mind that perhaps Peter no longer wanted her physically as he had always done. She'd kept away from him all this time because one couldn't deceive Peter: he could always pick out pretence and that was exactly what her approach to him would have been. Complete pretence. Well, she was sincere now, right from the soles of her feet to the top of her head. Totally genuine. He'd shown no signs since he'd come back of how he felt about her, except just now when he'd come in and kissed her with rather more urgency than for a long time.

Sometimes it might be better if they didn't expect so much of each other, that they simply came together because they wanted sex with someone, or because of outright lust for each other. Right now a dose of honest-to-goodness lust would fit the bill and they could leave the high and mighty motives of adoration and worship, devotion and loving-till-death-us-do-part for another time.

Caroline looked to see how much wine was left in the bottle. She was reaching out intending to top up her glass when Peter said, 'Is there anything left for me?'

Startled, having thought him asleep, Caroline looked up at him, her passionate thoughts plainly written on her face. His strangely phrased question didn't appear to relate to the wine, but just the same he was holding out his glass to her and she filled it for him.

Almost inaudibly Peter asked, 'Am I to have it all?'

Because at that moment she didn't want soul-searching between them only plain honest need, she shied away from answering him directly and instead showed him the empty bottle and simply nodded.

The challenge in his next question was unmistakable though. 'Are you sure?' This question was not begging a reply, it was demanding one. Now he was gazing steadily at her and somehow it unnerved her. There could be no pretending he was talking about the wine. Now she had to say it and say it she did, eagerly. 'Yes, I am.'

Peter didn't look at her again or speak until every drop of his wine had gone. It seemed to Caroline it took him an age to drink it. At last he put down the empty glass on the table, and very slowly took out his cross from his belt, looped the chain over his head and placed it on the table beside the glass. She watched the fingers she had so admired a few moments ago begin unfastening the buckle on his belt. Having removed it he neatly arranged it in a circle around the cross and the wine glass. His clerical collar he laid down to make a smaller circle within the belt. He undid his cassock and dropped it on the floor beside the hearth.

Peter came to kneel in front of her. Lifting her bare feet, one in each hand, he kissed them in turn, savouring the way the heat from the fire had warmed her flesh. With the same heat burning the skin of his back through his shirt, and with his eyes on her face, he slowly began to unfasten the row of buttons that ran from hem to neck of her dress.

'Caro! You're stark naked underneath!'

'I was determined there would be nothing to prevent me having my wicked way with you tonight.'

'You wanton woman, you!'

Caroline was in the kitchen making breakfast when Peter came back from his morning run. He stood in the kitchen doorway breathing heavily, rubbing the sweat from his face with the hem of his running vest. 'I'm back!'

Beth moved her mouthful of Weetabix to one side and mumbled, 'We know, Daddy, we can hear, and we can smell all that sweat.'

Alex smacked his spoon down in his empty dish and said, 'Wait till I'm old enough to go running with you, Dad! I'll get home first.'

'I've no doubt you will! I shall be past my prime by then.'

Caroline looked up at him. 'Darling!'

'Yes?'

'Nothing. Just, darling.'

'I see. Be down in ten minutes.'

'Your dutiful wife will have your boiled eggs done to a turn.'

'Think I'll have scrambled this morning.'

'Scrambled? Why break the habit of a lifetime?'

Peter shrugged his shoulders, winked at her and disappeared upstairs.

Beth, having closely observed the exchange between them, said, 'Daddy's happy this morning.'

'Isn't he always?'

'No. Not lately.'

Caroline recognised a woman's intuition in Beth's comment. 'Well, he is and let's be thankful.'

'I don't like it when Daddy isn't happy.'

Alex cleared his mouth of marmalade and toast and said, 'I don't either.'

Acutely aware that the children had sensed all too well that the atmosphere between their parents had not been of the best these last months, Caroline remained silent. When she heard Peter walk into the bedroom overhead Caroline began to cook his scrambled eggs.

He returned to the kitchen dressed and shining new. Beth lifted her face for a kiss. 'That's nice, Daddy, I don't like you when you smell.'

'Honestly! Good honest sweat never did anyone any harm. Good morning, Alex.' Peter bent to kiss the top of his head.

'Morning, Daddy.'

Caroline turned from the Aga to place Peter's breakfast on the table. 'Off you go, the two of you, and let's have those teeth cleaned really well this morning for once. Please.'

Beth protested, 'I always do.'

Alex answered, 'You don't.'

'I do.'

'You only brush at the front.'

'I brush longer than you do.'

'You don't.'

The sound of their bickering trailed away up the stairs. Caroline went to stand behind Peter's chair. She placed her arms around his neck and with her cheek resting against his head she hugged him.

Peter put down his knife and fork and bent his head to kiss her wrists. 'My darling girl.'

'You haven't said Grace.'

'So I haven't. I'm topsy-turvy this morning.'

'So am I. That's what happiness does for you.'

Peter looked at the clock. 'You're going to be late for surgery.'

'I know. Give me a kiss before Sylvia comes.'

'I'm wishing it wasn't Sylvia's day.'

'So am I.'

'I'm wishing we had the house to ourselves for the day. Hang the parish for once.' Peter glanced at the clock, contemplating the possibility of holding back the hands. 'Much as I regret it, you really must go.'

Caroline grunted her agreement and bent to kiss him once more. 'You do realise I've fallen in love with you all over again?'

'I guessed as much last night.'

The front door clicked shut and they heard Sylvia calling out, 'Only me.'

While Sylvia hung her coat in the hall cupboard and put on her apron, Caroline kissed Peter yet again, said, 'Love you,' and went into the hall. 'Hello, Sylvia, I'm running late, I'm afraid. Can I leave everything to you?'

'Of course, it's what I'm here for. Nice morning.'

'Oh, it is. Wonderful! You'd never think it was almost the end of October, would you?' Caroline raced up the stairs and Sylvia went into the kitchen.

'Good morning, Rector.'

He looked up at her lost in thought, a forkful of scrambled egg half-way to his mouth. She saw that the terrible strain, which had been evident in his face for months now and which he'd striven so hard to disguise, had utterly vanished and been replaced with profound happiness. Sylvia rejoiced.

Peter, in his endeavours to swing the tide of opinion towards preventing Tom continuing as verger, wandered into the Store later that morning.

Jimbo looked up from the till as Peter's tall shadow fell across the counter.

'Why, good morning, Peter, what can I do for you?'

'Have you a minute? To spare for a chat?'

'In five minutes Bel will be here and then I shall. Is it important?'

Peter nodded. 'I'll pour myself a coffee, may I, while I wait?'

'Of course, help yourself.'

The five minutes stretched to ten and then in bustled Bel. She was barely recognisable nowadays, having lost such a great deal of weight. Gone were the dresses constructed like tents, and the heavy flip-flops she'd always worn at work. Now she wore flip-flops which no longer needed to be built like barges to accommodate her large fat feet, and instead of the tent-like dresses a slim skirt and a sweatshirt with Turnham Malpas Stores emblazoned across the front.

'Right, Bel, on the till for a while, if you please, shelf-stacking as and when.'

'Sorry I'm late, someone was sick just as I was leaving.' She smiled that captivating smile of hers, which lit up the whole of her face and instantly Jimbo saw no need to point out how her being late angered him. He ruefully acknowledged that had it been Linda he would have been bound to say something to aggravate her.

'I see. The Rector needs a word with me. Bring your coffee through, Peter.' He poured one for himself, black no sugar, his one stringent discipline in his fight against the flab.

Jimbo took him into his office, put his straw boater on top of a filing cabinet, pulled out a chair for Peter, then settled himself on a stool. After taking a sip of his coffee Jimbo said, 'I guess I know what this is about.'

'You do?'

'It's Tom, isn't it?'

'It is.'

'You know, usually, Peter, I see eye to eye with you on everything. We've been through a lot together in one way or another, you and I, but on this I shall not be moved.'

'You won't?'

'No.' Jimbo drained his cup. 'That's not hot enough, the damn machine must be on the blink again. What's yours like?'

'Fine, thanks. I really would like you on my side in this. We must have a verger whose word we can trust, and I can't trust Tom any more.'

'That's as may be. But I shan't change my mind. So your well-known persuasive powers will not work this time, I'm afraid.'

'But, Jimbo ...'

'But, Peter ... Is that all?'

'I haven't finished yet.'

'But I have.'

'Please, Jimbo, listen.'

'He won't.' This was from Harriet, who had stopped in the doorway on her way to the kitchens. 'I've tried, and what's more he's doing his best to persuade everyone else to insist on Tom being reinstated as verger.'

Peter stood up as she came in, as did Jimbo who offered her the stool. 'No, thanks, Jimbo, I'm too busy to sit down. All I can say is, Peter, I'm very disappointed in my spouse, as you must be. He's a stuffed shirt and a moral blot on the landscape.'

Peter would have laughed if the matter hadn't been so serious. 'People respect your opinions, you know, Jimbo, and it would be tremendously helpful to me if we were both on the same side. It's very important that the post of verger is filled by the right person, and Tom is not the right person as well you know. Willie admits he is beyond the job now, but even so one doesn't employ dishonest vergers just because there is no one else.'

Jimbo huffed and puffed for a moment and then said 'What about the Church and Christian forgiveness? Isn't that what it's supposed to be all about?'

Faced with that kind of challenge Peter was silent. Then he broke his silence by saying, 'To be honest I hadn't looked at it from that point of view.' He paused again. 'However, I still feel the same. I cannot trust him any more.'

Jimbo shook his head. 'Then I'm sorry, we're still on opposite sides.'

Harriet sighed. 'Well, I'm on Peter's side. I'm sorry but I am.'

Peter pressed his argument. 'The fact remains that he knew what Kenny and Terry were up to and never split. Morally he was in the wrong and he knows it. He's hiding behind Evie's skirts begging for his job back but –'

'Peter!' Jimbo turned to pick up his boater, intending to leave. He made a move towards the door then turned back to say 'OK, OK. We'll both have another think about it. Must press on.' He tossed his boater into the air, caught it on his head, adjusted the angle and left Peter and Harriet looking at each other.

'I'm so sorry, Peter. He has a lot on his mind at the moment, you know, but really that's no excuse.'

'The trouble is, on the face of it he's right. Maybe I should bend over backwards to accommodate Tom, but I do not want him back, despite Jimbo's attitude.' Peter twisted his paper cup round and round in his hands too miserable to look at Harriet.

She sighed. 'It's not only him, it's Ralph, Arthur Prior, Neville Neal, and loads of people not on the council.'

'Those not on the council don't matter. I didn't realise Ralph still didn't agree with me?'

'He doesn't want to stir up trouble, you know how protective he is about the village, so he's willing to go along with it if that will preserve the peace, but at bottom he does want him as verger and, of course, Muriel is appalled at Tom's deceit but goes along with Ralph. She does consider him so brave to have done what he has.'

'I see.'

'Must love you and leave you. I'll work on Jimbo tonight, OK?'

'Thank you.'

Peter went off to call at Orchid House. It was Evie who answered the door. A strange Evie with a nervous tic that made her whole body shudder every few seconds. Her hair, with its striking resemblance to a bird's nest, and the curious outfit she was wearing reminded Peter of a bag lady he knew in his previous parish. Evie looked at him with blank staring eyes. 'Good morning, Evie. I've called to see Tom, is he in?'

Evie nodded, opened the door wider and let him in. She left Peter standing in the hall and disappeared through the door into the garden. Tom came in without Evie.

'Tom, Evie doesn't seem well this morning.'

'No, she isn't. Have you come to say I haven't got my job back?' Peter didn't answer him straight away so Tom continued, 'Make no mistake about it, if I haven't then so be it, I shan't lay blame at anyone's door because I can understand why.'

'To be frank none of the council agree with me at the moment.'

'I see.'

'It's the deceit, Tom, that's what I don't like. A position of trust and you didn't come clean, and you should have done. You should have confided in me at the very least.'

'I know that now, but you see the state Evie's in? I did it to avoid this very thing happening. The signs are there again, and I can't bear it. She's argued herself into thinking that if I get the job back that means we're safe here. She loves it here, you see, and now she's going to have the embroidery class, well . . .' Tom's eyes filled up with tears.

Peter nodded. 'Curiously enough, it isn't the threat of someone else getting beaten up, it's not being truthful that's my stumbling block.'

Tom nodded. 'Living two lives for so long, the odd bit of not being truthful is kind of what I'm used to, if you see what I mean.'

'Give my regards to Evie and send her round to see Caroline any time. She's excellent at talking to people, being a doctor you know.'

Tom opened the front door saying, 'Thank you for that, be seeing you.'

'Indeed. God bless you, Tom.'

'And you.'

Next he called on Ralph, whom he found sitting in the big armchair which had so impressed the missing Kenny.

'Take a seat, Peter. Coffee? Muriel's not in but I am, despite what she believes, quite capable of making coffee. Please allow me to?'

'Thank you, no.'

'In that case let's get down to business.'

'I will. I was under the impression you agreed with me that we couldn't possibly have Tom back as verger. But I understand that's not so.'

'I don't think we shall find a better man for the job. He's efficient, meticulous, punctual, hard-working. In this day and age where would we find someone as good?'

'As Muriel isn't here we can speak quite frankly just between these four walls.' Peter looked at Ralph to assess his state of mind; he appeared amenable so he plunged on. 'You weren't here when Muriel had her breakdown. It was heartbreaking to see her so defeated, so withdrawn, sitting there in the hospital, dreadfully isolated and quite literally unable to speak. If you had seen her you would have been devastated. *Anything* that you could have done to protect her or to make her better you would have done, believe me, and I mean *anything*. Well, Tom cares as much for Evie as you do for Muriel, and that's why he acted as he did, because he desperately needed to demonstrate to her that they could put down their roots. Despite *all that*, I can't stomach his return.'

Ralph sat looking at his hands. He studied the backs and then turned them over and looked at the palms.

After the silence had lasted more than a minute Peter said, 'Well?'

Ralph looked up at him. 'One needs to remember that the ordinary fellow in the street has emotions just as powerful as one's own; his reasons cannot be ignored. But I do understand what you mean. When all is said and done it goes against the grain, doesn't it? The damned fellow even lied to Muriel one day. Told her she couldn't go in the church to polish the brass because he'd been spraying for spiders so she waited outside for ten minutes or more. Of course, it was really because Kenny was in there doing whatever he was doing with my family tomb. So he was downright lying to protect Kenny, that I can't forgive. You're right, of course, as usual, I see that now.'

Peter stood up.'Thank you for that. Evie is ill again, so to salve my conscience I just hope we can find Tom a job here in the village. Thanks again, Ralph. I've still got Jimbo, Arthur and Neville to persuade, though.'

Ralph grunted, 'Leave them to me, I'll persuade 'em. They'll all agree by the time I've finished with them, believe me.' He smiled rather grimly at Peter, who smiled thankfully back.

Ralph got up to see Peter to the door. 'Thank you for making me see sense. You've a gift for it, you know, though some would call it emotional blackmail.'

Peter grinned down at him. 'Me? Emotional blackmail! Never!'

They shook hands and Peter went home still feeling very uncomfortable at what might be the outcome of his objections, but determined to stick to his guns.

19

The rubbish outside Don and Vera's cottage was finally removed by Barry and some of the labourers from the estate. Don swept up, viewed the plants that had been flattened by it, straightened a couple of them up and heeled them back into the earth again then went inside to prepare himself.

First he stripped and used the newly installed power-shower, the pride of his life, then he shaved. He'd already had his hair cut very short so that only the tips were black and the rest was growing iron grey, like Vera preferred. At the thought of Vera his insides quivered. He'd staked his all on her having him back. What more could a chap do but make a complete fresh start? The bedroom furniture had gone to the auction rooms along with Ralph's washstand, all the old rotten stuff was up at the Big House awaiting 5 November, he'd sold his motorbike, and what greater sacrifice could a woman ask than for a fellow to sell his BSA Gold Star motorcycle, which he'd ridden with such joy for more than thirty years?

He tied his third new tie since he'd renovated himself, inspected the state of his shirt collar. Ah! He'd forgotten those new stiffeners to keep the points straight. There, that was better. Right then, he'd be off. A bit of sly questioning of Rhett had established that this was Vera's Saturday off and there was no way he, Don Wright, was going to miss her.

He roared up the driveway of the nursing home at exactly nine o'clock. He saw through one of the big windows that the old dears who were mobile were breakfasting. Don rang the bell. The door was opened by a bright young thing wearing a cheerful golden yellow tabard over her white uniform.

'Good morning!'

'Good morning to you, young lady. I'm calling to see Mrs Wright.'

'Oh, Vera! Come right in. Do you know the way?'

'Yes, thank you, right to the top and turn left.'

She nodded.

Rhett answered his knock, gave his grandad a huge wink, admired the chocolates he was carrying and shouted over his shoulder, 'Gran! You've a gentleman caller.'

Don heard Vera calling out, 'Don't be daft! Is it yer grandad?'

'Come in, Grandad. We're just going to have some breakfast, want some?'

'Won't say no.'

Vera appeared. Don searched for a word to describe how Vera looked this morning but he didn't know the one he needed. If he had known it he'd have described Vera as vibrant. From the top of her well-groomed hair down to the naughty-looking gold slippers she was wearing she looked, well, great.

'Rhett's invited me to breakfast. Here, these are for you.' He held out the box and she took them from him.

'Thanks! My favourites. Rhett, set another place.'

They exchanged small-talk while they ate, a meal Don enjoyed for the kitchen was welcoming and the gay little posy of flowers Vera had placed on the breakfast table suited his mood.

Rhett pushed his chair away and stood up. 'I've a day's work to do. Will you be all right without me?'

Vera said, 'I didn't know you were working today.'

'Well, I am. They asked me yesterday.'

'Who?'

'The Bissetts. Neither of them are well enough to garden yet and they're worried about winter coming on and the garden needing tidying so I said I would. Then, on the proceeds, I'm going into Culworth with Michelle to the cinema and a meal.'

'Oh, all right, then. Take care of that girl, you know what I mean?'

'Gran! She's only fifteen.'

'Exactly!'

Rhett blushed bright red. Shortage of girls his age limited his choice. As for hanky-panky as his gran called it, he respected her too much for that. Besides, her step-dad Barry Jones was a man to be reckoned with and he didn't fancy getting at odds with him.

Rhett gave his grandad the thumbs up as he passed behind his grandma's chair. 'Will you be here when I get back, Grandad?'

'Don't know, do I?'

Vera didn't say whether he was welcome or not. Faced with this new Don whom she could scarcely recognise she was nonplussed. Chocolates? Flowers? Car! He must really mean business.

'Is it your day off?'

'You know it is, you old devil.'

Don laughed. 'Long time since you called me that.'

'Long time since you paid me any attention.'

Don lavishly spread butter on his last piece of toast. 'You know, Vera, I'd no idea how tired I was. All those night shifts. Tired right through to my bones I was. Dragging myself about. In winter I hardly knew what daylight was. I seemed never to see the blue sky, or hear the birds singing, it was just as if I was deaf and blind. Since I've been just doing days 'cos of them cutting back, and not working twenty-four hours I've caught up on sleep. Given me a whole new outlook. It's no excuse, I know, but for what it's worth there it is. The house, when I see it now, all shining and new, it's still the same house, you know, where I was born and where I want to die. I'd got in such a groove I thought if we changed it it wouldn't be the same, but it is and I don't mind. In fact I wish I'd done it years ago.'

Vera nudged his elbow. 'Get on with yer, yer daft thing.'

'But we couldn't have afforded to do what I've done now, then.' He winked at her, folded his last remaining slice of toast in half and pushed it into his mouth. When he'd finished munching it, and had rinsed his mouth with another drink of his tea, he patted his pocket. 'In here I've got a surprise for yer.'

Vera didn't show much delight, better not look too keen too soon. 'Oh!'

'A weekend away. Your choice.' He dragged a well-thumbed

holiday brochure from his jacket pocket. 'You decide when and where and I'll fall in with it.'

'I've always fancied London.'

'London!'

'Yes, a good musical on the Saturday night and a chance to see some of the places you only read about.' Vera smothered her excitement as best she could. New horizons opened up in an instant. Strolling down Piccadilly past Fortnum and Mason's, peering through the railings at Buckingham Palace, eating in a restaurant in Leicester Square, climbing up to the Whispering Gallery at St Paul's Cathedral where the Princess had married, bless her. All the brightness, all the thrill of the place, all the lively noise of it was so vividly in her mind, she could almost be there already. Suddenly she realised Don was speaking. 'What did you say?'

Now he had to repeat those difficult words as if it hadn't been hard enough to utter them the first time round. 'I was saying, I'm more than willing to come and live here. I did all those improvements to get you to come back to the cottage, but I've realised you won't, so I'll have to come here and we'll rent out like you said. It's the most sensible thing to do.'

'I see.'

Don reached across the table and let the tips of his fingers touch her hand. 'That's if you'll have me, which is what I want, if you will, that is.'

Vera filed his request at the back of her mind and dealt with more immediate matters. 'It seems to me you must be living in an empty house.'

'I am, almost. I couldn't bear to put all that old kitchen stuff in those nice drawers and cupboards so I'm afraid I went two or three times to the tip the other day and got rid of it all. Most of it belonged to my mother, God rest her soul.' Amen to that, thought Vera. 'So apart from one chair and the telly, Rhett's bed and that built-in cupboard in his room, and a new kettle, yes, it is an empty house.'

'So what about yer meals?'

'Willie and Sylvia are very good. Jimmy asks me round and Mrs Charter-Plackett.'

'I'd heard but I didn't believe it. What's she like as a cook then?'

'Brilliant.'

Stirrings of jealousy manifested themselves in Vera's insides. 'So about this holiday, if we book it and I don't go, Grandmama Charter-Plackett could have my ticket, could she?'

Don spluttered his disgust. 'Look, she's grand and we get on very well, and it's her's inspired me to press on, and she has good ideas about colours and what's right, but I have to be on my best behaviour all the time and it gets wearing.'

'Oh, I see. I count as nothing then. You can burp or fold yer toast up in front of me and bung it in, but not in front of her, oh, no!'

'Could you enjoy eating meals with her day in day out? I've got to put a stop to it.'

'Dear, dear, you are in a fix.' She stood up and began to clear the table. 'Well, I don't know what you propose to do all day, but I'm not wasting my Saturday off.'

'Where did you intend going?'

She'd no idea and had to come up with an answer quickly. Vera plumped for the bus into Culworth.

'Don't bother. I'll drive you in and we'll go rowing on the lake and we'll have a look at the shops and have some lunch out. How about that?'

'Sounds interesting.'

'And while we're there we'll book this weekend away.' He pushed the brochure back in his pocket.

They got back about half past five having achieved the major objective of booking the weekend away. It was to be in two weeks' time, in London as Vera had requested. Don had been a courteous escort, which had gone a long way to persuading Vera that she might, just might, have him back seeing as she was getting all her own way, and above all they had enjoyed each other's company, which they hadn't done for years.

She'd forgotten that Don could row with such smoothness that the boat glided easily through the water, and the weather was so beautiful, sunny and warm with just a slight breeze. The trees had the first of their autumn colours and she lay back enjoying herself.

'I'll have a rest, we'll tie up under that willow there, while I get my breath back. I'm not the man I was.'

Vera studied him as he skilfully drew the boat under the tree and tied the painter around one of its stout trunks. He was right, he wasn't the man he was when he was seventeen but . . . 'Shall we sit in the boat or get out?'

'Sit in it. That bank looks too wet and slippery to stand on.' He lay back and spread his arms out so he was gripping the sides of the boat.

'I'd forgotten you could row.'

'Either you're a natural or you're not.'

Vera looked out over the lake and pondered again about having him back. 'I'm not having you falling into your bad ways again.'

'Bad ways? What do you mean?'

'Like being idle, and not washing enough. Sitting in front of the telly for hours not speaking. Refusing to get dressed up when we go out, that is if we go out. Not being nice to me.'

'It's all self, isn't it, Vera? I've slaved to put things right these last weeks and still it isn't enough.'

'After thirty years and more of not putting yourself out you owe me something.'

'I'm only human. You're perfect, are you?'

Vera almost answered yes. She couldn't think of a single fault. 'So what are my faults, you tell me.'

Neither could Don. He caught her eye and magically they both burst out laughing. The boat rocked dangerously and Vera had to cling on. They hadn't laughed together like that in years. Somehow it cleared the air between them. Don looked at his watch.

'The time! They'll be charging us extra.'

'So?'

Don looked at her. 'So! What the hell?' They lounged there mostly in silence with Vera giving him covert looks to help her decide about him. From time to time they studied each other without speaking, finding this fresh development in their relationship both pleasing and satisfying.

'We'll have a coffee in that little coffee shop by the boathouse.' Don untied the boat and rowed them back. Now when he caught her eye she smiled, and all he'd done was row a boat that had cost him five pounds. When he thought of the money he'd spent already on the house . . .

But the coffee shop was dingy and unkempt, and whereas at one time it would have sufficed for Don, he turned his nose up at it today. 'This won't do, come on, let's go.'

They drove into the centre of Culworth and parked in the multi-storey. He took her arm and guided her through the sweet wrappers blowing about, round the cigarette butts scattered by a hundred feet, and the urine-soaked stairs, all things he would never have noticed before, out into the sun. 'The George! What about it?'

'The George? I'm not dressed well enough for there! What about the Belfry Café?'

'No, the George it is.'

They'd stayed so long drinking coffee that they had lunch there too. She was surprised by how well he conducted himself in the restaurant, there was a new finesse about him which, she decided, had come from dining with Grandmama Charter-Plackett. While Don paid the bill Vera went out to watch the swans go by, so Don begged bread from the waiter and took it out to her, and together they fed the water fowl, and laughed at the cygnets and Don took her arm and squeezed her hand. There were moments when Vera felt the old Don was back but mostly it was the new Don and she began to feel better disposed to his return. They went out to look at the shops and returned to have afternoon tea at the George too. When they got back to the nursing home Vera said, 'That's cost a packet that has.'

'As you would say. So?'

'You're right, why not?' Vera went to look out of the window, not trusting herself to look at him while she spoke. 'I've talked to Jimbo about renting out the cottage and he says no rent book. You have an agreement, a lease he called it, and you keep renewing it if they're satisfactory. That means you can get them out quick, if need be.'

'I see.' Don began to feel hopeful.

'So how about it?'

Don stood behind her, put his arms around her waist, and locked his fingers so there was no escape. 'I'd like that very much.' He gave her a squeeze as he said it.

Vera chuckled. 'Then go get your stuff.'

'Yer mean it then? Yer serious? It's what I would like more than anything.' He looked round the room. 'I like this place, there's a feel about it, we could be happy here.'

'I mean it.'

Tentatively, not wanting to push his luck, Don asked, 'I'll go get me bits and pieces then, shall I?'

Vera squeezed around in his arms and, clutched stomach to stomach to the new slimline Don, she said, 'Fresh start. Eh?'

'Fresh start. Car. Money in our pockets, a nest-egg building up. A weekend in London. A brand new wife. What more can a man ask for?'

'Brand new wife?'

'Well, you are. You're different from the old Vera.' He whispered in her ear, 'And them gold slippers is real sexy.'

Vera pushed him away. 'Get off! I'll sort out some drawer space and that till you get back.' But she was laughing and he laughed too.

Vera, left to herself, didn't sort out anything at all. She stood quite quietly by the window looking out over the garden, wondering if she'd done the right thing. This might well be something she'd regret, but having learned out of desperation how to be strong, then maybe from now on she'd be an equal partner. Come to think about it, that was how it should be. She twiddled her engagement ring with its minuscule diamond, round and round, and thought about being sixteen and having to marry him willy-nilly. No, she'd done the right thing. Rhett would be leaving home soon and she'd be on her own and that was no joke. Now she'd have Don and she'd have to keep reminding herself how hard won her triumph had been.

Into her mind came a picture of him laughing with her in the boat when neither of them could think of a single fault of hers. Vera moved across to the mirror and winked at Don's brand new wife. 'Go for it, girl,' she said out loud. 'Go for it.'

Don drove home elated, a new man in every way. The birds sang louder, the sky was bluer, the country lanes more beautiful than he had ever seen them. He had the sun roof open and he put his clenched fist through it and punched the sky. What a day! Briefly, just for a moment, he did wonder whether he would not have had such an expensive day if he'd played his cards more circumspectly; perhaps there'd been no need for the lunch and then the tea because it seemed to him that while he was rowing her on the lake she'd had her change of heart ... No, he was being mean and miserly again. Scrooge! He mentally cursed himself for so quickly returning to his old ways and shut the door on them with a bang.

When he went into the cottage he found a note from Mrs Charter-Plackett on the mat asking him to an evening meal. So he knocked and told her, and to his embarrassment she embraced him on the doorstep. 'I'm so pleased, Don, so very pleased. I shall miss you. We've had a good time, haven't we, doing up your cottage?'

'We have and many thanks, Missus, for helping, and the meals and that.'

'You're most welcome, it was a pleasure. Now, go on, hurry or Vera might change her mind!'

20

'Willie Biggs, will you ever grow up? You're the same every Bonfire Night.'

Willie grinned at Sylvia and rubbed his hands together. 'Why not? It's a bit of harmless fun and a chance for once to get something for free from old Fitch.'

They were slipping through the little gate at the back of the churchyard, which had been made many years ago to accommodate the family at the Big House when they came to church. No one was supposed to use it now but Willie had never bothered about such dictums. Bother old Fitch and his rules. Why walk all that way round when . . . Behind him he heard footsteps. Someone else taking a rise out of Mr Fitch? It was Sheila and Ron.

Willie whispered, 'What you doing 'ere?'

'Same as you, taking a short-cut.' Sheila had a torch, which she shone in Willie's face. His red wool hat and matching fingerless mittens combined with the excited grin on his face gave a distinct impression of a little boy up to no good.

Sylvia said good evening and how were they both, and Ron replied they'd never been better and were looking forward to a good night.

Together they ambled across the field towards the crowds. There was no mistaking the direction they had to take for the whole area in front of Turnham House was floodlit. Smack in the middle of the field waiting to be lit was the highest, widest, biggest bonfire they'd ever seen. To one side was the refreshment marquee, close by the smaller beer tent, and on a platform made of pallets was the Scout band, playing as though their lives depended on it.

Everywhere fairy-lights were strung, providing a magical touch to the whole scene.

'Well, I never! Half that stuff on the bonfire is Don and Vera's. Look at the size of the marquee, by Jove, he's really gone to town this year.' Willie rubbed his hands again in joyful expectation.

In the shadows in front of the huge kitchen-garden wall was all the paraphernalia of a massive fireworks display.

'This is his big apology to us.' said Sheila. 'That's what this is.'

Sylvia, nonplussed, enquired, 'Apology? What about?'

'Mr Fitch, feeling guilty about Jeremy Mayer. Could have killed him, you know. Very close brush with death Jeremy had, when they had that row. And guilty about the hedge. We got him there though, didn't we? Eh? Nipped his little scheme in the bud good and proper. His language! It was disgusting! Like Lady Templeton said, he'll never be a gentleman, but if this is him not being a gentleman then I'm all for it! Perhaps this time he'll have learned his lesson.'

'What lesson's that?'

'That you can't beat this village into submission. We've been here far too long for some newcomer to get the better of *us*. United we stand! Oh, yes.' She punched the air and laughed, and the others had to join in.

'They weren't the only ones to have a close brush with death, were they?' Sylvia took Sheila's arm and patted it sympathetically.

Sheila sobered and after a moment agreed with her. 'Still, we're all right now. Fit as fleas we are, Ron and me. Aren't we?'

Ron gripped her arm to lead her round a puddle and then said, 'We are indeed. I only hope Tom gets his job back, Evie's sore in need of assurance.'

Willie answered, 'Well, I think it's wonderful how you two have rallied round Tom and Evie. Real Christian forgiveness.'

Sheila was embarrassed at being awarded such lofty motives when all the time she was glad to have Evie as her friend, for truth to tell she hadn't got any real friends at all; acquaintances and associates but not real *friends*. For some reason she was the only person Evie felt free to speak to, well, not exactly free, but at least she did speak from time to time which made friendship easier.

They'd reached the edge of the crowd by now and all four of

them gave themselves up to greeting everyone and waiting for Mr Fitch and Sir Ralph and Muriel and his guests to come out from the Big House to make speeches and light the bonfire.

There was always a big ceremony at this moment, Mr Fitch taking the opportunity to garner every ounce of publicity for himself and his good deeds. But the villagers took care not to let him see their mirth because it wasn't courteous and, besides, they all knew which side their bread was buttered, regarding Mr Fitch. Sir Ralph's family had put the light to the bonfire for generations and now, with the sole survivor having returned to his roots, tradition had been revived, despite Mr Fitch's attempt some years ago to get a celebrity to do it. And yes! Here they came! A cheer went up as Mr Fitch mounted the platform with his specially invited guests.

Mr Fitch held up his hand for silence. 'Sir Ralph, Lady Templeton, ladies and gentlemen, children, it gives me great pleasure to be here this evening to participate in the celebrations. Before he goes up in smoke look closely at the guy on top of the bonfire. As you can see he bears a very strong resemblance to the real Guy Fawkes. In fact, he is the most splendid guy we've had in years.' A small cheer of agreement went up. 'Watch out when the flames reach his head, because it's been filled with dozens of jumping crackers! He was made by Evie Nicholls, the wife of our esteemed verger. Three cheers for Evie.'

A buzz of consternation flew round the crowd. 'Our esteemed verger'? But he wasn't, they hadn't agreed, or had they? Well, they hadn't up to yesterday.

Willie said under his breath to Sylvia, 'Not that I know of.'
'Me neither.'

They saw Ralph whisper in Mr Fitch's ear. After a moment of throat-clearing Mr Fitch said, 'Well, I thought it had all been decided but apparently it hasn't, so someone get their finger out and get it decided, for we can't do without them, can we?'

A ragged half-hearted cheer of approval went round the crowd, and then Mr Fitch continued his speech. 'All this,' he waved his arm encompassing the whole field as he did so, 'is due to the diligent application of one man, namely Jeremy Mayer. Where is he?' From the edge of the crowd a voice said, 'Here!'

'Step forward, old chap, with that dear wife of yours.' Now there really was a buzz of consternation, Dear wife? What was this? Something they'd missed and no mistake. 'Yes, I knew you'd be surprised! Jeremy and Venetia were married this morning, here in our church. One of the best-kept secrets this village has ever known. They didn't want any fuss, just a very quiet wedding. Well, then, step forward so we can congratulate you! Come on, up on to the platform!'

So Jeremy and Venetia climbed up and stood side by side waving. The cheer wasn't ragged now it was full-throated and they called for a speech. Venetia nudged Jeremy and he took a step forward. Though he couldn't yet be called slim, Jeremy had lost so much weight since his heart-attack that he was barely recognisable. While he spoke Venetia looked at him with pride and admiration, giving a very good imitation of an American political wife. More than a few sly remarks were made amongst the onlookers, on the lines of not before time, and what a change in him and in her, for she no longer advertised herself so blatantly, being dressed tastefully and with only half the makeup she normally wore, and her hair was not its usual outrageously dense black.

Jeremy got a cheer, but by now the crowd was wanting to see the bonfire lit because until then the refreshment marquee wouldn't be opened, nor the free beer tent. So Mr Fitch, sensing the growing impatience of the crowd, signalled for silence.

'Now, ladies and gentlemen, the moment we've all been waiting for. Sir Ralph! May I ask you to do us the honour of lighting our bonfire?'

Ralph stepped forward, took the flaming torch from Barry Jones and went, as generations of his family had done, to light the Guy Fawkes bonfire. He walked round it lighting it at the various places pointed out to him by Barry and as the flames took hold a final roaring cheer went up.

Don and Vera, in the middle of the crowd, watched as their old life crackled and sparked its way to extinction. 'You know, Don, I have to admit I'm blinking glad all that old stuff has gone. Somehow it was never my home. It was always your mother's with all her old stuff in it.'

'She did give us a roof over our heads when we couldn't afford one of our own.'

'Oh! I know she did and we were grateful, but it was always her home not never ours. I once lost some money down the side of the sofa and when I dug about for it I came up with a pair of her old glasses, and that was years after she'd died. Turned my stomach it did.'

'You never said.'

'There's a lot I never said.'

'Such as?'

'Doesn't seem to matter now.' Vera tucked her hand in his and followed the flames up into the dark night sky. The floodlighting had been turned off as soon as the fire took hold, and the flames were leaping so high you had to tilt your head back to see their topmost points, and it made it seem as though the flames were lighting up the very stars. 'I wish we'd had more children.' Of a sudden the flames reached Guy Fawkes's head and, as Mr Fitch had said, it really was filled with jumping crackers. They darted and cracked all over the place and more than one landed amongst the crowd and they had to leap about to avoid them. 'I wish we'd made more of ourselves.' Slowly, very, very slowly, the fire began to collapse. Nearest to them was that old wooden chair from their bedroom, its four legs pointing uselessly now towards the sky. She'd had her alarm clock stood on it for more years than she cared to remember. 'We've lost a lot of years, you and me.' The wooden chair, its rush seat already gone, the varnish on it now severely blistered, became enveloped by the scorching flames and crumbled. 'Shan't have to lose any more. Got to make up for lost time.'

'Well, now,' said Don slyly, 'I thought that was just what we were doing.'

Next to go was that cheap wardrobe that had been their Rhett's and before that their Brenda's. What a hopeless failure she'd been. Married to a useless man, well, no more than a boy when they married, and he'd disappeared within three months, leaving her with Rhett. Where was she now? Lucky if they got a card at Christmas, and no address on it. So what did she care? Well, now it was up to Don and her to make the best of it. She turned to look at him and was surprised to see he looked almost handsome in the warm glowing light of the fire. Vera recalled his last comment, and kicked his ankle. 'You cheeky devil, you, I heard that.' But she had to laugh.

Don smirked. 'I've been thinking I might have a liking for a winter sun holiday. February, just when you're getting sick of the winter. Cheer us up. Could you get a week off?'

'I dare say.' Excitement bubbled, yes, bubbled up inside her.

'You choose the place.'

'I've a fancy for Tenerife.'

'Good idea. Tenerife it shall be. But a hotel, not self-catering, eh? It's the auction next Friday, we'll see how much we get for the bedroom suite. 'Spect it'll be only a few hundred pounds if that, but it'll go towards paying for the holiday.'

Vera turned to face him, feelings surging up inside her that she hadn't felt in years and so could scarcely recognise. 'I have to say it. Right at this moment, I love yer, Don. The feeling might not last for long so you'd do right to enjoy it while you can.'

If she didn't know better she might have thought she saw tears sparkling on the edges of Don's eyes.

Round the other side of the fire stood Evie and Tom. 'Never mind, love, never mind.' Tom pulled his old school scarf more closely round Evie's neck. 'It'll all sort itself out. I knew it couldn't be true, because no one had told me. I'm sure the Rector will sort it for us. He has a wonderful way of getting people to do as he sees fit, you wait and see. I've every confidence in him.'

Evie didn't answer. She just stood there, twitching, her eyes lit from the outside by the fire, but dead within.

Tom pointed out that the guy was finally burnt. 'You did a good job there, Evie. Excellent. I don't know where you get all your ideas from, I really don't. Shall we go in the refreshment tent?'

She shook her head.

'Go on, love. A hot drink would fit the bill just right. How about it?'

'No, Tom. I just want to enjoy the fire. You go.'

'I tell you what, I'll go get something and bring it out to you.'

'If you want.'

'Don't move from here. Right?'

Evie nodded, watched him stride away and then turned back to watch the flames. All she had to do now was step forward, what, thirty paces? How quickly did you die in a fire? Would that be the best way? The quickest, cleanest way? Like cremation, except you were alive, like wives had to do in India years ago when their husbands died. Tom. Tom. He tried so hard to understand, but he couldn't. No one could, not this desolation so deep inside herself; this arid, shrivelled desert she carried around all the time. Perhaps that was the price she had to pay for having been given a talent. Maybe if she threw all her pictures, all her threads, all her fabrics, all her needles, on this fire, cleansed herself of all her skills, the desert within would flower instead and she'd find peace again.

She felt a touch on her arm. It was Sheila. Sheila, with her gutsy acceptance of what life threw at her. Sheila, who lacked charisma but was so warm-hearted. Sheila, who frequently made unforgivable gaffes but had an unexpected blundering insight. Sheila, who was the first friend she'd had in years and thus accepted her for what she was. Uncomplicated Sheila, who talked and filled her silences and made it so she didn't have to speak.

'Hello! There you are! I've been looking for you. I think it's been the best Bonfire Night we've had in years and you should see the refreshments! It's cost old Fitch a packet I can tell you. They're all in there stuffing their faces as if they were expecting a seven-year famine like in the Bible. I've come to get you, my Ron and your Tom are in the queue. Come on, let's join them.'

Evie half shook her head but changed it to a nod. Sheila put her hand in the crook of her arm and hustled her off before she wavered again. The marquee was packed. Long tables groaning with huge silver salvers piled high with all manner of savoury delights filled the length of the marquee. The queue wound its way around the other three sides, circling a few tables and chairs for those who couldn't stand and the drinks table serving soft drinks and tea and coffee. Jimbo had brought in serving staff from outside the village, but in charge was Barry Jones' wife Pat; they were all working with a will under her stern eye. Sheila squeezed Evie through the crowd and finally found Ron and Tom still nowhere near the head of the queue.

'Here we are! I've found her! We shall miss the fireworks at this rate. But what an evening. And we still haven't had the jacket potatoes and the children their toffee apples.'

'I love toffee apples.'

Sheila looked indulgently at Evie. 'Then you shall have one, even if I have to ask Mr Fitch himself.'

The delighted look on Evie's face was reward in itself.

Sheila couldn't cope with silence, and when she found the four of them standing there with nothing being said she piped up with 'Isn't it wonderful how well Evie's classes are going? We've had to close the list now. Twelve's quite enough if we're going to get our share of Evie's attention. She and I have come up with the idea that when we've all got more ... What was that word you used, Evie?'

'Proficient.'

'That's right, more proficient, we're going to start a project, all of us together. We don't know what yet, though, do we?'

Evie agreed. 'No, we don't.'

'But it'll be something inspired I've no doubt, knowing Evie. She's very talented your wife, you know, Tom, I'm just glad I discovered her. Ron and I got asked to eat with the posh people in the Big House but this is much more fun and you don't have to watch your manners quite so much, and you can be greedy without anyone noticing! Oh, look it's us next. Grab a plate, Evie, and help yourself. There's plenty to go at, so don't hold back. It's free. Go on. Go on.'

In the hall of the Big House Ralph and Muriel were talking to Arthur, Neville Neal and Jimbo. Balancing plates and drinks and making conversation always taxed Muriel, so she kept her concentration on eating rather than talk but her attention was caught by hearing Ralph say, 'So my accountancy firm has been bought out and it's now a massive concern and I'm not best pleased. One loses the personal touch, don't you know? Would you be too busy for me to come to the office to see you and we could have a discussion?'

Neville Neal's thin, almost emaciated face stayed expressionless. He swallowed the piece of quiche he had in his mouth without chewing it properly and he knew, just knew, he'd have severe indigestion before the night was out. 'Too busy? Why, of course not, Sir Ralph, not to see you. Delighted at any time. We at Neal, Parsons and Watts pride ourselves on our personal service. Any time. Any time.'

Ralph nodded. 'Good. I'll ring to make an appointment.'

'What a good idea. Look forward to seeing you. Very pleased. I'm sure we can be of service.'

Jimbo, listening to this, felt there were undertones to Ralph's proposals to which he was not privy. Then Ralph almost immediately turned to him. On the *qui vive* though he was, Ralph's comment to him caught Jimbo unawares. 'I've been elected to the committee of the county hunting, shooting and fishing lot, my title, I suppose, helps, you know, they think. They've become very dissatisfied with the caterers they've used up to now: changed hands and they're not up to par. Christmas Ball and such, you know. I expect perhaps you'd be too busy to quote.'

Jimbo almost shouted Bingo! out loud. He'd been after the contract for years. It meant, if he was successful, not just catering for the usual social functions but because people with the countryside at heart were often high-powered and they had weddings and twenty-first birthday parties and . . . 'I could quote, of course. Be delighted to. But I'm not a cheap option. If they want first-rate food and service they'll have to pay. But yes. Gladly. You can put our name forward.'

'Good. Good.'

Then Ralph offered to refill their glasses, which he did with charm and élan and he included Muriel in their conversation for a moment then addressed Arthur Prior, his illegitimate cousin twice removed and not unlike himself in looks, and turned on the charm. 'I was having lunch at the Conservative Club in Culworth the other day, Arthur, and I overheard something which might be of interest to you.'

'Oh, what was that, Ralph?'

'You know the two fields on the east side of your farm between you and Wallop Down Wood?'

Arthur nodded. 'I do indeed.'

Ralph's face was full of innocence as he sipped his wine and paused solely for dramatic effect. 'They're for sale. Coming up for auction in Gloucester in February.'

Arthur's face lit up. 'For sale! I don't believe it. I've been after those two fields for years, but I've never found out who owned 'em. They've been neglected but with good husbandry they'd make rich pasture for my cows and no mistake.' He gave Ralph a friendly nudge with his elbow and said, 'Thanks for letting me know. Forewarned is forearmed, brilliant. That's made my day.'

'Not at all, Arthur, pleased to be of service.'

Arthur, positively hopping with delight, turned to Muriel and gave her a kiss. 'This husband of yours is worth his weight in gold.'

Muriel smiled and said, 'I know.'

Jimbo said he'd better wander off to find Harriet as he was neglecting her but Ralph called him back: 'This business of Tom . . .

All three of them said, 'Ahhhhh . . .'

'Excellent chap, but to be quite honest I've had a change of heart. I've decided that Peter is right. We can't condone deceit, nor dishonesty, nor the fact that he permitted polluted money to be kept on church premises. In this day and age we have to take a stand against the slackening of moral standards, and whilst it would be courageous and right to allow him to be verger after all that has happened, ultimately it quite simply cannot be.'

His statement was greeted with complete silence by the three of them.

'I mean it. We've got to reconsider our position. Seriously reconsider.'

They were in a cleft stick and they knew it. Not so much Arthur, who could buy the fields without reliance on Ralph – all he felt was gratitude for being told something he could well have missed – but both Jimbo and Neville sensed that their agreement to Tom not being reinstated was a necessary requirement for Neville to become his accountant and for Jimbo to get Ralph's support for the contract for the country-pursuits lot. If they refused they stood to lose and they knew it.

Ralph could almost measure the tension between the four of them: it quivered and quavered in the air as they pondered his request. Would they or wouldn't they? He wanted them to agree with him and hoped none of them would mention Evie, which would put his own determination not to reinstate Tom in jeopardy. He knew Jimbo would be the last to agree, if indeed he ever did, but Ralph guessed it would be Neville who would capitulate first and it was.

'I have great respect for your judgement, Sir Ralph, and if that's how you think it should be, then I for one won't stand in your way. I'll fall in with Peter's decision.' He flashed his self-satisfied smile at Ralph and then at Muriel, who almost felt he was inviting her to pat him on the head for being such a good boy.

Arthur, with nothing to lose, agreed. 'Why not? I'm sure Peter knows better than me how these things should go. I agree.'

Jimbo, angry at being outmanoeuvred and quite deliberately so, didn't answer for a moment. Ralph offered him more wine but Jimbo put his hand over his glass. 'No, thanks.' He glanced across the hall and saw Harriet, head back, laughing at some remark of Peter's and guessed what she would have to say if he told her he'd refused yet again to change his mind about Tom. 'Very well. Peter's got my vote. You can tell him straight away, if you like.'

'Good! Good! Now somehow between us we must find a job worthy of Tom which will keep him in Turnham Malpas. So please apply your not inconsiderable intelligence to solving the problem for him, and most especially for Evie. We must be seen to be compassionate which at bottom, of course, we really are.'

Ralph made a point of smiling at Jimbo, but Jimbo turned away, unhappy to realise that his relationship with Ralph would never be quite the same again, and angry with him for having taken advantage of his Achilles' heel so mercilessly. But Jimbo cheered up when he reached the conclusion that maybe Ralph might turn out to be proved right. How could anyone really know? As he reached Harriet's side she beamed at him and he winked at her and felt his good humour restored.

Muriel wasn't entirely sure she agreed with Peter about Tom but she had bowed to his superior understanding of the moral dilemma with which they were faced. Feeling forlorn she left the men to their conversation and wandered off outside. A jacket potato eaten by the bonfire suddenly had more appeal for her than socialising.

The potatoes were being distributed by the Scouts and it was Fergus Charter-Plackett who jokingly offered her one. 'There's a napkin too. Look, here.'

'Oh! yes, please. It's no fun eating one indoors. Thank you, Fergus, very much. I'm looking forward to the fireworks. Are you?'

Fergus was puzzled by her almost childlike appreciation of the fun of Bonfire Night. 'I am, Lady Templeton. Yes.'

Muriel wandered away tossing the scorching hot potato from hand to hand, grateful she had her gloves on. The crisp night air brightened her spirits and she decided to eat her potato away from the crowd, because one couldn't be discreet when eating them and she wanted to enjoy hers without regard to good manners.

She went to stand in the shadow of the refreshment marquee, from where she could observe the fire but not be seen. When she'd finished, she wiped her mouth with the napkin and was debating what to do with the potato skin, because she'd never liked them and had never eaten one in her life and wasn't going to start now, when she heard a rustling behind her. I'll ignore it, it'll be someone having a kiss and I don't want to know. But the rustling turned into a voice saying, 'Lady Templeton! Lady Templeton!' A man's voice which she thought she recognised but couldn't quite place.

Startled Muriel said, 'Yes? Who is it? Who's there? Well, make yourself known.' A close footfall and there he stood behind her. Muriel fumbled in her pocket for her torch and shone it straight in the face of the intruder.

She gasped out loud. 'Ohhhh! I don't believe it! Kenny Jones! I thought ... we all thought you were ... dead! You did give me a fright!' Her hand on her heart to stay its thudding she said, 'What are you doing creeping about like this?'

In a hoarse whisper Kenny said, 'I'm sorry to frighten you, Lady Templeton, but you being sympathetic like I thought you'd be the best to ask. I need a word with my mum.'

'Well, she's here. Go find her. She was heading for the ... powder room the last time I saw her. Kenny, she'll be delighted to see you, she's been so worried.'

'Trouble is, I don't want no one else to see me, it's a bit difficult as you might say. But it is very urgent.' An anxious hand on her arm, he begged, 'Can you get her for me? But not a word to a living soul, mind. It's very important that, for no one to know I'm here. Promise?'

'I promise. Kenny! What have you been up to?' While Kenny

framed a reply Muriel made up her mind to do as he asked. 'No, don't answer that. You wait there. I could be a while but I will get back to you. Take care, Kenny, the two of you have broken your mother's heart. Try not to hurt her any more. Good luck with whatever you do. I won't tell.' She patted his arm, twinkled her fingers at him and strolled away.

Muriel went round the front of the refreshment marquee and ventured in, thinking this would be the best place to try first, and there Mrs Jones was, in the midst of a laughing crowd from down Shepherds Hill, a plateful of food in her hand, enjoying herself. How to get her out without too much fuss, that was the question. Well, she'd better be truthful and come right out with it, it was the only way. Some silly trumped-up excuse would sound ridiculous.

'Mrs Jones! I'm sorry to interrupt you but there's someone outside asking for you.'

'Asking for me? Who?'

'I don't know them at all,' she hoped she'd be forgiven for that white lie, 'but it's you they want.'

'Well, whoever it is, Lady Templeton, they'll have to wait till I've finished eating.'

'They can't. They're in a hurry.' Muriel became agitated, she really was no good at this cloak-and-dagger stuff. 'Really in a hurry.' Muriel tried winking at Mrs Jones but only managed to distort her face and look foolish.

Finally Muriel saw from her face that Mrs Jones had got the message.

'I see. Well, then. I'll come.' Her face a picture of studied nonchalance, Mrs Jones told her friends to keep an eye on her food, and she'd be back.

Outside the marquee Muriel whispered, 'It's your Kenny come to see you. Come with me.'

'Our Kenny? Oh, thank God! Where is he?'

'He's just round the back here. Call his name, he'll come.'

Muriel walked away with tears in her eyes.

Mrs Jones called out quietly, 'Kenny! It's Mum.'

When Kenny emerged from the shadows Mrs Jones wrapped her arms around him and hugged him close. 'Oh, love! Where have yer been? All these weeks, wondering. Our Terry, is he here?'

'No, he wouldn't come.'

'Why ever not?'

'Too scared.' He released himself from her grasp. He stood listening for a moment: the sound of laughter and happy voices could just be heard and then as he listened the band struck up again, and briefly he felt a deep sadness that he would no longer be part of this kind of life. 'They're having a good time, bully for them. Now, listen to me. In the morning Terry and me, we're going to Canada.'

'Canada!'

Kenny put his hand over her mouth. 'Shush! Out of the way. As soon as we get settled I'll let you know. Then in a while you and Dad can pretend to discover a long-lost cousin out there and you can come out to us.'

'To escape the police really, isn't it?'

'Well, them and other things. But we'll be safe there.'

'How will you find the money?'

'Money's no problem, believe me.'

'Oh, Kenny, what have you been up to?'

Kenny tapped the side of his nose. 'Don't ask. Give our love to Dad, and tell him not to worry.'

Clutching at straws she exclaimed, 'But you haven't got passports.'

'We have now.'

Her heart was fit to burst with joy that her Kenny had come specially to see her before he left. In the dark she wasn't able to see the expression on his face but she sensed he was different, and that he'd done something terrible and she wished she hadn't realised it.

Out of his pocket he took a wad of notes. 'I've counted it, it's to pay Sir Ralph the rent for the rest of the six months, and there's some extra for you and Dad. Sir Ralph had faith in me and I can't let him down. All the furniture is yours so take it, Dad'ull like that leather chair. But most important of all don't tell anyone where we are. You don't know a thing. Right?'

'Right. Take care, Kenny. Look after our Terry, he's not so sharp as you.'

'I will. I had to come, couldn't go without seeing yer. Got to go now.' They hugged and Mrs Jones so far forgot herself as to give him a big kiss. Kenny gruffly remarked as she was leaving him, 'Take care of yerself.' That was the nearest he got to endearments: and the nearest he got to Canada was New Zealand. After all, he knew his mother well and was absolutely certain he mustn't tell her the whole truth. Specially about ... He turned to walk away down through the trees towards his car, his heart more desolate than he had ever known. He'd made some bloody big mistakes in his life and recently done some dreadful things to save his skin, but somehow leaving Turnham Malpas for ever was the most painful of all.

Sylvia had been looking for Willie and in desperation had called in at the beer tent to see if he was still in there, though what state he'd be in, after all this time, she really didn't know. She couldn't go inside because she had the twins with her, having volunteered to look after them while the Rector and Dr Harris were in the hall having their refreshments with Mr Fitch.

They turned back towards the dying bonfire to continue their search. Hand in hand with the two of them Sylvia marched purposefully across the field. Alex and Beth were now getting very tired and if it hadn't been for the fireworks they would have gladly gone home.

Beth tugged at Sylvia's hand. 'I want my mummy.'

'So do I.'

The Scouts, having been resuscitated in the refreshment marquee, had reassembled and were playing an overture before the commencement of the display.

'Can we go find them?' Alex began to whine, and Sylvia decided she'd find Willie much quicker without two tired children in need of their mother.

'We'll go find them and I'll look for Willie by myself. He can't be far.'

Somewhat tentatively Sylvia stood in the doorway of the Big House hoping to catch Caroline's eye but the twins rushed in to look for her themselves. 'Mummy! We've lost Mr Biggs. Is he here?'

She took their hands and led them back towards Sylvia, standing in the doorway. 'No, darlings, he isn't. Thanks for looking after them, I do appreciate it. Can you really not find Willie?'

'Well, obviously it's not serious, he must be somewhere about, it's just that I haven't seen him for a while. They're both very tired, Dr Harris, they need to be in bed.'

Alex and Beth both protested loudly, stamping their feet and showing all the signs of going into serious tantrums. 'We're not going to bed! Not now. We want to see the fireworks.'

'Of course you shall. I'll get Daddy and we'll find a good place to stand. Hush now! Hush! That's enough.' Caroline put an arm round each of them and hugged them tightly to her.

Peter came across and together they all went out into the dark. The only light was provided by the vast pile of glowing embers, for the floodlights had been switched off again in preparation for the display.

Peter lifted the pair of them on to the stone wall surrounding the terrace and he and Caroline stood on the grass between them. Peter was wearing his heavy winter jacket and Caroline slipped a hand inside one of its deep pockets. In the hushed silence before the first rocket went up Peter took hold of her hand in his pocket and squeezed her fingers. Caroline looked up at him and smiled, 'Love you.' Peter looked down at her, his face radiant with the deep love he had for her, and then he kissed her smiling lips. They lingered over the kiss until Beth called out, 'Daddy! Stop kissing Mummy! I don't know what the parish will say and what's more she's going to miss the fireworks!'

Jimbo's firework displays had been considered truly wonderful but this . . . One moment the whole sky was heaving and tumbling with red light then turquoise, then yellow, then green, then a mass of multi-coloured swirling, then a sky-sized fountain of blues. They were all gasping with amazement. What a show! What a spectacle! Three cheers for Mr Fitch! Would this extravaganza never end? The finale was huge rocket after huge rocket firing off in all directions, higher and higher, filling the whole panoply of the heavens with myriad man-made stars. They cheered Mr Fitch at the end of the display spontaneously and gladly. What a night!

Reluctantly they made their way home; the entire village sated with good food, good companionship and Mr Fitch's brilliant final tribute. Tired children, weary parents wandered off, some to their cars, others on foot to find home and bed and sleep.

451

Ralph took a tray of tea with him when he went upstairs to bed. Muriel, having enjoyed every single moment of her evening to the full, was already sitting up in bed waiting for him.

'I don't think I have had a lovelier Bonfire Night in all my life. Wasn't it spectacular, Ralph?'

'It most certainly was. Don't pour yet, it's not ready. I'll do it when I've finished in the bathroom. You still haven't told me what you were doing when you disappeared.'

Cautiously Muriel replied, 'I've told you the truth. I got bored with the social chit-chat and went outside for a jacket potato and then I wandered about a bit.'

Ralph looked sceptically at her. 'My dear, you would never have done for the diplomatic service, you can't tell fibs to save your life.'

Muriel blushed. 'I know I can't, but I promised. I truly did promise not to say a word and I have a dreadful feeling that I did something quite wicked this evening because I should have told the police, which would have been very easy for they were about ... but I didn't.'

'The police!'

'Yes.'

'My dear!'

'So it's best if I don't tell you, then you can't be blamed if it all comes out. But I helped a mother ... and a son. Other than that my lips are sealed. Another bonfire been and gone. The years slip by so quickly, don't they?'

'I won't ask you again. I'm quite sure that whatever it was you did, it was with the best of intentions. Yes, they do slip by when you're very happy.'

'And I am very happy. It's been such a year. Who would have thought that I, Muriel Templeton, would lie down to stop a digger tearing up my village's heart all because I met a wren? I was so terrified.'

'A wren! I do love your mind, Muriel. I'm glad I'm privy to your thoughts, it is such a delight.'

He was still standing by the bed and she looked up at him and smiled. 'I did, and we looked each other in the eye and I *knew* I had to save his homeland, for he was relying on me to do it on his behalf. Wasn't it exciting about Jeremy and Venetia getting married this morning? Such a surprise. I'm so glad. Peter never said a word, the naughty boy, I would have loved to have gone to it.'

'It's a pity Tom didn't realise that Peter knows how to keep a confidence. I felt acutely embarrassed when old Fitch made that blunder about him being verger, I doubted all over again about not supporting Tom.'

'Peter would have won the day anyway, dear, now, wouldn't he? He is so upright in his moral judgements, and I've become sure he's right. The only black spot for me is worrying about Evie. I do wish we could find him a job round here. It wouldn't even have to be in the village, just so long as he could travel to it from here. Then perhaps Evie might have a chance.'

'I have had a word with old Fitch and so has Peter. We think he may have found something suitable for him.'

'Oh, I'm so glad! Have you noticed Peter and Caroline are all right again?'

Ralph raised an eyebrow. 'No, I hadn't. How do you know?'

'Well, I just do. They are, you can feel it. I think that one of the big highlights this year was your birthday party. It went so well. We'll have another party next year to celebrate our tenth wedding anniversary.'

'Ten years! It seems an age.' Ralph groaned.

'Ralph!' Then Muriel looked at his face and saw he was teasing. 'As for this year we've still got Christmas to look forward to, and I do love Christmas.'

A Village Dilemma

Inhabitants of Turnham Malpas

Nick Barnes	Veterinary surgeon
Roz Barnes	Nurse
Willie Biggs	Verger at St Thomas à Becket
Sylvia Biggs	His wife and housekeeper at the Rectory
Sir Ronald Bissett	Retired Trade Union leader
Lady Sheila Bissett	His wife
James (Jimbo) Charter-Plackett	Owner of the Village Store
Harriet Charter-Plackett	His wife
Fergus, Finlay, Flick and Fran	Their children
Katherine Charter-Plackett	Jimbo's mother
Alan Crimble	Barman at the Royal Oak
Linda Crimble	Runs the post office at the Village Store
Georgie Fields	Licensee at the Royal Oak
H. Craddock Fitch	Owner of Turnham House
Jimmy Glover	Taxi driver
Revd Peter Harris (Oxon)	Rector of the parish
Dr Caroline Harris	His wife
Alex and Beth	Their children
Mrs Jones	A village gossip
Vince Jones	Her husband
Barry Jones	Her son and estate carpenter
Pat Jones	Barry's wife
Dean and Michelle	Barry and Pat's children
Jeremy Mayer	Manager at Turnham House

Venetia Mayer	His wife
Neville Neal	Accountant and church treasurer
Liz Neal	His wife
Guy and Hugh	Their children
Tom Nicholls	Retired businessman
Evie Nicholls	His wife
Anne Parkin	Retired secretary
Kate Pascoe	Village school head teacher
Sir Ralph Templeton	Retired from the diplomatic service
Lady Muriel Templeton	His wife
Dicky Tutt	Scout leader and bar-manager at The Royal Oak
Bel Tutt	School caretaker and assistant in the Village Store
Don Wright	Maintenance engineer (now retired)
Vera Wright	Cleaner at the nursing home in Penny Fawcett
Rhett Wright	Their grandson

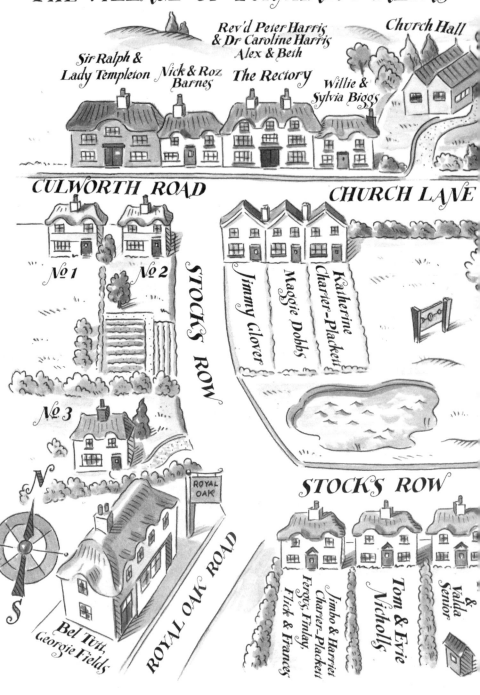

THE VILLAGE OF TURNHAM MALPAS

Rev'd Peter Harris
& Dr Caroline Harris
Alex & Beth

Church Hall

Sir Ralph &
Lady Templeton

Nick & Roz
Barnes

The Rectory

Willie &
Sylvia Biggs

CULWORTH ROAD

CHURCH LANE

No 1

No 2

STOCKS ROW

Jimmy Clover

Maggie Dobbs

Katherine
Charter-Plackett

No 3

ROYAL
OAK

STOCKS ROW

N
S

ROYAL OAK ROAD

Bel Tutt
Georgie Fields

Jimbo & Harriet
Charter-Plackett
Fergus, Finlay,
Flick & Frances

Tom & Evie
Nicholls

&
Valda
Senior

1

Jimbo, observing the growing crowd collecting in Church Lane, said, 'Harriet! What am I doing dressed like this?'

'Enjoying participating in village life.'

'I'm not, though. I feel an absolute idiot.'

Harriet appraised his appearance, taking in the dishevelled wig she'd insisted he wore, the old leather sandals long abandoned by him at the back of his wardrobe and, most genuine-looking of all, the scratchy, brown, muddied shift affair she'd crafted out of a length of hessian she'd found at a sale. 'Actually, you look very peasantlike. I'm quite proud of you. Especially your tights.'

Jimbo inspected the thick brown tights he wore. 'Proud?' He turned to look at her and, noting the twinkle in her eyes, couldn't help himself laughing. 'OK. OK. Point taken. Why I ever allowed myself to be dressed up I'll never know.'

'Because you're a darling and a sucker for country ways.'

'No, it's because you can twist me round your little finger, that's why.'

'Never once have you joined in the parade, you always find an excuse for being busy, busy, busy behind the counter and not participating; well, this year you are, so cheer up. Oh, look! There's the twins. Suddenly they look so grown-up.' Harriet waved to Beth and Alex. 'Come and walk with us, or the girls are up at the front if you prefer.'

Alex spoke for both of them. 'We'll join the girls, thanks.' Instead of leading Beth by the hand as he'd done since the day they could both walk, Alex gave her a push in the direction of the head of the procession, and she willingly accepted his decision and followed him.

Harriet watched the two of them press their way forwards. 'Strange how Beth is really the more outgoing of the two and yet she accepts Alex's lead without a murmur. Can't believe the two of them will be leaving the village school next year. Doesn't seem two minutes since they were born.'

'The piper's tuning up. Am I ready for this? No, I am not.'

'Yes, you are.' Harriet grinned at Jimbo's discomfort. 'Right! Here we go. I get all primeval and go like jelly inside when I'm doing this. Maintaining a six-hundred-year tradition really makes me feel as though I *belong*. Doesn't it you?'

Jimbo considered how he felt. 'I suppose. But I do feel a complete idiot.'

Movement began at the head of the procession, the piper, at the very front, began to play a melancholy tune on his ancient silver flute and they all started to move off towards the village green with Jimbo still feeling all kinds of an idiot.

Into view, as they reached the green, came the stocks covered to the very top with dead flowers. Standing beside it was the Rector dressed in his devil's costume, the horns on his headgear glinting in the bright June sun. There came an eager mumble as soon as the dozens of sightseers gathered in front of the houses surrounding the green caught sight of them. The press were there in force, as always, and Jimbo desperately hoped that they wouldn't recognise the urbane, stylish, man-of-the-world Store owner, seeing as he wasn't wearing his striped apron and his straw boater. The wig was beginning to itch his bald head. Surreptitiously he scratched as best he could without disturbing the damn thing. God! It irritated him. Why had he ever allowed himself ... but now, having walked all the way round the green, it was his turn to beat the dead flowers off the stocks. He surprised himself by beating the living daylights out of them and suddenly he was a village peasant angered by the vagrant who had brought the plague to the village and thus killed all his children, or his wife, or his mother. He looked up at the Rector as he straightened himself and saw one of his bright-blue eyes close swiftly in a wink. Jimbo grinned back. So at least, maybe,

Peter was participating with his tongue in his cheek, as indeed any sane member of a twenty-first-century village must. Although . . .

Harriet thrust his bunch of fresh flowers into his hand. He glanced at her and saw with surprise how distressed she was. 'Darling!'

'It all seems so real, Jimbo. So real. God! Just think how you would feel if you really had lost . . .' Tears sprang into her eyes.

'I know, I know . . .' And he did. But his two girls were up at the front with the other village children, his two sons at Cambridge and beside him was his beloved Harriet, and his mother was somewhere in the procession, no doubt beating the dead flowers from the stocks with her usual gusto as though her ancestors had been born and bred here for centuries. Thankful that he'd had the foresight to move his family from London and that blasted rat race, Jimbo stepped smartly round the green for the second time, his flowers clutched tightly in his hand. When he reached the stocks he saw Peter was divesting himself of his devil's costume and was revealing the white cassock he wore only today, Stocks Day, and when conducting weddings. Jimbo placed his fresh flowers on the stocks to symbolise a new beginning, a laying aside of death and destruction. The plague had finally gone. Death had been beaten.

Peter's prayer of thanksgiving for the survival of the village and his blessing of everyone taking part rang out across the green, the long, mournful dirge of the piper subtly changed to a lively, bouncing tune, signalling that the villagers could feel safe from disaster for yet another year.

Cameras flashed, voices called out, 'Look this way.'

'That's right.'

'One more! You two stand together. That's it.'

'One more! One more!'

Jimbo obliged, his wig askew, his hessian costume now also itching like fury, but a bright, relieved smile on his face brought on by doing his bit like everyone else.

'Your name? Your name?' Looking more closely when he didn't get an immediate reply the photographer said, 'Oh! It's you, Mr Charter-Plackett, didn't recognise you.'

Inwardly Jimbo groaned; his reputation had just bitten the dust well and truly. Grumpily he said to Harriet, 'I'm not wearing this for the rest of the afternoon, you know. I'm going home to change.'

'Spoilsport.'

'This wig is flea-ridden.'

'It never is.'

'It is. It itches.'

But Harriet's attention was elsewhere. 'Jimbo, look! I could swear that's Bryn Fields over there.'

'Where?'

'Over there by the oak. His back's to us, but I'm sure it's him. Well, that's a turn-up for the books. How many years is it since he did his moonlight flit?'

'You're imagining things. He'd never dare come back, not after what happened.'

Harriet stood on tiptoe. 'I'm sure it is. He's turned round. Look, there! There! Talking to Willie Biggs.'

'Nonsense! That chap hasn't a flying officer's moustache like Bryn had.'

'It's very like him even so. He's very tanned, which he would be, wouldn't he, if what they say is true.'

'Maybe he has a brother. I'm going home to change.'

'I'm not. I never do. I'm going to the fair with our children and then having my tea on the green like all self-respecting villagers.'

'I'll check the Store, give a hand and come along for tea when I see the tables out.'

Harriet, still agog at the prospect she might be right about Bryn Fields, didn't notice that Jimbo was looking at her. She ignored the jostling by the crowds too as they pushed past to get to the spare land where the annual joys of the fair awaited them, and tried to keep her eye on that tall, distant figure. She was certain it was him. It must be. She became aware of Jimbo and glanced at him to see why he was still there. Raising her eyebrows she said, 'What is it?'

'This Stocks Day thing must be getting at me. I'm so grateful I still have you.' Despite the hustle and bustle of the crowd he kissed her.

'Oh! It has got to you, hasn't it? It always does to me. Glad you joined in?'

Jimbo nodded, smiled and went home, feeling gratified deep

down that he'd done his bit for the village. He shook his head. What was he thinking of? How could beating dead flowers from the churchyard off the stocks and then heralding a new beginning by laying fresh flowers there possibly have any effect on anything at all, especially when the plague had died out years ago? How could a rational, educated man, an entrepreneur, a man of means, a man getting ahead in the world believe in such a thing? No, not *getting*, he *was* ahead. His chest swelled at the thought. He pushed his key into the front door with pride. Nothing, but nothing would stop further successes this year. He'd just seen to that by doing what he'd done.

He took the precaution of standing in the bath while he undressed and left his clothes and his wig soaking in it in hot water and disinfectant, just in case. The Store was extremely busy when he got there and he had to stay to help. They were selling everything from rolls of film to fresh fruit, from sweets to sticking plasters. Mentally Jimbo rubbed his hands with glee; this was how it should be, the till whirring itself silly and his special bell jingling joyfully each time the door opened. He became lost in the clamour and forgot to look out on to the green for when the open-air tea was ready, but he wasn't allowed to forget for Flick and Fran came bursting through the door shouting, 'Daddy! We're saving you a seat! Come on!'

They were so alike, these two. Seven years between them and Fran looked like a miniature of Flick, but even so he had to admit in his heart that Fran was by far the most beautiful of the two. But Flick! So grown-up now. A woman, no less, at just fifteen.

'Coming! OK, Bel? Back in half an hour. Right.'

Bel, at the till, smiled her beautiful relaxed smile, which lit up the whole of her face. 'Fine. See you. Next! That'll be two pounds twenty-nine. Thank you. Have a nice day. Next!'

Jimbo spared a thought for her as he crossed Stocks Row to take his place beside Harriet and the girls on the wooden benches borrowed from the church hall. Dear Bel. So willing but he always felt that at the heart of her she was very lonely. Some people got dealt rotten cards where life was concerned.

A large area of the green had been covered with trestle tables and benches, and every place was taken. The tables, half an hour ago laden with plates of food, were being rapidly cleared. One could almost have thought that the villagers had purposely not eaten anything all week. The simple old wooden benches they all sat on added to the illusion that it was the day six hundred years ago when the entire village had sat down to celebrate their victory over the plague, but then there would have been far fewer people for they had been decimated by the disease. Some families were entirely wiped out, in others only the most robust were left to tell the tale.

He sat between Flick and Fran, and ate a hearty tea. He sank his strong white teeth into a sausage roll, ate a slice of quiche – the cheese and broccoli one which was the most popular on his delicatessen counter – he munched his way through a ham sandwich, the flavour of which he definitely recognised, and finished it all off with a hefty slice of Harriet's special mail order fruit cake. Jimbo washed it down with a mug of cider, then sat back to survey the scene.

It never ceased to amaze him that this quiet backwater could galvanise itself into such incredible activity on special days. They might have television and mobile phones and e-mail but they were still a centuries-old village at heart. Even the ones the villagers disparagingly called the 'weekenders' made sure they were down for the weekend when anything special was on. He looked across at the old oak tree, still coming into full leaf each spring as though five hundred years of doing it were a mere nothing in the span of time. Jimbo had to admit to himself he loved the old place.

'Daddy!'

Jimbo roused himself to answer Fran. 'Mm?'

'Daddy,' she whispered. 'Is Mummy my mummy?'

'Of course she is. Why do you ask that?'

'Beth asked me if she was. I said she was but I wanted to be sure.'

Realising he was on delicate ground, Jimbo answered cautiously but positively, 'Well, you are, definitely.'

'I'm not borrowed, then?'

'No. You are not.'

'She's my real mummy, then. I grew in her tummy?'

'Yes, darling, you did.'

'Good.' Fran picked up her drink, finished it right to the bottom and said with a nod of her head towards the fair, 'Right, then. Come on, Flick, you promised.'

Flick raised her eyes to the heavens. 'All right, then. But this is the last time. I never get a chance to be with *my* friends, I'm always looking after you. One ride, that's all, because we've spent almost all the money Mum gave us.'

Jimbo winked at her and gave her a five-pound note.

Fran's bottom lip trembled. 'You've got to look after me, haven't you? You are my sister, aren't you?'

'And don't I know it. Thanks, Dad.' With a sigh Flick swung her legs over the bench and dashed to catch up with Fran already zigzagging her way through the crowds to the roundabout.

Harriet waited until they were out of hearing and then said quietly to Jimbo, 'Whoops! That sounds like one ten-year-old girl we know is asking about her parentage and desperately wants to know. Must be those sex lessons they've been having at the school.'

'Poor Beth.'

'And poor Alex, too. One might be tempted to quote "Be sure your sins will find you out".'

'Harriet!'

'Well, let's hope Peter comes up with something to explain it all.'

'Have they never been told, then?'

'Not the whole truth. I understand they know Caroline couldn't have children so she's not their real mother, but as for the rest . . .'

'Well, watch out, you may be getting some questions too.'

'I can't tell our girls the truth before Peter and Caroline have told the twins, can I?'

Jimbo accepted another glass of cider from the vast earthenware jug one of the helpers was hoping to empty before clearing up and said, 'No, definitely not. I'm going, Bel will be at the end of her tether.' He sank his cider at one go and squeezed his thickset frame off the bench.

'So am I. I feel quite queasy after going on the roundabout and then eating a big tea. I'll come and help in the Store, but I'd better go home to change first. I'll catch up with you.'

As they made their way to the Store, Harriet glanced up Stocks Row before they crossed and was sure she saw Bryn Fields again, walking down Church Lane. But it couldn't be him now, could it?

467

Still open to a charge of attempted murder, he wouldn't dare show his face, would he?

Always hectic on a normal summer Saturday evening, Stocks Night usually beat all the records in the bar of the Royal Oak. There weren't enough chairs to seat everybody inside, so many of the customers were sprawled on the green or luxuriating on the garden furniture that Georgie in her wisdom had placed in a new outside garden made from a section of the car park. Hedged about as they were on the new fashionable green chairs by the excess of cars, her customers still managed to enjoy the late evening sun.

Willie Biggs wrinkled his nose at the smell of fumes from the exhaust of a car, which had just sidled into a vacant space too close to his table for comfort. 'This new idea of Georgie's would be all right if we didn't have these 'ere cars so close.'

Sylvia knew he liked nothing better than a good grumble but decided the day had been too good to be spoiled by one of Willie's grumbling sessions. 'Come on, Willie! Don't grouse. It's been a great day, the sun's shining and we're breathing God's good air.'

'No, we're not, we're breathing His air made foul by man.'

'Oh, dear! We are in a mood.'

Willie looked into her laughing grey eyes and gave her half a smile. 'I am. I'm worried sick.'

Sylvia studied his thin, lined face and noted the stern set of his lantern jaw, and wondered what petty irritation had brought on such gloom. 'Tell me. I expect it's all something and nothing.'

'You wouldn't say that if you'd spoken to who I spoke to this afternoon.'

Sylvia, alerted by his tantalising statement, sat up and leaned towards him saying, 'Who?'

Willie took another sip of his ale before he replied. 'Someone who I thought we would never see again.'

'Well, who, then? Not Kenny Jones come back?'

Willie shook his head.

'Terry Jones?'

'No. Someone closer to where we are now.'

'Not Betty MacDonald?'

'You're getting close. You're on the right lines.'

'I can't think of anyone else who might ... not poor old henpecked Mac?'

'Close.'

Finally Sylvia grew tired of the guessing game and gave him a shove on his shoulder. 'Tell me, then.'

Willie glanced around to check no one was within hearing and whispered in her ear, 'Bryn Fields.'

Sylvia's mouth dropped open with shock. 'Get on. You're pulling my leg.'

Willie flatly denied any such thing.

When finally she got her voice back Sylvia said loudly, '*Bryn Fields!*'

'Sh! They'll hear.'

'But ... you couldn't have. He wouldn't dare.'

'Well, he has. Large as life.'

'I didn't see him.'

'You didn't see a lot of folk, seeing as you were in the church hall helping with the catering. But I did. I spoke to 'im.' He leaned back again in his chair enjoying taking centre stage with his piece of hot news.

'What had he to say for himself, then?'

'He was miffed, he hadn't realised it was Stocks Day.'

'I'd have liked to see him. So what's he like after ... what ... four – or is it five years since he disappeared? Did he say why he'd come back?'

Willie shook his head. 'Tanned, he is, and you'll never guess what!' He sipped his ale again to prolong his moment.

'What?'

'He's shaved his moustache off.'

'Never. Well, I don't know, he won't be the same without it. Anyway, I don't suppose he'll hang around long. No one will want him.'

'Oh, he will. He's staying at Neville Neal's.'

'Neville Neal's! That figures. They're both troublemakers. They make a pair. Well, we don't get far but we do see life as they say. Bryn Fields! Well I never.'

'So now you can see why I'm worried.'

Sylvia thought over the possibilities for trouble. Counting them off on her fingers she said, 'Georgie, for a start, though at least she might get a divorce at last, and then Dicky can make an honest woman of her. Dicky! My good heavens! He'll be frightened to death. Poor Dicky. The Rector won't take kindly to it either, considering the problems Bryn caused.'

'With his temper, we'd better all look out. I never look up the church tower without thinking about poor Dicky coming close to being pushed off the top. It's a bloody long way down.'

Sylvia shuddered. 'Oo! Don't remind me.' She shuddered again. 'I can't think why he's here. Maybe it's to make things straight for Georgie. He did love her, you know. He really did. I expect that Elektra was more fun to run away with but only for the moment. But she'd never stay ... She's not with him, is she?'

'Not so far as I know. I don't think even Neville Neal would want a tart staying, not with his two lusty boys.'

'Willie! What a thing to say. Anyway, there's one thing for certain. He won't dare show his face in here.'

Willie stood up, holding his empty glass. ''Nother one?'

'Yes, please. See if there's a table free inside, it's starting to get cold out here.'

'OK.'

Well, Bryn Fields. Of all people. She remembered the madness in his eyes when they finally got him down from the church tower and the rage in every shaking limb. Like something out of a film on telly, that was. What a mess there'd have been if he really had pushed Dicky over. Smashed to smithereens he'd have been, even though he was only the size of a jockey. Sylvia didn't like the idea of never hearing Dicky's cheerful voice again or not seeing his jolly laughing face; nothing ever fazed him ... Well, except when he was white as a sheet and sweating buckets being helped down the spiral stairs. How he ever got down ...

Willie caught her eye, signalling to her to come in. She picked up his jacket and went in, to find him already seated at their favourite table. 'Dicky's giving one of his comic turns in five minutes.'

'Oh, good! I could do with a bit of cheering up.'

Dicky Tutt, a sprightly little man, pillar of the Church Scout Troop and the light of Georgie's heart, stepped from behind the bar at precisely ten p.m., pushed a couple of tables closer together to make a space, clapped his hands and started his Saturday night comic turn.

'Good evening, ladies and gentlemen. I won't say anything at all about what a wonderful day we've had, the sun in the right place and a happy, busy day for all of us. Nor will I mention how wonderful the tea was, provided as usual by the ladies of the village and made possible by the great generosity of our esteemed Village Store owner, namely Jimbo Charter-Plackett, nor will I talk about the wonderful performance our Scout Band gave prior to the start of the procession. Whoever is in charge of those Scouts deserves . . .'

'Give it up, Dicky!'

'We've heard it all before . . .'

'Get a move on!'

Dicky laughed and began a story about the Royal Navy being billeted in a girls' school during World War Two. He had reached the climax with the line '. . . so this notice on the dormitory wall said "Please ring this bell if you need a mistress during the night . . ."' The roars of appreciation drowned the sound of the outside door opening. In fact, there was such a crowd standing by the door listening to Dicky that for a moment no one could see who'd come quietly through the open door as Dicky had begun his comic turn. It was only when the newcomer had pushed his way through the crowd to get to the bar and they saw Dicky's face had gone drip white that they all turned to see what was up.

He was a good six feet in height with dark hair going white at the temples and a well-tanned face with strong, severe features. He was wearing a smart tropical suit and sandals, which marked him out as someone from abroad.

Georgie looked across to see what had stopped the laughter so abruptly.

Someone coughed.

Someone gasped.

Someone said, 'Never.'

The man said jovially, 'Good evening, everyone' and, squeezing between the tables, went straight to the bar. 'Now, Georgie, busy as ever! I'll have a whisky on the rocks.'

Georgie out of habit automatically poured his drink and pushed it across the bar to him.

He tossed it back in one gulp, slid the glass back to her and asked for a refill. He didn't take his eyes from her but after the first recognition Georgie never once caught his eye.

'As lovely as ever.' Bryn shot the second whisky down and then, leaning his forearm nonchalantly on the bar top, surveyed the customers. 'Same old faces, too. Nothing changes. That's what's so good about this place, nothing changes. That's what I like.' He nodded to a few faces he recognised, then turned back to look at Georgie. 'Nothing to say to your dear husband come back to make things right?'

Georgie's face was no longer pretty; it was twisted and distorted by venom. In a voice totally unlike her own she snarled, 'How dare you! How dare you come back here, you nasty, thieving, no-good, cheating, lying womaniser. You're a thief! A no-good thief! Get out and get back under that stone you've just crawled out from under. Out! Out! Out!' To emphasise her point she banged her clenched fist on the counter and leant towards him.

The customers reacted as though she were about to spit in each of their faces. They recoiled as one.

But Bryn never flinched. 'My, you're lovely when you're in a temper.'

'You've seen nothing yet. Just go. I don't want you in here.'

'I see that obnoxious little tiddler is still sniffing around. I would have thought you'd have sent him off with a flea in his ear long ago.'

The little tiddler in question was keeping such a tight grip on his fear that he seemed to have reduced in size, if that were possible.

'Still telling his pathetic jokes and you're all still laughing at them I see.'

At this insult to his theatrical abilities Dicky flushed, the first sign of life in him since Bryn had walked in. All eyes were on him. He saw they were and it gave him strength.

He stalked stiffly across to stand in front of Bryn, and despite the cost to him and the terrible fear he felt at facing this monster who had come so close to killing him, drawing on reserves he didn't know he possessed he looked up at Bryn and said quietly, 'The licensee has asked you to leave. Git!'

'Oh! So now the little bantam cock has fluffed up his feathers, has he? Going to turn me out, eh? I don't think so.'

Keeping his eye on Bryn, Dicky said, 'Shall we ring for the police, Georgie?'

'No, no, that won't be necessary. We don't want them here. No. I'll leave the bar to you and Alan for half an hour. You come with me.' She beckoned Bryn, then disappeared without a backward glance through the door marked 'Private'. Bryn followed.

A collective sigh of disappointment flowed after them. But the door was shut firmly behind Bryn.

Georgie took him into their sitting room, which in Bryn's day had always had boxes of crisps and the like stacked in corners because it was used as an overflow from the stockroom. Now it was as elegant as it was possible to make a room at the back of a public house.

Georgie waited until he'd chosen a chair to sit in, then stood facing him. 'Well, what does all this mean? Not a word all this time and now you turn up. She's left you, has she?'

'Elektra's done very well for herself. Married a rich American self-made man. All money and no style. But he's besotted ... for now. She'll get plenty of alimony; she'll be set up for life.'

'Bully for her.'

Bryn studied her face. 'The years don't show.'

'I'm happy, that's why.'

'Happy? Come on, Georgie! Happy! With that little squirt.'

'He has more love and consideration in his little finger than you have in all your great hulk. I've brought you in here, not because I wanted you here, but because I didn't want you showing him up with some sort of macho behaviour. He's been my strength, has Dicky, and I won't have him done down.'

Bryn stood up. 'I'll use the toilet if I may.'

She stood aside, knowing full well he was going to take the opportunity to take a look around the bedrooms. Georgie waited and smiled to herself as she heard his footsteps above her head. Outwardly she hoped she looked calm and in control, inwardly she was shaken to the core. He looked so different, so outgoing, so *positive.* She could hear him coming down the stairs and took the premier chair in the room to give her the upper hand when he returned. 'Satisfied?'

'Surprised.'

'He doesn't sleep here, you see.'

'Who does, then?'

'Bel Tutt.'

'You've had our bedroom done up and a single bed.'

Georgie nodded. 'Why not? Life doesn't stop because you've done a bunk. Anyway, since Dicky joined me as manager, profits have soared.'

'Right.'

'He does the books, orders the stock, serves behind the bar, keeps Alan under control, all with the lightest of touches. Such a pleasing man to work with, you see.'

'I see. And you two . . .' He jerked his elbow as though nudging someone and winked.

'That's my business. Nothing to do with you. What have you been up to?'

'Bar work on cruise liners. Then Elektra met this passenger and before I knew where I was she'd gone off with him.'

'That's why you've come home, is it?'

'No, it isn't. It's two years since she went. I have to confess she hadn't your style. Common, you know.'

Georgie burst out laughing. 'Surprised you didn't know that first off.'

Bryn enjoyed her delight even if she was laughing at him. He was doing better than he'd hoped. 'Devastated, I was, by that dwarf . . .'

Georgie wagged a stern finger at him. 'I've warned you. There'd have been no business to come back to if it wasn't for him.'

Bryn saw he was doing much much better than he'd hoped, but he wouldn't take her up on that for the moment, mustn't push his luck. 'I'm glad you had help. I didn't want you to go down.'

'You *shot* me down, taking all our money with you.'

Bryn looked suitably contrite. 'I didn't want to. Elektra saw a bank statement and argued that seeing as I was leaving you with a viable business I had a right to the money.'

'She's not just an ugly face, then.'

He had to smile at that. 'You're right. Without her warpaint she was damn ugly. Come to think of it, she was ugly *with* her warpaint on. God, what a sight.' He brooded for a moment on the image that had been Elektra, then looked at Georgie. She might be older, but she still had that something special for him. 'I'm staying with Neville and Liz.'

'I see.'

'They invited me. I didn't realise it was Stocks Day. It still pulls the old heartstrings, doesn't it?'

'Didn't realise you still had a heart. Be frank. Why are you here?'

Too early yet to spill the beans.

Georgie wondered why he took so long to answer. 'Height of the cruise season so have they thrown you out for fiddling the till or something?'

'Got sick of it, to be honest.'

Georgie doubted that word honest, there was something behind this reappearance and she couldn't fathom what. He'd changed a lot since he'd left, become more of a man of the world, more . . . she couldn't put her finger on it. She stood up. 'I can't leave those two much longer and it's almost closing. Go out the back way.'

Bryn put his hand in his pocket and brought out the key to the back door. 'I've always kept it. Sentimental reasons, you know.'

He looked wistful, but Georgie didn't fall for it. 'That was a complete waste of time.'

'You mean you don't want me here.'

'In a nutshell. Out now, if you please, or I really will get the police.'

'All right, all right. You look good enough to eat.'

'Maybe, and it's flattering, but for now, hop it.'

As she was closing the back door after him she said, 'By the way, you might as well throw that key away, I've had all the locks changed.' After she'd bolted the door she stood leaning against it for support. Georgie's heart was racing. Thud. Thud. Thud. Why had that thieving, lying toad made her heart beat like this? He meant nothing to her at all. Nothing. But . . . there was something there which hadn't been in him before; a certain suaveness, a kind of polish. Shaving off his stupid greying moustache had definitely taken years from his age. She heard the door to the bar being opened cautiously. 'All right, Dicky, he's gone. I'm just coming.' It really was too cruel of Bryn to call Dicky a dwarf, he was a love and, more important, *her* love.

When 'time' was called the customers made a concerted rush to get out and spread the news. By Sunday morning the story of Bryn's surprising return had spread like wildfire through the village and to friends and relatives in the adjoining villages. Ancient rivalries between Turnham Malpas and Little Derehams surfaced, and there were scathing remarks passed about the notoriety of Turnham Malpas and an underlying envy that nothing of such a spectacular nature ever happened in Little Derehams. In Penny Fawcett the inhabitants made a note definitely to attend the Monday morning farmers' market in their village hall to hear the latest scandal direct from the lips of any of the Turnham Malpas people who regularly deserted Jimbo's Village Store on Mondays in search of home-grown food bargains.

The return of Bryn Fields kept everyone talking for more than a week. Wherever he went, whatever he did was the big talking point; the car he bought, the people he visited, the outrageous clothes he wore. But by the end of the week they were no wiser as to his reasons for being there than they had been when he'd first arrived.

2

They all knew Bryn had been to see Willie Biggs on several occasions but no amount of treating him to a pint of his favourite ale in the Royal Oak, or confiding in him bits of news of their own to draw him forth, would make Willie tell what Bryn had been seeing him about. Some had even resorted to trying to get Sylvia to spill the beans but to no avail; she was as tight-lipped as he. More than one said, 'That's what comes of working at the Rectory. She's sworn to secrecy about who comes and goes, and now she can't let it out not even for a winning lottery ticket.'

A week to the day of Bryn's surprise arrival he appeared once more in the bar at the busiest time. Willie, gathered with his cronies at his favourite table, gave Sylvia a wink to warn her. Jimmy, downing his last pint before going out to do his Saturday stint with his taxi outside Culworth station, caught the wink midstream as it were and said slyly to no one in particular, 'Bryn keeps himself busy.'

Willie deliberately ignored his remark and said, 'Cricket team's doing well this season. Should be the top of the league if they keep it up.'

'Never mind about the blinking cricket team. What's going on?'

Willie took his time to answer. 'How should I know, he doesn't confide in me.'

'Oh, doesn't he? Well, why does he keep calling? Is he fancying Sylvia?'

Sylvia blushed right to the roots of her hair.

Willie made a fist and threatened Jimmy. 'One more word and that's what you'll be getting right between the eyes, make a right mess of that hawk nose of yours. Can no one do anything in this village without someone casting aspersions?'

'Aspersions! What have you done, swallowed a dictionary?'

'No, Jimmy Glover, I have not. Just let it drop.'

Sylvia muttered, 'Oh Lord, he's coming across.'

Bryn made his way over to them, carrying a loaded tray. 'Been some time since I had the pleasure of buying you all a drink. I hope after all this time I've remembered your favourite tipple. He put down the tray and the five of them inspected it. 'Orange juice for Don, gin and tonic for Vera, ale for Jimmy and Willie, and for you, Sylvia, a Martini and lemonade.'

'Martini, oh no! That's not me. I like a snowball; you know, advocaat and lemonade.'

Bryn groaned. 'Of course. Sorry. I'll have this and I'll get you a snowball. Does the dwarf know how to make one I ask myself?'

'That's cruel, Bryn. Don't call him that. We all like him,' Sylvia protested.

Jimmy interrupted by stoutly defending Dicky. 'He stood by Georgie and kept this pub going for her in the first few weeks after you hopped it. Thanks for the drink, I won't be so churlish as to refuse it but don't buy me another. I can buy my own.' He half turned his back to Bryn, clinked his glass with the others and sat brooding about whether he should be friendly with Bryn.

When he came back with Sylvia's snowball, Vera and Don thanked him graciously and, after a nudge from Don's knee under the table, Vera started up a conversation with Bryn with the positive intention of finding out why he'd come back. 'It's no good, I've got to come right out with it. We're all wondering why you've come back, Bryn.'

Bryn tapped the side of his nose with his forefinger. 'Ah! That would be telling and I'm not ready to say anything until my plans are all in place.'

'Plans! What kind of plans could you be having for this sleepy old place?'

'You all need waking up, there's no doubt about that. And I'm the man to do it. You wouldn't be averse to earning an extra bob or two, would you, Jimmy?'

'Might.'

'I'll call round then.'

'I might listen – then again, I might not.'

Bryn twisted round in his chair and shouted, 'Dicky! Same again over here, and don't hang about.'

'Don't order any more for me, I'm driving tonight.'

'One more won't harm, I'm sure.'

Jimmy's heavy-lidded eyes rested on Bryn's face. 'You won't soften me up, not even with a whole gallon of ale. I can't forget your behaviour before you left. It was only the Rector being so strong that prevented you from murdering Dicky. I don't know how the poor chap can bear you in the same room as him. Why you haven't gone to prison for it I'll never know. Anyway, time I was off.' Jimmy strode out, leaving behind him an uncomfortable silence.

Sylvia pretended to check her watch, cleared her throat and said, 'I've a programme to watch on TV, if you'll excuse me.' She picked up her bag from the settle and squeezed out. 'Goodnight.'

Willie followed, glad of an excuse, leaving a half-finished pint on the table. Vera and Don felt uneasy. If he wasn't going to tell them why he was there, what was there to talk about? They were saved any further embarrassment by Georgie coming to the table with the tray of drinks Bryn had ordered.

Georgie looked at Vera and Don but avoided Bryn's eyes. 'Oh, dear! What a surprise,' she said, 'your guests are disappearing one by one. What do you want me to do with this lot, Bryn?'

'Oh! We'll drink it, won't we, Vera?'

Vera blushed. Don grunted and made to take his orange juice from the tray, but Georgie stepped back so the tray was out of his reach. 'I've a better idea.' Without any warning she tipped the drinks over Bryn's head. Ale and orange juice and gin and tonic ran all over him and the glasses crashed to the floor around him. All he could do was to sit there gasping, soaked to the skin, wiping away drink from his eyes with his well-tanned hand.

Between clenched teeth Georgie snarled, 'Another time don't you ever dare shout for Dicky to bring you drinks in that nasty way. I run a well-mannered pub here and I won't stand for it. You'd speak to a dog better than that.'

Bryn stood up and came as close as he had ever done to striking

Georgie. He brought his arm back to do that very thing, but the savage glint in her eye and the thought that he wouldn't get what he wanted from her by alienating her stopped him just in time. It was difficult to be taken seriously when wet through and smelling like a brewery, though, but he tried. 'I'm very sorry, Georgie, love, I shouldn't have asked like that. Forgetting my manners.' He paused to wipe the trickles of drink running off the end of his nose. 'Won't happen again.'

'In future remember what I've said. I won't have you speaking like that in here. And you can pay me for that lot before you go.'

Bryn spread his hands wide in a placatory gesture. 'I'd better get changed first. I'll be back.' He threaded his way between the tables, causing customers to snatch at their coats to avoid getting them wet. A long wet trail was all that was left of Bryn when the door closed behind him.

'Vera, let's be off. I don't want any more of him embarrassing me. Don't know what's got into him. He's not the same man at all. Come on.' Don took her elbow to assist her to rise, and in a gentlemanly fashion picked up her bag from the floor and tucked it under his arm.

'Thanks. 'Ere let me carry that.' They stepped around Dicky who was mopping the floor after Bryn. 'Don't know how you put up with it, Dicky, 'im coming in here. Just don't do anything daft, mind.'

Dicky looked up. 'I won't. If we knew why he'd come back it would help.'

'There's a reason, but none of us can fathom it yet. But believe me, we're all on your side.'

'Thanks.' Dicky stopped mopping to watch them leave. He leant on his mop handle and silently cursed Bryn. When he thought about it the worst scenario would be that this newly revitalised Bryn might take Georgie away from him – after all, they were still married, it was no problem. Then Bel would be back in Glebe Cottages with him and he'd be back to that old boring job. A sister wasn't quite the same as a lover, still less was a lover as good as a wife and a wife, namely Georgie, was what he wanted most of all. He finished the mopping, emptied the bucket in the grate outside and was storing them away in the cleaning cupboard when Georgie appeared.

'Dicky!' Georgie put her hands on his shoulders and, looking into his eyes, said, 'Don't be afraid. I won't go back to him, no matter what. I'm asking him for a divorce tonight. That's God's truth.' She gave him a peck on his lips, gently placed her finger on his mouth for him to kiss and then went back into the bar to help deal with the rush.

Uncanny, that, thought Dicky, she even knows what I'm thinking. But then Georgie always knew what he was thinking, it was typical Georgie, it was. His insides ached with the pain of loving her. A terrible paralysis crept over him when he considered perhaps having to face the rest of his life without her. The thought made him shudder deep inside; it didn't bear thinking about. It wasn't at all what he wanted, having snatched moments, sneaking off for weekends away, all because tongues wagged too freely in this close community. It had its advantages, though: they'd welcomed him and Bel with open arms and when they'd found out their secret – that he and Bel were brother and sister – no one really minded. But the Rector had made his opinion absolutely clear on the matter of him and Georgie: 'While you are the leader of our Church Scouts I will not tolerate you openly living with Georgie. I know it's not in line with current thinking, but there you are. Added to which, in the eyes of the boys you would become the object of unseemly mirth and sniggering, and with it all the hard work you've put into establishing the largest and most successful Scout group in the county would be gone, never to be regained. You are brilliant as leader, I could challenge anyone to find a Scout leader better than you. Don't lose all that, for your sake or the boys'.'

Dicky pottered about in the cleaning cupboard tidying this, reorganising that, until he could find nothing more to tidy. He gave a great sigh. Peter always saw the greater good, the long term, what was best for all concerned and after all he did have to be grateful to him for his very life. If it hadn't been for Peter being so very fit, Bryn would have had him over the top of the tower and he, Dicky Tutt, would have been strawberry jam. It struck him in a flash. Of course, that was it! Insist on prosecution. Of course! That would get rid of him sharpish. Bryn would be discredited for ever, Georgie could get a divorce, no sweat, and they could marry and he could live at the pub . . . Why had he allowed Peter to persuade him not to prosecute?

He perched on a case of carpet shampoo in the dark and his heart sank. He knew full well why. It was as Peter had said at the time, the whole story of Bryn, and Georgie and Bel would be open to public view and to distortion by the press. Let's face it, thought Dicky, I did torment Bryn with all the tricks I got up to. Anyway, Peter was right. It really wasn't in his nature to want revenge. He'd got Georgie's love and that counted for a lot. But hiding behind her skirts by leaving her to deal with Bryn . . . he had to laugh, though – pouring the drinks over him; what a woman!

'Dicky! Can you come?'

That was Alan wanting more help. He got up, shut the cupboard door and marched into the bar with a grin plastered on his face. 'Who's next?'

It was Bryn, a very smart Bryn. Dressed more suitably for the Caribbean than Turnham Malpas, he certainly made heads turn, no doubt about that. Dicky steeled himself not to go white at the implied threat of Bryn's presence. 'What can I get you, Bryn?'

'Whisky on the rocks . . . please.' He dug out his wallet crammed with notes, peeled off a twenty and said, 'Take for that tray of drinks that got spilled as well.'

'Thanks.'

Bryn threw the whisky down his throat and asked for another. He took that to a table and sat down to wait. It unnerved Dicky having to work with Bryn's eyes on him all the time. He felt like a goldfish swimming round and round its bowl, with a cat poised for whisking him out with its paw if he swam too close to the top of the water.

Bryn sat there until closing time, then went to the bar and asked Georgie if he could have a word.

'I can't leave all this mess. Wait ten minutes.'

'I'll give you a hand.'

'No, thanks.' But he did. He collected the empties and put them in the wheelie bin. He found a cloth and wiped a few tables, he collected some crisp bags off the floor and finally got out the cloth bag, which they'd always used to put the takings in the safe until the morning.

Georgie snatched it from him. 'That's my job. Go in the back, the door's unlocked.'

She and Dicky said a quiet goodnight to each other by the outside door. 'I won't let him persuade me, honestly, Dicky. I will not have him back. Believe me.'

'Are you sure?'

'Yes, I'm sure. I'll let you know tomorrow.'

'Right. I'll come straight after communion. Right.'

Georgie smiled at him. Their eyes were on a level and she could look straight into his and loved him so. She said, 'Right. I'm sorry about all this, but at least we might get a chance to sort things out. Goodnight, love.'

'Goodnight.'

Georgie turned out the lights and made her way across the bar and upstairs to Bryn.

She found him seated in a comfortable chair in the sitting room waiting for her. He stood up as she entered and it gave her heart a turn. He hadn't done that for years. 'I'm going to have a cup of tea.'

'Like you always did after a busy day. Can I make it for you?'

'Bel will be in the kitchen making herself a drink, so I'd better do it.'

'Very well.' He relaxed back into the chair and shuffled his shoulders about as though making himself comfortable for a long time.

'You want one?'

'No, thanks. Tea's not my tipple any more.'

When she came back with her tea she had the odd feeling that he'd been out of the chair poking through her belongings. The desk drawers were closed, the papers on top apparently undisturbed, all the same . . .

Georgie sat down and sipped her tea, expecting that Bryn would be the one to open the conversation. But he didn't. She heard Bel unlock the bathroom door, listened to a car roaring up the Culworth Road. Then the deep silence of the countryside descended. Eventually she said, 'I thought you wanted to talk.'

'I've a proposition to make.'

'Spill the beans, then.'

'While I've been managing bars on the cruise liners I've come into contact with a lot – and I mean a lot – of Americans, Americans who travel a great deal. Many of them want to come to Europe but haven't the know-how to make a successful job of it. They want to see the real England, what makes us tick, what makes us what we are, to get the feel of our heritage. I've an address book crammed with names and telephone numbers, and I've planned a tour, an off-the-beaten-track kind of tour. When they come to London they'll have two or three days there doing the Tower, Buckingham Palace, a performance at the Globe Theatre et cetera, then we'll travel to Bath, on the way...'

'You're not thinking of bringing them here, are you?'

'I'm coming to that. I shan't have them staying in the kind of hotel that can be found all over the world and they could be waking up in Hong Kong or Sydney or New York. No, that's not for me. They'll be staying in typically English country house hotels, hotels with ambience, ones just that bit different from the usual tourist dumps, so I thought...'

'Yes?'

'I thought that on their way to Bath and Stratford they could call here for lunch.'

'Here meaning here?' Georgie pointed to the floor to emphasise her point.

Bryn nodded. 'That's right, lunch here at the Royal Oak. They could have a tour of the church, call in at the Store for souvenirs, feed Jimmy's geese, finish off here for lunch: typical old pub, talk up the history a bit, you know the kind of thing. Perhaps even visit a cottage for some more atmosphere. What do you think? It could be a real money spinner for everyone. Us included.'

'Us? Who's "us"?'

'Well, you, I mean.'

'How many?'

'Groups of twenty, no more than twenty-five or the exclusiveness would be lost.'

'How often?'

'Well, this summer I've got one planned for August, one for

September. That's all. But it could mushroom. They'd be here Thursday, which is never a good day for lunches in our dining room, is it?'

'You keep making the mistake of saying "us" and "our". It isn't yours, Bryn. You took the money, remember, and I got the business and my name is over the door.'

'Sorry.' Hastily Bryn spread his hands in a placatory gesture. 'Habit, you know, you and me, a team for years, it's hard to drop the habit.'

Georgie sat sipping her tea, thinking about his plans. Twenty-five people for lunch on a Thursday would certainly be a boost. 'If I decided to do it, I'd have to consult Dicky first. It would have to be the same menu for everyone, I don't think the kitchen could cope with twenty-five people all wanting serving at once with different dishes.'

'Absolutely. Typical old English menu. Windsor soup, steak and ale pie with home-grown vegetables, spotted dick steamed pudding with custard, coffee and liqueurs.'

'What's Windsor soup when it's at home?'

'Anything you like, just sounds impressive. Drinks, of course, would be up to them, wine, beer, whisky, whatever they wanted. These people are rich, Georgie, real rich. I'll have them eating out of my hand. Two hours we have here, that's all. Should be enough. What do you think?'

'I'm too tired, Bryn, to get my mind round it, but it's definitely an idea. The problem I see is will you have a full load each week to make it worthwhile? That will be hard, making up the groups.'

'No sweat. I've got contacts you wouldn't believe. I cultivated them, you see. Didn't know why, then the whole idea burst into my mind and I realised the possibilities. I'll come back in a day or two when you've had time to think.'

'OK. Make it Tuesday. But you must understand' – into Georgie's eyes came a hard look – 'it is strictly a business venture. I want paying before the group leaves. They'll be escorted of course?'

'That goes without saying. You'll be paid on the dot and I shall be escorting for the first couple of seasons till we get the ball rolling. This tour scheme of mine could be a money spinner, personal touch and all that, and I shan't stop at just this one tour. I intend expanding as fast as possible. Visiting prime English gardens, castle tours, you name it.' Bryn rubbed his hands together in anticipation. 'You and me, together we'll show 'em.'

Georgie became caught up in his enthusiasm and allowed herself to smile. 'Sounds good; in fact, very good. Personal contact as you say. Now, I've got to get to bed. I'll let you out.'

'Thanks.' They both stood up at the same time and Bryn very lightly took her arm. 'Good to see you. I've lived to regret my treatment of you. I really have. Should have had more sense, not neglected you.'

Georgie stiffened and drew away from him. 'Too late now.' She led the way to the back door and let him out.

Bryn stepped outside and turned back to say, 'We could still make a good team, Georgie, I can feel that old something between us. Can you not feel it?'

'No. Goodnight. See you Tuesday.'

Bryn smiled to himself as he turned into Church Lane. He called out a cheerful friendly 'Goodnight' to Jimbo who was just leaving his mother's cottage. He'd be calling at the Store tomorrow. Jimbo'd be as easy as pie to influence, him being always ready to make money, so long as it was legal.

Bryn was at the Store as soon as the morning rush of mothers from the school had finished their shopping. He gauged that around half past nine would be about the best time.

He couldn't believe that Linda was still at the post office counter. 'Good morning, Linda. How are you? Still here I see. Thought you'd have gone long ago.'

'Why, Mr Fields. I wondered how long it would be before you called. How are you? My, I hardly recognise you, you're so . . . brown and, well, years younger without that moustache. No need to ask how *you* are!' She grinned ruefully from behind the grille and finally answered his question quietly. 'I think I've been sacked a total of four times now, but he always comes crawling back asking me to return, because he can't find anyone who can do it as well as me.'

'Watch it! The next time might be the last.'

'Oh, don't say that! It's so handy being able to drop Lewis off at the childminder and come straight here. Are you wanting something?'

'Just to see Jimbo. Is he in?'

'I'll give him a shout. Hold on.' Linda unlocked the door of her cage, as she called it, and carefully locked it after her. She excused her caution by saying apologetically, 'Can't be too careful!' She slipped into the back of the Store to find Jimbo.

Bryn looked round as a preliminary to his conversation with Jimbo. He preferred to be well armed before a business discussion. He noted the picture postcards of the area, especially the ones of the church and the village green, then he progressed to the jams and marmalades, remembering Jimbo had a line called 'Harriet's Country Cousins' whatever. Now that would be a good line for souvenirs. The title was perfectly splendid for his needs. Of course, he'd want a percentage when the sales grew. Which they would. He picked up a beautifully evocative jar, a six-sided pot with a red-and-white gingham cover on the top and an elaborate label saying 'Harriet's Country Cousins' thick-sliced Grapefruit Marmalade, made to a recipe from an old notebook found . . .'

'Yes!' Jimbo stood beside him resplendent in his striped apron and with his bow tie matching the ribbon around the crown of his straw boater. 'What can I do for you this bright morning? You wanted to see me?'

Bryn was instantly aware of the belligerent tone of Jimbo's voice, so he set himself out to charm and by the time he'd finished his spiel about his rich tourists and the money that could be made, he had Jimbo eating out of his hand.

At least he thought he had, until Jimbo suddenly said, 'And what is there in it for you, if I'm selling doodahs to your tourists?'

Bryn hesitated in order to demonstrate delicacy of feeling. 'Well, perhaps when we get things really going you could see your way . . .' He tapped the side of his nose and winked.

Jimbo said, 'I make no promises. I'm not here to make you a rich man, you know, Bryn. Margins are tight in a set-up like this, I've to watch every penny.'

'Oh, I can see that.' Bryn gazed around Jimbo's well-equipped, stylish set-up. 'Margins are very tight.' His right cheek bulged with the pressure of the tip of his tongue.

Jimbo was forced to smile. 'I'm still not promising you a percentage of my profits on anything I sell as souvenirs. Accounting for it would be difficult.'

Bryn nodded gravely. 'Of course, of course it would. You need to expand what you have on offer, though. Little framed pictures of the village houses. A small model of the church and perhaps the school, and of course a model of the Royal Oak. Now they would sell. Oh, yes. They would sell. Tasteful, of course.'

Stung by the implied lack of good taste on his part, Jimbo answered, 'Absolutely.'

'Think about what else you could sell. Once the old brains get going, who knows what we might come up with. I specially like Harriet's jams et cetera, they would go down a bomb with the tourists.'

'Are we to expect tourists every week?'

Bryn laughed. 'Not to start with, but I've every intention of directing as much business as I can to this village.'

'Let's hope they thank you for it.' Jimbo touched the brim of his boater. 'Must get on. Be in touch. When's the first lot?'

'August.'

'Right. I'll be in touch as I said.'

Bryn extended his hand. 'Thanks for your attention, I'm going to make sure it works. I've got quite a few ideas which, if they come to fruition, will put Turnham Malpas on the map. Ye olde yokel sitting by the pond, et cetera, you know the sort of thing. It's those little touches that really make a tour.'

Jimbo shook his hand and Bryn left with a satisfied smile on his face.

3

After their evening meal Jimbo explained to Harriet the purpose of Bryn's stay in Turnham Malpas. 'In addition he's going to have what he describes as an olde yokel sitting by the pond.'

'That's you, is it?' Harriet asked.

The two girls shrieked with laughter. Fran asked what a yokel was and Flick told her between gasps of laughter. 'I can just see you, Dad! Have you still got that old smocked thing, Mum, you bought in that sale? You know, the Victorian farmer's thingy?'

'I have. He could wear it, couldn't he? Very authentic.'

Jimbo said, 'Less of the mirth. What he wants us to do is expand our range of souvenirs.'

'We haven't got any souvenirs.'

'We've got your jams and marmalades.'

'Of course, I never thought of them in that light.'

'We've got postcards.'

Harriet thought for a moment and suggested, 'Turnham Malpas pencils with those dear little rubbers on the end.'

Flick said, 'Framed pictures of the village.'

Fran proffered the idea of sweets in Turnham Malpas tins.

Flick scoffed at her idea. 'Trust you to think of sweets, you'd eat all the profits.'

'I wouldn't, would I, Mummy?'

'No, darling, in fact you've come up with a good notion there. We could also put our Belgian chocolates in Turnham Malpas tins.'

Flick was appalled at such duplicity. 'That is outrageous. Dad, don't let her. She mustn't. That's cheating.'

'Definitely cheating.' But he winked at Harriet, which further outraged Flick.

Fran, being too young to understand what they were meaning, asked, 'Is there anything Flick and I could do? We'll be off school in August. I'd like to dress up.'

'We'll see.'

Harriet checked her watch. 'Come along, Fran, time you were off to bed.'

'I really want to talk business with Daddy.'

'You've talked enough. You had one of the best ideas so far, so that's sufficient to be going on with. Move!'

Tucked up in bed, the curtains drawn against the light, Fran said, 'Sit down to talk.'

Sensing there was something on Fran's mind, Harriet did as she asked. 'Two minutes, that's all.'

'Mummy.'

'Yes?'

'How can you be someone's little girl if she's not your tummy-mummy?'

'First, you're not worrying about yourself, are you? Because, let it be clearly understood, I am your tummy-mummy.'

'I know that because Flick remembers me being born in the hospital car park.'

'And you've been in a hurry ever since. However, there are some ladies who would love to be a mummy but they've got an illness or something and the doctors say they won't be able to have a baby growing in their tummy, so-o-o they can make a solemn promise to care for a baby who has no mummy or has a mummy who can't look after it and that's called adoption, and it's just as if the baby is theirs, except it hasn't grown in their tummy.'

'They look after someone else's baby.'

'That's right.'

'So is that what happened to Beth and Alex?'

'Yes, because Caroline isn't able to have babies.'

'So whose tummy did they grow in, then?'

'Someone's who couldn't look after them and gave them away to Caroline and Peter when they were tiny, tiny babies, because they thought it was for the best.'

'Did you know them?'

'I knew them when they were tiny.'

'No. I mean did you know their real mummy? I wonder who she is. Beth wants to know. I thought you might be able to tell her.'

'Fran, it's something very personal for Caroline and Peter, and I honestly think you shouldn't get involved. It's for them to tell her, believe me.'

'Beth keeps on and on about it. Every time I see her. She's asked loads of girls.'

'It really isn't any of our business.'

Fran turned over on to her side, closed her eyes and said, 'I think you know, but you won't tell me. It's not fair. Goodnight.'

'It's not my secret.'

'I shall tell Beth to ask Caroline.'

'You'll do no such thing. You'll mind your own business. Goodnight. I mean what I say. It's all too private.'

'Mm.'

Just as Harriet left her bedroom Fran called out, 'Teaspoons with a tiny church on the end. How about that for an idea? Or doorstops made out of wood with one of Jimmy's geese painted on.'

'Fran! I'll tell Daddy, but switch off now, please.'

Harriet found Jimbo in his study doing rapid sums on his calculator. 'I wish you'd never mentioned this idea just before Fran went to bed. Her head's full of souvenirs. She'll never settle and you know how much she needs her sleep.'

Jimbo looked up, lost in thought. 'I know this idea of Bryn's is only a possibility. It may or may not work depending, but we do get lots of other visitors from all over the place so whatever we decide on could be a year-round line. Why on earth I haven't thought of it before I don't know.'

'Teaspoons and doorstops she's come up with now. Heaven alone knows what she'll have thought of by morning.'

'She's a true daughter of mine, is Fran. I'll put those on the list. In the scheme of things this is only a small matter, but every penny counts. I tell you who'd be good for the doorstops: Vince Jones. He's a wizard with wood, remember?'

'And for framing the pictures. But has it occurred to you that you haven't spoken to the Jones family since Mrs Jones went steaming through the Store casting all before her?'

Jimbo laid down the calculator and leaned back in his chair. 'Ah! I'm getting carried away here.'

'I also remember all the cursing you did about the Jones family when their Terry and Kenny had to disappear quick sharp before the police caught up with them, or worse, those gangsters. Think of the outlay for all these things! The returns could be quite slow and we've no guarantee that Bryn's idea of tourists would work.'

'Agreed, but . . . the idea grips me and if an idea grips me then most often it turns out to be a good one. I'm going to play around with it, see what comes up. Doesn't cost much to have two hundred pencils embossed with Turnham Malpas Store, does it? You're not listening to me.'

'No, you're right, I'm not. I'm off to see Peter and Caroline.'

'Why?'

'Because Beth is obssessed with where she came from. They've always known, the two of them, that Caroline isn't their mother but that Peter is their father, but now apparently she wants to know the rest and those two should do something about it.'

'They'll deal with it when the time is ripe.'

'It's ripe now, believe me. Fran says Beth's asking everyone at school and before long some child is going to spill the beans.'

'Harriet, is this wise?'

'I'm going. Won't be long.'

Jimbo stood up. 'Please, think about it.'

'I'm *going.* I won't have Fran getting all upset, it's not right. What's more, the whole situation means I can't tell my own daughter the truth and that's certainly not right.'

'Very well, but tread very carefully, please.'

Hand on heart Harriet answered, 'I am the soul of discretion.'

Peter came to the door when she knocked at the Rectory. 'Hello, Harriet, come in. If it's Caroline you want to see she's out, I'm afraid.'

'Well, it was both of you, but maybe on second thoughts I'm quite glad it's you on your own.'

'Had we better go into my study?'

'All right, then, yes.'

Peter opened the door for her and she went in and flopped down in an easy chair. Peter sat at his desk and waited for her to speak. She was struck as always by his commanding presence – his height, the breadth of his shoulders, his fresh complexion and thick reddish-blond hair – he was very handsome in any woman's eyes. But his penetrating blue eyes made him intimidating, for they seemed to see straight through you, and it felt as though all your smallest and most unworthy thoughts were exposed to his scrutiny.

'Peter, I have a problem. Well, at least it's not my problem, it's yours and I don't quite know how to phrase it.'

'Mine? What are we talking about?'

'Your Beth and Alex.'

'Have they been misbehaving?'

'No. Never. They're always well-mannered and never any trouble. No, it's not that.'

Peter waited a moment, then said, 'Well?'

'You know they've been having sex lessons this term . . . well, it has caused them both, I think, but mainly Beth to . . . to be honest, it's time you and Caroline came clean about . . . well, not clean exactly, that's not what I meant to say, but it's time you and she spoke to the twins about their origins before someone else does and makes a balls of it. Because if that happens the twins could be irreparably hurt.'

Harriet thought it must have been at least a whole minute before Peter replied but of course it wasn't, it was seconds. 'I see. She's never said anything to us about it.'

'Well, it will be difficult for her, very difficult for them both, won't it? They won't want to hurt Caroline for they love her so, but they ought to be told, because it's causing Beth such anguish. Fran tells me she's asking everyone if their mother is their real one, hoping, I expect, to find someone else who's been adopted so she can compare notes or something. But what's made me come tonight is the fact that Fran asked me who their real mother is. And I don't like not being able to tell the truth to my children.'

'We shouldn't have made it so you can't be straight with your children. I'm deeply sorry about that. Obviously the moment we've avoided thinking about has come at last.'

'I know they know Caroline isn't their real mother, but I think if you told them the whole truth they'd be able to face it at their age. It doesn't mean they will want to go charging off to find . . . Suzy . . . does it?'

Peter got up and went to stand at the window. 'She longs to see them.'

Harriet was glad they weren't face to face or he would have seen the shock written there. She'd no idea they'd been in touch since Suzy left the village.

'That was long ago when she came to visit Michael while she thought we were on holiday. I told her, no, I couldn't allow it both for Caroline's sake and for her own. Her conceiving my children was one moment of shame, my shame, which I shall carry with me to the grave. Yet from it Caroline and I were blessed with the children we both needed.' Peter gave a huge sigh. 'It was Caroline who asked Suzy if we could have the children, you know. And when she told me what she'd done I said no. Caroline said, "I see. So we can adopt children we know nothing of but you won't let me adopt your own flesh and blood." She told me Suzy wanted us to have the twins as soon as they arrived, because Suzy wouldn't allow herself to see the children as they were being born in case she weakened. Such courage.'

Peter turned from the window, his eyes full of tears. 'I saw her immediately after the birth, you know; her pain at relinquishing them to Caroline and me was terrible to witness. But she knew she couldn't keep them, a widow with three little girls already, it would have been impossible for her. Yet she was so brave . . . she even asked me for my blessing. Can you believe that?'

Harriet shook her head, too emotional to speak, grateful he was looking anywhere but at her.

'When Caroline told me that Suzy wanted us to have the children and I'd said no, I told her I couldn't face looking at them every day and being reminded of my shame. I considered only myself with never a thought for what I'd done to *her*. I threw all her love and self-sacrifice back in her face. I have never met such forgiveness in a human being either before or since.'

'Peter! Should you be telling me all this?'

He shook his head but carried on to say, 'How Caroline coped with what I did, I shall never know.'

'So Suzy wasn't the only one to be brave.'

'Indeed not.' He paused for a moment, then his head came up and he looked her straight in the face. 'Thank you for telling me, Harriet, I appreciate it. I've always been intensely grateful for the way the village has kept our secret. Deeply appreciative.'

Harriet stood up, crying inside herself, longing to get away. 'I'll go now I've said my piece. It was only in your best interests and the children's. I hope you'll forgive me for speaking out.'

'There's nothing to forgive. God bless you, Harriet.'

'If anyone mentions anything to you from this conversation it won't be me who's told them.'

She left Peter to his heartbreak, made her escape, and went home to Jimbo and the no-nonsense world in which the two of them lived.

But stupidly the first thing she did when she saw Jimbo still working at his desk was to fling her arms round him and weep. 'Darling! Oh, God! You wouldn't believe.'

'Harriet! Were they angry with you? Tell me. Here, sit on my knee.' He gripped her tightly and let the tears run their course. 'Here, look! A clean handkerchief. Wipe your face and tell your Jimbo.' He wiped it for her and hugged her tight. 'I did say don't go.'

'I know but I'm glad I did.'

'Doesn't sound like it.'

'I think I'm not nearly as brave as I believe myself to be. Those two over at the Rectory, well . . .'

'Go on.'

'They're an example to us all.' Harriet told him everything she'd learned and finished by begging him not to say a word to anyone.

'Cross my heart and hope to die.'

'Promise?'

'Promise.'

'I never think about how lucky we are to have had four children as easily as we have done, and nothing wrong with any of them, but tonight I am. Peter and Caroline are in such a mess about this. If only they'd been able to have children of their own . . .'

'It's their problem, Harriet. I do feel very sorry for them but there's nothing either you or I can do anything about, except be good friends to them both.'

'I know, but what a predicament. I wish I could wave a magic wand and make it all right for the four of them. Heaven alone knows what the children's reactions are going to be.'

'I'm not often given to fanciful thoughts but I always think their love is something quite different from ours. Theirs is like a skittish, highly strung horse, all temperament and searing passion. It must be hell to live with a love like theirs, all up and down and sensitive and touchy. We're like a couple of shire-horses, confident and strong.'

'You make it sound damned boring, Jimbo.'

'Boring! No, not boring, more beautifully comfortable, kind of. However, as I said none of it is our fault. It's Peter's.' He slid her off his knee and turned to his desk. 'Look, I've made a list of souvenirs I fancy selling. I've decided to be magnanimous and restore the Jones family to the bosom of our enterprise.'

Harriet was astounded. 'After all you've said about them? I can't believe this.'

Jimbo gave her a conspiratorial smile. 'I know, I know, but business is business. Mrs Jones can come back to do the mail order business, because none of her replacements has measured up to her and Vince can do the doorstops et cetera and the picture framing. Now he's retired they need a helping hand and I'm in a position to give them it, so I must.'

'So that's how you justify it. Well, you can ask them because I shan't, it's all too embarrassing.' Harriet gave a huge sigh as she finished speaking.

He heard her sigh and said, 'Harriet! Don't worry about the twins; you've done your bit, just leave it to them. I can't bear for you to be unhappy. I love you, you see, and what hurts you hurts me.' Jimbo caressed her hand and twisted round to look at her standing behind him.

She smiled down at him and bent to kiss him. 'And I love you, even if I am a shire-horse.' They both laughed, Harriet picked up his sheet of notes from the desk and they began discussing Jimbo's souvenir scheme. But for Harriet it didn't entirely block out her worry about Peter and Caroline.

Peter was sitting in his study brooding on the problem when Caroline came home. She put her head round the study door and knew even before he spoke that Peter was troubled. 'Darling! What's the matter?'

'Harriet's been to see me.'

'Yes?'

'Apparently Beth is asking all round the school about . . .' Peter hesitated, unsure how to phrase Harriet's news. 'Well, to be blunt, about her real mother. She wants to know who she is.'

'Oh, God!' Caroline sat down abruptly on the sofa.

'Caroline! We knew it would come some time and it's come *now*, so we have to face it.'

'Not yet, not now. Please. I need time.'

'We've had ten years of time to think and all we've done is amble along from day to day, putting it off, thankful for their ignorance.'

'I won't face it. I just won't. I'm not ready for it.'

Peter's answer to Caroline's anguish was not the sympathetic one she'd hoped for. 'I'm sorry, darling, but they *are*, even if we're not, and something must be done about it.'

'No, we don't need to. We can just amble along as you say, and wait and see. They haven't asked *us*, so it can't be that serious.'

'That's probably because they don't want to hurt us, especially you. Harriet pointed out to me the strong possibility that others might tell her and that could be catastrophic.' Peter paused for a moment while he searched for the right words. 'You see, other people might be . . . cruel . . . you know, and Beth and Alex can't fight that kind of cruelty without having a strong bond with us about the whole matter. I know it's painful, my darling, but we're the grown-ups in this and we've to smooth their pathway.'

Caroline shook her head vehemently. 'I know they need to know, but not yet, they're so little. So innocent.' As she said 'innocent' she gave a great agonised sigh.

Peter went to sit beside her on the sofa. He put his arm round her shoulders and held her close. 'I know, I know. We don't need to tell them today or even tomorrow, but we must very, very soon. Deep down, you know I'm right. If they have a need to know then now's the time, isn't it? Otherwise it puts us on the wrong foot and makes us appear deceitful, and . . . Suzy herself didn't want that. She begged me to be truthful and we both know she was right.' Peter gave her a gentle shake. 'Eh? Don't we?'

'But what will they think of you?'

'That's my burden, not theirs.'

Caroline shrugged his arm from her shoulders and turned to face him. 'My absolute dread is if they want to see her.'

'I don't think they will, not yet anyway, but we can't blame them if they do, can we? It's only natural. Think it over, seriously, please.'

'I will. But how shall we . . . kind of . . . do it?'

'Heaven knows. We'll think of something. We're not entirely bereft of brains, are we?'

'I wasn't thinking of brains, it was heart and feelings and . . . things I'm most concerned about.'

'Ah! Yes.'

Never one to allow the grass to grow under his feet, Jimbo had Mrs Jones installed in the mail order office and Vince doing practice runs with doorstop designs in less time than it takes to tell. Mrs Jones glowed with satisfaction the first morning she was allowed back in the Store.

Linda waved cheerfully from behind her post office grille. 'Hello, Mrs Jones. Quite like old times. I expect you'll be glad to be back, just like me.'

Mrs Jones's normally grim face was creased with smiles. 'You've no idea! Things have been very tight since Vince retired, but now the sun is out as you might say and I'm back doing what I was cut out to do.' She looked around the Store, glad to know she'd be able to shop in here again instead of trailing to Culworth for everything she needed.

She bounced into the back of the shop and went straight to the mail order office, closed the door behind her and breathed a sigh of delight. There was a pile of orders waiting for her so she flung off her coat and hat, dug in her bag for her reading glasses and waded in. She reached out and took down a jar of 'Harriet's Country

Cousins' Seville Orange Marmalade' but, before she parcelled it up for the post she ran her finger round the label, stroked the red gingham cover, teased the neatly tied bow of the gold cord encircling it and read out the description of the contents, then held the jar up to the light and enjoyed the golden orangey glow of it. There wasn't a single jar of home-made marmalade on the market to compare. She felt a surge of contentment run through her veins, decided the jar was the most beautiful thing in her life at that moment and set to work as though she'd never been away.

Jimbo, with an ear to her office door, listened to her banging away with the stapler and rejoiced at the old familiar sound. He really would have to stop sacking staff the moment they displeased him because it always meant him eating humble pie and he was growing tired of the taste.

Harriet caught him listening to the ripping sound of parcel tape being dragged off the reel and poked him in the ribs whispering, 'Satisfied?'

'I am. Music to my ears, that is.' With a smug smile on his face he went on. 'She's promised not to lose her rag ever again and she says I can call her Greta now.'

'Oh! Who's a lucky boy, then?' Harriet, grinning from ear to ear, went towards the kitchen to face a day of making puddings and cakes to fill the freezers. Halfway through the morning she remembered about the twins and Peter's distress, and it took the edge off her pleasure.

Dicky Tutt had the edge taken off his pleasure in the Store that same morning but not because of the problem at the Rectory. He had called in for a copy of the *Culworth Gazette* for Georgie on his way to the pub for his morning stint and found himself facing Bryn right by Jimbo's news-stand. The hairs on the back of Dicky's neck stood up and his scalp prickled.

'Good morning, Dicky! Nice day.'

Dicky picked up on the mocking tone in Bryn's voice. Remembering how he'd hidden behind Georgie's skirts the night she'd poured the drinks over Bryn's head, Dicky decided to stand his ground. 'The morning would be a lot nicer if you weren't here.'

'Don't be like that, I mean no harm.'

'Don't you? Just go back where you came from and leave us all alone. Georgie's had enough of you and so have I.'

Bryn took hold of the lapels of Dicky's jacket. 'See here, you stunted little specimen, you miserable little dwarf. I'm still Georgie's husband and it's staying that way. She and I are business partners, right? I'm going to bring big business to the pub and that's what she wants. See? So your Georgie this and Georgie that means nothing.' Bryn snapped his fingers in Dicky's face and disdainfully dusted off his hands as though he'd been touching something unseemly.

Linda rang her panic button.

Dicky snapped. He grabbed hold of Bryn's shirt at chest level and jerked his face down towards his own. 'See here, matey, Georgie is mine and I'll move heaven and earth to keep it that way. So you can take your miserable pathetic business elsewhere. Find another pub and use that for your pie-in-the-sky plans. Any more of you aggravating me I'll go straight to the police, and talk about church towers and such. They'll listen to me. After all, I had plenty of witnesses and they've all got long memories.' Dicky relaxed his hold on Bryn. 'So git before I do my worst.'

Jimbo appeared by the news-stand.

Dicky saw by Bryn's eyes that he was alarmed, but only for an instant. Then they changed and Bryn sneered, 'You! A little squirt like you? Ha!'

'Yes, a little squirt like me. Any more sniffing around Georgie and I will, God help me, I will.'

Something in the sparky way Dicky defied him triggered the idea that Dicky was intending to marry Georgie. 'I do believe you're thinking of marrying her, aren't you?' Bryn roared with laughter, holding his sides, his mouth wide open, his eyes screwed tight, his head thrown back. The sound of his amusement bounced from wall to wall. He got out a handkerchief and wiped his eyes. 'Oh, God! What a laugh. You and Georgie! Oh, my word!'

One customer crept round to the front of the meat counter to get a better view, another put down her basket and abandoned all pretence of shopping to stare, and Jimbo prepared to roll up his sleeves and break up a fight. But they were all disappointed because Dicky, red in the face with rage, drew himself up to his full height, all five feet four of it, and said, while prodding Bryn's chest with a forefinger, 'That's my intention. I want Georgie as my wife and she wants me. And by God, we will be together one day if I have to *kill* you to get her.'

Dicky stalked out of the door with such dignity that the observers almost clapped their approval, but then they looked at Bryn and saw a frightening mixture of hate and fear in his face which boded ill for Dicky. Poor chap.

Linda had stopped her pretence of counting her stock of stamp books. Mrs Jones, having come out to see the fun, scuttled back to her office in panic. Jimbo heaved a sigh of relief and the customers got on with their own affairs, mindful as they did so to give Bryn a wide berth.

He was rooted to the spot, apparently unaware of his surroundings. Jimbo watched Bryn almost shake himself and focus his eyes on Jimbo himself. Bryn laughed. 'Did I imagine that or did the little dwarf actually threaten to murder me?'

'He did.'

'My God! I'd like to see him try.' Bryn smoothed the front of his shirt and said, 'Right, Jimbo. Have you had any more thoughts about what we talked of yesterday?'

'Come into my office.' Jimbo jerked his head towards the back of the Store and strode off in front of Bryn.

Jimbo took off his boater and, carefully placing it on a shelf, slowly turned and said in measured tones, 'The next time you want to have a fight don't choose my Store as the venue.'

'Get on with you! You know full well it's good for trade and that's what matters to you, isn't it? They'll all be in here tomorrow hoping for a further instalment and what does that mean? More money in your tills. It's your Achilles heel, isn't it, Jimbo? Profit and more profit. You don't fool me. This morning's little episode will do this place no end of good.'

'Bluster doesn't impress me. So listen and get the message. I'm going along with the idea of souvenirs because I want to do it. Not because you've persuaded me but because it makes sound commercial sense. It'll be a long time before I see fit to give you a slice of the action. Right. Got that straight. If there is a repetition of this morning you'll never get a percentage no matter how big it is.

That man has a right to threaten you and I'd back him one hundred per cent. Not as far as murder, but certainly where his ambitions for Georgie are concerned. So . . . watch your step.' This time it was Jimbo's forefinger prodding Bryn's chest.

Bryn looked seriously disconcerted and backed off. 'OK. OK. I get the message. That's the trouble with this damned village: everyone thinks they have a right to take sides.'

Jimbo ignored him and moved on. 'Mm. This is a list of the ideas we've come up with and I'm getting organised.'

Bryn studied Jimbo's list and felt heartened by his enthusiasm. 'Excellent. Excellent. I like the idea of sweets in Turnham Malpas tins. And the pencils. And the doorstops.'

'Must press on. Be seeing you.'

'Can I keep this list?'

'You can.'

Jimbo watched him walk out of his office and shook his head in amazement. How could the chap dare to return? Attempted murder was the least of the charges the police could get him for. Yet here he was, throwing his weight about and expecting them all to be on his side. Scoffing at Dicky was idiotic and bound to cause bad blood. Only Harriet could settle his ruffled feathers, so he went in search of her.

4

The next morning was idyllic. It had been a wonderful spring and now the summer was living up to its name. Each morning dawned bright and warm, so much so that there were constant threats of reservoirs in danger of running dry and the possibility of hosepipe bans, but everyone was determined to enjoy the weather and ignore the warnings. Jimmy Glover went out early to inspect the pond and found it now only half full at the most.

His geese clustered round him, honking for food. He had ten fully grown ones and nine goslings, and they were a picture. Jimmy knew that there was some opposition to him keeping them, but there'd been geese belonging to the Glover family on the green for one hundred and fifty years and more. It said so in some old parish records and, though there were no more Glovers left to keep them after he'd gone, he'd every intention of finding someone who would take them on. Made a mess indeed. Threatened visitors indeed. Fouled the road. Huh! Grazed on the blooms in the tubs outside the cottages. Wandered into Neville Neal's garden and ate his ornamental flowers. So what if they did?

He sat himself down on the seat kindly provided by the council, opened up his plastic bag, and began pulling out pieces of bread and tossing them on the grass.

'Mr Glover! Mr Glover! Wait!'

Across the green came Beth Harris. A bonnier sight he couldn't hope to see. Her lovely ash-blonde hair in plaits today, her bright-blue eyes, so like the Rector's, sparkled with anticipation, and those lovely rounded cheeks of hers, rosy with the heat of the day, reminded him so much of ... She was wearing her white shorts with the cornflower-blue shirt that matched her eyes. What a treasure! 'All right, Beth, there's plenty left for you.'

'I thought I was too late. Isn't it a lovely day? Mummy's taking us into Culworth today, and we're going boating on the lake and taking a picnic. Do you like boating on the lake?'

'Not much. Can't swim.'

'I can. Daddy taught us both years ago. Alex is better than me, he swims like a fish, Mummy says, and he can dive. I can't.'

'You will one day. Here's another piece.'

Beth concentrated on feeding the geese. She liked the goslings best, their parents were so huge and got so angry if something didn't suit. When she was little she used to stand on the seat to feed them she was so afraid. 'Don't you think geese on the green is a lovely idea?'

Jimmy nodded.

'I do too. It's like an old-fashioned picture of a village, isn't it?'

'It is an old-fashioned village, that's why.'

'You're right. I hope the geese will always be here, for ever and ever, don't you?'

'I do that.'

'Have you got any children who can look after them when you are too old?'

'No.'

'I didn't think you had. I could look after them for you. That is, if you wouldn't mind.'

'That would be a grand idea.'

'You've no wife either, have you, Mr Glover?'

'Well, I don't talk about it much, but I did have a wife and I did have a baby but they both died when the baby was newborn.'

'I'm so sorry. I shouldn't have pried.'

Jimmy looked at her contrite face. 'That's all right. It happened a long time ago.' And somehow, talking to her, it didn't matter as much as it used to do. In fact, no one had mentioned it to him for donkey's years; perhaps no one except him remembered. He stared across the green thinking about the old pain and how time healed.

Beth sat on the seat beside him admiring her new trainers. She stuck up a foot and asked, 'Do you like these? As soon as I saw them I loved them. They were expensive but Daddy said I should have them.'

'He's a good chap, is your dad. We're all glad he came here.'

'He can get cross sometimes, you know, specially if we're mean. I hate it when he's cross, he makes me feel so bad.'

'Quite right. You shouldn't be mean.'

'No.' Beth sat silent for a moment, then she said, 'Mummy's lovely too.'

Jimmy nodded his approval. 'She is that. Always got time to listen, she has, even though she's busy with church and the practice and your dad and you two.'

'She's not actually my real, real mummy, you know.'

'I know.'

'She couldn't have babies so she adopted us.'

'That was a lucky day for you. You couldn't have a better mother, not anywhere in the whole wide world.'

Beth, still admiring her trainers with half her mind, banged her feet together to hear again the delicious clumping sound they made, and startled the geese. The goslings fled to the pond for safety, while the older geese stood their ground. 'We did have a mother, but she couldn't keep us.'

'I see.'

'Did you know our proper mummy?'

Jimmy unexpectedly found himself at the sharp end and terribly exposed. He'd walked right into that one and not seen it coming. He shooed away a goose trying to sneak off with his plastic bag, then made a pretence of fastening a bootlace to give himself time to think. 'I never lie, but I'm giving you fair warning that I am about to. No, I didn't know her.'

Beth studied Jimmy's statement. So he must mean he did know her but he wouldn't tell. Was she some dreadful person, then, whom no one wanted her to know about? Pictures of witches took form in her mind, dreadful people with chins that almost met their noses and wicked, cold grey eyes and blackened teeth. She shuddered. 'I'm going home; it's cold.'

'That's right. You go home and give that mummy of yours a kiss and hug her tight. She's worth it, she is. I wish she was mine.'

With eyes wide open with surprise Beth looked at Jimmy saying, 'You do?'

'I most certainly do. If I'd had a mother like yours I could have conquered the world.'

'You could?'

'Oh, yes. Mine, you see, didn't want me, so I was always a nuisance. Always telling me I was no good, and look where that got me? Long-time poacher and now part-time taxi driver. But I'd always fancied sailing the world, exploring and that, and writing books about it when I got back.'

'Really!'

'Oh, yes. The thing I would have liked to do most was to find an island no one else had ever seen and tell everyone about it, and they'd have to alter their maps to make room for it. Paradise Island I'd have called it.'

'Would you have lived there?'

'Possibly.' Jimmy stood up. 'Remember, with a mother like yours you can do anything in the world. She's a treasure, think on. And don't forget what I said about giving that mum of yours a hug as soon as you get in. It's time I took Sykes for a walk. Now I'm going to stand out here in the lane and watch you to your door. See you safe home.'

Beth said, 'I can take myself home now I'm ten.'

'I know that, but there's always cars come unexpected and I'd never look your mum in the face again if anything happened to you, you being so precious.'

''Bye, then, Mr Glover. Why do you never bring Sykes with you when you feed the geese?'

''Cos he's a bad lad and chases them, and they hate him for it and try to peck his tail.'

'Why does he chase them?'

'Jealous, that's what. Plain jealous, because he thinks I might just love the geese better than 'im.'

'But you don't, do you?'

Jimmy rubbed his chin and thought for a moment. 'All in all, I think Sykes might just have the edge.' He grinned down at her. 'I can talk to him and he understands, but these geese don't understand a blasted word I say.'

When Beth got to the Rectory door she turned to wave to him. He touched his cap to her as if she were a proper lady and shouted, 'Have a good day on the lake.'

'I will. The geese must be silly, Sykes hasn't got a tail.'

Jimmy had to smile. He went indoors hoping his mother would forgive him his outrageous fib about her. Still, it was in a good cause. Though the part about exploring and writing a book had been true; he'd just been too idle to get round to it.

He was about to set off with Sykes when there came a knock at the door. He heard it open and it was Bryn Fields, bright and breezy, dressed to kill. 'Come to see you about this scheme of mine. Have you a minute?'

Sykes ran at him, not knowing who he was and fancying he was a burglar at the very least. 'Sykes! That will do. He's a friend. I think.'

Sykes stopped barking and went to sniff Bryn's trouser leg.

'Five minutes, that's all, I'm just off out with Sykes.' He drew up a chair at the table for Bryn and sat himself down on the other one. 'Sit here, seeing as it's business.'

Jimmy listened open-mouthed to Bryn's plans, not letting on that he'd already overheard the drift of them in the Store one morning.

'And you want me to dress up and have a basket of bread to feed the geese and let them have a go.'

Bryn nodded. 'That's right, but not only that. I want you to tell them about your geese having been there for centuries and that yours are the descendants of geese the village had at the time of the plague . . . well, your family had, unbroken for fifteen generations, that kind of thing. I'm going to make a thing about it on the way here on the coach microphone you know, tell them how devastated the village was and about Stocks Day. "Same as that tree," you say and point to the old oak, and tell them that if the tree dies so will the village and how old it is.'

'Sounds a bit dodgy to me.'

'Not at all, they'll lap it up. Willie's going to mug up on the church history, and put on his old verger outfit and take them on a guided tour of the church.'

'Willie is?'

'He is. No doubt there'll be something in it for him.'

Jimmy thought over what he meant. 'Tips, yer mean?' He rubbed his thumb and forefinger together as though handling money.

'Exactly.'

'I see. Dress up, you said, you mean in my funeral suit?'

'Certainly not. No, I mean in some kind of old smock thing like old farmers used to wear.'

'I haven't got one of those. I'm sorry.'

'Pity. I'll have to apply my brains to that, then.'

'In a basket yer say.'

'Well, you can't have it in a plastic bag or something, can you. It wouldn't be in character.'

'You're not making me out to be the village idiot, are you? I'm not having that.'

'Certainly not. Simply a chap who's a real villager, a genuine memory they can take back with them to the States. I'm determined this is going to work. We'll all be making money at it, believe me.'

Jimmy stroked his chin, a habit he had when he was going to come out with some remark which would set the cat among the pigeons, as his old mother used to say. 'How about if I don't get any tips? I'm not doing it for nothing, not for no one.'

'I tell you what. You tell me what tips you get and if they don't add up to enough I'll add some to make it right.'

'And what if they add up to more than we expect? I'm not having you ripping me off.'

'Jimmy! I wouldn't do a thing like that. You know I'm as straight as a die.' Bryn looked affronted.

But Jimmy ignored that. 'Straight as a die. Oh, yes! That's why you took all Georgie's money, is it, when you flitted with that tart. That was very straight as a die. Don't take me for a fool.' Jimmy tapped the table sharply with his knuckles to emphasise his point.

'That was a big mistake on my part and has nothing to do with what we're talking about now. I'll think about it and come up with a sum of money I think will be fair.'

Jimmy frowned. 'It's all off if you don't play fair and square with me. I'm not having it. Come back when you've had another think.' He stood up, tucked his chair under the table, and indicated his

intention by taking his old poaching coat from the peg on the back
of the door and putting it on ready for walking Sykes.

'That's it! Poaching! You could tell some of your poaching tales.
I never thought about that.'

'How long have they got here, then?'

'Ah! Two hours and they've to eat lunch, go in the Store for
souvenirs, look around the church, listen to you.'

'Heck! They'll have it all to do at a run.'

'Leave it to me. I might squeeze in another half-hour. I'll look
into that. But I take it I have your co-operation, then? You'd like to
do it?'

'I think so. Twice this summer you say?'

Bryn nodded. 'That's right, more next year when I really get the
ball rolling. It's going to be a money spinner I can tell you. This
village is amazing, you know. No road signs, no street lights, no
house numbers, a real genuine backwater it is. They'll love it. We
live here and don't value it enough. It's normal to us, you see. To
people who live in New York it's a piece of living history.'

'*It is.*'

'I know, we need to remind ourselves, though, just how left
behind we are. Wonderful.' Bryn went to stand at Jimmy's front
door. 'I mean, just look at it. Where in the world would you see
houses still looking like they did the day they were built? Not a
single house out of character. The only eyesore is the bus stop
outside the Store. There's nothing else to spoil it, is there?'

'That's right, if yer don't look at Neville Neal's house. Or at Sir
Ralph's Hipkin Gardens.'

'I know, but even those have been sensitively designed.'

'I'll give you that. Right, I'm off.' Wryly Jimmy added, 'I've no
doubt you'll be back.'

Bryn found himself being turned out, but he didn't mind. He'd
won his case, so another piece of his jigsaw was falling into place.
He paused for a moment, watching Jimmy and Sykes wandering off
down Stocks Row towards the spare land. No need for a lead for
Sykes, just the right kind of freedom for a dog, but only this village
could provide it. Imagine that, no zebra crossings, no one-way
signs, nothing to mar the beauty of it. Bryn closed his eyes and felt
himself to be back centuries, then the peace was disturbed by the

sound of a car. When he opened his eyes he saw it was Sylvia Biggs, driving past the Royal Oak and on to heaven knew where. He glanced at his watch, half past nine, Georgie wouldn't be downstairs yet, give her another half-hour and she'd be having her morning coffee and he'd join her, with a bit of luck, and they could discuss their plans in more detail. Frankly, at the moment he found her presence enjoyable in a way he'd never found Elektra's. What a fool he'd been not to have seen the signs earlier and done something about winning Georgie back before it was all too late. Well, in his book it was never too late.

He found himself outside the Store where Jimbo was standing gazing at his new window display. 'Good morning, Jimbo.'

'Oh, right, good morning. What do you think then? Give me your opinion.'

'Absolutely excellent. If that doesn't empty your freezers of ready meals I don't know what will.'

Jimbo stepped further back and looked up to assess the impact the headquarters of his empire was making.

Bryn, in order to ingratiate himself, said, 'It's so good, I'm surprised you don't open another one in a similar situation.'

'With mail order and catering and this, I've enough on my plate. Another outlet would spread me too thinly and I'd spend too much time running back and forth, till in the end I'd finish up doing nothing well. No, we do better with just this. I've a couple of sample souvenirs to show you.' He strode off into the Store without bothering to see if Bryn was following, but he was right behind him, glad Jimbo was so enthusiastic.

When he emerged again into the front of the Store he found Georgie paying for some groceries. Bel had them packed into two bulging bags. Bryn said, 'Allow me. I was just coming across to see you.'

'Only to talk business.'

'Yes, and a coffee. I know there'll be one going about now. You see, I haven't forgotten your little ways, have I?' He heaved the bags from the counter, Georgie opened the door and the two of them went off down Stocks Row.

At that moment Dicky was outside at the front of the pub watering the window boxes with the hosepipe. He bent down to test the compost in the tubs and as he straightened up he caught sight of Georgie's bright-orange top. He made to wave but saw that Bryn was with her. They were both absorbed in conversation and hadn't noticed him. Damn him. The two of them had a togetherness he didn't like. A kind of companionableness which even four years of separation hadn't dented. Dicky snapped off the hosepipe and began winding it up on to his forearm. He disconnected it from the tap on the wall and carried it into the bar, leaving the door propped open, thinking Georgie and Bryn would follow.

He only had to see Bryn and the few doubts he had about Georgie's love surged to the front of his consciousness. She'd promised to ask Bryn for a divorce but he knew full well she hadn't. Dicky went to put the hosepipe away by the back door and found himself an unwitting eavesdropper. The two of them were standing just outside the back entrance talking.

'It's no good, Bryn, I don't object to doing business with you but as for anything else, well, it's Dicky you see, we want to marry.'

He heard Bryn gasp. 'So it's true, then. What are you thinking of, Georgie? For heaven's sake. The man is a twat. A runt. He's got no business acumen, nothing. And what about my share of the business? Eh? What about that? Our partnership has never been dissolved and I know he couldn't buy me out in a month of Sundays. Come to your senses, woman.'

'Don't you "woman" me. The money is no problem, he has the promise of whatever's needed for buying into the partnership and that's what I want him to do. Buy you out! Not that you deserve it considering how much money you took with you when you went off with that tart. You can try your best, Bryn, but I am marrying Dicky and I want a divorce *now*, or the lunch business is off.'

Dicky considered coughing in order to let them know he was there but the chance to hear the outcome of this conversation was not to be missed and he stayed where he was.

Bryn began laughing, that head-thrown-back, loud, mocking laugh he'd used before. When he calmed down he said, 'You wouldn't do that to me. Not to me! We mean too much to each other.'

'Now I know where you are I shall instruct my solicitor. I've plenty of evidence. I want a divorce immediately. Then Dicky and I can marry. He'll move in here and Bel will go to her house, which she longs to get back to. I can't wait to get my life straight. OK?'

'I don't want a divorce.'

'Well, you're getting one.'

'So where's he getting the money from to buy my share?'

Quickly Dicky dropped the hosepipe on the stone floor, swore loudly, picked it up and meandered through the door as though he'd just that moment arrived. He'd always known he was cut out to be an actor. He smiled at Georgie and said, 'Alan's made the coffee, when you're ready' and brushed past Bryn as though he didn't exist, hung the hosepipe on the bracket ready for another time and calmly went back into the bar. So she did want him. She did. He punched the air, triumphant. A triumph tinged with a bitter hatred of Bryn.

But Bryn wasn't aware of the rage burning in Dicky and after he'd had an enjoyable chat with Alan and a quiet word with Georgie he set off back to Neville's to use his computer for writing some business letters. On the way he noticed the church door was open so he decided to go in and have a look around to value its potential for a conducted tour. As he went up the church path he felt goosepimples coming up on his skin and didn't look up at the church tower. He must have been mad at the time, absolutely mad. He went in and began walking about. There appeared to be no one around so he assumed he must have the church to himself.

Some long forgotten memory surfaced as he looked at one of the tombs. Surely tombs were supposed to lie from east to west in a church, but this one lay north to south; how odd. He'd get Willie to look it up, there was definitely some history attached to it. He studied the carved screen, stood for a moment in the war memorial chapel looking at the names on the roll of honour. My God! Biggses and Joneses and Neals and Parkins, and *four* Glover brothers, and that was the list for the First World War. Sobering thought. He made a note in his little book to remind Willie to point out to the tourists about the four Glovers and then they'd meet one of their descendants on the green. What a touch. They'd be eating out of his hand in no time. Brilliant! On a special plaque of its own he read of the Templetons of Turnham House who'd also given their all for their country; in the American War of Independence, the Crimea, the Boer War and the two World Wars. What a history! What a sacrifice! For one brief moment Bryn wondered if he really should be making money from such tragedy, but quickly comforted himself with the thought that as they were all dead, and had been for years, they wouldn't be any the wiser.

The lights were on, but it was gloomy in the church because the storm clouds, which had been gathering over and beyond the bypass all morning, had finally arrived. The rain began clattering against the windows above the altar, beating a strange rhythmic tattoo on the stained glass, then lightning filled the church with a blaze of startling blue-white light, followed by the most enormous clap of thunder Bryn had ever heard in his life. Directly overhead, it appeared to make even the foundations of the building shudder. It was closely followed by another flash of lightning, which illumi-nated the whole of the window behind the altar and made the figure of Christ appear to move. In horror, Bryn sucked in his breath through clenched teeth. Thunder followed immediately, just as loud and close as the first clap. Bryn, who couldn't remember having been as frightened ever before, not even as a kid watching a horror film, grasped the end of the nearest pew for support. For the first time in years he prayed. For the first time in years he felt a need to cower and hide. However, in the nick of time the man in him resisted. But the storm didn't abate for ten whole minutes by which time he was a wreck. The thunder and lightning passed over, the glowering skies lightened, gradually the rain reduced to a gentle pattering and the church once more became the friendly, secure place it always was. He sat down in a pew, wiped the sweat from his face and hands, and pulled himself together.

'All right, Bryn?'

Bryn almost shot out of his skin at the sound of the voice so kindly enquiring after his health. He turned, dreading whom he might see. It was Peter. Relief. What a relief. That was odd, Peter was completely dry so if he'd only just come in how could he be . . . ?

Bryn held out his hand. 'My, what a storm! Never known the like, not even a tropical storm.'

Peter shook hands saying, 'How are you? I've been going to call.'

'I'm well and you?'

Peter nodded. 'Fine, thanks. You've come back to make things right for Georgie then?'

Bryn was about to say yes but as always Peter's blue eyes saw right through him and he couldn't tell a lie – well, not a serious one anyway. 'I've come back to help make amends, yes.'

'Good! May I sit down? Have you time to talk?'

'Oh, yes.' He moved down the pew a little and Peter sat beside him.

'What do you propose?' Peter rested his elbow on the back of the pew and waited for a reply.

Bryn knew all about Peter's ability to leave a silence, which one felt compelled to fill immediately and which often made one fall right into a trap of one's own making, but he thought for a while before answering. 'I'm bringing some business to Georgie and the pub, and the rest of the village if they want it.'

'This American tourist business.'

'That's right.' Bryn got carried away explaining his plans, embroidering his spiel here and there to make it more appealing, mentioning the tour of the church and his hope that the tourists might contribute to church funds. He'd thought about a collection plate or something . . .

'I'm not sure I like the idea of people paying to enter a house of God.'

'There wouldn't be a fixed charge, just . . .' He searched for the word. 'Donations.'

'I'll think about that. Sounds an excellent idea, but I wasn't meaning your business plans at all. I meant making things right so Dicky can marry Georgie.'

Again that dratted silence of his.

This time Bryn had no defence against it and, fumbling in his mind for a reply, said the first idiotic thing that came into his head. 'Let's be honest here, padre, she won't do herself any good at all marrying that little squirt. What does he know about business? He's a non-starter, he is. No, I'm doing her a favour by *not* divorcing her.'

'I don't believe in divorce, Bryn, but I have come to realise that if life is hell then something has to be done about it. I can think of not one single thing in your favour that could persuade me you are not under a moral obligation to release Georgie.'

After he sorted out what Peter meant, Bryn's jaw dropped open.

Peter got to his feet. 'I mean it. In my view the cards are all stacked against you. Give it some thought. If you need someone to talk it over with, my door is always open.'

Bryn watched Peter walk towards the choir vestry and hardened his heart to his advice. Divorce? Not likely. Perhaps things wouldn't get back entirely to what they were – after all, he'd be travelling to the States drumming up business and then he'd be going round England escorting his tours – but divorce was out. Bryn stood up and decided to go into the churchyard for a breath of air now the rain had virtually stopped.

He stood under a tree and looked over the wall towards Turnham House. Magnificent building, that. One day, you never knew, he might be living in such a house. He mused on the subject for a while, realising that it would be no fun without Georgie.

The moral dilemma Peter had presented to him niggled away at the back of his mind. What the hell, she was still his legal wife and he would resist divorce with every fibre of his body. Her marrying that ... he cringed at the prospect of Dicky being Georgie's husband. It was like something out of one of Dicky's joke books. He focused his eyes on the figure crossing the field between him and Turnham House. It was Jimmy returning from his walk. Way behind him came a flash of white and black: Sykes hurrying to catch up. Bryn thought, he's going to get back into the village by crossing Rector's Meadow and then climbing the gate into Pipe and Nook.

But Jimmy changed direction and appeared to be heading for the little gate in the churchyard wall. Well, he couldn't be bothered with Jimmy at the moment, he'd too much on his mind, so Bryn set off down the church path, into Church Lane and turned through the gates of Glebe House.

Jimmy had changed his intended route because he'd seen some people emerge from the little copse which backed up to the churchyard wall and wondered what they were up to. There'd been gypsies about for a while and he thought maybe they were them, making a reconnaissance of the church with a view to theft. But as he drew closer he recognised Gilbert Johns. Jimmy waved. Gilbert called out, 'Hi!' The three young people who were with Gilbert also waved. They were carrying papers and clipboards and measuring tapes and, despite sheltering in the copse, were soaking wet.

'What you up to, Gilbert? Thinking of buying this place, are you?' He jerked his head in the direction of the Big House.

Gilbert laughed. 'No. No. These three are archaeology students; they're working in my department for a few weeks. We're looking for the possible site of a plague pit somewhere close to the church wall. We know there is one and we think it might be in this copse.'

Jimmy stood stock still. Sykes, who by now had caught up with him, bristled and growled and, when he saw Jimmy looking as though he intended to walk forward towards Gilbert, he flattened himself to the ground showing his teeth in a nasty snarl and then, apparently overcome by terror, fled under the gate into the churchyard and disappeared.

'You're not thinking of digging?'

'We might, if we decide it's the right place.'

'You'd better not, all hell'll be let loose.'

Gilbert smiled and the students sniggered, hiding their laughter behind their clipboards.

'You can laugh. No one goes in that copse. See my dog? He gives that copse a wide berth every time we come past. I couldn't *drag* 'im in there even if I wanted to, which I don't. Take my advice and leave well alone. We all do, that's why it's so overgrown. The groundsmen never touch it.'

'Come on, you know more than you're saying. Tell all.'

It was the long pause before Jimmy answered that made the students want to laugh out loud. Gilbert repeated, 'Tell all.'

'Old people around here, *if* they mention it at all, call it . . . Deadman's Dell.'

The students shouted, 'We're right, that'll be it.' They almost danced a jig at the prospect.

Gilbert raised an eyebrow. 'Deadman's Dell? Really? That sounds hopeful.'

Jimmy backed off. 'You're not thinking of . . . like . . . digging there, are you?'

'We very well might.'

'It's not right, it's irreverent, that is, digging for bones. Didn't them poor devils suffer enough before they died, never mind digging 'em up now? Them could be ancestors of folk who still live hereabouts. It's not right. No, grave robbing's not right.'

The students looked scornful. Gilbert said quietly, 'As county archaeologist I can guarantee that whatever we do – if, in fact, we do anything at all – would be done with the greatest respect.'

Jimmy backed off a little further. 'It'll be safer if you do nothing at all. We don't want that copse digging up; tempting fate, that is, tempting fate.' Jimmy wagged his finger at them. 'It's already started. What do yer think that storm was about? It was a warning, that's what. Leave well alone, do you hear me? Serve yer bloody right if you all get the plague yerselves.' He walked off towards the little gate, put his hand on it, briefly turned back to look at them, wagged his finger again, and shouted, 'Take heed! You'll be cursed!' Then he went through and disappeared from sight.

The students at first doubled up with laughter and then fell silent, suddenly feeling concerned.

'Cursed?'

'Where have we come? I mean, don't they know in this village that it's the twenty-first century. We haven't gone into a time warp, have we?'

Gilbert assured them that no, they hadn't, and that Jimmy was being incredibly naïve and of course they weren't cursed; there was no such thing as being cursed and with Mr Fitch's permission they'd investigate. Mr Fitch, he knew, would give the go-ahead without hesitation, because he was a practical, down-to-earth man who would love nothing better than . . .

'But should we be disturbing ancient bones? After all, they've been buried there more than six hundred years. What would we gain when all's said and done?'

Gilbert placed a finger on his temple. 'Knowledge. A paper published. Progress.'

'And afterwards?'

'To appease everyone we'd have the bones interred in the churchyard with a headstone or a plaque, and we'll have a funeral service, which they wouldn't have had at the time of the plague. No priest, no time.'

'Gilbert, be honest, you must be feeling a bit of concern because you used the word "appease".'

'Only because these people are superstitious beyond belief. They'll imagine all kinds of terrible things will happen, which could have happened anyway even without us opening up that pit. Right? I'll see the Rector, too, on Sunday and make it right with him.'

Jimmy had expected to find Sykes waiting for him outside his cottage door, but he wasn't there. Eventually he went looking for him in the church, it being Sykes's second home, and found him shivering and afraid, hiding under a pew in the very darkest corner. Jimmy knelt down and peered under the seat. 'Come on, Sykes, old chap. Jimmy'll take you home. Come on, now.' But Sykes wouldn't come and had to be dragged out by his scruff, and carried home because he refused to walk. Sykes cowered in his bed for the rest of the morning and only came out when Jimmy, in desperation, offered him a saucer of warm milk sweetened with a spoonful of honey which, in Sykes's opinion, came a very close second to Dicky's home-brewed ale.

5

Jimmy didn't go to Culworth station to work his taxi that night; he went to the pub instead and hoped to find as many local people as he could to whom he could relate his experience of the morning. With Sykes tucked under the settle, he had a small crowd gathered round him listening avidly in no time at all. 'So-o-o, it has to be stopped.' Jimmy took a pull at his ale, banged the tankard down and waited for some reaction.

Vince Jones, now doorstop manufacturer and picture framer to Charter-Plackett Enterprises, scratched his head and said a little scornfully, 'I reckon you're making too much of this thunderstorm business. It wasn't that bad.'

'You should have been out in it. I was. I know.'

'It was pure coincidence, that's what. Wasn't it, Willie?'

Willie, who had experienced funny coincidences in the past with a tomb in the church, didn't dismiss Jimmy's argument quite so decisively. 'He could have a point. There's some funny things happen because of the past. But what's the use of digging up old bones, what would they do with 'em when they'd got 'em? Nothing. Rector won't agree anyway, believe me.'

Jimmy looked towards Sylvia and asked her what she thought.

'Well, that would be for the Rector to say, he knows best. But I think they should be dug up and buried right.'

'It's not on holy ground, though, so it's got nothing to do with 'im. If anyone can protest it's old Fitch, it's on his land.'

Mrs Jones piped up, 'I reckon Willie is right, what does it matter anyway? There's more important things than a few old bones, Jimmy.'

'Not much more important if it brings destruction down on the village. It doesn't do to interfere with the past. Just think, Vince, they might be ancestors of yours.' Certain he'd thought up a reason which would bring Vince out in support, Jimmy had another long drink of his ale and waited for Vince's reaction.

'You've backed the wrong horse there, Jimmy. My great-grandfather came from the Rhondda Valley way back, but definitely not as far back as them bones. So they're not my relatives.'

'No, Vince, but they could be mine.' Mrs Jones suddenly discovered a deep empathy with those bones in Deadman's Dell. 'There's been Flatmans in the parish records for years. I think I might have a right to a say what happens to 'em.'

Vince snorted his disdain at her fanciful idea. 'Get on, yer daft beggar, what the hell does it matter?'

Willie, brought abruptly to life by Sylvia's championing of the bones burial question, demanded, 'You mean you'd go against me?'

'Well, yes, I think I would. They've a right to Christian burial, they have.' Sylvia shuddered as though she were being asked to be buried in unholy ground. Sensing a row brewing, however, she said, 'Anyways, they could dig and find nothing at all, so I'm not going to worry myself about it till it happens, if it ever does. Willie, go get the drinks in. Will you join us Mrs Jones, Vince?'

They'd just got themselves nicely settled with their drinks at Jimmy's table when in came Bryn Fields. Jimmy debated as to whether or not Bryn would support him and decided that he didn't want him on his side anyway, so he'd keep quiet. But he hadn't bargained for Alan Crimble having overheard their conversation while he'd been going round collecting empty glasses.

Alan served Bryn his drink and then, leaning confidentially on the bar counter while Bryn downed his first whisky of the day, he confided what he'd heard.

Bryn listened with great concentration, wondering how he could turn this to his advantage. Of course! Willie could show the tourists the site of the plague pit and make the point about bones interred there being those of ancestors of people still living in the village. It all fitted in beautifully. Maybe they could put up a plaque, 'Here lie victims of the Black Death', in old-fashioned writing. My word!

Things were coming together better than he could ever have hoped. 'Thanks, Alan. That might come in useful.'

'O' course, Jimmy's convinced that storm was caused by them students poking about in the Dell. Reckons we'll be in right trouble.'

Bryn pushed his glass across the counter and intimated he wanted a refill. That storm. He still felt distinctly iffy about it. Could Jimmy be right? God! This place was getting to him. He'd got a turnip for a head if he thought like that. By the time he'd drunk his second whisky he'd got things under control. This was a real gift, oh, yes! An absolute gift. Well, he'd bide his time and play the long game. Talk about a stroke of luck. By Jove! Things couldn't be better.

The question of Deadman's Dell became the main topic of conversation in the bar. It spread to the dining room to people wholly unconnected with the village, people who only saw it as a quaint place to eat on a summer's evening, but they also had opinions on the matter. Roughly, had there been a head count, they were divided fifty-fifty as to whether or not the Dell should be the subject of an archaeological dig.

Gilbert Johns, in the choir vestry the following morning organising his collection of choirboys into an angelic chorus, remembered that he had to speak to Peter after the service about the Dell, as he chastised one boy for his crumpled surplice, another for his unruly hair, held out a tissue to a third, demanding he remove his chewing gum, reminded the youngest member not to rustle sweet papers during prayers and asked for silence.

Twenty pairs of eyes looked up at him and Gilbert said, as he always did, 'Good morning, chaps. We'll run through our exercises, get ourselves in trim. Ready?' He raised his hand, gave them their note and started them off on a pattern of chords and scales they could have done in their sleep. They'd sung in cathedrals and won choir competitions under his tutelage, and next to archaeology the choir was his passion. Gilbert was so proud of them all, and they in their turn worshipped him. He had the knack of treating them as equals, yet keeping control, of bringing out the best in them but not demanding more than they had to give. This September two of them would be going to cathedral choir schools, and there weren't many village church choirs could boast of that. All in all they were a brilliant bunch and what was so encouraging was the list of boys waiting their turn to join. They came from Turnham Malpas, Penny Fawcett and Little Derehams, and even from as far away as Culworth.

Gilbert checked his watch: nine fifty-nine precisely. He cocked an ear for Mrs Peel's final trill before ... there it was. 'Ready. Quiet now. Here we go.' He snapped a thumb and finger twice, his signal for them to adopt what he called their 'church face', and opened the door. Whether it was the ruffs around their necks or the glowing red of the choirboys' cassocks or their shining morning faces, the hearts of the congregation always lifted when the choir appeared and quite a few female hearts fluttered at the sight of Gilbert processing down the aisle. He had his choirmaster face on and didn't even see his Louise, freed from their three little ones by the crèche to sit for an hour in comparative peace.

Once the service was over and he had dismissed the choir he went in search of Peter. He found him in his vestry removing his surplice. 'There you are.'

Peter said, 'I am. I expect you've come to see me about the Dell?'

'You know, then.'

'I do. They're all talking about it and expecting me to stop you doing it. Shall I?'

'Do you want to?'

Peter sat on the edge of the table, folded his arms and asked 'Do you want me to?'

'In fact, you can't, because if we're right it isn't on church land.'

'Somehow, though, overnight, bones have become my responsibility.' With a wry smile on his face Peter asked, 'You tell me what is really happening.'

'As opposed to rumours and counter-rumours.'

'That's right.'

'We think there's a pit, dug at the time of the plague, where they buried people because they had no priest to hold services and they were dying so fast they'd no one to dig proper graves so they did the next best thing: dug a big hole outside church land and bunged them all in. If we are proved right, which we can only do by digging, we shall examine the remains, find out what we can. Then what I propose, with your approval, obviously, is to hold a service and bury them in the churchyard. That way they'll have had a funeral service and be buried on consecrated ground even though it's … what? … six hundred and more years late.'

Peter sat thinking for a moment, head down, staring at a worn patch in the vestry carpet. 'No doubt I shall be harangued from Little Derehams to Penny Fawcett for agreeing but yes, I think you should, mainly because I prefer the idea of them being buried in consecrated ground and only for that reason, and you can tell everyone I shall conduct the funeral service.'

'Thanks. You know we'll deal with everything with the greatest respect.'

'Of course. I wouldn't expect anything other. Mr Fitch will be delighted, he loves anything like this. I hope you'll make sure for his sake that it gets into the papers.' He grinned at Gilbert who raised a finger in acknowledgement of Peter's understanding of the workings of Mr Fitch's mind.

'I shall be seeing him tomorrow. He'll be glad of your approval, likes to be seen nowadays "doing what's right by the village". Must go. Louise will be champing at the bit to be off.'

'Your brood OK?'

'Fine, thanks.'

'Good. Doesn't get easier the older they get.'

'Thanks for the warning. Talking of warnings, there's going to be a lot of opposition. Apparently that storm we had was solely a warning to me for poking about in the Dell and worse is about to fall if we continue. Just thought I'd say.'

'I can see what they mean, though.'

They both laughed.

Gilbert left, then came back and, putting his head round the vestry door, said, 'By the way, thanks. Grateful for your support.'

As he went to gather up Louise and the children he met Bryn who had paid one of his rare visits to church that morning. He was lurking by the lych-gate clumsily clutching the baby, while Louise was playing a complicated chasing game between the gravestones with the two older ones. Bryn handed the baby to him saying, 'Here, this is yours. I was waiting for a word.'

'Be my guest.'

'I want you to know you have my full support over the Dell. I've been thinking, if you find what you think you'll find, how about a plaque, say, on the church wall by the little gate explaining all about it?'

'Where my hunches are concerned, I've learned to wait and see until I'm proved right. Everything points to us being right but one never knows. However, it would be Peter who would have to give permission for that.'

'Well, I just wanted you to know that at least you have *my* full support. We should know about these things, it's important to the village's history.'

Rather sourly, for him, Gilbert replied, 'To say nothing of your tourist scheme, eh?' The baby began to stir fretfully. 'This baby is about to scream for his food and my mother-in-law will be frothing at the mouth; she's expecting us for lunch. Will you excuse us?'

Bryn opened his mouth to protest that he was only thinking of the good of the village, but Gilbert shouted, 'Louise! Come!' and she did, scooping up the two gravestone chasers as she came, so before he could explain himself properly to Gilbert they were already crossing the green.

By Saturday a fire was burning near Deadman's Dell. The students had arrived that morning in a dilapidated old car equipped with rakes, billhooks and thick gloves to clear the undergrowth before commencing their dig.

A small group of onlookers had gathered, among them Alex and Beth from the Rectory, having spied the activity from the attic window, Bryn who tried to pretend he hadn't a vested interest in their success but seriously failing to do so, going so far as to offer to supervise the bonfire, Willie leaning on the church wall, Fran and Flick who'd had a phone call from Beth in case they were at a loose end, and Mrs Jones who'd walked up to the village to go to a coffee morning in the church hall but couldn't resist taking a peek, having no doubts that numerous Flatman ancestors were about to see the light of day.

Willie, concerned that the children were getting far too close to the fire, called out, 'Beth! Alex! You'll have a better view if you sit on the wall.' He patted the top of the wall and hoped they'd come; the two of them could come up with some devilish arguments for doing exactly as they wished, arguments which defeated his powers of reasoning. Fortunately for him they saw the merits of his idea and came running. Beth, to her fury, couldn't get up onto the wall and he had to lean over and help her, but Alex had sprung up without assistance. Beth put out her tongue at Alex, then settled herself after she'd found a smooth piece of coping stone on which to sit. The two of them talked non-stop to Willie and he had to admit to a sigh of relief when he spotted Sylvia arriving with a bag of sweets.

Beth spied the bag immediately. 'Sylvia! Are those sweets for Willie?'

'They were, but I dare say he's kind enough to share.'

They were assorted sweets from the pick'n'mix in Tesco's, and Beth loved the Turkish delights. With her mouth full of chocolate and Turkish delight, Beth asked Sylvia if she thought she might have ancestors in the pit.

'I doubt it. My great-grandmother came from far, far away.'

'How far?'

'Scotland.'

'That's a long way. What about your great-grandfather?'

'Same. Came to work on Nightingale Farm.'

Beth considered this for a while, watching the great piles of brushwood the students were heaping on the fire, and helping herself to another sweet from Sylvia's bag. 'Just think, if we'd got seven children in our house like the Nightingales . . .'

'Thank heavens you haven't, I don't think I'd have coped. Think of the ironing.'

It was almost possible to hear the workings of Beth's mind. 'Did you work at the Rectory *before* we were born?'

There was a cautious note in Sylvia's voice when she replied, 'No, I started when you were about four weeks old.'

'So you remember us being born, then?'

'No. I've just said you were about four weeks old.'

'Does Willie remember?'

'They'll be needing a saw for them thick branches. I'll go and get one for 'em.' Willie beat a quick retreat, and Alex in his absence dropped down off the wall and went to help Bryn with the fire.

Beth turned her guns on Sylvia again. 'Did you know my mummy isn't my mummy?'

'Yes, but if you're going to ask me if I knew your real mummy, I didn't. It's like I said, you were four weeks old when I came to live in. Now watch the fire, it's getting bigger and bigger, isn't it?'

Beth agreed. She felt the urge to know about her mother much more than Alex did. They'd discussed it a lot these last few weeks when no one was about and he'd refused to try to find out. But she couldn't help herself. Something kept rising in her chest, something she couldn't make go away, a need to *know*, a need to feel, a need to talk about her real mother. Daddy was Daddy and Alex was like him, so much like him it was unbelievable and the bigger he grew the more like Daddy he looked. But Beth Harris didn't look like anyone she knew. It certainly wasn't Harriet or Miss Pascoe at school, or any of the mothers who gathered at the school gate or taught in the Sunday School or helped with the Brownies or walked the streets of Culworth. She was always on the lookout and had not yet seen anyone with her rounded cheeks, her fair skin, or her thick ash-blonde hair, or her sturdy legs, no one at all. So where was she, this mother of hers and Alex? Maybe she'd died when they were born. That could be it! Having twins must be hard work. As Miss Pascoe had said in those lessons they'd had, mothers had to push their babies out and she'd had it to do twice!

Willie came back with the saw but took care not to stand anywhere close to Beth. She knew why. He didn't want to tell her anything if he could avoid it. Nobody did. She wasn't a logical person at all, she left all that to Alex, but like a flash of light she realised that the only, only person she could ask who really would know and would give her a truthful answer was her daddy.

So one day she would take her chance. He didn't bath her any more now she was grown-up. In the past that had always been a good time to talk, so she'd ... the fire was out of control, smoke was billowing and blowing straight at her, Sylvia was coughing and waving her arms, shouting, 'Children! Come with me. Alex! Where's Alex?' It caught the lower twigs of a tree growing inside the churchyard wall, the breeze aiding and abetting its spread. 'Alex! Where are you?'

Beth stood up on the wall and screamed, 'Alex! Alex!'

Sylvia pulled her down and hurried her away, insisting she stood by a gravestone well away from the fire and didn't move. Then Beth saw flames leaping, smoke rising in great clouds, voices shouting; that was Willie, that was Bryn, that was Sylvia. Flick and Fran joined her and they stood huddled together, horrified; the tree which had given up its lower branches to the scorching heat now took on a fire all of its own and the flames crackled and licked up the branches.

Willie raced by calling, 'Go home, out of the way.'

Flick tried to move her away but Beth refused to go. 'Alex! Alex!' she kept shouting. 'Alex!' Great sobs exploded in her chest. 'Alex!'

With her eyes squeezed tight with fear she didn't see him come running through the little gate. 'Isn't it a great fire? It's caught two trees in the churchyard now.' His face was aglow with excitement. 'Willie's gone for the hose.'

Beth opened her eyes, truly saw him standing there in front of her, unharmed and ready to burst with excitement and, fuelled by relief, all the fear balled up inside her went into the beating she gave him. Her fists flying, her feet kicking, her voice hoarse with shouting, she charged him time and again, and it wasn't until Caroline came running and took hold of her that she stopped.

Willie fastened the hose to the tap in the wall, Bryn and one of the students heaved the reel over into the field and unwound it as fast as they could, Willie turned on the tap but the flow from one hose made little impression at first. Gradually it began to get the fire under control. By then, though, everyone from the coffee morning and most of the villagers living around the green were in the churchyard watching.

Caroline was sitting apart on a flat gravestone, hugging Beth, with Alex standing beside them, puzzled by her onslaught. 'I didn't do anything, Mum, honestly I didn't. It was her.'

'I know you didn't. She was frightened, that's all.'

'It's a brilliant fire, isn't it? It happened whoosh! Just like that. I was throwing twigs and things on and then whoosh! Up it went. I was there right in the middle of it all. Did you see the flames?'

'All right, Alex, that will do. Yes, I did, that's why I'm here.'

Beth wriggled free of her mother's arms and looked at Alex through her tears. 'I thought you'd been burned up.'

'No-o-o. Not me. I was too quick.'

'I shouted and shouted.'

Brimming with excitement, Alex told her he couldn't hear her shout for the crackling of the flames. 'You should have seen it.'

'I did!' Fresh tears rolled down her cheeks. She put her arms round Caroline's neck and buried her face in her shoulder. 'Go away, you *stupid* boy.'

Caroline began to laugh, as much with relief as anything else. 'Oh, darling, I do love you. I'd have wanted to do just the same.'

'Hit him?'

'Well, perhaps not quite so hard as you did, but yes. It's being glad they're all right, isn't it? After being so frightened.'

'I thought he'd b-b-burned up like a guy.'

'Here, let's wipe your face.' Caroline took out a tissue and dabbed Beth's face for her, smiling with love while she did. 'There we are, you're all presentable now. Better?'

Beth nodded. There was nothing quite like a good hug when you're frightened and Caroline knew just how to hug her to make her better. Perhaps she'd leave finding out about her own mother till she was bigger. Then, looking over Caroline's shoulder, she saw her daddy striding between the graves towards them, looking both relieved and angry at the same time. He'd given her his blue eyes, she could see that. She squeezed Caroline's neck more tightly. There was no doubt that he was their daddy. He came over and gave them both a hug and a kiss. 'I couldn't get off the phone. Thank heavens you're all right. Where's Alex?'

Beth answered him, 'The stupid boy is in the field.'

'Whose fault is this?'

Caroline, her hand cradling his as it gripped her shoulder, said, 'No one's. I think it just happened.'

'I'll go and see. Coming, Beth?'

She shook her head in reply and held tight to Caroline, content to wallow in security and love for a while longer. 'You're the best mummy ever.' Gradually the excitement of the fire got to her and, filled with curiosity, she disentangled herself and stood up. 'I'll just go and see what he's up to, the stupid boy.'

He was standing by, listening to his father tearing a strip off the students and Bryn.

'Didn't it occur to you that the fire should have been made much further away from the wall. I am surprised at you. Where is Gilbert?'

'Coming.'

'Is he indeed. Well, I suppose we have to be thankful it didn't spread to the church hall. There's one thing about it, you won't have to clear the Dell any more, the fire's done it for you.'

Deadman's Dell was now a charred mess. The trees were only blackened and scarred on their trunks, leaving the twigs and leaves more or less untouched and would soon recover, but the undergrowth was totally burned away exposing rich-looking soil undisturbed for centuries and, once the sun had done its job and dried the blackened grass and weeds, digging would be easy.

Peter stood gazing down at the soil wondering what secrets it might or might not reveal. He turned his attention to Alex. 'You've learned a lesson this morning. Tell me what it is.'

'Fire's dangerous?'

'And unpredictable.'

'And *strong*. Whooosh!' Alex imitated the flames with his hands, swooping them here and there in wild, excitable gestures.

'Powerful's the word. Never to be tampered with. Never to be regarded lightly.'

'I see that.'

'Good. So long as you've learned to treat it with respect. Like the sea, when it's out of your control it's your master not your friend.'

'Fire's a friend when it keeps you warm. Fire's a friend when it cooks your dinner. It's a friend for a blacksmith ... and a glass blower.'

'Because they don't let it get out of hand, do they? Life's precious and you're precious. I wouldn't want to make you afraid of life, but if you take risks, Alex, then make sure they're calculated risks.' Peter put a protective arm round Alex's shoulders.

Taken off his guard by finding himself unexpectedly in the midst of a confidential talk, Alex took a step he never intended to. 'Man to man, Dad, are you my dad?'

'I am.'

'Then who's my mother? It's not Mum, is it? I remember she said so years ago.'

'No. As she told you, she can't have children, so someone else had you for us. You'll have to be content with that for now.'

'All right. But . . .'

Seeing Beth skipping towards them, Peter answered sharply, 'Enough, Alex.'

'But . . .'

'Enough.' He despised himself for not being truthful, he who valued truth so highly in all his relationships. 'If you want to see the start of that film, we'd better go home for lunch right now. Has Mummy gone home, Beth?'

Beth nodded. 'Will they really find bones, Daddy?'

'Gilbert hopes so.'

'I shan't be a bone person.'

'Neither shall I. I'm going to be a fighter pilot.' Alex zoomed off, arms outstretched whirring about Rector's Meadow lost in thought.

Beth shouted, 'Come back, you stupid boy.' Staring scornfully at him as he wheeled about she said, 'You wouldn't think he was ten, would you, Daddy?'

Peter looked down at her and thought, she's older than we realise. She'll have to be told. They'll both have to be told and the innocence of childhood, which he and Caroline had striven so hard to preserve for them, will be gone for ever. And worse, what would their opinion be of him? As he'd said to Caroline that night when they'd discussed what Harriet had told him, their opinion of him was a burden he had to bear.

Alex came back to join them and they made their way home, along with the people who'd rushed out of the coffee morning to see the fun.

One said, 'That was a fire and a half, wasn't it, Rector? You didn't see the worst of it.'

Another said, 'Wouldn't mind, but they haven't even lifted a trowel yet and it's caused trouble. They shouldn't be doing it.'

And yet another, 'Don't be daft. It wasn't them bones that caused the fire.'

'I'm surprised at you, Rector, encouraging 'em with promises of a service and burial and that.'

'So am I. Downright asking for trouble.'

'Downright irresponsible of you, Rector, if you ask me.'

Peter stopped to confront his accusers. 'When they died they were deprived of the services of a priest and of burial in consecrated ground, so I shall see they get it, just as I shall make sure, if I am still here, that when you enter eternal life you too will have a service in this church and be buried here as is your right.'

Gasps of astonishment at his forthrightness could be heard, but Peter ignored them and continued home through the lych-gate.

Alex muttered, 'Good for you, Dad.'

But they weren't to escape because just as Peter put his key in the door of the Rectory Bryn hailed him.

Peter said, 'Go in, children, I won't be a moment. Yes, Bryn, what can I do for you?'

'Just want to say thanks for standing up to them, and for promising to support the dig. I'm all for it. Important for the village and all that.'

'No, Bryn, be honest, important for *you* and your tourist scam. My motives have nothing whatsoever to do with that. It would be a whole lot better if you paid attention to the matter I discussed with you the last time we spoke. If you'll forgive me, my lunch is ready.' Peter went inside leaving Bryn angry and upset.

Jimmy called across from his front door, 'Put that in your pipe and smoke it, Bryn Fields. Serves yer right.' He went into his cottage, hooting with laughter.

Bryn made a rude gesture at him and went back to Glebe House to lick his wounds.

6

One of the best places for catching up on the latest gossip was by the tinned soups in the Store. There was something comfortable and private about that small area and many were the tales told in the confines of that secluded spot which proved totally untrue, but also there were many which proved startlingly and unbelievably accurate.

Mrs Jones, getting her shopping after finishing her stint in the mail order office, had decided to treat Vince, now he was working, to a nice tin of cream of chicken soup. She browsed along the shelves debating whether or not to pay over the odds and get a really tasty one with white wine in it, or whether his doorstops and picture frames really did merit such madness. Behind her she heard footsteps and turned to see who it was.

Linda Crimble was doing her shopping.

'Who's looking after the post office, then?'

Linda sprang indignantly to her own defence. 'Mr Charter-Plackett. It is my lunch hour you know.'

'Who's rattled your cage?'

'Nobody.'

'Somebody must have, snapping at me like that. I only asked a civil question.'

Linda put her wire basket down on the floor. 'Sorry, it's Alan, he's all at sixes and sevens.'

Mrs Jones raised an eyebrow and waited.

Linda drew closer. 'Heaven alone knows what's going on at the pub; Alan can't make it out. Every night when he comes home he goes on and on about it.'

Mrs Jones's eyebrow rose a little further.

'Bryn's . . .'

Someone brushed past in a hurry, snatching a Scotch Broth as they went.

'Bryn's causing such ructions, you wouldn't believe.'

'With Dicky you mean.'

Linda nodded. 'Well, Bryn's like . . . courting Georgie.'

'Courting?' Both Mrs Jones's eyebrows went the highest they ever could.

'Sh! He's making up to her like nobody's business; there every night, flirting and that. Dicky's fit to boil.'

'No!'

'He is. Bryn never gives him a chance to talk with Georgie, private like.'

'But I thought Georgie was wanting a divorce.'

'She is. But he's so charming to her, is Bryn, you wouldn't believe.'

'Well I never.'

'Alan says you could cut the atmosphere with a knife some nights and Georgie's been quite sharp with Dicky a time or two.'

'Well . . .'

'Alan says one night there's going to be a bust-up, and you can't quite forget, you know, that Bryn did try to . . .' Linda drew a finger across her throat.

'Exactly. Well, you never know, do you?'

'You don't. Dicky's always so pleasant, it's not fair to 'im. He's not been so good with his comic turns as he usually is, bit quiet like, but there's no wonder, is there? Bryn was so against him doing it when his name was over the door. My Alan says sometimes Georgie really falls for Bryn flattering her.'

Mrs Jones folded her arms across her chest, her big brown eyes agog with interest. 'Really! Yes, well, I dare say he can be a charmer when he wants, though I've never noticed it. It must be difficult for your Alan, being in the middle of it all so to speak.'

'It is. Alan reckons there'll be murder done there before long.'

'Does he really?' Hoping to learn more, Mrs Jones bent her head a little closer to Linda and prompted her with a question. 'Bryn doesn't stay the night, does he, by any chance?'

They both heard Jimbo clearing his throat and Linda looked at her watch. 'Whoops, that's me. Time's up.'

'Keep me posted.'

Linda winked. 'I will.'

That same night Dicky was at Scouts so Bryn saw his chance. He'd been working up to it for days and now was his moment to take steps. He didn't know where they would lead him but he knew where he wanted them to lead: straight into Georgie's bedroom. He debated the choice of cravat or bow tie and decided that the cravat in Turnham Malpas would look out of place, but would give a more relaxed impression. He smoothed the grey hairs above his ears, wondered if he should dye them, but decided the grey added a touch of dignity and authority, checked his trousers were pin neat, notched his belt a little tighter, thrust back his shoulders and decided that, yes, how could she possibly resist him. He'd noticed a definite softening in her attitude over the last few days and . . .

When he'd tossed back his second whisky he leaned confidentially across the bar counter and said to Alan, 'Georgie?'

'Broken a nail. Won't be a minute.'

'New girl working out OK?'

Alan's habitual deadpan face broke into a slight grin. 'Trish is great. Thumbs up, as you might say.'

'Like that, is it?' Bryn looked across and watched her weaving between the tables, wiping spills and collecting glasses. Trim bottom she had, no sagging there. Mm . . . he could see what Alan meant. Bright as a button she looked, so they weren't all dunderheads in Penny Fawcett, then. He ordered a third whisky while he waited for his prey to return to the bar.

When she did, Bryn was overcome with genuine admiration for her. Tonight Georgie wore a black suit, with a white shirt in a fine material which had a soft, frilly, waterfall sort of collar. Her blonde hair, mercifully still not needing assistance from a bottle, was kind of bubbly and frothy around her still pretty face and he felt a gut-wenching he hadn't felt in years. The cold, scheming plan he'd had back at Glebe House fell apart; just as he had when he'd very first met her, he fancied her like hell. A lump came into his throat at the memory.

He held up his half-empty glass and toasted her, calling out, 'Pretty as ever, Georgie, I don't know how you do it.'

Georgie, who'd thought she had the problem of Bryn well sorted in her mind, noticed the jaunty cravat below the well-tanned face and thought how handsome he looked. Such presence he has tonight. I'll have to watch my step. She answered, 'Less of your cheek, Bryn Fields. How many of those have you had?' She nodded towards the whisky he held in his hand.

'My third.'

'Didn't know you drank at this pace. Nothing to do?'

'Plenty, but I try not to work in the evenings. Too much work makes Jack a dull boy.'

'We can't have that, can we?'

Bryn smiled at her, sensing again the softening of her attitude. 'Quiet in here tonight.'

'Often is, Mondays.'

'I see Georgie's little helper isn't about.'

'No. Scouts.'

'You're looking very attractive tonight. Haven't seen that outfit before.'

Surprised to find that the mild flirting they were doing was exceedingly welcome, Georgie said, flicking a finger at the waterfall collar of her shirt, 'It's new, glad you like it.'

'Oh, I do. That collar softens the severity of the suit.'

'Just what I thought.'

'A feminine touch, so to speak.'

'Exactly.'

Georgie realised that the few customers at the tables had gone very quiet and were avidly listening to them. She flushed at the thought that they were giving their audience such entertainment.

Bryn noticed her blush and felt elated. 'I'll give you a hand at closing, I know how much there is to do.'

A week ago she would have refused him point blank but not tonight. 'Thanks.'

'My pleasure, I assure you.'

Georgie served a lone customer who'd strayed in and as she slotted the money into the drawers of the till said, 'Alan! You and Trish can manage for half an hour, can you?'

'Of course.'

'Just need to talk business with Bryn about the tourists.'

Alan gave her a wink, which Georgie didn't find amusing. She unlocked the door marked 'Private' and nodded to Bryn to follow her.

Bryn carried his whisky through into the sitting room but didn't sit down. He waited for Georgie to invite him to, feeling it looked more gentlemanly, which was the approach he'd planned before he came but which now came naturally because of the sudden eruption of his feelings for her. More than he ever had, he regretted neglecting Georgie to the point where she fell out of love with him. 'Georgie, I . . .'

She gave him the full treatment of those large blue eyes of hers and his insides melted. 'Yes . . . you were saying . . . ?'

Bryn cleared his throat. 'I was going to say that I hope for your sake as well as mine I pull off this tourist business.'

'So do I.'

'Did you know they've found what they were looking for in Deadman's Dell? Bones and bits and pieces. I've been to have a look. A bit gruesome, but I'm thrilled. Really thrilled. It'll make all the difference for my groups. These idiots who say we shouldn't do it, the worst will happen et cetera, they're mad. Completely mad.'

Georgie had to smile at his enthusiasm. 'We could do with some nice steady lunch trade on Thursdays. If it comes off it will be brilliant. Clever of you to have thought of it.'

Bryn somehow, but he didn't know how, began to tell her about life on board a cruise liner and before he knew it they were both laughing their heads off, pouring another drink, wiping tears of laughter from their eyes and enjoying themselves so much they didn't notice the time. Georgie crossed those elegant, slender legs of hers and Bryn caught a glimpse of a lacy petticoat.

'My God, Georgie, you still have that something that makes a man's insides turn to liquid gold.'

'Bryn!' She sat up straight and uncrossed her legs.

'I mean it. How about it? We're still man and wife you know.' He bent forward and gently caressed her right knee with his thumb.

She pushed his hand off her leg but understood what he meant by liquid gold. At the same time her brain said no. No! No! 'This won't do, Bryn.'

'Why not? Both you and I still have rights. There's no one to say we shouldn't, now is there?' The persuasive tone of his voice was almost her undoing.

Georgie hesitated and then remembered Dicky. 'There's Dicky.'

Bryn sat up. 'Dicky!' He only just managed to keep the scorn out of his voice. 'Come on, Georgie. He'll never know if you don't tell him and I certainly shan't.'

Georgie smiled. 'You wouldn't be able to resist! A feather in your cap you'd see it as.'

Bryn saw he might be in with a chance. 'No, not a feather in my cap, not a conquest, just the need of a man for his lovely wife. It's been a very long time, Georgie, love.' He placed his hand on her leg just under her skirt hem and found she didn't resist. While he talked he rubbed her leg with his thumb. 'You have to admit to a certain feeling for me tonight. I'm no longer the thieving blackguard you saw me as at first, am I?'

'There's Dicky,' Georgie protested and found herself weighing up how she'd feel about Dicky if she did fall for Bryn's charms just this once. As he rubbed her leg she knew he was a very different man from the one who'd left her four years ago. Very different, and she seriously fancied a taste of this very different man. She leaned towards him meaning to kiss him but somewhere a door banged and a voice called out, and she drew back.

Bryn's hand stayed on her knee, though, caressing and enticing, his eyes never leaving her face. 'Come on. Upstairs. Eh?' Georgie half rose as though intending to lead the way, Bryn leaned over and kissed her lips and she returned the kiss in full measure.

Georgie murmured, 'This is not on.' And kissed him again. 'We mustn't.' He stopped her protests with another kiss, gentle and yet urgent. He took her elbow, helped her up and held her close, enjoying the smell of her hair and the feel of her body pressed so willingly against his. 'Oh, Georgie, I've been such a fool. Such a fool.'

Like the crack of gunfire the door burst open and there stood Dicky, his face flushed with anger. In his hand was the cricket bat Georgie kept for emergencies. He held it with both hands as though about to hit a six, and silently lunged towards Bryn. Georgie screamed, 'No!' She sought to release herself from Bryn's arms, he began to lose his balance and, as he tried desperately to regain it, Dicky swung the cricket bat at Bryn's head and felled him like an ox.

Georgie didn't know she was still screaming 'No! No! No!'

Dicky let go of the bat and it thudded to the floor.

Bryn lay in a tangled heap between the cupboard and an easy chair, the whisky decanter and two glasses splattered across the carpet around him.

The only sound was that of Georgie's breath racing in and out of her lungs in great noisy, hysterical gulps. Dicky was carved from stone. Alan and Jimmy stood in the doorway also carved from stone.

It was Jimmy who broke the spell. 'What the hell's going on here?'

'I said I'd do for 'im and I have.' Dicky's voice was grotesquely unlike his own.

Georgie knelt down, her breath rasping in her throat, and felt for Bryn's pulse.

'Is he dead?' Alan asked.

Georgie shook her head.

'I'll go for Dr Harris.' Jimmy fled on winged feet.

Georgie nodded.

Dicky dropped into a chair, all the fight gone out of him.

The three of them remained speechless, frozen in their positions, staring mutely at Bryn until they heard a woman's swift footsteps.

Georgie sat down, Dicky stood up and Alan moved away from the door so Caroline could get in. She knelt down beside Bryn and as she did so Bryn began to stir. 'Bloody hell! Ah! My head!'

Caroline rested a firm hand on his shoulder. 'Lie still for a moment, Bryn, till you come round properly. You're going to have an almighty bruise and a lump. Could we have an ice pack or frozen peas or something, Georgie, to keep the swelling down. Don't worry, Bryn, you're going to be all right. You must have cracked your head on the corner of the cupboard as you tripped.'

Dicky looked at Georgie and saw a warning in her eyes.

'Too many whiskies, that's the trouble with him. I did tell him.'

She somehow got up from the chair and walked as quickly as she could out of the room. Jimmy caught her eye as she passed him and winked. She squeezed his fingers in thanks.

Alan, remembering that he'd left Trish to manage in the bar on her own, disappeared. Bryn sat up. Dicky still didn't speak, but he did see the bat lying just where he'd dropped it.

'I'm sure you should go to hospital. You could have it X-rayed. I can't tell whether or not you've cracked your skull.' Caroline helped Bryn into a chair.

Dicky moved closer to the bat.

Georgie came back with some ice cubes in a plastic bag. 'Will this do?'

'Splendid.' Caroline applied the ice bag to the side of Bryn's head and he winced.

'That's painful!' He tried to jerk his head away but even that hurt.

Dicky got the toe of his shoe to the bat and edged it under the coffee table. 'Got to get back to Scouts.' He sidled out of the room, leaving Georgie with Jimmy and Caroline and her patient.

Jimmy said he'd better be going, or he wouldn't get another pint in before closing time.

Caroline felt puzzled by the secretive atmosphere and decided to remain out of it until she'd worked out what had really happened. If Dicky thought she hadn't noticed him pushing the cricket bat under the coffee table he was sadly mistaken. 'Bryn, you should go to hospital.'

'I'm not. I'm going back to Glebe House as soon as maybe. A night's sleep is all I need. Feel better in the morning. In fact, I feel better already. This ice is doing the trick.' He took it off his head to rearrange it and winced. 'Wow! Some cupboard. I don't remember falling.'

'Perhaps you will tomorrow when your head's settled down. I'll walk with you to Glebe House. Tell me when you're ready. I still think you should go to hospital, though.'

Bryn said no and tried standing up. 'There you are, you see, you're too cautious, Dr Harris, too cautious. Sorry to have bothered you.'

'That's OK.'

Georgie said nothing at all except, 'Thanks.'

But she had plenty to say when she walked round to Dicky's house after she'd closed up and she knew he'd be home from Scouts. She let herself in with her key and found him standing with one foot on the bottom step of his spiral staircase, as though making up his mind to go to bed.

'Dicky, love!' Georgie, arms wide, intended kissing him but Dicky was having none of it.

He backed away from her. 'No, Georgie. No.'

'It was all nothing what you saw, it was the whisky talking.'

'I'm not a fool.'

'I know you're not.'

'If that's how you feel you'd better go back to him and have done with it.' His face crumpled and she thought he was going to weep.

'Don't, Dicky, please don't.'

'Don't be upset by what I saw? What else can I be? Eh? What else? You stood there in *his arms*, the man who tried to murder me. Or had you forgotten? I've watched him this last few days trying to get closer and closer to you, and he has, Georgie, he *has*. You've let him.'

She knew she was guilty of that. 'You shouldn't have hit him like that, though, you know. You could have killed him, then where would the two of us be? Thank God you didn't. I couldn't bear the thought of you being in prison after all we've been through.' Then a thought occurred to her. 'How did you know to come right then?'

Dicky looked away. He fiddled with an ornament on the mantelpiece. Then he said quietly, 'Alan doesn't like Bryn, you see, but he and me, we're mates, so he rang me on my mobile, on a thought-I-ought-to-know basis. He was damn right too, I did want to know. I'd do the same all over again. I've threatened to kill him and I will because he's not having you. I had thought you loved me.' He turned to face her to see her reaction.

She did love him. She did. She must have been crazy this last week. Hang what the village thinks, I'm staying the night with him. 'Dicky! Love!' She held wide her arms and this time he came into them and hugged her tight.

*

She was ready for off before seven the next morning but hadn't bargained for Peter's early-morning run. She stepped out of Dicky's door, shut it quietly behind her, went down the garden path and set off down Church Lane to find herself facing Peter as he turned out of the lych-gate after saying his early-morning prayers in the church. He made a handsome figure in his old college rugby shirt and shorts. She could have sworn that briefly there appeared to be a halo of light round his fair hair.

'Good morning, Georgie, another beautiful day.'

'It is indeed, Rector.' Not a word or a hint of criticism but Georgie felt shabby. She knew those penetrating blue eyes of his had seen how she felt. He might not have said anything but, after all he'd done to preserve her standing in the village, she'd let him down and no mistake. Well, there'd have to be an ending to all this hole-in-the-corner sneaking about. She'd have that divorce from Bryn and she and Dicky would have things put right by a register office wedding, though she'd have loved Peter to marry them in the church. At the flick of a net curtain to her left she knew Grandmama Charter-Plackett had watched Peter greeting her. Damn and blast!

Linda, of course, knew the whole story, having listened to it until after midnight, with Alan describing in full his part in the night's happenings. She couldn't wait for Mrs Jones to come to work. Straight up on nine she was there, unaware of the gossip Linda was about to impart. Linda opened the steel door to the post office section and beckoned her for a word.

'What's up? I'm in a hurry.'

'You'll never guess what happened in the Royal Oak last night.'

Mrs Jones's eyebrows worked overtime. 'What?'

They were so absorbed in their gossip that neither of them noticed Jimbo had returned to the front of the Store and was busy rearranging the cards on the Village Voice notice board.

'Your Alan *rang* him?'

'On his mobile.'

'The miracles of modern science.'

'Exactly. So he arrived . . .'

Neither of them noticed that Jimbo had found some writing pads on the stationery counter in need of straightening.

'Without saying a word he went behind the counter, picked up the cricket bat Georgie keeps there in case of trouble and went straight through to the lounge and fetched Bryn one.'

Mrs Jones almost fell from her perch with shock. 'Dicky hit Bryn with a cricket bat! I don't believe it, wait till I tell Vince, he won't half laugh.'

'Well, he did, as true as I'm here. Course Alan wasn't right behind him so he didn't know what they were up to when Dicky burst in, but it must have been something serious, mustn't it, otherwise why hit him with it? Out for the count he was. They got Dr Harris to see to him and she wanted him to go to hospital but he wouldn't.'

'He should've.'

By now Jimbo was openly listening.

'He should, but he didn't and Dr Harris saw him home.'

Reluctantly they had to put an end to their conversation as the rush of mothers from the school had begun. Jimbo went to the till, Mrs Jones to the mail order office and Linda to opening up the post office and sorting out her cash for the morning's business.

Gradually the story of Dicky's foolhardy bravery infiltrated the village houses and spread via the milkman and the postman as far as the outlying districts. If Georgie had hoped that Caroline's idea of Bryn having hit his head on a cupboard as he slipped would carry the day she was to be sadly disillusioned. What was worse, Grandmama Charter-Plackett, making her early morning call at the Store before departing for Culworth, let out by mistake what she'd seen at seven that morning.

Her nose pressed to the grille, Linda said, 'So the Rector knows they've been ... you know ...'

'I didn't say that. I said the Rector spoke to her just as she left Dicky's cottage, that's all. Nothing more. For all I know they could have sat up talking all night.'

Linda stared into the distance, lost in thought. 'Given the choice, I know who I'd prefer.'

'Linda! Really. What would your Alan think to that.'

*

542

At this precise moment Alan was doing a lot of thinking as, out of Dicky's hearing, he was getting his comeuppance from Georgie. 'I may have known you a long time but you have nothing to do with my private life and I won't stand for you putting your pennyworth in. Do you hear me? If he'd killed Bryn last night how would you have felt? Tell me that.'

'I didn't know he was going to do that, did I? It's not right, you and Bryn, he'll be . . .'

'What's right and what's wrong is my business, so you keep your long nose out of it in future and leave me to sort things out for myself. Right. Or else you'll be out on your ear.'

Alan blenched. Lose his job. Get thrown out. He knew nothing else but bar work with Bryn and Georgie. Nothing at all. Briefly he saw destitution looming, little Lewis homeless, and Linda looking to him for answers and him having none. Hurriedly he declared he would not interfere again and Georgie was free to do as she wished.

Grimly Georgie replied, tapping his chest with her finger as she did so, 'Thought that might remind you where your loyalties lie. Remember, he tripped and caught his head on a cupboard.' She saw the look of guilt in his eyes. 'You told Linda, didn't you? You did. I don't believe it. Blast it, I might as well have put an advert in the *Culworth Gazette*. That's it, then.' She threw her hands up in despair.

Alan cringed. Anything but that. 'I-I-I'm out, then?'

Georgie saw how cruelly she'd behaved towards someone who didn't deserve it. Poor inadequate Alan. It wasn't his fault. Only hers, for letting that thieving, conniving louse persuade her to . . . 'No, Alan, you're not out, but I warn you, one more piece of interference and you will be. Lock, stock and barrel. Understood?'

Alan nodded in gratitude. He'd have licked her shoes if she'd asked him to. He knew Linda would have told everyone she met, even though he'd said keep it to yourself. She was like that, was Linda. Well, he'd tell her at teatime just how close to losing their livelihood her chattering to customers had brought them and might still if she didn't watch her Ps and Qs. In future he wouldn't warn anyone about anything and then he couldn't be in trouble. Women! God save him from bossy women.

7

Caroline and Harriet had a Christmas Bazaar to organise so they arranged to have their inaugural meeting at Harriet's. Coffee being the first item on the agenda, Harriet was pouring it out into some new mugs Jimbo had had designed for what he now called his tourist trade.

Caroline admired her mug. 'These are very attractive. I like the colour and the picture. He doesn't hang about when he has a new project in hand, does he?'

Harriet had to laugh. 'No, he does not. You know Jimbo, anything new and he moves heaven and earth to achieve it. That's what makes him so successful.'

'Which he definitely is. Let's hope Bryn's new project does as well. More business in the village can't be anything but a plus.'

As Harriet offered Caroline a biscuit she said, 'These are new. I'm thinking of selling biscuits mail order, I want to know what you think.'

The slightly misshapen biscuit, misshapen as in home-made, was a tempting golden mound of cinnamon and . . . and . . . syrup or was it honey? It smelled delicious and lived up to its promise when she bit into it. 'This is gorgeous! Absolutely gorgeous. How do you do it?'

Harriet showed her delight on her face. 'Trial and error. It's an old recipe I found in a book of Mother's when I sorted through her belongings. It's purported to have been handed down from the seventeenth century, but I daren't put that on the packet as I'm not totally sure it is.'

'Well, it's lovely. A real treat.'

'Good. Wait till Bryn tries one. He's in and out of our door like a yo-yo at the moment, bursting with new ideas for his tourists. Let's hope it all comes off.'

'He's in Bath checking out hotels for his tours.'

'So he's well enough to travel, then?'

'I went to see him yesterday and he appears to have recovered. Still all black and blue but the swelling's gone down. It was an almighty bump he had.'

'Not surprising. I'd have an almighty bump if someone had swiped me with a cricket bat.'

Caroline, in the act of picking up her mug, paused, put it back down again and asked, 'Who hit him with a cricket bat?'

'Thought you'd have realised. It was Dicky.'

'*Dicky hit Bryn with a cricket bat?*'

'He did.'

'So . . .'

'Yes?'

'I thought he'd tripped and hit his head on the corner of the cupboard. I said so and no one denied it, but I knew there were undercurrents I couldn't pick up on. So that was it.'

'Also my dear mother-in-law saw Georgie coming out of Dicky's cottage the following morning.'

'No!'

'And she saw Georgie meet Peter going out for his run.'

'He's never told me.'

'And they've been away for a weekend together.'

'Bryn and Georgie . . .'

'No, of course not. Georgie and Dicky.'

'I see. So why did Dicky hit Bryn?'

'That's what no one knows.'

Caroline picked up her coffee and sipped it while she thought. 'Harriet! We really mustn't speculate, must we, that's how rumours start.'

'No, but isn't it fun?'

Caroline had to laugh. 'Yes. You know there's trouble about the dig, do you?'

'Can't work in a village store without hearing all the rumours.'

'Everywhere Peter goes he's being blamed for it when he couldn't stop it if he tried to. It's not on church land.'

'He shouldn't have offered to have a service and burial. That's what's got under everyone's skin. I wonder . . .'

'What?'

'I wonder, should I tell you that there's a protest meeting tonight.'

'Where?'

'At Willie Biggs's.'

'He hasn't told us.'

'Well, no, I don't expect he has.'

Caroline became indignant when it occurred to her that Sylvia had not said anything either. 'Sylvia hasn't said a word to *me*.'

'Apparently she's furious and is refusing to have anything to do with it.'

'Oh, dear. Are you going?'

Harriet shook her head. 'Of course not.'

'What time?'

'Er . . . well, *I* didn't tell you, right? Half past seven.'

'Right.'

Sylvia's opposition to Willie's determination to challenge the dig and the burial had boiled up inside her until she could no longer hold her peace, so two hours before the meeting was to begin she finally told him how she felt. 'You've known all along I agreed with the Rector, all along, and you've the gall to decide to hold the meeting here. Well, I'm sorry, Willie, but I'm leaving you to it.'

In a soft, wheedling tone Willie said, 'Sylvia! Now, this isn't like you.'

'Don't take that tone with me, because it won't get you your own way.'

'But I need help with the refreshments and things, and arranging the chairs and . . .'

'I'm quite sure you're perfectly capable of seeing to all that. You're not helpless. You managed for years on your own.'

'Sylvia, please!'

'You can wheedle all you like, I'm not staying for the meeting. Wild horses wouldn't make me.'

Willie watched her pick up her handbag and cardigan. When she went to the drawer where she kept her car keys, he knew she meant business. 'You don't mean you're really going out while the meeting's on.'

Those fine grey eyes of Sylvia's, which had attracted him to her from the first, looked at him with scorn. 'I have my principles. How can I be here? If I am, it means I'm in agreement with you, which I am not. And never will be. I honestly can't see why it's wrong to dig up the remains and give them a decent Christian burial. It's their right.'

'It's only because you work for the Rector, that's all. You're taking his side because of that, not because it's a principle.'

'Anyone would think I hadn't got a mind of my own. Well, I have. I won't oppose him on this.'

'But he won't be here; he doesn't know about it.'

Sylvia tapped the side of her nose. 'Don't you be too sure about that. He sees and knows more than we think.'

Willie cringed at the thought of a confrontation with Peter, for whom he'd always had the deepest respect. Goosepimples broke out all over him at the prospect.

'Sylvia! You haven't told him. Have you?'

'I may be against you, Willie, but I wouldn't do a trick like that. I need an apology from you for thinking such a thing.'

Willie realised how much he'd hurt her but he felt it counted for nothing in comparison with how he felt about her withdrawing her support from him. 'Sorry. But it's not like you, isn't this . . .'

'I'm sorry too, more sorry than you realise, but I will *not* stay for the meeting.'

Thoroughly cowed by her adamant refusal to give in to him, Willie asked sadly, 'Where will you be?'

'In Culworth at the pictures.'

Horrified, Willie stuttered, 'All by yourself?'

Sylvia nodded.

'Do I get a kiss before you go?'

Sylvia studied his woebegone face. 'Very well.' She gave him the merest peck, conceding in her own mind that she'd make it up to him when she got back.

*

At exactly eight o'clock Peter knocked at Willie's door and walked in as he always did in village houses, calling out, 'It's Peter from the Rectory,' as he entered.

He was greeted by stunned silence. To a man the conspirators couldn't meet his eye, but he looked at each of them and said a cordial 'Good evening, everyone. Sorry I've arrived late.' Several of them blushed with embarrassment, others found their shoes more interesting than meeting Peter's eyes. They were occupying easy chairs, dining chairs and in some instances stools, which Willie had collected from various rooms in the cottage. The small living room meant they were shoulder to shoulder in as much of a circle as Willie could devise. No one moved a muscle.

Willie, from years of treating him with deference, leapt to his feet and offered him his stool.

'Thank you, Willie, but I'll perch on the end of the table if you don't mind.' Sitting there gave him an advantage, which crouching on a low stool wouldn't have done. 'Please continue. Just sorry I arrived late.'

Naturally Peter's arrival had taken the wind out of their sails and no one had the courage to continue. Finally Grandmama Charter-Plackett spoke. 'You know why we're here, Rector?' Peter nodded. 'We've all agreed we don't want the dig and we certainly don't think it quite right for you to be supporting it by offering burial. Already we've had a fire, which could have got out of control if it hadn't been for Willie's swift action, and we all dread what might happen next. I've been keeping an eye on it. They've only scratched the surface so far and found a few bones, but we want it closed up now and perhaps when they've done that you could say a few words appropriate for the circumstances and then we can forget about it.'

'You all know perfectly well that I have no jurisdiction over that land. It belongs to Mr Fitch. And then there's Gilbert.'

Jimmy spoke up. 'Look! Gilbert would dig anywhere whatever if he thought he could find something of value. Look at the trouble we had over the Roman ruins when we wanted to hold the Show. He didn't care a button that all our hard work would be in jeopardy. All he could think of was what he might find. He just gets carried away, he does. Also my Sykes knows a thing or two about that Dell. He won't go anywhere near it. Wild horses won't get him in there, not even if he thinks there's rabbits there. Animals is wiser than you think.'

There was a general nodding of heads at Jimmy's last statement.

Arthur Prior from Wallop Down Farm added his opinion. 'Two of my granddaughters have come down with violent attacks of chickenpox. They've blisters the size of a two-pence piece and they're very poorly. I just hope to God it is chickenpox and nothing more sinister. They've very high temperatures.'

Gasps of horror could be heard all round the room. A couple of the weekenders who'd been persuaded to stay on for the meeting voiced their protests too. 'There you go! You see, and this is only the start. Heaven alone knows what might happen next. Please, Rector, will you stop it?'

'I can't.'

Vince Jones had his say. 'You could, sir, please, have a word with Mr Fitch. We're all so afraid. They've got to stop.'

Arthur Prior got to his feet. 'I propose we make a deputation to Mr Fitch and go up to see him. The Rector's quite right. He can't stop the dig but Mr Fitch could, and he's been much more amenable lately, so he might listen.' He sat down again, feeling that he'd exonerated Peter from any blame, but the others would have none of it.

Miss Senior's woolly hat bobbed again as she shuddered and, with a nigh hysterical tone in her voice, said, 'Think what might 'appen if they's buried in our own churchyard. I shan't fancy finding myself next to 'em when my time comes, believe me.'

A muttered 'hear! hear!' came from most of the people squeezed into Willie's tiny living room. A silence fell while they all looked to Peter for support.

'Those bones have been there for over six centuries already, and for most of that time they've been there unknown to anyone. Can any of you give me a sound reason for suspecting the bones are responsible for anything at all, either evil or good?'

'Don't think reason comes into it.' This from a weekender who guessed he was about to be persuaded by Peter that their protest was foolish.

Willie spoke up. 'Well, Rector, we know it doesn't make sense but it's how we all *feel*. It's not right and we want it stopped.'

'I'm afraid you haven't my support. I am still willing to see their remains decently buried in hallowed ground and so, too, should you be. They could be your ancestors, don't forget.'

Grandmama Charter-Plackett said firmly, 'You're a clergyman and I can see where you're coming from, but it won't wash with us. We want it stopped and I for one offer myself as a member of the delegation.'

'Hear! hear!'

'Who's willing to go with me?'

When it came to the point of standing up to Mr Fitch there was a marked reluctance on everyone's part to volunteer. In the end Arthur Prior said he would go with her and Peter realised he'd lost the debate. 'I'm certain in my own mind that Mr Fitch will say he wants the dig to go ahead, and quite rightly so. There's no harm in it, none at all, take my word for it.'

But they wouldn't be moved. They even begged Peter to head the deputation but he refused. 'I'm sorry I can't be at one with you about this, but there we are. I assure you, you are worrying unnecessarily about the situation and I have to say I'm disappointed in you. I thought you would have had more Christian understanding in you than to deny people a respectable burial. I'll leave you to it.'

Peter turned to leave but not before Miss Senior had said, 'And what about the chickenpox, a high temperature and sinister? What about that? I think it's very suspicious.'

There were grunts of agreement from almost everyone in the room.

'I'll say goodnight, then.' Peter left, feeling ashamed of them all and especially of Willie, of all people, spearheading it.

Despite high words between Mrs Charter-Plackett and Mr Fitch when he met with them in his office, he refused to withdraw his approval of the dig and both Arthur Prior and she were left in no doubt that their interference was nothing less than idiotic, and they weren't to come bothering him with prejudices and complaints more suited to peasants.

At this Grandmama Charter-Plackett drew herself up and gave him a piece of her mind, which left him in no doubt either that, although he might have money now, his origins were no better than theirs. 'Peasant? Huh! If we are, then so too are you. You can't pull the wool over our eyes, believe me. You're a self-made man, without that much good breeding in you.' She held up her thumb and forefinger scarcely half a centimetre apart. 'Good morning to you, Craddock. Let's hope nothing of a sinister nature happens to you in the next few weeks. If something does happen, such as you being run over by a bus, I for one will not be sending you a get well card. Come, Arthur, we're wasting our time here.' She sailed majestically out of Mr Fitch's study and stormed out on to the gravel drive. Looking up at the beautiful Tudor building which was Turnham House she said, 'This place deserves someone better than him. Had Sir Ralph still been in possession he would have treated us with dignity.' She remembered a word she'd heard one of Jimbo's boys use, which at the time she had thought distinctly common, but it fitted the occasion now. 'Mr Fitch is a scumbag, that's what he is. A scumbag.'

To emphasise his support of the dig Mr Fitch turned up at Deadman's Dell the same afternoon. He'd forgotten how distant and unmoved by money or titles Gilbert could be and he was received with no more ceremony than the local dustcart operator. This riled him and when he bent to pick up one of the bones with his bare hands intending to examine it, he received one of Gilbert's broadsides. 'Put that down immediately. Have you no sense, man? They've not to be touched.'

Mr Fitch straightened up and looked at Gilbert with a nasty glint in his eye. 'I've a good mind to refuse you permission to carry on.'

'Have you? Too late. I've got your letter saying we can.'

'I can withdraw it.'

'You might be interested to know I've got the *Culworth Gazette* coming this afternoon. They should be here any minute.' Gilbert, head down, squatting in a shallow trench, smiled to himself.

Mr Fitch didn't answer. He watched the delicate process of removing earth from around a find, the gentle scraping away, the sensitive handling of the minutest scrap of material and became absorbed: the quiet throb of excitement was palpable. Just as he crouched down to get a closer look at something one of the students had found, the photographer and a reporter from the *Gazette* arrived. 'Excellent, Mr Fitch, stay right there and I'll take a picture.' The camera clicked and whirred, and Mr Fitch pointed and smiled until his knees gave out and he had to stand up.

'We understand you're funding this dig, Mr Fitch?' the reporter asked.

'Well, not exactly but ... should the occasion arise I would be more than willing. Such happenings as this are very important to an ancient village like this one and if money can help in any way then I'm your man.'

'Excellent!' He scribbled on his notepad.

The reporter addressed Gilbert's back. 'Mr Johns, isn't it?'

Gilbert looked up and nodded. 'That's me.'

In all, Mr Fitch had an interesting and worthwhile interlude down at the dig, and felt justified in ignoring the stupid, childish pleas of Arthur and that old harridan Grandmama Charter-Plackett. Under a bus, indeed. Fat chance. He never went anywhere near a bus.

Bryn, when he came back from Bath, was horrified to discover how frightened the village was about the dig. There were now four of the Prior granddaughters suffering from severe chickenpox. The teachers at the school were finding their class numbers dwindling daily until, on the morning Bryn returned, only three-quarters of the school was present.

Beth and Alex were disappointed to discover they'd had chickenpox quite badly when they were very small, so their chances of being away from school for a couple of weeks were very slim.

Beth asked, 'Were we properly poorly, Mummy?'

'Very. Your spots were so close together I couldn't find a space to put my finger.'

'Really? Mum, did we have a temperature?' Alex remembered having a severe sore throat when he was eight and how funny his head had felt and how hot he'd been.

'You did. Daddy couldn't bath you, because he couldn't bear to see your spots.'

'You bathed us, though, didn't you, Mummy?'

Caroline nodded. 'I did indeed, Beth, just to help you stop

itching. We used bottles and bottles of calamine to cool your spots down. You even had spots in your ears.'

Beth contemplated the thought and said sadly, 'So there's no chance of us getting it, then?'

'None, I would have thought.'

'Oh, well.' She'd quite fancied the drama of being really ill but apparently it was not to be. 'We'll be off, then, and see who's next to have got it. Come on, Alex, or we'll be late. They're all saying it's the dig that's made everyone ill, but it isn't, is it?'

'Of course not.'

Alex said, 'They're blaming Dad.'

'Are they?'

'Yes, they say he shouldn't have said what he did about a service.'

'Are they?'

'I nearly had a fight about Dad, Mum, in the playground yesterday.'

'I hope you didn't?'

'No, but I wanted to.'

'Well, don't. Please. It will all calm down in a day or two, you'll see.'

Quite out of context Beth remarked, 'Janine nearly got run over yesterday.'

Caroline broke off from clearing the table to say, 'Where?'

'Outside school, before school began. She wasn't being silly. There was a terrible screech of brakes.'

Alex said, 'There was, Mum, she isn't exaggerating. Poor Janine. They had to let her lie down for a while.'

'I'll leave this and go with you to school. It's getting beyond a joke, all those cars.'

Caroline had firmly believed that the crisis over Peter's decision to have a service would subside shortly but it didn't. Gilbert's two older toddlers caught chickenpox and so did Louise, who'd never had it as a child. Then Fran Charter-Plackett developed it and two days later Harriet went down with it. Even though there were columns in the papers about the epidemic of chickenpox in Culworth and the surrounding areas, none of the villagers believed anything other than that the dig was responsible for the Turnham Malpas chickenpox. Common sense quite simply did not prevail.

When Bryn next went into the Royal Oak, Georgie refused to serve him. 'I'm sorry, Bryn, but that is my decision. You are banned.' She stood, arms crossed, and waited for him to go.

But he didn't. He leaned on the bar counter and said confidentially, 'If Dicky hadn't come back the other night you know exactly where we would have been and don't try to tell me we wouldn't.'

'But he did and we didn't, and I don't want to, and you cause him too much upset and you're not welcome in this bar.'

Bryn tried putting on the charm. 'Come on, I'm not that bad. You were very close to me that night. Closer than we've been for years.' He leant over the bar and put a gentle hand on her arm. 'I rather thought you liked the new me.'

Georgie hesitated. He was right there, but . . . 'I don't, not at all, and buzz off or . . .'

'You wouldn't call the police, now would you?'

'Just go, before Dicky comes in.'

'Sir Galahad to the rescue, eh?'

'Do as I say.' At this point Alan came up from the cellar, saw Bryn, put down the crate of lagers, did a swift about turn and disappeared. He'd been told not to interfere so he wouldn't even give himself the chance.

'Just serve me a whisky and I'll be gone.'

'No. Alan, come please!'

'Please, just one and I'll be gone.'

'No. Alan!'

'Can I have a meal in the dining room?'

Georgie almost relented and opened her mouth to say it was all right but changed her mind. 'No. Now shift yourself or I really will call the police.'

'And there I thought you and I were business partners.'

'I promised Dicky . . .'

'Oh, well, if it was only that little squirt you promised that means nothing . . .'

'Right, that's it. Out!' Georgie started to walk round the end of the bar, calling 'Alan!' as she did so.

'OK! OK! I'll be off. How long am I banned for?'

She couldn't resist his chirpy smile nor the wink he gave her. She'd meant to ban him until his group came in August but she hadn't the heart. 'One week.'

'Right! Jug and Bottle here I come.'

Someone sitting at a table shouted, 'Watch out for that barmaid with the chestnut-coloured hair. She'll have anyone in trousers, she will.'

Bryn gave a thumbs up and went out with a final wink at Georgie, who was already regretting banning him. Alan appeared again as though by magic and she took her anger with herself out on him. 'Where the blazes have you been? I wanted you to help turn Bryn out and I called but you didn't come.'

'You told me I wasn't to interfere in your private life again, so I didn't.'

'Oh, I see. So that's how it is. I'll remember this.' She retired behind the bar again and continued serving as though nothing had happened but inside she wished Bryn were there. She enjoyed his flirting and the changes in him more than she liked to admit, and frankly couldn't understand how she could love Dicky and yet find the new Bryn so intriguing.

Dicky walked in to begin his evening stint behind the bar and immediately her heart burst with love. Of course this was him, the man of her heart. They didn't kiss in public but she wanted to so much. That divorce. She'd put things in motion immediately. First thing tomorrow. Dicky smiled at her with such love in his eyes and unknowingly his smile strengthened her resolve.

Unusually for them, Jimbo came in with his mother. Several people called out to him asking how Harriet and Fran were. 'Beginning to turn the corner, thanks. A slight improvement. We've just popped out to celebrate Mother's birthday. Can't stay long.'

The two of them chose a quiet table and Jimbo went to order their drinks. The flow of conversation went back and forth around the tables, people came and people went.

When Jimbo returned to their table with the drinks, Mrs Charter-Plackett said quietly, 'I see Bryn isn't in tonight.'

Jimbo raised his glass to her. 'Happy birthday, Mother, and many of them.'

'Thank you, you darling boy. I'm so proud of you, so proud.'

'And I of you. Still so full of spark and energy.'

'Less of the "still". I'm not that old!'

'Of course not. Of course not.'

'I can see you're worrying about Harriet and Fran. Well don't. Like you said, there's a slight improvement today. Harriet was quite chirpy when I took her a cup of tea before we came out.'

'This business of the Dell. I see they were digging again today. Craddock Fitch was there too.'

'Blast that man. Thank heavens he didn't marry Harriet's mother. I couldn't be so vituperative about him if he had. He is so *rude*, in a way which leaves one with no alternative but to be very rude back. Which I was. I even said if he got run over by a bus I wouldn't send him a get well card.'

Jimbo laughed. 'It was a close-run thing, you know. She had more or less decided to say yes to his proposal.'

'I was sorry she died how she did, so suddenly. Terrible shock for Harriet and for all of us. Life is so short, one never knows, does one, when it will be one's own turn to be called.'

Seeing she was succumbing to what he called the birthday syndrome Jimbo said, 'You don't think like everyone else that the chickenpox is a result of the dig, do you?'

His mother snorted her contempt. 'Of course not! I'm not a fool, but then again . . .'

'I know just what you mean. Your head says it's ridiculous but the heart says something quite different. By the way, Mother, this business of Bryn and Georgie's divorce.'

'Yes?'

'I understand Bryn's trying to find out who is going to finance Dicky buying into the pub when Bryn and Georgie get their divorce. Thought I'd warn you, just in case he came fishing for answers from you.'

'He'll get no change out of me. In any case he'll be more likely to think it will be you offering, not me. He's a scumbag. That's what he is.'

'Mother!'

'He's trying to get his feet under Georgie's table, the devious beggar. She's better off with Dicky. Lovely man, he is, makes two of Bryn.'

Amused by her close involvement in village matters Jimbo asked, 'Glad you came to live in the village?'

'Of course. I know I behaved badly when I first came but I have improved, haven't I?'

For fun Jimbo didn't answer immediately, then he said, 'Ye-e-e-s-s,' as though he had to weigh up the matter.

'You get more like your father every year. You bad boy.' Jimbo went to replenish their glasses and when he got back to the table his mother said, 'I'm not a superstitious person, but with all this going on about the ghastly effect the dig has had on everything, I must be off my head worrying about saying what I did about Craddock going under a bus. I should never have said it.'

'For heaven's sake, Mother, if something did happen to him how can it be your fault? You wouldn't be to blame at all.'

'No, but it does make you wonder sometimes just how much influence what you say has on people. I shall have to keep my tongue in check, I really will.'

'Well, that wouldn't be a bad idea.'

'I do hope so. I do hope so. I feel quite dreadful.'

'Are you ready? I've left Harriet for long enough.'

Fran was fast asleep but Harriet was awake when he got back. 'Hush, darling, don't wake her, I want her to sleep as long as possible. Oh, Jimbo, I can't remember feeling so ill before. Can you get me a fresh drink? Did you have a nice time with your mother?'

'I did. She's getting quite mellow in her old age. 'Nother drink you said?'

8

A feeling of impending doom permeated the village as the chickenpox epidemic continued to rage and the school numbers dwindled to a new low, trade at the Store dropped and attendance at church also suffered. It rained, too, day after day, with a relentlessness that seemed it would have no end. The pond on the green flooded and parts of the churchyard also went under water. Surrounding fields, good pasture and arable land alike, were flooded and the beck that ran through the spare land flowed wider, deeper and faster than had been known in living memory. Leaden skies became the order of the day and with them a depression descended everywhere. Somehow it made getting over the chickenpox harder than ever. Some sceptics said, 'Chickenpox! That's nothing, it can hardly be counted as a disease, that can't,' but this particular strain appeared tenacious in its infectiousness. Grown-ups and children alike fell victim to it.

In church on the Sunday morning Peter prayed for those who had been stricken so badly with chickenpox and that soon the village would be restored to its usual quiet everyday calm.

'Fat chance of that,' whispered Mrs Jones to a neighbour who nudged her and answered in a loud whisper, 'He doesn't know the half.'

A worshipper in the pew in front said, 'Sh.' While someone in the pew behind leaned forward and asked, 'What do you know that I don't know?'

The neighbour replied *sotto voce*, 'There's to be a demonstration at the dig.'

'No!'

'Really?' asked Mrs Jones.

'There is.'

'Sh!'

'When?'

The worshipper in the pew in front turned round angrily. 'Sh! Have some respect.'

Mrs Jones winked at her neighbour and said, 'Tell me later, Annie.'

After church she was told that the demonstration was to be the next morning and they'd be ready and waiting for the students when they arrived. 'I'm going to support the demonstration. It's downright disgusting what they're doing, disgusting. You'll be there, won't you? We need all the help we can get.'

'Come rain or shine, I'll be there all right.'

To Mrs Jones's embarrassment the neighbour insisted on making a 'Protest against the dig' placard for her.

Next morning it was raining harder than ever. Great fat raindrops fell incessantly, the dark-grey lowering clouds made it seem like an early January morning not a July one, so a lot of people who had promised to support the demonstration duffed when the time came to take their stand. Annie from church, Willie Biggs, Alan Crimble from the Royal Oak and Vince Jones were there, and the two Misses Senior but no one else.

Mrs Jones, Sylvia and Bryn arrived to represent the supporters of the dig. It all felt rather like a damp squib and the dejected representatives on each side of the debate huddled in two opposing groups.

Bryn yelled, 'It's pointless you standing there. The dig's going ahead come what may.'

'Not if we can help it,' Willie shouted in defiance. Sylvia blushed at his vehemence.

'You might as well go home right now.'

'We shan't till you've gone.'

'Look! They've almost finished, you know. They don't expect to find much more.'

'If that's right, why are you here?'

Mrs Jones piped up with, 'Because we got wind of what you were going to do, that's why we've come.'

Willie sniggered. 'I can see you've got lots of support.'

Sylvia felt ashamed of herself, but stuck to her guns. 'You're not much better.'

Willie, broken-hearted by their differences, didn't reply to her, but Vince did. 'We've got plenty of support as you well know. They're all frightened to death, what with this rain and the chickenpox and that.'

'Rubbish!' shouted Bryn. 'You're talking absolute rubbish. You all need a good shake-up. You've lived here too long. You're too set in your ways. Here am I, trying to bring business to the village and this dig will be a highlight and all you can think of is that it's evil.'

'It's not the dig,' declared one Miss Senior. 'It's the Rector threatening to bury the bones in the churchyard. We don't like it at all, do we?'

The second Miss Senior shook her head and muttered under her breath, 'I'm in agreement, fully in agreement. It's the work of the devil.'

Bryn roared with laughter. What fools they were. 'We've got to move with the times, you daft old biddies.'

Sylvia protested at his rudeness.

Mrs Jones said, 'Hey, hold on, there's no call for that.'

'Well, they are! We've got to move on, get modern. Onward and upward. So what if there's a few old bones in a coffin buried deep. What harm can they do, for heaven's sake?' Bryn laughed aloud at their dyed-in-the-wool attitudes.

'Doesn't look as if they're coming today,' Willie said. By now his faithful anorak, which he normally only wore in winter, was letting in the wet.

'They're usually here by now.' Vince adjusted the angle of his umbrella and it dripped down his neck. 'Blast!'

Alan Crimble spoke up for the first time. 'If you ask me . . .'

Bryn interrupted him. 'Nobody's asking you and what's more you should be on this side not that, you being an employee of my pub.'

'Your pub! That's rich.'

'Yes, my pub.' Bryn began to boil with temper. 'I gave you a home and a job when you'd nowhere to go, just you remember that. By rights, Alan Crimble, you should be standing shoulder to shoulder with me.'

'Well, I'm not, and I wouldn't be if it was the last job on earth.'

'You snivelling little . . . pipsqueak.' Bryn closed up his umbrella, laid it on the church wall and put up his fists.

'Oh, "pipsqueak", is it?' Alan shaped up to Bryn.

Willie said, 'Alan, stop it. We don't want a fight.'

Bryn shouted, 'I don't mind. Not at all. I'm a match for anyone.' Huge drops of rain fell from the branches above his head. He glanced up at the sky and wondered what the blazes he was doing here in weather like this, losing his temper with a fool like Alan Crimble. He lost all his fight at that moment and decided to leave. 'To be honest, there's not much point in us all standing here getting pneumonia. They're obviously not coming today. Let's agree to go home, shall we?'

There was a general nodding of heads from both sides and what had been intended as a fight to the death on the part of the objectors ended with them creeping home defeated and soaked to the skin.

Bryn rallied his troops. 'Round one to us, I think?'

'Definitely,' agreed Mrs Jones.

'But no more threatening to fight, Bryn, I don't want Willie hurt,' Sylvia begged, conscious that this was the first rift ever between her and Willie and not for the world did she want him injured.

'Pity there weren't more of us here, but it can't be helped. Thanks for turning out, you two.'

Bryn went home to change and decided there would be no more confrontations on his part. It was a complete waste of time. The dig would go on regardless of what they did and perhaps, once the bones were buried, life would get back to normal. Oh, God, now he was bestowing on the bones powers they most definitely had not got. Or had they? Nothing seemed to have gone right since the dig started. He'd better be careful or his wonderful plans would not materialise. If only the rain would stop. And if only the chickenpox epidemic would stop too.

*

561

Jimmy was one of the last to become infected and he lay for three days in his house, alone and ill, until it occurred to Grandmama Charter-Plackett that she hadn't seen him about and she went to investigate.

'Hello-o-o-o! Jimmy, are you there?'

She could hear Sykes scuffling behind the door. 'Hello! Jimmy?'

Sykes began to bark: his odd little noise which came between a yap and the bark of a much larger dog. Then he started to whine and scrabble at the edge of the door.

Mrs Charter-Plackett cautiously tried the doorknob and found to her surprise that the door wasn't locked. She spoke to Sykes so he could recognise who it was. 'It's me, Sykes. All right?' She pushed open the door and bent to pat him. There'd been no fresh air in the house for several days, she could tell that; the air was stale and smelt of dog. There was no water left in Sykes's bowl either, and not a sound from upstairs. She went to stand at the bottom of the stairs and called up, 'Jimmy? Are you there?' He must be, his car was parked at the end of his garden as usual.

Having reached the top of the stairs, she peeped into one of the bedrooms and found Jimmy fast asleep in a seriously tousled bed. The air offended her sensibilities so she crossed the room to open the window. It creaked and groaned and the noise woke Jimmy. She didn't think she'd seen anyone with as many spots as he had. Not even little Fran.

'Why, Jimmy! I didn't know you were ill. I hope you don't mind, but I hadn't seen you about and thought I'd better investigate.'

Jimmy lifted his head from the pillow and groaned. 'It's Sykes. I haven't been able to feed him.'

'I'll see to that. It seems to me you need seeing to, too. First things first. I'll attend to Sykes and then you. A cup of tea. Eh?'

Her patient croaked a thank you and laid his head gratefully back on the pillow.

'You should have rung me, you silly man.'

Jimmy nodded a little impatiently. He was in no mood for Mrs Charter-Plackett's vigorous brand of jollying up.

By the time she'd fed and watered Sykes, and he'd rushed out of his cat flap into the garden and back in, and up to see Jimmy and generally decided life might have got back to something like normal, had the kettle boiling, had found a packet of porridge oats and made Jimmy a bowlful, Jimmy had been to the bathroom and flung some cold water on his face and dabbed it dry and run a comb very tenderly through his hair, desperate to avoid the spots on his scalp, and was back in bed.

'Why, that looks better. Now sit up and eat this. No argument. I like my porridge with golden syrup so I've put some on for you.'

She left him and went downstairs to do some bits of washing up he'd left. She wrinkled her nose at his carefree bachelor ways but manfully battled on with her tidying up.

A quarter of an hour later she was seated on his bedroom chair, watching him drinking the last of his tea. 'There, you must feel better. So you've got chickenpox.'

'I had every ailment under the sun when I was a boy but never chickenpox. Now it's finally got me. By Jove, but I've felt ill and not half. It could kill anybody, it could.'

'You realise why you've got the chickenpox, I suppose?'

'No.'

'Because you've opposed the dig. That's why, according to all the pundits who reckon they know it all.'

'It could be that. It could, yer know. There's stranger things 'ave 'appened, believe me.'

'You're soft in the head if you think that, Jimmy Glover.'

Jimmy smiled. 'You can scoff, but I bet they're right. Anyway, thanks for helping. I should be up and about tomorrow.'

'You haven't got rid of me yet. I shall cook a nice meal this evening and you shall partake of it. A nourishing chicken casserole, I think. On my way back from walking Sykes I'll call in at Jimbo's and see what he's got.' She stood up, brushed down her skirt, picked up his tray and noted with satisfaction that he'd eaten all his porridge. 'You look as if you need a sleep. Snuggle down. Sykes and I shan't be back till the casserole's ready, so you can relax. I won't lock the front door. Your cupboards look a bit bare of the essentials so I'll take the liberty of getting a few things for you. Jimbo will put it on the slate. Take care.' She didn't tell him he was as white as a sheet between his spots, nor that his long thin face was even thinner; he really was a sickly sight.

After she'd taken Sykes for his walk and become thoroughly wet, even though she'd worn her waterproofs, she tied him up outside the Store and went in.

Linda gave her an extra polite 'Good afternoon', having in the past been at the receiving end of her sharp tongue and regretting it.

'Good afternoon, Linda. I can't be long, I've tied Sykes up outside and he's not best pleased.'

'Sykes?'

'Yes. Jimmy's ill with the chickenpox so I'm caring for him. Is Jimbo about?'

'He is, he's in his office, he said to call if it got busy.' She pressed her thumb on her emergency bell. One press for Jimbo's presence, two presses for a serious emergency. Jimbo came bustling through from the back immediately. 'Mother!' He kissed her on both cheeks as she preferred and said, 'Thank heavens we've got a customer; it's been so quiet this morning.'

'No wonder with this chickenpox. Jimmy's got it now and he's been very poorly. The silly man didn't ring anyone so I've only just found out. I can't be long, I'm soaking wet. I'm making a chicken casserole for Jimmy, so have you fresh chicken today?'

Just as she was about to pay for Jimmy's groceries Sylvia came shopping for the Rectory. She shook her umbrella vigorously and put it in the umbrella stand so kindly provided by Jimbo. 'Good afternoon, Mrs Charter-Plackett. The weather doesn't improve, does it. They've had to stop the dig, everything being so wet.'

'Oh, good! I'm glad.'

'You're one of the ones who doesn't approve, then?'

'I was at Willie's meeting.'

'Were you indeed?'

'Didn't you know?'

'No.' Sylvia intimated by the shrug of her shoulders that she didn't want to know anything at all about 'that' meeting.

'So you agree with the Rector, then.'

'I suppose I have to say yes to that.'

'Of course, what else can you do when you work at the Rectory? You've got to be loyal.'

'I'm old enough to have my own opinions. I've never discussed the matter with him.'

Mrs Charter-Plackett looked askance at her.

'It's true. I never have, nor with Dr Harris. I just believe it's only fair to those poor unsettled remains for them to come home.'

'They should be left in peace.'

'Who says they're at peace where they are?'

'Well, they're certainly not at peace now they're being dug up. It's disgusting and it's irreverent.'

'You're not one of those idiots who thinks all our misfortunes are due to the dig. I would have thought you would have had more sense.'

'Well, really!'

'I mean it. More sense.' She looked up at Jimbo's clock above the door. 'Must fly. Shopping to do and the twins will be home soon.'

The discussion was abandoned by Sylvia just as Mrs Charter-Plackett was warming to her subject and she felt cheated. She exclaimed 'Well, really!' again and marched through to the back to find Jimbo. 'Some people are getting above their station.'

Jimbo looked up from his computer and said, 'I could hear you from here. I do wish you wouldn't be so antagonistic. "Above their station", honestly, Mother, it's no longer the rich man in his castle and the poor man at the gate, or hadn't you noticed?'

'Of course I have, but speaking to me like that, saying I should have more sense.'

'Well, perhaps you should have more sense. We both agreed the other night that our heads told us one thing and . . .'

'Our hearts another. So I'm listening to my heart '

'Don't, it's causing too much trouble. Willie and Sylvia aren't speaking, you know, all because of this . . .'

'Still? I thought they'd patched it up.'

'Vince and Greta Jones aren't either. It's causing an awful lot of trouble and you're adding fuel to it. Please don't.'

'I will not have my son telling me what I can and cannot say. If I feel strongly about something then I shall speak my mind and I shan't ask your permission.'

'I was only appealing to your good sense, but obviously, as Sylvia found, you haven't any.' He turned back to his computer and, because of being thoroughly rattled by his mother's intransigence, deleted some figures by mistake and swore.

'Jimbo! That is disgusting! In front of your own mother. Really!'

'You are exasperating, Mother, and if you anger me much more I shall say even worse. Don't come to my Store if all you can do is upset the few customers I have left.'

'I won't, then. I shall condemn myself to travelling into Culworth for everything. I'm sure Jimmy will appreciate the business.'

'You've forgotten he has the chickenpox.'

Realising she had made a complete fool of herself, she drew her shoulders back, marched out of the office and stormed through the Store, remembering her shopping but completely forgetting poor Sykes who by now was soaked to the skin. Consequently, as soon as she got home she put down her shopping and began to take off her wet things, remembered Sykes and had to go all the way back again. The jerk he got on his lead as she set off home once more hurt Sykes's feelings, and he sulked and refused to walk properly so she carried him home, fuming at her strong-headedness and the mess she'd got herself into.

'Thank God he's not a bull mastiff,' she muttered as she put the key in her door, only to find she hadn't locked it in the first place. 'I really will have to pull myself together. Casserole first, cup of tea afterwards.' Then she saw Sykes's wet footprints on her beautifully polished floor and the marks on the wall from his wet coat as he tried to rub himself dry, and knew he had to be dealt with first. This was not a good day at all. Those bones had a lot to answer for. Bryn was delighted by the episode in Deadman's Dell only because it suited him for his groups, not for any other reason. Damn him. She'd have to sort him out because it was obvious no one else was going to.

9

For the moment Bryn had more important matters needing his attention; primarily making sure that under no circumstances would Dicky get Georgie to the altar. He'd only another three weeks before he'd have to leave and go to London to meet his first American group flying into Gatwick. Therefore time was not on his side. His ban from going into the Royal Oak was up and he made free with his opportunities. Dicky didn't work every day, so he made a special point of being in there on his days off. But more significantly, he went in when Dicky *was* working, fixing him with a nasty glare, perfected in his bedroom mirror, at every possible chance he could. A threatening glare first, which he knew got Dicky's back up, then he'd set himself out to flirt with Georgie. The best of it was he sensed that Georgie enjoyed the flirting.

'Bryn! Behave yourself. You've seen me in this suit before. I've had it years.'

'But you've never filled it quite like you're doing tonight.'

'Bryn! That's cheek, that is. I don't weigh one ounce more than I did the day we married.'

'No! I hadn't realised. You were magnificent that day, Georgie. Truly beautiful.'

Dicky went to stand beside Georgie. 'She still is.'

'I didn't say she wasn't. I *meant* she still is. I remember it like it was only yesterday.'

'So do I.' Georgie went quite weepy at her memories.

Dicky sensed he was losing the game. 'Another whisky, Bryn?'

'Thanks, Dicky, I will.'

He tossed it back with a practised lift of the elbow. 'Tell you what, Georgie, my first group is up to twenty-five, a couple already booked are bringing two friends with them, I've had to close the list.'

This time Dicky took his glass from him without being asked and poured him another double. As he pushed it across the counter he gave Bryn a mean, challenging look. Man to man. Eyeball to eyeball. Bryn recognised the gauntlet Dicky was throwing down. 'And another.'

Dicky solemnly handed him his third and then his fourth. 'You're running up quite a bill. We don't have a slate here, you know. Remember, you wouldn't have one when your name was over the door.'

'That's right, I wouldn't. Here, barman.' Bryn laid a twenty-pound note on the bar counter, taken from a thick wad. 'Have one on me.'

'No, thanks, not when I'm working.'

By mistake Bryn said, 'The landlady won't mind.'

If there was one thing guaranteed to anger Georgie it was calling her the landlady.

'That's enough, the pair of you. I won't stand for it. Don't serve him any more tonight. He's had enough.'

'No, Georgie, I haven't had enough. 'Nother one, barman.' He sent his empty glass skittering across the counter and Dicky only just managed to stop it crashing to the floor. With a poker face he refilled the glass and handed it to Bryn. Seated now on a bar stool, Bryn accepted the glass and steadily downed the lot. The small area of his brain that from long practice could keep him in control no matter how much he drank swung into the arena. For that was what it had become: a gladiatorial confrontation, in public, for possession of the woman they both wanted. He downed his sixth and then his seventh glass, and Dicky, still poker-faced, poured him his eighth. The rest of the customers in the bar watched with breathless anticipation. Every eye was focused on Bryn and Dicky. The strange thing was that by the eighth glass neither of them was speaking. It had become a silent game of filling and emptying, filling and emptying. Georgie cringed with apprehension. He must have done some hard drinking in the past to withstand all this whisky. Someone's inane high-pitched laugh shattered the silence and should have broken the spell they were all under, but it didn't.

Suddenly Georgie banged her fist on the counter and said, 'Dicky! Don't serve him another glass. That's an order.'

The ninth and then the tenth glass, and still Bryn wanted more.

Bryn pushed his glass across the counter towards Dicky and signalled with a crooked finger that he wanted yet another double.

Georgie shouted, 'Don't you dare serve him. Do you hear me?'

But Dicky ignored her. Dicky who'd always been so . . . well . . . so *obedient* to her smallest wish. Bryn tossed back his eleventh double.

Dicky refilled Bryn's glass but instead of handing it to him he placed it well away from Bryn's side of the counter, making Bryn reach right across if he wanted it. Bryn crooked his finger again and beckoned for it to be given him. But Dicky, with a grin on his face which almost reached from ear to ear, didn't obey. Bryn overreached himself, almost caught hold of the glass but missed, overturned it and shot every drop of whisky down the front of Dicky's shirt, and he himself fell off the bar stool and on to the floor, unconscious. He lay flat on his back, his mouth wide open as though waiting for another whisky to be poured down his throat.

The entire bar erupted in hysterical laughter. They held their sides, wiped their tears, nudged each other, rolled about, pointed helplessly and roared with laughter all over again. As for Dicky, he simply spread his hands wide, shrugged his shoulders and looked as innocent as a newborn baby. The staff waiting on in the dining room came through to see what was the matter; some diners left their meals to see the fun.

Georgie stormed round the counter and knelt beside Bryn. 'Come on, Bryn, wake up. You've got to get home. Come on.' She shook him by the shoulders, slapped his face twice, to no avail. 'Dicky! Jug of water please.'

Without a word Dicky filled a large jug with water and handed it to her.

'You ought to have had more sense. I told you to stop serving him. What were you thinking of?' She threw the jug of water over his head and face, but to no effect.

Dicky said loudly, enjoying his audience, 'Round one to Dicky Tutt.' Everyone clapped their approval.

'Good on yer, Dicky!'

'Good for you!'

'Just what he deserved.'

Georgie snapped out, 'Get me a towel.'

Dicky found a not particularly savoury one from the bottom of the towel cupboard and handed it to her.

She vigorously rubbed his head and face dry. 'It's no good, he's completely out. He's not going to get home in this state.' She took hold of the front of his shirt and shook him briskly. 'Bryn, wake up! Come on!' But Bryn didn't.

Dicky laughed. 'Not much of a Romeo now, is he?' He got a round of applause for his remark.

'It's nothing to the credit of either of you. You call yourselves grown men. Huh! More like two little boys. I'm disgusted with the pair of you. It's all your fault, Dicky.'

Georgie's indignation soon turned to laughter and when Georgie and Dicky looked at one another they laughed louder still. So did the spectators – there hadn't been such an hilarious night in the Royal Oak for years.

'Them whiskies looked more like triples to me,' someone shouted.

Dicky gasped out, 'The last two were!' and everyone laughed louder than ever.

But they still had the problem of what to do with Bryn. 'We'll drag him into the back and he can sleep it off. I'll ring Neville and let him know.'

Bryn's planned night of romance had an ignominious ending. Dicky took one leg, Georgie the other, Alan caught hold of him under his armpits and between them they hauled him off stage into the back storeroom. Georgie found a blanket and covered him over. So Bryn spent the night squeezed between cartons of Tortilla crisps and toilet roll twelve packs from the cash and carry and not between the sheets with Georgie.

When he woke next morning Dicky was standing over him reliving his last night's triumph. 'So, you've woken up at last.'

'Oh! What are you doing here?' Bryn clutched his head with both hands and moaned.

'I work here, remember?'

Bryn opened his eyes and saw the word 'Tortilla' written only five inches from his eyes. His voice thick with sleep he asked, 'Where am I?'

'In the storeroom, sleeping it off.'

The events of the whole evening flooded back to him. 'You little sod. It was you.'

Dicky shook his head. 'No, it wasn't me. You did the drinking. Not me.'

Bryn tried to sit up. 'Ah! Get me a drink.'

'Hair of the dog?'

Though he was in agony, Bryn was sharp enough to see through Dicky's game plan. 'No. Black coffee. That's best.'

Georgie called out, 'Send him upstairs for a cold shower.'

Bryn shuddered. Cold shower. What did she think he was? He was far too frail for a cold shower.

'There's still some of your clothes in the wardrobe, Bryn. Put fresh on.'

Dicky didn't know this and he felt Georgie was disloyal to him, keeping Bryn's clothes as though she expected him back any minute. He half kicked Bryn's leg. 'Get up, then.'

'Steady on.' Bryn heaved himself up and, towering over Dicky, said, 'Don't for one minute think you've won. You haven't. Right?'

'Says you.' Dicky strutted out of the storeroom saying, 'Shall I show you where the bathroom is? Oh, of course, you know.' He grinned, considering he'd won another point. But at bottom he was bitterly angry. All he wanted was to get his and Georgie's and Bel's lives sorted out. They'd been in limbo far too long. He got through his routine with one ear cocked for Bryn. He heard him come down from the bathroom, caught a glimpse of him in an outfit he'd worn before he'd hopped it with Elektra, which did him no favours, listened for him talking to Georgie and then to his delight saw him cross the car park and go out into Church Lane. Good riddance to him. He'd thought she might give him breakfast but she hadn't. He just wished he'd died last night from all that drink. Obviously that wasn't the way to go.

He went to look for her. 'Georgie! There you are.' Dicky took her hand in his and said, 'There's something I need to know.'

'Fire away.'

'The divorce, is it going ahead?'

'Of course it is. I want rid of him as soon as possible after last night. I can't stand all this macho squaring up to each other. All this testosterone. Give me a kiss.' They kissed joyfully. 'Oh, Dicky, I do love you.'

'And I love you. Just let's get it all straightened out and then . . .'

'I can't wait. But listen to me, no more trying to finish him off with stupid tricks like last night. You mustn't, you know, it might backfire.'

'I know, I was daft, but the chance was too much to pass by. He knew exactly what I was doing and thought he'd win, but fortunately for me he didn't. It is stupid, the whole situation is stupid, and I want no more of it, believe me.'

'For the sake of the business I can't pass up those lunches on a Thursday, but from now on that's all it will be, him turning up from time to time with his punters. If he wants to put business our way then so what! All the better for us. That's all it will be and I mean it.'

'His clothes . . . get rid of them.'

Georgie had to laugh. 'OK. The new Bryn looked ridiculous in them, didn't he?'

Dicky hugged her tight. 'That's the problem, the *new* Bryn.'

'You've no need to be jealous, love. There's nothing there for him any more.' Georgie knew he needed reassuring about her love for him and she said what he needed to hear, but somewhere deep down came that hankering again, nudging at her, worrying at her. She sighed.

He sensed her hankering, felt she was wanting to be loyal to him but finding it difficult; just that little bit of conviction missing. But then again when he said he wanted no more of Bryn and his sparring he too didn't entirely mean it; well, almost but not quite. Just that little bit of conviction missing, the same as it was for Georgie. They'd been all right till Bryn turned up again, opening up old memories, looking more handsome then he'd ever done. Well, he for one wasn't giving Georgie up without a fight. Like he'd said once to the Rector, she was everything to him; on that matter he didn't lack conviction, not one jot.

'Coffee time?'

'Yes, please.'

Bryn kept a low profile the morning after his humiliation in the bar. He'd been an idiot, a complete idiot taking up Dicky's challenge. The only one to come smiling out of it had been Dicky himself. It simply wouldn't do. He had to have the upper hand not only in Georgie's eyes but in the eyes of the whole village. Damn and blast, he thought, as he showered yet again in the hope of restoring some semblance of equilibrium to his shattered body. He was getting too old for the kind of drinking he'd done last night. He carefully arranged the bath towel on the rail in Neville's guest bathroom and walked into the bedroom. He looked at the clothes he'd just removed and thought, where on earth was I coming from to be wearing a shirt and trousers like that? I even thought I looked good in them. Huh! No wonder Georgie had gone off him, no wonder at all. He must have been an idiot. Bryn bundled them up ready for the bin and selected a matching set of shirt and trousers from his extensive wardrobe. Then he settled himself in a chair by the window and looked out on to Neville's well-manicured garden, intending to take time reappraising his future.

He was right about doing this tourist business. Hour upon hour serving cruise guests on those damned liners had honed his skills to a fine point. He'd been out of his depth to begin with but by the end of the first year he'd found he could have them eating out of his hand. A combination of flattery and a good memory for faces and what drinks the punters preferred had earned him more in tips than his wages and that was the way to go with his tourists. Barely three weeks and he'd be off to London to meet his first group. He rubbed his hands together in glee. From a file on the bedside table he took his list of Americans for the first group and sat lost in thought.

But somehow Georgie's face kept intruding, and instead of the words he saw an image of her laughing up at him on their wedding day, crying when she'd found she wasn't pregnant when she'd been confident she was. That had been a blow, that had; no children. But it had been a long time since he'd grieved about it. A long time. Down below him he spotted Guy and Hugh, Neville's boys, standing smoking by the summer house. Two huge great boys, well, men really, confident, well-educated, Oxford or somewhere similar now behind them, both heading out into the world. They'd only themselves to blame if they didn't succeed. Unbidden came the thought: if only he'd had their chances.

Somewhere below a door opened and he heard Neville calling for Liz. He wished he'd never thought to ask the slimy toad to help finance his scheme. In a rare moment of clarity he knew Neville would bleed him dry if he didn't watch it. That was what happened when you'd made your money, you could just sit back and do nothing and in the returns would roll. Well, damn moneybags Neville. He'd pay him his loan back as soon as he could, even if he had to go without to do it. He and Georgie together would conquer the world. He needed Georgie to enjoy the fruits of his plan, there'd be no point in being rich just for himself. Somehow he had to have her, come hell or high water. He'd never thought he could fall in love all over again but that was exactly what had happened to him. He only had to see Georgie and the blood was gushing through his veins, his heart making that leap it used to do whenever she walked into a room when they were young and starting out.

Bryn checked his watch. They'd be opening soon. He strolled downstairs, called out he wouldn't be needing lunch and left for the Royal Oak. He turned out of the gates to go down Church Lane and saw a surveyor standing on the pavement taking a bearing through a theodolite. He gave him a cheery 'Good morning' and a salute, and meandered past. Then Bryn stopped in his tracks. He turned back and went to pass the time of day with the chap. Friendly, kind of, the new Bryn. The new hail-fellow-well-met kind of Bryn.

'What are you up to this fine sunny morning, might I ask?'

His assistant some yards away glanced up. The surveyer answered, 'You can ask.'

Bryn thought aye, aye! Something's going on here he doesn't want us to find out about. 'Just wondered, you know, why you were here. Realigning the road or something?'

'No.'

'What then?'

The surveyor tapped the side of his nose with his forefinger. Bryn began to smell a rat. 'I see. Mum's the word.'

He nodded.

'Surely we've a right to know; we are all ratepayers.'

'Look, I'm trying to do a job of work here. Would you mind moving on? Please.'

Bryn tried several diplomatic approaches but the chap remained annoyingly silent.

'There is such a thing as good manners when someone's speaking to you.'

'Look! I'm here to do a job. Just go away.'

Bryn was tempted to kick a leg of his theodolite, but decided against it. He wouldn't learn anything that way. He turned on his heel and went back to Glebe House.

'Neville!'

'Yes. I'm in the study,' came the reply in that reedy voice which could irritate so very quickly.

Bryn pushed open the door and there Neville sat in his gleaming study, at his obsessively tidy desk, fingers poised over his keyboard, peering at him over the top of his gold-rimmed half-glasses.

'In your position as councillor do you know anything at all about these chaps out here surveying the place?'

Neville paused only for a moment but Bryn picked up on it, then Neville said, 'Not a thing.'

Bryn thought, you liar. You absolute liar. You do. 'I'm surprised you don't, you being on the council.'

'I may be on the council but I don't know every jot and tittle of what's going on in other departments.'

'I thought you were in planning?'

'I am, but this isn't my kind of planning.'

'I see.' Bryn rubbed his chin while he considered. 'Do you know who might know? The chappie himself isn't forthcoming, which is suspicious in itself.'

Neville had returned to studying his computer and looked up impatiently. 'Sorry, Bryn, must press on. I'll ask around.'

I bet, thought Bryn.

Reluctantly he left Neville to his work and wandered off to the Royal Oak.

It was lunchtime and only Alan was about.

'Georgie not in?'

'Getting ready to go out. Her day off.'

'Ah! I'll have a whis— No, I'll have a tonic water. Choose something for yourself, anything you fancy.'

'No, thanks, too early for me.'

Bryn settled himself on a bar stool and quizzed Alan about where Georgie was going.

'I've been told not to interfere in her private life, so I've no idea.'

Bryn chuckled. 'Whoops!' He laughed some more and saw Alan beginning to go red in the face. 'How's the kid? Louis, or whatever his name is.'

'Lewis, actually. He's doing great.'

'Time you had another.'

'You can't rush these things.'

'Young virile chap like you.'

'These things take time and it costs money to bring up a kid. Two might just finish us off.'

'I bet. Tips you get in here. Cruise liners are even better for tips. I could earn more than my wages every week on the liners.'

Alan perked up at this, but then knew for sure that Linda would never tolerate his absences. 'Here's Georgie.'

She came through from the back, dressed for off, and what a picture she made, thought Bryn.

'My taxi'll be here in a minute. You can manage, can't you, Alan?'

'Of course.'

Georgie saw Bryn. 'You've turned up. Feeling OK?'

Bryn nodded. 'I'm just planning to go into Culworth. Can I give you a lift?'

He saw her hesitate, ponder and dismiss the idea. 'No, thanks.'

'Why not? I won't pester, I'll drop you off and we'll arrange a picking-up time.' He gave her a winning smile, saw her hesitate, than make up her mind.

'All right, then, but I'll have the taxi to pay.'

'Leave me to attend to that.' They heard the horn tooting outside. 'Won't be a tick.'

Bryn came back in and realised that Alan and she had had words; Georgie was flushed and Alan was sullen.

'I'll go and pick up my car. Won't be a minute.'

'I'll wait outside in the yard.'

'OK.'

After he'd settled her in her seat in the most gentlemanly way, Bryn roared off down the Culworth Road delighted to be able to show off his new car to her.

Georgie settled back on the luxurious leather seat and that nagging annoying feeling buried deep down struggled to the surface again. When she'd been so sickened by Bryn for so long, how could she possibly have any feelings left for him? But she had. They surged to the forefront of her consciousness and she revelled in them. He made her feel a million dollars. She glanced at him and he caught her eye.

'Watch the road, for heaven's sake!'

Bryn could only laugh, out loud, boisterously, joyfully. 'Let's lunch first, then we'll go our separate ways.'

'I don't know about lunch.'

Bryn nudged her. 'Go on.'

'Well . . . all right, then.'

'Good! The George for Georgie. Heh!'

'You've changed.'

'I needed to. Alan giving you grief?'

'Not really. Just thinks he's my guardian. Well, I've got news for him. He isn't.'

They drove in silence for a while, Bryn exulting in the chance to show Georgie what he was made of and Georgie enjoying the pleasure of escaping briefly from her workaday life. She looked at Bryn's profile and thought he wasn't the best-looking of men but there was something about him nowadays which had been lacking before. He'd become prepossessing, almost attractive. She said, 'It seems to me you're a hardened drinker. I didn't appreciate that performance last night.'

'Neither did I. It won't happen again. I'm not a hardened

drinker, don't think that of me. It was Dicky's challenge that made me make a fool of myself.'

'Too right, you did make a fool of yourself. Why can't you just leave Dicky alone?'

'He annoys me, thinking he can whisk you off to the altar as soon as the divorce comes through. What's more, like I've said before, I shan't agree to it.'

'Hard luck, I'm going through with it.'

Bryn, having to pause at the traffic lights at the bottom of Deansgate, took his chance. He laid a gentle hand on Georgie's knee and said, 'That night...'

'Yes?'

'You and me in the lounge. You were very tempted. You and me making music together.' The lights changed and he drove on.

'I may have been tempted, but I'd never have forgiven myself. I'm marrying Dicky.'

Her throat seemed to fill up with emotion and tears were very close. What was the matter with her? Blowing with the wind, she was. When she was with Dicky it was Dicky, with Bryn, out of the blue, she discovered emotions long since dead.

'You don't sound as convincing as you did.'

'Oh, but I am.' Liar, she thought, liar.

When they walked from the car park into the George she noticed one or two admiring glances directed at Bryn. His manners and bearing in a place like the George were exactly right, and she couldn't help thinking that Dicky would not have carried the whole situation off with quite the same style as Bryn was doing.

All through the meal Georgie endeavoured to keep the conversation as general as she could, avoiding all mention of Dicky or Bel or the pub, but after an hour of sustaining that Bryn inevitably turned the talk to Dicky.

'It's quite simple, Bryn, I love him and I don't love you.'

He looked keenly at her, noted the slight flush the wine had brought to her cheeks, the way her lovely blonde hair curled and swirled so naturally about her face, her mouth so sweet and yet showing strength, and he wished so very much that she were his. What an idiot he'd been.

'I sense doubt. I sense there's indecision.'

'Do you indeed.'

'I do.'

Georgie's eyes filled with tears. 'I do. I do. I do love him.'

'And me? What about me?'

A tear spilled over and ran down her cheek. Georgie found a tissue and wiped it away.

'Well, what about me?'

'Stop putting pressure on me. Stop behaving like a lunatic. I know what you're capable of. You make me afraid of myself.'

'What do you mean?'

'You make me not know my own mind. I want you out of my life. I want you to go. I don't want your lunch business and I don't want you in the bar. Right!' She stood up and marched from the restaurant blinded by tears.

He rushed after her, leaving two twenty-pound notes on the till as he went. Bryn caught her as she headed away from the hotel towards the station taxi rank. 'Look here, this is ridiculous. At least let me take you home.' With his arm round her shoulders he lead her towards his car and they sat there for a while until Georgie had command of herself.

'I was going to see my solicitor again with some papers he needs, to do with the business. You know, for the divorce. I'll tidy myself up and I'll go. I can't waste a day. I get few enough days off as it is.'

'Why bother, when you're not sure? I've found a whole new love for you, Georgie, a whole new love. I admit to being a fool in the past, but I've come to my senses now. I want you to leave things as they are. I'll do this tourist thing now I've got them planned and then after this summer I'll forget it and we can go back to being husband and wife running the pub, and we'll employ more staff so it's not so intense. You know, more time off. What do you say?'

Her answer was to stare out of the windscreen saying nothing. Bryn waited. And waited, until eventually he said, 'Well, all right then, you think about it.' He turned the ignition and started reversing out of the parking space.

'You're asking too much of me.'

Bryn stopped the car half in and half out. 'I'm only asking for the status quo.'

'Too much water under the bridge for that.'

'I don't see why.'

'How long till you become what you were before? How long till you kill what I have for you like before? How long till you forget the love bit and fancy the new barmaid? How long, I say, how long?'

Silenced by the obvious truth of what she said, Bryn drove her to the solicitor's office and remained outside like a condemned man awaiting his sentence. When Georgie came out and got back in, neither of them noticed the car which went past them in the busy street, nor did they see the wave the driver gave them.

10

'Caroline! You'll never guess who I saw in Culworth today, outside a solicitor's office would you believe, you know, the one in the side street off Deansgate?'

'No?'

'Bryn and Georgie.'

Caroline turned from the cooker and looked at him. 'How odd, him driving her to the solicitor's to get a divorce from him.'

'It's curious, isn't it? It looked as though he'd sat outside and waited for her. She was getting into the car just as I passed.' Peter went to put his communion case in the study and came back into the kitchen closing the door behind him. 'Darling, we must come to some decision about ... what to say to the children. We did say we would. Have you given it any more thought?'

'A little. I think I can face up to it better now than I imagined I would. But I still haven't thought out how to introduce it.'

'No, neither have I. What I don't want to do is give them the idea that their arrival was some dreadful murky underhand happening of which we are completely ashamed. I am ashamed of what I did, and rightly so, but I don't want them to feel that.'

'Even so, if it was rather less beautiful than we would have wished, neither of us has regretted it, have we?'

She turned round to look at him and he couldn't quite decipher what she was asking him, so he avoided a straightforward answer by saying, 'From the moment I first saw them I have loved them.'

'Me too.'

They were both silent for a while, then Peter said, 'It's amazing how one can help others with their problems and yet, with one's own . . .'

'Photographs. How about photographs?'

'Which?'

'In the parish albums. There must be some of her in there. Surely?'

'I don't know.'

Caroline answered quite clearly, 'You do, you know.'

Peter flushed. He poured himself a glass of water from the jug on the table and took a long drink before he said, 'I'll check that.'

'It will hurt me more than you to see them. Remember that. Tell the children, darling, they need to wash their hands.'

By the time the children had responded to this request the meal was on the table. 'Grace.' Peter waited for them to close their eyes and put their hands together, then said, 'By the grace of God we have food to eat, clean water to drink and a loving home. Praise God the Almighty. Amen.'

'I had hoped Bryn and Georgie might get together again. What about you?' Caroline asked him.

'I hoped so too, but considering the tales we've heard of the goings on I very much doubt it.'

'Oh, well! We'll have to leave it to them; there's nothing we can do about it. It's Dicky I feel sorry for.'

Beth enquired, 'Doesn't Mrs Fields want Mr Fields for a husband any more?'

Caroline answered her with, 'It's all very complicated, Beth, but I'm sure one day they'll get it all sorted.'

Alex said, 'I like Mrs Fields. She's nice, and I like Mr Tutt. I can't wait to get into Scouts proper, then we'll have him for our leader. He's always good fun.'

Beth emptied her mouth before asking, 'Where are Mr and Mrs Fields's children?'

'They haven't got any.'

Beth looked at Caroline as she said this and came out with, 'Perhaps she's like you, Mummy, and can't have children.'

'I expect that's so.'

'Will I be the same? Because you're my mummy?'

Caroline cupped Beth's lovely rounded cheek in her hand and

skirted round the situation as usual by saying, 'Not necessarily. You'll probably have dozens of children.'

'Oh, I wouldn't want dozens, but four would be very nice, thank you. Think of all the washing. And the ironing.'

Alex said, 'I'm not having any at all, I'm going to explore the world in my plane, I shan't have time.'

For quite a while Beth ate her food without speaking. Caroline cast a few glances at her and, knowing her as she did, suddenly realised she was going to produce some devastating piece of information and felt sick to her stomach.

She did just that. 'But if you're not my mummy, and my tummy-mummy could have Alex *and* me, then perhaps I *shall* be able to have babies.'

Peter answered on Caroline's behalf, 'Yes. It's very likely and I shall be proud to be their grandfather.'

Alex burst out laughing. 'Grandad! Grandad!'

Beth giggled. 'Granny! Granny!'

'Who is my granny?'

Peter looked at Alex and said, 'There's your Granny and Grandad Peterson who are Mummy's mother and father, but unfortunately my mother and father died a long while ago, so you've never known them.'

Beth declared, 'Those two sisters at school who dance, they don't know where their daddy is. They've only got a mummy. And there's Janine, she's only got her daddy and sometimes her mummy because she's usually in hospital. And there's Sean, he's got a dad at the weekends.'

Caroline asked Beth how she knew all this.

'Because I listen.'

Alex snorted his disbelief. 'Because you're a nosy parker. I've heard you asking.'

'I do not.'

'You do.'

'I don't.'

'You do, so there!'

Peter rapped on the table. 'Children, this won't do. Finish your dinner.'

Beth burst into tears. 'I don't want mine. He's horrid. I only wanted to know.'

Peter reached out to pat her arm. 'Of course you did. You needed to get it sorted out, didn't you. It's very sad that so many children haven't got both their mother and their father at home. Very sad indeed.'

Alex said in a belligerent tone, 'They look all right.'

Caroline murmured, 'But some of them must hurt inside.'

'Definitely. I'm sure they must. Now dry your tears, young lady, and count your blessings.'

This silenced Alex and Beth but it did nothing to quell the fear in Caroline's heart. Week in week out she felt as though she'd actually given birth to them both, she loved and adored them so dearly. So much so that for years she'd been able to dismiss from her mind the time when Alex and Beth would need an explanation of their origins, but as Peter had said only a few short weeks ago, the time had come. Whether it was harder for her than for him she wasn't quite sure. Whether or not they would fully understand the situation she didn't know. What she dreaded most of all was them wanting to know all about Suzy and their three half-sisters, Daisy, Pansy and Rosie. Their names were engraved on her heart. Even worse, though, would Alex and Beth still feel the same about her after they'd been told? She remembered the searing pain of the day when, thinking they were all away on holiday, Suzy had come back to the village. In her mind she could still see Alex running out into the road in his pyjamas and her snatching him up, and seeing Suzy standing by the lych-gate looking up the church path waving to Peter. It didn't bear thinking about.

Caroline looked at Peter and he saw how troubled she was. 'Children, if you give Mummy and me ten minutes I'll come and play a game with you. Your choice.'

'Lose Your Shirt,' shouted Alex.

Beth suggested Scrabble.

'Not Scrabble, I don't like Scrabble.'

'That's because you always lose.'

'I don't.'

'You do!'

'I don't!'

'Make up your minds. Ten minutes, then.'

He closed the kitchen door after them and began clearing the table.

Caroline asked, 'Just how far shall we go?'

'Play it by ear. They're both intelligent; they'll soon understand the whole picture. I've had a thought.'

Caroline said, 'Good. Because I haven't.'

'I think the photograph album is the best approach. We can casually find one of her and begin the explanation from there.'

'Oh, God!'

'You've nothing to fear.'

'Haven't I?'

'No, why should you? I bear the burden of guilt, don't I? They may never want to speak to me again, but that's for me to cope with.'

'Do they *have* to know everything?'

'As I said, I'll play it by ear. Go as far as they want to go. They know the mechanics. Believe me, Kate Pascoe has left no stone unturned in her sex education lessons. I know because she thrashed it all out with me before she started them.'

Bent over the dishwasher filling the racks, Caroline almost groaned aloud with anxiety at the prospect. She turned to face him. 'You must impress on them that they are adopted by you and me. That there's no going back. That Suzy wasn't able to keep them because she couldn't cope, with her husband dead and three children already. Don't let them think she didn't want them, because she did. I think maybe I'm not ready for these revelations.'

'Is one ever completely ready? For something on this scale? But what I shall emphasise is that the two of them answered your prayers as well as mine. I don't want them to think Suzy and I foisted them on you. It was you who asked her for them, remember.'

The doorbell rang. It registered with neither of them so at the second ring it was Beth who opened the door and found Georgie Fields on the doorstep, looking distraught.

'Is the Rector in?'

'Yes, he is, Mrs Fields. Will you come into the study and I'll go and get him.'

Georgie crept in to the study, where Beth invited her to sit down and went to find Peter.

'That's our game cancelled.'

'Why?'

'That was Mrs Fields at the door. I've shown her into your study, Daddy.'

Peter put down the tablecloth he was folding and left the kitchen. He found Georgie sitting on the study sofa, weeping. Closing the door behind him, he seated himself at his desk and asked quietly, 'Now, Georgie, what can I do for you?'

Georgie couldn't answer. All she could think of was coming back from Culworth in silence because she was so confoundedly mixed up about everything and then finding herself alone in the lounge with Bryn.... she sobbed again at what she'd done.

'I'm sorry for interrupting when you're busy. I don't even know if I should have come. But I'm so mixed up. I can't ever, ever forgive myself for what I've done.'

Peter waited.

'I could kill him, I could.'

Peter waited.

'I've made such a mess of things.'

'There's an answer to be found to most problems.'

'Not to this.'

'Tell me.'

'I can't.'

'There's nothing I haven't heard about the frailty of human lives. The foolish, the downright evil, the absolute depths of depravity. I don't expect for one minute that your problem is any more dreadful.'

'It is to me.'

'Ah!'

Georgie dried her eyes. 'I should never have come here. I can't tell someone like *you*. Never. I'm an idiot, an incredible fool. I quite simply can't tell *you*. I'll go.' She stood up.

'That's all right by me, but sometimes it helps to speak to an outsider. Gives a new dimension to things, don't you know.'

'I . . .'

'Anything said in this room is entirely confidential; I don't even tell Caroline. You have my word about that.'

Peter waited.

'It's Bryn.' She sat down again. 'It's Bryn. Before he came back I was absolutely clear about Dicky. All I wanted was to get face to face with Bryn, sort out the business side of things, you know, the money side, get the divorce, marry Dicky and live happily ever after.'

'And ... what's stopping you doing just that?'

'Me. I'm stopping me.'

'I see. How does Dicky feel?'

'Well, that's just it.' 'It' was Dicky finding out that they were in her bedroom with the door locked when he came to start his shift. He'd been looking for her and as he had free run of the upstairs rooms he thought nothing of going up there to find her. He'd tapped on her bedroom door as a last resort and found it locked, and had known instinctively what was afoot. She and Bryn were sleeping in each other's arms and they'd woken with such a jolt when Dicky had rattled the doorknob.

'He's ... we've ... Bryn and I have ... slept together today and Dicky's found out.'

He'd stood hammering on the door, shouting and shouting. They'd both dressed and eventually Bryn had unlocked the door. Dicky must have heard the key turn because before Bryn could open the door he had pushed it open and was facing them, eye to eye, hands clenched by his sides. Georgie didn't think she had ever seen Dicky so wild with temper. She'd honestly thought murder would be done. He'd looked past them and seen the bed so obviously slept in, and he'd given Bryn a stare which had made her blood run cold. His face was contorted with such fearful anger, such terrifying despair, such horror. She shuddered at the thought.

Georgie heard Peter say something, but didn't know what it was. 'I'm sorry, I didn't hear.'

'I said I'm so sorry to hear that. So sorry.'

'So am I. I've run away to you because I'm so frightened. Just tell me what to do.' She remembered how Dicky had stormed off downstairs, leaving her and Bryn in shock. She'd hurried Bryn down the stairs and out through the back, and then she'd gone to the bathroom and showered and changed and redone her make-up and tried to pull herself together but she hadn't been able to face Dicky so, like a coward, she'd run to a safe haven hoping for some answers.

She mistook Peter's silence for an inability to give her an answer so she stood up again and made to leave. 'I'm sorry to have troubled you.'

'Wait, just a moment. I can't tell you what to do, that's for you to decide. There's nothing quite like removing oneself from a situation in order to get a perspective on it. Be honest, tell them or write them a note and tell them the *truth* of why you're going. When you're by yourself, think about what you want, not just for this year or next, but for *the rest of your life*. You won't have the answer the first day and maybe not even the second but eventually you will. When you've decided, come back and be absolutely up front about your decision.'

Georgie looked up at him. 'Do you know, I think you're right.'

'People might think it's running away from your problems, but it's not. What it is, is taking charge of your life again. Go today, tonight, straight away.'

'I will. Thank you. Yes, I will.'

'God bless you, Georgie, I shall remember you in my prayers.'

'Thank you for that.'

Peter opened the study door for her and saw her out. He watched her walk away towards the Royal Oak and thought, what a mess human beings make of their lives. Then he thought about his own problem of the twins' birth and knew he was no different from the rest of humankind.

Dicky had walked down the stairs knowing he was capable of murder. He imagined the feel of his hands round Bryn's neck, sensed his own inhuman strength, slowly, slowly strangling him, almost felt Bryn's body suddenly lack resistance as he collapsed at his feet. A grim smile crossed his face and a tear trickled down his cheek. He stood at the foot of the stairs gripping the newel post, trying to come to terms with what he'd found out. His mouth felt like a piece of arid desert, his teeth so dry they stuck to the insides of his cheeks. He could hear Trish and Alan talking, the sound of laughter from the bar, the clatter of cutlery and china in the dining room; none of it made any sense. Dicky felt black inside, emptied, voidlike. From upstairs came sounds of life, voices and movement. He couldn't bear to be standing there so numb when they came downstairs, so he hurried to the storeroom and, leaving the door ajar, sat down on a case of something or other to brood and listen.

But he heard nothing except scurrying feet and haste, the bolt shot back, the door open, shut and the bolt refastened, and Georgie's feet climbing the stairs again. He remembered how he'd loved to massage those same feet for her when they ached after a day behind the bar. But there was one thing for certain: he, Richard Tutt, wouldn't be massaging her feet ever again. When he could hear the water running in the bathroom, moving like an automaton he went to where he had hung his jacket, took it down from the peg, laid it over his arm, took hold of the knob of the door bolt and thought he could feel the warmth of her hand still there, so he caressed it for a moment, a lump rising into his throat as he did so, then he opened the door and left the Royal Oak, vowing it was for the last time.

He flung himself down on the sofa in his tiny cottage living room, lying there for what felt like hours, filled with black despair. His mind racing and racing through what had happened, trying to find reasons, while all the time his imagination shied away from thinking of them in that bed, together, touching, thrilling . . . everything which had belonged to *him* now besmirched by Bryn. Such an agonising betrayal, he couldn't believe Georgie was capable of it. But she was. He groaned out loud and wept.

He woke when he heard Bel's voice saying, 'I've got away for half an hour, Dicky, love.'

He didn't answer her. There wasn't anything to say.

'She's gone. There was this letter on the mat. It's from her, I recognise the writing. I'll put the kettle on.'

It seemed only one tick of the clock when Bel came back in with the tray. She poured out his tea and pushed it close to him.

Dicky picked up the cup of scalding tea and burned his lips trying to drink it.

'Silly boy, it's straight from the pot. Put it down. Have you read the letter? No, I can see you haven't. You'd better read it. I can't, it's got your name on it. I'd like to know what's happened.'

'You don't know?'

'No. I might be your sister but I'm not a mind reader. All I know is she's packed her bags and gone. For a few days, I understand. I've been too busy in the dining room to get away any sooner. I do know she's been to see the Rector and then come back and said she was taking a few days off. She didn't tell me, it's only what I've learned from Trish and Alan.'

'She and Bryn have . . . slept together today.' He spoke as though he was having to prise the words out of his mouth.

Bel gasped with shock. 'Oh, Dicky, love, I'm so sorry.'

'As far as I'm concerned that's it. I'm finished with her. The love of my life. Over. Done. Finished.'

'Oh, Dicky!' She kicked off her shoes and lay back in the easy chair, lost for words. All she longed for was his happiness. His total happiness. And here he was, broken to pieces. Gently she prompted him into action. 'See what she says in her letter.'

Dicky handed it to her. 'You read it.'

'I can't, Dicky, I can't. I mustn't.'

'Read it!'

'I . . .'

'Do as I say.'

Bel opened the letter and swiftly read it through.

'Out loud!'

'Out loud? But it's private.'

'See if I care. Read it, please.'

Bel cleared her throat and in a shaky voice read out:

Dearest Dicky,

Can you forgive me for one moment of wrongdoing? It didn't mean a thing to me, you're all I care about. I'm so muddled. Peter said go away and think, and I am. But it's you all the time.

All my love,

your Georgie

Dicky snatched the letter from Bel and read it through for himself. 'Hah! "*I'm so muddled.*" She's not the only one. Muddled? I should say. So am I. I can't understand the signals I'm getting. Does she or doesn't she love me?' Dicky's voice broke as he asked that last question.

'Oh, Dicky, I don't know the answer to that one and neither does she apparently. Like she says, give her time.' She went to get some biscuits from the kitchen, desperate for something to do to cover her distress. How could Georgie do this to him? Her loving, kindly Dicky didn't deserve this. So patiently waiting for a divorce which never materialised and this was his reward. But sleeping with that creep, Bryn. God! How could she? How could she? Bel peeped round the kitchen door and saw that Dicky was still clutching the letter, lost in thought. He needed something to do. 'They'll be glad for you to get back to work; they were busy when I left. We'll walk back together, eh? What do you think?'

Dicky refused a biscuit, looked up at her and said, as though making a public announcement, 'I, Dicky Tutt, am not setting foot in that pub again.'

'Dicky! Don't be ridiculous. You must.'

'There's no must about it. I'm not.' He swung himself round on the sofa and laid his head on one arm, his feet not quite touching the other. 'See yer.' He put his arms across his chest with the letter still in his hand. Briefly she thought he looked as though he'd been laid out.

Out of fright she said, 'Dicky, don't do this to yourself. The only one to lose out will be you. You've got to hang on to something. You can't go back to that dreary, boring job you had, you hated it. In any case you've been too long away, it won't be waiting for you, not now.'

Dicky ignored her.

'Do you hear me?'

Dicky still ignored her.

'Right, well, I've got to go. I'll sleep here tonight, I'm not leaving you on your own. So if you want to go to bed before I get back, make up the sofa bed. Right?'

Dicky nodded. Bel threw up her hands in despair and set off back to the Royal Oak with a heavy heart.

*

At Glebe House Bryn had just been handed Georgie's letter. Guy gave it to him with an amused smile on his face. Bryn didn't give him the satisfaction of opening it in front of him.

'A billet-doux from the wife, no doubt.'

'Probably.' He tossed it on the table without so much as a glance, but he knew whom it was from and longed to open it. He'd no idea what the situation back at the Royal Oak was, because Georgie had whisked him out in a trice after Dicky had seen them both. Bryn had a prickly feeling down his spine still, after that glare Dicky had given him when he'd twigged what they'd been up to, the two of them. My God, there was still the old magic there. He couldn't help a satisfied smile, forgetting that Guy was still watching him from the door.

'Looks to me as though the cat has been at the cream. Good luck to you, man.'

Bryn waited for the door to close behind Guy and aimed a rude gesture at it. That Guy got more like his father every day. He opened the letter from Georgie and read:

> *Bryn,*
> *I'm going away for a few days. When I come back I shall have made up my mind what I want to do. The situation is tearing me apart.*
> Georgie

In Bryn's mind there was no quandary for Georgie: he, Bryn Fields, was the obvious and only choice. Women! Ah, well, nothing but good would come out of her being away.

He turned his mind from Georgie and thought about the men he'd seen in the village street earlier that day. A visit to the pub might prove valuable. He was skilled at turning a conversation in the direction he wanted it to go and he remembered that when he'd lived in the village, before Elektra, there'd been someone down Shepherds Hill who had a son in the council offices. What was his name? He dredged his memory and came up with Kevin. That was it, his mother called him 'our Kev'. If Dicky was there, well, so what, he presented no serious threat with the pub full of customers, not likely.

He heard Liz calling everyone for dinner. He sprang to his feet shouting 'I'm coming' and went downstairs to yet another of Liz's beautifully prepared meals. He really couldn't take advantage of their hospitality much longer. Maybe when Georgie came back she'd be ready for him to return to live above the pub.

When he got to the bar he found his luck was in. There, to his total delight, was Kevin's mother ensconced on the settle, everyone's favourite seat because it gave such a good view of the bar. He stood in front of her and said, 'Can I buy you a drink for old times' sake? What will it be?'

'Why, it's you. Throwing your money about, aren't you?'

Bryn shrugged his shoulders. 'So long as you're on the receiving end I shouldn't worry too much. Well, can I?'

Kev's mother nodded. 'A double vodka, please.'

'Orange with it?'

'No, ta. I like it neat.' Her small, brown, closely set eyes watched him march across to the bar counter. She knew only too well she wasn't getting the drink for the good of her health; there'd be a catch somewhere. But what? she asked herself.

She toasted him and downed half the glass in one gulp. 'Excellent.' Bryn could see he was in for an expensive night if he didn't watch his step.

'They seem short-staffed tonight. They say Georgie's gone off for a couple of days. And Dicky! Well, he's nowhere to be seen, let's put it like that. So I expect he's gone with her. I don't suppose you know anything about it, do you?'

'Nothing.'

'Have they gone together?'

'Shouldn't think so. How's your ... what was his name? ... the one who works at the council offices. I know ... your Kevin.'

So that was it. He was after some information from their Kev. Well, he'd have to pay for it.

'He's doing fine. Been promoted. He's in media and communications now.'

'He'll need to know everything about everything then, won't he. A good chap to know.' Quite by chance his fingers strayed to his wallet, which now lay on the table beside his glass. He fingered it delicately and looked at our Kev's mother with a single raised eyebrow.

'He's well informed, oh, yes.' She emptied her glass and put it down in the middle of the table.

'Fancy another one?'

'That's very kind of you, Bryn, very kind. I don't mind if I do.'

At the bar he asked Trish where everyone was tonight. 'Dicky's not turned in and Georgie's gone to the coast, last-minute thing.'

It hit him like a massive clout on the side of his head. Dicky missing! They hadn't gone together, had they? Surely not! He'd ignored what Kev's mother had said about Dicky, but she might be right after all. Perhaps they had gone together. But not after he and she had ... he'd left his wallet on the table alongside Kevin's mother. In his confusion he grabbed the wallet, tried to take a note from it and fumbled it so out spilled the whole wad of fifty-pound notes and twenties. Kevin's mother eyed it with relish.

Bryn paid for the drinks, took them to the table and said, 'Shan't be a minute.'

He fled to the dining room and found Bel clearing a table. He caught hold of her elbow and spun her round. 'Your Dicky, where is he?'

Bel looked at him, hating every bone in his body, and said, 'Are you worried about him, then?'

'No ... well, yes, well, no, not really, just tell me where he is.'

'That's his business. After what you've done to him I wish I could crush the life out of you with the heel of my shoe. You're scum.' She picked up the loaded tray and stalked straight past him.

'Don't walk away when I'm speaking to you.'

Over her shoulder she said, 'Well, I'm not speaking to you' and pushed open the door into the kitchen.

Bryn ground his teeth with annoyance, remembered Kevin's mother and hastened back to sit with her. 'Sorry about that. Where were we? Oh, yes. Your Kevin's promotion. I'm wanting to know why those council chaps were round the village this morning.' Was it only this morning? 'A chap with a theodolite and an assistant taking measurements. Surly, he was, and wouldn't answer my questions.'

Kev's mother eyed his wallet, still prominently displayed on the table. 'I could ask him, of course, but I can't guarantee he knows the answer.'

'You bring me the answer and then . . .' His own eyes deliberately wandered to his wallet. He picked it up. 'I'll make it worth his while to find out,' he told her.

The small brown eyes sparked with an avaricious glint. 'I see. He's no fool, our Kev. Hope you're not thinking small.'

Greedy woman. 'Of course not. I just need to know. After all, in the interests of the village we don't want changes, damn signs and things. No, definitely not, so we've to be prepared, haven't we?'

'D'yer think that might be it, then? By Jove the toffee-nosed around here won't want that, will they? Spoiling their precious village. Eh?' She grinned.

'No. That was what I was thinking. Sir Ralph and the like won't take kindly to it at all. We, you and I, we'd be doing them a good turn.'

Kev's mother stood up. 'Don't make it sound as though you have the interests of the village at heart, the only thing in your heart is worrying that double yellow lines and road signs will spoil the village for your tourist scam. You can't kid me. I'll ring soon as I get home. I might be in here tomorrow night if I've got anything for you.' She squeezed out from the settle, went to speak to a neighbour and left.

Bryn finished his drink while he applied his mind to finding out if Dicky had gone away with Georgie. His stomach churned with the thought that they might have gone together. But she had said she needed time to think away from them both, so she wouldn't have written that if she didn't mean it, though she might have if she didn't want him to know Dicky had gone with her. Red-hot pokers seemed to burn their way into his guts at the thought of them together.

He leapt to his feet, called out 'Goodnight' to Alan and Trish, and left. As he approached Glebe Cottages he looked to see if there were any signs of life in there. He couldn't tell. So he began cautiously creeping up Dicky's path. He looked towards the front window and could see nothing. He crept closer, slowly, carefully, until his nose was inches from the window. Was that a figure lying on the sofa? He shaded his eyes and peered in with his nose now almost touching the glass. It was. It was Dicky! Staring into space, totally helpless and so, well, so lifeless. Relief flooded through his body. Thank God. They hadn't gone together then. But there was something terribly defeated-looking in Dicky's posture. He looked like a whipped dog, thrashed almost to death. Completely crushed.

Bryn slipped softly back down the path and went into the garden at Glebe House. He sat for a while on the seat in front of the summer house and lit a cigarette. It wasn't often that he smoked but tonight he needed one. Bryn dragged on it, drawing the smoke into his lungs with relish. He rejoiced in his knowledge that Dicky wasn't with Georgie, but underneath that came a sense of sorrow, a deep regret for Dicky's plight. The poor chap was ... was ... destroyed, and it was all down to him, Bryn Fields, for wanting to satisfy his own selfish pleasure with Georgie. A small voice inside him argued and why not; after all, she was his wife. Then his conscience kicked in and he knew he'd no rights where Georgie was concerned; it was he who'd gladly exchanged her for that dreadful Elektra. He must have been mad, completely mad to have fancied that tart.

Someone called out from the open French windows, 'Drink, Bryn?' It was Neville. 'Whisky?'

'Thanks.' Bryn stubbed out his cigarette, picked it up and took it to the outside bin, remembering even in his distress about Dicky, not to litter Neville's immaculate garden.

'Coming.' Bryn realised that losing Georgie wouldn't affect him nearly so badly as it had Dicky. He, Bryn, would bounce back far quicker, being a different kind of person from Dicky. The poor chap was in pieces. With a heavy heart he joined the family for a nightcap and hoped he'd be able to sleep tonight, but he was aware it wasn't a certainty.

11

He went to bed to think. He'd some e-mails to send off tomorrow, courtesy of Neville, to his lunch and coffee stops on the tour confirming numbers, and reconfirming the hotels en route. Check with Jimbo about the souvenirs. Check with Willie about the tour of the church. See Jimmy about the geese and rehearse what he had to say. Stroll round to Deadman's Dell to see what progress was being made – if no one was there he'd ring the county offices and speak to Gilbert himself. See Bel about the dining room and the meal. Ring the coach company confirming times and dates et cetera; probably send them an e-mail to make sure they had no excuses for being late at the airport. Decide what to do about Georgie.

He turned over and thought about her in bed that afternoon in the bedroom which had always been theirs. She'd responded to his need for her so willingly, so wholeheartedly, he'd been over-whelmed. Much of the cherished feelings of their earlier years had returned to them both and he came close to worshipping her. Him, Bryn! Feeling like that about a woman. Surely not. It wasn't part of his psyche to come even close to worshipping a woman. But he had. He shouldn't have, though; seeing Dicky so destroyed had cut right to his heart and taken most of the joy out of his encounter with Georgie.

If he took Dicky out of the equation then how did he feel? Pleased, elated, thrilled, triumphant even. But taking that peep at Dicky had affected him more deeply than Bryn cared to admit. That secret view of him lying on the sofa had made him realise he couldn't play with other people's feelings, couldn't carelessly meddle in their lives without a qualm.

With Dicky in the equation he felt selfish, inconsiderate, thoughtless. If he truly loved Georgie he should want her happiness, so if that meant her marrying Dicky, so be it. He wouldn't stand in their way. When she came back he'd tell her that. It would mean selling his share of the pub to Dicky. It would mean he had no permanent home. It would mean depending on his tours for income and that seemed exceedingly shaky. No, he'd have to get another pub. Settle for second best with someone else, a hard worker, and the two of them would make a success of it. He finally closed his mind to a reunion with Georgie. It would be so much easier to have that reunion with her, though: a ready-made business, settling back into the old routine, familiar faces. Just before he fell asleep he'd reverted to the idea of making a new start, for Dicky's sake. Dicky obviously loved her and desperately needed her . . . for once in his life he'd do the right thing, no matter how hard it would be.

Kev's mother was, as she had promised, seated on the settle with an orange juice in front of her when Bryn entered the bar. He waved to her, mouthed 'vodka' and she gave him the thumbs up.

'Thanks for this.' Again Kev's mother tossed back half her vodka in one gulp.

'Have you any news for me from your Kevin?'

'Ah, well. It's not definite. What was the word he used? Yes, exploratory it was. There's been complaints, yer see, about all the traffic round the school gate mornings and when they finish. Such a jumble, which it is, cars parked all over the place, on the green, in the road. So-o-o they're thinking of double yellow lines and one-way traffic, street lighting and a zebra crossing across the top of Shepherds Hill.'

Bryn almost choked at the prospect. 'Street lighting! Zebra crossing! My God, have they gone mad?'

'It's true, though, they need something at school time, or there'll be an accident before long. They can't help coming in cars from Little Derehams and Penny Fawcett, can they, since the education cancelled the school minibuses. Scandalous, that was. It's too far for children their age to walk and there's no footpaths neither, so they'd be walking in the road round all them blind bends. Dangerous. Spoil the village, though.'

Bryn sipped his whisky.

'It's Miss Pascoe what's asked for the one way.'

Bryn took another sip of his whisky while he had a good think.

'Loads o' signs they'll put up. Them postcards showing ye olde Englishe village won't be no more. There'll be bloody great one-way arrers all over the place.'

'Not if I can help it. No, siree. They're not riding roughshod all over Turnham Malpas. We've got some big guns, you know, to fight this. Mr Fitch for a start.'

Kev's mother added the name of another big gun: 'His nibs, Sir Ralph.'

'Exactly. They neither of them will want the village spoiling. If the council want a fight, a fight they are going to get.'

'Miss Pascoe at the school 'ull have a lot to say about that.'

'Who else besides her will want it, then? I can't think of a living soul.'

Kev's mother sniffed derisively. 'Nor me. Damned waste of time, the council. Don't know why we bother to vote 'em in. Street lights might be a good idea, though, you know. Help people to get home safe who've had too much to drink.' She said this with a sly smile on her face, which let Bryn know they were all talking behind his back about his night with Dicky and the double whiskies. He wished he hadn't been reminded of Dicky, it only recalled his pledge to give Georgie back to him. Make amends to the poor chap.

Kev's mother said, 'Well?'

'Well?' Bryn saw her rubbing her thumb and forefinger together. 'Oh! What I promised.' He dug in his back pocket for his wallet, and slipped her a fifty-pound note. 'Say thanks to Kevin for me. Much appreciated.'

'That all?'

Bryn raised his eyebrows.

'I went to a lot of trouble for you and I didn't need to.'

Bryn thought about the cost of her vodkas and her delight at the news she had to impart, and weighed it against the cost of the local phone call she'd made and thought, stuff you. But his newly awakened conscience pricked and he took out a ten-pound note, folded it and put it into her hand as he patted it. 'Pay for the phone call. Thanks for all you've done. Would you be on side if we started a campaign?'

'Might, but then again . . .' Kev's mother picked up the ten-pound note and pushed it into her pocket. 'Thanks, anyway. If I've any further news I'll let you know.'

'Good. I'll be glad to hear. There's more where that came from if it's useful news.'

Kev's mother tapped the side of her nose, slid out from the settle and went to join a neighbour over the other side of the bar.

Bryn looked at his watch. Still quite early. He eyed his empty glass, almost went to get another and thought this new Bryn with his spanking-new conscience is having only one tonight. Purposefully he marched to the bar with his glass, paused as though debating something in his mind, decided to leave and, calling a loud 'Goodnight!' to everyone, left and headed for Glebe House. As he approached the cottages he slowed his steps. There were no lights on at Dicky's, though it was still only twilight, so maybe . . . Bryn went up the path, as he had the previous night but instead of peering in the window he tried the door handle. It wasn't locked. He put a foot on the doormat and called softly, 'Dicky! Dicky!'

He walked into the living room and saw Dicky lying on the sofa, just as he had been when he'd last seen him. 'Dicky?'

Getting no response, Bryn went to sit in an easy chair, facing Dicky. There was such a terrible stillness about the chap he could almost have been dead. He hadn't shaved, that was obvious, he hadn't combed his hair and by the grey, drawn look on his face he hadn't washed either. In front of him was the coffee table with sandwiches, a mug and a flask on it, which, as far as Bryn could see, were untouched. Presumably Bel knew, then, that at least he was alive.

I owe him a lot, he thought. I nearly murdered the fellow; would have done, too, for murder was in my heart at the time. The least I can do is put his life back together again, if he'll let me. Bryn must have sat an hour while the twilight deepened into real darkness. With no street lights to illuminate the room it had become pitch-black and he could no longer see Dicky. He heard a stirring sound of cloth against cloth, a slight creak of bones, a small cough.

'Don't be alarmed, Dicky, it's Bryn. I'll put a light on.'

He drew the curtains and fumbled his way to the light switch. The bright light showed to what depths Dicky had sunk. It emphasised the shadows on his cheeks, the world-weary look of his eyes and the appalling fragility of the man. It had only taken him twenty-four hours to shrink to a shadow, his bustling energy completely gone.

'I've been waiting for you to wake, Dicky. I've something to tell you. Will you listen?'

Dicky simply stared.

'I want you to know that Georgie is for you. I've always known, but I wouldn't acknowledge it. But I do now. She belongs to you. She hasn't belonged to me for a long time.'

Dicky slowly raised a hand and gestured his acknowledgement of what Bryn had said.

'When she comes back in a day or two I shall tell her I want a divorce.'

It was hard work telling someone life-changing things and getting no reaction. Bryn tried again. 'Have you heard me? Do you understand what I mean?'

But Dicky didn't respond.

'Look here. Let me pour you a drink. What is it? Coffee? Get this down you.'

Bryn opened up the thermos and poured some coffee into the mug. He put it within reach and waited. Dicky half rolled on to his side and looked at the steam coming off the top of the coffee.

'Sit up. You'll manage better.'

So Dicky did and drank from the mug. Slowly at first and then in great gulps. But he still wasn't for speaking.

'You see, Dicky, I'm a greedy beggar, always wanting more of whatever it is I can't have. Well, I've been doing a lot of thinking and I'm going to change. I have changed I should say. If marrying you makes Georgie happy then ... so be it.'

'I *can't*. Marry her.'

Bryn cast him a startled look. 'Why ever not? What do you mean?'

'Not after what she's done. She's yours. She betrayed me.'

'Damn it, man, it was me betrayed you. I persuaded her. I made it so she couldn't say no.'

'I wanted everything between us to be honourable, without stain. Perfect. Beautiful. After what you did, all that's been destroyed. There's nothing left between her and me.'

'Without stain? Honourable? Destroyed. What are you talking about, man? She's sure to come back and beg forgiveness and go ahead with the divorce, and then you and she can settle down at the pub to married life and a business partnership. I understand you can find the money to buy a half-share.'

Dicky shook his head.

'Go for it, Dicky, please. Make her happy.'

'No. It's all too late now.'

Bryn saw him look with interest at the generously filled sandwiches, so he leant forward, took the cling film off them and handed him the plate. 'Go on. You'll feel better. You've nothing more to fear from me. I've treated you rotten and it's all stopped. I've called you names that I shouldn't have and I'm ashamed.'

'Squirt. Dwarf. Tiddler. Stunted little specimen.' Dicky stirred uncomfortably against the cushions as if saying the words brought back all his pain. 'Well, I'm not setting foot ever again in that pub. Not for anything.'

There was such finality in his voice that Bryn was forced to believe he meant it.

'I walked out after I'd opened the bedroom door and seen what I saw, and I said to myself, "I'm leaving the Royal Oak for the last time." I've spent the happiest time of my life in there these last four years, but they've come to an end. I know now you can't expect lifelong happiness.'

'But they need you. You and your jokes. You're good on the stand-up comic bit, much better than I ever let on to you. It was jealousy made me object to you doing a turn, sheer jealousy. They need you still. Georgie needs you.'

'No. Not any more.' The last of the sandwiches consumed, Dicky lay down again. He closed his eyes and ignored Bryn. Bryn stood up and looked at Dicky thinking, he might say that now but wait till Georgie comes home. He'll change his mind. At least Dicky looked less of a dead man than when he'd come in. 'I'll go, then, I'll leave Georgie to persuade you. I can't do any more than say what I've said.'

Bryn closed the front door behind him thinking, he'll come round to my way of seeing it, he can't do any other. By tomorrow, that's right, by tomorrow he'll be feeling better when it's sunk in that I mean what I say. He didn't know how wrong he was.

Georgie came home at lunchtime two days later, her first priority being to speak to Dicky as soon as time would allow. But of course he wasn't working. 'Trish, where's Dicky?'

'Well, he hasn't been to work since the day you left. Bel says he won't come.'

'Won't he, indeed? I'll soon sort him out with what I've got to tell him. Soon as this rush slows and you've had your lunch, I'll buzz round there to see him.'

'Don't tell Bel. She'll likely bite your head off.'

'Ah, I see. Right. Mum's the word.'

So Georgie slipped out quietly by the back door at about half past two and sped down Church Lane to Glebe Cottages. There was no need to use her key, the door was unlocked. The living-room curtains were drawn and when she peered through the gloom she saw Dicky lying on the sofa in his dressing gown. 'Dicky, what's this? Still not dressed. Are you ill?'

There was no reply. Dicky could have been waiting for the undertaker he was so still; not even by so much as a flutter of his eyelids did he show recognition of her presence.

'Dicky, love.' Georgie bent over him to kiss his cheek. Which she did, but it was like kissing a marble statue. 'Dicky! I've come to tell you that I'm still divorcing Bryn and marrying you like we've wanted all this time. Come on, love. Stir yourself.' She stroked his hair in the way she'd always loved to do; his thick, springy hair, so extravagant on a man of his size. 'Come on, love, speak to me, your Georgie. They're all wondering where you are. Bel says you won't go to work. Now that's not right, is it? You know how we depend on you.'

Dicky heard but chose not to reply.

'I've done my thinking, love, and of course I know and you

know that we were made for each other. You and me. Together. Married. A good business. Equal partners. Like we said. Perfect. Just beautiful.'

At the words 'perfect' and 'beautiful' Dicky gave a choking kind of groan so full of anguish that Georgie's eyes brimmed with tears.

'Oh, Dicky! I know what wrong I've done you, a terrible wrong, worse than I would ever have thought possible of myself, a moment of madness I hope you can forgive me for. Please, Dicky, please forgive me.'

'I can't.'

'You must. You must. Please.' Georgie knelt beside the sofa resting her forearms on the cushions alongside Dicky. 'Please, love.'

'Just go away. You betrayed me. The thought of you with *him . . .*' He groaned again. 'I can't bear it. Go away. Back to Bryn.' His right arm flicked sharply at her arms where they rested on the cushion beside him and the glancing blow made her take her arms away from his side.

'Dicky!'

'I loved you more than I've ever loved anyone in all my life. Like first love. The love of a much younger man, really. Such passion I had for you, you were the light of my life, the beat of my heart. You knew that and still you did what you did. You dirtied our love for each other with that man. It's finished.'

'Finished? What do you mean? Finished! You can't mean that.'

'I do.'

'This is ridiculous.'

Dicky sat up. 'Don't lay the blame on me by belittling how I feel. It is not ridiculous, it's the truth, Georgie, the absolute truth. I told Bryn and I'm telling you, I am not going back into the Royal Oak ever again.' He lay down and closed his eyes once more.

'You've seen Bryn? What for, for heaven's sake?'

'Ask him.'

'I'll talk to Bel first, right now. She'll talk you round if anyone can.' Georgie got up and left the house.

On the sofa where he'd lain since that first terrible day, Dicky wept.

*

Georgie set off for the Royal Oak, then spun on her heel and returned past Glebe Cottages to Glebe House and rang the doorbell for the first time ever.

Liz came to the door. 'Oh, hello, Georgie. What a lovely surprise. I've just put the kettle on, do come in.'

'Hello, Liz. It's Bryn. Is he in?'

'Yes, he is. He's in the garden enjoying the sun, smoking.'

'Can I go straight to see him? I'll go through the side gate if you don't mind. It's personal.'

'Right. OK, then. It isn't locked.'

Georgie opened the gate as quietly as she could, wanting a glimpse of Bryn before he saw her. There he was, as Liz had said, seated in front of the summer house, smoking. Not so tanned as he had been at first, though still much more prepossessing than when he'd gone away. She carefully latched the gate and went towards him. He heard her footsteps crunching the gravel and looked up. His face broke into a restrained smile and he moved up to make room for her on the seat.

'You're back, Georgie.' He patted the seat beside him, inviting her to sit with him.

'Yes.' She sat down, leaving a space between them.

'You've decided.' He stubbed out his cigarette in the flower pot beside the seat, and as he flicked soil from his fingers, he asked somewhat cautiously, Georgie thought, 'Which one of us is it to be?'

Georgie nodded. 'I've decided. Yes.' She took a deep breath. 'It did me good getting away. It was Peter's idea and he was right. Away from the pressures, you learn what really counts. He said, "Think about what you want not just for this year or next, but for the rest of your life" and, of course, I've chosen ... Dicky.' Georgie expected a huge explosion of temper from Bryn but he sat quite still and there was nothing but silence. 'Bryn?'

'Have you told Dicky?'

'I have, but ...'

'He isn't interested.'

'You knew.'

'I've been to see him. That's what he told me.' Bryn explained about his visit.

Georgie was appalled. 'You mean you don't want me?'

'To be honest, I do in a way, but not like I did. When I saw what I'd done to him I knew I couldn't take you from him.'

'I see.'

'He's being so stubborn, so damned stubborn. He can have all he wants on a plate, and he won't take it because of some stupid idea about perfection and beauty in your relationship. He's a romantic.'

For a moment Georgie didn't reply. She appeared to be admiring a rambler rose ablaze with blossom, but in her heart she was loving Dicky for being a romantic and hating Bryn for being so scathing about Dicky's ideals. 'But then, of course, you wouldn't know anything about his kind of loving. He's all heart and you've none.'

'I'm changing all that. I've found my heart while you've been away. Or maybe it's my conscience I've found. I do know you belong to each other and I've no rights whatsoever. Elektra saw to that.'

'Hm, I see. Well, I don't know what we're going to do to bring him round. He's desperately hurt. We were terribly wrong.' Georgie stood up and bent to kiss Bryn. 'Thanks for finding your conscience.'

'It's Dicky you should thank; he found it for me.'

She walked away from him, paused by the rambler in full bloom and turned to wave goodbye. A frightening lump came into his throat at the sight of her looking so lovely against the flowers but he managed to smile and wave in return. God! Was he turning into a romantic too? Heaven forbid. He'd the tour to lead. Money to make. Things to do. Things to do. Mr Fitch to get on side when he returned from the Far East. Sir Ralph to persuade. A campaign to organise. A whole new career to tend. But as he listened to Georgie crossing the gravel drive the other side of the gate he pondered the might-have-been, which had now become the never-will-be.

12

Bryn went to London to collect his group of tourists and left the situation about Dicky still in limbo. The sole good news was that he was eating again, just small meals under persuasion from Bel but it was a matter for hope. He kept the bolts on the doors so Georgie couldn't get in and watched television for most of the day, only getting up to open the door when Bel peered in at the window.

They were eating their evening meal and Bel couldn't hold back any longer; she had decided to speak her mind. 'You can't go on for ever like this, Dicky. You can't expect Georgie to keep paying you to work when all you're doing is lying flat on your back ignoring everyone and everything. Bryn's gone now, so you can come out from under and show your face.'

Dicky carried on eating. He still hadn't shaved but he was looking better and was showering and dressing each day, but he refused to go out.

'When the money runs out, how are we going to pay the mortgage on this place? You know we need both our wages to keep going.' Then she played her trump card and wondered why she'd never thought to mention it before: 'There's no Scouts next week.'

Dicky hadn't been listening properly but suddenly it registered. 'No Scouts?'

'No, Gary told you he'd be in hospital having his foot done and you said you'd be there, no need to worry.'

'We can't have no Scouts.'

'Well, apparently you can, because there isn't.'

Dicky sat silently shaking his head and repeated abruptly, 'We can't have no Scouts.'

'No, we can't, but we have.' Bel quietly went on eating her dinner. Balancing it on her knee wasn't very easy, but to encourage Dicky to eat she'd taken to having her meal in front of the television too.

Dicky cleared his plate, laid his knife and fork side by side, took a drink from his glass of water and said, 'It's Scout night tonight, isn't it, Bel?'

A wicked kind of grin crossed her face. 'Yes. But you're far too ill to go. Puff of wind would blow you over. It's quite chilly out. Before I go back to the dining room I'll get a blanket for your legs. Don't want you to catch a cold.'

'Anybody would think I was in my dotage.'

'They'd be right, wouldn't they.'

'I'd have to shave.'

Bel put her empty plate with Dicky's and handed him his dish of stewed plums and custard. Silently she ate hers, leaving him to come to his own conclusions.

'Tea or coffee?'

'Have I time?'

'Just about.'

Dicky thought for another moment. 'Neither, thanks.' He hauled himself off the sofa and went gingerly upstairs. She heard the bathroom taps running and rejoiced.

He came back down after twenty minutes, dressed in his uniform, scraped as clean as a new carrot from head to foot, his clothes immaculate, his face solemn.

He explained himself: 'Well, you know, I can't just turn up next week and not know what's going on, can I?'

'No, no. Don't forget your key. I might be late tonight.' Bel watched him pick up his Scout file and head for the door. 'Your key! See you.'

Dicky hesitated. 'Should I go, Bel?'

'You might as well, you'll feel an idiot sitting watching television all night dressed like that.'

'I can't let them down, can I?'

'Not you.'

'Not when it's all I've got left.'

As he closed the door behind him Bel clenched her fists and shook them at the ceiling in triumph.

Dicky, by exerting enormous self-control over his feelings, endured the whole evening with, outwardly at least, his usual style; a healthy mixture of authority, laughter and camaraderie.

They were putting all the equipment away in the Scout cupboards and preparing to leave when Peter came in. 'Good evening, boys, Gary. You look to have had a good evening.'

Gary answered, 'We have, sir, very good indeed. We won the canoeing at the weekend, by the way. Did anyone tell you?'

'No. I'd no idea. Well done. Second year running. Full marks.'

'County championships next month.'

'Excellent. Good luck. Let me have the date and I'll try to get there. All the best for your op next week, Gary. Is Dicky here?'

'Locking up at the back. Goodnight.'

'Thanks. Goodnight.' Peter found Dicky bolting the back door. 'Hello, Dicky. Time for a word?'

Dicky had realised Peter had come in and hadn't known what to say to him, so he'd dallied by the back door. He still didn't know. 'Yes.'

'Let's sit on the bench out here. Everyone's gone.'

There was no gainsaying Peter. He opened the inner door and held it open for him. Dicky was tired. Keeping control of his feelings and on top of that this being his first night out of the house for over a week had taken a lot out of him.

'Here, sit down. You look exhausted. It won't take long.'

Dicky collapsed rather than sat beside Peter. He rested his elbows on his thighs and, clasping his hands together, stared at the floor.

Peter went straight to the nub of the matter. 'Church hall, funny place for a heart to heart, but you're not out and about and I've tried your door a few times and it was locked. I've seen Bel. Well, rather she came to see me. You've got her very worried.'

Dicky stared at the floor.

'And me. I'm worried.'

Dicky shifted his weight a little but didn't answer.

'I'm glad to see you out, though. That's a start, isn't it.'

Dicky clasped his hands a little tighter to stop them shaking.

'You see, love is the strangest thing, Dicky. It takes us by surprise and then when we've got it, sometimes we don't know what to do with it. It should make us strong, happy, loving, forgiving. It should make life a joy, it should be a pulsing, throbbing thing which colours every hour of our day. Then something cuts right across that and love makes us unhappy, bad-tempered, jealous, envious, revengeful, murderous, to name but a few. Sometimes we have love offered to us and for whatever reason we reject it, and then we reach the deepest of depths and feel the worst it's possible to feel, but pride or resentment or distrust makes us stubborn and we suffer.'

Dicky straightened up. 'I can't bear it. You know they ... one afternoon ... well, they got it together?'

Peter nodded.

'It's broken my heart.'

For a while the two of them stayed silent, then Peter said, 'Some time ago I had my heart broken too. But I realised that I had to learn to forgive, generously, if I was ever to regain what I had almost thrown away. Georgie's offered you a lifetime of loving. Don't you throw it away.'

'He says he's the one to blame. He persuaded her to. No one seems to remember that he nearly murdered me and yet she could let him persuade her to ...' Dicky surreptitiously rubbed his eyes.

'They haven't forgotten, not really. I certainly haven't. But that has nothing to do with Georgie loving you, has it? It's not Bryn, it's Georgie who wants to marry you and heal the wounds.'

Dicky nodded and almost smiled at the memory of her.

'I remember meeting you in the Store at the start of it all and you saying, "She's the cream in my coffee, the fizz in my drinks, the sherry in my trifle, the icing on my cake." I've never forgotten those words. So simple, but so meaningful. Think about what life without her will be like if you don't forgive her and wipe the slate clean.'

'Terrible.'

'Only good can come from a love as great as yours, Dicky. So let it. Love given freely, despite everything that happens between you, is a wonderful, worthwhile thing.'

Together they got up and walked towards the main entrance. Peter waited while Dicky turned off the lights. They stood there for a moment in the darkness. 'Do you know, Peter, I've had some of the most rewarding times of my life in here at Scout meetings.'

'Good. That's excellent. It's what makes for quality of life, isn't it? Just think how many lives you have influenced for the better.'

'I hope so.'

As Dicky locked the outer door Peter said, 'Glad to see you picking up the threads again, Dicky. If you need to talk confidentially, you know where I am. The Rectory door's always open to you. Any time. Goodnight. God bless you, Dicky.'

Dicky watched his tall figure striding away down the path and remembered how Peter had almost lost his marriage over that actor fellow and Caroline fancying each other, and yet now they were as one again as though it had never happened. Maybe they were more emphatically one person than before; as Peter had said, forgiving had made their love stronger than ever. Georgie! Georgie! His hand reached out to touch her and for a moment he thought he could feel her hand in his. How he loved her. But he couldn't quite, not quite . . . bring himself to . . . perhaps in time.

Dicky went home to find Bel already making herself a bedtime drink. 'How's things, Dicky? Go all right?'

Dicky tossed down his file and keys on the sofa with a gesture more like his old self and said, 'Fine. Absolutely fine. I'll have hot chocolate, Bel, please.'

'Great.' She came into the living room, planted down his drink on the table and flopped into her favourite chair, cradling her mug in her hands.

Without looking at her Dicky said casually, 'I think it's time you went back to keeping Georgie company at the pub at night.'

'You do?'

Dicky nodded. 'I do. I've talked to Peter tonight and I'm feeling better. In fact I might . . . just . . .'

'What?'

'I might, just might, start work at the pub on Monday.'

'Sooner than that. She's thinking of finding someone else.'

'See how I feel tomorrow, then. I can't go back to my old job, couldn't face all that boredom. In any case the money's not as good.'

Bel sipped her hot chocolate for a while, then said tentatively, 'I wonder if Mrs Charter-Plackett is still of the same mind.'

'I didn't say I was going to buy that half-share. That's a whole different ball game.'

'Oh!'

'Don't push me, Bel, I'm not ready for it.'

'Never mind, then. Sorry. I'll move my things back to the pub tomorrow if that's all right.'

He nodded firmly. 'It is. Got to pull myself together.'

'Can I ask?'

Dicky looked hard at her.

'Can I ask if going back means anything? You know, should we draw some conclusions from it?'

Wide-eyed with innocence Dicky said, 'None.' But in his heart he knew differently. As Peter had said, you can't carelessly throw away the offer of a lifetime of love. Maybe, just maybe, he'd been too hasty.

It was Alan's late-turn shift and Georgie was wondering how on earth she and Trish would manage without some muscle on the premises to heave the bottled drinks in and bring supplies up from the cellar.

'Don't worry, Georgie. You and me, we can manage. We don't need men, they're just handy from time to time.'

'Are they, indeed? Well, we'll have to, we've no choice. I just hope we can cope tomorrow with Bryn's group coming. Twenty-five all at once. I'm starting to get nervous about it. I wish, in the circumstances, I'd never agreed to it, but I did and we need the trade. Bel says the kitchen is all organised so all we've got to do is keep the drinks coming. Anyway, I'll make a list of what we want for today.' She found a crumpled piece of paper right at the back of a drawer, smoothed it out and laid it on the bar counter. 'Right. Mixers. Yes.' As she wrote 'mixers' at the top of the paper the back door shut with a tremendous bang. If she hadn't known it couldn't be, she would have thought that was Dicky. He always managed to let the heavy back door get caught by the wind. She wrote down 'sparkling water' and glanced around to see which other shelves needed filling up. She smelt his aftershave first of all; that fresh lime and tea tree she'd given him on his birthday. Her heart gave a lurch and began to beat erratically. Slowly she turned round and found she was right. It *was* Dicky. Thinner, leaner, more grave, but Dicky. 'Hello, love.' His eyes didn't light up when she spoke, but there was something there, a kind of strength, she thought, which she hadn't noticed before.

'Realised it was Alan's morning off. Thought I'd better give a hand.'

If that was how he wanted it, unemotional, casual, then so be it. 'Thanks. We were just debating who'd be getting the beer up from the cellar.'

'Right. Done the list?'

'Almost.'

'I'll wait, then.'

Trish decided to pretend it was no surprise to see Dicky there. It was easier than having to find something embarrassing to say. 'Morning, Dicky. Put Coke on that list, Georgie, there's hardly any on the shelf.'

'OK.'

'It's the hot weather.'

'Not before time. We deserve it hot.' Georgie looked at Dicky from under her eyelashes and found he was covertly weighing her up. She gave him a cautious smile, but he didn't respond. No wonder, Georgie thought, no wonder, after what I've done to him. 'There's the list, I don't think I've forgotten anything. Thanks.'

They worked all day like this, saying the minimum, pressing on, till Georgie thought she might burst with frustration. She was relieved when he went home for his meal at five, but he came back to work an evening shift, which he wasn't scheduled to do.

By closing time Georgie couldn't take it any longer, making up her mind that enough was enough and she was having it out with him. As she opened the safe to put in the cloth bag she used for storing the takings overnight she said, 'Dicky Tutt! I want a word.'

Alan said a hasty 'Goodnight!' and disappeared.

Dicky stood silently, waiting while she locked it.

'There was no need to come back tonight; you weren't due on.'

'I know, but I've got to make up for my absence somehow.'

'No need.'

'I feel there is. If you pay me a wage, then I've to work for it. It's only right.'

'We can't avoid what's happened between us. We can't ignore it, disregard it. Someone has to say something.'

'No, they don't.'

'Yes, they do.'

'I'm off. See you lunchtime tomorrow.'

Georgie daren't say she didn't want him to come tomorrow because of Bryn, but she had to say something to stop him coming in. 'Dicky!'

Before she could come up with a credible excuse he'd said 'Goodnight', turned on his heel and closed the door sharply behind him.

At eleven thirty precisely the following day, right on schedule, the tour coach pulled into the village to disgorge its load. It had begun as one of those eternal village mornings blessed by peace and serenity as it had been for more than a thousand years, the only sounds those of the geese on the green honking at a feral cat, the delightful singing of the children in the school floating out through the open windows and the spasmodic chatter of the people in the queue outside the Store waiting for the lunchtime bus into Culworth. But the quiet was to be blown apart by the thrum-thrum of the coach engine and the noisy, excited babble of its occupants.

They disembarked from the coach with an eagerness amazing to behold. They scattered hither and thither like a host of vividly feathered parrots just released from captivity, exclaiming at the green, the houses, the pub, the geese. Best of all for the queue at the bus stop was the sight of Bryn marshalling his flock. Over white trousers and shirt he wore a navy blazer. They could just see a badge of some sort on the pocket and the regimental tie which completed his outfit. The white moccasins on his feet induced a burst of giggled comments from the queue. 'What does he think he is?' 'Looks the part, though, don't he?'

Then they spotted Jimmy emerging from his garden on to the green. He was carrying a basket they were sure they'd last seen displayed in Jimbo's window full of Easter eggs, but what he wore was the most amusing of all. It was a very old Victorian farmer's smock, a work of art to the eye of a collector but to the people in the bus queue he made a highly rib-tickling picture. On his feet he wore a pair of old boots from his poaching days and to top it off a soft black felt hat with a wide wavy brim.

They watched Jimmy walk steadily towards the seat beside the pond, observed him touch the brim of his hat and call out a greeting to the tourists. 'Good morning to ye all. You be welcome to feed my geese, you be.'

All twenty-five of the tourists leapt at the opportunity, cameras flashing: 'Hold the bread. Merle, turn this way.'

'Hi, sir. Can I photograph you for my album?'

'Sue-Ellen, smile!'

'What a souvenir! So genuine!'

Jimmy turned this way and that, obliging the Americans. The geese took exception and began to hassle one of the men by noisily pecking at his trouser seat as he crouched to take a picture.

'Hey, Marlon, watch out!'

Before Jimmy could distract his geese with another chunk of bread, Marlon was racing across the green with two of the geese in full pursuit, the man's huge stomach shaking and shuddering like a firm jelly as he ran. By this time the queue was having hysterics, but the twenty-five Americans were wielding their camcorders and their digital cameras as fast as they could, loving every moment of the chase.

Bryn was boiling with temper. Between clenched teeth he bent over Jimmy's shoulder and muttered, 'Stop those damn birds, or else.' Jimmy leapt up and, putting his fingers to his lips, he emitted a piercing whistle. To his surprise it worked, the two geese put on their brakes and came racing back half flying, half running, leaving Marlon to stagger back as best he could.

Finally Bryn got his tourists assembled and suggested they might like to hear from Jimmy, whose ancestors had lived in the village for something like six hundred years.

'Gee! No!'

'Can that be true?'

'Really.'

'Amazing.'

Unfortunately the queue couldn't quite hear what he was saying and only occasionally a snatch of his well-practised discourse drifted across the green: 'My family name's on the memorial plaque in the church ... given their lives for old England ... so we been 'ere my ancestors all them years, poachers mostly. I've poached these wood man and boy ... this 'ere is my dog Sykes ... my family's bred Jack Russells for generations.'

'The liar! His dog's a stray!' muttered someone in the queue. 'What a load of rubbish.'

'See that old oak tree yonder ... a hundred years ago ... terrible storm ... it lost a third of its branches ... but it survived ... once the old oak dies so will the village.' He used such sepulchral, doom-laden tones that the tourists were reduced almost to tears. Some took notes, others filmed Jimmy sitting lost in gloom.

Unfortunately the lunchtime bus rumbled into the village at that moment and the queue had no alternative but to climb aboard and miss the fun.

Bryn decided Jimmy would soon be over-egging the pudding if he didn't move everyone on pronto, so he assembled his charges and suggested they wander across to the church, where they would be treated to a talk on its history, a history going back over a thousand years.

'*You mean that very church?*'

'There's been a church on that site for well over a thousand years. The present church has parts going back to the eleventh century, the rest is fourteenth century. But let's go and hear all about it. You can find Jimmy's ancestors' names if you like.'

Jimmy called out as they left, 'Don't forget to visit the plague pit,' his voice once more laden with doom. Once they all had their sights set on the church, Jimmy threw all the leftover bread in the pond and went as fast as he could to the pub for a restorative drink.

Georgie had to congratulate him on his costume. 'You look so authentic, Jimmy. Absolutely right for the part.'

'Thanks. Like the smock? Genuine, you know. Harriet's lent me it, and the basket.'

'Did it go well?'

'They were delighted. Nice folk. Very nice. I shall be on all their pictures.'

'Talk go well?'

'Oh, yes. Very well. They've gone across to the church now, so half an hour and they'll be ready to eat.' Jimmy took his real ale over to the settle and Sykes crept under it as he had always done, ever since he'd adopted Jimmy.

He was still sitting there when the Americans came in for their lunch. Three of them offered to buy Jimmy another drink, two of them sat on the settle with him for photos and they enticed Sykes out for his share of glory. Another asked if he knew where they could get a smock like his. 'How long has it been in the family?' The moment had come when he either lied or told the truth and spoiled the fantasy. It was a question he hadn't quite prepared himself for. 'Being poachers, we didn't own things like this to pass down the generations, but this belongs to someone in the village who comes from farming stock.' Half-lie, half-truth and he got away with it.

Bryn took them through to the dining room, got them settled and came back into the bar for a word with Georgie. 'Going like a dream. Like a dream. They're paying for their own drinks, you know, apart from the half-bottle included with their lunch. Pour me a whisky quick, I need it.'

He tossed back the whisky, slapped down the glass on the bar, then spotted Dicky talking to a customer at one of the tables. Bryn glanced at Georgie and raised an eyebrow. In reply she very slightly shook her head.

Bryn watched Dicky for a moment and went across to speak to him. There didn't seem to be quite so much naked hate in Dicky's eyes as there had been and Bryn took hope from that. 'OK, Dicky? Glad to see you picking up the threads. One step at a time, eh?'

Dicky looked at him but didn't respond to his question.

Bryn put out a hand and patted his arm, but Dicky dusted off his sleeve where Bryn had touched it. 'Too soon yet for the friendly gesture. Just keep out of my way.'

Bryn stood back. Palms exposed and held up in reconciliation he said, 'Fine. Fine.'

'Bryn! Hi, baby!' One of the American tourists approached them. 'Hi, Lalla! How can I help?'

'Marlon's wanting souvenirs. Where do we go?'

'The Village Store. We'll all go across there in a moment.'

'Right! I'll be powdering my nose. Don't go without me.' Lalla pattered off, twinkling her fingers at him as she went.

They were all charmed by the Store and most especially by Jimbo. A real English gentleman, they declared, and were exceedingly impressed when Bryn let out that Jimbo had been to Cambridge. He did a roaring trade with his souvenirs and items of food they bought to keep them sustained while on the coach.

'It must be wonderful living here.'

'You've made us all so welcome, fancy living here all the time. Great!'

'Everyone's been so kind. Just another picture! That's it!'

'I don't want to leave.'

'I guess it's like going back in time.'

'Nothing's changed, ever.'

'Not a road sign in sight. Wonderful!'

'And the church ... well ... I can't wait to get back home and tell them all about it. So old. And the tombs! And the ghost! They'll be so envious.'

'That lovely man who guided us round. Such a wonderful tale to tell.'

'You won't let them change it, will you? Keep it as it is.'

Bryn wholeheartedly agreed with these sentiments and, catching Jimbo's eye, said, 'We'll keep it like this, won't we, Jimbo?'

'Of course.'

'Not even an advertisement of any kind. Marvellous.'

'We'll be telling our friends. They'll all be coming.'

'Come along, Bryn, baby.' Lalla, clutching her two Turnham Malpas Store carrier bags to her chest, hooked her free arm through Bryn's and led him out of the Store, the others following reluctantly.

Georgie had decided to wave them off and took Trish and some of the customers out with her into the car park.

''Bye! 'Bye-bye!'

She came in for some serious embracing before they all left, and compliments about the food and the ambience of the Royal Oak flowed back and forth.

Lalla squeezed Dicky's arm and said, 'That joke! You naughty boy. I could come back just to hear some more. Only wish I could squeeze you into my case. Be seeing you!' She climbed up the coach steps and turned to wave for the last time. ''Bye, everyone. You lucky people!'

Before he climbed into the coach Bryn put his hand on Georgie's shoulder and whispered, 'Brilliant! Absolutely brilliant. Food wonderful, they're all so impressed. It's the start of something big for you and me, I'm sure.' Georgie smiled up at him, pleased by his success as well as her own.

Dicky's hand closed in a vicelike grip on Bryn's elbow. 'Unless you're wanting to do the rest of the tour with a black eye, let her go and get on your way.'

Bryn prised Dicky's fingers from his elbow and said quietly, 'When I get back, you and me's going to have a talk. Man to man. Clear the air. Right?'

Dicky shrugged his shoulders.

'See you both. Thanks for everything you've done. We've made a great start.'

As the coach backed up and swung round to leave the car park Georgie waved brightly to them all. The Americans responded enthusiastically and Georgie had the feeling that some of them at least would be back. The moment they were out of sight she turned on Dicky. 'Dicky Tutt, grow up! He's trying to made amends. He wants the divorce and he's going to get it. Whether or not you want to marry me afterwards is up to you, but I want to marry you, remember.'

13

'Caroline, I'm home! Just got some things to put in my study and I'll be with you. Good day, darling?'

Caroline felt that lift to her heart which only Peter's presence could bring about. 'Fine, thanks, and you?'

'All right. Tell you later.'

Caroline brought the Bolognese part of their evening meal out of the oven and called the children to wash their hands. 'It's ready, don't delay.'

Peter, Alex and Beth all arrived at the table at the same moment. Beth said loudly, 'You haven't washed your hands, Alex.'

'I have.'

'He hasn't, Mummy.'

'Only Alex knows if he has or not, so if he hasn't, he can wash them at the sink.'

As she drained the spaghetti Alex came to turn on the taps and run his hands underneath.

Triumphant Beth exclaimed, 'You see, I knew he hadn't. You've started telling fibs, Alex.'

'That will do, Beth. Alex's conscience is his own responsibility.'

Caroline served the spaghetti Bolognese and after Peter had said grace she asked him if he'd seen the Americans.

'No. I didn't leave Little Derehams until well after lunch, but Willie told me almost every word of what he'd said on his guided tour. They were deeply impressed by the war memorial plaques and all the names on there, and seeing Willie's uncles and grandfather and Jimmy's four uncles, and our wonderful banners and the architecture and how old the church was. He seemed to have thoroughly enjoyed himself, to say nothing of the tips he got. He told them everything, even to the ghost he vows is there by the tomb.'

Beth shuddered. 'I've never seen a ghost in there.'

'Neither have I, but I'd like to.' Alex made ghost noises and waved his arms at Beth, who hit him hard on his leg. 'That hurt!'

'Good, you know I don't like scary things.'

'Stop it the two of you! I want my meal in peace.' Caroline soothed Alex's leg with her hand and mouthed a kiss to him.

Peter said, 'After we've eaten I'm going to catch up on the parish photo album. I'd be glad of some help.'

Both Alex and Beth volunteered.

With his mouth full of food Alex muttered, 'It's ages since we did it, Dad. Mr Prior came the other day with a load. He likes being our photographer. He said he'd been taking parish photos since he was twelve. That's positively historical.'

Peter laughed. 'Well, that means he's been doing it for about sixty years.'

'Sixty years! He's seventy-two, then. That's old.'

'We did have a lady called Mrs Gotobed and she lived to one hundred. She died about a year after you were born. Now that really is old.'

Peter noticed, but the children didn't, that Caroline had gone quiet. Without her the three of them chattered on about age, and grandparents and what changes Mrs Gotobed had seen in her lifetime. Without speaking Caroline served the cheesecake Sylvia had made for them before she left that afternoon. When the time came to clear up she said, 'We'll clear the table and then you can start on the albums in here. I've some letters to write. I'll leave you to it.'

Quite deliberately and with every intention of getting his own way Peter said, 'I think it would be nice if you helped us, darling. The children and I haven't seen you all day. How about it?'

'I'd rather get the letters written.'

'I know you would, but they can be done any time.'

'No, really, I must get them written.' Caroline folded the tablecloth and went to switch on the dishwasher. 'You always do it, the three of you.'

'Get the albums out, children, and find Mr Prior's envelope. They're on their special shelf in the study.'

As the children darted off on their errand Peter went behind Caroline to put his arms round her. He nuzzled her hair and held her close. 'It's got to be the two of us. It mustn't look like something you can't talk about. It needs to be in the open between us all.'

'You've sprung it on me; it's not fair.'

'I just feel the moment is ripe.' Peter turned her round to face him. 'It has to be faced.'

Alex came back in, staggering under the weight of the albums, with Beth coming up behind carrying Mr Prior's envelope.

Peter released Caroline and went to pull out a chair for her. 'Here you are, darling, you sit here.'

She couldn't refuse, it would be too obvious. But when you've kept a secret for more than ten years ... 'OK, then.'

'Is there a photo of old Mrs Gotobed, Daddy? Which one will it be in? This newest one?'

'No, the last full one.' He stood up and heaved the one he wanted out from the bottom. 'Here we are. This one.' Eventually he found Mrs Gotobed in a Harvest Festival photograph taken, he guessed, about two years before she died. 'There she is with her daughters, Lavender and Primrose. Both very dear ladies.'

Alex burst out laughing. 'Lavender and Primrose. Help!'

Beth peered at the photograph through Peter's magnifying glass. 'I think they're very pretty names. Look how old she is. Just look. All wrinkly and thin. She looks like a little bird. Like a wren.'

They played a game of guessing who all the other people were in the photo and then Peter let them ramble along through the pages till they came to the page he wanted them to look at.

'These are of the village show. Nineteen ninety-one, I think. Yes. Can't quite read it.' The two of them identified several people, including Lady Bissett wearing an astonishing hat, and Venetia from the Big House when she was going through her Quaker dress period. Then Peter said casually, 'There's someone there who belongs to you.'

'Belongs to us?'

'Yes.'

'Just us?'

'Yes. You and Alex.'

Alex looked hard at the picture. 'Is it Grandma and Grandad? I can't see them.'

'No. It's this lady here.' He pointed to someone with long fair hair, wearing a smart red-and-white dress and obviously serving behind a stall.

Beth protested she didn't know her. 'Do I know those three girls sitting on the grass in front? They don't go to school.'

'That's their mother standing behind the stall. They'd be too old now for your school, wouldn't they, Caroline?'

Alex asked, 'Who are they? What are they called?'

Caroline answered his question. 'Daisy, Pansy and Rosie. That's Daisy, that's Pansy, I think, and the little one kneeling up is Rosie. They'll be something like eighteen, sixteen and fourteen now.'

Beth found the tone of her mother's voice oddly unlike her normal one, but still she had to ask, 'But they don't live here. I've never seen them, so how can they belong to us.'

Peter took the plunge. 'They were three lovely girls, so sweet and pretty and shy. I expect they still are. They are actually related to you, they're your half-sisters.'

'Really? Honestly?' Beth was intrigued.

Alex was more cautious. 'What does that mean?'

Caroline was sitting with her hands resting on the table, gripped tightly together, her head down. Suffering. 'They have the same mummy as you.' Alex hid his shock while he worked out whether it meant what he thought it did.

Beth thought this over for a moment, took the magnifying glass and carefully inspected the girls and the lady standing behind the stall. 'So where's their daddy? Is he here somewhere?'

'He didn't used to join in things. He was a scientist and always preoccupied.'

'So there's not just Alex and me. There's Daisy, Pansy and Rosie. That's five of us.'

'I expect you could say that.' Peter added, 'They left the village, though.'

'Where have they gone?' It was Beth doing all the asking; Alex had withdrawn from the conversation.

Caroline, in fear she might ask to go to see them, said, 'A long way away.'

Still peering through the magnifying glass Beth said, 'The mummy looks pretty. I like her hair. It's the same colour as mine and her cheeks are round like mine. Oh! Just like mine!' She glanced at Caroline as though assessing whether or not there was anything of Caroline in her own face.

Alex, by now, was standing beside Caroline, his face inscrutable.

Peter said, 'Yes.'

Then Beth asked the question Caroline had been dreading. 'Daddy, could we see them some time?'

'Perhaps when you're eighteen.'

'You always say that. You said the same when I wanted my ears pierced and when I wanted to wear make-up. Well, I shall wear it before I'm eighteen, Daddy. I'm sorry but I shall.' Still scrutinising the photograph, Beth came to a splendid conclusion. 'I wish we could see a photo of those flower girls' daddy, then Alex could see if he's like him.'

'He wouldn't be like him, though, would he?'

Beth stared hard at him. 'Why?'

'Because I'm your daddy.'

'Oh, of course you are. I'm getting awfully muddled.'

Peter was trying to lead them to their own understanding of the situation but felt he was floundering. He turned to Alex and said, 'You're very quiet, young man.'

'Just thinking.'

'I see. Come and have a look at the flower girls. Come on.'

Alex shook his head and pointed to Beth. 'No, thanks. They're not really my sisters. She's my sister.'

Beth, still greatly intrigued by her discoveries, ignored him and asked, 'So what's her name?'

'Whose?'

'The flower girls' mummy.'

'Suzy Meadows.' There, it was out, thought Caroline. She'd said the name she'd dreaded to hear on the children's lips.

'Suzy. Suzy. Suzy Meadows.' Beth repeated it time and time again until Caroline's head swirled with it and she blurted out, 'She was a lovely, kind, generous person.'

'You knew her, Mummy?'

'Of course. I asked her if I could have you both. She knew there was no way she could feed and clothe three children and look after two new babies and earn money for them all.'

Beth, who'd been kneeling on her chair to get a better view, shuffled down on to her bottom and looked set for hearing a story. 'Go on, then.'

'Well, I knew she was expecting twins and I knew her husband had died and she already had three girls to bring up, so I asked her if she could possibly let us have you.'

Alex, ever sensitive to his mother's mood, put a hand on her shoulder to comfort her and leant his weight against her.

'She said that was what she had planned and she wanted us to take you.'

'So she gave us to you.' Beth's eyes grew wider. 'Did she love us?'

'I know she did.' Caroline put an arm round Alex's waist and hugged him, as much for his comfort as for her own. 'You were born first, darling.'

'Then me?'

'Alex was screaming his head off, really screaming.'

'Did I?'

'No, you were all quiet and composed, and you were sucking your thumb even then.'

Rather smugly Beth reminded her she'd stopped now.

'I know, but you were then. You were small and neat and beautiful.'

'What about me?'

'Alex, I remember thinking what big feet you had and that you were long and gangling. I thought to myself, he's definitely Peter's boy and he's going to be just as big.'

Alex posed as he'd seen strong men pose and Beth laughed. 'I was beautiful! You weren't.'

'He was, just as beautiful. You were both beautiful.'

'Did the Suzy person think we were beautiful?'

Caroline was instantly back in that delivery room witnessing Suzy's bravery. Felt again her own extreme joy mixed with the terrible fear that Suzy wouldn't be able to part with thcm. How had Suzy lived through it? Should she tell them Suzy couldn't bear to look at them, fearful that she wouldn't be able to give them up if she did? Caroline hesitated while she weighed up the merits of telling or not. 'She was so full of pain at giving you up to your daddy. So full of pain.' Without warning Caroline was crying. Unspoken and unrecognised anxieties tore to the surface and ten years of persuading herself that now she had the children it didn't matter about not being able to bear children of her own, that it didn't matter about Peter's unfaithfulness, all came pouring into the open along with her tears. She was inconsolable. Her heart-rending, gut-wrenching sobs shocked them all.

'My darling girl! Hush! Hush!' Even Peter's arms round her gripping her firmly didn't assuage her distress.

The children clung to her and Beth wept. 'I'm sorry, Mummy, I didn't mean ... '

'Come on, Mum. Don't cry. Don't cry.'

But she did cry. She'd been too brave all along. In her gratitude for the chance to take the children for herself she'd been too accepting of what had happened. She should have raged and stormed, and made Peter's life hell. She'd no idea that all of it, the whole terrible mess, had been secretly boiling and bubbling in her and the tears pouring down her cheeks, for herself and for Suzy and for the children, wouldn't stop coming.

'Darling, you're frightening the children. Please. Please.'

Alex couldn't bear to hear her anguished weeping. He closed up the flower girl photo album with a bang and carried all the albums back to the study. But instead of putting them neatly on the shelf where they always sat he flung them to the floor and kicked them across the carpet. Then he went back into the kitchen and picked up the envelope with Mr Prior's latest contributions, took it into the study, shook the pictures out all over the floor and stamped on them in a wild frenzy. If Beth didn't understand what had happened he did. Stamp. Stamp. Dad had done with Suzy what you did to get children, like Miss Pascoe had explained, like Dad had explained, too, very simply, years ago. Stamp. Stamp. Stamp. Which Beth seemed to have forgotten all about. Stamp. Stamp. Who cares about half-sisters and all that rubbish, they were old anyway. Stamp. Sta— He stuck his fingers in his ears so he couldn't hear his mother's sobbing. She loved him tons more than someone who could give him away. His heart felt as though it had broken into a thousand pieces. Slowly his own tears surfaced and ran down his cheeks, and he locked the study door so no one could discover him crying. Alex felt so alone; more deeply distressed and perplexed than he had ever been in all his life.

Peter, later that evening, went to his study and found the albums and the photographs lying where Alex had left them. He realised then, as he had suspected, that this was Alex's reaction to understanding fully the implications of what he'd learned, whereas Beth had only accepted without appreciating what was behind it all. Caroline was in bed, exhausted, and at last he'd got the children to bed too, though whether they would sleep . . . The trauma, brought about by the disastrous revelations, was mind-numbing.

He knelt down and began to pick up the pictures, straightening out the more crumpled ones and wondering what on earth he could say to Arthur Prior about them. Small matter, compared with what he had to face now. A son who probably loathed him and a daughter more confused than she deserved. And a wife . . . it didn't bear thinking about how she felt. Peter paused for a moment and felt again the pain of Alex not being able to look him in the eye.

There was the sound of someone on the stairs. At the moment he didn't think he could cope with anyone, but they were coming down whatever he thought. Standing in his navy-and-white pyjamas in the study doorway was Alex. 'I can't sleep, Dad.'

'Come and sit on the sofa. I won't be a moment doing this.'

'Sorry I made that mess. Beth's asleep in your bed and Mum's asleep too.'

'That's good. They'll feel better in the morning.'

'Dad . . . '

Peter reached across to put Arthur's envelope on the shelf and then stood up. 'Yes.'

A frightened face looked up at him. 'Did you do it on purpose? To get a baby for Mum?'

'That's how it turned out.'

Alex didn't allow his eyes to look at his father. 'So it wasn't on purpose for a baby for Mum?'

'No.'

Vehemently Alex declared, 'I don't want to see them, those girls, nor that Suzy person, even if Beth does. You won't make me, will you?'

'Of course not. Only if you wish. For Mum's sake . . . I'm glad you don't.'

'Dad . . . does everyone in the village know? About us.'

'At the time they didn't, then they did, but they never say a word and for that I have always been very thankful.' He sat down on the chair at his desk. 'You couldn't be loved more by your mum and me, you know that, don't you? You're properly adopted, no one can take you from us, you are ours for ever and a day. Praise be to God for that.'

'I . . . you don't love this Suzy person, do you, instead of Mum?'

Peter shook his head. 'I loved her only for the moment. Mum is the one I truly love and always will, no matter what.' He went over to sit beside Alex on the sofa. 'Do you want to know anything else? I'd rather you asked now than kept worrying.'

'Not right now.'

'If Beth wants to talk to you about it all, be careful what you say. I'm certain she hasn't realised as you have.'

'I'll have to be truthful to her?'

'Of course. How about hot chocolate, you and me, mm?'

'Will Mum be all right? I've never seen her so upset.'

'It will take a while, I'm afraid.' He got up and asked again about hot chocolate.

'Yes, please. Mum's great. I never think she isn't mine . . . you know . . . it's like for real.'

'What you have learned about tonight is not for discussion outside this house. It is an entirely private matter which Mum and I *never* talk about to anyone, for your sakes as much as our own. We can talk about it between ourselves, of course, if we wish, so you and Beth are absolutely free to discuss it with either Mum or me or each other. And your grandma and grandad know about it too, so you can talk to them absolutely freely if you wish. You understand?' Alex nodded. Peter bent over, looking as if he were intending to kiss him but Alex dodged away so he couldn't.

Peter left Alex to drink his hot chocolate in bed and turn out his own light. He went into their bedroom and found, as Alex had said, that Beth had gone to sleep with her mother's arms round her. He stood, looking at them both. As he watched, Beth sat up and said 'Toilet'. She climbed out of bed, disappeared to the bathroom and didn't come back. He found her fast asleep in her own bed.

So he was left with Caroline. He drew the duvet up around her bare shoulders and lay on his side looking at her. Her eyelids were still red from weeping and they appeared swollen, too, and there were shadows where there hadn't been shadows before. She stirred in her sleep as though searching for Beth. 'She's gone back to bed, darling.'

Caroline stretched, clutched her head and muttered, 'Aw! I feel terrible.'

'I'm so sorry. Can I get you anything?'

She shook her head. 'Alex, is he all right about it?'

'So-so. His problem is he has understood, which Beth hasn't. She's just intrigued.'

'She's not a fool. She will in a day or two.'

'It didn't go quite as I intended.'

Caroline turned away from him saying, 'I'd no idea I would react like that. I've always thought I had it under control. Accepted it, you know.'

Peter pulled the duvet around her shoulders again. 'I didn't want them to think their conception had been something . . .'

More sharply than he had ever known, Caroline snapped out, 'You can't find the word, can you? You honestly can't find it. Well, I'll find it for you, shall I? Sordid? Would that fit the bill? Or how about shoddy, or shameful? No, I think sordid was the word you were looking for.'

'Caroline!'

'Caroline nothing! Whatever brought it about?' Her question was met with stunned silence. 'Well? Lost for words? It's time we talked about it. I was so thrilled at the idea of at last having babies and ridiculously pleased that they were yours and not a stranger's that I never bothered to enquire or even think how it had come about. I simply closed my mind to stop myself getting hurt any more than I was.'

'My God.'

'Well? I'm waiting.'

So quietly his voice was almost inaudible Peter said, 'I . . . do you really want to know?'

'I wouldn't have asked if I hadn't.' Caroline turned back to face him. 'Well?'

Peter rolled over on to his back and stared at the ceiling. 'I noticed her at my first service here. Then I saw her passing the study window and couldn't believe how devastatingly attractive I found her. I took you out to lunch to make myself stop thinking about her; to help me cling to sanity. Her face seemed to be everywhere I looked: on the page, in the mirror, on the computer screen. I went to sleep with her face inside my head. She would not go away. Then the police arrived to tell her Patrick had committed suicide. Her parents arranged to take the children out and I was to pop round to discuss the cremation and such with her because she didn't want the children to overhear. So I did.'

'And . . .?'

Ever so quietly he murmured, 'It was lust, Caroline. Sheer lust.' He saw Suzy's beautiful sad face and felt the touch of her hand on his arm as she begged him to comfort her, her intention absolutely plain. Remembered his own overpowering surge of sexual appetite. 'Alex asked me tonight if I loved her still. I never loved her, only craved her.' He recalled the sweet, scented smell of the palm of her hand as he'd kissed it. 'Craved her.'

'That was a sin.'

'Yes. Over, literally, in minutes, because our need for each other was so powerfully urgent. But a sin nevertheless, which I shall take to the grave.'

Caroline absorbed what he said, then replied, 'So that night when she rang very late for your help and you wanted me to go too . . .'

'Because I couldn't risk being in the house with her alone.'

'I must have been completely naïve not to have sensed that in the air. Talk about rose-coloured spectacles.'

'Saying how sorry I am is totally inadequate. But I don't know how else to apologise.'

In a dangerously strained voice Caroline answered, 'It makes me sick to my stomach to hear all this. If she hadn't conceived then, you wouldn't have told me about it, would you?'

'No, I don't think I would. But it would have been to save you the pain.'

'And that's he who values truth so highly. Well, I've nothing to confess about Hugo. We never made love. I wanted to, but didn't, for your sake. There was always that something indefinable which held me back.'

'I'm eternally grateful for that. I sensed you hadn't made love, but it's wonderful to have it said. You must be a vastly better human being than I.'

'Mm. It's half past one and I've surgery tomorrow – no, this morning. Goodnight.'

'God bless. Thank you for your love and for your loyalty. I certainly don't deserve you.' Peter switched off his light.

'No, you don't. Strange thing is I still adore you. How does that come about?'

'Don't know, but I am deeply grateful. Goodnight, my darling girl.'

Minutes later he said, 'I adore you. Utterly. Can you ever forgive me?'

It must have been a whole minute before she replied, 'As I said at the time, I forgave you soon after I learned you were their father. I had no option, because I wanted them so much and I couldn't allow myself to be in a position of you being grateful to me on a daily basis. But tonight I ask myself what you would have done if I had *not* asked Suzy to give them both to us. If I'd said definitely *no* to that and you'd had to watch her leave with your children. Would you have gone with her?'

Peter gave her her answer immediately. 'No. She said herself that you were the one for me, that you were my soulmate. I can say with my hand on my heart that, without any hesitation, I know I would have had to let them go.'

'You would never have asked me to be a mother to your children either?'

'Never. I love you too much to ask that of you.'

'Thank you for that. I love you too, so very much. No matter what.' She saluted his love with a gentle kiss on his forehead.

*

Next morning when the twins came down for breakfast it appeared as though last night had never happened. They entered the kitchen to find everything as normal: the kettle singing on the hob, the table laid, their mother pouring milk into the huge jug they used at breakfast time, the one patterned all over with spring flowers, their chucky-egg egg cups with their very own chucky-egg spoons, the special cereal bowls they'd bought when they were holidaying in Portugal. They could hear Dad above their heads singing in the shower. Their mother appeared to be as she had always been until last night, happy and cheerful.

Before they knew it Dad was sitting down to eat his breakfast, and they heard Sylvia's key in the front door and her calling out as she always did, 'It's only me.' To Beth, last night had become a strange dream to be thought about another day. As for Alex, he was glad to find things appeared to be back to normal, when he'd thought nothing would ever be the same again.

14

The day Bryn came back to Turnham Malpas after seeing off his American group at Gatwick happened to be the day that, unknown to him, Mr Fitch returned from the Far East. Bryn had a hurried lunch in Liz and Neville's kitchen, and went off to the Big House, not knowing, but hoping against hope, that Mr Fitch might be back.

Bryn pulled up with a screech of brakes, sending the gravel flying. Just as he leapt from his sports car, full of his success and desperate to find an influential ally to stop any possibility of the council deciding to modernise Turnham Malpas, Mr Fitch came out of the front door. 'Good afternoon, Mr Fitch. Very, very glad to see you home safe and sound.' Bryn shook hands vigorously. 'I must say you're looking in excellent health for a chap who's just put in hours of flying time.'

'Thank you, Fields. I must say I'm very glad to be back. If you've come to talk to me let's walk about the garden for a while. After all those hours in that damn plane I'm longing to see some countryside, my countryside. You know . . . come through into the rose garden, it's my favourite place. When I first came to live here, had the flat made and got the staff training school organised, it was simply a place to live. Now, well, I love it. I've had a lot to learn, a lot, but I think I finally know how privileged I am to live in such a place as this.'

'It's certainly a lovely estate now.'

Mr Fitch's icy blue eyes became angry. 'I don't just mean the estate, I mean the whole place. I just wish I owned every house in the village and then . . .' Mr Fitch's thin, severe face and those ice-cold eyes of his warmed for a moment. He touched a glowing rose in full bloom and savoured its splendid scent. He looked at Bryn with such joy in his eyes that Bryn became embarrassed as though he'd been privy to some tremendous secret to which he had no right at all. 'You see, it isn't just money. It's knowing that one is only a trustee of land like this and it, the land, is far more important than anything else. I hold it all very close to my heart.' He picked up a handful of rich, crumbly soil and let it trickle very slowly through his fingers.

Besides being unaware that Mr Fitch had a heart, Bryn had never seen him in such a mood and was at a loss to know what to say. Finally he answered, 'I suppose after being abroad so much you're more than glad to be home.'

'I am, I am, but I wasn't meaning that. I was meaning that the land itself affects you after a while. I learned about how to care from Ralph, you know. Great chap. His heart belongs to the land. Oh, yes. A man of powerfully sympathetic understanding where the land is concerned. I admire him.'

Mr Fitch looked almost mistily into the distance and Bryn, considerably surprised, blurted out, 'I thought you two were sworn enemies.'

'Certainly not, Fields. What gave you that idea? We're the best of friends, he and I. Let's have a look in the glass houses. Follow me.'

Mr Fitch chattered on with such enthusiasm that Bryn became almost enamoured of the vines and the peaches and the ... 'You see, it's the seasons, coming one after the other never mindful of man, just doing their own thing. There's such a reliability about the seasons, don't you think? Such an assurance.'

'Oh, yes. There is.'

'Century after century, always the same and it doesn't matter what man does or doesn't do; it happens. One's part of history, you know. Had you ever thought about it like that?'

Suddenly Bryn realised that with Mr Fitch in this mood it wasn't going to be difficult to persuade him to become a powerful ally. As they turned to leave the glass house Bryn said, 'Talking of history and centuries and such, I have a mole in the council offices and he informs me that the council are doing exploratory investigations into modernising the village.'

If he'd drawn a gun on Mr Fitch he couldn't have looked more horrified. 'Modernise the village? My God! What do you mean?'

This was more the Mr Fitch he knew and Bryn took a step back. 'One-way signposts, street lighting, numbering the houses, yellow lines . . .'

'Yellow lines! Lighting! Never! I won't allow it.' Mr Fitch began to boil. His snow-white hair almost sparked with indignation and horror. 'One-way signs! What are they thinking of? They'll be putting up advertising hoardings next. Traffic lights! What brought this about?'

'Miss Pascoe at the school saying how worried she was about all the cars pulling up to drop the children off in the mornings. She's been on about it for months. Mayhem, she claims. Parking on the green and such.'

'I'll give her mayhem, the bloody woman. This is what comes of giving women positions of authority. Wait till I see her! I'll give her mayhem.'

'If I might suggest, I wouldn't use that argument.'

'What argument?'

'The one about women in positions of authority. It doesn't go down well in the present climate.'

'Well, you may be right. Diplomacy, eh?'

'Exactly. In any case it's the council we need to get at, not Miss Pascoe. I wondered if you had any influence?'

'The last time I tried my kind of influence, Sir Ralph shamed the officials into changing their minds with no one ever taking up battle stations. Have you tried him?'

'They're in Singapore and then they're going on to Japan. The whole job could be done and dusted before he gets back.'

'Pity. These people with their inherited titles seem to get their own way in the countryside in the most gentlemanly fashion. Scarcely a word in anger and Bob's your uncle, the whole matter is cleared up apparently to everyone's satisfaction, and both sides believe it's they who have brought it about. I admire that.' He stood, hands in pockets, gazing across the lawns towards Sykes Wood. 'This mole. It wouldn't be our Kevin, would it?'

Bryn had to smile. 'Yes. Our Kev.'

'I classify him as a rat rather than a mole. However, needs

must . . .' Mr Fitch turned on his heel and began to walk towards the house. 'Surprised to find you of all people interested in preserving the village. It couldn't be a vested interest because of your tourists, could it?' He looked up at Bryn with an amused grin on his face.

This old codger saw more than was good for him, he'd have to admit it. 'That's right. Just got back from a very successful trip with my first group of tourists. They loved it. Second group next month. I'm really on to something big.'

'Back with Georgie, then?'

'No. I've given up all rights there. That damned Elektra . . . burned my boats, you know.'

'Women can be the very devil. Leave it with me. Need some sleep to bring me round. Jet lag, you know. Don't bother me again with this, Fields. I'll ring you.' Mr Fitch abruptly dismissed him with an impatient flick of his hand and disappeared into the house.

Bryn became distinctly disgruntled when he thought about that final piece of arrogance. And there was he, thinking for a while that he and Mr Fitch were associating on level terms. Bryn felt he'd been dismissed with less grace than Mr Fitch would have spoken to a dog of his. 'Fields' indeed. Did he need Mr Fitch's help with the entire village just waiting to shoulder arms to prevent their enemy from modernising their precious village? Well, better two strings to one's bow, so he'd stir up the villagers and see what happened.

He tried the Village Store first, running into Mrs Jones who was picking up a jar of 'Harriet's Country Cousins' Lemon Cheese' made with real lemons and fresh barnyard eggs, from the preserves shelf. 'How would you feel about it? Could I count on your support?'

'To be frank, in letters of one syllable, no.'

'No?'

'That's what I said. It's nothing short of criminal the chaos on Sunday mornings at morning service and during the week at the start of school. There's cars all over the place. Do we have to wait for someone to get run over before something's done?'

'But do you want yellow lines and road signs all over the place?'

'If it saves lives, yes I do.'

'But there has never been an accident nor anything anywhere near it since the year dot.'

'What about Flick Charter-Plackett and that little Janine outside the school the other day?'

'As you well know that wasn't because of chaotic traffic, but little girls running out into the road without looking.'

Mrs Jones came down from her high horse. 'Well, maybe you're right about that, but the fact remains it all needs organising.'

'So I can't count on you?'

She shook the jar of lemon cheese in his face. 'I've something better to do than stand here arguing.' She marched off to attack her parcel tape with renewed vigour.

Next he tried Sylvia who was shopping for the Rectory. 'What do you think about this business of yellow lines and one-way traffic?'

'To be honest I shudder to think about there being accidents outside the school. I hardly dare let the twins go on their own, just in case. So one-way traffic and some yellow lines would go down well in my book.'

'And in mine.' This was Jimbo joining the discussion. 'We always take Fran to school and put her right inside the gate. There's so many cars coming from all directions.'

It wasn't until Bryn spoke to Jimmy that he found an ally. 'I'm on your side, definitely.' He nudged Bryn and gave him a conspiratorial wink. 'Can't have our little scam spoiled can we?'

'So how much did you get in tips?'

'That'd be telling. But quite satisfactory, thank you.'

'So if we hold a protest outside the council offices you'd be with me?'

'Count me in.'

'They all thought you were great. If your tips don't come up to scratch one time don't come looking to me for recompense.'

'OK. OK. I enjoyed it. Easy as pie it was. Nice people, too.'

'Only don't go on about the plague pit quite so long, just enough to whet their appetites.'

'Right. Did they go to see it?'

Bryn nodded. 'I spun a bit of a tale there, actually. When is the burial taking place? We need a headstone up.'

'Ask the Rector. He'll know better than me.' Jimmy whistled up Sykes and left Bryn standing alone in the middle of the road.

Suddenly Grandmama Charter-Plackett's cottage door snapped open and there she was, beckoning him in. 'Time for coffee?'

Now she really was a formidable old bat and he needed her on board. 'Good morning! I have indeed. Just what the doctor ordered.'

'I've got the kettle on.'

Her kitchen was at the back of the house overlooking her charming garden. While she busied herself with the cafetière he stood at the back door admiring the view. 'By the looks of this you're a gardener, not just someone who gardens.'

'What a delightful compliment. I consider myself just that, a real gardener. It's so rewarding.'

Bryn took in the whole of her view, noticing she could see the old oak tree as well as the stocks if she stood on tiptoe, and the whole lovely vista of some of the best houses in the village as well as the Village Store. 'You've a lovely view of the green.'

'Exactly. I keep intending to *buy* a house when one comes vacant, but then I'd lose this view. I don't think there's a single house with a better view. Some are as good but definitely not better. Come and sit down.'

She went out through the back door to her small group of table and four chairs on her little terrace. 'Some people call this my patio, but that's so common. It's a terrace.' She put down the tray on the snow-white wrought-iron table and sat down.

'You wanted to see me?' Bryn asked.

'Yes. About Dicky.'

'Ah!'

'Is he marrying Georgie?'

Bryn shrugged his shoulders. 'Who knows? Dicky certainly doesn't.'

'I hear it's all your fault.'

'Dicky thinks it is.'

'I'm very fond of Dicky. Lovely little chap. He and Georgie are well suited.'

'If he does marry Georgie I understand there's someone in the village willing to help him buy my share of the pub.'

Mrs Charter-Plackett organised her cafetière and carefully filled his cup. 'There we are, cream and sugar? I would have thought that the money you took from your joint account when you skipped with that hussy would have been enough for you. You left Georgie in a mess.'

Bryn was surprised she knew as much as she did, but he didn't miss the fact that she hadn't taken up his remark about someone lending Dicky the money. Could it be her?

'I've felt sorry about that. You could be right. But the stubborn fella won't have anything to do with her. He's gone back to work because he needs the money, but he reckons that Georgie and I . . . well . . . I have besmirched their love.'

'Hm. I heard about that. You were an idiot.'

'Maybe. While I'm here, I'd like to ask if you approve of this business of the yellow lines, and street lighting et cetera.'

'No, I do not, and if you're starting up some opposition then count me in, as they say. It would ruin everything. Imagine! Huh!' She shuddered.

'You're the first one I've spoken to, apart from Mr Fitch and Jimmy, who's against it.'

'Oh! He's back? I'll do some campaigning for you. That Kev everyone talks about . . .'

Bryn tapped his jacket pocket. 'I've got him right there.'

'Good. Good.'

They drifted on to talk about all manner of things and Bryn found her an entertaining woman. Eventually she signalled that he should be moving off so he stood up and carried the tray inside for her, but before he left she said, 'I'll have a word with Dicky. See what I can do.'

'Thanks.'

'You're not interested in staying married, then?'

'No. Divorce is going through.'

'Good man. I've enjoyed your company.'

'And I yours.'

Bryn's luck was in that day for he found Peter at home. He was sitting in his study reading a prodigious tome the size of which quite intimidated Bryn. 'Sorry if I've interrupted . . .'

'Quite glad of an excuse, actually. Sit down. What can I do for you? I hear your tour went well.'

'It did. Yes, it did.' Bryn sat on the sofa wishing Peter were wearing mufti. This clerical collar bit and the cassock felt like a barrier to normal conversation. He'd be confessing his sins if he didn't watch it. 'It's like this. You know the plague pit; well, are we any nearer to having a service and a burial? If so, will there be a headstone saying who – or is it what? – is buried there?'

'Two weeks today. I'm paying for the stone, I feel so strongly about it.'

'That's more than kind, that is, more than kind. I just wondered because those Americans of mine were fascinated by the pit and the idea of a burial. Yes, indeed they were. Does everyone know?'

'It will be in the weekly newsletter on Sunday.'

'Right. I see.'

'How's Dicky?'

'Working. He said he'd never set foot in the Royal Oak again, but he has, so maybe there's hope for him and Georgie.'

'I sincerely hope so. They need each other. I'm just so sorry it all went wrong.'

Here we go, thought Bryn, confession time again. 'He's being stubborn.'

'With good cause, I think. But I have talked to him and tried to get him to see reason.'

'Well, old Grandmama Charter-Plackett is on the case so watch out. With her . . .' They both laughed. 'The other thing is did you know that the council are thinking of modernising the village? Zebra crossings by the school, lighting et cetera?'

'I had heard rumblings.'

'How would you feel about that? For or against?'

'Half and half, actually. Lighting. Zebra crossings, possibly even one-way traffic . . .'

'But not the whole hog surely? Think of the signposts. And whatever kind of lighting standards would they put up? Ruin the . . .'

The telephone rang and Peter lifted the receiver. 'Turnham Malpas Rectory, Peter Harris speaking.'

Bryn watched his face change to complete puzzlement, then

concern. 'No, no, you're all quite busy enough. I'll come. Tell her I'm coming right away.'

Bryn stood up. 'I'll go. I can record you as half and half, can I?'

Peter didn't appear to know what he was talking about. 'Got to go. Sorry. Do you mind?'

'Not at all.' The two of them left together and Bryn stood in Church Lane to watch where Peter went. Mm, he thought, I wonder what's happened?

Then he had a stroke of luck: one of the weekenders staying over for the week was setting off for a walk. He called a cheery 'Good morning to you!' as he passed.

'Good morning! You won't know me . . .'

'I do. Bryn, isn't it, used to be landlord at the pub. How's things?'

'Fine, fine.'

'Coming back to take over again, are you, though that Dicky's doing a great job.'

'No, just back for a few days. I wondered . . .' Bryn explained his mission and the weekender nodded his head in agreement. 'Oh, I wholeheartedly agree with the protest. Disgraceful. We're sick to death of government interference, sick to death. It's diabolical what they think they can do with the country nowadays. Your life isn't your own. We haven't bought this cottage to find ourselves in a wilderness of signposts and traffic lights. Certainly not. You've got my support, definitely.' The weekender strode away in his imitation Barbour jacket and walking boots towards Sykes Wood with a cheery wave and a thumbs up shouting, 'Leaflets, leaflets, that's what you need. And a big protest meeting to discuss strategy.'

Bryn rubbed his hands with glee. He appeared to be having a more profitable morning than he had first thought. Leaflets, though. He went back to Glebe House to rough one out. Perhaps even posters for windows.

Peter could hear Beth screaming as he crossed the school playground. He lengthened his stride and arrived full pelt in the hall, where he found her having the most terrible tantrum he'd ever seen her have. Miss Pascoe was struggling to calm her down but to no avail. The classroom doors were open and children were spilling out to witness this phenomenon.

Peter scooped her up and carried his grunting, snarling daughter into Miss Pascoe's office. He closed the door behind him with his foot, sat in the chair and hugged her hard. 'Hush! Hush, my darling child, calm down. Hush! Hush!' He tried to rock her but she was fighting him like a hell-cat. She beat her fists on his chest, grabbed his hair to pull it, pushed at his chest with her fists to be released but none of her strategies worked because he held her so firmly. Finally her strength ran out and she burst into tears, flushed and exhausted by her outburst.

Peter stroked her hair and gently rocked her, allowing the tears to flow. Slowly the crying lessened and he was able to get a tissue from Miss Pascoe's box on the desk to wipe her eyes. 'There we are. There we are.' The two of them sat quietly hugging each other until Beth relaxed against him, shielding her face with the tissue. She'd laid it fully open so that it completely covered her face. He could feel her shuddering as she strove for control. 'There we are. That's better. How about going home for the rest of the day, eh?'

He thought he detected a nod.

'What do you think, eh?'

He got a positive nod this time.

'They're all out playing, your class. Shall we wait till they come back in?'

Beth nodded again from under the tissue. She laid her head on his chest and enjoyed the security of his arms round her helping to make everything right. Gradually the love he felt for her reached her innermost turbulent being and she began to relax. 'Daddy?'

'Yes, my darling.'

'Sorry.'

'You must have had good reason.'

Beth nodded.

'Are you able to tell me?'

'No.'

'I see. Does Miss Pascoe know why?'

'No.'

'Is it something you've done and shouldn't have?'

His answer was a shake of Beth's head.

'Well, then. I think she'll be needing her room. Let me dry your eyes again and we'll leave. Blow everyone out playing. Head up and we'll march home. How about it?'

'They'll all see me.'

'Of course they will, but who cares? You and I, we're tough.'

Beth took the tissue from her face and he could have wept at the sight of her distress. Her sweet rounded cheeks were streaked with dusty tears, her eyelids swollen, her lashes still dripped a tear. Carefully he reached out and wet a fresh tissue under the washbasin tap and cleaned her face. 'There, that's better. Let me straighten your hair. Now you look like new. I think we'll say sorry to Miss Pascoe tomorrow, shall we?'

Beth nodded. She got off his knee, and prepared to show herself to all and sundry.

Peter opened the office door and found Miss Pascoe in the book corner picking up the books Beth had apparently flung about.

'There you are! Going home? What a good idea. We'll talk about it another day, shall we, Beth?'

Peter answered for her. 'Thank you. I'm so sorry.'

'Don't worry, Rector. We've seen worse, believe me.' She patted Beth's cheek. 'See you tomorrow, Beth, bright and shining new.'

Beth refused to look at her because she was so embarrassed. How could she explain to Miss Pascoe that she'd realised that very morning what it was her daddy had been trying to tell her on the evening with the parish photo albums? Tell her that she'd seen a photo of her real mother but at the time hadn't understood what it meant, but now she did? That they had the same colour hair and the same rounded cheeks. Tell her how she'd made her mummy cry like she'd never cried before, tell her she, Beth Harris, wasn't what she thought she was and that she'd three sisters she hadn't known about. That when she looked in the mirror she didn't know who she was. Was she Elizabeth Caroline Harris any more? Now she *knew* she wasn't normal would they let her sit the exam for Lady Wortley's after Christmas? Maybe they wouldn't want her, not when they knew she didn't belong. If she'd got it right her daddy must have done what you did to get babies ... So was she Beth Meadows, really, and one of those flower girls? But she couldn't be because Elizabeth wasn't a flower name. So she didn't even belong to them either. Her daddy slotted his key into the Rectory door and together, hand in hand, they went in.

'Would you like a nice cold drink, darling? You must be thirsty.'

'Yes, please.' Daddy went into the kitchen, poured two glasses of that fizzy real lemonade they both liked, and together they went into the sitting room to sit on the sofa and drink it. Daddy pulled the coffee table closer so she could put her glass on it when she'd finished. She'd better say it. Might he be cross? She glanced at him and saw he wasn't cross, only hurting. 'Sorry, Daddy, for screaming.'

'That's all right. I feel like screaming sometimes when things get too much. The thing is to get out in the open *why* you screamed.'

Daddy was so gentle when things were upset. He always understood. She couldn't bear making Mummy cry again as she had that night; she had to sort it out with him, not her. Very softly she told him why she'd screamed and cried and thrown the books about. It had boiled up inside her into a huge balloon and it burst at school. 'I was crying because all of a sudden I understood what you meant.'

'I thought perhaps it might be so.' Daddy was being so careful not to hurt. But he had hurt her that night, though she hadn't realised at the time. She needed to get Daddy to sort it out. He'd always said they could ask anything they wanted and he'd try to answer truthfully.

'Daddy, you're my real tummy-daddy, aren't you?'

'Yes.'

'But Mummy isn't my tummy-mummy?'

'No, because Mummy's place for growing babies till they're ready to be born isn't there, so she can't. It's like I said when you were very small.'

'So instead, this Suzy person had us.'

'Yes.'

'I see. So was my mummy pleased when she knew?'

'She wanted you both so very much.'

'So am I a Harris or a flower girl?'

'You're a Harris because Mummy and I adopted you, for ever and ever and ever. You are ours by law. It's all written down.'

'I'm glad about that. I'm glad I'm a Harris.' She felt a sharp pain of fear in her heart. 'That Suzy person can't come and get me, then?'

'No, she can't.'

'I don't think I'll bother to see the flower girls and the Suzy person. I won't have to, will I?'

'Definitely not.'

She'd asked as much as she could. She couldn't be bothered to try to understand any more of it at all. She was worn to a shred with the whole thing. 'I'll watch TV now.'

Beth switched it on quickly to put him off explaining any further. Oh, good, that was the phone ringing again. As her daddy went to answer it she lay back against the cushions and prepared to forget the whole thing. But couldn't, at least not quite. This *Teletubbies* was ridiculous. There was nothing on. Maybe she'd go back to school after lunch. But what would they all think? They'd tease her. No, she'd go back tomorrow when she felt better. Mummy would be home before long. Mummy. Mummy. Mummy. Mummy. The word ran like a well-beloved tune through her head.

Having run off far more copies of his leaflet than he'd any right to do on someone else's computer, Bryn set off to push them through every village door. He was surprised at how vicious some people's letter boxes were; his knuckles became quite tender. At some doors a dog snatched it straight out of his hand, which served to remind him not to let his fingers linger the other side of the letter boxes for too long. It was quite soothing wandering along in the sun stuffing the leaflets in every door. The blasted council mustn't succeed or it would ruin everything he'd planned. Bryn decided to give our Kev a call, ask him about further developments. Now the council had changed their routines and become less keen on allowing the general public to attend their meetings it was becoming increasingly difficult to learn about future plans, so our Kev had to be kept sweet. As he reached the bottom of Shepherds Hill and was crossing over to do the other side and so back to the village he thought about inviting our Kev out to a meal. But he felt that was going too far. No, he'd simply hand over more dosh, that was the best way. Money spoke to rats.

He met quite a group of mothers coming home with their

children from the school. 'Good afternoon, ladies, would you be so kind as to take time to read one of my leaflets. You may live outside the boundary of Turnham Malpas but it will, I'm sure, be of interest to you, with your kiddies attending the school.' He smiled sweetly at the children; he even chucked one little boy under the chin as he'd seen politicians do and began handing out leaflets, but he hadn't bargained for their vigorous reaction. 'We want some traffic control, it's our kids' lives that are at risk.' He thought this particular mother was about to strike him.

'Is that what it's about?' another asked.

'Thank you, but no.' The third mother stuffed his leaflet down his shirt neck.

Bryn protested. 'I say, I say. Please.'

'We'll stuff them all down your neck if you want.'

Bryn backed off. 'Sorry, ladies, but it's a free country . . .'

'Not so's I've noticed. Buzz off.'

Disconcerted by their opposition, Bryn finished putting leaflets in letter boxes when he arrived at the last of the new cottages in Hipkin Gardens. He was hot and sticky and thirsty. He'd done every house including those down Royal Oak Road and Church Lane and the Culworth Road. Was it worth it? Honestly, was it worth it? Then he thought about the delight his group of Americans had expressed about the village and decided, yes, it was. So he popped into the Royal Oak for some much needed refreshment and while he was there distributed the last of his leaflets to what turned out to be several very enthusiastic supporters of his protest, and felt tremendously heartened.

15

It had been mentioned twice in the weekly church newsletter that the funeral service for the bones was being held on Tuesday morning at ten o'clock and that afterwards there would be coffee served in the village hall. Peter rather suspected that he would be the only person present apart from Mrs Peel at the organ and Caroline. He'd written a special funeral service as there were large parts of the normal one which would be inappropriate, and he'd laboured long and hard to get the wording exactly right.

'Caroline! I've finished it. Would you read it through before I print it out?' Getting no reply he went in search of her. He found her in the attic looking through small baby clothes belonging to the twins.

'Do you remember when we bought these? No, of course you won't, but I do. I was so excited. The twins were coming home from hospital and I was hurrying to get things ready.' She held up two very small premature baby sleep suits, each with a tiny rabbit embroidered on the front. 'I loved these. Still do. They are lovely, don't you think?'

Peter took hold of them and held them up to the light. 'Indeed they are. Beautiful. Weren't we excited?'

'Oh, we were. And these! Remember these?' She was holding up a pair of bootees she'd made for Beth because her feet were always cold. 'I loved every stitch of these, every single stitch.' She kissed both bootees before she replaced them in the box along with the other early baby clothes and put on the lid. 'I'm sorry for all those tears that night. It spoiled the telling, didn't it?'

Peter had to smile. 'A little, but it was understandable. They were horrendous times.'

'They were, but at the same time so joyous. I wouldn't have had it any other way, though. After all, I've got the babies I wanted and you've got children of your very own.'

'I have. Thanks be to God.'

'Exactly. Poor Suzy. I wonder if she ever thinks of them and what they're doing. It hurts me still thinking about how brave she was, but they are turning out to be terrific people, aren't they?'

Peter kissed the top of her head. 'They are.'

'What did you want me for?'

'To read the funeral service I've written for the remains.'

'Ah, right. I doubt there'll be anyone there but thee, me and Mrs P.'

'I know, but we've got to do it right whatever.'

'Of course. I'll be down when I've tidied up. Really all these things should go to someone in need.'

'Keep them a while longer.'

'I think I will.'

'Why not bring the children up here and let them see? Make them feel as though they belong ... or something, I'm not quite sure.'

'That's an idea. By the way, this afternoon we're going boating on Culworth Lake. Might as well take advantage of the good weather while we can. Are you able to come with us?'

'Sorry, urgent sick visiting.'

'OK, then. I'll be down in a moment.'

Peter went down the narrow attic stairs and on to his study, and left Caroline to her memories.

The sun was even hotter that afternoon. Caroline packed plenty of drinks and sunhats, which the two of them hated but being so fair she had to insist upon, and with the sunroof open to its fullest extent they set off for the lake. It was on the Turnham Malpas side of Culworth so the journey there was not lengthy. In no time at all they were parked beside the lake and getting their hats and drinks out of the boot.

Alex had a favourite boat, and he ran down the slipway to search for her and found her tied up as he had hoped. She was called the *Mary Rose* and shone with layers of marine lacquer, over a lovely golden-brown stain. On her side the words *Mary Rose* were painted in bright royal blue with a Union Jack sticky transfer alongside her name. The brass oar locks seemed to shine more intensely than the other boats' and, well, he just plain loved her.

Beth arrived beside him. 'I want to go in that other one called *Elizabeth*.'

'We're not. It's this one and no other.'

'You always get your own way.'

'It's our boat is this. Ours. See.'

'Mummy! Alex wants to go in the usual one.'

'We will today and next time we'll go in the *Elizabeth*.'

Seeing Beth beginning to work herself up into a rage, which had become more frequent since the night of the photo albums, Caroline hastily gave her the money and sent her off to the boat office to pay.

The boatman came down to see them safely aboard and to shove them off. 'Nice day for it, Dr Harris.'

'It certainly is, Tony. Looks busy.'

'Yes, thank goodness. It's a short season.'

He shoved off the *Mary Rose* with his bare foot and they splooshed out on to the lake. Caroline had become very proficient at rowing and they were soon speeding down the centre of the lake heading for the long arm off to the right where the trees bent down to the water and where the children loved to tie up under a particular willow which dipped the ends of its twigs into the water to form a delightful secret hideaway.

They sat there under its cool canopy sipping their drinks and talking about school starting soon, and it being their last year at the village school, about beginning at their new schools and about uniform and new friends and a myriad other things of interest. After a little while Caroline decided to untie the boat and row back into the main part of the lake.

They were smoothly making progress round the big open area at the far end where the water was deep and where sometimes the two of them spotted fish in the dark depths when a crowd of youths in a bigger boat than theirs came racing down the lake yelling 'In . . .

Out ... In ... Out ...' at the tops of their voices. Caroline, trying to keep to the rules of the water and pass on the right, became worried that they were taking no notice of where they were going. She shouted to them and so did Alex but they couldn't hear. She swiftly directed the boat to pass them on the left, then saw another boat approaching her and before she knew it she was trapped between two boats both heading straight for her, one from the front and another from the rear. The second boat took evasive action and pulled away but the boat with the youths in it kept going and Caroline couldn't row strongly enough to get out of their way. They hit her full on with their surging bows and rocked the *Mary Rose* so that Beth, who'd been covering her eyes with her hands from fear of what might be going to happen, suddenly tipped out of the boat, hitting her head on the edge before she disappeared from sight.

An oar slipped from Caroline's grip.

Alex stood up.

'Sit down. Sit down.'

He did.

Caroline looked into the depths of the water.

No Beth.

Terrified, she could hear Alex bellow, 'Beth, Beth.'

Caroline saw Beth's fair hair rise to the surface.

Too far to reach.

'Stay in the boat.' Caroline carefully lowered herself over the side into the water.

Alex by now was screeching, 'Help! Help!'

Caroline swam to where she'd seen Beth's head come to the surface and dived.

One of the youths jumped into the water and swam to help.

Can't find Beth. Too dark.

Have to go up for air.

Go down again.

Too dark.

Go up for air, there's Beth going down yet again, further away.

Swim towards her.

The dark waters closed over her again.

Find her. Find her. Find her. There!

Grasp her.

Hoist her to the top.

Hold her head out of the water. Lungs bursting.

One of the youths swam towards her, took hold of Beth, swam with her to the boat and heaved her in.

Beth lay in the bottom, frightened and exhausted, choking and spluttering.

Desperately Alex held out the oar for his mother to grasp.

But the youth came up behind her and gave her the most tremendous push up so that she was half in and half out of the boat. Caroline pulled herself up but was too paralysed with fear and too heavy with water to manage the last push up into the boat. 'Oh, God! Oh, God!'

The youth came behind her and manhandled her into it, grabbing her body anywhere at all to achieve his objective. She collapsed in the bottom of the boat alongside Beth. By now they were floating well away from the lost oar and all she could think about was how to get back to the shore with only one oar. 'Beth! Beth?'

As they tried to get themselves seated without upsetting the boat, Caroline heard the phut phut of a motor boat engine. Thank heavens! It was Tony coming.

He circled round, rescued the oar and came alongside. 'Dr Harris! Young lady! OK? I'll tow you back. Hold tight. Sit up. That's it. On the seat. I've got you, don't worry.'

Caroline began to shake, not so much with the chill of the water on her skin but the full horror of what might have happened. Beth was unable to speak. Alex was deathly white from shock.

Tony switched off his motor boat engine, tied up and then tied up the *Mary Rose*. 'Come on, now. I'll switch the fire on in the boat office. Warm you up. Just wait till I get hold of those bu— beg your pardon, Dr Harris.' He hustled them into the boat office and turned on the fire. Out of a cupboard he brought towels somewhat the worse for wear and a collection of dry clothes kept for the purpose. Tony went out, shutting the door behind him, and they could hear him ranting and raving at the top of his voice and using fearful bad language at the youths. They heard their boat bump into the side and Tony still raving at them.

Caroline stripped Beth of her clothes and rubbed her hard with Tony's rough towel. She still hadn't spoken. Alex was channelling his fear into looking for something suitable for Beth to wear. 'Here we are, look, shorts and a shirt with dolphins on it. You'll look all right in these, Beth. Bit big but . . .'

Caroline was quickly becoming chilled right through to the bone. She left Beth to dress herself and began stripping off her wet clothes. 'Look for something for me, Alex, please.'

'There's not much, just this funny dress or a pair of man's shorts and a football shirt.'

'They'll do.'

They were much too big but she wasn't going to let that bother her.

'Look! I've lost a sandal. My best sandals!' Beth began to wail. 'My best sandals!'

Caroline put on the shorts and football shirt saying, 'Never mind about your sandal. We can always buy another pair, but we can't buy another Beth.'

Beth took hold of her hand.

Alex grasped the other. 'Let's go home,' he said.

'That's the best place. I'll get my bag and we'll go straight home. But we'll thank Tony first.'

Tony knocked at the boat office door and shouted, 'The wife's made a cup of tea for you. Sit on this seat out here in the sun. She'll be out in a minute.'

Beth wanted home more than anything. 'I want to go home.'

'Hush, darling, we will when we've had a nice cup of hot tea.' They emerged into the sun, thankful they were all alive. 'Thank you, Tony, that will be lovely. I found a plastic carrier bag in the office and I've borrowed it to put our wet things in. Where's the young man who jumped in the water to help us? I'd have liked to thank him.'

'They've all gone. I gave them a telling off and no mistake. They won't be back here for a bit. Idiots. I'd no idea they had drink in the boat. It's forbidden, really, but the moment your back's turned . . . Ah, here's your tea.'

The tea was welcome, it was sugared but it didn't matter, because it tasted like nectar.

'Ring Dad, tell him.'

'He's sick visiting, darling.'

'Please ring Dad, he'll want to know.'

'I don't want to worry him, it'll keep till we get home.' Caroline put an arm round Alex and hugged Beth with her free arm. 'Feeling better?'

Beth held up her feet. 'One sandal's no good.'

'Never mind, you can wear your flip-flops for a day or two. We can't go into Culworth to buy new sandals looking like this, can we?'

Alex looked at the two of them and burst out laughing. It was infectious. Both Caroline and Beth joined in and laughed till their sides ached, but it was such a relief. Laughing took some of the fear away.

They drove home singing silly songs from when they were small. Caroline put the car in the garage at the end of Pipe and Nook Lane and they went into the Rectory by the back door so no one would see them looking like freaks.

Peter was back and the children ran into the study to tell him their adventure.

His first words were, 'Whatever are you wearing, Beth?'

She explained, with Alex putting in his pennyworth where she hadn't explained clearly. 'And when I was under the water I could see fishes and nasty bits and the water tasted dreadful!'

'Beth! My darling! Where's Mummy, is she all right?'

'She's putting the kettle on. The water was so cold and dark, Daddy. I've never thought about water being dark before.'

'Did you try to swim?'

She shook her head.

'Why not? It's because of accidents like this that we taught you to swim.'

'I tried but I was so frightened. I kept going up but then I went back down again. I felt so heavy. I couldn't stay up and I couldn't see Mummy anywhere. It was so cold.' She shuddered at the memory. 'Worse than the swimming pool. I've got a huge, huge bump on my head, Daddy, look.' Beth pushed her hair away from her face to show him a black-and-blue patch close to her temple. I bumped it on the edge of the boat when I went in. It really makes you so you can't think.'

'Thanks be to God, you're safe and sound.' Peter hugged her.

Alex declared he'd tried to help. 'Mum wouldn't let me dive to find Beth. She told me to stay in the boat.'

'Very wise, else she'd have had two of you to rescue, wouldn't she.'

'*I* could have swum back to the boat and climbed back in, Dad.'

'I expect you could, but it's as Beth says: it's very different from the swimming pool.'

Caroline came in still dressed in her borrowed clothes. 'Peter! Am I glad to see you.'

Peter stood up and put his arms round her. 'And I'm glad to see you too. There I was, visiting my housebound sick, totally unaware of the danger my entire family were in. Darling! I'm so sorry I couldn't come with you. Are you sure you're feeling OK? It must have been a terrible shock. You were so brave.'

'I jumped in without thinking. She kept coming up and going down again. I was scared to death. I don't call that being brave.'

'Well, I think you were brave anyway.'

Beth said, 'She was. She dived dozens of times to get me, didn't she, Alex? Dozens. She was brave. I'll need new sandals. I've left one of my best ones in the lake.' She held up her bare foot to show him.

'I'm hungry. Is it nearly time to eat? It must be.' Alex wandered off into the kitchen.

Peter volunteered to start the meal while Caroline changed, so she and Beth went upstairs to find fresh clothes. They sat on Beth's bed, had a long cuddle to comfort themselves and giggled at their outfits. 'Mummy, I was so scared. I thought I was going to die.'

'Don't, darling, don't even think about it.'

'But I did.' She curled her arm more tightly round Caroline's neck. 'It's terrible down there. I go under the water in the swimming pool with my eyes wide open but under there, under that lake . . . there's swimmy things and black bits, and it's so dark you can't see, and even when I went down I didn't touch the bottom. I couldn't even *see* the bottom.'

'I know, darling, it's very deep at that end of the lake.'

'Have you ever drowned?'

'Not even nearly.'

'Has Daddy?'

'Not that I know of.'

Beth kissed her cheek very hard, again and again. 'I love you, Mummy. I truly do.'

'And I love you.' Caroline wound her arms round Beth and hugged her more tightly. 'I love you so very much.'

'And me you. And I love Daddy. Do you love Daddy?'

'Of course I do. You know that.'

Beth sat up and loosened her hold on Caroline. 'I love you like you really were my mummy. Which you're not, but you are and I want you to be for ever. Daddy says no one can take me from you. They can't, can they, if it's written on paper?'

'No. Never ever. Was that what the screams were all about at school the other day?'

Beth nodded. 'Yes. All of a sudden I understood. But I want to live with you all the time. Mr Glover said he wished you were his mother too, because you're so lovely. Well, that's how I want it to be. I'm going to be yours for ever. I'm not going to bother about those girls with the flower names, not for now anyway.'

'Thank you, darling, I like the sound of that very much. But you can when you wish, you know, when you're older.'

Beth shrugged her shoulders. 'Perhaps.' She stood up. 'I think I'll put on my blue shorts and that white top.'

'Fine. I'd better get changed myself.'

'I've got things sorted out now.'

'Good, I'm glad.'

'I'm your girl because I must be because you said you jumped in the water without giving it a thought, so you must love me the very bestest. Mustn't you?'

Caroline smiled at her. 'I expect I must.'

'Well, I *know* you do.'

Beth disappeared into the depths of her wardrobe searching for her favourite blue shorts and said no more, so Caroline crossed the landing to her own bedroom, overwhelmed with joy.

*

There'd been rain over the weekend, for which every gardener in the neighbourhood was very grateful, but on the morning of the bones service – for that was what everyone called it whenever it got a mention – a weak sun appeared and bathed the village in a kind of mystical hazy light from first thing.

Peter was approaching the service with trepidation. Not because he wasn't well prepared for it, but because it had occurred to him that he could very easily have been conducting a funeral service for his own daughter. As he tucked his cross into his leather belt and made the chain comfortable round his neck he looked at his reflection in the bedroom mirror. Behind him he could see Caroline standing by the dressing table putting on a necklace.

'Caroline, come here, darling.' Through the mirror he watched her come to stand beside him. They looked gravely at each other in the glass and Peter said, 'Thank you for being utterly wonderful and for loving me.'

'Thank you for loving me. Because I do love you. This funeral is getting to you, isn't it?'

Peter nodded. 'The thought occurred to me that but for you I might have been conducting Beth's . . .' He felt as well as saw her shock.

'Oh, my God! Don't even think it. And don't let her hear you say that. She really thought she was going to die.'

'I'm sorry. Sometimes, though, it is salutary to remind ourselves to be grateful for His mercy.' He found her hand, grasped it and took it to his lips to kiss. 'Thank you for coming with me this morning. Is my congregation ready?'

She smiled back at him, checked her appearance and said, 'It is.'

They got downstairs to find both Beth and Alex ready and waiting. 'We're going to be late.'

Caroline asked, 'Why, where are you going?'

'To the bones service, Mum.'

Peter protested, 'I'd arranged for you to stay with Willie while . . .'

'We're going. We want to.'

Peter saw that determined look in Alex's eye which experience had taught him meant he, Alex, was set on having his own way and that nothing, but nothing, would change his mind.

'We're both going, aren't we, Beth?'

'Oh, yes.'

Peter couldn't face the ensuing battle if he refused to allow them to be there; he was in no mood for an uproar. 'Very well. Pop next door and tell Willie. I've got to go. We'll see you in church.'

Alex knocked at Willie's and Sylvia's door, pushed it open and put his head round it, just as he'd seen his father do, saying, 'It's Alex from the Rectory.'

Sylvia was standing with her handbag on her arm, obviously about to leave for the service. Willie was ensconced in his chair by the fireside trying to read the paper.

'Willie! We're going to the service. Dad says we can, so we shan't need to stay with you. Thank you all the same.'

Willie nodded his agreement without looking at the pair of them.

'Are you coming with us, Sylvia?'

'You go on. I'll follow in a moment. I need a word with Willie.'

Alex left without closing the door. Sylvia pushed it shut and went back to stand in front of Willie. 'This has gone on far too long. Get up and come with me.'

'I shan't.'

'You will.'

'I won't.'

'After all you've said in the past about how Peter is so close to God he knows the rightness of things without even having to debate about it, and you're *still* flying in the face of his decisions. How can you? How can you?'

'Because I can.'

'Willie Biggs, you've been fooling me all these nine years we've been married. I thought you were a good, upstanding man, a man young in mind and body with modern ideas. I can see how wrong I've been.'

'Just a minute!'

'You're a silly, stubborn old man, that's what. I'm disgusted with you. What Peter will think I can't imagine.' Sylvia marched towards the cottage door with tears brimming in her eyes.

'Hold on a minute, then, and I'll come.'

She had her hand on the catch and didn't look back to see if he followed because she knew he would; he was as tired as she was of their conflict. Arm in arm they hastened up the path into the church and arrived just as Peter announced the first hymn.

Peter's beautifully chosen words, the tremendous feeling he imparted with every sentence he spoke, lifted the heart. 'God of peace and compassion, make bright with Your presence the path of those who have walked in the valley of shadows.' Mrs Peel played 'Abide with me', with such soulful passion no one could fail to be moved. Peter's closing words brought tears to their eyes, so powerful and heartfelt had been the service. 'Father God, they have journeyed beyond our sight many years ago, but we, Your children of today, entrust them to Your keeping, with complete and utter faith that in Your infinite mercy, You will transform the fearful terror of their deaths into a bright new healing dawn in Your everlasting Kingdom. Amen.'

The service had been difficult enough, but the sight of the coffins being lowered into the grave was almost his undoing. He said the final blessing with tremendous relief and was able at last to see who besides his own family had come, for he'd been aware the moment he'd walked into the church that there were far more people present than he had ever hoped for. He realised as he blessed them that there was a representative from almost every family in the village and felt a huge sense of triumph. So, despite half the village setting themselves against him so vehemently, they'd finally come round to his way of thinking. He smiled at them all and they all smiled back.

Duty done they went from the churchyard into the church hall for their coffee. Mrs Jones laid a firm hand on his arm. 'One thing's for certain, Rector, they'll be resting in peace now. We shall have no more troubles, not after that beautiful service. How you think up all those lovely words I shall never know. Like poetry it is, sheer poetry. Gets you right there.' She thumped her chest as she spoke. 'As I say, we can look forward to peace now. Ever since Gilbert dug up them bones there's been nothing but trouble but I can feel right here' – she thumped her chest again – 'that things are going to be right now.'

'Thank you, Mrs Jones. Thank you. I'm glad you approve.'

'Of course I do. It could well have been Flatman bones you've just laid to rest. You know, my family go back a very long way.' Her large brown eyes scanned the crowd. 'I notice even Willie turned up and he was dead against it. Mind you, I understand Sylvia's had a lot to say about his attitude. She must have won!'

'I was a bit surprised, I must say. Here's a coffee for you ... Greta.'

It was the first time he'd called her Greta and whereas at one time she would have been indignant at his familiarity, today it seemed a lovely friendly gesture, a kind of acceptance that she belonged to the inner fold. 'Thank you ... Peter. No sugar. I'm quite sweet enough! About the council and the road safety, how do you stand on that?'

'I certainly don't think things should stay as they are. We need something, unobtrusive certainly, but something, because one day there's bound to be an accident; it's unavoidable.'

Smugly Mrs Jones declared, 'Then we're on the same side, Peter.'

'Good. I'm glad.'

Bryn came to talk to him, so Mrs Jones moved away. 'Thank you, Rector, for the service. Excellent. Lovely hymns, too. I'd like to go halves with the headstone if you'd agree.'

Gravely Peter studied Bryn's face and pondered his motives. 'Why?'

'Why? ... because, well, because I feel I should.'

'Why should you?'

'Because I think everyone in the village should donate money to it. It belongs to all of us. You can see that, all those people turning out for it.'

'I have to confess to being surprised at how many attended the service. I just wish I could believe your motives, Bryn.'

'I know it looks as if I've only come because my tourists love the idea of it, and that it enhances their tour, but I really want at least to give some money towards the headstone.'

'Greta Jones, for instance, Greta Flatman that was. Descendant of an old village family, it could be one of her ancestors we've buried today. She has genuine reasons for being interested. But you ... ?'

Bryn didn't like the sceptical expression on Peter's face. He'd as much right to be here as anyone else. 'I'm still very fond of the village. I've lived here – what? – ten years.'

Peter sighed. 'Oh, Bryn!'

'Will you let me go halves? Please.'

'Very well, then. I've ordered it. I'll let you have the bill, then you can do as you wish. Who am I to deny you your heart's desire? Talking of heart's desire, have you done anything about your divorce?'

'It's going through; takes time.'

'Good chap.'

'Though there's not much point in it. Dicky won't even talk about marrying her. So it might be that Georgie finishes up with neither of us. And a lonely life that will be.'

'He'll come round, given time. I've read your leaflet. I'll be at the meeting, not on your side, though.'

'We need open debate. I'll be glad for you to put your side.'

'Good, because I shall.'

16

On the day of the meeting Mr Fitch went to school. He was there by eight forty-five. Propped against the school wall, he watched the children arriving. He saw the chaos of drivers trying to pull up to let the children out, the haphazard parking, the difficulty of pulling away without bumping into another vehicle and the risk the children ran if their parents couldn't find space close to the entrance. He was given the occasional 'Good morning' by parents taking their children on foot through the school gate and certainly got some odd looks when all he did was acknowledge their greeting with the briefest of nods. All in all, though, there was no hurried screech of brakes or even the slightest chance of one of the children being mown down.

He stood there, still propped against the school wall looking at the village, listening to the joyous sound of the children's hymn singing coming through the open windows. Back to school. Those were the days, he thought, those were the days. He thought about his own two boys and realised he'd been so remote from them that he'd never even once taken them to school or gone to a school occasion to support them. Sad, that. He'd been a fool. Too busy concentrating on his career. He'd missed out there. Missed out on everything of any real value. Precious lives passing by him till they'd gone for ever. The singing stopped and he could hear the tramp of feet, the closing of classroom doors, the rustle of paper, the squeak of chalk. Those were the days.

No good facing her until break. Or was it still called playtime? Such a happy word, 'playtime'. Tag, and chain tig, and hopscotch. Marbles! Remember marbles? Then on dry days in the summer the headmaster teaching cricket. He must be turning in his grave now at the thought of rigged cricket matches. Pity that. Pity. We had such fun. He fancied coffee so he went into the Store to see if they'd got their coffee pot on the go. Couldn't remember the last time he'd been in there, either. As he opened the door Jimbo's bell dinged a cheerful ping and the aroma of baking assailed his nostrils. Jimbo must have studied psychology: he'd created such an ambience it became compulsive to shop, one must, one couldn't help it, one needed to have a share of ... what? Happiness? Comfort? A slice of childhood?

Mr Fitch felt out of place. He was at least twenty-five, maybe thirty, years older than the other customers. Well, he needn't let that worry him, he still had a contribution to make. He still made things tick, if not tock!

'Coffee, Jimbo!'

Heads turned. Turned back when they saw who it was. What the hell did he want?

'Good morning.' Jimbo raised his boater. 'Coffee in the jug freshly made. Help yourself!'

So he did. Added half a teaspoonful of multicoloured coffee sugar – such a nice touch, he thought – and seated himself on the chair by the side window to watch the world go by.

The rush subsided and Jimbo took a moment to speak to him. 'Are you needing a word?'

'Not really. You've a little gold mine here, Jimbo. Such style.'

Jimbo raised his boater for a second time. 'We have.'

'Ambience, that's what you've created. I do believe your customers feel better for having been in here. You've made them feel up-to-the-minute, in-the-swim, with it, as they say.'

'That's our aim.'

'This meeting. About the council and their crackpot ideas for modernising us. What do you think?'

'Something needs doing, but quite what I don't know. It is chaotic.'

'Yes, but only for about ten minutes, then we're back to the peace and quiet. Is it worth spoiling the village for the sake of ten minutes twice a day, for three-quarters of the year?'

Jimbo took off his boater and smoothed his bald head. 'You have a point. But you haven't a small child going to school. We have and we worry.'

'Easy to take her across Shepherds Hill and pop her into school. Better than traffic signs everywhere. How about a voluntary code?'

'That would work for about a week and then...'

'You're right. This coffee's good. Could we get by with the bare minimum?'

'Who defines the bare minimum? Wasn't too bad when we had two minibuses picking up the children from outside the village. The council claim they can't afford it any longer, so now we've more cars than ever.'

'Even Nightingale Farm's tractor and trailer.'

'Exactly. Well, there you go, the Nightingale children were picked up, you see, by one of the minibuses, so that made life a lot easier all round. Two vehicles but twenty or more children, now it's perhaps the same number of children but it takes at least ten or twelve cars to get them here. However, I'll be at the meeting tonight.'

'So will I, Jimbo. I'm not having this village ruined by any damn council. They claim they can't afford the minibuses, yet they've money for all this traffic control nonsense. It doesn't add up.'

'Must press on. See you tonight.'

Mr Fitch placed his empty cup in the waste bin by the coffee machine, wandered around the Store looking in the freezers, assessing the quality of the goods on display, fingering the ripe plums, the glowing peaches, the bright, super-fresh vegetables and eventually left when he heard the children out playing in the schoolyard.

Miss Pascoe's class were out in the yard and Miss Pascoe herself was in her room opening her post. She heard the light knock at her door and called out, 'Come!'

So he did.

'Why, Mr Fitch! How nice of you to call. Please take a chair.'

'Good morning, Miss Pascoe.'

'And a very good morning to you. How can I help?'

'About this traffic business.'

Miss Pascoe's hackles rose. 'Yes.'

'I've been watching.'

'I saw.'

'It's the number of vehicles that is the problem.'

'Exactly.'

'But it's only for three-quarters of the year and only for about ten minutes twice a day.'

She sat in her chair, braced herself against the back, put her fingertips together and said, 'It only takes a split second for a child to be killed. A split second. A nano-second.'

There'd been an alteration in the tone of her voice. A stiffening of her attitude. A summoning of her resources. Mr Fitch realised she was one of these new women who were the bane of his life in business. They got things done but did they need to be so aggressive? Why couldn't they acquiesce as women used to do? 'I agree, but . . .'

'No, Mr Fitch, I'm having the one-way signs and the yellow lines and the lights.'

'Who says?'

'I do.'

'What if we oppose you?'

'Then the death of a child might well be laid at your door and if you want that kind of burden on your conscience then . . .'

'Eh?'

'Then I certainly don't. Something has to be done and quickly. The council have done the preliminary work and are all set for agreement.'

'Who says?'

'The county chairman of traffic planning.'

'It's county level, is it, already?'

Miss Pascoe nodded.

'I see. Well, I too have friends in high places. I shall see what can be done.' He stood up to leave. 'Don't think you've got the better of me. There's dozens in this village who don't want it ruined.'

'At what cost? A child's life? I have only the interests of my children at heart, Mr Fitch, and I can hardly be blamed for that when I'm the head teacher of the school. Can I?'

She fixed him with a stare which almost, but not quite, intimidated him. Standing up, she said, 'Excuse me, that's the bell and I have a class to teach. The children, you see, always come first with me.'

And she left him standing there! Alone, in her poky little office. She'd humiliated him. Yes, she had. Humiliated him. As he'd said to Bryn, women in authority. They didn't know how to use it. Well, she'd met her match.

He had to make an uncomfortable passage through the hall with the children springing about doing their Physical Education, climbing wall bars, balancing along an upturned bench, jumping over a horse. In his day they'd had half a dozen beanbags and some hoops, and been thankful. Indulged, that's what, indulged. He stormed across the playground, narrowly averting a disastrous stumble over a nursery child pedalling like fury on a little trike. They damn well weren't going to have their own way about this, not if he had anything to do with it.

He was one of the first to take a seat at the meeting that night, on the front row, determined to have his say. Unfortunately, unless he turned round frequently, he couldn't see who'd showed up, but judging from the babble of conversation there were plenty there, and most of the voices he didn't recognise so they must be parents from the school.

Bryn took his place, feeling exceptionally confident that his arguments would sway general opinion. However, ten minutes before kick-off, when he saw the size of the crowd already gathered, he did wonder if it would be as easy as he'd first thought. It felt close tonight, the windows needed opening. But he had to succeed. His tourists wouldn't be half so enamoured of Turnham Malpas if all they could see were one-way signs and huge street lights. Three-quarters of the romance of the place would be gone. And Miss Pascoe confidently picking up a chair and placing it beside his own didn't help matters either. Honestly, you brought money to the village and what thanks did you get? None. Bryn loosened his tie a little, mopped his top lip and sipped some water, hoping to allay a touch of indigestion. That was better. He'd put a bright, confident face on the matter and he'd win through. Peter was there too, so he'd see nothing went wrong.

But the entire evening went disastrously awry. The parents were

665

vociferous in their declaration that something must be done. Some even went the whole hog and demanded signs shoulder to shoulder along the roads, the green fenced off, yellow lines outside all the houses and around the green. By the time they'd finished the whole centre of the village was to be a no-go area for cars. No longer would you be able to pull up outside the Store while you shopped and any question of parking outside the school was completely ruled out, and you certainly couldn't park outside your own house, not even while you unloaded your shopping. As for lighting, Mr Fitch was convinced that Stocks Row would be akin to Piccadilly Circus if they had their way. He waited until they'd run out of further restrictions to impose, then he stood up, beating Miss Pascoe by a whisker.

'Mr Chairman, ladies and gentlemen. I wish Sir Ralph and Lady Templeton were here, but they're not. If they were, Sir Ralph would be appalled by your road safety ideas. But in that wonderfully gentlemanly way of his he would explain to you why they couldn't be allowed. He would talk about his village, a village with a Templeton at the head of it for more years than I know of. Certainly five or even six hundred years. Oh, yes, he has history and tradition at his very fingertips. Would that I had it too. We cannot, we must not, defile the village with such twenty-first-century trumpery as traffic lights and yellow lines. It would be sacrilege. We are here on this earth for only our allotted span, no more, and we must hand on to our children and our children's children a village fit for human beings to live in. Leave the trappings of modern society to the big cities. Here we have a haven . . .'

Someone at the back stood up and shouted, 'Haven! It won't be a haven if a kid gets killed. Never mind your poetic humbug, we're living in today's society, not blinking hundred years ago. Shut up and sit down, you old faggot.'

Bryn recognised the woman who'd tried to stuff his leaflets down his shirt neck. 'I think it would be better if . . .' But his voice didn't carry over the hubbub Mr Fitch's speech had caused.

While Peter had a word with Bryn, Miss Pascoe made up her mind to speak but Peter got to his feet while she was still thinking about it. His powerful voice carried right across the babble and he got the silence Bryn had tried for.

In reasonable tones he argued his case. 'Losing our tempers will achieve nothing. Mr Fitch is quite right. I would hate to lose our wonderful backwater; it would be criminal to allow anyone to destroy it. There are all kinds of reasons for preserving our heritage and I'm quite sure that with a bit of common sense we can overcome this problem. A little give and take on both sides, a modification of plans, a certain subtlety, a large amount of good will and we would arrive at an amicable solution. I propose we form a committee . . .'

'Reverend! Please, not a committee. They cover a lot of ground but get nowhere, as you well know. We want action. Action! Action!'

A steady drumming of feet on the wooden floorboards and the shouting of 'Action! Action!' began, and there was nothing to be done about it. It was like some kind of primeval chant: a hate thing compounded by a wish for instant capitulation. Peter was appalled. Bryn was beginning to panic. Mr Fitch was on the verge of washing his hands of the whole matter.

Grandmama Charter-Plackett stood up at the back and stepped firmly to the front to take her stand beside Bryn. She banged on the table with the gavel Bryn had brought but never used. 'Silence!' If she'd been on board ship in a violent thunderstorm the very waves would have ceased their pounding. The noisy opposition, surprised by her reckless intervention, fell silent. You could have heard a pin drop. They expected that she would shout but she didn't. She spoke so softly they had to strain to hear.

'All this matter needs is some clear thinking. None of us is a fool, we all have brains, and I for one would like to have something done about the cars because I have a precious grandchild attending the school and believe me, your cause is mine.' She pressed a hand to her heart to emphasise her feelings. 'Precious to me here,' she said, patting her chest again, 'as I know all your children and grandchildren are precious to you. We all have their welfare at heart. The Rector is the man to chair the committee and have you ever known anyone more able? Level-headed, understanding, persuasive. What more can you ask? And he too has children at the school, don't forget, so who could have your interests at heart more than he? I propose Mr Fitch as another member, for his business brain. I propose Bryn because he found out what the council were up to and apparently has friends in high places . . .'

'Oh, yeh? Our Kev! High Places! Huh!' This from that uncouth woman Bryn had met after school down Shepherds Hill.

In her most superior tone Grandmama asked, 'And you, madam, your name is . . . ?'

'Angie Turner. Shepherds Hill.'

'You could be another member. Your forthrightness would be welcomed, I'm sure. We need people with plenty of get-up-and-go on a committee like this. After all, we're taking on the whole council.'

Miss Pascoe tried again to speak but Bryn overrode her. He objected to Angie Turner on the committee most violently. He stood up to put his point. 'I honestly feel that Mrs Turner wouldn't be quite . . .'

A man leapt to his feet, a big brute of a man with forearms built like ships' hawsers and a huge shaved head. 'Not out of the top drawer eh? Is that what you meant?'

'Well, no, of course not, far be it from me to . . .'

'Well, I'm Colin Turner, Angie's husband, and I'd like to know why she can't be?'

Unfortunately Bryn couldn't think of one possible *acceptable* excuse for her not being on the committee. His hesitation was his undoing.

'Well, I'm waiting for the answer. You toad, we know you've not called this meeting because of the children's lives. It's because you want to retain the status quo for your own objectives; namely American tourists.'

Peter stood up again. 'Mr Turner . . .'

'With the very greatest respect, Reverend, this is not an argument for someone like you to be involved in. I'm well aware you'd have her on the committee without a second thought because you're not biased; you have respect for each and every one of us. I simply want an answer as to why he, *that toad* – he stabbed a thick finger at Bryn – 'doesn't want *my wife* on his committee. It's as simple as that. Well?'

Bryn opened his mouth and nothing came out. Absolutely nothing. His mind went numb. He looked bleakly at Grandmama

Charter-Plackett for inspiration. He opened his mouth again and still nothing came. He cleared his throat and uttered some fateful words. 'We'll be dealing with councillors and planning officers at the highest level and your wife ... well ... she has the children to think of ... and it's not easy to find the time ... and ...'

Peter saw he was having difficulties, sensed he was totally flummoxed, but at the same time knew Bryn had to extricate himself or he'd lose face. But he didn't. Bryn looked wildly round the hall, searching for answers, saw Colin Turner leave his seat and begin to march purposefully towards the front. Bryn's eyes bulged, he ran a finger round his shirt neck, beads of sweat appeared all over his face. Grey-faced, he gripped the edge of the table, gasped audibly and crashed to the floor before Colin Turner reached him.

There was an instant of total shocked silence, as though someone had pressed 'pause' on a video, before Peter leapt up and went to kneel beside Bryn. The moment he got close Peter sensed he was dead. There was such a pallid stillness about him: as though his soul had gone away.

'Give him some air,' someone shouted.

'Ring nine-nine-nine.'

'Glass of water. Quick.'

Peter pressed both hands on Bryn's chest and counted one, two, three, four, five presses. Paused, pinched Bryn's nose and breathed into his mouth. He did it again, and again, and again. Even before he'd begun he'd known it was too late, but he had to try. He tried once more but to no avail. Bryn had been stone dead the moment he touched the floor. Peter looked up at Grandmama Charter-Plackett and slowly shook his head. She went white, looked at Colin Turner and signalled the message to him with her eyes that it was too late: Bryn had gone.

Colin dropped to his knees and began the process all over again. 'He's got to live. He must. He must. He must.' Five times, five grunts, nip his nose. Breathe! Breathe! Breathe! Colin covered his face with his hands and wept. Grandmama put her arm round him. That was one sound she couldn't bear: a man weeping. Men's tears were so excruciatingly painful to listen to.

'I wasn't going to hit him. I wasn't, honest. I only wanted to address the meeting. I wouldn't have hit him. Not me.'

Peter took off his cassock and laid it over Bryn. 'Could someone go and get Georgie, please.'

Colin Turner said, 'Dr Harris! She'll help.'

Gently Peter told him, 'Bryn was dead when he hit the floor, Colin. It's too late.'

All Angie Turner could say was, 'Oh, Colin! Oh, Colin! Oh, Colin.'

Peter addressed the gathering. 'In the circumstances we'd better bring the meeting to a close. There's nothing anyone can do for now. Thank you for coming. Pray for Bryn before you sleep. It's a sad day. Goodnight. Goodnight. God bless you all.'

Bewildered and appalled, they all slowly departed, except for the key players in the drama. Angie was still saying 'Oh! Colin!' time and time again. She hadn't an ounce of fight left in her. Colin was rigid with distress. Willie had gone immediately Bryn had collapsed to alert Caroline, who had to push her way through the crowd that was leaving so sorrowfully.

'Give me some space.' Caroline knelt down, pulled back Peter's cassock, felt the pulse in Bryn's neck, which had been throbbing only moments before, placed her ear close to his mouth but could neither feel nor hear any breath whatsoever. She shook her head and looked up at Peter.

He whispered, 'He was dead before he fell.'

Colin groaned loudly, 'Oh, God!'

Caroline gently covered Bryn's body and stood up. Though not knowing the circumstances, she realised from his distress that Colin Turner must be involved. 'You weren't to know. There'll have to be a post-mortem; unexplained death, you know. Don't blame yourself.' She rubbed one of his powerful forearms in sympathy.

His eyes again filled with tears, his head shaking from side to side in disbelief, Colin said, 'We tried, the Reverend and me. We did try.'

'I'm sure you did. Has anyone called an ambulance?' Peter nodded.

At this moment Georgie came in. They all made space for her. Caroline had straightened Bryn's limbs, closed his eyes and rested his forearms across his chest, so even before she saw that the whole of him was covered Georgie didn't need to ask. She drew back the cassock and stood gazing down at him. Without looking up she asked, 'I know you've a quick temper, Colin, did you hit him?'

'No.'

Peter expanded Colin's reply. 'No, Georgie, he didn't. Bryn couldn't find the answer he was searching for and suddenly he pulled at his collar and then dropped ... dead. I'm so sorry.'

'You're sure he's dead?

Caroline answered, 'Yes, I am.'

'I shall want Beck and Beck from Culworth to bury him. They did my mother and were most considerate. Dicky, where's Dicky?'

Colin Turner said, 'I'm so sorry. So sorry. I never touched him. I never meant to.'

'Can't be helped. These things happen. Where's Dicky? I want Dicky.'

They'd heard the hall door open just after Georgie came in but hadn't noticed it was Dicky coming to look after her. He was standing alone at the back of the hall. 'I'm here, if you need me.'

'Dicky, ring Beck and Beck and tell them I want them. Straight away. I want him in their chapel of rest.'

Caroline interrupted her train of thought with a gentle reminder. 'We'll have to wait for the ambulance. Sudden death, you know. There'll have to be a post-mortem.'

Georgie looked up at her, puzzled. 'Oh, of course. I didn't think. What do you reckon, Caroline? Heart attack?'

'Seems likely. But of course I can't say for sure.'

'At least he didn't know. Did he?'

'It was too sudden.'

'He'd have hated being ill. Not being all that brave. Dicky?'

Dicky went to stand beside her. He longed to hold her but knew instinctively it wouldn't be seemly. Georgie stood quite still, her arms held grimly to her sides.

'Would you like a chair, Georgie? Take the weight off your feet.'

The answer to Dicky's question was 'Go and close the bar. And the dining room. For tonight. Tell them why. Respect, you know.'

Dicky left without a word. So they stood there not knowing what to do next. None of them was heartbroken, except perhaps of them all it was Georgie who felt the worst. She'd left his face uncovered but no one had the courage to cover him up again. It seemed intrusive to take the initiative.

Peter asked, 'Has he family, besides you?'

'A couple of cousins. That's all. Distant. Card at Christmas, you know. There'll be no one to mourn. Except me.'

For long minutes they all stood silently apart, gazing fixedly at the dead face; despising themselves for thinking *there but for the Grace of God go I.*

Only the ambulance arriving spurred them into action. Caroline went into a huddle with the ambulance crew, speaking softly out of respect for the dead and the bereaved. Peter began quietly praying. Grandmama and Colin and Angie stood mute, their eyes drawn, despite their resistance, to the ambulance men and the stretcher, and the blanket and the return of his cassock to Peter, the removal of the body.

Georgie, choked by the immediacy of Bryn's extinction, looked to Grandmama for help. A stalwart in adversity, Grandmama murmured gently, 'Come, my dear, I'll take you home.'

'Not to the . . .'

'No, no. To my home if you wish . . . you can have the same bedroom that you had before.'

'I thought of Dicky's . . .'

Firmly the reply came: 'No, my dear, that wouldn't be quite . . . right.'

'No, perhaps not.' Georgie allowed herself to be shepherded away.

Peter spoke to Colin and Angie. 'In no way at all were you to blame, Colin, remember. We were all witness to that.'

'Thank you, Reverend, thank you.'

'You're a star, Rector. A star. We're so sorry.' Angie dabbed her eyes with her tear-soaked tissue. 'We've got to go. Mum's sitting for us. She'll be cut up. She liked Bryn in the pub, you know.'

'So did we all. He'll be missed. Goodnight.'

'Goodnight.'

'Peter! Darling! Can we go home?'

17

Dicky had gone straight back to the Royal Oak as Georgie had asked, but they already knew because some of the people who'd left when Peter had closed the meeting had gone straight to the bar for a stiffener and to spread the news. So when he walked back in, consternation was the order of the day.

Dicky was so stunned about Bryn dying that he hadn't given it a thought that his death freed Georgie to marry him. So when someone said with a nudge and a wink, 'Well, Dicky, he's played right into your hands,' he couldn't understand what they meant.

'Behave yourself,' someone else said angrily.

Dicky looked around, bewildered, his mind focused on closing up. 'Georgie, she's asked me to close early. In respect, you know. If you don't mind.'

There was a general mumble of agreement. A voice said, 'I propose a toast to Bryn. Raise your glasses! To Bryn, God rest his soul.'

'To Bryn!'

'To Bryn! The old dog!'

'To Bryn!'

Dicky didn't drink to him. Dicky wouldn't drink to him. Not on your life. The damned fellow couldn't possibly be dead. He'd be back, couldn't have had his life snuffed out as quickly as he had. Oh, no, he couldn't possibly have gone for ever. He'd be back if only to plague him. Dicky couldn't think what to do, so he went to find Bel.

She was taking an order for puddings in the dining room. Bel caught sight of him with his ashen face and stiff gait and her heart went out to him. She abandoned her customers and enveloped him in a bear hug. 'Don't worry! Don't worry!' She patted his back, smoothed his hair, held him close, whispered, 'He's gone now. Gone for good. He can't haunt you any more, love.' Out loud she said, 'I'm serving the puddings to this table and then I'll close up. You go and close the bar.'

Dicky found Jimbo clearing used glasses, urging the customers to leave, organising Alan and Trish. 'There you are, Dicky. It must have been a terrible shock. I came straight from the meeting; thought you might need a hand.'

'Oh, thanks.' Dicky had had one too many shocks of late, first Bryn coming back, then the incident of the cricket bat, then finding Bryn and Georgie in bed and now this. Dumbly he watched as Jimbo deftly rid the bar of its last customer, bolted the door, stacked the dishwasher with glasses, emptied the till, went to check the kitchen for Bel, carried the waste bin bag round emptying ashtrays, collecting empty nut packets, asking Trish to wipe out the ashtrays, did this, did that.

It slowly began to register in Dicky's overloaded mind that Bryn was out of the picture completely and absolutely. There'd be no more taunting from Bryn, no more heartache over him. He'd been blotted out. Georgie! How must she be feeling? He'd go and see. Fully expecting that she'd be back upstairs, he set off at a gallop to find her. But the rooms were empty. Abandoned almost. Deserted. Where was she? He ran all the way to the church hall to find Willie locking up. 'Where's Georgie?'

'I don't know, Dicky. Everyone's gone.'

'She can't have disappeared.'

Dicky, at a loss to know what to do, stood just inside the main door so Willie couldn't lock up. 'Is she at the Rectory do you think?'

Dicky looked at Willie. 'Do you think so?'

'Well, I don't know. Just a guess.'

'I see.' He couldn't face Peter, not tonight. No. Slowly Dicky wandered back to the Royal Oak, still badly in need of Georgie.

Jimbo was just saying goodnight to Bel. 'Mother's been on the phone, Dicky, in case you're wondering where Georgie is. She's sleeping at her cottage for tonight.'

Dicky turned tail and ran.

Bel said, 'He doesn't know whether he's coming or going. It's all been too much. And now this.'

Dicky hammered Grandmama's front door knocker. He pushed open the letter box and shouted through it, 'I need to speak to Georgie.'

The bolts on the door were pulled back and there was Grandmama beckoning him in.

'Where is she?'

'I'm just taking her a nightcap. You can take it up if you like, but don't stay long, she's exhausted. I want her to have a good night's sleep. Well, as good as she can get in the circumstances.'

Dicky started up the steep staircase.

Grandmama called after him, 'First door on the right.'

The door to her room stood open and Dicky could see her sitting up in bed in a voluminous white nightgown that certainly wasn't her own. The light from the bedside lamp drained all her colour; Georgie appeared to be white all over. He paused for a moment, thinking of what to say. Words didn't seem much good at present. 'I've brought you a nightcap. Don't know what it is.'

'Put it here.' Georgie moved the lamp a little to make room for the small tray.

'I don't know what to say.'

'Neither do I.'

Dicky laid a hand on the bed post and looked down at her, longing to give her a kiss. 'I'm here for you.'

'I know that.'

'It's not the time to be making promises.'

'No.'

'But I've been a fool.'

'No. You're the last of the great romantics, Dicky.'

'Am I?'

Georgie nodded. 'I've got to clear the old wood, so to speak, and then we can talk. I can't see beyond the next few days.'

'Neither can I.'

'Say goodnight, Dicky.'

'Goodnight.' He longed to hold her in his arms, feel her comfort, comfort her.

Georgie took hold of his hand and squeezed it. 'That's all for now. I've got to think. It's been so sudden. Whatever can have caused it? He seemed to be in good health. Never ailed a thing for years.'

'Heart gave out, I expect.' He held her hand in both his. 'See you in the morning. Don't worry about the pub. Bel and I will keep things going. You can rely on us. Goodnight, love.'

Georgie picked up her drink and began to sip it as though he weren't even in the room. So Dicky left, numb with heartache.

He remained numb with heartache for what seemed like an age. They had to wait for the result of the post-mortem, yet keep the pub going as cheerfully as they could, order this, cancel that, pay wages, pay bills, this and that, that and this, all of it pointless or so it felt. The least that could be said for it was that it occupied his mind and, for a while, stopped him brooding. Dicky didn't dare talk about the future, nor the past come to that; in fact, he didn't dare talk about anything at all to anyone. Georgie stayed on at Grandmama's so they never got a chance to talk in depth. He couldn't, not with Grandmama's eagle eye on him. She didn't say it but he knew she was thinking that she wouldn't put up with any hanky panky under her roof. Not that he and Georgie ever got near it. There seemed to be something strange and alien keeping them from being close. Maybe it was the ghost of Bryn ever present between them. Perhaps after the funeral his ghost would go to rest.

Dicky was right. Bryn's funeral closed a chapter in his life, in all their lives and at last the way forward felt clear. As Georgie had said, the old wood had been done away with. Overnight Dicky got back his bouncy happiness and Georgie looked as though a huge weight had been lifted from her shoulders. She was more lively than she had been for a long time and regained a lot of her old sparkle. Two nights after the funeral Georgie moved back into the Royal Oak, and she and Bel and Dicky kept to the old routine: Bel sleeping at the pub and Dicky in number one Glebe Cottages.

There was plenty of nudging and winking going on behind the tinned soups in the Village Store as they had all fully expected that Dicky, now Georgie was a widow, would move in with her, but he didn't. Somehow Georgie wasn't ready for it, not yet. She'd explained to Dicky how she felt. 'I want to make a completely new start with you and I'm not quite ready yet. Bryn dying like he did, so suddenly, I didn't have time to get used to the idea and I haven't yet. I won't have you marrying half a person, because that's how I feel at the moment, only half a person.'

Dicky, being the romantic he was, could understand that and he didn't want half a person either.

'I've cleared his wardrobe and removed all his things from Liz and Neville's but I haven't quite got rid of *him*.'

Dicky, fearing his clothes might turn up at the Scout Jumble Sale, asked, 'Where have you taken his things?'

'To Oxfam. Where else?'

Dicky nodded. 'I see. It won't be long, though, will it? Before we marry?'

Georgie put her hands on his shoulders. 'No, it won't be long. But we'll have a very quiet wedding, very early in the morning, just us, and after we'll slip away for a few days' honeymoon. Then I shall have to get used to being Mrs Georgina Tutt.'

'Blessed day.'

'You see, if we marry too soon after Bryn, people will think we were glad to see him go. Which I wasn't in a way, because he was doing everything we asked of him and you must admit he had changed a lot. He was much nicer to know, the divorce was going through and he was doing his best to make things right for you and me.'

'I admit he did seem to have discovered his heart.' Dicky grinned at her.

'He did discover it and all because of you. And he regretted so much that afternoon when, you know, we . . . he really was very cut up about how badly you felt about him and me . . .'

Dicky placed a finger on her lips to stop her going any further. He really couldn't take the wraps off that particular discovery, it still hurt. 'I don't want to hear about that. Let's put that behind us for ever, right now. There's only you and me to think about now, no one else.'

'You're right. Just you and me. But there is also Bel. Dicky, will she be all right, do you think, living back in Glebe Cottages on her own?'

Georgie saw a twinkle in Dicky's eyes. 'I've an idea she won't be living there on her own for very long.'

Surprised, Georgie asked, 'She won't?'

'Remember the chap called Trevor who used to deliver the bread and then got taken on in management? Well, Bel and he' – Dicky crossed two fingers – 'they're like that and I think there'll be wedding bells before long.'

Georgie was aghast. 'I'd no idea. She's kept that quiet. How's she going to fit in a husband as well as working at the Store, helping here and school caretaking? She'll never manage it.'

'No, I think you'll be looking for a new dining-room manager and the school a new caretaker.'

'Well I never. She never mentions him.'

'Made a mess of it first time round and it makes you cautious, doesn't it, I expect.'

'Give me a kiss.'

'What for?'

'For being such an understanding man.'

After the disastrous meeting about modernising the village no one had the heart to pursue the matter with the council, nor even to call another meeting, but Mr Fitch hadn't allowed the problem to disappear from his agenda. He knew the wheels of local government turned slowly but like an elephant they never forgot, and one day they would arrive with all the paraphernalia of modern city life on a couple of wagons, and he'd worried about it on and off ever since Bryn's sudden demise. Then all at once, in a flash of inspiration, he saw a part solution which might satisfy Miss Pascoe and also Angie Turner, and deter the council from going completely off the rails.

He set about the scheme the very next day. It involved, to begin with, getting Angie Turner on side. He debated whether or not to tackle our Kev too but decided he'd had enough backhanders recently and that he was getting far too greedy. No, he'd have to go direct, straight to the top with a generous plan, nothing to do with road safety at all on the face of it. But it would help the environment. After all, the main problem was the number of vehicles. Cut down on those and what possible reason could there be for large-scale capital investment in traffic control? Then he remembered Miss Pascoe. Drat the woman. She was a stumbling block and a half, and no mistake. He spent a distracted morning with the question of Miss Pascoe at the forefront of his mind. Then inspiration! Of course! Tactics.

So that lunchtime he arrived at the school and reorganised the supervisory duties so that Miss Pascoe was free to lunch with him at the Royal Oak. She brusquely refused alcohol of any kind as she was teaching in the afternoon, but she did listen to his plans. A complete refurbishing of the computer situation at the school, which he knew was dear to her heart, and also he, personally, would subsidise a reinstated minibus service to bring the children in from outlying villages and farms. 'One from the Little Derehams direction and the other from Penny Fawcett. How about that for an idea?'

'And the computers?'

'No more second-hand gear like that I gave you before. Up-to-the-minute technology. Cross my heart. Scanners, whatever you want.'

'All this is if I agree to the minibus idea?'

Mr Fitch had to smile. 'Well, fair's fair. This way everyone gets satisfaction.'

'You are a rogue. An absolute rogue. No minibus, no computers.' Her eyes twinkled, which took the sting out of her uncompromising statement.

'Something like that.' Mr Fitch grinned like a cheerful schoolboy caught out in a scam. 'Say yes!'

Miss Pascoe placed her knife and fork side by side, dabbed her lips with her napkin, then looked into those frosty light-blue eyes of his and said, 'I see nothing changes with you, you're always the same year in year out, nothing stops your scheming, evil mind from working overtime.'

'I take exception to that last remark. I'm only trying to do my best to help everyone. The village, the school, the children. Be fair.'

'If the staff agree, then yes. They feel just as strongly as I about the safety of the children, you know. They back me every step of the way.'

'Good! I've got to get the parents on my side. I'm sure they won't mind paying a small fixed sum to save them having to turn out twice every day to get the children to school and home again. That Angie Turner has a long walk, poor girl, having no car.'

'She's a firebrand, but nobody's fool. Been very upset by Bryn's death.'

'Haven't we all?'

Miss Pascoe looked at her watch. 'Got to get back.'

'No time for pudding?'

'Sorry. No. Must go. I think we can say yes to your diabolical scheme.'

He smiled to himself. 'I thought you would. I'm off to give Angie Turner a ride to school in my car.'

'Take her home too, it's only fair.'

Mr Fitch hesitated. 'You're a dragon, that's what you are. I'll be seeing you.'

'Thanks for lunch! An even bigger thank you for being so generous.'

'Not at all. My pleasure.'

Miss Pascoe got to her feet, picked up her bag and said mischievously, 'Just hope Angie's two-year-old twins haven't got sticky fingers.'

'Eh, what?'

Miss Pascoe laughed when she heard Mr Fitch groan as she left the dining room.

Jimbo stood tidying his souvenir display and thinking about poor Bryn. Such plans, cut down in a moment. Massive blood clot finding its way to his heart. Maybe he'd better start running again with Peter, but he'd begin slowly and build up. Jimbo recalled those early-morning winter runs, when the fields were covered with a light frost and the trees bathed in icy crystals, like a winter wonderland for fairies. He picked up one of the tins of sweets and studied the picture on the lid of the beck on the spare land and the little footbridge over it, and the huge beech trees in the background, and loved it. He smoothed his hand over a framed picture of the church with the words 'St Thomas à Becket, Turnham Malpas' on a small label attached to the mount. He chose a red pencil from the display and lovingly read the words on the side. 'All in such good taste,' Harriet had said with her tongue in her cheek, when she saw them for the first time. He chuckled. What would he do without her?

One of Vince Jones's doorstops caught his eye next and he stroked the decorative knob stuck to the end of it. He held it in his hand as though about to place it under a door when the thought struck him. Good grief! It was the third week in September! Third week! That rang bells. What on earth was it? He slapped his forehead with his open hand. Of course! My God! Bryn's tour. He checked the date on his watch. Four days and they'd be here.

But no one to meet them at Gatwick. No one to conduct the tour. 'Linda! Got to go. Won't be ten minutes. Hold the fort!'

'But the mothers will be in soon, I can't . . .'

She was too late. Jimbo had gone, running across the green as though the devil himself were in hot pursuit. He hammered on the back door of the pub. 'Georgie! Georgie!'

He heard the bolts being dragged back and the key being turned, and there in front of him stood Georgie still in her dressing gown. 'Sorry! Sorry! But I've just had a thought.'

Georgie stepped back to let him in. 'It'd better be good.'

Jimbo answered, 'Depends on how you look at it. Georgie, Bryn's tour, aren't they due in four days' time?'

Georgie looked at him as though he'd said the Martians were due any minute. 'Tour? Oh, good grief. Yes. You're right. They are. Never gave it a thought.'

'Paperwork. Was there any paperwork with his stuff at Neville's?'

Georgie tapped her head with her fingers. 'Can't think. If I find it what are we going to do? I can't conduct a tour.'

'I'll do it.'

'No, no, we'll have to cancel.'

'Too late. We've scarcely time to let the customers know, anyway. Meals, theatre tickets, no, it's easier to run the tour. The hotels will want paying in full, at such short notice, and they weren't cheap hotels, were they?'

'No. My God! They weren't. What are we to do?'

'First, find Bryn's paperwork, then we'll decide. Must fly, Linda's on her own.'

'Right.'

'When you've found his files give me a buzz.'

Jimbo fled back to the Store, his head whirling with ideas. If push came to shove he'd conduct the tour himself. He would. Yes, he would. Could be fun. Give him a break.

Harriet, having delivered Fran to school, was already in the kitchens behind the Store making the icing for a wedding cake order. She turned to smile at him as she heard his footsteps. 'Where've you been, might I ask?'

Jimbo explained. Harriet listened open-mouthed. He concluded with, 'So I shall do the tour for him.'

'You will?'

'Yes. Can't be that difficult. Just need to read his files, get to grips with the itinerary, ring ahead and away you go.'

'Poor Bryn. Poor Bryn. He intended making his fortune with his tours. Probably would have done, too.' Harriet stood gazing out of the window on to the garden. 'Remember Stocks Day? Me saying I'd seen him? It was such a shock. Poor Bryn.'

'God rest his soul. He'd be delighted to know we were going ahead with it, though, wouldn't he?'

Harriet smiled. 'Yes, of course he would. Yes, that's the best thing to do. A kind of tribute to him, wouldn't it be?'

Jimbo nodded. 'Yes, he'd have liked the idea of that.' Jimbo dipped his finger into the icing. 'Yes, Bryn would be delighted.' He licked his finger clean. 'That's good.'